BAD BLOOD

Kris Lillyman

For Netty, Scarlett and Dexter.

PART ONE

One

I was laying on my bed in the dark just listening, waiting for the noise of the car outside, just as I had on many nights before. It was one in the morning but I was fully dressed, fully conscious. Ready for what I knew would happen when my old man finally came home. At fourteen, I considered myself to be a man already, not in appearance maybe, but in mind and experience. My boyhood had finished years ago, extinguished mercilessly by George Reilly, the man I was ashamed to call my father.

Out of the silence, I heard the first unmistakable sound of the car and listened intently as it grew louder, travelling up the war torn street that was once lined with more than two hundred terraced houses. Now though, amongst the rubble, which was still evident in many places even three years after the war, only fifty or so still stood. Fifty red-bricked monuments to those that had died; sons, brothers, husbands and fathers. I was only sorry that my father wasn't one of them.

The car pulled up outside and I had the familiar feeling in the pit of my stomach; a mixture of hatred, dread and anxiety. As my old man shouted his goodbyes to the driver of the car, not caring that he might be waking the neighbours, I slipped off the bed and quickly nipped along the landing to Mum's room, to put her on alert. To give her the three minute warning.

The driver of the car was a man named Benny Mottola; a nasty piece of work from the East End. A hard case, a villain and a black-hearted thug, just like my dad.

George and Benny were wartime buddies who, in the three years since their return from France, had lived their lives with scant regard for anyone else. They were drinkers, womanisers and trouble makers. Violent men with vicious tempers and I hated them both.

George was a big, powerful Irishman with a bald head and a thick black moustache. He was also a heavily tattooed brawler with a quick, unpredictable anger and even quicker fists. Benny was a twenty-five year old, second generation Italian, fifteen years younger than his friend, with slicked-back black hair and a broken nose. He, too, was a big man and mean with it - meaner even than George. The word was that he was connected to some crime syndicate in the States but no one had ever dared to ask him about it. The two of them were big pals, but Benny, even though he was much younger than George, was undoubtedly the boss.

Dad had turned up with Benny on the day he returned from the war - four years after me and Mum had last seen or heard anything from him. But George Reilly didn't care about us, in fact he barely even acknowledged us as he marched into the kitchen and took the small amount of money that Mum had saved, which she kept in an old tea caddy in the cupboard.

After stuffing the notes into his pocket and tossing the tea caddy aside, George strode back out the front door. His triumphant homecoming from the war and the reunion with his family had lasted less than a minute. At the time, I was barely ten and had little memory of my father before then, but Mum remembered and had hoped that the war may have changed him. She had hoped that the violence and cruelty of the man had all been spent on fighting the Germans. But in less than sixty seconds, those hopes had been dashed forever and were immediately replaced by despair.

Outside, Benny was leaning against his car, and, like my dad, wearing his demob suit. He looked swarthy, tanned and menacing, a smouldering cigarette dangling carelessly from his thick lips.

As the old man walked towards him, Benny turned his head to me, his eyes deep set and cruel. He smiled, but there was no warmth to it and I was glad that my dad had left him outside.

George jerked a thumb backwards, 'Benny, meet Rita and Sean - ain't they just the most wholesome thing you ever saw?' The sarcasm was thick in his voice, the disdain for us both undisguised. I knew what Mum had been hoping for, as she had as good as told me, and now my heart broke for her.

Benny tipped an imaginary hat, by way of acknowledgment, but said nothing.

'George, aren't you staying?' Mum asked with trepidation, remembering her husband's temper as well as his right hook. 'You've only just got back. What about us—?'

'What about you, Rita?' Said George.

'I just thought—' Mum began.

'Look,' snarled the old man, 'I don't care what you thought. Benny saved my life over in France and I'm gonna buy him a drink if, of course, that's okay with you?' I couldn't tell if what he said was true or not, but guessed by the way Mottola sniggered that it probably wasn't.

Benny laughed with a throat like rough gravel, 'He's right y'know luv,' he said with a wink as the pair of them got into his car, 'I saved 'im from gettin' the pox in France - and I'll save 'im from gettin' it 'ere too! Ain't that right, Georgie Boy?'

Mum and me could still hear them laughing as they sped off down the road, Mottola pamping the horn all the way to the junction.

In the three years since that glorious homecoming, things

had gone from bad to worse and I'd now come to know my father all too well. To know him and despise him.

I inched open Mum's door, knowing that she too would have heard the voices of Dad and Benny below, knowing that she, even more than me, would be dreading the moment when the car pulled away and her husband entered the house. Mum was sitting bolt upright in bed, the covers pulled up under her chin, her pale blue eyes wide and frightened. I could tell that her greying, strawberry blonde hair had not even touched the pillow as she sat there waiting, shaking. Knowing.

Benny blasted the car horn as he pulled away. A moment later the front door crashed open and Mum let out a small whimper. The old man was home and her regular nightmare was about to begin.

'Rita!' George shouted. He was drunk, standing in darkness at the bottom of the stairs, bellowing at the top of his voice. 'I'm hungry. Come get me somethin' to eat!'

Mum obediently got out of bed, as if in a trance. I noticed, not for the first time, how thin she'd become and remembered how attractive she had once been. Even as a young boy I'd been aware of the admiring looks she'd received from men as she walked down the street. But now that woman was gone, replaced by the drawn, worry-worn creature before me. The only looks Mum got now were from those concerned for her health.

'Be careful,' I said. It was no good me telling her not to go, or to stay out of the old man's way, as we both knew neither of those would work. 'I'll be listening. I'll be there if anything happens.'

Mum looked at me with panic in her eyes. 'Stay here, luv. It'll do no good, you know it won't. You'll just get hurt again. I'll be fine. He'll be—'

'Woman! Did you 'ear me? I want some bloody food. Get your arse down 'ere, now!' George was getting angry.

'I'll have to go. Stay here. Please Sean. Just stay put.' With that she slipped on her housecoat and raced down the stairs, desperate to appease her husband.

Fifteen minutes later, I could smell cooking, but the aroma didn't make me hungry, it made me feel sick, because I knew what was coming next. Almost as if on a timer, the shouting started. Something, as usual, wasn't right and within seconds I heard a crash of pots and the smash of plates and then I heard my mum scream.

Without heeding her warning, I leapt down the stairs and darted through the sitting room into the kitchen. The old man's first punch had knocked Mum down and I arrived just a moment too late to stop a follow-up kick to her stomach.

Fuelled by rage, I sprang onto my father's back as my mum writhed in agony. 'No, Sean!' She shouted, but I ignored her as I flung an arm around George's thick neck and battered his massive bald head repeatedly with my free fist. But it was a futile attack. 'Is that the best you can do boy?' My father growled, rearing backwards like some great bear, smashing my back between him and the kitchen cupboard, forcing me to lose my grip.

Reacting quickly, I immediately sprang up to attack again, but the old bastard had already anticipated the move and as I leapt, he span around and grabbed me with his huge hands. He held me for a second, crushing me in his grip, then, as if deciding I wasn't worth the effort, he tossed me, like a rag doll, back against the wall. I cracked my head but somehow I remained on my feet. 'Leave her alone!' I shouted as I staggering forward, still reeling from the blow.

'It's my house, boy—,' George snarled, '—and in it, I'll do exactly what I fuckin' well like!' Then he launched the hammer blow - so fast that I barely saw it coming, and just a split second before everything went black, I briefly felt the pain.

5

I woke up sometime later, my head throbbing badly. Several strands of unruly blonde hair hung messily over my eyes. Wearily, I brushed them aside and glanced around the devastated kitchen. The cupboard door was hanging off, a chair lay broken on the tiled floor along with the remains of a meat pie and a saucepan that had spilt its contents of boiled potatoes across the floor.

Mum was slumped in the corner of the room, weeping, her face purple and bloody, and streaked with tears.

Cautiously I climbed to my feet, suddenly aware of the pain in my nose and the blood dripping from it. A slight touch told me it was broken. The second time in two years.

Mum looked dreadful, like the survivor of a car crash, and for the millionth time I cursed my father. She was clearly in a great deal of pain, with her midriff being the main point of concern. I suspected that she had cracked a rib but couldn't be sure, whatever it was, it needed a hospital. Sitting her carefully on a chair, I quickly checked the house, but George Reilly had gone; gone to find his pal Benny or some whore who got paid to take his beatings. I didn't know and didn't care, I was just pleased he'd gone.

After that I ran up to the telephone box on the corner of the street and called an ambulance, then set about packing a few of Mum's things in an overnight bag. It was a well practiced procedure.

Within a quarter of an hour, the ambulance was parked outside and Mum was being stretchered onto it. As I climbed in beside her, I noticed neighbours staring out of their bedroom windows, some were even outside in their night clothes, blatantly gawping at the proceedings without the slightest trace of shame. I stuck up two fingers and mouthed an obscenity at them, then watched with relish as they visibly recoiled.

Mine and Mum's lives had turned into a circus and I was playing to an insatiable crowd. The people in the street pretended to be shocked but I knew that they were really savouring every minute, already relishing tomorrow's gossip.

The Reilly family never failed to put on a good show.

*　*　*

Just a short distance away from where we lived, my best friend, Joe Cassidy, was awoken by a scream coming from his twin sister's room. Immediately alert he darted from his bed and rushed to help.

As he threw open Sarah's bedroom door, he saw the man on top of her; his big frame writhing hideously, fully dressed but with his trousers pulled down to his knees. Sarah was fighting, just as she always did, but the man was too powerful and had already slapped her into near submission, but still she fought. The man raised his hand again, but before he could strike her, Joe was on him. Using all his strength he pulled him off Sarah and flung him to the floor. Vic Cassidy hit the ground and glared up at Joe, his son, the boy who was the image of him. Tall, strong and good-looking with the jet black hair that all his family had. Vic should have been proud of his fourteen year old son, but instead he resented him. Joe had all the promise that Vic never had; courage, compassion and an inner strength which would be forever out of Vic's grasp. And for that he hated the boy.

Vic was scum. A sadist and a paedophile who wallowed in the repulsive glory of what he was, which he had long ago come to terms with, but in Joe he saw all the promise that could once, perhaps, have been his, and each time he looked into the boy's eyes he was reminded of it.

He smiled up at Joe. A grin so wide, so white, so sinister that he looked like the devil himself. 'Ah, first the daughter, now the son. The perfect night,' he said.

'Leave her alone,' Joe said, his eyes burning as black as coal as the hatred smouldered within them.

7

'Oh, I've finished with her. Now it's your turn.' Vic's cravings were two-fold and, even to him, very odd. He got his kicks out of young girls, particularly and most peculiarly, his own daughter, a desire which he couldn't quite fathom. Of course, she was a most striking girl, slim and extremely pretty, but she was, after all, his daughter. Secondly, and again, to his mind, most confusingly, he enjoyed the fights with his son, which to him, in some strange way, were equally as erotic and maybe even more satisfying. Years ago, there was little fight to be had, Vic used to beat Joe and that was that. But more recently, as Joe had grown, he'd been able to put up a much better show and even though the boy was just fourteen, the two of them had become much more evenly matched and Vic now got much more pleasure from the fights than he ever had before.

Joe hated his father. Could barely even look at him for the disgust he felt. How could he and Sarah be of his loins? How could a father treat his children in such a way? The creature sprawled on the carpet before him was no man, but a monster; a vile, loathsome animal that had somehow crawled into both their lives and had stayed to antagonise them purely for the thrill of it. Even the merest glance at Vic made Joe want to vomit.

Fortunately, Vic was rarely at home. When he wasn't doing time in prison he was out on the streets, ducking and diving. He was a well-known figure in the underworld, disliked by most, despised by many for his unusual tastes, but respected nonetheless, as man who could get things done. Indeed, there was no end to his talents; burglar, fence, debt collector and pimp were all trades at which Vic excelled. But he'd always remained at the lower end of the criminal ladder, among the filth and the dirt which was where he was happiest. He knew he'd never rise above the squalor. Joe and Sarah had the potential to, but Vic never would. The realisation of this, when he was a younger man, was a bitter pill to swallow, but now he accepted it. Enjoyed it. It was his domain, his world, and in it he was the master.

Joe and Sarah only saw him once or twice a month, when the craving took over him, when no power in the land could prevent him from satiating that need. But Joe would always try, as he would on this night.

He stood over Vic, his fists clenched and ready for battle. His young body was firm and well formed, he was a tough kid, always had been, although 'kid' was hardly the word to describe him. Childhood had passed Joe by, as both he and Sarah, his younger sister by half an hour, seemed to have been born adults. The choice had not been theirs, it was just a fact of life.

Joe knew that his body was changing; it was physically maturing as his mind already had. He also knew that in time this new adult physique would give him the strength to finally defeat his father. Joe was going to be taller, broader, tougher. He could see it and so could Vic. The clock was ticking, but the winner of this night's bout was already a foregone conclusion. All Joe could hope to do was hold Vic off and prevent any further molestation of Sarah.

'You think tonight could be the night, boy?' Vic said as he slowly got to his feet, his eyes never leaving Joe's. 'You think this could be the night you finally get the better of me?' As he spoke he eased up his trousers and prepared himself for battle. 'You might be right. I'm tired, it's been a tough week and your sister really took it outta me.'

Joe said nothing. He was not going to play Vic's mind games, not going to rise to the bait.

'I quite fancy your chances tonight,' Vic continued, 'I reckon that you stand a pretty good chance. What do you think? You up to it, tough guy? You reckon you can do it? Let's see shall we?'

The two circled carefully, Joe being the more guarded, always aware of Sarah, the defence of her uppermost in his mind. It was his one weakness and Vic used it to full advantage. As Joe risked a quick glance to his sister, Vic spotted his moment and with a growl pounced forward.

*   *   *

At the hospital, my nose was reset, which hurt like hell but I refused to let it show. Mum was being kept in for observation; she had two broken ribs, severe bruising and a mild concussion. It was bad but it had been worse.

As I waited in the corridor for the nurses to finish with Mum, I checked my reflection in a mirror on the wall and was horrified by what I saw. My face was a mass of bruises and my nose swollen and bloody. A few girls had told me I was good-looking, although I'm not sure I believed it - I don't think they would either if they could see me now. I had my mum's strawberry blonde hair and her blue eyes, but unfortunately the rest was my father's and when I looked in the mirror, he was who I saw - even with the bruises. I was proud of my physique though. It was lean and hard and my frame broad. In time I knew I would be able to take on my father as an equal, maybe even one day give him the beating he so badly deserved. But that time seemed a long way off. Too long.

Depressed and weary, I took out a crumpled packet of Woodbines and lit one up. I took a long drag and tried to relax, to clear my head and put the hatred I felt towards my old man to the back of my mind but at some level it was always there, always with me, and I hated that too.

Suddenly, there was a commotion in the next corridor; there were raised voices and one, in particular, that I would have known anywhere, as it belonged to my best friend, Joe Cassidy.

At first, I thought that maybe Joe had come to the hospital to be with me and Mum, but then, as Joe came around the corner, I saw the true reason and my heart sank.

Like me and Mum, Joe and Sarah were also regular visitors

to the hospital and, invariably, it was me and Joe who were left in the corridor smoking, whilst those we had tried to protect were worked on by the medical staff. It was an all too common situation, but it had united us and bound us tightly together.

Joe and me first met when we were just three, in a children's home in Bermondsey. Back then Mum was in hospital with a fractured skull and a broken leg - a parting gift from George, who'd pushed her down the stairs the day before returning to his unit. Joe and Sarah's mum was a prostitute who'd stuck around just long enough to give birth before vanishing, forever, into the night. The twins had been born at a convent and the nuns, convinced they were doing the right thing, managed to track down their father and persuade him to take them in. Vic dragged Joe and Sarah up with the help of a few of his working girls. They had no fixed home for the first two years of their lives, just brothels and bedsits and doss houses.

Then their luck changed for the better, as Vic was arrested for burglary and sent down for a five year stretch. Sarah was taken back in by the nuns, but Joe was sent to the children's home in Bermondsey.

Whilst there, Joe and me grew as close as brothers. Once Mum was healed, I was sent home, but Joe became a regular visitor at our house and in the five years leading up to Vic's release, Rita became like a mother to him too. One of my fondest memories is of Mum, Joe and me all going to the picture house every Saturday afternoon to watch the matinee. Joe loved gangster movies starring Edward G. Robinson and James Cagney but I loved westerns with the likes of Randolph Scott and John Wayne and Mum liked anything but particularly films starring strong sassy women such as Jane Russell and Louretta Wild.

Afterwards we would always go to a cafe for a cup of tea and a bun to chat about what we had just seen. It was wonderful and I know it was one of Mum's favourite things.

In those years, I had only met Sarah a few times and, even then, only briefly as the nuns were incredibly strict about who visited her.

Unfortunately, when Vic was released from prison, the authorities gave Joe and Sarah back to him, which was when their troubles really began. Vic started interfering with Sarah when she was just eight and beating her when she was ten. Joe had been fighting him since the night it started and had even more bruises from his father than I had from mine.

Now the twins were fourteen, like me, but our battle still continued. Here we were, once again, at the hospital, where we had all been so many times before.

Joe was half carrying Sarah and I ran to their aid. A nurse was tailing them, insisting that they wait their turn to see a doctor, but Joe was having none of it.

Joe showed no surprise that I was there. 'Rita okay?' He asked quickly.

'Yeah, just about,' I replied. 'What about you two?'

'I'm fine. Sarah's not so good though, I didn't get there quick enough.' Joe always blamed himself but it was never his fault. Then he turned to the nurse and said, 'Listen, if you don't get a doctor out 'ere in five minutes, I'm gonna go and find one myself. And when I do, I'm gonna drag 'em out 'ere and blame you for it - geddit?'

I didn't doubt it, as Joe was well capable. The nurse apparently thought so too, because she quickly caved, 'Oh, very well. Wait here then,' she snapped, 'I'll be back in a minute.'

As she disappeared through a pair of heavy swing doors, we eased Sarah onto a chair.

She was a real beauty, even in her present, injured, state. Jet black hair and smooth, tanned skin, with finely carved features and lovely dark, almond shaped eyes. From the very first moment I saw her at the convent I'd loved her, but she didn't know it, no one did. It was my one secret from Joe, as I'd never told him and couldn't imagine a time when I ever would. Joe was fiercely protective of his sister and I didn't know how he might react. Joe's temper was phenomenal and when he was angry there was no telling what he could do.

Two minutes later the nurse was back with a doctor and they led Sarah off for an examination. Joe wanted to go too, but stayed with me at his sister's insistence.

'Make sure he doesn't punch anyone, Sean,' she said.

'Like I could stop him,' I said with a smile.

I tapped out another couple of cigarettes and gave one to Joe. For a long time, we both sat there and smoked. Both bruised, both battered, both injured trying to protect the ones we loved.

Another night of hell. Another night of violence. Another night at the hospital. Just like the many that had come before. I watched the smoke curl slowly up to the ceiling. Perhaps next time I wouldn't be sitting in a hospital corridor but standing over my mother's grave. After all, the odds were surely getting slimmer all the time.

A thought had been buzzing about in my head for sometime, one which, for a long time, I had been reluctant to acknowledge. But it was there and it had been steadily growing stronger.

The thought was of murder, or, more specifically, the murder of George Reilly.

I had tried to think of another way, to cling on to some forlorn hope that his beatings would end and that he would eventually tire of persecuting my mother. I had tried to put the thought of murdering him to the back of my mind, but it kept resurfacing, growing stronger and stronger until it was almost impossible to ignore.

Now, with the events of this night, I could finally see the truth of the matter and the reality hit me with a jolt. This hell would never end. It would go on and on until Mum was dead. Unless I did something to stop it. Forever. And there was only one permanent fix. My father had to die.

'I'm gonna kill my dad,' I said. It was more to myself than to Joe, but he heard and, as he took another drag of his cigarette, he turned to look at me, 'You are?' He said.

'Yeah, I am.'

Joe blew out the smoke in a long, smooth stream. 'And I'm gonna kill mine,' he said.

* * *

Even though the war had been over for three years, it was difficult to notice it in Peckham, South London where we lived. Times were tough, money was scarce and work was hard to find. Food was still on ration and rubble from destroyed homes could still be found on a number of streets. Many families were struggling to make ends meet, as were we, but somehow we got by. Mum had a couple of cleaning jobs and took in washing, she also did a bit of sewing to further her income. Joe and me stacked crates part-time at Smithfield market and picked up a bit extra running errands for a local bookie called Ernie Elmore.

Ernie also did a nice little side line in house-breaking and, occasionally, we would go with him on a job, operating as look-outs or bag men, if it was a big haul. More recently, he had been sending us in alone, choosing the less taxing look-out role for himself, although still keeping the lion's share of the takings. This did not sit well with Joe and me and we had been meaning to have a word with him about it, after all, if we were doing most the work, surely we were entitled to the bigger cut.

However, the night after the hospital, when we had just completed another successful job for Ernie, neither of us felt in the mood for a row with him. So after he paid us our share, we just went on our way.

Some time later, Joe and me were sitting around a fire we'd built in an old abandoned warehouse. It was the place where we normally went to count our meagre earnings and to moan about how lazy Ernie had suddenly become, but tonight was different. Neither of us were saying much at all as we watched the flames, both alone in our thoughts of the night before.

'Did you mean that last night. What you said?' Joe suddenly said.

'What about?'

'You know, about killin' your old man.'

'Yeah. I meant it.' I said. Then glanced at Joe, 'Did you mean it about killin' yours?'

'Yeah.'

There was silence again for a short time as Joe lit a cigarette, then he said, 'How you gonna do it?'

'I don't know how yet,' I replied, 'but I know I've got to. He'll kill Mum if I don't.'

'Same 'ere.' Joe said. 'Sarah's cracking under the strain, I can tell. If I don't do something soon she's gonna lose it, y'know, in the head. She's gonna have some sort of break down. Killing Vic is the only way to stop it. Same with your old man. Death's too bleedin' good for 'em, but it's the only bloody way.'

'I know. And I'm gonna do it,' I said.

'No, we'll do it, 'Joe said. 'You kill your dad and I'll kill mine.' Then he spat on his hand and offered it to me. 'Deal?'

'You completely sure?' I said.

'More sure than I've ever been of anything. Some how, some way, those bastards are gonna die.'

'Okay then,' I said, spitting on my palm and clasping Joe's hand tightly to seal the bargain. 'It's a deal.'

'You swear it?' He said.

15

'Yeah. I swear.'

In that moment we sealed the fate of George Reilly and Vic Cassidy.

We were fourteen and it was a childish oath, but in the years to come, it was going to mean everything.

Two

We were fourteen year old tearaways. Tough kids living in one of London's toughest neighbourhoods. Our friends were tough too; a proper bunch of reprobates always looking for the main chance. We stole and we fought and we generally raised hell.

It was the environment we lived in or, at least, that was the excuse, and survival was the name of the game. Everyone lived on their wits and crime was an almost accepted way of life. From my viewpoint, and Joe's, it seemed that the honest, hard working types were ironically the ones who were struggling the most, with almost all finding it nearly impossible to make ends meet.

However, those who were a little more shady, a little more dishonest and not so bothered about staying on the right side of the law, seemed to fair much better. It wasn't right, but it was a simple fact of life and if they could do it then so could we.

These were the people who, to us, represented excitement and risk. They had nerves of steel and weren't frightened of anything. If they wanted something they took it and to hell with the consequences. These were our role models; the villains and gangsters of post-war South London, and foolishly we hoped to, one day, be just like them.

We liked their tailored suits and silk ties, and their hair which was slicked down with Brylcream. We too wanted to chain-smoke Navy-Cut and frequent night clubs and drinking dens. To live in the seedy, nocturnal underworld with all of its danger, glamour and excitement. To have women hanging from our arms who wore figure hugging dresses that showed their ample charms.

The men we admired so much always seemed confident and cool and drove around in shiny black cars. The tools of their trade were knives, razors, bats and chains, but somehow, in a strange kind of way, that all added to their appeal.

Unbeknownst to me, George Reilly and his brutish pal, Benny Mottola, were deeply involved in this underworld scene I admired so much. They were two of the main enforcers for an up and coming firm in the East End - one which they had ambitions to soon run for themselves.

My dad gave no outward signs of being a gangster; he wasn't a snappy dresser, nor did he have a flashy car - at least not one that I ever saw and he certainly wasn't generous with his cash. The only tangible thing which really should have pointed the way for me was his cellar; a permanently locked hole in the ground hidden beneath our under-stairs cupboard, accessed by a trap-door. George had dug this hole himself in the weeks after his return from the war, and had forced Mum and me to transport the earth and rock excavated from it to our small back yard, to form a now completely overgrown and baron vegetable patch. In this cellar, my father stashed crates of stolen cigarettes and booze and any black-market goods he could get his hands on. It was his own private lock-up which not even Benny knew about, and, of course, Mum and me knew what we'd get if we ever mentioned it to anyone.

But even the cellar with its stock of illegal contraband didn't really make him a gangster, it just made him a bit of a crook - just like a good percentage of other people trying to make a quid in these tough times. Having a cellar certainly wasn't glamorous, it didn't have style or intrigue. If anything it was a bit squalid and dirty and what I considered in those days to be small time. What I didn't get was that this was just what George had creamed off the top; an emergency stash in case things turned sour. His and Benny's true operation was a much bigger enterprise and they were pulling huge jobs all over London and the south of England. They were on the up; the men to know or to stay away from; men with ambition who were steadily scaling the lofty heights they aspired to.

But I was ignorant of all this. There was no real sign to help me recognise the truth; no visible clue to tell me what my father really was. But had someone told me, I'd have been physically sick, knowing that I had been unwittingly trying to emulate the one thing I hated most in all the world.

If only I'd known, things might just have been different.

*   *   *

Like my father, Vic Cassidy was also embroiled in the world of crime. He ran with an outfit known as The Twenty Ones, so named because they operated out of a club near the docks called The Pontoon. The Twenty Ones were a small time bunch of hoods controlled by Big Jack Anderson, one of the main players in the South London underworld, although he was nowhere near as influential as his cousin, Vinnie Reece, who, at that time, was the undisputed king of organised crime in London.

Vic Cassidy looked after one of Anderson's cat houses. The kind of establishment where the girls on offer were the low class, low budget type, but he made a reasonable living from it.

However, for a bit of extra income, Vic did a spot of debt collecting for Jack. A task that he would have gladly performed for nothing - payment was just an added perk of the job.

What he liked most about this kind of work, was when people couldn't pay, because that meant he was free to inflict some pain which, as a sadist, he had a particular penchant for.

Vic had not gone to war because he had lost three of his toes in a childhood accident and had walked with a slight limp ever since. This as it turned out, was enough to keep him out of the forces, which suited him just fine.

In August 1949 Vic Cassidy killed Ernie Elmore; sliced him up with a razor beyond all recognition.

Ernie, it transpired, in his role as bookie, had owed Big Jack a lot of money after a sizeable win on the horses, but he hadn't paid up. After Elmore promised and failed to come up with the money on three previous occasions, Anderson finally lost his patience and sent in Vic.

With Ernie gone, Joe and I continued on with the house-breaking alone and with no more third man to pay, it was a much more lucrative arrangement. For the first time in Vic's life, he had inadvertently done Joe a favour. Although both of us chose not to dwell too much on what had happened to poor Ernie. Everything just boiled down to money, and this was just another chance to get hold of some.

Using one of Ernie's contacts we fenced out the gear we stole, and by Christmas we were making a good enough living to quit our part-time jobs at Smithfield. A life of crime seemed a much better option.

*　　*　　*

By the summer of 1950, Joe and I were sixteen years old and on the way up. Things were especially good for me as I hadn't seen my father for three months due to a six month stretch he was doing for assault. Not as it turned out on me or my mother, but on some bloke he'd nearly beaten to death in a back alley.

The first I heard of this was the day after he had been sent down, but I didn't care; he was gone, at least for the time being and that was all that mattered.

Although not wanting to, my mother felt it her duty to visit

20

George in prison, only to be told by him that she was not to go back there as he had *'no wish to see her disgusting face.'*

As it turned out, this was the best thing he could've done for her, it meant that she didn't have to see him - he'd actually ordered her not to and the relief in her was obvious. Six months without the worry of being beaten, abused or living in fear. She was free to do just what she wanted with no one to tell her otherwise. When she returned from the prison, she was humming a tune, and for the first time in years, she was genuinely happy. Joe and me even started taking her to the pictures again whenever we had time, which she loved.

* * *

Vic Cassidy had also been spending less time at home, which was solely down to Joe, who had grown into a six foot two powerhouse, more than capable of dealing with his father's sickening advances towards Sarah.

Vic was wise enough to stay well clear of the house for he knew that if he so much as looked at Sarah in anything other than a fatherly way, Joe would kill him. However, Vic was content to bide his time.

Needless to say, neither Joe nor I hadn't so far had an opportunity to carry out the details of the pact we made over eighteen months before. But it had not been forgotten.

* * *

House-breaking was okay, but the hours were shitty and the thrill of it had worn off. More importantly, although lucrative, the profits no longer out-weighed the risks. It was a sure ticket to prison and neither of us planned to end up there. Besides, we wanted a crack at the big time, and the man who could provide us with that chance was Vinnie Reece.

Reece was the main man, the guv'nor, and South London was his manor. If we were to make it, it would have to be with his backing. If we could get in on the ground floor of his firm, serve our apprenticeship and work our way up through the ranks, impressing a few of the faces along the way of course, then surely success and wealth would be quick to follow. Maybe in as little as ten or fifteen years, we could be running things alongside Vinnie, perhaps even being awarded our own piece of the pie, just like Big Jack had - and then we really would be kings.

*   *   *

The guy we fenced our gear through, got us in with a man called Alfie Noakes, who owned The Golden Gloves pub in Camberwell. Alfie was well known all over London, not just as one of the main faces, but also for his role as Vinnie Reece's right hand man.

Alfie was responsible for collecting the revenue from all of Vinnie's enterprises. He was a villain, no doubt about it, but he was one of the good ones. His pedigree was undeniable; an ex bare-knuckle fighter with a reputation earned from blood and sweat, not just from his association with Vinnie Reece, who was also his best friend. Yet although Alfie was one of the most feared men in London, he was also a generous family man with six kids; a real genial sort of guy - at least until someone crossed him, which few rarely did.

He commanded respect, but also respected others, especially when they fought for what they wanted and worked hard to achieve it. If Alfie liked you, you could go far, and, as luck would have it, he liked Joe and me.

We started off running errands for Alfie, menial work that paid far less than burglary, but we knew if we kept our heads down and did all that was asked of us, that we'd soon move onto better things. Sure enough, once Noakes decided he could trust us, we were finally deemed fit enough for more taxing work, which entailed collecting what Alfie called *parcels* from all over South

London.

You didn't need to be Einstein to work out that these parcels were stuffed with large wads of cash, but we never so much as peeked. To interfere with these packages in any way would destroy the faith Alfie had placed in us - which would be very stupid and very hazardous to our health.

It was also a test, from his point of view, of our character, which we both understood well.

There were two elements to this kind of work which were very important to the likes of Alfie Noakes and Vinnie Reece. The first of course, was to return with the money - not an easy task when you have always known poverty. The temptation to take the money and run was almost overwhelming as the contents of just one parcel could have taken us a long way from Peckham. The second element, and by far the most important, was collecting the money in the first place - as at such a youthful age, getting some of the hard cases to take us seriously was no easy feat.

Joe and I gave this a great deal of thought. We knew if we were to be successful, we'd have to be treated as adults, which meant we'd have to act as adults did, letting the people with whom we dealt know that we meant business, not giving them the opportunity to treat us like a couple of naive kids playing at being gangsters.

We made a conscious effort to dress older by buying a couple of second hand demob suits that Sarah altered for us. We wore them with starched white shirts and dark sombre ties, a uniform which helped mc look perhaps eighteen, and Joe a young twenty. We also adopted a morose, almost funereal demeanour when dealing with people, which helped to detach us from any childlike qualities. Physically speaking, both of us looked tough and well capable of taking care of ourselves, which was the one thing we could thank our fathers for, so there was no need to work on that.

The first few times we went out, Alfie accompanied us,

mainly so people would know that we worked for him and that we acted on his behalf, but it was also to see how we operated.

We always worked it the same. I was the mouth, he was the muscle, which is to say, it was me who did the talking, whilst Joe stood behind me and looked menacing. If I was given any excuses, or, as was quite often the case, any abuse, I would take the rearguard position and Joe would step up and leave the person in no doubt about their options, completely unfazed by their size or age. Several times I'd seen Joe deck a man for refusing to part with the cash, but they only did it once. One run in with Joe was more than enough to persuade most people that the boys with whom they were dealing meant business - and believe me, the men we were up against weren't the sort you could convince easily.

Alfie was obviously confident in our abilities, because after two or three stints as chaperone, he sent us out on our own. Me as the voice of reason, Joe, as the enforcer.

At first, we only visited what Alfie called 'the low riskers.' Collecting rent from small businesses and domestic houses. The work although not particularly ethical was legal and not too dangerous, however, there was always the odd nutter who'd rather get a slap than pay up but that just came with the turf.

This was our proving ground and it served us well enough for a short time but we soon out grew it. Alfie realised this even before we did and steadily began to increase our workload, giving us more responsible assignments with higher elements of risk attached. This involved making pick-ups from rowdy pubs and seedy gambling joints as well as dockside bars and sleazy brothels. Rough dives mostly, in tough districts, which didn't make it the easiest work in the world, but Joe and I loved it. The adrenaline was constantly pumping and we had to live on our wits.

Our methods were amazingly effective and within just a few months the investments that Alfie had made us responsible for became the most profitable and hassle free of the entire Reece organisation, which didn't go unnoticed by our employer.

Our reward was to have three more pick-ups added to our roster; the difference being that these were Vinnie's own personal babies, those he had either a specific interest in, or ones he wanted to keep a watchful eye upon. For him, it was his way of saying he trusted us enough to chance his luck. For us, it was our big break and we were determined not to squander it. If we did a good job who knew what could happen and at this point, we were a good ten years ahead of schedule.

The names of these venues were The Acropolis, Red Ruby's and The Pontoon.

*   *   *

To the casual observer, The Acropolis was a busy and fashionable restaurant, which had a clientele ranging from the more affluent middle classes to the lowlier members of London society. But in reality, that was merely a front for the far more lucrative gambling den which could be found in the back room on almost every night of the week. Mostly it was high stakes - strictly for major players only and a nice little earner even without the revenue from the thriving restaurant, which Vinnie also took half of.

His unlikely business partner in this enterprise was a flamboyant queen known as Greasy Phil; an ageing peacock who strutted around with a long cigarette holder clamped between his teeth and wearing a crushed velvet smoking jacket. He was camp, gushing and effete, but his wealthy patrons loved him.

Phil lived above the restaurant in luxurious style with his ninety-two year old mother and a yappy little dog of the terrier variety that was more like a pampered rat. However, underneath all the fluff, Phil had a razor sharp mind and excellent business sense, which had made him very rich and very well connected, which is exactly why he was so important to Vinnie.

The parcels we collected from The Acropolis, which contained Vinnie's cut of the takings, were always wrapped in pink flowery gift paper, which the little Greek did purposely to annoy Vinnie, but to Phil, that was all part of the game.

*   *   *

Vinnie Reece owned Red Ruby's lock, stock and barrel, but what made it such a success was the person who ran it.

Ruby Walsh took enormous pride in the fact that her house was the best in London. Her girls were all gorgeous - not just for whores - but truly beautiful and Ruby treated them as if they were her own daughters - that is if you ignore the fact that she let men screw them for cash.

To compare Ruby's house to the one Vic Cassidy ran, would be to compare a vintage Chardonnay to a bottle of ginger ale. Ruby's clients included the rich and famous, showbusiness personalities, politicians and the aristocracy - it was even rumoured that certain members of royalty had sampled the delights to be found at her establishment.

Ruby herself was warm, vibrant and full of fun, and still very sought after by the more discerning gentleman - although nowadays Ruby only performed herself on very special occasions, or if she took a shine to someone in particular.

She had bright red hair and a very pretty face that just showed the first signs of ageing. Always immaculately made up, she had eyes the colour of emeralds and a wide, welcoming smile, although the first thing men always noticed was her vast bosom that was usually on display in a low cut evening dress that made the very best of her womanly figure. She tottered around her self styled empire in impossibly high stilettos which, if used as a weapon, could inflict more damage than a switch blade.

One rumour had it that Ruby and Vinnie had once been

lovers, another suggested it was not Vinnie, but his brother Ray who she had loved. But whichever it may have been, Vinnie insisted that she be treated with the utmost respect and gave her a large amount of leeway in all dealings. Neither Ruby nor any of her girls were ever, under any circumstances, to be mistreated and any problems, of which to my knowledge, there were none, were to be reported directly to Vinnie. Only he was allowed to determine the best course of action, and only the very privileged and most tactful were deemed worthy to collect revenue from her, so it was indeed a sign of trust that Alfie had put us in charge of such a special investment.

Ruby's place was a very profitable operation for Vinnie Reece but it could have been even more so had he not given her such a free reign. She didn't ever skimp on furnishings or clothes, either for herself or the girls, and they all lived in grand style - but as long as she was happy, then so was Vinnie.

Ruby was ever pleased to see Joe and me and even though her package was usually ready for collection she would always insist we stayed for a drink with her and the girls, who'd fawn and flirt with us mercilessly. We'd be led through to Ruby's extravagant private chambers, seated in one of her best arm chairs and encouraged to stay as long as we liked.

Girls had always been attracted to Joe and those at Ruby's were no different. Compared to the usual specimens that walked through the door he looked like a film star. With his smouldering looks, dark brooding eyes and hard, fit body, he epitomised manhood in its prime. Joe could have taken his pick of the beauties on offer without having to pay a penny, and occasionally, with Ruby's permission, he did so.

I too was undoubtedly in good shape physically, but nowhere near as handsome as Joe; just an average looking sixteen year old with a mop of dusty blonde hair and a broken nose but surprisingly even I drew some admiring glances. However, unlike my friend, I was far too shy to act upon them. Besides, I was in love with Sarah, not that she knew it of course.

After a few months though, I noticed that Joe was no longer interested in going off with the girls either, choosing instead to sit downstairs with Ruby and me. For a while, I couldn't quite understand why this was but then, all of a sudden it dawned on me - with more than a little help from Ruby.

Ruby had recently appointed a new maid; employed to dust and clean and, if necessary, to provide refreshments to waiting clients during busy periods. Her name was Rose Mason. She was barely seventeen, but very pretty and slim with auburn hair and chocolate brown eyes.

On one particular evening, Rose was on hand with a plate of cucumber sandwiches and after both Ruby and I had taken a couple, she offered the plate to Joe, 'Care for a bite, sir?' She asked innocently.

Joe coloured up, 'No thanks' he replied huskily, looking longingly into her elfin face.

'Oh, you fancy a nibble, don't you Joe?' Ruby leered suggestively, nudging me hard in the ribs, 'Just not of a cucumber sarnie, ain't that right?'

Joe, for the first time ever, was clearly embarrassed. 'Come on Sean,' he said irritably, climbing to his feet and heading hastily to the door, obviously expecting me to follow, 'Let's get going.'

Without another word, he bolted from the room. I hadn't even had a chance to move and was still sitting there, balancing a cup of tea and a half eaten sandwich, absolutely dumbstruck. Ruby, meanwhile, was in hysterics and Rose was standing beetroot-faced in the corner. It was clear to every one of us that Joe Cassidy was in love.

*   *   *

The Pontoon was situated near the river in Rotherhithe, at the end of a one way street. It was a dump, but a fully operational club nonetheless, complete with the obligatory stripper on a Saturday night.

A sleazy joint with a sleazy clientele, consisting of a few faces and many local villains, mostly of the small-time variety. In addition to them of course, was the thirty strong outfit who liked to call themselves the Twenty Ones and the club was their base.

The leader of this motley bunch of crooks, and owner of The Pontoon, was Big Jack Anderson.

Jack had made his money on the black market during the war. Even though he had been young enough and fit enough to fight for his country, he had somehow managed to avoid being called up. Instead, he had built up a thriving business supplying contraband and restricted goods to those who were willing to pay the highest price.

The person who had fronted the money for this operation was the same man who had lent Jack the money to buy The Pontoon; none other than Vinnie Reece, Big Jack's cousin.

According to Ruby, Vinnie had done this at the behest of his dying mother, who had also asked him to accept a very low monthly repayment in return. Vinnie had never been comfortable with this, knowing how untrustworthy his cousin was, but it was his mother's last wish, so against his better judgement, he had reluctantly complied. But he knew it was a mistake.

Sure enough, nearly ten years later, Jack had still only paid back a fraction of the debt, just as Vinnie suspected. It wasn't that Jack couldn't afford to pay, he just didn't see why he should. Vinnie was already rich so why should he make him even more so?

Consequently, getting money out of him was like getting blood out of a stone as Jack knew that Vinnie would never welch on the promise he'd made to his mother. Reece was a man of honour, whilst Anderson was most definitely not. However, had the two men not been related, things would have been very different. Jack had a lot to thank his aunt for, because if it hadn't been for her, he would have undoubtedly wound up dead; nobody took advantage of Vinnie Reece and got away with it.

*   *   *

Since the war, Big Jack had expanded his interests to encompass virtually every illegal money spinning enterprise possible. Gambling, whores, smuggling and racketeering were just some of the schemes he had a hand in and the revenue from them financed his lavish lifestyle. Flash cars, fancy women and above all, gold. His most prized possession, and his trademark, were a pair of custom made sunglasses which were gold-plated and had tiny diamonds set into the stems. The glasses, set-off by his bottle black hair, served two purposes; the first was that they hid his shifty dark eyes; the second was that they enabled him to observe all things around him, without anyone actually knowing it.

The dog track, horse racing and cards - poker in particular, which he of course played at The Acropolis, were yet more ways he got rid of his income.

All this high spending kept Jack strictly small time. However, he had ambition in abundance and resented the fact that it was Vinnie, not he, who had control. Jack thought himself to be the bigger man and one day he was confident he would prove it.

For the present, he was content to put on a genial face, but in private, behind closed doors, and to his true confidants, he would plot the overthrow of Vinnie Reece, and, when that happened, when the time was right, there would be a new king in South London. King Jack.

*   *   *

The Pontoon was a lion's den; everyone in there armed to the teeth - knives and switch blades mostly, but the odd one would have a gun. Joe and I wouldn't have stood a chance if things turned nasty. One on one perhaps, but not as a group.

We were perfectly safe though, Alfie knew that Jack would display his purely public face of affection to any members of the Reece mob, to which we now most certainly belonged.

He would always greet us with a smile and a joke, but you could never see his eyes, which I suspected were as cold as stone.

'Siddown boys, have a drink on the house' he would say 'I trust Vinnie is well - give him my regards the next time you see him.' This would always raise a smile from anyone within earshot as they all knew that nobody as lowly as us would come into contact with Vinnie himself. They were right, Joe and I had never even seen Vinnie Reece, let alone spoken to him. But Jack was no fool, he knew we were Alfie's boys and suspected we were being groomed for greater things. To insult us would be to insult Vinnie and Jack had no wish to do that, at least not yet.

We'd share a drink with Jack, and pretend to laugh at his jokes, but as soon as we'd collected his parcel - which would never be soon enough - we'd make our excuses and leave.

*　　*　　*

At the end of our long day, usually well after midnight, we would always report back to Alfie's pub in Camberwell where he would pay us for the work we had done. He always settled up with us on a daily basis, because as he used to say, 'You never know what's gonna happen tomorrow.'

Which was true, but we didn't care; we were young, we had money in our pockets and life was good, and at the time, that was all that mattered. But Alfie was right, we didn't know what was going to happen, which with hindsight, was probably a blessing.

31

Three

With my father away in prison, our house became a far more relaxed place - so much so in fact, that Joe came around every morning for breakfast. He'd sometimes even bring Sarah, which for me, was the perfect way to start the day.

Since my father had been away, Mum had almost returned to her old self. She was using make-up again and taking time over her hair and her clothes, and generally making herself attractive. She would get involved in most conversations and took an active interest in how best Joe should take care of his sister. When Sarah wasn't present, Joe would solicit advice from Mum, about womanly things that he felt he should know, in case Sarah should ever ask. He wanted to be there for her always and was preparing himself for any eventuality.

After breakfast Joe and I would usually go to the Golden Gloves Gym for a work out. The gym was directly above Alfie's pub and also owned by him. It was a boxing club in the most part and Alfie was the coach; a very good one, and the club had won numerous trophies.

On the clean white walls there were photographs of all the contenders that Alfie had once trained and one in particular was of great interest to me; it was of my father.

The picture had been taken when he was around sixteen years

old and showed him from the waist up in a typical boxers pose, wearing a vest with Golden Gloves Gym printed on it. Underneath the photo was a caption which read:

'*George Reilly - 1926 Amateur Boxing Association Heavy Weight Champion, South London and District Under Eighteen's*'.

He looked just like me, only with dark wavy hair, which looked strange because I could only ever remember him with a bald head. Also in the photograph, his arms were unblemished and now they were covered in tattoos, all of which had turned blue and indistinguishable with age. He looked tough though, even back then, with powerful arms, wide shoulders and a lean, muscular torso. All the right equipment for the line of work that he eventually chose.

It seemed that I not only looked like him, but also boxed like him. I turned out to be a natural although, unlike George, I was never a real contender as I just didn't have the determination or the commitment. But I did have talent. Alfie knew it the first time I stepped into the ring. Within just a few short weeks at the club, with Alfie's coaching, I was taking on all comers at The Golden Gloves - and winning. Even against Joe.

Boxing and street fighting are two very different things. I was a boxer, but Joe was very much a brawler. In the street, Joe could beat anyone, myself included. But in the ring, he just couldn't come to terms with all the discipline. Every time Joe got in, Alfie would try to instruct him according to the Marquis of Queensberry rules; 'Feet, Joe— Keep your gloves up Joe— Watch your guard Joe,' he'd say, time and time again. But Joe just got mad and fought the only way he knew how, which was when most of us who had any brains, got out of the ring - including Alfie himself. Joe didn't just get angry, he very nearly exploded and when that happened no power on earth could stop him.

'You're good, Kid' Alfie once told me 'But don't ever get on the wrong side of Joe - he's a fucking nightmare.'

*   *   *

George Reilly was released from prison three days earlier than expected, on the fifth of December 1950. I remember the date well for two reasons. The first was it happened to be my seventeenth birthday and Ruby had thrown a party for me, which even Alfie attended; the second was that my mother spent the night in hospital with suspected internal bleeding and a fractured wrist - a welcome home present from her loving husband.

Had I known that George was being released early, I would never have gone to Ruby's. I had intended to be with Mum when my father got out, knowing how much she was dreading his homecoming. In the days leading up to his release, she had started to withdraw again, and the nightly sobbing which I hadn't heard for eight and a half blissful months, had once again resumed. I knew she was scared and I wanted to be there to protect her. In the time my father had been inside I had grown into a man and was ready to prove to him that I would no longer be brushed aside. If he wanted trouble, I was going to give him a whole lot. In fact, I was going to kill him.

When Joe and I returned from the party it was to an empty house. Mum's friend and neighbour, Ivy Reynolds, was waiting for us when we arrived and told us what had happened. She was a very caring woman, who knew exactly what had been happening over the years; it would have been impossible not to as the wall that separated her house from ours was paper thin. In fact, in our street, Ivy was the only one who genuinely cared about Mum and me - to everyone else we were just a sideshow.

Both Joe and I raced to the hospital, where we found Mum; bruised, bloodied and looking dreadful. She had two black eyes and a split lip, but was sitting up in bed trying hard not to cry. When she saw us, the tears she'd so bravely been holding back

34

welled up and spilled down her face. She flung an arm around both of us, pulling us tightly towards her and wept uncontrollably. Her deep breathless sobs piercing my heart and heightening my guilt for not being there in her moment of need; each salty tear feeding the hatred I felt for my father.

Knowing how much Joe cared for my mother, I glanced across at him and saw an expression on his face that I'd not previously witnessed. It was like staring straight into hell. His lip was curled and his teeth were clenched and he wore a look of such anger and blood lust that, just for a second, I wished George Reilly would walk through the door.

As we hugged her gently, I asked her what had happened but she was unable to properly respond. Each time she tried to tell us she would breakdown in a state of hysteria, so I decided to let her rest, I could pretty much guess what happened anyway.

Eventually we managed to calm her and after some time she finally fell asleep.

Joe and me spent the night on the wooden benches in the corridor outside her ward. I told Joe to go but he wouldn't. Mum meant as much to him as she did to me.

In the morning, the doctor deemed her fit enough to be sent home. Her injuries although painful weren't as serious as at first thought and provided she had plenty of rest with no strenuous activity she could be released.

A taxi dropped us off outside our house and as we stood on the pavement my mother spoke. In a barely audible whisper she said, 'Sean, I can't. I can't go in there, he'll kill me next time.'

Ivy Reynolds came out of her house and almost immediately read the situation. 'Don't worry Sean, luv' she said, 'Rita can stay with me until she feels better.' I felt the tension leave my mother's quivering body instantly.

Ivy was a very sweet little woman, perhaps slightly older

than Mum, who had lost her husband and both her boys in the war. She lived alone in a house filled with the memories of those she'd loved. Her whole life had been dedicated to looking after her family and now it was gone. She was the ideal person to nurse my mother back to full health. I worked all afternoon and evening and needed to bring in the money. Ivy was a seamstress who worked at home, she could be with Rita all day where as I could not. My father would never make a scene at Ivy's. He knew she would call the police. Besides, to make a scene would be to say that he cared and he didn't.

Until I was able to find a permanent new home for Mum, Ivy's would do just fine.

My father needless to say, was nowhere to be seen. In fact, I didn't set eyes on George Reilly until two months later, and after that, I would never see him again.

* * *

In the years that had passed, my feelings for Sarah had not diminished, in fact, if anything, they had grown, yet I still hadn't acted upon them and it was steadily driving me insane. But I had begun to notice that my feelings may be reciprocated. Most notably on the night of my birthday party at Ruby's. When I went to call for Joe, Sarah answered the door. She was normally warm and friendly and on this night I had expected perhaps a little more; a kiss perhaps, or at least a 'Happy birthday, Sean.' But she was anything but warm, in fact, she was downright hostile. 'Oh, it's you,' she said, 'I suppose you're off to celebrate your birthday with a bang'.

Not catching the true meaning of what she said, I replied, 'I certainly hope so,' and grinned broadly.

'Disgusting!' She spat, as if she'd swallowed something horrible.

Joe came up behind her just as I was wondering what I'd

done wrong. 'Don't worry, Sis,' he said smiling wickedly. 'I'll make sure he doesn't catch anything.' He kissed her on the cheek, then turned to her seriously and said 'Any trouble, get in the bathroom and lock the door, I'll be home by midnight.' This was Joe's usual procedure and he was always home when he said he would be. It made Sarah feel safer.

Joe only came home later than promised once, which was that night. The night he spent with my mother and me at the hospital.

On the way to Ruby's I asked Joe about Sarah's strange mood, his response was, 'Don't worry, she's only jealous.' I took this to mean jealous because we were going to the party and she wasn't.

With all that ensued that night, I forgot all about what Sarah had said and indeed what Joe had said about her being jealous. It wasn't until about a week or so later, that I suddenly remembered.

'It must have been because we were going to the party' I thought. But then again, Sarah knew what Red Ruby's was and she would never want to go to that sort of place, so why would Joe say she was jealous. Did he know something I didn't?

I had to find out.

*   *   *

On the morning of Christmas Eve, Joe, Sarah and I were at Ivy Reynolds' house as she'd invited us all for lunch. Joe and Mum were in deep conversation in the kitchen and Ivy was upstairs looking out yet more photos of her boys. Sarah and I were alone in the living room.

It was now or never.

'I'm sorry you couldn't come to my party' I said. 'It was thoughtless of me to have it at Ruby's and besides—' I took a deep breath and threw caution to the wind, '— I missed you.'

Sarah looked at me with her dark, round eyes, her face truly beautiful. At seventeen she'd grown into the woman I always knew she would. She was silent for a long moment, registering the meaning of what I'd just said. Then, just when my nerve was starting to break, she whispered, 'I missed you too.'

For a second I was taken aback. She did have feelings for me and that was surely proof of it. With my confidence wavering, I decided to take a bolder step before my courage deserted me entirely.

'I wondered if you'd like to come out with me sometime?' And then, just to save face, in case of instant rejection, I added, 'Just as friends of course.'

That last bit seemed to sour her mood and suddenly she sounded irritated, 'Oh, you mean you, me and Joseph?' She asked almost scornfully.

Sensing I'd upset her, I blurted out rashly, 'No, just you and me! Perhaps we could go to the pictures?'

'What? And not invite Joseph?' She teased, her mood lightening again, and clearly enjoying my discomfort 'But surely that would be classed as a date, wouldn't it?'

I had been rumbled. She knew exactly what I'd meant but wanted to hear me say it, 'Well, yes. I suppose it would - will you come?' I asked sheepishly.

Sarah smiled widely, 'Sean Reilly, if you only knew how long I've wanted you to ask me. Of course I'll come.' She giggled, took hold of my shaking hand and kissed me quickly on the cheek. Then added mischievously, 'But you'll have to clear it with Joseph first.'

Sarah stood up, almost as if to let me examine the prize that would be mine if I passed the test, smiled at me again, and with a knowing twinkle in her beguiling dark eyes said 'Don't worry, he'll be a pushover.' With that, she turned and glided innocently into the kitchen.

After she'd dropped her bombshell, I sat on Ivy Reynolds sofa and stared blankly at the wall, trying to come to terms with the enormity of the task Sarah had set me; I'd got to ask Joe if I

could date his precious sister, I might just as well have killed myself
there and then.

*   *   *

I had rehearsed what I was going to say to Joe a thousand
times, but as yet hadn't had a good chance to ask him. Every time
I got close something would happen to divert his attention or, if
I'm completely honest, on the odd occasions that I did have an
opportunity, my bottle had failed me.

It was the first week of January 1951 and Joe and I had just
celebrated the last New Year we'd spend together for a very long
time - not that either of us knew this on the cold Wednesday
morning at Alfie's gym, when I'd finally plucked up the courage to
inform Joe of my intentions. It was now or never.

Joe was holding the punch bag for me and I was banging
away at it wearing a pair of old leather boxing gloves. I figured that
if things turned nasty, at least I was in a position to defend myself.
I was pumped up with adrenaline, ready for the onslaught, should
it go the wrong way.

'Joe?' I said.

'What?' Replied.

'What would you say—' I thumped the bag, grateful for the
pause as I tried to summon up the words. 'What would you say
if—.' Again I smashed at the bag, I was drawing out the inevitable,
making it worse, 'Get on with it, man!' Screamed the voice in my
head, 'Just bloody say it!'

'For Chrissakes, Sean, spit it out! What would I say if what?'
Joe already sounded pissed off.

'What would you say if— if I was to ask Sarah out on a date?'
The deed was done.

Joe instantly let go of the punch bag and for a split second
glared directly into my eyes. Then, inexplicably, without further
confrontation, he turned away from me and hung his head low as

if in defeat. He walked slowly to the line of lockers that dominated the back wall of the gym and silently opened the one in which his kit was stowed. He started to take out his clothes, not once looking back and I felt like a traitor. Of all his possible reactions, I'd least expected this.

It had not gone as planned, I'd blown it completely and destroyed our friendship in the process. Not to mention ruining any chance I might have had with Sarah in the future.

Christ I was a fool; I knew how much Sarah meant to him, so what on earth was I thinking?

Looking at Joe's back as he got dressed, I felt terrible, as if I had betrayed his trust. Why couldn't he have just punched me and forgotten that I'd ever asked?

I walked up behind him, but not too close, just in case he started swinging. 'I'm sorry Joe' I said pathetically, 'I love Sarah, but I know what she means to you, If you don't want me to see her then that's...' Suddenly I noticed Joe's shoulder's shaking. I walked around to the side of him so I could see his face, which he was trying to bury in his locker but it didn't work, I could still see it.

He was laughing. Not just chuckling, but very nearly guffawing. 'Christ, Sean,' he said, with tears rolling down his face 'It's taken you since Christmas Eve to finally ask me - Sarah and me thought you'd never get around to it!' Suddenly the reality of the situation finally dawned on me - he already knew.

'You bastard!' I exclaimed, 'How long have you known?'

Trying to get himself under control, but not really succeeding, he laughed, 'I've known for ages - it's been bloody obvious!'

Now starting to feel very stupid indeed, I asked, 'Did Sarah know?'

'Don't worry, Sean, Sarah didn't have a clue, not until Christmas Eve. I didn't even know she felt the same way until about an hour before your birthday party.'

'You mean, she told you!' I was appalled.

'Of course she told me. We're twins, we tell each other everything - you should know that!'

'And you don't mind?' I asked incredulously.

'Of course I don't mind. My best friend going out with my sister, I couldn't be happier. If I can't trust you, then who can I trust? - I know you'll look after her.'

My heart soared. I felt so relieved, so happy.

*   *   *

Later, on the way back from the gym, Joe became more serious. 'Listen, Sean,' he said, 'Sarah's been through an awful lot in her life, some of which you already know about. But there are other things you don't. Things that you probably can't even imagine. It's not my place to tell you what they are, if she wants you to know, then she'll tell you - when she feels ready. But, for now, just take it slow, okay. Be gentle with her, she deserves it.'

*   *   *

That night, I took Sarah out for the first time. Just me and her and no one else.

We went for a drink in a quiet little pub in Camberwell where the lighting was soft and we could just sit in one of the dimly lit corners and talk.

We talked about many things; about our hopes and dreams; about our plans for the future. Her father was never mentioned and when she spoke of family it was only of Joe. Like it was only them, as if their father, and, indeed, their mother, never existed.

As twins, Joe and Sarah's bond had been naturally close, but their upbringing had forced them to become more than that, almost as if they were one. Now I was on the scene, disrupting that bond, but in a good way I hoped. When I suggested this to Sarah, she giggled musically and her eyes sparkled with mischief. 'Yes, Mr. Reilly,' she said, 'I have noticed that you have a very distracting way about you.' Under the table, she took my hand and squeezed it, 'But it's very welcome,' she whispered.

Suddenly our eyes were locked together and so badly I wanted to kiss her, and I suspected she was willing me to. But I couldn't, not there, not in the pub.

I suggested that we should perhaps finish our drinks, then maybe take a stroll, and she eagerly agreed.

Outside, the night air was chilly and Sarah snuggled into me, tucking her arm underneath mine and taking hold of my hand; her smooth, delicate fingers linking perfectly with my rough, calloused ones.

We walked together for an uncertain length of time, our destination unknown and not discussed. We talked sporadically, when the mood came over us and at other times remained quiet, completely at ease in each others company and not at all awkward with the lengthy silences. It was as if we were meant to be together and both of us knew it.

We bought chips from a shop near the river, smothering them in salt and vinegar, then ate them out of soggy newspaper as we strolled arm in arm by the dark waters of the Thames, the lights of the city glittering like a Christmas tree upon its surface to conjure up a magically romantic setting.

And then it happened.

As we leant on the railings over looking the river, I glanced down at Sarah to see her staring up at me. God she was beautiful. Her gorgeous dark eyes, her long lustrous hair, and her plump red lips, just waiting to be kissed and I could resist no longer.

At first, when our lips touched it was tender and gentle, tentative even, as each of us responded to the others kiss. Her lips tasted of salt and vinegar and shandy. Delicious. Added to that was the sweet aroma of her light perfume, making it an utterly intoxicating cocktail from which I would want to drink again and again.

A second passed, in which, I suspected, a psychological barrier came down allowing her to succumb fully to the moment, then her mouth opened and I felt her warm tongue searching for mine. I responded eagerly. Suddenly, as our passion intensified, the remains of our chips were discarded onto the cobble stone ground and we embraced with all the desire that had for so long, been hidden.

'I love you,' I blurted. I couldn't help it. It was true and I had to tell her.

'I love you too, Sean,' she gasped breathlessly, before smothering my mouth with hers once more.

* * *

My world was in a whirl and I couldn't believe my good fortune. As I left Sarah at her door, a little before midnight, the light in her front room still burning brightly and the shadow of Joe's anxious figure standing inside, I wondered how come it was that I was born to be so lucky.

Four

Vic Cassidy was starting to cause trouble; word around the manor said that he was bad-mouthing Alfie and Vinnie, a situation which was wholly unacceptable. The main source of irritation was the fact that Vic was refusing to make protection payments, a crime which could not go unpunished.

Although the house Vic ran was owned by Big Jack, protection still had to be paid to Vinnie as part of the conditions he and Anderson had agreed upon prior to the place being set up. Which in Jack's view, was an unnecessary and demeaning proviso which had always rankled.

However, according to Jack, he no longer had any control over Vic and had washed his hands of both him and the whorehouse completely. Not a very likely story, but one that was difficult to disprove.

The upshot of all this was that Vic owed money and with Anderson suspiciously and uncharacteristically reluctant to do anything about it, the matter was left up to Vinnie to sort out.

At first, Vinnie had instructed Alfie to send a team in to collect the revenue, but they returned with no money, just a number of cuts and bruises - courtesy of some heavies who, it was rumoured, had been supplied to Vic by a firm from the East End.

Vic was getting above his station and had to be put back in

his place.

Alfie wanted to make a statement. He intended to send a full crew - which meant at least six of his best. And that included Joe and me.

Alfie didn't question Joe's loyalty, but Vic was still his father, so wanted to be sure that Joe was comfortable with what was about to happen.

He took Joe aside and asked him if he would be willing to go with the rest of the crew to Vic's; if he was not there would be no hard feelings, he would understand. Joe just looked at Alfie square in the eyes and said with meaning, 'I've wanted to see that bastard squeal for the last seventeen years and there's no way I'm gonna miss it.' That was all Alfie needed to hear. Joe was in and so was I.

The crew was led by Alfie and a guy called Dog Tooth who was Noakes' number one. Tooth towered over most people and was built like a brick shithouse - to get on the wrong side of him was most definitely not a good idea. Four more of Vinnie's hardest came along too.

We pulled up outside a row of three dirty, red brick terraced houses from which Vic ran a stable of over twenty whores. All the rooms were squalid and filthy, but the clientele that frequented them were not the sort to care. On the door of the centre house were two burly guards who none of us recognised. The rumours so far seemed to be true; Vic did indeed have outside help.

As we got out of the cars and marched up to the entrance, the two doormen automatically stepped closer to each other, attempting to block our way. They had obviously been primed to expect trouble, and looked the sort that could handle it. However, they had not been warned about Dog Tooth.

Tooth just wandered up to them and quick as a flash, before they had time to react, banged their thick heads together with a sound similar to that of two eggs cracking. As they fell, he grabbed hold of their collars, lifted them off their feet and effortlessly flung them aside. He then smashed open the door and stepped through into Vic's office-cum-living room, the rest of us following in his wake.

Seated in two shabby sofas were three large men, another two, both with half dressed women on their laps were sitting in arm chairs. Again, none of the men familiar to us. Before the men could stand, Dog Tooth and the rest of the boys flooded into the room and forced them back into their seats, with both the whores being dumped unceremoniously on the floor with their breasts and underwear on full display. Alfie glared at the girls and jerked his thumb in the direction of the stairs. Neither needed any coaxing and made hasty getaways.

'What the fuck's all the noise?' An angry voice shouted from behind a door that led off the room. The door swung open to reveal a man naked from the waist up, trousers undone and no shoes or socks on his feet. He was tall, with jet black hair and tanned skin, he was also clutching a sawn-off shot gun; the preferred weapon of the London underworld. His looks were unmistakable and I knew without doubt, that I was staring at Vic Cassidy.

'Alfie Noakes, as I live and breathe' Vic said, feigning pleasure, 'I'm honoured, I didn't think I was good enough for the likes of you. What brings an old married man like yourself, to a place like this I wonder? Surely ya can't be bored of that lovely wife of yours after all these years? Mind you, she must be gettin' on a bit now. S'pose you fancy somethin' a bit more lively'

Alfie could feel his hackles rising 'Shut up, Vic!' He snapped.

'Come on, Alfie. There's no need to be like that, no need for animosity - see, I'll even put the gun down - sort of a good will gesture shall we say?' Cassidy leant the shotgun against the wall closest to him.

In the room that Vic had just appeared from, Alfie could

see a young girl, not much older than twelve or thirteen. She was sitting up in the grubby bed that her pimp had just vacated.

'Still up to your old tricks, I see' Alfie remarked as he nodded toward the young prostitute in the adjoining room.

'Well, y'know how it is Alfie,' Cassidy smiled leerily, 'Fresh meat's always the best.'

Alfie ignored the remark and continued as if Vic hadn't spoken 'I've heard that you've been learning some new tricks, Vic - tricks which Vinnie don't like the sound of.'

'Ah yes, Vinnie.' Said Vic thoughtfully 'How is poor old Vinnie? Not too good I shouldn't think, if he's reduced to hiring snot nose kids still wet behind the ears,' Vic gestured in Joe's direction, who was standing behind Alfie. Joe lunged forward, but I grabbed his arm to restrain him and Alfie put his hand up, a signal for him to stay calm. Joe shrugged off my grip and stood down.

'I see your having about as much luck taming him as I did' Vic laughed.

'Cut the crap Vic,' Alfie said, nearing boiling point 'You're finished here. Get your stuff and piss off - but before you go I'll take what you owe Vinnie.'

'You're wrong Alfie, this is my place, and I'm not going anywhere,' Vic replied, 'And as for the money, I figure it's only what I'm due for all the hard work I've put in over the years - so I'm keeping it - and that's final.'

'The only thing that's final around 'ere Vic, is you messin' us about. It ends now, and no matter what, you lose' Alfie snarled.

'Oh, I don't think I'm gonna lose anything, Alfie. Nothing's gonna happen cos I've got my boys to look after me.'

'Looks like your boys have got their own problems' Alfie nodded to the men in the chairs.

'Not those boys, but those boys' Vic pointed in the direction of the street. Outside a group of about seven men, all armed with bats, knives, chains and the like, had gathered just beyond the front door. They had obviously been waiting in one of the adjoining houses, primed for an attack and somehow Vic had raised the alarm. Seven men outside, six inside. Thirteen against eight. Long odds but I was betting on us.

'You slimy piece of shit!' Alfie shouted as he charged toward Vic, 'I'm gonna fuckin' kill ya!'.

Cassidy hadn't anticipated this, he stupidly assumed that Alfie would back down when faced with a stronger opposition. Vic's error was to judge his enemy by his own shortcomings.

Faced with the option to either stand and fight, or to make a run for it, Vic made his choice instantly; it was automatic and without hesitation. Faster than lightning, he ran back into the bedroom and bolted the door before Alfie could even get close to him.

In pursuit of his prey, Alfie ran up to the door and attempted to open it, but it wouldn't budge. Desperately he tried again, this time throwing his shoulder into it but still it didn't shift. Then he noticed Vic's shotgun leaning against the wall. He snatched it up, took two paces backwards and blasted the door open. Still holding the shotgun, he then hurled himself into the room.

The young girl in the bed was screaming hysterically with the bed clothes pulled defensively up to her chin. She pointed wildly at the open window, the curtains flapping in the breeze. 'Don't shoot, don't shoot!' She cried 'He went out of the window!'

Alfie ran to the window where he saw Vic Cassidy, still with no shoes on his feet and naked from the waist up, scrambling over the waste ground at the back of the house. Alfie hurriedly lifted the shotgun, took aim and emptied the other barrel but a sawn-off is not an accurate weapon for distance, especially at night and he only managed to clip him. Vic shouted with pain, snatched hold of the arm in which he'd been hit and carried on running, his stride already hampered by his deformed foot.

'Your fuckin' dead, Cassidy!' Alfie shouted 'If you ever show your face this side of the water again, you're a fuckin' dead man - understand?' Whether or not Vic heard this, Alfie couldn't be certain, as he'd already vanished into the night.

Meanwhile, in the house and out in the street, it had all kicked off. Dog Tooth was fighting with two men, both armed with switch blades, Joe had already taken two others out and was in the process of disposing of a third, and the other four of our men seemed to be fairing well enough against a pretty good opposition. I was having a little trouble with the big bastard on me, but a couple of well timed kidney punches and a knee to his groin were starting to take effect. As he finally dropped to the floor, I heard Joe shout 'Alfie, look out!'

Alfie had stepped out of the bedroom straight into the fray and unwittingly into the sights of a man aiming a murderous looking dagger directly at him. Seeing the danger, Joe launched himself into a flying dive, landing on the man and knocking him to the floor just a fraction too late to prevent him from throwing the knife.

As if in slow motion, I saw the knife leave the man's hand and watched in horror as it flew through the air toward its unsuspecting target. Without thinking, I hurled myself in front of Alfie, thrusting him back into the bedroom and forcing him off his feet.

I landed hard on the cheap stained carpet, hitting my head on Alfie's knee as we crashed to the ground, momentarily knocking myself out. I awoke after a minute or two, dazed by the blow, with my vision a little starry and it took a few seconds for me to recover. But slowly, as my eyes cleared, I saw that we had won. Those of Vic's men who were not lying prostrate on the ground had fled; our boys giving half-hearted chase.

I looked behind me, into the bedroom and saw Alfie sitting up on the floor. He was looking at me with a grave expression on his face, Joe too, who had come to my side, was also looking concerned.

'Help me up Joe' I said 'I can't lie around here all night,' but as I moved, I felt an excruciating pain in my side and looked down to see what had been troubling Alfie and Joe. The stiletto blade of the knife had buried itself up to the hilt between the middle two ribs on my left hand side and a slow trickle of blood was seeping from the wound, staining my white shirt bright red.

'Oh shit.' I said quietly, suddenly feeling woozy. I attempted to sit up, but as soon as I did so, I promptly passed out.

*   *   *

I awoke in the back seat of Dog Tooth's Ford Prefect, a car which was ridiculously small for a man of his bulk. Alfie Noakes was in the passenger seat, his body and head twisted round so he could talk to Joe who was sitting on the back seat, with my head in his lap. I was laying across the seat, my knees bent up and my feet resting on the door handle. Joe was pressing a now extremely bloody rag - which turned out to be his one and only jacket - hard against my wound. 'Listen Joe,' I said in a rather limp attempt at bravery, 'I know we're close, but don't y' think Sarah might get a bit jealous?'

Joe looked down at me and smiled 'Stupid bloody git' he said.

'Don't worry son,' Alfie shouted down to me, as if being stabbed had caused me to go deaf 'I'm gonna get you the best medical attention money can buy.'

I obviously couldn't be taken to a hospital, too many unwanted questions about how my wound had been inflicted, so Dog Tooth was driving me to a safe house where a doctor on Vinnie's payroll would tend to me. 'I'll never forget what you two boys did for me tonight,' Alfie went on, 'You saved my life, and I won't ever forget it - I'll make sure Vinnie knows it too.'

The safe house was in Wandsworth; the doctor who lived there had, at one time, managed to get himself into a bit of trouble with the law - performing illegal abortions for girls too young, or too scared to go to the proper authorities. Vinnie Reece had bailed him out by calling on one of his influential friends, who had magically made the charges disappear. Since then, the doctor had returned the favour by performing services such as the one he was about to do for me.

He informed me that my wound, although serious, was not life threatening as miraculously the blade had somehow missed all my vital organs. I would however, require bed rest for a week, maybe two and after that to refrain from any strenuous activity for another month.

Alfie stayed long enough to make sure I was comfortable then Dog Tooth took him home, with the instruction to keep him informed of my progress.

Joe stayed with me the whole time. The doctor cleaned the deep hole in my side and sewed me up using ten neat stitches, then he and Joe helped me upstairs to a crisp, freshly made bed, which is where I remained for the next five days.

Each day, Joe, Sarah and Dog Tooth would visit. Sarah at first, had been inconsolable, convinced I was going to die - probably due to Joe's elaborate distortion of the facts. Finally, I made her ask the doctor, who explained that I was going to be fine, which caused her, rather touchingly to cry with joy. To my eternal shame, I found this emotional response very gratifying - she obviously felt as deeply about me as I did her.

Sarah would stay with me in the evenings whilst Tooth and Joe would turn up at different times throughout the day - whenever work allowed. Alfie also visited twice, the first time bringing with him a basket of fruit that his wife had prepared.

On the day before my release, Joe was with me when the doctor came rushing into the room. He started making a fuss around me, plumping up my pillows and straightening the bed clothes. 'What's going on Doc?' I asked 'It's only Joe, not royalty.' The doctor's response left Joe and me stunned.

'Mr. Reece is downstairs, and he wants to see you.'

*   *   *

Joe and I stared transfixed at the bedroom door, awaiting the imminent arrival of the legend we'd heard so much about. We had never seen Vinnie so didn't quite know what to expect, but when the door finally swung open, it certainly wasn't the smiling matinee idol that entered.

Vinnie Reece stood at the bottom of the bed. He was tall, slim and impeccably dressed in a pin-striped tailored suit. Looking supremely fit, he had chiselled features which were healthy and tanned and a pencil thin moustache that was trimmed to perfection; his black wavy hair was sprinkled with silver at the temples and brushed neatly back with Brylcream. The only thing that marred his otherwise perfect features was a long scar that started on the bridge of his nose and finished in the centre of his right cheek, a thin line which remained white against his golden skin.

Vinnie Reece in all his impressive glory cut an extremely dashing figure. A figure that now stood smiling down at Joe and me as I lay in my makeshift hospital bed.

As he spoke, his voice was deep and warm, the South London accent betraying his Peckham roots. Roots which he was determined never to forget. Under different circumstances, it could be the voice of terror, but on this occasion, it was thankfully amiable and cheerful.

'So you're the two lads I've heard so much about,' he said, shaking both our hands firmly. 'Alfie's told me, and he doesn't lie.

He's also told me that he owes you his life. That means a lot to me personally. Him and me go way back. Best friends, I suppose you'd call us. Kinda like you two.'

Vinnie sat down on the edge of the bed and thought for a second, then continued 'Listen boys, I know George Reilly and Vic Cassidy, and I'm sure I won't upset you when I say I think they're both pieces of shit - but that's between me and them.' He paused again, 'Whatever I think about your fathers doesn't reflect on you.' He looked directly at us, a serious expression on his face, 'Understand this. If there is anything I can ever do for you boys, just ask. If it's within my power, I'll do it. I'm in your debt - and I never forget who I owe.'

Joe and I were stunned into silence, neither of us knowing what to say to follow Vinnie's last statement. Luckily, Vinnie lightened the mood for us, 'So, Sean, when do you get to escape?' He asked. We chatted with Vinnie for five or ten minutes, answering all his questions and telling him about ourselves, and he seemed genuinely interested. Then, when at last there was a lull in conversation, he almost reluctantly stood up and made to leave. He shook both our hands again and said sincerely, 'Look after yourselves boys - and remember, if you need anything, anything at all, just ask.' He then turned, walked to the door and left.

We had known of Vinnie Reece for most of our lives, but apart from the fact that he was obviously very rich and powerful, had never really fully understood why people held him in such high regard. But now, after meeting him, we most definitely did.

Five

Eventually my stitches came out and I was deemed fit enough to go home, on the understanding that I was not to do anything physical which could result in my wound re-opening - a thought which didn't really appeal.

Joe had finally asked Rose out for a date amid whoops and hollers from Ruby and the girls. She had said 'yes' and they had been inseparable for the couple of weeks since. It turned out that they had many things in common and Joe even made her laugh - something which he did with very few people.

They made an extremely attractive couple. Joe, tall and darkly handsome; Rose, slight and delicate with a beauty that was fresh and irresistible.

To celebrate Joe and Sarah's eighteenth birthday, the two of them, together with Rose and me, went for a slap up meal at The Acropolis. We were seated at the very best table and drank champagne all night. We were even served by Greasy Phil himself, who couldn't have been more accommodating - especially now the word was out that we were tight with Vinnie Reece.

The night was a great success. Rose and Sarah hit it off straight away and we all ended up getting more than a little drunk. I'd never seen Joe so full of fun; teasing Sarah and myself mercilessly about when we were getting married; telling jokes - which was certainly out of character; and generally having a good time. He appeared to be carefree, whilst being very attentive to Rose and openly showing his obvious affection for her. It was probably the happiest I've ever seen him.

*   *   *

Our work routine returned to normal, although I let Joe take care of any trouble if it arose. My side was healing nicely, the scab that had formed was hard and crusty, although still quite sore to touch but another couple of weeks and I'd have been back to normal. Unfortunately, I suffered a set back which both Joe and I would remember for the rest of our lives.

*   *   *

My mum had spent the last couple of months at Ivy Reynolds' place where she had been well taken care of. She had recovered from her injuries, but was still in a very fragile state of mind, knowing that my father could return to the house next door at any time. This made her constantly on edge. She jumped at every sound and still had trouble getting through a whole night without having a nightmare.

I took it upon myself to find her new accommodation, and did so with the help of Alfie. A small terraced house near his pub had recently become vacant, the tenant having died a few weeks before. The house was owned by Vinnie, and on his say so, Alfie had agreed to let my mother live there under the protection of the Reece mob as a special favour to me. Living there, right in the heart of Vinnie's territory, there was no way that George Reilly could get at Mum - not without risking his own life anyway, so it was the perfect solution.

Whilst Joe and I were sorting things out at the new house, Mum and Ivy went around to the old one to gather all Rita's knick knacks that she had accumulated over the years. Nothing of any value, just personal things that were special to her. Mum was very reluctant to go into the house, but with Ivy's coaxing and the promise of a new home, she eventually set foot over the threshold.

Wishing to spend as little time there as possible, she and Ivy set about their work quickly - Ivy never leaving my mother's side for a moment, just in case her courage failed her.

They had been in the house for about an hour and had filled four large cardboard boxes with Mum's personal things, which they had stacked in the kitchen, when they heard the back door bang open. Then they heard the destructive sound of Mum's boxes being thrown to the ground, the delicate items within smashing into tiny pieces as they landed on the hard tiles.

When she heard the noise Mum's resolve crumbled. She began to shake violently and her whole body involuntarily shrivelled away from the sounds in the kitchen. She caught hold of the sofa to prevent herself from collapsing. Slowly, her face contorted in a silent scream and, induced by panic, a small trickle of urine ran down her legs and formed a puddle on the living room carpet. The tears that she'd bravely held back all morning were now streaming down her hollow cheeks, her worst fears having become terrifying reality. George Reilly had returned. Two months away and he'd chosen that precise moment to come back; a moment, I would find out in months to come, which was more than just a cruel coincidence.

'Where are ya then, you fuckin' whore,' his brutish voice yelled out, 'Think you can fuckin' leave me do ya? Well you've got another thing comin' my girl - nobody leaves George Reilly - nobody, understand?'

My father was in a foul rage; one which my mother knew from bitter experience would leave her either hospitalised or dead. Ivy knew it too and was determined to protect her friend. She tentatively opened the kitchen door from the living room and walked bravely in.

'Now George, please calm down, Rita is coming with me—' Ivy began.

'Shut your fuckin' interferin' face you old cow and get out of my bleedin' house.'

'I.. I... I'm sorry George, but I won't—' Ivy continued defiantly.

'Yes you bloody well will, you nosy witch' George shouted, and slapped Ivy hard around the face with the back of his hand sending her lurching backward over the kitchen table.

'Get out!' My father shouted once more, showing her his hand for a second time, threatening to hit her again. But even though Ivy was stunned by the blow, she somehow managed to remain calm and clear headed. Seeing her opportunity, she swiftly ducked under my father's raised up arm and darted towards the door.

'Hang on Rita!' She shouted 'I'm going for help.' Then she directed her gaze at the big man bearing down on her and hissed, 'And you, you evil bastard, can rot in hell!' With that, Ivy ran from the kitchen, down the hall and out through the open front door into the street.

* * *

I had just laid a bit of old carpet in the parlour of Mum's new house and Joe was in the process of painting the kitchen. However, with nothing else more for me to do, I decided to go on to Mum's old place ahead of Joe; he was almost finished and would meet me there shortly.

On the way back alone, I took a slight detour, calling in at the greengrocer's to buy myself an apple, which meant that I approached our house from the rear instead of the front. It made no odds though as all I had to do was nip down the alley and hop over the fence into our tiny yard, entering the house through the back door.

However, before I even got to our fence, I heard her scream.

*   *   *

When Joe had finished, he took off his grubby overalls and placed his brush into a bowl of white spirit to soak. Then he put on his jacket and left the house, glancing at his watch as he locked the door. He had completed the paintwork sooner than expected and was pleased to see that he was only about ten minutes behind me. Joe smiled, he should arrive just in time for a nice cup of tea.

After a brisk walk, Joe eventually turned onto the street where we lived, passing the bright red telephone box that stood on the corner. As he became level with it, its door opened and Ivy Reynolds stepped hurriedly out, almost crashing straight into him.

'Whoa, there Ivy' Joe said, as he caught her arm, stopping her from falling over 'What's the rush?' But the moment he looked into her tear filled eyes, noticing the purple bruise that was beginning to form on her cheek, he instinctively knew.

'Rita?' He asked softly.

Ivy could do no more than nod. She eventually managed to whisper 'I've called the police' but it was too late, Joe was long gone.

*   *   *

I vaulted over the fence and cleared the distance to the back door in two strides. Bursting into the kitchen, I saw my father standing right in front of me, an evil grin on his face like some demented Cheshire cat.

'Well, well, well. The return of the prodigal' he sneered. I was horrified to notice that the white vest he was wearing was speckled with tiny drops of blood, which I had a nauseating suspicion belonged to my mother.

'Where is she, you bastard, what have you done to her!' I demanded.

'That's not very nice now, is it?' He replied calmly 'Surely no way to greet your old man after all this time.'

'Fuck you!' I spat 'What have you done to Mum?'

'Oh, your mother's fine, just taking a little lie down - ain't that right Rita?' He directed this into the living room and I caught the sound of a very faint groan. 'See?' He continued 'She says she's fine.'

'You sick bastard, what have you done?' I demanded again, this time marching forward with my fists clenched. My father pushed me back violently with both hands, slamming them hard against my chest, sparking a twinge in my side that reminded me I still wasn't healed.

'Don't you want to stay and chat with me?' He mocked.

'Fuck you!' I shouted again.

'That's no way to talk to your father now is it boy?' He taunted, obviously enjoying himself, 'It's time I taught you another lesson.'

He had barely finished speaking before he swung his big round fist toward my face - but I was ready and blocked it effectively with my left arm. I countered quickly with a right upper-cut which landed squarely underneath his wide jaw, making him stagger backwards, and I was delighted to see the look of total surprise on his face. I had stunned him for the first time ever, and in doing so, noticed just the slightest element of doubt flash in his demonic eyes.

However, he recovered quickly and tried to find my face again with his other fist. This time, I just ducked out of the way and punished him with a heavy shot to the kidneys.

'I see you've been practising' he winced 'But you've got a long way to go before you get the better of me, boy.'

I was well up for it now, with adrenaline pulsing through my veins feeding my hatred, 'Come on then, arsehole - show me what you've got,' I invited.

George launched a full scale attack, throwing punch after

devastating punch. He was similar in height to me, but bigger physically which he used to good advantage. I noted that age had slowed him a little since we had last fought, which gave me just enough time to block or swerve some of his most damaging blows and counter with my own. I was conscious not to expose my injured ribs, which made my guard a bit one-sided and quite a few of his shots managed to get through but my anger made me almost impervious to the pain. He was a hard bastard who loved to brawl and I sensed that he would be even more dangerous if I hurt him, but I was more than holding my own and was gratified to see, after matching him blow for blow for what seemed like an eternity, that he was finally, visibly, tiring. He was thirty-six and had the beginnings of a gut, I was seventeen and at the peak of physical fitness and the difference was starting to show.

Slowly, just like Alfie had taught me, I started jabbing to the head and body with shots designed to exhaust him further. 'Come on, boy,' he taunted, 'I've taken worse than this from girls - is that all you got?' His words were brave but his voice was hoarse and his breathing laboured. I didn't answer. His goading would not distract me from the task I had set myself.

Even though George wasn't going to go down easily, I could almost taste victory - for the first time in my life, I knew I would walk away the winner. I was going to beat him. I was pretty sure too, that I was going to kill him, just like I promised Joe I would three years before. George Reilly's time had come and so had mine.

He was weakening now, quickly, the power draining from his punches and I sensed he had nothing left. But I did. And I let him have it all.

The sheer ferocity of the assault I launched caught him off guard, and his tired expression changed to one of disbelief as he finally realised that he was going to lose.

My final attack was an expelling of hate, an unleashing of

vengeance for all the abuse that my mother and I had suffered at his hands - a barrage that had lasted all my lifetime and most of hers. Now it was time for pay-back.

I moved forward all the time, pummelling his face and body with a shower of crippling punches. Blow after blow of hard, well aimed jabs that quickly turned his face into a red and bloody mass. I heard his nose shatter and watched with glee as his eyes became puffy and swollen as he fought desperately to keep them open under the swelling.

Finally, his massive arms dropped limply to his side in defeat and he rocked on legs barely strong enough to support his weight. He was finished.

Unable to restrain myself I launched the final hammer blow that landed like a wrecking ball on the side of his face. Instantly he dropped to his knees, then slowly rolled forward. My father's forehead smashed onto the floor and his front teeth made a sound like fingernails on a blackboard as they slid along the tiles before snapping off. He was out cold. I had beaten him fair and square. But my anger was still raging, I wanted to kill him. I was going to kill him.

Then, I heard a groan from the living room and my anger evaporated in an instant, with all thoughts of my father vanishing from my mind as I turned to look through the doorway I saw what I had desperately hoped never to see.

My mother lay on the living room floor with her legs crumpled awkwardly underneath her. A small stream of blood was trickling from her open mouth; her eyes were wide open and her breathing was quick, like a panting dog. There were lacerations on her neck and chest and her collar bone was protruding, obviously broken. Her face was covered in bruises, most of which had already turned black and she looked dreadful, like she'd been through hell, which I'd no doubts that she had.

61

'Oh my God, Mum!' I cried, as I ran to her and fell to my knees by her side. 'What's he done to you?' I went to lift her, then thought better of it for fear of causing more damage.

'Sean?' She said in a barely audible voice 'Is that you?'

'It's me Mum' I said, choking back the tears which threatened to overwhelm me 'I'm sorry... I'm so sorry - if only I'd been here with you—'

'It's alright luv' she whispered bravely, her leaking eyes finding their way from the ceiling to my face 'It doesn't hurt now, not any more.' I looked at her, unable to speak, the emotion bursting inside of me. For long seconds I fought to compose myself, but I couldn't prevent the tears from dribbling down my cheeks. I knew she was dying. 'Stay with me Mum, please... stay with me—'

Suddenly, her eyes darted away to a place behind me, 'Look out!' She tried vainly to scream, but her voice was too weak and I was unable to properly grasp what she had said until it was too late.

Just as I turned, a large hobnail boot connected with my damaged side and an excruciating pain shot violently through my whole body. With his astonishing strength and miraculous resilience my father had somehow managed to rouse himself, climb to his feet and stagger up behind me. Then, focusing on a small patch of blood on my shirt, which had seeped from my weeping stab wound, he had aimed a kick hard at it.

I reeled in agony, clutching my side desperately, but he kicked again, unleashing an explosion of pain that left me defenceless. His face was a grotesque mask of blood and bruises, but if his injuries hurt him, he certainly didn't show it. The only thing that was plainly evident was that his rage had returned, and as I tried in vain to retreat from him, I cursed myself for believing him finished.

Again, he kicked and I felt my head spin as I fought off the blackness that was threatening to wash over me.

'Thought I was done for, didn't you boy?' He growled. 'I'm

twice the man you'll ever be - no one fucks with me and lives to tell the tale.'

As I lay sprawled, utterly helpless on the floor, writhing in agony, my father staggered to the drinks cabinet and selected a bottle of Vodka. He considered it for a moment, almost as if deciding whether it was worth wasting, then took hold of the neck and slammed the base hard against the teak cabinet, smashing the bottom off it and letting the contents escape onto the carpet. What was left was a lethal weapon with long, razor sharp teeth, that he waved menacingly in my direction.

I somehow crawled to the corner of the room and pushed myself painfully up the wall onto my feet, leaving a wide smear of blood on the patterned wall paper as I did so. I had to ready myself for his attack.

My father grinned at me, exposing the bloody gap where his front teeth used to be, 'Now boy' he said, spitting pink saliva as he spoke 'It's time for your final lesson.'

Suddenly, with a loud crash, the lounge door burst open, very nearly coming clean of its hinges and Joe, with a face as black as death, hurled himself into the room. Pausing only briefly to take in the horrific scene, he leapt over the sofa in a single bound and flew towards my father, who had turned to face his new opponent.

George Reilly, held the broken bottle out in front of him in an effort to impale Joe's racing body, but Joe's lightning quick reflexes allowed him to swerve aside, away from the pointed shards. In the same movement, he grabbed hold of my father's wrist and tried to force the bottle from his grip, but George held fast. Even in his damaged state he was still incredibly strong.

The two men wrestled each other for a few moments, neither giving much ground until Joe head-butted George, catching him hard across the bridge of his already shattered nose but, although dazed, he kept a tight hold of the bottle.

With his wrist still being held, my father tried to swing the broken bottle in between him and Joe, his last chance to determine the outcome of a battle he was otherwise destined to lose. As he did this, he pushed the bottle as hard as he could towards Joe's stomach.

Joe was ready. He twisted aside and used the momentum of my father's thrusting arm to his advantage, directing the serrated spikes of the broken bottle up and round into George's exposed throat. It pierced deeply into the soft flesh of his neck, puncturing the Adam's apple and making a soft squishing sound like a ripe tomato being crushed.

Joe took a step back, instantly releasing his hold on my father. It had not been his intention to inflict such a dreadful wound, it had merely been an instinctive reaction for self preservation and he was shocked by what he had done.

George stood there paralysed for several seconds, a gasping, gurgling sound emanating from his throat and a look of utter disbelief on his face. The glass bottle was sticking hideously out of the spurting wound, as his body suddenly went into uncontrolled spasm, and then, abruptly it stopped and he slowly fell backwards into the drinks cabinet. The glass doors of the wooden unit smashing around him as he slid slowly to the floor, dead.

Joe raced over to me, took my arm around his shoulders and helped me over to where my mother lay. He carefully lowered me to my knees; the agony in my side burning like a hot iron. Joe knelt down on the other side of my mother and together we delicately lifted her head and held it in our hands.

Her breathing had now slowed and her face was calm. There was a slight smile on her swollen lips as she gazed up into our faces. 'Mum, Joe's here,' I said, 'We're both here.'

Her lips pursed together briefly, as she told me to 'Ssh' and then she smiled again. 'My two brave boys' she mouthed, her voice less than a whisper 'Thankyou for loving me... it meant so much.'

As she slipped away, I could hold back no longer. My shoulders started to shake and I wept unashamedly for the first time in twelve years.

As I looked across at Joe, I noticed a solitary tear rolling slowly down his cheek. We didn't speak, words were not needed.

Six

The police, called by Ivy, arrived some minutes later to find Joe and me bent over my Mum's dead body. My father's blood spattered corpse lay over on the far side of the room, the broken bottle still jammed in his throat. The police, upon witnessing this macabre scene, immediately grabbed hold of Joe and me, slapped us in handcuffs and carted us swiftly off to the station.

My memory of the next few hours, is all a bit blurry as I was still reeling from the dreadful events of the afternoon, but one thing is for certain; at no time did I consider either myself or Joe guilty of a crime. We had acted in self defence and my father had died as a result of his actions, not ours. Besides, there was no guilt in killing an animal like him.

However, I was soon to find out that in the eyes of the law, even with mitigating circumstances, the death of George Reilly had to be accounted for, and we were going to have to stand trial in order to clear our names. Furthermore, if found guilty, we faced lengthy prison sentences.

*   *   *

After my wound had been re-stitched, I was led down to the holding cells to join Joe, who had been taken there ahead of me. We would be held there on remand for three days, until our court appearance.

Although we were not sure what the outcome of the trial would be, our brief, supplied courtesy of Alfie, suspected the jury would take my case into consideration. Having lost both my parents in such horrific circumstances he thought it unlikely that they would punish me further by sending me to prison.

However, Joe's case was not so clear cut. We were hoping for a verdict of manslaughter and if not a suspended sentence, then perhaps a lenient one. But it could be construed by a jury that Joe had in fact intended to kill George Reilly, and that his was a pre-meditated act, fuelled by the need for vengeance. This would make it a verdict of murder which would carry a much stiffer, maybe even a life, sentence. Whatever the outcome, we thought that Joe would have to serve some sort of time, so set about working on a contingency plan based on this eventuality.

Our main concern was for Sarah's safety. If Joe was imprisoned, then Vic Cassidy, if he ever returned, could become a very real threat to her. So, on the assumption that I would go free, we agreed that I should move in with Sarah, as her guardian not her lover. Our relationship, at this point, was not a sexual one - I was waiting for Sarah to be ready and had no wish to push her, which Joe knew and respected. For the time being I would sleep in Joe's room.

We discussed the possibility of Sarah moving into the house that Alfie had offered my mum but decided that she would be happier where she was and if I had the locks changed she would be secure enough there.

We could have moved into my house but at that time it held too many bad memories and I needed to be somewhere other than there.

The only thing we couldn't immediately find a solution for was my impending National Service, which was looming rather rapidly on the horizon. Who would look after Sarah while I was away in the forces? This, we both agreed, needed a lot of thought.

* * *

Joe and I said our goodbyes in the cells below the courtroom, just in case we didn't have an opportunity later. Then, as we at last heard the guard coming to collect us, Joe turned to me and said, 'I'm sorry about Rita. She was sort of like my mum too y'know? At least, I loved her like she was.'

'I know.' I replied.'She loved you, too.'

'I was too late to save her though wasn't I.' Joe said bitterly.

'We both were.'

'Yeah.'

'But at least my old man got what he deserved,' I said.

'Yeah, I suppose.' Joe said, then added, 'You remember that night a long time ago, when we made that oath - about you killin' George and me killin' Vic?'

'Yeah. I remember.' I replied.

'Well half of it's sort of come true, ain't it. Your old man's dead ain't he?'

'I know. And I know what you're thinking. Vic's still out there - he's still a threat.'

'Yeah, he is. And I don't want you to do anything stupid. It's just that I'm worried about Sarah, that's all. She needs protecting from him.'

'Listen. If I walk free from the courtroom, don't worry. I'll look after her. And if Vic comes sniffing round, well, I'll take care of it. I promise. I'll complete the deal we made - even if it hasn't gone exactly as we planned. I'll finish it.'

'Thanks, Sean.' Joe said, 'I know you will.'

'Don't worry about it. I'm just sorry for the way it's turned out, that's all.'

'Hey, I'll be fine' he grinned, and just before the guards took us, he added with a wink, 'The bastards won't know what's hit 'em.'

When the verdict was delivered, mine was read first.

'Not guilty,' was all that I remember them saying, and although tremendously relieved, I was not surprised. I was far more anxious to hear of Joe's fate.

I glanced across at Sarah, who sat prettily in the audience, wearing a smart blue dress. I nodded to her, trying to give her strength and she managed an uncertain smile back, but I could tell she was falling apart inside.

Then Joe's verdict was announced.

On the charge of murder; *'not guilty.'*

Thank God. Not murder. Joe, myself, Sarah and everyone who knew us breathed a huge sigh of relief.

On the charge of manslaughter; *'guilty.'*

That was what we expected. Our QC suspected that to be the most likely decision. Again I glanced at Sarah, and saw that she, like the rest of us, was waiting anxiously to hear the sentence.

The Judge cleared his throat and in a dull, monotonous tone, began to speak. Right from the start the signs were ominous. He pointed out that although the crime was one of passion, and an act of self-defence, it was still a very violent crime which could not be atoned for lightly. He even said, which I thought to be almost laughable, that even though George Reilly was a very unsavoury character, he was still a father, whose son had been robbed of a parent. When I heard this, I wanted to shout out, to tell the Judge that if it wasn't for Joe, it would be me who was dead and not George Reilly, but I knew it was too late. The sentence had already been decided upon and I felt a surge of dread in my guts as at last it was delivered.

Nine years.

For a moment the court was stunned and there was absolute silence whilst the severity of the sentence sank in. Nine years.

Joe was eighteen, even with good behaviour, he wouldn't be out until he was at least twenty-five. I couldn't believe it, it was inconceivable. Slowly I turned and looked over at Joe, but he just stood there proud and erect. No expression on his face to betray the bitter disappointment I know he felt.

Suddenly, Sarah let out a long wailing cry and began to sob inconsolably. Rose was there also and she too was crying. After a few moments the whole assembly erupted, with everyone shouting at once, even our QC who, infuriated by at what he'd just heard, picked up a whole wad of papers and threw them into the air to show his utter disgust.

I noticed Vinnie Reece sitting alone at the back of the court, massaging his forehead with the palm of his hand, the shock on his face clear to see. Alfie and Ruby, who had also come to wish us well, stood up and began hurling abuse at the Judge and a bailiff had to manfully force them back into their seats.

Such was the commotion that the Judge had to use his gavel several times to restore order.

As Joe was escorted from the dock in handcuffs, he turned and looked back at me and stared hard into my eyes. He nodded and I, understanding his meaning, nodded back. 'Take care of Sarah,' he was saying, 'Keep her safe.'

He saw that I understood and allowed himself to be led from the court room.

*   *   *

Sarah was devastated. She'd already taken the death of my mother badly, who she'd grown extremely fond of over the past few years. Rita had become like an older sister to her, someone to whom she could go to for advice and confide in, not least about her feelings toward me.

Then there was Joe, who was the only constant in her life. He had always been there to care for her, to provide for her and to protect her. Theirs was a tight bond which had been, until now, unbreakable.

Now he was gone, her world was shattered.

I was the only person upon whom she could rely and if I showed any signs of weakness or wavered even slightly, I knew she would crumble. I'd always known that she was fragile, but until now, I hadn't realised just how delicate she really was. What Sarah needed was security. She needed to know that I'd be there for her no matter what and I was determined that I would be. I had given my oath to Joe and I fully intended to keep it. The simple truth was that I loved her, and the role I had been forced to play, was one that I gladly accepted.

The other truth is, that if I'd not had Sarah to look after, I may well have gone to pieces myself. The death of my mother still haunted me and caring for Sarah would help to ease the pain of her loss.

*   *   *

I moved in with Sarah and had all the locks changed as Joe and I had agreed. I even took the added precaution of fitting bolts to all the windows as being too careful was not something that applied when dealing with Vic Cassidy.

As the days passed, we slowly came to terms with the absence of Joe. Life simply had to go on, even though Sarah found it terribly hard at first, but as the days turned into weeks, she at last began to brighten.

Living together felt right for both of us and the love we had, grew into something even deeper. It still wasn't a sexual relationship, but there was no rush. After all, we had the rest of our lives.

*   *   *

Once things had settled down, and Sarah's anxieties had eased, I returned to work. Alfie assigned me a new partner; a nice enough guy in his middle thirties, who what he lacked in brain power, made up for in brute force.

Eddie Carter was certainly not the most intelligent bloke under the sun, but he was amiable enough, although lacked the necessary tact and diplomacy to deal with Big Jack and Greasy Phil. Eddie's methods tended to border on the thuggish so, at Alfie's insistence, I took the lead in all business matters. Eddie had no problem with this, even though he was by quite a few years, both in age and experience, my senior.

Eventually, things started to get back to normal. Sarah and I had settled into a comfortable routine and Eddie was proving to be a reliable and physically capable partner.

Time was beginning its healing process and Sarah was starting to smile once more, showing the first signs of returning to her old self. Even the threat of Vic Cassidy turning up unexpectedly was looking less likely and our previous vigilance became gradually more relaxed.

We visited Joe as often as we were allowed, and kept him up to date with life on the outside. He appeared to be fit and well, and assured us that he was fine, convincing neither of us fully, but Sarah always felt happier after visiting.

*   *   *

It was several weeks before I felt able to return home, to the house where Mum had died. But it had to be done as things needed to be sorted out.

I took a deep breath and stepped inside. The house smelled of her and it surprised me to find it comforting. I let the aroma fill my nostrils for a few moments, savouring the memory of Mum.

I braced myself before going into the kitchen, wary of what I might find. But as I looked around the room, I saw no evidence of the mess I'd been expecting. No blood, no broken crockery, no remnants of my last visit. I should have realised that Ivy would never have let my mother's always tidy house stay in the state it had been on the night Rita was murdered.

I wandered cautiously into the living room and glanced anxiously at the spot on the carpet where Mum had passed away and was relieved to find no trace of her blood on the carpet. Ivy had been thorough and considerate, I would make it up to her, I promised myself. My neighbour's efforts made me feel much more at ease than I ever thought possible, making my homecoming far less painful than it might otherwise have been.

What was left of my mother's personal belongings had been placed carefully into a cardboard box and left neatly in the middle of the floor. I carefully inspected the contents of it and found memories of my mother attached to each item I touched. Articles of no value except to the people who had loved her. They needed to be with someone who appreciated them, someone who understood their worth.

I removed two items that held special memories for me personally. The first; a gold crucifix on a thin golden chain, which I placed around my neck. Mum had worn this every day for as long as I could remember. The second, a pair of small solid silver stud earrings, which had once belonged to my grandmother, that Mum had worn only on special occasions. These I intended to give to Sarah on our wedding day.

The remaining items, I left in the box, which I took around to Ivy's. 'Thanks for everything Ivy' I said, 'I thought you might like to have these. I know Mum would be happy if you did.'

'I don't know what to say luv,' Ivy replied, obviously quite touched, 'It would be an honour.'

I stayed for a cup of tea and a chat, and told her that I would be keeping hold of the house, although not actually living there. I also asked if she would keep an eye on the place for me, and offered to pay her for this. Ivy agreed but would accept no money,

'It would be my pleasure,' she said.

I thanked her once more and returned to my house, which of course it now was with both my parents gone. I was not sure that I would ever live there again as it held too many bad memories for me but I knew that I didn't want to sell it. Although for what purpose I should keep it I had no idea. I suppose it was that I always saw the place as Mum's and mine, not my father's, and for that reason alone I couldn't bring myself to part with it.

I was just about to leave when a thought occurred to me. Had George left anything in his cellar? I went to the under-stairs and peeled back the carpet that concealed my father's secret lock-up. It was padlocked, as expected, but the police had given me my father's set of house keys and together with them, on the bunch, was the one to the padlock. I inserted the key and the lock snapped open. I then lifted the trap-door and reached for the light switch, which was just below the lip of the opening. The naked bulb of the cellar illuminated the small room, revealing it to be empty. The old bastard had cleaned it out but I didn't care as I wanted nothing of his anyway, although it occurred to me that the cellar may prove handy one day.

I closed the trap-door and re-locked it, then covered it carefully again with the carpet, to make it completely invisible. As I tucked my father's keys back into my pocket, instinct told me that it would be a good idea to keep this hide-away secret.

Seven

Joe was sent directly to Wormwood Scrubs and processed into the prison system. His civilian clothes and possessions were confiscated and packaged into a cardboard box, which would be kept in storage until his release.

Wearing a sombre grey prison uniform and carrying the bedding supplied to him, Joe was escorted to his new home on 'E' wing. Every door and gate he passed, slamming closed behind him and the metallic sounds of the keys turning in the locks reminding him that he was now in a closely guarded cage.

As Joe was led through into the prison's vast interior, the loud jabbering of the inmates suddenly fell silent and all eyes focussed on the new prisoner - the young kid with the impressive reputation who had killed a big time villain.

Joe kept his gaze firm and steady. He'd anticipated a reaction, it was only to be expected and they were clearly sizing him up. Then, as he and the prison guard made their way up the metal staircase, toward the second floor landing where Joe's cell was located, a loud wolf whistle broke the silence. This immediately signalled a torrent of heckling, which resounded deafeningly around the whole wing. The noise drowned out even the heavy clang, clang, clang of both the guard and Joe's shoes as they struck the iron mesh flooring of the galleried landing, on route to their destination.

The guard eventually stopped outside the designated cell with its thick metal door already open.

'Right, Cassidy, in you go,' he said loudly, trying to make himself heard above the din and pointing the way with his lovingly polished side stick. 'Pick a bunk, and store your kit in the cupboard - and no talking after lights out.' He then turned and left Joe alone, the other inmates still jeering loudly.

After a while, the furore started to die down allowing Joe to concentrate more on familiarising himself with his new home.

The cell was tiny, far smaller than he'd imagined, with whitewashed brick walls and a cold concrete floor. At the far end was a small barred window that was set just above head height and the only thing visible through it was the dull grey sky. Along the right hand wall was a bunk bed, each bunk with its own thin pillow and stained beige mattress. The wall opposite had a small writing desk with a wooden chair tucked underneath and adjacent to this was a little wooden cupboard.

Joe opened the cupboard and was surprised to find someone else's belongings already in there. For the first time it struck him that he wouldn't have the cell to himself and was curious as to who he'd be sharing with. After making some room, he stowed his spare clothes and unfolded his bedding then proceeded to make-up the top bunk. When that was done he leapt up onto his new bed.

Stretching out, he considered his new residence for a few seconds. It certainly wasn't the Ritz but the bed was reasonably comfortable with only the odd spring sticking out of the thin mattress. He decided that it could have been much worse and said out loud with a smile on his face, 'That's it Joe, keep those standards high.' Then he closed his eyes and went to sleep.

*   *   *

'Hey, that's my bunk!' Joe heard the voice shout which roused him from his slumber. He turned his head toward the sound and opened one bleary eye.

There was a skinny little man standing a few feet away from him. The man had an unruly moustache and big yellow teeth with an unlit roll-up dangling limply between them. He looked fidgety and very nervous.

'Eh?' Joe murmured sleepily.

'I said, that's my bloody bunk you're lyin' on,' the prisoner repeated but without much conviction.

Joe opened his other eye and gave his new cell mate one of his long meaningful stares as he considered the creature standing before him. He was not impressed.

'Not any more it ain't,' Joe replied, and once again closed his eyes.

*   *   *

Billy Finn was a habitual criminal who'd spent most of his life in and out of prison. He'd been arrested many times, for burglary mostly, but with a bit of shoplifting and car theft thrown in for good measure.

He was a weedy, insignificant character but the inmates very rarely harmed him because he was amiable and eager to please. They certainly didn't respect him as he was too willing, too subservient, a glorified slave who was constantly at their beck and call. It didn't matter what they asked him to do, he was always happy to oblige. It was Billy's way of surviving, the least painful way of serving his time, and it worked. Nobody gave him any trouble, he just wasn't worth it.

Because Billy was so inconsequential to the other prisoners, he was privy to many clandestine conversations and secret dealings. Often he was the runner between one inmate and another, passing on details that were deemed too risky for the conspirators to be seen discussing in person. Even though many weren't aware of it, Billy became the eyes and ears of the prison and what he didn't know, wasn't worth knowing. In his head he stored a wealth of accumulated knowledge and if someone had bothered to take an interest in him, to actually get to know him, they would have found a loyal and devoted friend, who held valuable information on nearly every prisoner and illicit scam in the Scrubs.

Billy was not an aggressive sort. He was placid, amiable and good natured. But when a new prisoner, and a much younger one at that, had moved into his cell, stolen his bunk and interfered with his belongings, he felt he had to try to exert some authority.

But that hadn't worked. The man lying on his bunk hadn't even flinched.

In fact, one look into his new cell mate's eyes told Billy that this was no ordinary prisoner. He had been around enough villains in his time to recognise those that had class and those that didn't. And this kid definitely had it. Strength, confidence and physical power, all the necessary requirements, but there was something else too, something that Billy couldn't quite put his finger on, but it set this lad apart from most others he'd met. He knew also that he wouldn't be the only one to see it and that could add up to a whole heap of trouble.

As his new cell mate began to stir once more, Billy slipped back into his far more familiar role, that of the amiable nobody.

*　*　*

Joe yawned and sat up on the bunk, swinging his legs around so that they dangled over the side. He rubbed the sleep away from his eyes with his fingers and when his vision had cleared he noticed the same skinny creature standing in front of him that had woken him earlier. This time though, the creature was smiling. A hideous grin that showed its big yellow teeth.

'Watcha, Mate. Sorry about before, you took me by surprise. I weren't expectin' no one. My name's Billy - Billy Finn. I'm ya cell mate.'

Joe jumped to the floor and stretched. He again looked at Billy, and considered him for a long moment. Billy stood looking up at him, smiling broadly with his eyes wide open and his head nodding slightly, rather like an eager dog waiting for his master to throw a stick for him. He looked almost comical.

Although Joe tried, he couldn't hold his stern expression. He shook his head and grinned in defeat. Joe held out his hand and Billy snatched it immediately, shaking it wildly.

'Pleased to meet ya, Billy. I'm Joe. Joe Cassidy.'

Suddenly, the colour drained from Billy's face, the smile replaced by a look of dread. In the last week he'd heard that name mentioned many times around the prison. This was the man who had killed George Reilly.

George had been a big man, a well known face, with many friends in prison and now those same friends were looking to get even.

'Oh, shit.' Billy said.

*   *   *

It was apparent, right from the start, that Joe's time inside wasn't going to be easy. Everyone seemed to know who he was but Billy had given him the low down on those who were known associates of George. Most of these were hard bastards whose intent could not have been more obvious. Every time Joe turned around he'd see one of them glaring at him or a group of them conspiring together. He knew they were just biding their time and waiting for the right moment to strike.

Over the weeks that followed Joe kept himself very much to himself, the only person he had any proper conversations with was Billy, who would jabber on about anything and everything. Joe didn't mind though. He liked Billy, perhaps because he was his polar opposite or that he was a bit like an over excited child. But he was good company and he helped the time pass a little more

79

quickly.

Every morning and evening Joe would exercise thoroughly - determined to leave prison in as good a shape as when he arrived. Twice a day he would do two hundred push-ups and two hundred sit-ups followed by a hundred squat thrusts, the work-out helping to focus his mind.

Even though Joe tried to keep out of trouble, it had proved impossible. Already he'd had three fights, although two with strictly second rate opposition and Joe had ended them with just one punch, both protagonists being knocked out cold.

The third fight though, was with much better competition, a big, heavily tattooed bull of a man with enormous muscles, who picked his moment well.

The man, who came at him with a razor in the showers, had a reputation for being tough and did put up a pretty good fight but in the end it had finished with his balls being crushed and his nose split in two, whilst Joe came out of it unscathed. This did much to improve Joe's standing amongst the general populace and the respect he was given, in the most part, was greatly increased. From then on many of the other inmates who had previously made their dislike for Joe blatantly obvious, seemed to under go a change of heart. Billy said the word on the grapevine was that they no longer wished to exact their revenge over the death of George, preferring instead to let bygones be bygones. The real reason though, he suspected, was that they had all seen what Joe was capable of and weren't keen to receive the same treatment.

There was one prospective challenger however, that Joe knew would be an entirely different proposition. His name was Frank Blades.

Blades was the big man in the Scrubs. The undisputed king. He was also the obvious leader of those conspiring against Joe and according to Billy, rotten to the core. Furthermore, Blades was known to have been a good friend of George Reilly.

Frank was a prime specimen of manliness. Almost exactly the same build as Joe, although just a few years older, with a powerful physique and an animalistic nature. He had a Mexican style moustache that stopped just short of his jaw line and a small 'V' of a beard which sat under his lower lip. His hair was an unnatural mahogany colour which, Billy said, he dyed with boot polish.

Blades was a prolific homosexual who was not picky about whom he targeted, although he particularly enjoyed it if his victims fought back. But when they finally succumbed - which, one way or another, they always did, they were left bloodied, bruised and broken. After Frank had finished, they were usually subjected to gang rape by his crew, who were all of the same sexual persuasion as their leader.

Being the dominant male was something that delighted Blades and proving his superiority among the prison population gave him enormous pleasure.

Joe was conscious of being watched by Frank and knew that he was being evaluated for strengths and weaknesses. Joe also knew it was just a matter of time before their paths crossed.

*   *   *

Joe enjoyed the visits by Sarah and myself although made no mention of his troubles, especially those relating to Frank Blades and the friends of George Reilly. All he would say was that he was doing okay and prison was not too bad.

Rose also visited Joe for a short time, but each time she saw him she became more and more distressed. She loved him so much and it broke her heart to see him in prison but no matter how she tried she could not bring herself to tell him what she so desperately wanted to - that she was pregnant with his child. Rose was just a young girl, only barely eighteen and the man she loved, the father of her baby, could not be with her. Her parents were good people, but they didn't understand. To them it was shameful and immoral. They said it was against God's will and if she insisted on keeping the bastard offspring of Joe Cassidy, then they would be forced to have nothing further to do with her.

Rose felt as though she had no one to turn to. She couldn't burden Sarah with her problems, not after all she had been through herself and Ruby, well she would understand, but there would be little she could do to help. So Rose kept it bottled up and pretended that everything was okay. But it wasn't.

She fretted over her predicament for several heart-rending weeks, her emotions in turmoil, before finally deciding on what to do. There was no way Joe could help her and if he should ever discover what she was hiding from him it would only make things harder for him. He had enough to contend with without a baby to worry about too. So, for Joe's sake, she knew she had to leave London. There was no other way. She had relatives in Northamptonshire, an aunt and uncle, who were more liberated than her parents. With them, she could start a new life - both her and her baby.

And so, three months into Joe's sentence, with no prior warning, Rose disappeared.

None of us had any clue as to why. She left no forwarding address and when I approached her parents on Joe's behalf, all they would say was that she'd gone away and would not be returning.

It fell to me to tell Joe of this and when I did, it came as a terrible blow.

For the first time since I'd known him, it seemed as though he'd finally been beaten.

Eight

Since Sarah and I had moved in together the work rate had been steadily picking up, with Eddie and me working all hours. It was profitable though and Alfie always saw us alright with a little extra cash here and there to make it worth our while, so neither of us minded. My only grievance was that because I was so busy I didn't get to spend as much time with Sarah as I would have liked. Nevertheless, I made certain that she was rarely alone and had Ivy go round to sit with her as often as possible.

However, Ivy couldn't be with her all the time, and on two occasions when Sarah had been all alone, I had come home to find her cowering in the bathroom with the door locked, convinced that a noise she'd heard was Vic Cassidy trying to get into the house. But those were in the weeks shortly after Joe was imprisoned and thankfully her nerves had eased somewhat since. Now, if Ivy could not be there for some reason and she was in the house by herself for an hour or so, she was far more able to cope. But I tried not to let it happen often.

On one particular occasion though, it was unavoidable. The reason for this was that Big Jack had done a vanishing act and I had been forced to wait three hours at The Pontoon for him to return. He had not been making his payments, deliberately fobbing Vinnie off with one excuse after another. Something didn't smell right and

Alfie wanted me to get to the bottom of it. However, by 1am he still hadn't shown his face, so Eddie and I called it a night. I went home furious, not only because I had wasted my time, but also because I knew that Sarah had been on her own for several hours and she'd be getting anxious.

Normally she wouldn't sleep until I got home, so when I put my head around her door to tell her I was back I'd usually find her in bed reading. Invariably when I did this she would get up and come downstairs in her dressing gown, where she would give me a kiss and a hug and then make us both a mug of cocoa, which we would sip whilst catching up on each other's day.

However, on this particular evening, I was disappointed to find Sarah asleep. Not wishing to wake her, I watched her lovingly for a few seconds, then quietly closed her door. Exhausted, I went straight to bed and as soon as my head hit the pillow I was out. I was a light sleeper, though, always on the verge of consciousness and ever aware that Vic Cassidy could return at any time.

It seemed as if I had only been asleep for a few seconds when I felt the weight of someone else on my bed. Immediately I awoke to see a dark figure looming over me. Convinced that it was Vic Cassidy come to murder me in my sleep, I quickly span around and grabbed him by the shoulders, pulling him straight over me and on to the floor on the other side of the bed. I threw myself on top of him, pinning him to the carpet with one hand clamped on his throat, my other fist held high about to be smashed down into his face. A split-second before I did so, I heard a voice scream, 'Sean, NO!'

Immediately the red-haze cleared from my eyes as I looked down and saw Sarah's beautiful face, partially obscured by the loose dark strands of her long hair. Her big dark eyes were full of terror and I quickly released the grip on her throat, and she gasped with relief.

'Sarah?' I said dimly.

'Surprise!' She croaked with a slightly mischievous smile.

'What are—?' I began, but she interrupted.

'I don't want to sleep on my own anymore, Sean - I want to sleep with you.'

Suddenly I realised that she too was completely naked and I found it impossible to avert my gaze. 'What—?' I began, but my mouth dried up with nerves and I had to swallow before I could continue. 'Are you sure? - I mean, do you want to—?'

'Yes,' she said firmly. 'More than anything, I want to.'

I tore my eyes away from her body and stared into her face with another question on my lips, but she gave me a look of such excitement and allure that it extinguished all doubt. 'I want to,' she said again, and as if to underline it, she took hold of my hands and placed them upon her. Her skin was so soft and smooth, like brushed velvet. I could smell her perfume, which was sweet and slightly musky and added fuel to the fire that was now burning in my loins.

Slowly, I moved my hands over her breasts which lay heavily against her. Sarah smiled again, as I explored them with my fingertips and I was unable to resist a peek as I felt her nipples spring out under my touch. My mouth watered at the sight of these ripe, round berries and I bent down and took one between my lips, working it with my tongue, until it stood proud and erect. Then, I did the same with the other and Sarah gasped with delight.

She reached out and placed a palm softly on the flat of my stomach, stroking it gently, gradually inching it downwards to find the proof of my arousal; her other hand slipping around behind me to caress my buttocks.

Straddling her nude, I could suddenly feel the warm curls of her womanhood tickling my scrotum, then the electric touch of her fingers as she found my fierce erection.

'I see you're properly awake now,' she whispered huskily.

'I love you,' I blurted.

'Then prove it,' she replied wantonly, seizing me hard and directing me downwards.

As I found her, she cried out passionately and I lowered my head and kissed her open mouth, taking away her voice but finding her hot tongue eager to greet mine.

* * *

That night we made love time and again but the first time was fast and quick, an answer to the animal passion that had built up in both of us, just wild, uninhibited sex. The months of waiting finally exploding in a crescendo of lust and wanting and when it was over, we lay in each others arms, revelling in the joy of our love.

We never wanted that night to end. It was as if, for those few hours, we were the only two people in the world.

When at last the dawn came and the first few rays of sunlight shone through the thin curtains, we lay together, our bodies entwined, Sarah's head resting on my chest, her breathing slow and calm, neither asleep nor awake. Gently stroking her hair, I quietly said, 'Marry me?'

Sarah, slowly lifted her head and stared lovingly into my eyes, 'Yes,' she replied, and once again covered my mouth with hers.

* * *

The following weeks were spent in a blissful haze and both Sarah and I were truly happy for the first time in our lives. Our happiness was tinged with guilt however. Whilst we were making the most of our life together, Joe was locked in his cell, away from those he cared for; unable to be with the woman he loved. Nevertheless, he was genuinely pleased to hear of Sarah's and my engagement and wholeheartedly gave us his blessing.

Tragically though, our happiness was to be short lived.

Nine

I found out what my father had been, or indeed who he had been within the East End underworld completely by accident, and the knowledge shocked me.

Dog Tooth had discovered that Vic Cassidy had, as previously suspected, hooked up with the new firm from across the river, who had ambitions to expand into Reece territory. A situation that would no doubt spell trouble. To add further fuel to the flames, Tooth also found out that Big Jack Anderson was having dealings with this new crew, too, and was, by all accounts, becoming one of the main players. This explained his absence over the last months and the increasing disregard with which he treated his debts to Vinnie.

I happened to be present when Dog Tooth was relating all this intelligence to Alfie, at the Golden Gloves. It was all very intriguing, but I'd had a busy night and was finding it hard to stay interested. All I wanted to do was get home and climb into bed with Sarah.

Then suddenly, Dog Tooth said something that piqued my interest immediately.

'Seems like Mottola's gonna go all out for Vinnie's turf,' he said. 'And if he does, I reckon we got a war coming.'

'Not *Benny* Mottola?' I asked, with dread.

'Yeah. Benny the Bull they call him — how do you know 'im?'

I told him that Benny was my dad's best friend and a light bulb flicked on in Dog Tooth's head as he suddenly remembered who my father was. 'That's right,' he said incredulously, 'That's what I was told, Benny and George were running this firm together! Sorry, Sean, I just forgot who your dad was - I mean with you and 'im being so different an all—'

'It's okay, Tooth,' I said. 'I'm glad I'm not like him.' Dog Tooth was a good bloke and there were few better to have standing next to you in a scrap but, with the best will in the world, he could sometimes be a bit dim.

I left Alfie and Tooth chatting as I headed home but I couldn't get the information out of my head, and couldn't sleep for thinking about it. It seemed incredible that the threat from across the Thames was being orchestrated by Benny Mottola, my father's best friend - the same man I'd despised from the first moment I set eyes on him.

A couple of days later, Sarah wasn't feeling particularly well, having picked up a bug from somewhere or other, so I went to visit Joe on my own. With his sister not around, Joe and I were able to talk more freely and I told him what I had learned about Benny. Then Joe told me what he knew and, more specifically, about my father being friendly with this man Frank Blades and the rumours that he, too, was linked to this firm from the East End. He then related what had been happening to him in prison and I didn't like the sound of it one bit.

On the way home, my head ached from what I had been told. I was concerned for Joe, of course, but I was also concerned with the situation as a whole. If Benny had now allied himself with Vic Cassidy and Big Jack, all the rotten apples were in one big, very nasty barrel.

I could also see now how George Reilly knew my mother was home on the day that he killed her. Joe and I had made no secret of the fact that we were helping mum to move and, in passing, I had mentioned it to Big Jack, a fact I had forgotten all about until now.

Anderson, in turn, must have related this seemingly trivial snippet of information to my father.

God how I cursed my stupidity. I knew that George's appearance on that fateful afternoon was just too much of a coincidence. The day that ended with the murder of my mother and my best friend being sent to prison.

I needed to speak to Vinnie, deciding that he should be aware of what I knew. Also, Vinnie was the one person I knew who could help Joe. If Mottola had a man like Blades on the inside doing his bidding then Vinnie certainly could too. Indeed, someone with Vinnie Reece's power could get anything done.

Two hours later I found myself in the passenger seat of Dog Tooth's car on route to the Reece residence.

*　*　*

Tooth turned his little car into a small but exclusive cul-de-sac made up of about six large three storey houses. The biggest of them all stood in the centre, with what seemed like every light ablaze. Both on the driveway and along the road expensive cars were parked nose to tail. Rollers, Bentleys and Jags, flash motors that belonged to rich people. All of them guests at Vinnie Reece's party.

After parking up, we got out the car and walked up to the entrance where Tooth rang the doorbell. As we waited, we listened to the muffled sounds of conversation and music coming from inside.

After a minute or two the door was opened by an attractive blonde woman in her early forties wearing a lot of jewellery and an off-the-shoulder evening dress. She looked every inch the sophisticated and well bred lady of the manor. Then she opened her mouth.

'Ello Toothie, luv' she gushed in broad cockney 'And you must be Sean. Pleased to meet ya darlin', she shook my hand lightly, whilst giving me the once over, 'Quite the looker aren't ya sweetheart', she said approvingly. 'I'm Peggy, Vinnie's wife. He's expecting you. Y'know where duncha Toothie?' Dog Tooth nodded and Peggy tottered away back to her influential guests.

I followed Tooth up the first flight of stairs, passed several elegant people in deep conversation. We reached the landing and Tooth tapped three times on one of the doors that led off from it. 'Come in!' Vinnie shouted from his inner sanctum.

We entered the plushest room I had ever seen. Oak panelled walls, ceiling high book shelves and heavy wooden furniture. It wreaked of money and good taste. Vinnie Reece was sitting in a green leather armchair, a brandy in one hand, a cigar in the other, which glowed as he took a puff. Once again he looked immaculate. Black evening suit, crisp white dress shirt and a thin silk bow tie.

'Thanks, Tooth' he said, 'Go get yourself a drink, while I have a chat with Sean would ya?' Vinnie waited for the door to close behind Dog Tooth before he continued. 'Hello, kid, good to see you again', he said. 'Sorry to 'ear about y' mum - she was a good woman, God rest 'er soul. I knew her years ago and she didn't deserve what happened to her.'

'Thanks' I said, a little surprised.

'Drink?' He asked, 'Whiskey, brandy?'

'Whiskey, thanks.' I replied, feeling a bit overawed.

He poured my drink into a crystal tumbler and as he passed it to me, waived me to another leather armchair 'Siddown, son and tell me what's on your mind.'

I sat down as ordered, wondering where to start.

'Come on, kid, how bad can it be?'

'You gotta help Joe,' I said suddenly. 'I'm sorry to be so blunt, Mr. Reece, but you did say if there was anything you could do to just give you a shout, well, I suppose now I'm shouting.'

'That you are, son.'

'Sorry, Mr. Reece. I really am, but it's really important that you help.'

'My name is Vinnie, son. And if it's that important that I help, then you'd better explain.'

'Okay. Well it all goes back to Benny Mottola and my father...' I began, then continued unswervingly to relate everything I knew.

Vinnie listened in silence, never taking his eyes from me, giving me his full attention and puffing periodically on his fat Cuban cigar.

When I had finished, I said, 'That's why Joe needs help. I mean he can handle himself, I don't know of no one better, but in there, with this Blades breathing down his neck and Mottola determined to—'

Vinnie held up his hand to silence me. A frown on his face, obviously deep in thought. After what seemed like an eternity, he finally spoke.

'It all adds up kid. I know of Mottola and he's a right evil bastard. I got a whisper that it was 'im an' yer dad who kicked one of my boys to death in Wandsworth a few years back. Just after the war. It was real nasty, real bloody. They just about had to peel the guy off the street. Blades is bad news. A fuckin' psycho who kills just for the thrill of it. I reckon he's sliced up more people than you've had hot dinners - although it weren't that that got 'im sent down, it were car theft. Got caught nickin' somebody's Jag if memory serves me right.'

'And Big Jack?'

'Jack's a worm. Always has been, always will be.'

'So you think what I said might be possible?' I asked.

'I don't just think it son. I know it. I never trusted Jack. And if he got wrapped up with Georgie Reilly then I 'ate to think what they was gettin' up to - especially now I know Mottola was involved too. All of 'em together. An' now Benny's runnin' the show and lookin' to take over my manor. You did good kid. Very good. Thanks for the warning.'

'What are you going to do now?' I asked.

'I'll handle it son but for now the only people you can trust apart from your girlfriend are me, Alfie and Dog Tooth.'

'And Joe,' I said.

'Yeah, and Joe. But he could be in a whole lot of trouble inside. He's the one who killed your dad and Mottola's gonna want blood.'

'Is there anything you can do to help him. I mean, there must be something—' again, Vinnie held up his hand to silence me.

'Don't worry, Sean, I'll give Joe a guardian angel - someone Benny's boys won't dare touch.'

'I hope it's someone you can trust,' I said, getting a bit above my station.

'I should fuckin' hope so,' smiled Vinnie, 'It's my brother.'

Ten

Joe was angry. Frustrated that he'd been unable to stop Rose from leaving. He needed an outlet for his anger before it consumed him and the target he'd chosen to vent this wrath was Frank Blades. Joe was sick of waiting for Blades to make his move and of having to constantly watch his back. Enough was enough. It was time for him to take control.

*   *   *

Frank Blades and his boys were standing in a group at the far side of the exercise yard, talking and joking amongst themselves as Joe and Billy eyed them from the opposite end.

'Are you sure about this Joe?' Billy asked for the hundredth time.

'I'm sure,' Joe replied, his eyes never leaving the huddle of men, his attention focused on the tall man with the Mexican moustache who stood at its centre.

'Take this then,' Billy said, pulling makeshift knife he'd secretly fashioned in the metalwork shop, disguising it from casual view by the flap of his jacket.

'Keep it, you might need it,' Joe said, 'cos if I lose, they might just come lookin' for you too.' He gave his friend a wry smile and a wink, before stepping off towards Blades. Billy just stared after him, open mouthed, the comprehension of what Joe had said slowly sinking in. The little man closed his eyes and said a silent prayer, not for Joe but for himself.

* * *

Joe strolled up to the pack that surrounded Frank Blades and roughly barged through them until he was standing nose to nose with Blades who didn't even flinch. Frank's gang made to retaliate but Blades calmed them quickly, 'It's alright, boys,' he said, 'I think he just wants to give me a kiss.'

Joe's black eyes stared directly into the pale blue of Frank's. 'You want me Blades?' Joe enquired menacingly.

Frank smiled, as if he was a tart being propositioned, 'Oh yes, Cassidy, I want you,' he replied with relish 'I want you very much indeed.'

'Fine. Boiler room then, in five minutes,' Joe said.

'I'll look forward to it,' Frank responded flirtatiously.

Joe held his stare for a moment longer, then turned and barged his way back through the pack.

* * *

Joe had already bribed a couple of guards to make themselves scarce for half an hour, ensuring that the boiler room was left unattended. The room was dark and humid, and smelled of sulphur. The ceiling was covered in a labyrinth of pipework that dripped boiling water onto the dusty stone floor. The walls were dotted with thermometers and temperature gauges, all of which suggested that something was about to blow. They were not wrong.

Joe stripped off his jacket and shirt and hung them on one of the gauges. Then chose a position in the centre of the room which would give him plenty of space for manoeuvre. As he stood there in his thin white prison issue vest, his muscles shining with sweat, the door opened and Frank Blades strode in - closely followed by six of his soldiers.

'See you brought the girls with you,' Joe said sarcastically.

94

'Just a little insurance Cassidy. Besides, I do so love an audience,' Blades replied, smiling confidently, his men sniggering like a pack of hyenas eager for their turn at the kill.

Blades also stripped down to his vest and handed his clothes to one of his goons. As he did this, Joe studied him. His arms were large and his fists were like cannon balls, he was a man of undoubted power who knew how to put it to good use. Joe had watched him in action many times in the exercise yard and had been impressed by what he saw. Blades was probably the toughest Joe had ever faced so he'd have to be extremely careful.

Blades took a moment to limber up. Stretching and twisting and touching his toes, then when he was completely ready, he raised his fists to signal that the fight had begun. Joe followed suit.

'Ave him, Frankie!' One of the onlookers encouraged.

'Kick his arse!' Suggested another.

Both fighters circled cautiously, anxious not to give ground, both lusting for first blood. As they came within reach of each other Frank released a lightning left jab which landed squarely on Joe's mouth, splitting his lip.

He was fast but Joe had seen the punch coming, although too late to duck out of its path. It was a good shot, well timed and well aimed. Even more powerful than he'd expected.

Another jab, this time to the right, but Joe just managed to move his head aside in time and Frank's fist whistled past his ears.

'Go on, Frankie!' More encouragement from the troops.

Blades then went for the body, missing Joe's ribs by an inch as he swerved clear and the heavy punch struck nothing but air, leaving Frank slightly out of position. This allowed Joe his first strike - a blistering upper cut which connected firmly under Frank's chin, sending him reeling backwards.

Blades recovered quickly and smiled with admiration as he rubbed his jaw, 'Not bad, Cassidy. Not bad at all,' he said patronisingly. But the confident manner with which he shrugged off Joe's punch was betrayed by the surprise in his eyes. This young scrapper was good.

Blades raised his fists once more, but immediately Joe threw a quick one-two and Frankie reeled backwards again. This time he was visibly shaken by the speed of Joe's attack.

Blades blinked his eyes to clear his head, but Joe launched a hammer blow into his ribs knocking him sideways and then another to the side of his face which sent Frank crashing to the floor.

'Come on Frankie, stop pissin' about, 'ave the bastard!' One of the crowd shouted.

Blades sat on his backside, looked up at Joe and smiled trying not to betray the shock of being knocked to the floor in a fight for a very long time. Never before had he felt such hard punches. The fight had just started but already he had a cracked a rib, he was certain of it. Frank was in the scrap of his life and it would take all his guile to win it.

There was blood in his mouth, and he could feel with his tongue that one of his front teeth was hanging by a thread, knocked loose by Joe's attack. Frank put his fingers in his mouth and pulled it free, leaving a bloody gap. He showed no pain, no emotion as he cast the tooth carelessly aside and wiped his gooey fingers on his trousers afterwards.

'Y'know boys, I think he means business,' Frank laughed, but there was no humour in his voice.

Joe stepped towards him, his fists clenched, willing Blades to get up. 'C'mon then, tough guy, I thought you were gonna give me a fight - thought you were gonna show me something a bit more than all the other wankers who've tried.'

'Oh, gimme time, Joey boy, gimme time. I ain't even started yet,' Blades replied menacingly. He was now in the squat position, about to stand, or so it seemed, when suddenly he shot out his foot and whipped it around the back of Joe's legs, forcing him over onto his backside. With deadly speed, Blades sprang on him, driving his knee forcefully into Joe's stomach as he landed and firing off several damaging jabs to his face. He grabbed Joe by the hair and wrenched his head upwards then butted him viciously on the forehead.

The crowd went wild. This is what they had come to see. This is what they had expected.

Blades jumped up with Joe laying dazed and winded at his feet and slammed a steel toe cap into his ribs. 'That's it, I'm gettin' nicely warmed up now,' he said, 'How's it for you, Joey boy, is this a bit more like what you wanted? Did those other wankers show you such a good time as this?' Again he blasted Joe in the ribs with his heavy work boot.

'Am I a disappointment, Joe? Do you find me so very—' he kicked again, '—very—,' and again, '—unsatisfying? Or am I putting on a good enough show for you now?'

The assembled crowd were laughing now, loving every second.

Joe was winded. He lay on the ground scrunched up in agony, his rib cage exploding with pain, his head pounding. But there was to be no reprieve. Blades reached down, grabbed him by the scruff of the neck and pulled him to his feet, butting him again for good measure, this time on the bridge of his nose. A violent burst of pain shot through Joe's head but he remained on his feet and forced up his guard to defend himself against Frank's ruthless onslaught. The shots raining down on him from every angle. Punches to the head, neck and body, kicks to the kidneys and groin. Joe was blocking well but still taking a heavy battering.

Moving defensively backwards, he finally came hard up against a wall, finding himself unable to retreat any further. There was no other way but to stand and take the beating.

'Is this good enough for ya, eh, y'snot nosed little brat?' Frank was in full force now, his adrenaline pumping, his anger at its peak. 'I'm gonna fuckin' kill ya, y'know that boy, don'tcha? I own this fuckin' prison. It's mine -understand? Mine. And no fuckin' killer of Georgie Reilly is gonna take it from me. You're nothin' boy and your arse is mine.' Frank was now holding Joe by the throat with his left hand and clubbing his face with his right.

But Joe was made of strong stuff and with iron will focussed his dark eyes on Blades. He'd heard enough of Frank's shit and had taken enough of his beating. It was time now to do what he knew he could. He put all his strength into his arm and forced Frank's hand away from his throat. Blades' long feminine finger nails ripping the flesh on Joe's neck as they released their grip, leaving four diagonal gashes across his Adam's apple.

With his other hand, Joe reached down, grabbed Frank firmly by the balls and squeezed. Hard.

Joe delayed his next move for just a second to witness the look on Blades' face as it contorted with pain. Then Joe head-butted him with such force that it made a sound like two rocks colliding. Frank's nose split down either side as the bone snapped and blood spurted from the hideous wound. He screamed in agony, silencing the cheers of the shocked onlookers immediately.

Blades staggered backwards, his legs wobbling like jelly and for a moment Joe thought they might buckle but somehow Frank stayed on his feet.

But it made no difference.

Joe unleashed a blistering assault which demonstrated to all watching his awesome superiority. Punch after punch that turned Frank's face into a blood spattered pulp and hard body shots that snapped two more of his ribs.

Finally, Blades fell to his knees. 'Enough, enough, I'm finished

- you win,' he pleaded breathlessly, barely able to speak as red saliva sprayed from his bleeding mouth. 'Just stop - please.' There were tears rolling down his face.

Joe stopped and stood poised over the pathetic blubbering creature begging at his feet. 'So you're the big man of the Scrubs,' he said contemptuously, 'You're the one that everyone's so afraid of.'

The audience were hanging on every word. Amazed by what they had just witnessed.

'Well not any more, Frankie boy. Now you're nothin.'

Joe walked over to where he'd left his clothes, and slowly, silently, put them on whilst Blades was still a crumpled heap on the floor, sobbing pitifully onto his blood stained vest.

Joe was battered and bruised, nothing more. Nothing that time wouldn't heal. It was a decisive victory, he knew it, Blades knew it and so did his cronies who were now doing their best to look as inconspicuous as possible, their heads all hanging low.

Joe turned to them with a steely glare, 'Anyone else fancy their chances before I go?' He growled. There was no reply, every eye staring at the floor.

'I'll take that as a no then,' he said, and made his way slowly towards the door.

Frank staggered to his feet, his face awash with blood and a psychotic glint in his eyes. There was no way he was going to be beaten, not by an eighteen year old brat. He was Frank Blades for Christ sake, the hardest bloke in the Scrubs and nobody was going to get the better of him. He nodded to one of his goons who had been instructed about what to do in the case of this eventuality. The goon pulled out a wooden handled kitchen knife with a serrated blade and tossed it obediently to Frank.

As Joe was within reach of the door, he heard the sound of footsteps behind him and turned quickly to find Blades charging full speed at him, the knife held out front aimed at Joe's belly. It was a last desperate attempt to save face and win the fight but it was too late, Frank's body was tired, his movements were slow and Joe had already anticipated the attack.

He lightly side-stepped out of the way and as Blades momentum carried him forwards, Joe brought his knee up and made firm contact with Frank's jaw.

Blades dropped instantly to the floor, his body sprawled out on the dusty concrete, the knife flying from his hand and sliding well out of reach. He was out cold.

Joe looked down at Frank's prone form, casually adjusted his collar and said coolly 'Like I said Blades, now you're nothing.' And with that, left the room.

*   *   *

Billy's expression changed from one of extreme anxiety to one of incredible joy as he saw Joe emerge from the boiler room. He bounded over to him like a dog with two tails and very nearly hugged him. Joe had to give him one of his meaningful looks to restrain him but nevertheless couldn't stop himself smiling at the little man's obvious delight.

'Jesus! You did it. You bloody well did it, Jesus!' Billy enthused still bouncing around with excitement. Then a shadow of doubt crossed his mind 'You did do it didn't you?' He asked quickly.

'Yeah. I did it,' Joe replied.

*   *   *

That night in the cell, Billy said, 'Of course, you know he won't forget it.'

'Who won't?' Joe asked sleepily.

'Frank Blades, of course. He'll never forget what you did. He's not the type - we'll have to be careful.'

This had already occurred to Joe. Blades wasn't the sort to take that kind of humiliation lightly, he'd want revenge and Joe's instincts told him he'd stop at nothing to get it.

'I know.' Joe replied.

*   *   *

Two days later, Billy burst into the cell 'Guess what?' He said excitedly.

'What?' Joe enquired, not really interested.

'Frank Blades is being transferred in a fortnight - our troubles are over!'

Joe was surprised by the news. Blades was in the hospital wing and would be for almost two weeks, which meant he'd only be back in the population for a day or two before he departed. Surely it couldn't be that easy, he didn't know why, but it just couldn't.

*   *   *

The two weeks passed without incident and finally the day came of Blades' transfer. Joe and Billy had remained on guard, but everything seemed to be relatively quiet. Joe had earned much respect since word of his decisive victory over Frank had got out and Billy too, by association, was also treated far better by the prison population in general.

They were strolling around the exercise yard with almost everyone nodding a greeting, which was quite a novelty considering the lepers they had once been, when Billy said, 'You know, Joe, I don't think I've ever enjoyed life so much.'

Joe smiled sympathetically at his friend; the little misfit of a man who had at last found some sort of happiness in his thoroughly unrewarding existence and said, 'Billy, you deserve it - and don't let anyone tell you different.'

Billy, beamed back at him, a wide grin that exposed his yellow tombstone teeth. Suddenly his smile disappeared, 'Bollocks, I've forgotten me ciggies' he announced, 'Back in a sec!' And with that he went scampering off, back to the cell, completely invigorated by his newly elevated status.

Joe waited a while, but Billy didn't come back, so when the whistle sounded he wandered back to the cell alone curious to find out where his friend had got to.

Joe reached the second floor landing and immediately noticed that his cell door was shut. 'Odd,' he thought. As he pushed it open, his foot splashed in a puddle of blood on the floor and the macabre scene that lay before him made him gag. He vomited and had to steady himself against the bed. What he saw was ghastly, and it took a moment before he felt able to walk over and kneel down by the side of his friend's mutilated body, which lay in a lake of dark red blood on the concrete floor of the cell. Joe's hands were shaking as he took Billy's head carefully in his hands. The little man's throat had been sliced so deeply that he'd almost been decapitated. The knife used was the one Billy had fashioned himself in the metalwork shop and it lay stained at his side. His eyes bulged hideously in a deathly stare and his tongue lolled limply out the side of his mouth.

Joe's emotions spilled over in a mixture of pain and anger, 'NO!' He shouted.

As Joe looked to the heavens, he noticed the ominous message scrawled on the whitewashed wall, crudely written in his friend's blood.

'It's not over,' it read.

Joe bowed his head, his eyes tightly closed, trying to stop the tears that welled up behind them as Billy's words echoed inside his head. 'Of course, you know he won't forget it.'

*   *   *

There was an immediate investigation launched to find Billy's murderer, but no one was ever charged. However Joe knew who was behind it and he swore that one day he'd make Blades pay.

Eleven

Joe's morale was at an all-time low. During his first few months in prison, his girlfriend had disappeared and the only friend he'd made had been brutally murdered. Everything had turned to shit and now, as the only occupant of his cell, with no one to help break the monotony, Joe was perilously close to cracking. Luckily, the ultimate antidote to his condition was on the way.

*   *   *

After another dull day, Joe trudged back to his cell dreading the thought of being locked away again with just his boredom for company.

As he entered his block, he noticed it was noisier than usual. The inmates were in good spirits; most laughing at a bawdy song that was being sung loudly and rather tunelessly by someone in one of the cells.

'Balls to your partner, arse against the wall,
If you don't get fucked on a Saturday night
You'll never get fucked at all...'

Joe couldn't help but smile, the person who was singing had a deep gravelly voice, which made it sound all the more raucous, and reminded him of a drunk at closing time.

As Joe climbed the stairs, the singing became louder and louder, and he soon realised that whoever was making this awful racket, was in his cell.

More than a little curious as to why someone was in there uninvited, Joe angrily banged open the door, the deafening sound of the metal being struck echoing loudly around the whole landing.

'Awww, Balls to your— Fuck me!' The large man lying on the top bunk very nearly jumped out of his skin as the noise of the door stopped him in mid verse.

'Jesus Christ, Joe! Whattaya tryin' to do - kill me?' He said, still in a state of shock.

'Do I know you?' Asked Joe, getting angrier by the second as he glared at the wild haired, one-eyed man who was now sitting up on his bunk.

'No, son, you don't. But I think you know my brother, Vinnie. My name's Ray. Ray Reece.'

* * *

Ray Reece looked every bit the wild man that Ruby had said he was, especially with the shock of bright red hair that stuck out like a toilet brush. Then there was the black leather eye patch which concealed the empty socket of his missing eye, lost in a knife fight in his youth. And the blazing ginger moustache waxed sharp at the ends along with the long, pointed goatee. A modern day pirate if ever there was one.

In looks, he was about as far removed from Vinnie as two brothers could possibly get, although in size and stature they were equals. Ray, like his elder brother, was famously tough with a legendary reputation and Joe was honoured to finally meet him.

Tales of Ray's exploits had become part of South London folklore; he was a villain and a rogue, but whenever anyone spoke of him they smiled affectionately. A colourful eccentric whose boisterous and rowdy antics always had a certain panache, a style of their own that you couldn't help but admire. He was an irresistible character with a charm that even juries weren't immune to. He had been arrested for many things, but this was the first time he'd ever been in prison, although the sentence he undoubtedly deserved, had been considerably reduced thanks to his irrepressible personality.

Ray jumped down from the top bunk and held out his hand which Joe shook firmly.

'Pleased to meet you son,' Ray said, 'I've been sent to help.'

* * *

In one of the many parallels that could be drawn between Joe's life and mine, it turned out that I too was going to be a father, although I, unlike my friend, was lucky enough to know it. Sarah was pregnant, about three months gone, but as yet it was difficult to tell as her figure was still beautifully slim and her belly showed only the slightest evidence of a bump.

We were ecstatic when the doctor told us the news and immediately started making wedding plans. Joe, whose dour mood had vanished since Ray's arrival, was over the moon when we told him and the thought of becoming an uncle delighted him.

Furthermore, now Ray was with him, Sarah was much less concerned about her brother's well-being, although sadly, because he was inside, Joe would not be able to act as my best man. Fortunately Alfie agreed to do the honours in his absence and even offered us the Golden Gloves for our reception as a wedding present.

But, as we planned for our wedding, Benny Mottola advanced ever further into Reece territory and Vinnie was having to fight tooth and nail to keep control of his empire. The necessary violence used to win these battles had reached a whole new level, with guns now being bandied about like toys. Pretty much everyone carried one, although not me. Perhaps it was because I was going to be a father, or because I'd seen enough death and killing to last me a lifetime, but guns were not what I'd signed up for. A life of crime -

a life of violence, I was fast beginning to realise, was no longer for me.

Things were getting out of control and I didn't like it one bit.

The incident that really brought it home to me was when The Acropolis was bombed, killing six people and injuring dozens more. Greasy Phil himself spent three weeks in hospital, the attack destroying everything he'd worked for. With his business in ruins and his fortune lost, he packed up his few remaining belongings and returned to Greece a broken man.

The attack was all over the newspapers and as usual, the police had no idea who was behind it, but Vinnie knew, as did the rest of us, it was the unmistakable work of Benny Mottola.

The war had started and it wouldn't end for many years.

* * *

The bombing of the Acropolis, along with many other similar incidents made up my mind and when I talked it over with Joe he agreed. We decided that I should leave London with Sarah and our unborn child to make a life for ourselves in a different part of the country. I had enough money saved to get us a small flat somewhere and keep us going until my National Service began. When it did, Sarah and the baby would come and live close to wherever I got stationed, free from the threat of Vic once and for all.

It would be a whole new beginning, away from the violence that both of us had known for all of our lives. We planned to leave as soon as I could arrange it but in the meantime we'd have to remain vigilant. As a precaution, and with Alfie's approval, Eddie now looked after Sarah in the evenings whilst Dog Tooth and I went out on the Firm's business.

I spoke to Vinnie of my plans, explaining all the reasons why I had to leave and he understood. He knew Sarah and I were possible targets and suggested that it was probably a wise decision.

We decided to leave straight after the wedding and our hopes soared as we dreamed of our new life together. In just a few short months we'd be free - or so we thought.

However, the dice of fate was still rolling.

Twelve

The worst night of my life began much the same as any other, with Dog Tooth and myself dropping Eddie off with Sarah before starting our round. We pulled up outside the house and I accompanied Eddie to the door. When Sarah opened it and saw me, she smiled widely with pleasure, her long shiny hair hanging loosely down her back and her lovely face glowing with health. Pregnancy definitely suited her.

'In you come Eddie, the kettle's on,' she said pleasantly as he strolled by her and into the kitchen. 'And as for you, young man,' she said to me, 'I want you home early,' she glanced around making sure Eddie was out of ear shot, and added seductively, 'I've got plans for you.'

'Sounds promising,' I replied, giving her a lascivious wink, 'I'll be back before midnight.' I kissed her on the lips and rubbed her belly, which was starting to grow rapidly 'Look after my boy,' I said as I turned to leave.

'You mean your girl' she laughed after me.

I got back into the car, and as Tooth pulled away, I glanced out of the window and saw Sarah's beautiful smile for the last time.

*   *   *

Elsewhere, Vic Cassidy had just pulled a job with a couple of his mates. It had gone almost exactly as Big Jack said it would, apart from a slight deviation from the plan, which Vic considered to be an 'on the job perk.'

Jack had been planning it for a couple of months; ever since he'd had the good fortune to play cards at The Acropolis with a very drunken and extremely wealthy aristocrat called Lord John Tailby - the Marquess of Devon.

After the game, with an eye for the main chance, Jack had taken Lord John back to The Pontoon for more drinks, which culminated in Tailby revealing that he kept a secret stash of money at his apartment in Hampstead which his wife knew nothing about. 'Play money,' he called it, used to bank roll his gambling and to buy his mistress expensive trinkets - which ensured her continued favours.

Apparently there was usually well over two hundred grand in the safe at any one time, which piqued Jack's interest considerably.

The combination to this safe was revealed after a few more shots of whiskey and a little gentle persuasion. Although the Marquess was careful to tap the side of his nose, and slur the words, 'Say no more, old boy. Nuff said, what?' As if this would ensure Big Jack's confidence - him being a man of honour and all.

When Jack said goodnight, Lord John couldn't even speak and it was doubtful he'd be able to remember his own name in the morning, let alone that of his drinking companion. Big Jack left Tailby slumped up against the door of his penthouse, snoring like a baby; his trousers drenched in urine and his shirt covered in fresh puke.

For Jack, it had been a very interesting night; the plan for how he was going to liberate the money from the Marquis' safe already forming in his head.

* * *

House-breaking was beneath Big Jack, no matter how much money was at stake, so he had been forced to trust Vic Cassidy, who for five grand, said he'd do the job for him. However, Anderson had omitted to tell Vic just how much cash was at stake, so when the safe clicked open and a torch revealed the contents, Vic and his cohorts were surprised to say the least. Although trying to suppress their whoops of delight, the intruders managed to wake Lord John and his mistress, who caught them emptying the contents of the safe into a large Gladstone bag. Not appreciating the disturbance, Vic and his boys fell on them like a pack of animals.

Tailby was viciously beaten then tied to a chair naked and forced to watch Vic's two accomplices savagely rape his mistress. Vic didn't take part personally as he was gearing up for something altogether better on his way home.

Eventually the intruders left the penthouse, leaving Lord John half dead and his girlfriend bound and gagged at his feet; her body covered in semen, her genitals weeping blood. Neither had seen the faces of their attackers as they had all worn balaclavas. It could have been anyone.

*   *   *

Once in the car, Vic opened the Gladstone bag which was full of Lord John's money. Big Jack's money.
Looking at it, he decided that there was no way was he going to accept a poxy five grand now. Fuck Big Jack. What risk had he taken? Why did he deserve all the cash? All he'd done was offer a pathetic five grand. Where was the gratitude in that? It was an insult, that's what it was.

Vic was suddenly angry, and seeing a telephone box on the side of the road, he yelled, 'Stop the car! - I'm gonna call the bastard!'.

The next minute, Vic was shouting down the phone, telling Big Jack that unless he gave him and his boys an equal share of the takings they were going to keep it all.

Jack stayed cool, trying to placate Vic, 'Why don't you come by The Pontoon tonight and we'll talk about it?' He offered.

'I won't be put off, Jack - we'll 'ave our rightful share - we ain't takin' a penny less than you.'

'Sure, Vic, sure. We'll get it all sorted I promise ya,' Anderson's voice was calm, smooth as treacle, 'Come round tonight and we'll all 'ave a chat.'

'Well, alright then,' Vic's voice was still terse, '—but I won't be there for an hour or so. I'm gonna go see me daughter for a while - I'm overdue a visit.'

Anderson knew he'd won the battle, 'Fine, Vic. But make sure you bring the money, okay?'

'I'll bring it, don't you worry, but first I'm gonna 'ave some fun.' With that Vic slammed down the phone and marched back over to the car. 'Boys,' he said, 'I think we've earned ourselves a little celebration. Take me home!'

*   *   *

Jack's stomach turned with revulsion as he replaced the receiver, he knew why Cassidy was going to visit Sarah and the thought disgusted him. But it wasn't that which concerned him; it was Vic's blatant lack of respect and the audacity in which he'd demanded an equal share of the money - who the hell did he think he was?

It was clear that Vic Cassidy had long out lived his usefulness. As soon as he arrived at The Pontoon Jack would kill him and take what was rightfully his. That would show the double-crossing bastard who was boss. As for Vic's subordinates; killing them wouldn't go so unnoticed. They were Benny's boys and Jack knew he'd have to tread carefully. He'd offer them an extra five grand each as a sweetener, that should do it.

*   *   *

Anderson waited as patiently as possible for two hours, but with still no sign of Vic after a third he was getting extremely pissed

111

off. He was tempted to send someone to drag Vic away from Sarah and to forcibly bring him back to The Pontoon but, with difficulty, managed to restrain himself.

Then, miraculously, two people walked into his club and the sight of them conjured up a delicious plan that would have Vic scurrying out of Sarah's bed faster than greased lightning.

*   *   *

After a busy night, Dog Tooth and I eventually arrived at The Pontoon at around eleven thirty. We were tired and wanted to get home. The last person I felt like seeing was Big Jack Anderson, who was sitting at the bar sipping whiskey with a curious expression on his face - almost as if thankful to see us.

We walked up to him and he gestured for us to sit down.

'No thanks,' I said. 'Have you got the money Jack? I'm tired and it's late,' I was past being nice.

'Bet you'd rather be at home with the little woman eh?' He winked.

'Let's just keep my personal life out of it shall we?' I retorted, my hackles starting to rise.

'Sure, but I thought your missus might be needing you, that's all.' Jack said, giving me a real meaningful look.

'What?' I barked, now getting seriously cross, 'What the bloody 'ell are you talkin' about?'

'She might not be alone, that's all. Someone we both know might be payin' her a paternal visit.'

I saw red and blew my stack 'What the fuck's it got to do with—' suddenly I stopped in mid sentence, the realisation of what Jack was trying to tell me finally sinking in. 'Oh Christ, Sarah.'

'Gimme the car keys Tooth' I demanded desperately.

'What—?' Tooth asked, not comprehending what was going on.

'Give me the fuckin' keys!' I shouted, my panic levels rising by the second. Tooth pulled out the keys which I quickly snatched from his hand before bolting for the door.

Jack began to smile. Vic would soon be back at The Pontoon. And so would the Gladstone bag.

*   *   *

I sprang out of the car and bounded up to the front door. In my hand I had a long bladed knife that Dog Tooth always kept in the glove box as back-up. However, as I reached the door, I pulled up sharp noticing it had been jemmied. I placed an ear to the gap and could hear the sound of two men talking in the living room. Silently I slid into the hallway. Eddie's body lay where it had fallen; his eyes staring glassily at the ceiling; his face frozen in a hideous death mask. The carpet around him was wet with blood from the deep stab wounds in his stomach.

But I didn't give him a second thought. He was a good man, but I didn't care, all I cared about, all I could think about, was Sarah.

I eased along the wall, passed Eddie's body and stopped beside the doorway to the living room. Taking a deep breath, I peered carefully around the door. The two men, neither of whom I recognised, were seated in the armchairs chatting casually, as if enjoying an evening at the pub. There was no sign of Sarah.

Tooth's knife was concealed in the palm of my hand, held by my little finger and thumb; the blade running up the back of my forearm, hidden from view. I took a beat, then entered the room.

'Where is she?' I said, in a forcibly calm growl.

The two men turned to face me, both startled by my intrusion but quickly regaining their composure as they rose to their feet in unison, preparing for the attack. They were big burly thugs, dangerous men, I sensed, who thrived on violence, and looking into their cold eyes I could see no fear.

'Well, well, well,' said the first, 'What've we got 'ere then?

Must be the boyfriend, whatta y'reckon, Jimmy?'

'Don't look much like the lover boy type to me Jez,' said the other, 'Looks more like a lanky streak of piss.' The first man laughed at his friend's humour.

'Where is she?' I said again in the same even tone, 'I want her now,' my muscles tensing, the anger coursing through my veins.

'No, sunshine, you've got it all wrong. You gotta wait your turn,' replied the first man, 'I'm next, then Jimmy, then, if she's not too knackered, you can 'ave a go - mind you, I doubt if she'll feel yours after Jimmy's been there, he's hung like a donkey - ain't that right Jim?'

'That's right Jez,' said Jimmy, 'And I do so like to hear 'em squeal when I play rough.' They both sniggered lecherously at the thought.

'Tell me where she is now, or die,' I ordered.

'Wrong again, son,' said Jez, matter of factly, 'I think you'll find it ain't us whose gonna be dyin'- it'll be you.' He opened his grey woollen trench coat and pulled out a large, murderous looking bayonet from the scabbard secured to his belt. The bayonet had the dried remains of Eddie's blood smeared along its length.

Jimmy too, pulled out a pearl handled cut-throat razor and flicked the shiny blade open.

'Your move I think, sonny,' Jez said to me, smiling.

Blood was racing at a furious rate around my body; adrenaline flowing through me, making me feel invincible as I charged forward. Jez lifted the bayonet and tried to stick me, but I was quick; my reflexes powered with hate and rage. Changing my grip on the knife in the palm of my hand, I blocked his thrust with the edge of my blade, making contact just below his knuckles and severing two of his fingers, causing the bayonet to go spinning from his grip. As he looked aghast at his three remaining digits, I swung the sharp steel of my knife around and slashed him across the throat. As our bodies collided, he fell backwards into the chair, a look of horror on his face.

I span around to face Jimmy, who'd barely had time to react in the second it took me to take out his friend. Looking at me dumbstruck, he jabbed the razor in my direction, but again I was too quick, and sliced him across the wrist. The cut-throat dropped from his fingers in a spray of red as my other hand fastened on his neck forcing him hard up against the wall. I squeezed his windpipe in a vice-like grip and put my face within an inch of his, 'Where is she?' I snarled through gritted teeth.

'She's upstairs - Vic's with her,' Jimmy mouthed, his voice barely a squeak. I carried on squeezing, unable to release my grip - wanting to kill him. Tighter and tighter until his face turned purple and he ceased to struggle. Eventually I let go and Jimmy's lifeless body slid to the floor.

I turned instinctively to check on Jez, ready to rip his head from his shoulders, but he was already finished, thick jets of blood pumping from the hideous gash in his throat. I felt nothing as I watched him die.

I ran from the room and leapt up the stairs four steps at a time, I bounded across the landing and launched myself against the bedroom door forcing it open with my shoulder.

As I landed, I knew I was too late.

Vic Cassidy was sitting on the bed. He wiped his mouth as he looked up at me with a crazed look in his dark eyes. I could see the madness in them as he smiled proudly, obviously pleased with what he had done. He was bare chested with his trousers undone, the remainder of his clothes scattered about the room. There were scratches over Vic's face and neck and long slashes across his torso, inflicted by Sarah's fingernails as she tried to fight him off. But she had failed.

My darling girl lay behind him on the bed, motionless. There was blood on her night dress and on her legs, her torn underwear draped over one knee. The night dress was around her waist with her stomach and private parts exposed. They too were bloodied, ripped in the vicious struggle with her father. Violated for the last time by the monster who had cursed her life. Now, at last, he had killed her.

I just stood there, stunned, unable to fully comprehend what I was seeing. The knife slipped from my grip and stuck in the carpet as I stared at the horrific scene before me. My girl dead. Her swollen belly exposed and the baby inside it dead also. My whole world gone.

I felt numb and hollow and useless. My body unresponsive as Vic gathered up his clothes and dressed himself. He was in no hurry, completely unrepentant, completely immune to the damage he had done and the pain he had caused. But my focus was on Sarah, my thoughts with her and the baby, my mind refusing to allow anything else in.

Then Vic was speaking to me, but it sounded distant and I could barely make out the words, but he was right there. Right beside me. 'I take it you took out Jez and Jimmy?'

I made no reply. The words meant nothing.

'That's pretty good going, kid. Them boys were tough - they were untrustworthy, devious fuckers, but tough all the same and the truth is, you've done me a favour. But I wouldn't wanna be in your shoes now, not for all the tea in China, not when—'

'You killed her.' I spoke, but the voice didn't seem to belong to me.

Vic sniggered and the sound penetrated my daze. 'You killed them two hard cases downstairs but you couldn't save her could ya? Well, let me tell you this, sonny, no one saves her from me. She is mine, she belongs to me and no one stops me from doing whatever the fuck I want with her, understand?'

'She was going to be my wife.'

Then I heard the laugh. Deep and gruff and evil. A mad, wild laugh that snapped me out of my trance. 'Who the fuck do you think you are?' Vic growled. 'She weren't never gonna be your wife or your lover or your woman? Not never! I told you. She's mine. I own her, and not you nor your new locks and ageing body guards, or even my arsehole son, can ever change that. Never.' Vic pulled on his jacket and stepped up to confront me, the insanity in his eyes clear to see. 'Now, if you would kindly get out of my fucking way,' he spat, 'I've got important things to do tonight that have already waited long enough.'

He made to barge past me, but I stood my ground. 'No,' I said. The anger at last breaking through the numbness.

'Don't test me boy, I ain't in the mood - an' I think you'll find me a bit more of a problem than Jez and Jimmy.' He attempted to barge past again, but this time I physically threw him back.

'You're not going anywhere,'I said glaring at him. The anger building to a crescendo, bubbling up like a volcano. More anger than I'd ever felt in my life, more than I knew how to deal with.

'Don't make me laugh. You're already dead son, you just don't know it yet. So, if I were you, I'd get going, before I have to kill you and earn myself a nice little bonus.'

'Try it then. Kill me. Do your fucking worst. Kill me you bastard or I swear to God I'll kill you!'

Vic eyed me for a moment longer, his stare like a rabid panther, mad and dark and dangerous. Then he charged, growling all the way and I hurled myself at him, the volcano within me exploding with rage.

Our bodies collided and I was aware of Vic's head striking mine, but I felt nothing. No pain, no injury, just hate as a red haze descended over my eyes and I began to fight more furiously than I ever had before. I know Vic was fighting hard too, fighting like the mad man he was, but I don't fully remember it.

For a time, I was insane too, more so than perhaps even Vic, but for how long I cannot be sure as everything in those minutes happened in a blur. As if in a dream, or a nightmare. All I know is that it was a violent, hard fought battle that seemed to last until every last ounce of my incredible anger was spent. I can't even be certain of the moment when Vic stopped fighting, but only that it was sometime before me.

Eventually, exhaustion got the better of me and my legs buckled. I found myself sitting on the floor, the anger now gone and the tragedy of the situation slowly sinking in. As the red haze of violence lifted, I was staring once again at Vic Cassidy, but he was no longer laughing, no longer moving at all, his smashed in face now just a bloody pulp. I had killed him with my bare hands. Murdered him. And I didn't care. All I felt for him was revulsion and if I could have killed him again I would have.

Then the grief hit me. It hit me like a spear driven deeply into my chest and I began to sob. I was crying for my beautiful dead girl and my unborn child, my head buried deeply in my blood-stained hands.

As I wept, a ghostly tune played in my head. It was the haunting, dreamy melody of the nursery rhyme, Rock-a-bye-baby. I tried to flush it from my mind; to rid it from my grief stricken thoughts, but found that I couldn't. Only after several seconds did I realise that the tune was not just in my head, but that someone was actually humming it softly. As this dawned, I stopped crying and looked up to the bed.

It was Sarah. She was alive.

With this realisation my heart leapt and I jumped to my feet. But she didn't see me, her eyes were locked onto something far away that only she could see and she was humming the lullaby to herself. Calming herself, soothing her baby, detaching herself from the reality of what had happened to her.

But she was alive and suddenly I didn't care about anything else.

'Sarah, it's me - I'm here my darling' I cried, sitting down by her side, but she looked right through me as if I was transparent. Her eye's were completely vacant with no recognition in them whatsoever, and she just continued to hum.

* * *

I sat there with her for a long while trying to make her hear me, trying to get through to her, but it was no good. Her mind, it seemed, had just shut down. Had she lost her sanity, I wondered. She was definitely in some kind of trance, physically, purposely, albeit sub-consciously, locking out the pain.

'Please God, let her and the baby be okay - help us please!' I wailed, praying earnestly for the first time since I was very small. My hands were shaking and I could feel the panic rising within me. I had to get a grip.

The woman I loved had been attacked and raped and only time would tell if there was still to be a baby. On the bedside table Sarah had collected a pile of baby things, a few of which she had made and a few which she had borrowed. On top of the pile was a solitary white bootee, which seemed to represent something good. Something pure and unblemished which had escaped the horror of the night's events and I picked it up and put it in my pocket. I could only hope that the child for whom it was made would somehow survive this dreadful ordeal.

I looked toward Sarah and touched her cheek, but she completely unaware of my presence, safe in her own peaceful world, away from any further danger.

I wiped the tears from my eyes and walked to the bathroom where I filled the washbasin and sluiced my face; scrubbing it with my hands in an effort to calm my racing emotions as well as to wash the blood from my skin.

After a long moment, I eventually stood up and looked at myself in the mirror; I was still extremely shaken but forcibly more composed. I towelled myself off and walked back onto the landing.

It was then that I noticed the brown leather Gladstone bag. Immediately curious, I picked it up and found it surprisingly heavy. I then tried the latch, but it was locked. Puzzled, I carried the bag back into the bedroom and knowing it to be Vic's, searched through his blood-spattered jacket for a key. I quickly discovered it in the right-hand pocket and instantly tried it in the lock.

As the key turned, the bag fell open and I gasped out loud when I saw that it was stuffed full with bundles and bundles of ten pound notes.

*   *   *

Each bundle of cash was well over two inches thick, and a very quick tally revealed there to be at least five thousand pounds in each wad. My head began to ache as I tried to calculate the total sum, but unable to think straight, I gave up, concluding the final figure to be staggering.

I knew that the money was stolen - no doubt the spoils of some robbery - and possibly en-route to Benny or Big Jack. Focusing on that assumption made the following decisions easier, although the choices I made now would determine the rest of my life.

*   *   *

The plan that I conceived was one which would be gut-wrenching to adhere to, but the only one that I believed would leave Sarah and the baby - if indeed, there was now to be one - in relative safety. Sarah needed time to recuperate, time for her mind and body to heal. It was a plan that aside from Sarah and myself, relied on trusting three other people, Vinnie Reece, Alfie Noakes and above all Ruby Walsh.

In the stillness of the hour, I could hear the slapping of shoes on the pavement below; someone was approaching at a run and immediately I was concerned. I rushed to the window and peered through a gap in the curtains, and saw Dog Tooth, slowing to a halt and panting breathlessly from his run. He looked up at the window with his beetroot face wet with sweat, but as he saw me staring down, his relief was instant as he realised I was unharmed.

Dog Tooth had run the three miles from The Pontoon, which was no mean feat for a man of his bulk - and a remarkable show of loyalty.

Thinking quickly, I picked up the Gladstone bag and stuffed it hurriedly into the bedroom cupboard. Even though Tooth was a good and reliable friend, I decided it best not to tell him about the money - at least not for the moment.

As I reached the top of the stairs, Dog Tooth entered the house. 'Jesus Christ - Eddie!' He exclaimed, still panting. 'He's dead, Sean, Eddie's fuckin' dead - what the bloody hell happened - is your missus alright?'

'She's alive.' I said, 'but she ain't alright.'

'Bastards!' Tooth spat 'I'll fuckin' kill 'em.'

'I already have - take a look in the front room' I replied. Tooth looked at me in surprise, and then did as instructed. 'Jesus Christ!' I heard him exclaim again.

I waited for Tooth to reappear from the room before I added, 'It gets worse, there's one more upstairs.'

'Who?' He asked.

'Vic Cassidy.' I replied flatly.

Dog Tooth shook his head slowly 'Y'know this means trouble, don't ya Sean?'

'I know.' I answered.

'But y'know who you've killed don't ya?' He pressed.

'Yes Tooth, I know; Vic Cassidy and two of Benny Mottola's worthless goons - and I'm glad about it, alright?' I said. Why was he asking such inane questions? What I needed to do was deal with the situation, not dwell on it.

'No, Sean.' Tooth replied in an effort to drum it home, 'What you've done is killed Vic Cassidy, one worthless goon and Jez Mottola - Benny's brother.'

Now I knew what Vic meant when he said I was already dead.

Thirteen

I frantically packed Sarah's clothes into a large suitcase, which Dog Tooth took out to the car. I then wrapped Sarah in a warm blanket and carried her down the stairs and sat her in the passenger seat of the small Ford.

I'd instructed Tooth to take Sarah directly to Ruby's and briefly outline to her what had happened, then I asked him to drive straight to Vinnie's house and bring him - no matter what it took - back to Ruby's, collecting Alfie on the way. I told him that under no circumstances should he tell another soul of what had happened and he assured me he wouldn't.

The time was now 2am. I figured I had until about mid morning before the search began. I would be wanted by the police, and if caught would face a hanging, or, at the very least, life imprisonment. That however, was an almost attractive prospect compared to what would happen if Benny got hold of me first; I had killed his brother and in doing so had written my own death sentence.

I had nine, maybe ten hours, to organise Sarah's future and make good my escape and every second was vital.

I watched Tooth's car speed away, then hurried back into the house. There was nothing I could do about the bodies and no way to hide the evidence of me being there as there just wasn't time.

The hall, living room and bedroom were all covered in blood and it would have taken days to get rid of it. Given another few hours, I could've organised the removal of the corpses, Vinnie would have been able to help with that. But it was too late and I just had to accept it.

It was then that the remarkable truth of the situation struck me. The tragic irony. Joe and I had finally fulfilled the oaths we had made at fourteen. But instead of us killing our own father's as we had planned, we had instead killed each others. For our actions Joe was now rotting in prison and I was about to embark on a desperate flee from the gallows. My home, my family, my life, as I'd known it until now, all gone.

Dwelling no more on these melancholy thoughts, I went to the airing cupboard and pulled out the Gladstone bag. Then, after throwing a few of my clothes into a holdall, together with the little box containing Mum's silver earrings, I switched off the lights and left silently by the back door.

* * *

Moving quickly and using the darkest roads and alleyways, I made my way to Mum's house. I hopped over the back fence and quietly let myself in. Going straight to the living room, I closed the black-out curtains, which had hung there since the war, then switched on the light.

Immediately, I opened the Gladstone bag and removed the contents. Laying each bundle of cash next to one another on the carpet, I noticed they were all the same height, so I chose one, removed the elastic band, and began to count.

Five thousand pounds exactly. Forty five bundles, all of which I assumed, contained the same amount. That totalled two hundred and fifty grand - a quarter of a million pounds! I was stunned, but intended to put it to good use.

I divided the cash into two equal piles. The first pile I put back into the Gladstone bag, which I then stashed safely away in my old man's hidden basement - his secret lock-up, which was perfect for my needs. In the bag was one hundred and twenty-five grand - money for Joe which he'd find invaluable upon his release from prison.

Then I turned my attention to the second half of the money, the remaining one hundred and twenty-five thousand. I divided it into two stacks; one containing a hundred grand, one containing twenty-five. The smaller amount I concealed at the bottom of my holdall; this would be my escape fund; money I'd need to build a new life - hopefully enough to buy freedom and evade capture.

The remaining stack I threw into my mother's shopping bag, which was still where she'd left it under the stairs. As I thought of her, I instinctively touched the gold crucifix that hung around my neck. Whilst I wore it, Mum would always be with me, and I felt comforted by that.

When everything was done, I looked for the last time around my home, the scent of my mother still in the air. Closing my eyes I said aloud, 'Watch over us Mum, take care of Sarah and Joe for me.'

Then I wiped my moist eyes, turned off the light, took the holdall and the shopping bag and left the house the same way as I'd entered.

* * *

I arrived at Ruby's at 4.30am, using the back door which led directly to her private quarters. Vinnie was pacing the floor impatiently and as he noticed me enter the room he said 'About bloody time! Are you alright, kid?' The concern in his voice was touching.

'I'm okay,' I replied, 'But I need you to sit down and listen to what I've got to say. We haven't got much time.'

Vinnie, Alfie and Ruby all took seats whilst Dog Tooth watched the door.

'Where's Sarah, is she alright?' I asked Ruby.

'Don't worry luv, she's safe upstairs asleep. I gave her a bath, changed her into a clean night dress and put her to bed. I also burnt that blood covered nightie she was wearing.'

'Thanks Ruby' I said, ' I appreciate it, I really do.'

'She's not right though Sean, her mind seems... er—' Ruby was struggling for the correct word.

'I know Ruby, I know.' I interrupted 'She's been through hell.'

'What exactly happened kid?' Alfie asked.

I stood in the centre of the room and related the whole story, and when I'd finished, I sat down exhausted; tiredness and shock eventually catching up with me. My audience remained silent for a long moment, until Vinnie finally spoke 'So where do we come in?'

I looked directly at them and said 'I want you to look after Sarah and our baby.

I paused for a second to let this sink in, then continued, 'Ruby, I know it's a lot to ask, but I'd like you to take them in.' Then I looked to Vinnie and said, 'I'm hoping you can get them new identities - perhaps as some kind of relatives of Ruby's.'

'No problem,' replied Vinnie graciously, 'But what about you, whatta you gonna do? You can't stay around here.'

'I know. I need a new name, a passport and passage on a ship - no questions asked - and I need to leave as soon as possible. Can you sort it?' It was less a question and more of a plea.

'I'll take care of Sarah and the baby,' Ruby spoke up, 'It'll be my pleasure, but you do realise that the baby might not—' she hesitated for a moment, '—Well, might not survive?'

'I do. I know you'll do what's best,' I said, managing a slight smile.

I turned to Vinnie and Alfie again, 'Can you sort it?'

'We can sort it kid,' Alfie replied, 'But to get you out of 'ere quickly is gonna take a lot of dosh. A *lot* of dosh. Forgers don't come cheap - not the good 'uns, and they ain't too keen on workin' quickly neither.'

'Don't worry,' Vinnie interjected, 'I know someone - owes me big time. I reckon I can persuade 'im to come up with the goods - that's if he fancies keepin' his fingers!' He smiled broadly but I couldn't be certain that he was joking.

'About the money—' I picked up the shopping bag and pulled out several bundles of notes '—Is this enough?' I asked.

'I'd say that should about cover it,' said Alfie with a grin.

'Whatever's left,' I said, addressing them all now, 'I want you to use to look after my family. Y'know, to help Sarah, and to get my kid a good education - if it, well, if it survives. Whatever they want - whatever's best. I know I can count on all of you.'

'Christ, luv, with all that money I reckon I could get 'em lined up for the throne!' Ruby said. 'But I'll be careful, don't you worry, I'll put some away for 'em. Invest it. Keep it safe, so they'll always 'ave enough and never go without - and your kid, well I'll treat it just like me own, I promise. But what about you luv, are you okay - have you got enough?'

'Don't worry about me, Ruby, I've got plenty. Just take care of my family.' I replied.

* * *

By 6.30am, we'd ironed out the details. If all went to plan, I'd be leaving England at seven that night. It appeared that Vinnie even had connections in international shipping - someone else that owed him a favour no doubt. I didn't care, but the clock was still ticking and my life now lay in his and Alfie's hands.

Before he left, Vinnie embraced me and patted me on the back. He then placed a firm hand on my shoulder, looked me in the eye and said, 'Don't worry, kid, I'll keep 'em safe, you can depend on it.'

I shook both Vinnie's and Alfie's hands and thanked them,

and they in turn wished me luck.

It was the last time I ever saw Vinnie, but as I watched him walk away, I knew I would never forget him.

It should have been the last I saw of Alfie also, but circumstances dictated otherwise.

*　*　*

I was to remain at Ruby's for the rest of the day in hiding, until Dog Tooth came to collect me at 5.15pm, he would take me to the docks and accompany me as I boarded the ship.

I spent much of my time with Sarah, just stroking her hair as I listened to the tune she repeatedly hummed, wishing that she could come with me. If only things had been different. I gently rubbed her swollen belly, my heart breaking at the thought of my child growing up without me. But I knew Ruby would take care of the baby, and of Sarah too. Furthermore, Joe would be released in six and a half years and he would undoubtedly protect them.

*　*　*

At around 3.30pm, Mottola and a crew of heavies turned up at Ruby's. Benny was seriously pissed off and was threatening to trash the place in his search for me. But Ruby was brilliant and just fronted it out like the old pro that she was. 'Listen darlin,' she said. 'You're welcome to search the place, 'ave a look in all me nooks and crannies if that's what you're after. But I gotta tell ya, I've got a couple of me regulars in from Scotland Yard - an' one of 'em's the Chief Inspector. I don't think he'll take too kindly to you catching 'im with his pants down - but it's up to you darlin.' You help yourself if you wanna take the chance.'

Benny didn't fully buy the bluff and for a moment Ruby thought he might just take her up on the offer. So she pushed it further to hopefully throw him off the scent. 'Course, you're welcome to wait around until he's done - 'ave a drink with me and the girls. Hell, you might as well take a couple of 'em for a test drive

128

- it's been a kinda slow afternoon.'

Benny wavered for a few more seconds, then said, 'Come on boys, he ain't here - just this sad old tart and her scabby whores.' But before Benny turned to leave, he grabbed a tight hold on Ruby's arm snarled, 'Course, if you do run into that murderin' Sean Reilly, you'll be sure to tell me, won't ya darlin? That's if you wanna keep that pretty face of yours. Understand?'

Ruby nodded and smiled through the pain. 'I will luv, I will.'

I watched through the net curtains as Benny and his boys got back in their cars and pulled away. Ruby had saved me, she'd kept me safe and I knew she'd do the same for Sarah while I was away. She was a good friend, but I needed to get away from her place before Mottola came back.

'Are you okay?' I asked Ruby when she came up to see me shortly afterwards.

'Christ, I'm fine darlin,' she replied, 'It takes more than a couple of bloody thugs to scare me! Mind you,' she added, 'that Mottola's a real nasty piece of work. We'd better prey Tooth gets here in time.'

My sentiments entirely.

It was only then that I noticed Sarah had stopped humming and was looking directly at me. 'Sean, what's the matter?' She asked as I raced to her side. Had it happened I wondered, had she snapped out of it?

'Nothing's the matter my darling. Everything's fine,' I lied, taking one of her delicate hands and kissing it gently. 'Everything's going to be just fine,' a tear rolled down my face, 'We're together, and I love you.'

'Where are we?' She asked.

'We're at a good friend's house, someone who's going to take care of you,' I replied, my voice cracking.

'The baby?' She said, 'Is the baby alright?'

'Yes, my darling, the baby's fine - nothing at all to worry about,' I lied again.

'But what about—?' her eye's glazed over again 'What about—?' As the memories came flooding back to her, she switched off again in a sub-conscious effort to blot them out. 'I was having such a lovely dream, I didn't want to wake up,' she said, her voice sounding detached once more. 'Why did you wake me Sean? I didn't want to wake up.'

'You must wake up Sarah. I love you - please wake up!' I was pleading with her, but Ruby placed a hand on my shoulder. 'It's no good Sean, she can't hear you, she's back where no one can harm her.'

'Sarah, please... please wake up, I've got to go away. I'm going away for a long time, I need you to understand, I need to say goodbye.'

Sarah roused slightly, and then said dreamily, 'Goodbye, my love.' Then she turned to the wall and began to hum softly.

I bowed my head, tears streaming down my face 'Goodbye my darling.' I said.

* * *

As I waited downstairs for Dog Tooth's imminent arrival, Ruby poured us each a glass of whiskey. 'To the future,' she toasted, and I raised my glass, then knocked the warm liquid back in one gulp. Ruby filled it again. 'To good friends,' I returned the toast.

Ruby put down her glass and gave me a long hard hug. 'Look after yourself boy,' she said 'I'll miss ya.'

'I'll miss you too, Ruby,' I replied, kissing her on her cheek 'And thanks for everything.'

'Oh, don't be silly - and don't you go worryin' about Sarah, I'll make sure she's well taken care of.'

'If she ever snaps out of it,' I said, reaching into my inside jacket pocket, 'Will you make sure she gets these - they were my mother's.' I put the small silver stud earrings into Ruby's hand.

'Of course I will, luv. It'll be my pleasure' and she hugged me again.

*　*　*

The time was 5.30pm. Dog Tooth was fifteen minutes late. 'Perhaps he's got held up,' Ruby offered.

'Perhaps,' I replied anxiously. I paced the floor, unable rid myself of the feeling I had in my gut. Something was wrong and I knew it.

Another forty minutes passed; I was in danger of missing my boat and Ruby phoned Vinnie to ask if everything was okay, but all he said was not to worry, Alfie was on the way.

Alfie was on the way - not Tooth. I began to feel sick.

Five minutes later, the Jag pulled up at the rear of Red Ruby's and Alfie emerged from it, a grim expression on his face.

'Where's Tooth?' I said as Alfie stepped through the darkened entrance.

'Tooth's dead, Sean.' He replied quietly.

'Oh, Christ. No!' I was aghast.

'Benny caught up with him this afternoon. Shot him in the eye, poor bastard.' Alfie was obviously devastated, Dog Tooth had been with him for years and, apart from Vinnie, was his closest friend.

'Oh, Christ, Alfie, I'm sorry. If it wasn't for me—'

Alfie held up his hand to silence me. 'It's not your fault kid. You didn't pull the trigger.'

'But—'

'Not your fault,' Alfie said again. 'Remember that. Always.'

'Did he talk?' I asked, my concern not for myself, but for Sarah.

'Never. Not in a million years,' Alfie replied firmly.

'Sorry, Alfie. I know he wouldn't have - I just had to ask

though, y'know, for Sarah's sake.'

He looked at me and shrugged. 'I know, kid. It's alright, I understand. But let's get outta here now before Mottola catches up with us.'

I gave Ruby a last kiss, then followed Alfie to the car. Before I got in, I glanced up at Sarah's bedroom window, 'Goodbye.' I said.

*   *   *

We travelled in silence, both of us lost in our thoughts. Alfie mourning the loss of Dog Tooth, and I the loss of Sarah.

Alfie brought the Jag to a halt on the docks next to a huge cargo ship named The Aztec Princess, which was emblazoned on the stern in chipped white lettering. She was old and weather beaten and I was doubtful if she'd make it to Tower Bridge, let alone out to sea, but she was to be my transport out of London and was therefore grateful.

As we sat in the car, the heaven's opened, the rain beating like a snare drum on the roof. 'This is it kid.' Alfie said.

'Yep.' I agreed, feeling a little lost for words, and watching as Alfie reached into his pocket and pulled out a brand new passport and birth certificate, both expertly forged.

'Vinnie's called in a few favours today - these would've normally taken at least a week.'

'I know. Thanks Alfie, I appreciate everything you and Vinnie have done for me.' I said.

'Ah, don't worry about it kid, just stay outta trouble and make somethin' of your life - that'll be enough thanks for us.'

I took the papers from him and glanced at the name on the birth certificate. 'Sean Noakes?' I queried, and looked at Alfie, but he was staring out of the window at the pouring rain, trying to hide his embarrassment.

'Well,' he said, 'We had to think of a name didn't we? And besides—' he added, 'I've got six kids, what difference does another one make.'

I felt decidedly choked 'Thanks, Alfie.'

'No problem. Now, let's get you on that ship before Mottola and his boys turn up.'

* * *

Alfie escorted me aboard ship and introduced me to the captain; a man who apparently used one of Vinnie's warehouses to secrete his less than legitimate cargo. He in turn, showed me to my quarters, which were tiny but perfectly adequate. More importantly, they were private and had a lockable cabinet in which I could store my holdall.

Back on the deck of the ship, Alfie and I said our goodbyes. We shook hands and wished each other luck and then I watched him walk down the gang plank and drive away into the cold, wet night.

As the ship set sail, I stood by the rail and savoured my last look at London, the place of my birth and the place where my heart would always belong.

Putting my hand in my pocket, I felt something woollen and when I pulled it out, I saw it was the single white bootee that I'd picked up from Sarah's bedside. Without thinking, I put it to my lips and kissed it.

'Look after them, Mum' I said.

* * *

In Barcelona, seven days later, I managed to pick up a week old copy of The Daily Mail that a tourist had dropped. My picture was splattered all over the front page and they were declaring me to be 'public enemy number one.'

It appeared that I was wanted not only for the murders of Vic Cassidy, Jez Mottola and the other gang member who was apparently named Jimmy Feathers, but also in connection with the brutal assault and robbery of someone called Lord John Tailby.

It was thought by the police that I had been with Vic when the Marquess' safe had been emptied, and that I may also have been involved in the rape of his mistress.

It was assumed that I had then betrayed my companions and, after murdering them, had run-off with the loot. Eddie, they deducted, had been in cahoots with me, but had been killed during the ensuing violence, possibly by one of the other dead men.

It was clear from the story that the press didn't care too much for Vic and his gang and that my far bigger crime was the assault and robbery of Tailby. I had attacked the establishment, the rock upon which England was built, and it was a crime for which neither Tailby himself, nor the press, would ever forgive. On that issue, I stood falsely accused, but at least I knew whose money I was spending.

The journalist had described me using words like evil, vicious and dangerous, but I didn't feel like any of those things. All I felt was empty, homesick and scared.

However, I was relieved to read that Sarah was thought to have escaped with me, although not suspected of the killings - which was the only good news in the whole newspaper. It seemed, for the time being at least, she was safe enough.

Back on the ship, heading for some other foreign port, I sat on my bunk feeling more alone than I ever had before. I knew not where I was going, nor where I'd eventually end up, just that home was far away and getting more distant with every day that passed.

* * *

Two months later, my son, Michael, was born. Sarah gave birth to him four weeks prematurely and didn't make a sound throughout the labour. He had ten fingers and ten toes, a shock of black hair and weighed in at three pounds, four ounces. A small, but healthy boy.

I wouldn't meet him until he was ten years old.

PART TWO

One

I fell in love with the motorcycle the moment I laid eyes on it; a 1951 Indian Chief that was second, maybe even third hand, but I had to have it. Big, shiny, powerful, a thing of such beauty that I just could not resist.

In seven years, I'd barely touched the twenty-five thousand I'd escaped with, somehow managing to survive on the wages of the many jobs I'd had since leaving England. But now, I found myself in San Francisco, with the ship that had brought me here departing without me. At twenty-five, I'd seen the world, or at least a great deal of it, and had enjoyed many of its varied cultures and experiences. I'd even tried to settle twice - once in Brazil, once in Spain - but each time, the wanderlust within me had moved me on. But now that urge had long since past. I wanted a home and America, I had decided, was going to be it.

Looking at the bike, I figured I'd laboured long enough and was due some reward for my years of enforced exile, so even though it cost a small fortune, I bought it and it was worth every dime.

The powerful, smooth engine hummed rhythmically as I cruised along the cliff tops of the coastal road, heading south, the sun on my back, the wind in my hair and the turquoise ocean glittering below me. For the first time in years I felt at peace with the world and very nearly happy. The canvas holdall, that had been a permanent companion, was strapped to the seat behind me and in it were my entire worldly possessions. But I couldn't have cared less, I was embarking on a new adventure, one which I felt certain, I was going to enjoy.

*   *   *

I headed for Orange County, LA where, I'd heard, the girls were pretty and the sun shone every day. The local scene was also fun and youthful and seemed like the ideal place for a guy of twenty-five to have a good time and to forget the horrors of his past, at least for a short time.

I ended up in Newport Beach, a surfers paradise full of young, friendly revellers. I slept wherever I could, although usually on the beach, which was just fine. The Indian parked right by my side, the holdall tucked under my head as a pillow. The night sky was crystal clear with every star shining as brightly as the lights on a Christmas tree and I'd lay there for hours, just staring upwards, awed by the majesty of it all. My problems dwarfing in the vastness of space, my thoughts of home temporarily washed away by the soothing sound of the ocean.

After a couple of weeks, I got talking to one of the local surfers in a bar; a guy the same age as myself called Virgil Nash. He was a typical beach boy with white blonde hair, blue eyes and bronzed, sun kissed skin. A guy who girls found irresistible and whose dream it was to become a movie star.

We got on very well and before too long he said I was welcome to bunk down at his place until I found a place of my own - an offer which I gladly accepted.

Virgil's apartment was small and scruffy and situated above a noisy diner, but it was cheap and cheerful and Virgil himself was great company. He and his friends were a lively crowd who partied constantly, with every night a mixture of dancing, drinking and screwing. The long hot days were spent either lazing in the sun or surfing, with no one ever seemingly having to work. It was a truly hedonistic lifestyle, but one which I couldn't help but enjoy.

The afternoon's were my favourite time of day as I had the apartment to myself and would spend hours sitting on the small balcony, reading through the letters I'd received from home. I'd kept every one, all tied up together with a ribbon and stashed along with the money in my holdall.

Whenever I received a new one I would savour every sentence, reading it over and over again, with no one to disturb me, my thoughts taking me back to South London and Sarah. Ruby, Joe and myself had written as often as my travels allowed. As soon as I'd settled somewhere for longer than a month, I'd write to inform them of my whereabouts and we'd correspond regularly until it was time to move on again.

Neither Ruby or Joe ever disclosed my location to anyone as to do so would be to sign my death warrant. Benny Mottola was still hunting for me and he'd not rest until I was dead; this he had made known throughout the London underworld. The reward he'd offered for my capture currently stood at ten thousand pounds, which was an incentive many would find irresistible.

Lord John had also made certain that my alleged crimes were not forgotten about, never allowing the police to relax their efforts in trying to track me down. His campaign ensured that I was still hot news, and my photo apparently featured regularly in the papers. Time, it seemed, had done little to ease the pressure.

Going home was not an option.

*   *   *

After weeks of lazing around and living on Virgil's pleasure, I decided it was time to get a job. Virgil said I should go with him to auditions, to try and make it as an actor. He reckoned I had the looks, but I was doubtful and besides, acting didn't seem to be the

139

life for me - too much exposure for a start, too many eyes staring. And, in truth, I had my mind set on a different career.

On my travels I'd become a surprisingly good horseman, having worked on numerous ranches - particularly in South America and Spain - in order to earn a living. During that time I'd developed a deep love for horses and had become quite skilful in their training; a talent I could never have discovered in South London. It was because of this newly acquired talent that I had purposely chosen California, which was littered with ranches and stud farms. Having decided I would like to work with horses full time, I thought I'd try my luck in the wealthy and extremely beautiful Palm Springs, east of LA, which, according to Virgil, had many surrounding ranches that may be hiring hands.

Virgil also said, that if things didn't turn out, he was fairly sure he could secure me occasional work as an extra in the movies. He himself made his living this way whilst waiting for his big break. The money wasn't great but it was enough to get by on and allowed him to surf pretty much every day.

In the few short months that I'd known him, Virgil and I had become very good friends. His generosity in letting me stay at his place had given me the chance to settle, to put down roots which would form the basis of my new life. His amiable manner and agreeable nature had made it much easier for me than it might otherwise have been.

It was my intention to find work with lodgings included, where I could stay during the week and return to Newport Beach at the weekend to party with Virgil and his gang.

Fortunately, I hit pay dirt on my very first attempt.

*   *   *

The ranch was an enormous spread called Wildwood, which it proudly displayed on the arch over the entrance. The entrance itself was finally arrived at after mile upon mile of white painted fence that ran parallel to the dusty road I rode in on, giving me some idea of the huge size of the ranch within.

As I drove the Indian slowly up the long tree-lined driveway, I gazed in wonder at the vast expanses of grazing land that lay on either side, which made for a lush oasis of greenery in a spectacular desert landscape. Horses of brown, chestnut, grey, sorrel, black and palomino roamed freely over the grassy terrain, allowing me a first glance of the fabulous animals I was hoping to work with.

Wildwood specialised in the breeding of quarter horses, which were a compact, muscled breed with a lovely, gentle nature. Their impeccable blood-line evolving from Arabians crossed with English and Irish horses in America during the seventeenth century. With long and distinguished pedigrees, they are suited to everything from rodeo to dressage and show-jumping to cattle herding, but they are especially known for their speed over short distances. They seemed to be horses of true character and in that, for me, lay at least some of their appeal.

At the end of the driveway, behind a huge, immaculately kept island of flowers, was a magnificent white house; colonial in style with shuttered windows, wrought iron balconies and hanging bougainvillea. The house seemed to belong more to the cotton plantations of nineteenth century Georgia than to twentieth century Palm Springs, with the neon lights of Vegas and the modern conveniences of LA equal distances away. But no matter where it was, it was quite simply the most impressive place I'd ever seen.

After swinging the Indian around the floral island and putting it on its stand, I nervously approached the grandiose front door, flanked on either side by two thick marble columns that supported the sheltering porch, and rang the doorbell. After mere seconds, the door was opened by a smartly presented maid in a grey cotton dress and white pinafore.

'Good morning, sir,' she said.

'Yes, good morning,' I replied, 'Is the master in?'

'No sir, there is no master, I'm afraid, only Miss Louretta.'

'Oh, right' I struggled for a second 'Is it possible to speak with her then?'

The girl eyed me up and down for a few moments and I suddenly became aware of my scruffy appearance; it seemed that riding a motorcycle along dry dusty roads in a white tee shirt hadn't proved to be such a good idea.

'What's it in connection with?' She asked suspiciously.

'I'm looking for work, and I thought there might be a chance—'

'Who is it Blanche?' A woman's voice asked from inside the house, cutting me off in mid sentence.

'It's a young man, Ma'am, says he's looking for work. I was just about to tell him we didn't have any,' Blanche said.

'Oh, yes we have,' the lady of the house responded, 'I've just fired Curly - caught that lazy sonofabitch sleepin' in the hay loft again - show the guy in!'

Blanche looked at me sympathetically as she opened the door, 'This way sir.'

I entered sheepishly.

'In here son!' Miss Louretta's voice boomed from the direction of a room immediately opposite the front door. I obediently crossed the vast black and white tiled entrance hall, trying to take in the staggering opulence of my surroundings, realising that the person who lived here was obviously very rich.

I entered the room and was immediately overwhelmed by its size and grandeur. It was light and airy with deep, wide windows that looked out on the marvellous landscape I'd just passed. There was a definite feminine touch to the decor; white sofas with lemon and green cushions and fine ornate furniture which I suspected

142

might be Italian. I knew nothing of good taste but guessed this place had it in spades.

Above the marble fireplace hung a large oil painting featuring a likeness of someone I recognised immediately.

'That's Louretta Wild,' I said unintentionally aloud.

'It sure is, honey,' her voice startled me and I span around to face her.

'You're... you're—' I stammered, first looking at her, then the painting 'You're Louretta Wild.'

'Last time I looked, I was,' she said, matter of factly.

'But you're—' I tried again.

'Old?' She interjected.

''No, you're a film star!' I said, pathetically star-struck.

'I was once, honey, now I'm just an old broad who breeds horses, my movie days are long gone.'

'But—' I attempted to disagree.

'Relax, kid - siddown, take the weight off - tell me about yourself, like what's your name for starters?'

I did as she asked, placing myself carefully in one of her white armchairs, trying hard to prevent any dust from staining it, but not succeeding.

'Sean Noakes' I said, '—I'm looking for a job where I can work with horses.'

'What's that accent, son - you're not from these parts are ya?'

'No, Ma'am, I'm from London - London, England' I replied.

'I know where London is, kid. What brings you to Palm Springs?'

Skipping neatly over the truth, I told her that I left home to travel the world, elaborating greatly about my knowledge and experience of horses in order to get the job.

As I told the story, I studied the woman who, as a kid, I'd worshipped every Saturday morning at our local cinema. Then, she was a goddess, with platinum blonde hair, an hour glass figure and long slim legs that glided across the screen. The characters she played were always sassy and sharp with a quick wit that would render any man speechless - a persona that I was soon to find out, was no act.

Her beauty had now faded, the hair had silvered and her figure had become more fulsome, but she was still a very striking woman.

When I'd finished my yarn, she remained silent for a long moment, then said, 'Alright, kid, you'd better show me what you can do. If you're okay, then you're in, if you're not, well there's another ranch down the road - you can try you're luck there.'

*　*　*

The corral was at the rear, a short distance from the house and looked like something straight out of a western. Five of her hands, all proper cowboys, wearing Stetsons and leather chaps were out there exercising the animals.

'Hank, bring out the grey!' Louretta ordered.

'Yes, Ma'am!' Hank obeyed, a smile on his face, he apparently knew what she had planned.

After a few minutes, Hank reappeared leading the most beautiful horse I'd ever seen; rich grey with a white nose and a creamy white mane that flowed gracefully in the breeze. Obviously agitated, the grey was snorting and whinnying, dancing excitedly on its long, white-socked legs, straining to be free. Quarter horses were supposed to be gentle by nature but this one seemed to make nonsense of that theory as it eyed me warily.

It was led into the centre of the corral where another hand carefully placed a saddle on its back. This in itself was a delicate procedure as the slightest movement caused the horse to buck and kick, but eventually the saddle was secured and Hank nodded to Louretta.

'Okay, kid. Impress me,' she said.

I ducked between the rails of the enclosure to face my opponent, then slowly walked to where Hank was standing and carefully took the reins from him. I waited until Hank was out of the pen before I began. All eyes were on me, certain of the carnage they were about to witness.

'Ssh' I whispered, gently stroking the Grey's nose and neck, 'I'm not going to hurt you.' Staying at the head for a short while, just talking and stroking, allowing us to become acquainted, I then moved around to its side. Again, speaking to it in the same quiet tone as I took hold of the saddle, caressing and comforting the horse as I put my foot in the stirrup. 'Thatta boy, that's good,' I said softly, lifting myself off the floor and placing my full weight on the metal loop. 'Good boy, there's a good fella,' I soothed as I swung my free leg over its back. 'That's it, that's it,' I said lowering my backside into the saddle. 'There we are, good b—'

All of a sudden, the horse erupted with such ferocity that I was nearly catapulted skywards, but I hung on. It bucked and reared and kicked and ducked, but still I clung on. It span around then darted for the edge of the corral and skidded to a halt just inches before hitting the fence, but I tightened my legs vice-like around its girth. It twisted and bolted in the opposite direction throwing me around as if I was a rag doll, up and down went the roller coaster, my backside crashing time and again into the saddle, jarring my backbone. My teeth crashed together catching my tongue between them and I felt warm blood flood my mouth, then, without realising, I was flying through the air, completely free of the animal, though I could still hear it snorting and growling below me. Suddenly my back slammed against the Grey's muscular buttocks and as I fell downwards, a wild hoof punched me hard in the ribs. I crunched head first into the dust and slid to a halt on my chin.

I'd been in the saddle for seven seconds, but it felt like an eternity.

Slowly, painfully, I stood up, every bone in my body aching, my ribs burning and bruised. I gobbed out a mouthful of blood. My head throbbed, my vision was starred and there was a loud ringing in my ears. After a few moments, my senses cleared and I became aware of the cheering from the gathered workforce. I looked up and saw Louretta walking toward me, she was smiling and shaking her head. 'Not bad for a limey,' she laughed.

'Do I get the job?' I asked breathlessly.

'Yeah, honey, y'get the job.'

*   *   *

Hank told me later, that no one had previously stayed on the grey for longer than five seconds. For the first time in my life, I felt like I'd really achieved something.

Two

Joe stood alone outside the heavy iron gates of the prison and took a long deep breath of fresh air, savouring the smell of freedom. He'd been inside for seven years, six months, but now he was free.

With Ray as his mentor, and with the undisguised backing of the Reece firm, Joe had eventually made many friends in prison. He'd also earned a healthy dose of respect since his total annihilation of Frank Blades and was highly regarded among his peers. So much so, in fact, that at just twenty-five years old he had become the most respected man in the Scrubs - by both inmates and screws. An achievement that had not gone unnoticed by those on the outside who took an interest in such things.

Now, however, Joe was out and waiting for Ray to pick him up, the old pirate having been released a few months earlier, but he was late. This was nothing that Joe hadn't anticipated as Ray never wore a watch, he said they only served to remind him of what little time he had left - not that he was going anywhere - but Ray liked to live life to the full and wanted to appreciate every second.

Joe had missed him, even his constant barrage of bawdy songs, crude jokes and roguish behaviour. Without him, prison just hadn't been the same and it certainly would be good to see him again - that is, if he ever turned up.

Just as he was thinking about finding a cab, Joe heard the

sound of tyres screeching and looked up to see the Bentley speeding round the corner. The face of the man behind the steering wheel unmistakable.

The horn blasted loudly as the car came alongside and skidded to a halt. Ray Reece sat in the driving seat, a wide smile on his face and a black, shiny peaked chauffeur's hat tilted at a jaunty angle on top of his wild red mop of hair.

'Need a cab, Guv'nor?' Ray asked, grinning at his friend.

'Yes I bloody well do - and not before time!' Replied Joe in mock anger.

'Well, that's gratitude for ya,' said Ray, 'Cleaned the bloody car an' all - still, Vinnie'll be pleased - if he ever finds out I nicked it out his garage!'

Joe couldn't suppress his laughter, it was good to see Ray again. 'Home, James!' He said, as he made himself comfortable on the back seat.

Ray drove Joe directly to Ruby's as he was anxious to see his sister; to judge for himself the torment she was in and to see if he could coax her out of her cocooned world. He was eager to meet his nephew too, who was now six years old.

When the car pulled up, Ruby rushed out to greet Joe, making a real fuss over him, and Joe hugged her tightly and gave her a kiss on the cheek, but then, unable to wait any longer, he asked, 'Where is she?'

'She's upstairs, luv, first room on the right,' replied Ruby, 'But Joe—,' she caught hold of his arm 'Don't expect too much.'

Pausing only briefly outside Sarah's door to brace himself for what he might find, Joe pushed it slowly open and hesitantly entered the room.

Sarah sat in a comfortable arm chair gazing dreamily out of the window. In seven years, she'd lost all trace of the girlishness she once possessed, her hair had been cut shorter for convenience -

Ruby brushed it for her morning and evening and washed it every other day. Her pallor had changed also, the once lovely, healthy olive complexion was now pale and drawn, her cheeks sunken and hollow and her eyes had lost the bright, intelligent sparkle.

'Hello, Sis,' Joe said nervously, but there was no reply. He walked around to the front of her and knelt down by the side of her chair. Looking directly into her face, he tried again, 'Hello, Sis. It's me, Joseph.' Still nothing. Joe swallowed down the lump in his throat, she looked worse than he'd expected.

Once more he said, 'Sarah, it's Joe - I'm here now, to look after you, like I always used to, remember? Just like when we were kids. I promise.'

There was no response, nothing whatsoever. It was as if Joe didn't exist. He tightened his lips and took a deep breath, attempting to quell his emotions. He shut his eyes and tried to control the anger, fear and deep regret that churned within him. If only he'd been around he thought, maybe he'd have been able to prevent this awful thing happening to his sister. But he knew thinking like that was useless, there was no use in contemplating what might have been, he'd primed himself to expect the worst, but nothing could've prepared him for the reality. His beautiful vivacious sister was gone, and in her place sat a woman whose mind was lost in a far away place, constantly evading the truth of her shattered life. Joe felt utterly helpless, his heart aching with the pain from his twin's suffering.

Joe kissed Sarah lightly on the cheek and said softly, 'Don't worry, Sis, everything will be alright, I swear it.'

As he stood up, Joe noticed a small boy standing in the doorway. 'Who are you?' The boy asked pointedly. Joe looked at him and instantly recognised his nephew. It was the eyes. They were unmistakably the eyes of a Cassidy. Joe had them, Sarah had them and so did Vic. Yet his complexion was pale in sharp contrast to the jet black hair and gave Michael a chilling appearance but thinking little of it he gave the lad a broad smile.

'Who am I?' He said, 'I, young Michael, am your Uncle Joe, and I'm pleased to meet you.' Joe offered his hand for the boy to shake, but Michael merely considered it for a second, no expression on his face, then turned and walked away. 'Obviously made a good impression there,' Joe said to himself, slowly shaking his head.

Whilst in prison, Joe had promised himself that he'd be a friend to Michael, to try and give him all the support that a father would, but somehow, after that first icy encounter, he suspected things weren't going to be that easy.

*   *   *

Michael was an introvert who had very few friends, preferring instead to stay alone in his room than to go out and play with the other boys in the street. He didn't fit in, not out there or at school and resented those who did. He was always the odd one out, but rather than to keep trying, he purposely distanced himself; becoming aloof and presenting an air of superiority. But his solitary existence made him lonely and subsequently ill tempered. He'd invariably take out his anger on anyone who got in his way which, unfortunately, was mostly Ruby.

Ruby had tried her best with Michael. She loved him like a son and had given him everything he'd ever wanted - perhaps too much, she realised - but she couldn't help it, he was the apple of her eye. She would do anything to please him, and when he was in a good mood, he was a very loving child, but when he was angry, he could be spiteful and say hurtful things which upset her more than she cared to admit.

Ruby had told Michael that Sarah was his mother, but he refused to accept it and simply referred to her as 'the mad woman upstairs' for which Ruby constantly reprimanded him, but what could she do? Since the age of three, Michael had insisted on calling

Ruby 'Mum' which pleased her, but it did not sit too comfortably. Nevertheless, as the years passed, she grew to accept it and loved him all the more for it. His surname after all was Walsh, not Cassidy or Reilly, as at the time of his birth, Vinnie, Alfie and Ruby all deemed it wiser to hide his true identity. On paper, Michael was her son, so why not in reality?

Ruby had long ago ceased taking an intimate role with her clients, yet still greeted them and took care of the finances. However, in order to spend even more time with Michael and Sarah, she had recently called upon Ray to handle the day to day running of things. It turned out that he and Ruby had rekindled a relationship they'd had many years before, ending speculation as to which of the Reece brothers it was that she had loved. There was now no question, as since his release from prison, Ray had breathed new life into her and she was a picture of health and happiness.

Ray had made something of a breakthrough with Michael too, who viewed him as a kind of surrogate father, even though the boy's hurtful jibes were occasionally aimed at him. However, Ray was a steadying force who Michael respected and rarely crossed.

When Joe was told by Ray of his relationship with Ruby he just smiled and said, 'Well, fancy that, you all loved up. I never thought I'd see the day - and a daddy too.'

Ray just glared at him.

'No, no I'm pleased for ya, honest I am,' Joe grinned wickedly, 'When are the pipe and slippers comin'?' Ray made a grab for him but Joe was too quick, 'C'mon, Daddy, let's go see Alfie.'

Ray grunted and cracked his knuckles with humiliation, he could see Joe was going to get a lot of mileage out of this.

* * *

They found Alfie behind the bar at The Golden Gloves. He was older and balder, but still the same loveable rogue. They embraced and sat down with a pint and chatted about old times, all of them smiling at the memories, but after a while the conversation became more serious as they discussed Big Jack and his involvement with Benny. They talked about Frank Blades too, who Alfie knew well and he warned Joe to stay away. 'He's an evil and unforgiving bastard,' he said, 'If ya cross 'im, he'll haunt ya 'til ya die.'

Alfie told Joe that Frank had been released a year ago, but had no idea of his current whereabouts, 'I don't know and I don't care - but the further away from 'ere the better if ya ask me!' He said.

Alfie's face then saddened and a hint of melancholy entered his voice 'Suppose Ray's told you about Vinnie?'

'No, what about Vinnie?' Replied Joe.

Alfie looked quizzically at Ray, who shook his head and croaked, 'I couldn't. I thought I'd leave it to you,' For the first time since Joe had known him, Ray seemed lost for words.

Alfie nodded his understanding, as he too had found the news hard to take.

'Vinnie's got lung cancer Joe,' he said flatly. 'Doc gives 'im six months at most, poor bastard, and there's nothing anyone can do.'

Joe was stunned. The last time he'd seen Vinnie, he had been a picture of health; tanned, strong and fit; a man who he'd been convinced could overcome anything.

'He wants to see you, Joe,' Alfie continued, 'He's got a favour to ask.'

'Sure—' Joe replied, still in shock, 'Anything he wants, whatever I can do.'

*   *   *

Vinnie looked dreadful; frail and hollow cheeked with a sickly pallor. The matinee idol looks that had made him so dashing had all but disappeared and he was barely recognisable as the figure Joe had known seven years earlier.

Vinnie was in his study, seated in his favourite armchair, a bottle of port and two crystal glasses standing on the table close by. He was wearing pyjamas underneath a smoking jacket, both made of satin.

'Hello, Joe,' he said, genuinely pleased to see him, noticing that he too had changed. Joe had always been tall and muscular, but in the years he'd been away he'd definitely grown into a man. He was the embodiment of manhood and strength; a man of relatively few words, yet when he spoke, people listened. He had natural presence and a leadership quality which others rarely opposed. Vinnie had recognised this when he'd first met him, but he noticed now that Joe realised it too. It was apparent by the confident way in which he carried himself, not arrogant, but self-assured and controlled; a real cool customer.

Vinnie couldn't help but smile at his own impeccable judgement. He'd made a good choice, one which could not have been bettered.

'Come in, son, and siddown,' Vinnie nodded toward the armchair opposite his, as he poured Joe a glass of port.

'How was life in the nick?'

'Aw, not too bad, thanks to you - and your brother - it's hard to get bored with Ray around,' Joe replied.

'Yeah, I know, y'don't have to tell me, I've had to put up with that mad bastard for years,' Vinnie smiled affectionately at the thought of his younger brother.

'I've been hearin' lots of good things about you, Joe. You done well in there boy. Very well. People speakin' very highly of ya. It's been good for me to hear.'

'Like I said, it's all down to you, Vinnie. Thanks.'

'Nothing to do with me son, I just made a few calls - you was the one who did the time. And you done it well.'

'Well, whatever it was, thanks anyway.'

'No problem son. No problem at all. Now what you got

153

planned now that you're out?'

Joe had been pondering this question for almost all of the time he'd been in prison, what would he do? What line of work was he suited to? His first priority was Sarah and her care was paramount. Ruby had it well in hand, especially with the help of the money I'd left her before escaping abroad, which she had used wisely. But Joe wanted to be there for her too, physically, emotionally and financially if it should ever become necessary. Where money was concerned nothing was ever certain and who knew what Sarah might need in the future.

Joe had discovered his brain in prison. He found that he was actually quite clever, particularly at matters related to money and finance and he read many books on investing and speculation, about stocks and shares and how to get a return on your money. He even took a couple of accountancy courses and found he was good at that too. With this knowledge, it had long been his intention to invest the one hundred and twenty-five grand that sat hidden under the stairs at Rita's house, in order to get a very healthy return that would not only benefit him but Sarah and me also. It was a plan that we had worked on, via letter, for many years. But to see any return, even on an investment of that size, would take time and Joe needed to earn now, whilst we all waited for these investments to pay out - if, indeed, they ever did. There was no guarantee, no promises, just his intuition which he hoped would serve him and all of us well in the years to come.

'Good question,' Joe replied to Vinnie. 'I'm not too sure yet. Ex-cons aren't exactly right at the top of an employers wish list. But something will turn up, I'm sure.'

'I know it will son, I know it will. Now have yourself another drink and let's talk for a while. We got lots to discuss, you and me.'

The two men chatted for a long time, pausing every so often for Vinnie to cough - a deep hacking cough that left red spittle on his lips. It troubled Joe to see Vinnie in such ill health, but he kept his sympathy to himself as Vinnie certainly wouldn't have wanted pity. They talked about many things; Joe described his time in prison and outlined his brief knowledge of Benny Mottola, he also mentioned Frank Blades and Vinnie nodded, knowingly.

After another glass of port, Vinnie confided to Joe his hopes for The Firm, his strategy for survival and his plan to crush the Mottola gang with whom he'd been at war for nearly seven long years. Vinnie had managed to keep a grip on nearly all his more profitable enterprises, but many of the smaller, more vulnerable ones had succumbed to pressure from Benny and his boys. Mottola was continually gaining ground, never easing up, fighting tooth and nail to gain a foothold on the turf he desperately desired, and slowly but surely he was succeeding.

Vinnie's illness accounted for much of the control Benny had gained, and in that lay his problem. Vinnie no longer had the strength to run his empire, his mind was still razor sharp but his health was fading fast. To run a firm such as his you had to have your finger on the pulse and be prepared to take decisive action if something or someone stepped out of line. Even with the ever reliable Alfie, who kept him up to date with everything, Vinnie could no longer be the dominating force he once was, he didn't have the energy or the enthusiasm, but more importantly, he no longer commanded the same degree of respect. His time was nearly over and people sensed that. The influence and power that he'd had over the last twenty five years was slipping and he was very aware that he was fast becoming a 'has-been.'

Vinnie needed to send a message to let everyone know that the Reece firm was still number one. For that, Vinnie needed a messenger; someone who could act on his behalf; someone that people would respect and listen to.

'It's you I need Joe,' Vinnie said at last, 'I want you to take over.'

'Me—?' Joe was incredulous. 'But what about Alfie, or Ray? Don't they—?'

'No, son. You're the one.' Vinnie had made up his mind already. 'Alfie'll retire when I'm gone. He's had enough of it, he's done it for too long, all he wants now is his pub and his gym. And Ray - well Ray's Ray. He'll never change. He's never been one for responsibility, it's not his thing. I 'ave asked 'im, but he don't want it - not enough fun he reckons. He says you're the man for the job and I agree.'

'Vinnie, I don't know what to say—' Joe began, but again the older man stopped him.

'Don't say anything for a moment, son, just listen to what I've got to say before you make a decision.'

Vinnie then went on to tell him how he wished to pass the reins over slowly, how he intended, over whatever time was left, to teach Joe all he knew. Teach him every trick, every scheme and every detail about all his varied and diverse enterprises and how to make them work profitably and how to make them grow. He was offering Joe the keys to the kingdom, a life of luxury, wealth and power, a lifestyle that would be accompanied by enormous responsibility and pressure, but a life that would allow him to pursue all his dreams. Vinnie also said that he hoped one day, with the right investments and the right decisions, that the firm would become totally legitimate, and outlined his plan to make this happen. It wouldn't be immediate, in fact it would take well over ten years, but eventually, with wise and careful guidance, it would get there.

Joe listened to all Vinnie had to say without interruption, then, when he'd finished, the room fell silent and Joe sat in the armchair resting his chin on his knuckles, deep in thought. He could see that the plan made sense and if he was honest with himself, he knew it was an opportunity he had been born for. It was the dream he and I had had all those years ago, when we were kids, and now it was being offered to him on a plate. But in our dream, no one got hurt or killed, except maybe Vic and George. But certainly not Rita or Eddie or Billy or Sarah and no one went to prison. The life on offer to Joe now was one that would almost certainly mean more violence, it came with the turf and if chosen, Joe would have to prove himself tougher than anyone else.

The reality was though, that he was an ex-con, with few prospects and even less qualifications, except maybe as a hired heavy or a night club bouncer. What Vinnie was offering Joe knew he could do, and with an apprenticeship served in the Scrubs, he knew he could do it exceptionally well.

Vinnie could sense the turmoil within his young friend, 'Concentrate on making it legitimate, son - that'll make the rest easier to live with. A few years from now and you'll be a respectable business man, squeaky clean, beyond reproach - and if all works out right, very, very rich.'

Joe, he could see, was still wrestling with his conscience, 'I would view it as a favour to me personally,' Vinnie added, 'You're the only one who can do it Joe. It's either that or Mottola takes over - 'im and his goons - men just like the ones who did that to your sister.' It was a cruel statement, but nonetheless, a fact and Joe knew Vinnie was right. He craved vengeance for what had happened to his sister, as well as what happened to Billy - who was killed by a member of the Mottola gang. Vinnie was offering him a chance for vengeance, a chance to destroy Benny Mottola and Frank Blades and he had to accept it. He owed it to Sarah and he owed it to Billy, but he also owed it to himself.

A wry smile appeared on Joe's face, 'Okay, Vinnie, you're on, I'm in,' he said.

'Good man!' Vinnie exclaimed, then reached over and

vigorously shook Joe's hand, 'Peggy!' He shouted, 'Bring us some champagne, we've got some celebratin' to do!' Then Vinnie erupted into a violent coughing fit which left him pale and breathless. Although it was unspoken, both men knew Joe needed to take over as soon as possible.

Three

Joe needed a way to get noticed. Something that would make everyone sit up and pay attention; a clear message saying that the debts that had been owed to Vinnie Reece, were now owed to Joe Cassidy - and he would be collecting.

Joe was already known as a hard case throughout the underworld, with news of his exploits in prison, particularly his annihilation of Frank Blades, spreading like wildfire across the whole of gangland. Blades was no pushover, maybe the best street fighter in London, so with his defeat, Joe's reputation had increased ten-fold. However, being good with your fists was one thing; running a firm was another.

If you were going to come out on top, you had to be the most vicious, hateful and most thoroughly scary bastard around. If you weren't, then eventually, the opposition would walk all over you.

Joe knew this, and saw the opportunity to make his mark with a fence named Harry the Louse, who had stepped seriously out of line.

Harry owned 'The Lucky Break Snooker Club' in Walthamstow which was a front for his money laundering and fencing operations, he also ran a few whores upstairs. Arms dealing was another of his sidelines; if you were looking to rub someone out, or just wanted to rob a grocery store and needed a gun for the job, then Harry was your man. He could supply anything from pistols to hand-grenades, and perhaps, given enough time, even a tank. But all at a price as nothing came for free.

Harry also had a big mouth, but with so many villains relying on his services, he thought himself indispensable and therefore, untouchable. This made his tongue loose and his talk not only careless, but also disrespectful.

Word had it that Harry had been slagging off Vinnie and Alfie; declaring them to be past it and boasting that if they ever came after their protection money, he'd send them packing. This information came via one of Alfie's lads, whose mates had been playing snooker at the club and had actually heard Harry say it.

Now Harry, was pushing forty and not what you might call fit or hard, but he had three minders and they were in a completely different class; all ex-boxers, all big, and all famously mean. Unofficially they were known as Huey, Dewie and Lewie, but it wouldn't have been wise to tell them.

When word got back to Alfie about Harry's slur, and subsequently, to Vinnie and Joe. The decision was Joe's to make and he didn't hesitate.

*   *   *

Deliberately, Joe chose to take only Ray with him, the theory being the smaller the force the greater the impact. Ray's job however, would be to merely watch the door, to stand guard whilst Joe made his impressive debut.

As they stepped into the club, Joe noticed that only two of the eight snooker tables were in use. It was a quiet night at the Lucky Break, or at least it had been.

'Right you lot!' Ray shouted at the four punters playing, 'Piss off now if you know what's good for ya!' They didn't need to look more than once at the piratical red-haired man to realise they would be better off doing exactly as he said. Quickly they grabbed their cigarettes and coats and made for the door. As they cautiously edged past Ray and Joe, Ray snarled, 'Remember, you've seen nothing here tonight. Not unless you wanna see me again anytime soon. Understand?' They all nodded in unison. Safe as houses.

Harry, sitting on a stool next to the bar at the far end of the room and sucking on a fat cigar, had been in deep conversation with his three burly minders, who had now all risen defensively to their feet, ready to protect their boss, who was still seated. Harry remained outwardly calm, but in his chest, his heart was beating faster; he knew Ray Reece and what he was capable of; the young man with him he recognised too, although he'd never met him. Instinctively he knew it was Joe, whose reputation was even more impressive than that of his companion's.

Harry didn't have to ask what the two of them had come for, so there was no point in trying to oil them up with any chit-chat; he'd stepped out of line and he knew it. As to whether he cared depended on what happened in the next couple of minutes. But he was pretty confident that his boys could take care of the situation.

'I've got no grievance with you Ray!' Harry shouted.

'Nor I with you, Harry old son. You and me are just tickety boo, but it's not my call.' Ray was clearly enjoying himself, 'Alfie's been hearing all sorts of rumours. Seems you've been bad-mouthin' 'im an' Vinnie - which I found very 'ard to believe. But then he tells me you're a couple of months behind with your payments too, which again I thought was odd. Now obviously, I see this as just a slight oversight on your part, but Vinnie, well he sees it differently. Says you've got no intention of paying. Surely that can't be right, can it Harry?'

'I've been payin' long enough, Ray - an' I'm sick of it. If Vinnie wants his money, tell 'im to come 'ere and geddit 'imself - my fight ain't with you!'

'Oh, don't worry, me old mate, I've got no quarrel with you

161

either, but I'm merely a spectator.' Ray was geniality itself, 'Like I said, it's not my call. Joe is number two now. All decisions are his. He's the one you need to be talking to, not me.'

Harry looked at Joe, whose dark eyes were burning into him. Surely the stories about him had been exaggerated, he couldn't be *that* good, at least not against Huey, Dewie and Lewie. No way. In the second it took for Harry to contemplate this, he made his decision.

'Fuck it then!' He announced. 'If it's just the errand boy I'm dealing with, then Vinnie can stick his money where the sun don't shine.' It was too late now, Harry was committed.

'If the kid wants the money, let him come and get it, my boys will 'ave great pleasure in kickin' his arse!'

Ray smiled, then said to Joe, 'That's it then, son. Looks like you're on, don't let your Uncle Ray down now will you?' The older man was just as anxious as Harry to see how Joe fared against first rate opposition. He'd seen Joe in action many times in prison but only against second-raters and he'd always regretted not seeing the fight with Frank Blades, so was looking forward to what promised to be a good show. He wouldn't be disappointed.

Harry snapped his fingers, and Huey, the hardest of his three goons, started walking towards Joe, who was striding through the wide avenue of snooker tables to meet him.

As they came together, Huey made a grab for him, but Joe slammed a hammer punch into his kidneys causing him to bend almost double. As he did so, Joe grabbed a handful of curly brown hair and smashed Huey's face against the heavy oak frame of the nearest snooker table. His nose split and erupted with blood as he collapsed unconscious to the ground. It had taken less than four seconds for Joe to despatch him and Harry's mouth dropped open with utter disbelief, the half smoked cigar he had been chewing falling to the carpet.

Ray gave a slight chuckle of paternal joy. 'That a boy' he said under his breath, 'Show 'em what your made of.'

Joe carried on walking as if the man hadn't even been there.

Now it was Dewie's turn, who with a sadistic smile on his face, walked purposely forward to the second table in the row of eight, several feet from where Harry sat at the bar, and picked up a cue. He wouldn't make the same mistake as his associate, he would show the young scrapper who was boss. He continued a couple more paces then stood his ground, waiting for his foe.

As Joe approached, Dewie swung the cue wildly at his head. But he ducked and the shot thrashed freely into thin air. Anticipating the shot, Joe was working several steps ahead and had already planned his next move.

As he ducked, Joe snatched up the other cue from the table and quick as a flash, sprang up and slashed it sideways like a samurai sword, catching Dewie hard across the jaw. Two teeth fired like bullets from his mouth followed by a trail of bloody spit. Joe then brought the cue up and round, swinging it furiously in an under-arm motion, powering the heavy end of it straight into Dewie's crotch, almost audibly crushing his balls. Ray winced in sympathy as the second minder fell to the carpet, utterly useless.

Again, Joe didn't even pause as he once more charged forward.

Harry felt his bowels shift with fear. Things weren't going to plan. Never would he have believed it possible for one man to take out Huey and Dewie so easily. But he'd witnessed it with his own eyes and Joe was now headed straight for him.

First though, Joe had to get past his final line of defence. Desperately Harry turned to his last man, and was horrified to see the same fear and astonishment on Lewie's face that must surely have been on his own.

'Get him!' Harry shouted, 'For fuck sake get the bastard!'

Reluctantly, Lewie stepped forward, hoping that somehow he could stop this charging mad man, but Joe's eyes were red with rage and Lewie knew he was out-classed.

Joe stopped for a split second, to break the well worn cue over his knee, then marched forward again, holding one half in each large hand.

Lewie quickly reached into his pocket, pulled out an ivory handled flick knife and simultaneously popped open the murderous looking blade. His confidence rose a little, but it was premature, because as he waived the knife at Joe he received a hard rap on the wrist from one of the cue ends and all too easily the knife span from his grip. It landed on the snooker table nearest the bar and skidded across the green baize.

Momentarily panicked, Lewie attempted to lunge forward and grab Joe around the waist in a bid to force him to the floor, but once again Joe was far too quick.

The last thing Lewie saw was a bright white light as the two halves of the snooker cue smashed into each side of his skull, knocking him senseless. He was out for the count, unaware that he'd even hit the floor.

Harry by this time, was completely shitting himself and had to resort to desperate measures. Unfastening his jacket, he pulled a shiny black pistol from his belt and pointed it shakily at Joe.

'Stop you bastard or I'll fuckin' shoot ya. I mean it, I'll fuckin' kill ya dead.'

Joe drew up sharply, about three feet from Harry, still holding the two halves of the snooker cue.

The gun was waiving unsteadily in Harry's shaking fist, but his fear was subsiding and his confidence returning fast. 'That's it you bastard. Not so fuckin' hard now are ya? Some big shot you turned out to be. The Great White Hope - pah! More like a jumped up streak of piss. Well, shall I tell you what you are now?' Harry grinned coldly, 'Yer dead son. Dead as a fuckin' door nail.'

Ray's heart sank. He thought it was over, but for the first and last time in his life, he had underestimated Joe.

Joe just stared back into Harry's pale eyes. 'I don't think so,' he growled, darting swiftly sideways out the line of fire and whacking Harry hard under the wrist with one of the cue ends. The blow forced the gun up into the air just as it fired, with the bullet burying itself harmlessly in the nicotine stained ceiling. But before its impact, Joe had already clubbed the other half of the cue into Harry's ribs, doubling him over in agony. Throwing the cue to the floor, Joe then grabbed hold of Harry's left arm and snatched the gun from him, tossing it over the bar out of reach before twisting Harry's arm round up behind his back, almost to breaking point.

'P..P..Please! Stop, for fuck sake stop' Harry squealed, the bravado he'd shown just a moment before vanishing instantly, 'I'll pay, I promise I will - just let go of me, please.'

'No deal. Where's the money?' Joe asked firmly.

'I haven't got it, I need some time, just let me go and I promise I'll get it.'

'Don't lie to me you piece of shit. You've got it. Now tell me where it is, before I break your fuckin' arm.' Joe pushed Harry's elbow another inch up his back and he screamed with pain, tears now running down his cheeks.

Alright, alright! It's in the safe behind the bar, now let me go for Christ's sake!'

Joe nodded at Ray, who casually strolled up the length of the room and around to the opposite side of the bar. He carried with him a black leather brief case which made him look like some eccentric city gent.

'Well whaddaya know, he's tellin' the truth. There is a safe 'ere,' he said, 'All we need now is the combination.'

'Well?' Joe raised Harry's arm another half inch.

'Five, seven , eight, one, three, four!' Harry was now crying.

Ray entered the combination. 'Bingo!' He said as the safe sprung open. 'Looks like it's all here - in fact, I'd say there was more than enough.'

'Take it all' Joe said flatly, 'I think Harry 'ere owes Vinnie something on account by way of an apology. Whaddaya say Harry?'

Harry was unable to answer, he was sobbing too loudly.

After Ray had transferred all the money from the safe into the brief case, Joe released Harry, who slumped forward onto the nearest snooker table, panting breathlessly.

He looked at Ray 'Please Ray, you know me, Vinnie knows me, I'd never do anything against either of you - you know that, don't you? Don't clean me out - leave me something, please.'

Ray was lighting a cigarette, completely unaffected by the man's pleading.

'It's not up to me Harry' he said matter-of-factly, 'Joe is the man. He calls the shots now and sadly old son, I think you've pissed 'im off big time.'

He was right. Joe wouldn't just let it lie, not now, and Harry knew he had to act fast in order to save himself. He scanned the room quickly for some sort of weapon; a cue or a ball or anything hard enough to protect himself with, then a flash of blue steel caught his eye, from the snooker table next to him, and he saw the flick knife was still laying where it had fallen, just two feet away. Recognising his chance, Harry made a desperate grab for it, but before reaching it, one of Joe's huge hands clamped firmly on the scruff of his shirt, and stopped him dead.

Joe threw him onto the snooker table, so that he was sprawled on his fat stomach across the chalk marked baize. He seized Harry's wrist and pulled his arm across the table so that his hand rested on the thick wooden framework, then picked up the flick knife. Suddenly Harry read his intent, the true horror of his fate hitting

166

home.

'Oh Jesus, oh no, please don't, I'll pay you anything I promise, anything you want!' He squealed.

Joe just looked at him coldly and said, 'You've got nothin' I need.'

'Oh God, oh God—'

'But maybe you need to remember who the boss is round 'ere - and this should help!'

In one swift, powerful thrust, Joe brought down the blade of the knife, skewering Harry's hand straight through the centre, pinning it to the oak of the table, the sharpened steel burying itself at least two inches into the wood.

As Harry shrieked in agony, Joe turned and walked away.

'Please, pull it out! Don't leave me like this, please, I can't move!' Harry screamed.

Joe ignored him. 'Torch it,' he said to Ray.

Opening the brief case once more, Ray pulled out a petrol filled bottle that had an old piece of rag stuffed in the top. Then, from his pocket, he pulled out a Zippo lighter and lit the rag.

Joe turned back to Harry and said, 'Well it's like this, Harry, pull the knife out or you're charcoal. It's your choice.' He then nodded to Ray, who threw the homemade bomb into the far corner. As it smashed, the flames took hold instantly and started to make their way across the beer stained carpet.

'See ya around Harry!' Joe said as he and Ray left the building.

*   *   *

Harry survived, as did his club after an expensive refurbishment. But he, and everyone else were left in no doubt that the Reece firm were once more back in control.

Joe's message had been received loud and clear.

Four

Joe hit gangland like a steam train, making his presence felt in every bar, every brothel, every night club and every gambling joint. For each business Benny had taken over, Joe took back two. For each soldier of Vinnie's that had been harmed, Joe hurt four of Benny's. For any man who'd changed their allegiance to Mottola, Joe gave them only one chance to come back. Neither would they be asked again, or be given the opportunity to go elsewhere if they declined.

He took control. Nobody disrespected him, nobody bad-mouthed him and nobody said no to him. That was the only way - any other would have shown weakness.

He increased his territory almost daily, raking in thousands a week from protection money alone. On top of that there was the cut from cat-houses, pubs, clubs, restaurants, haulage, shipping and numerous other enterprises that all turned a healthy profit. He owned property in upmarket locations such as Kensington, Chelsea and Knightsbridge, as well as the less prestigious areas like Rotherhithe, Peckham, Tooting and Walthamstow. He had shares in clubs in Soho, Oxford Street, Carnaby Street and Covent Garden all of which were frequented by the young, trendy and rich.

Joe made certain that half of all takings went to Vinnie, no matter how much or how little. That was the deal. Upon Vinnie's death, Peggy, his wife, would continue to take a smaller percentage. She would be a rich widow, but that would be scant compensation for losing the man she loved. But Joe would watch over her, as would Ray and Alfie.

With his own share, Joe did various things. All illicit income was used for The Firm; to fund its growth, to pay the troops, to refurbish, to buy-off, to bribe, to negotiate and to deal. Joe personally did not take a penny. The only money that he ever had in his bank account, safe, wallet or hand came by way of his legal ventures, like the restaurants, clubs and night spots - which all pulled in thousands of more pounds. Joe poured a large amount of this revenue into a new investment company which, although operated by him, was jointly owned by both of us - me being the silent partner, for obvious reasons. We called this company Ironclad Investments. Initially, this was set up using the money I had stashed at Rita's house, the one hundred and twenty-five grand from the Marquess of Devon's safe - with which Joe bought sizeable shares in various growth companies that he speculated would do well in the years to come. As time passed, and as the company flourished, he bought more shares - as many as possible - all in the name of Ironclad. These investments quadrupled their initial worth in no time, making us both a great deal of money. My share, however, I entrusted to Joe, because for the life I was leading, money was, at present, of little use. Even though I was incredibly happy at Wildwood, I could not assume it to be permanent. At any moment I could be back on the run and, if so, I needed to be able to travel quickly and leave no trail to follow. That meant having no bank accounts, no businesses and no fixed abode. Just me, the Indian and the holdall.

*   *   *

Vinnie fought the illness much longer than anyone believed possible, but after a brave battle, he died two days before his fifty

169

fourth birthday, in the June of 1960, nearly eighteen months after Joe had been released from prison. It was the end of an amazing reign, but the crown had already passed to another.

Alfie was gutted. He and Vinnie had been closer than brothers for over forty years, so when Vinnie died, Alfie retired, reasoning that without his friend, it just wouldn't be the same. He still had his pub and his gym and, of course, his large family that worshipped the ground he walked on. Alfie would certainly not be lonely or unhappy in his retirement.

Ray was also devastated and went on a drinking spree that lasted over a week, but eventually, when he'd come to terms with his brother's death, he came back to the comforting arms of Ruby who knew only too well what he was going through.

Ray would always be Joe's strong right arm, but with Vinnie's passing, Joe promoted another man who had been with the firm for several years; a reliable sort who was very wise to the London scene. His name was Carl Napier. Although not handsome, he was suave and stylish, with dark slicked hair and a pencil moustache; a poor man's David Niven, but harder edged and without the Sandhurst accent. He had charisma and charm in abundance which made him very popular with the ladies.

Joe had known Napier for quite a while and had always thought him to be a good man, not some gangland thug, but a clever, resourceful operator with a smooth line in patter that could get him almost anything. He was a man of ambition and to hear him speak you would think the glowing future he saw for himself was preordained - you would also be mad to bet against it.

Joe knew too, that Carl had been approached by Benny, who had offered him a better deal than he got with Vinnie, but Napier had declined, preferring to stay with Reece and take his chances. This proved he was loyal and not easily bought, a trait which Joe also admired.

Joe made his base at The Golden Gloves pub, which was not ideal but would do for the time being and meant he could work out regularly in the gym upstairs. Since his very first day in prison, exercise and fitness had become something of a religion.

Astonishingly, another regular habit of Joe's was letter writing. He and I had always corresponded as often as my travels allowed, but since settling in California, we'd been writing at least once a month. It allowed us not only to keep up to date with what we each were doing, but also served to gain a different perspective on a particular subject that may be concerning either one of us. Because our lives were now so different, we could offer opinions without bias, which was often helpful in finding a solution to a particular problem.

Face to face, Joe could appear cold and unemotional and certainly far from talkative, but writing allowed him to express himself, to vent his feelings which he felt unable to do verbally. Often his letters were three or four pages long and I would read them with relish, hungry for knowledge about the people and places I missed terribly.

I was deeply saddened by the death of Vinnie and wished I could have returned for his funeral; I owed him a great debt, which I could never repay. However coming home was out of the question, so I wrote a letter of sympathy to Peggy, which I asked Joe to pass on.

I always addressed my letters to Ruby, which Joe would then collect, which was a safe system, or so we thought, designed to keep my whereabouts secret, but it very nearly brought about our downfall.

* * *

Gloria Coombs was a whore who had worked at Ruby's for six months. She was a beautiful girl but ruthlessly ambitious and neither Ray nor Ruby fully trusted her. But she was very sought after by the clientele so, reluctantly, they put up with her.

Only a select few of the girls knew Sarah's true identity; those who had been there on the night she was brought in, but these had been with Ruby for years and, in the most part, were like daughters to her. They could be trusted and their loyalties to Ruby were unquestionable. To the others, of which Gloria was one, Ruby had maintained the story of Sarah being her troubled cousin.

However, unbeknownst to Ray and Ruby, Gloria also worked for Benny Mottola, who had told her to find out anything she could about either Joe or myself.

Gloria saw in Benny the route to power and money and, in her wildest imaginings, she even contemplated a life of pampered luxury as his wife. But for Benny it was purely a convenience. He recognised her potential and, sensing her greed, had easily coerced into the role of spy.

For months Gloria's efforts had been fruitless and Benny was starting to believe her presence at Ruby's to be futile. But then, due to an oversight in Ruby's normally vigilant regime, Gloria finally struck gold.

Five

Ruby was looking forward to seeing her sister, who was making one of her rare visits to London from her home in Scotland. Michael however, was not so enthusiastic, and had chosen that morning to vent his displeasure. He hoped, by this difficult behaviour, to make Ruby cancel her appointment, which was a technique that had proved successful many times in the past, but not on this occasion as she refused to give in. Even if she had to drag him kicking and screaming behind her, she would not miss the chance to see her sister.

The letter from California arrived that morning, and Ruby placed it on the mantelpiece, intending to slip it into her handbag before she left. But with Michael's tantrums, she found herself running late and all thoughts of the letter vanished from her mind. Nevertheless, after keeping the taxi waiting for twenty minutes, she and Michael did eventually manage to leave the house.

*　*　*

Ray was out with Joe, and Gloria knew he wouldn't be back until after dark, so decided to take a gamble. She crept away from the other girls and slipped silently through the door into Ruby's private quarters without being seen. Once inside, she worked swiftly, searching every drawer and cupboard, looking under each chair - even lifting the Persian rug to make sure nothing had been hidden underneath. Meticulously she replaced everything, careful not to alert Ruby to her intrusion and when satisfied, she moved to go upstairs. But as she turned, Gloria noticed the light blue envelope sitting on the mantelpiece and berated herself for not seeing it before. She rushed to the letter and saw at once it had been sent via Air Mail from California. Clutching it like a prize, she read the name out loud, relishing every word, 'Mr. J. Cassidy, c/o Miss R. Walsh,' she said. Unable to contain herself, Gloria tore open the envelope and hurriedly read the letter inside, but it was only when her eyes fell on the signature at the bottom that she realised the value of what she had discovered, and immediately imagined a reward to equal it.

The letter was signed simply, your friend always, Sean.

*   *   *

Benny chuckled wickedly as he re-read the letter for the third time. In it, he discovered not only the whereabouts of his brother's murderer, but also the whereabouts of Sarah, who he previously assumed had fled the country as well. He also delighted in reading about Michael, whose very existence, until that moment, was unknown to him. It was almost too good to be true.

Benny had waited nearly ten years for news such as this and he was going to savour every morsel. At last he was going to have his revenge. And, in the process, finally take control of South London.

*   *   *

After reading the letter through one more time, Benny picked up the phone and called Frank Blades. 'Go buy a plane ticket to California, Frankie,' he said with a wicked smile on his face, 'There's someone there I want you to take care of.' He then began to outline his plans for retribution.

As he talked, he studied Gloria, who was still standing in front of him awaiting her reward, and not for the first time Benny thought how sexy she was. She revelled in the attention as he eyed her up and down, his gaze wandering lustfully over her pushed-out breasts and tight round arse in the sprayed on dress. She smiled; a wanton, enticing smile, knowing exactly what he was thinking. He grinned back, his loins stirring and stretching the front of his trousers. What was it about whores - why couldn't he resist them?

The grin was all the come-on Gloria needed as she stepped over to him and knelt between his legs, keeping eye contact as she unbuttoned his straining fly. A moment later she had him in her mouth and Benny had to summon all his powers of concentration as he swiftly tried to wrap up his call to Blades.

Finally he managed to do so and was able to give Gloria his full attention. He watched with delight her bobbing head in his lap and felt the pleasures of her practiced art, which she had mastered to perfection. All too well in fact, as within mere seconds it was over.

Her eagerness riled him and suddenly he was angry, just as if someone had popped a switch in his head. That was all it took; the slightest disappointment, the stupidest of reasons, but the blue-touch paper had been ignited.

He cursed her silently, 'Typical whore, the sooner they get it over with, the sooner they get their money!' He regarded her with disdain as she knelt beside his chair, her bright red lipstick now smeared hideously around her mouth, making her look like a grotesque caricature of her true self. No longer did he want her, or to feel her on him - now she disgusted him; just another scheming little bitch after his power and money. Why did these women always attract him and why wasn't he ever strong enough to rebuff them. He felt sick and dirty, she had ruined everything and he needed to be rid of her before he vomited.

Gloria looked up and smiled at the man she assumed had taken her as his lover, but in his eyes, where she'd expected to see adoration and desire, she saw hate and loathing. A chill ran down her spine and fear filled her belly but before she had time to move, Benny stood up, banging her head against his naked torso, forcing her back at an uncomfortable angle. He made her wince as he snatched a handful of her golden hair and crudely wiped himself with it.

Gloria's lower lip began to quiver as she craned her neck to stare terrified at the figure standing menacingly above her.

Benny's teeth clenched together and his lip curled as he placed one powerful tattooed hand over her face, 'You filthy fuckin' whore,' he growled, 'You disgust me.' Then pushed her sharply away, jarring her head backwards. But he was stronger than he knew and she was at an awkward angle, her neck already strained to the full. Mottola heard the snap, then watched without the slightest trace of emotion as Gloria's lifeless body slumped to the floor.

So much for her reward.

Benny had not meant to kill her, but now she was dead he felt no guilt, she wasn't worth it. As far as he was concerned, she got what she deserved. He would get Jack to dispose of her as he was always discreet, although it usually came at a price and rarely was it cheap. Big Jack was a man who knew what he wanted, and what he wanted was a bigger piece of the game - a game to which Benny had a golden ticket.

*   *   *

Benny re-arranged his clothing, telephoned Jack then dragged Gloria's body behind the sofa so it could not be easily seen. He then strode purposely out of his office and locked the door behind him. He clumped heavily down the narrow staircase and stepped into the men's bar of the Black-eyed Pea, the pub where he conducted all his business. Several members of his crew sat chatting and smoking, but as soon as Benny entered the room they fell silent, as to disrespect him was to commit a very grave error.

'Meathook, Dino, Russ!—' He barked at three of the men, '—get yourselves tooled up - we're goin' across the river to do a bit of business. He then turned to another, 'Stutter, you're drivin' - but make sure y'take a shooter too.'

*   *   *

Michael had done his best to ruin Ruby's day, his surly behaviour proving to be a constant source of embarrassment both during lunch and throughout the rest of the afternoon. It ended when, after a disastrous tea at Harrods, again courtesy of Michael, Ruby decided to call it a day. She left her sister at the station and got a cab home, arriving back just after six.

*   *   *

Ray arrived an hour later, but the moment he pulled the Bentley up outside the house, he sensed something was wrong. The lights were off, even in Sarah's room which was odd as she hated the dark. Ray smelled danger, and cautiously got out of the car, aware that he was possibly being watched. He brushed his hand against his side, feeling the reassuring bulge of the .38 in his belt that his jacket concealed. The gun was loaded as always.

Casually, he made his way to the rear of the car, trying not to look too conspicuous, and flipped open the boot. The sawn-off shotgun was wrapped in a red tartan blanket and a box of cartridges sat in the hub of the spare wheel. Ray unwrapped the gun and loaded both barrels; the car shielding his actions. Then, after stuffing a handful of cartridges into his pocket, he straightened up and expertly slid the shotgun butt up under his armpit, letting the shortened length of it run down his inner arm, disguising it from view, a move he'd perfected on many prior occasions. Ray then lifted out his gym bag with his free hand, making that seem to be the purpose of his visit to the boot, which he then slammed shut. Afterwards, he sauntered to Ruby's door, appearing not to have a

177

care in the world, certain that hostile eyes were watching his every move. He turned the handle and stepped into the hallway. His fears were now confirmed; the landing light, which Ruby always left on for Sarah just in case she got scared or needed something, was switched off - the only time in over ten years.

Carefully Ray placed the gym bag on the ground and adjusted his grip on the shotgun. Holding it with both hands now, he pointed it into the darkness and with just the slightest of clicks, cocked both barrels.

He eased himself into the living room, but the moment he crossed the threshold, the lights came on and the shooting started. Ray dived behind the sofa, but was just a split second too late, and a bullet ripped into his shoulder as he crashed painfully to the carpet.

Shot after shot blasted around and through the sofa as Ray forced himself flat against the floor. Another bullet caught his upper arm on the same side as the last wound and still the firing continued. Handfuls of wadding and cotton fibre filled the air around him and a metallic tune was being played as the bullets hit the coiled springs of the sofa. Again Ray was hit, this time through the back of his left knee shattering the bone and he screamed in agony. As he did so, the top of his right ear was blown away, the shot passing so close to the side of his head that it severed the elastic of his eye patch causing it to twang violently off.

Blood was now pouring down the side of Ray's face soaking his white cotton shirt, his jacket sleeve and trousers were also wet and gluey from his other wounds and all he could do was wait for the bullet that would finally kill him, but as he lay there, his face pressed hard into the carpet awaiting certain death, the shooting stopped.

Ray heard the muffled voices of the firing squad. He couldn't make out much, but the gist was that Benny thought him to be dead and was sending a volunteer to check.

Ignoring the pain, Ray silently rolled onto his back; his shotgun poised and ready. Moments later, a man's face appeared over the back of the sofa. It belonged to a villain named Russ McAllister, who Ray recognised from years back. McAllister was a horrible, weasely sort who'd shoot his own mother for five bob and certainly wouldn't object to finishing off one of the famous Reece brothers.

Confident in finding a dead body that resembled Swiss cheese, McAllister casually looked down behind the sofa. But the cocky expression on his face turned to one of terror as he found himself staring down the barrel of the sawn-off. Before he had a chance to pull back, Ray fired, blowing the man's head clean apart, splattering it like a melon being hit by a truck. Blood, brains and skull fragments rained down on Ray, but he didn't have time to worry about that.

McAllister had also been carrying a sawn-off, which fell from his grip as his body was forced into the air by the blast. Quick as a flash, ignoring his injuries, Ray grabbed it; he now had a matching set. Using his good arm, he pushed himself up to a squatting position, resting his weight on his undamaged leg. He could hear the panicked enemy hurriedly reloading and knew he only had a matter of seconds before they unleashed another volley. There was no time to think, just to act.

McAllister's headless torso was slumped like a horrific rag doll over the back of the chair, his arms dangling limply down. Sliding a gun barrel under each of the corpse's arm pits, Ray pushed himself awkwardly to his feet, with the dead body rising up with him, acting as a shield. As Ray reached his full height, he peered over the top of McAllister's spurting neck and spied the opposition. There were four of them - all known killers; Eric 'Meathook' Murdoch, Dino Rosella, Stutter Bagshaw and the unmistakable figure of Benny Mottola, in all his glory. Across from them, tied to chairs by the wrists and ankles were Ruby, Sarah and Michael - thankfully still alive.

Almost instantly the firing started again, and Ray felt every thud as the bullets ripped into the corpse shield. He made the first shot count, aiming between Benny and Murdoch, hoping that the spread of shot at that range would kill both men. It killed one, unfortunately not Benny, but it did knock him down and rendered his shooting arm useless. Ray staggered slightly as he turned unsteadily to face the other two men and unloaded the second barrel of the first shotgun into Rosella's chest, killing him on the spot. Dropping the spent weapon, Ray aimed the fresh one but, before firing, a bullet clipped his good ankle and sent him sprawling to the ground, the headless corpse he was supporting landing heavily on top of him.

Ray could no longer see Stutter Bagshaw or Benny the Bull from where he lay on the carpet, and with his injuries was unable to manoeuvre himself quickly enough to locate their whereabouts. But then he heard a voice behind him; it was Stutter, 'It's okay, Boss,' he was saying, 'I'll take care of you, I'll get ya outta here.' Then, in response, Ray heard Benny's deep gravelly voice, agonised and straining, 'Get the boy,' he gasped, 'Whatever ya do, get the boy.'

Ray's body was beginning to cease up. He found the corpse on top of him almost impossible to shift as he was weak with blood loss and injury. He heard Michael struggling as Stutter untied him, which fuelled his resolve, and with a huge effort, he pushed the dead man's body off him.

Clutching the shotgun, he scrambled desperately round and saw Bagshaw pulling Benny's arm around his shoulders, forcing him to his feet. Michael was being held too and was kicking and screaming with Stutter's hand clamped on his throat. Ray couldn't risk the shot as the spread might have killed Michael, and he threw the weapon aside. Stutter glared at him, glad to see the shotgun out of harm's way on the carpet - with both arms full he was in no position to protect himself. But as he eyed Ray, sprawled and bloodied on the floor, he considered the threat to be over, and smiled smugly at his beaten adversary.

However, as Bagshaw turned for the door, Ray pulled the revolver from his belt and slowly, pulled back the hammer. He pointed it at Stutter, his vision starred and blurry, the barrel waiving like a feather in the wind, but he had no choice other than to pull the trigger. He'd tried for a head shot, but the bullet caught Bagshaw in the hip, making him stagger backwards and cry out with pain. But amazingly, he remained standing, neither letting go of Mottola or the boy. Ray cursed and aimed again, squeezing off another round just seconds after the first. But it was too late, Stutter had somehow managed to throw himself and his captives through the door opening into safety and the shot hit the wall with a loud crack.

Ray was now struggling to stay conscious and looked around to find Ruby, still tied to her chair.

He stared hard into her tear filled eyes, 'It's alright, luv' he said, 'Joe'll get 'im - everything will be alright' and with that, his eyes closed and his head fell to the floor.

Six

Big Jack was depressed. His dreams of becoming number one were evaporating fast and it seemed there was very little he could do about it. He sat gazing into space, pondering his predicament, blaming Joe, the one who had prevented him from achieving his rightful status. If it wasn't for Cassidy, Jack felt certain that Vinnie would have offered The Firm to him.

However, Anderson had always despised having to answer to Vinnie, the cousin he believed unworthy of such power and status, who, even after death, had managed to rob him of the position he'd been born for. Without so much as a thought for him, Reece had handed the crown to some young scrapper, not even attempting to keep it in the family where it rightfully belonged.

It was this act of treachery, this blatant lack of respect, that had forced Jack to join forces with Benny, who'd offered him all the things that his cousin had not. At first, he'd felt a twinge of guilt but as time went on, and with no deal on the table with Cassidy, he became bitter, allying himself and the Twenty Ones with Mottola.

But it had proved to be a very bad decision.

Mottola had become increasingly unstable in the last few months, with wild mood swings and a savage temper that many fell victim too, some suffering animal like beatings. His sexual appetite had changed also, he'd become violent, particularly with the whores that Jack had been ordered to obtain for him. Some of the girls had been scarred for life, and things were going from bad to worse. Jack had to change his luck.

The Mottola gang was on the way down, the Cassidy Firm on the way up and Jack felt as though he was going nowhere fast. And he blamed Joe. If it was not for him things would be so much better as Jack would have already achieved his goal. He would be in charge of Vinnie's firm, the most powerful firm in London, and not some jumped up errand boy straight out of the nick.

The only way forward was for Jack to personally take control of the Mottola gang, but for that, he first had to get rid of Benny. As he sat in his grubby office at The Pontoon contemplating this, the phone rang. It was Mottola informing him of his 'little accident' with Gloria, and ordering him to dispose of the body.

'Better make it quick,' Benny demanded, 'I've got business on the other side of the river - but I'll be back in a coupla hours and when I get 'ere, I want the corpse of that whore gone. Understood?'

Jack understood alright. He understood that he'd got to do something about Mottola pretty damn quick before both of them were sent down.

The call was the last straw. That was it, he could take no more.

* * *

Every so often, the police raided The Pontoon, The Golden Gloves and The Black-Eyed Pea - all the gangster strongholds in fact - no matter how much the likes of Jack, Joe or Benny paid them to stay out of their businesses. It was something that was unavoidable, as Scotland Yard, the government and the media all demanded such action, but rarely was anything found or anyone arrested. Normally, this was thanks to tip-offs from coppers on the take, who would be rewarded handsomely for their information. However, there had been occasions when notification of a raid was not given, and in these cases, arrests had been made.

Jack got to thinking about this, and wondered what the consequences would be for Mottola if the police stormed The Black-Eyed Pea and found Gloria dead in his office. It certainly wouldn't look good for him that was for sure. What a terrible coincidence; Benny killing a girl and the police catching him red-handed. Nevertheless, a coincidence it would be, or at least, that is how it would be perceived.

Anderson despised the law, hated coppers and it went against the code he lived by to be an informant. A grass was the lowest of the low, the scum of the earth, but in this case, he could see no other way. Within a few short hours, he could be rid of Benny for good, all it would take was one simple phone call.

Jack smiled and picked up the receiver once more; perhaps the police did have their uses after all.

Seven

After Rose left, Joe never thought he'd fall in love ever again; but there he was, staring at a woman of such staggering beauty that he knew, without doubt, that she would only have to snap her fingers and he'd be hers, body, mind and soul.

Rose had been pure and innocent and naive, but this woman was sexy, confident and worldly wise. She knew how to use what nature had given her in abundance, and use it she certainly did.

Joe admired her as he sat in the car waiting for Carl who was speaking to her and making her smile. Making her look even more beautiful. Joe's eyes travelled upwards from the girl's long shapely stockinged legs and narrow waist, over her firm, round breasts and on to her irresistible face. He found himself day-dreaming about running his hands through her lustrous auburn hair and kissing her soft red lips. But then cruelly, all too quickly, he was snapped out of his dream as Carl leaned in and kissed her. And she kissed him back.

For a second, Joe felt his anger prickle and the emotion took him by surprise; it had been a long time since a woman had aroused his passion so strongly. But Rachel Davenport was Carl's girlfriend and, as such, completely off limits, yet she had awakened feelings within Joe which he knew to be very dangerous. Feelings which he knew would have to be satiated.

Joe and Carl were on their way back to Ruby's from The Golden Gloves, where they, along with Ray, had been discussing business with Alfie. Somehow Carl, anxious for his boss to meet the love of his life, had managed to talk Joe into taking a detour to where they now were; outside Rachel's flat.

Ray had gone on alone in the Bentley; Joe and Carl agreeing to follow along fifteen minutes later in the Jag.

When Rachel answered the door, she stood with Carl, talking softly and canoodling the way lovers do. Carl was obviously smitten as his almost claustrophobic attentiveness loudly declared, but Joe sensed that her feelings were not quite so intense, and guiltily, he felt pleased, although the ease in which he disregarded his friend's happiness did not sit easily.

As Carl and Rachel walked over to the car, Joe opened the door and stepped out, buttoning his immaculately cut Italian jacket as he did so. Vinnie had taught Joe the importance of good clothes and stylish dressing. He'd said it presented an image of success and power, and, on first impressions alone, could give the vital psychological edge. He was right.

'Joe, meet Rachel - the girl I'm gonna marry,' Carl said excitedly, and Joe felt another knife in his heart. 'Rachel. This is Joe. My best friend and boss, and a better man you couldn't hope to meet.' Once again, the guilt washed over Joe as he held out his hand.

'Pleased to meet you, Rachel,' Joe said, 'I've heard a lot about you.'

'All good, I hope?' Rachel replied, a lovely, beguiling smile on her face.

As she took his hand, Joe could have sworn he felt an electric shock, and as their eyes met, he knew that she had felt it too.

As Rachel looked into his face, she was immediately attracted to his darkly handsome features and dark shining eyes, which sparkled irresistibly as they stared into hers. She almost felt feint, a little weak at the knees, surprised that feelings so intense could spring up so quickly. Never before had she experienced such an instant attraction, such an overwhelming desire, and it quite literally took her breath away.

Joe looked hungrily back at her, his expression betraying his wanting, unintentionally telegraphing his inner most thoughts.

Magnetically, they were drawn to each other, neither one wishing to relinquish the grip on the other's hand, almost if they were fused together.

'Hey, Joe! Let go of my woman, will ya?' Carl exclaimed with only a slight trace of humour, breaking the spell and bringing Joe and Rachel back to reality with a jolt.

'Sorry.' Joe apologised, as he quickly let go of Rachel's hand 'I was lost in a world of my own then. Yes, it was good–, I mean Carl, has told me about you—.' He was babbling, trying to brush away the awkwardness of the situation. '—All good. It's very nice to finally meet you.'

'And you,' Rachel replied, 'It's nice to meet you too,' her voice was suddenly husky.

Joe saw her eyes flash with meaning. She felt the same way as him. He knew it, but he desperately hoped Carl didn't. Sadly though, he did.

*　　*　　*

They left Rachel and drove quietly toward Ruby's place, neither man feeling at all comfortable with what had just transpired. Joe was wrestling with his conscience, never would he betray a friend, but at the same time, he found himself mad with desire for the woman he'd just met.

Carl meanwhile was not sure what he'd just witnessed. He felt shaken, his confidence dented. The woman he loved, who he was going to marry, had shown obvious signs of attraction to another man. A man who was not only good looking and powerful, but one who he also looked upon as a close friend. Surely it was all in his mind, or at least, that's what he forced himself to believe.

Both locked in their own thoughts, neither man suspected anything awry as the car pulled to a halt outside Ruby's. But had they been just two minutes earlier, they would have witnessed Benny and Michael being bundled into a car by Stutter Bagshaw, who then sped them away into the night.

Nothing could have prepared Joe or Carl for the carnage they saw as they strolled innocently into Ruby's living room.

Ray lay face down on the carpet in a pool of blood, the corpse of a headless man lying beside him. The bodies of two other men lay where they had fallen amidst the blood spattered frenzy that had occurred just minutes earlier.

Sarah sat bound and gagged in a dining chair, her emotionless eyes raised to the ceiling, her mind switched off from the bloodbath she had witnessed. Ruby was tied to an identical chair, although hers was laying on its side and she was trying desperately to hotch towards Ray, tears streaming down her face. The sound of her hysterical sobbing was muted only by the handkerchief that was still stuffed firmly in her mouth.

Horrified by what he saw, Joe noticed immediately that his nephew was missing. The ropes that had bound him still hanging from the chair he'd been tied to.

Joe ran to Sarah's side and quickly untied her, whilst Carl did the same for Ruby.

Holding Sarah's head between his large hands, Joe swiftly examined his sister's face for any sign of bruising. 'Are you okay, Sis, are you hurt?' He asked desperately. But she merely stared through him, as if he was transparent, a vacant look on her face and humming the haunting melody of Rock-A-Bye Baby, the tune she sang to escape.

'It was Mottola!' Ruby cried, spitting out the gag, 'He's killed Ray and taken Michael!'

Joe turned to face Ruby, the full horror of what had transpired sinking in. 'You've got to stop 'im Joe,' Ruby pleaded, 'Kill the bastard and bring Michael back safe. Kill 'im for what he's done to Ray.' She was crying loudly, inconsolable with grief.

Joe ran to Ray's side, as did Ruby, who threw her arms around her lover's lifeless body and sobbed into his spiky ginger hair, kissing him repeatedly. Her wailing giving voice to the pain in her heart, with the salt of her tears mingling with the blood from Ray's half severed ear.

'My God, Ray. What have you done?' Joe's voice was full of sadness as he looked upon his friend; the man who had saved him from self destruction in prison; the man who'd taught him so much; the man who had died trying to save his family. 'What am I gonna do without you?' Joe asked quietly.

A moment passed, the atmosphere heavily laden with sorrow as Joe contemplated the death of his trusted lieutenant. Then suddenly, out of the grief, someone spoke. 'I tell you what you can do—' the voice was low and husky, '—You can get this woman off me and go and get the bastard who shot me - that's what you can do!'

Ray was alive. Somehow, by some miracle, he'd survived. Ruby's tears turned to those of joy, as she smothered him with kisses 'Alright woman! That's enough.' Ray protested, 'Carry on like that an' I will be bloody dead!'

Joe smiled with relief, his delight undisguised, and he squeezed Ray's forearm in a gesture that conveyed the unspoken affection and high esteem he felt for his injured friend.

Ray turned his head slowly, every muscle aching as he looked up at Joe and said, 'I mean it boy, don't worry about me, I'll be fine. Just go and save Michael.'

Joe had to think fast as Michael's life depended on it. He phoned Alfie and briefly filled him in, asking him to get over to Ruby's as soon as possible to organise the clean up operation and pay-off the law, which would buy the time needed to dispose of the bodies and destroy the evidence.

Carl would take care of Ray, get him to the doctor's house in Wandsworth where he'd receive immediate medical attention. The doctor was more than equipped to cope with Ray's wounds, as his association with the underworld assured him of a steady stream of similarly injured patients.

Ruby, although extremely worried about both Michael and Ray, agreed to stay with Sarah, who, after the night's events, would need her care more than ever. What damage Mottola and his boys had done to Sarah's fragile nerves was anyone's guess, but they could have set her recovery back years.

When Joe was certain that he'd covered all eventualities, he took the car keys from Carl, jumped in the Jag and headed as fast as he could towards East London. He'd had no time to assemble a crew, no time to devise a tactical strike or to contemplate the huge dangers of what he was about to do, he just knew he had to get Michael back. And for that, armed only with a six-shot revolver and a set of knuckledusters, he was charging alone into the lion's den.

*   *   *

By the time Benny arrived back at the pub his wounded right arm had turned a fierce purple and he'd lost all sense of feeling below the elbow. He had six pieces of shot buried deep in his forearm, a further two in his upper arm and four more in his chest. He felt tired and weak, but knew he had to remain alert, certain that the Cassidy mob would soon be paying him a visit.

The man who had saved Benny's life was also in a bad way.

190

Having driven all the way back from South London with blood pumping from the nasty wound in his hip, Stutter was sitting in a sticky red puddle, his trousers, socks and shoes all soaked and his face a ghostly grey from blood loss. As soon as he brought the car to a halt, Stutter could fight no more and slumped, unconscious, over the steering wheel.

For the entire journey, Michael had lain terrified on the floor of the car with Benny's foot pressed hard on his chest. Only when they had reached the Black-eyed Pea was the foot removed and replaced by Benny's hand as he grabbed Michael roughly by the scruff of the neck and forced him out of the car. Using the boy for support Mottola pulled his own huge bullish frame from the vehicle, but his head was swimming and he had to fight to stay upright. Placing his good arm around Michael's shoulders, Benny rested his immense weight on the lad to help support himself, and without giving his dying driver a second thought, thrust Michael forward and staggered with him, unsteadily to the back door of the pub.

Michael found it impossible to hold back the tears as Benny forced him through the doorway and up the stairs, his body being thrown backwards and forwards to balance Mottola's vast bulk. But finally, with his young legs buckling under the strain, they eventually reached the office. After locking the door, Benny threw Michael onto a battered settee then staggered across to his ancient desk and eased himself into his chair.

Michael gasped in horror. The settee upon which he lay, was positioned opposite a sofa that stood on a set of carved wooden. Behind it, Michael could clearly see Gloria's lifeless body, her open eyes staring directly at him. The boy was transfixed, frozen with terror and unable to avoid her deathly gaze. He began to shiver violently, never, in his whole life, had he been so scared and was certain that, at any moment, he too would be killed.

Benny was badly wounded, unable to think straight and slipping uncontrollably in and out of consciousness. He was on the verge of delirium, chuntering under his breath and jumping at shadows, although his reflexes were slow and cumbersome. To make matters worse, none of his crew knew he was back; he had entered by the back door, which was the quickest and least painful way to his office. But his men weren't aware of what was happening and he was far too weak to go downstairs and put them on guard. He had left himself unprotected and vulnerable and it was his own stupid fault.

Benny slid open the top drawer of his desk and took out a revolver and six bullets. His injured right arm was completely useless which was going to make loading the gun difficult. But with his left hand shaking like a leaf, and a great deal of effort, he managed to do it, all the time fighting the urge to pass out. When done, Benny laid the pistol on the desk and placed his good hand over it. He was now as ready as he could hope to be. Glancing up at the clock on the wall, he desperately tried to focus on the hands with vision that was blurred and starry, but he could just make out the time, it was seven fifty-five.

* * *

Joe looked at his watch. Seven fifty-five. By his reckoning he was just fifteen minutes behind Benny. He drove through the streets of the East End and finally turned onto the road that led to the Black-eyed Pea, parking up about two hundred yards from the pub. He couldn't chance being seen, even though leaving the car that far away would make escape more hazardous. But it was night and the street was badly illuminated, which he hoped would be enough to keep him from getting shot.

Joe looked at his watch again. Two minutes past eight, time to make a move. He ran the two hundred yards and stopped behind a car parked haphazardly at the rear of the pub. He carefully peered in and saw Stutter's body slumped over the steering wheel, quite obviously dead. Then Joe noticed a trail of blood leading from the car to the back door of the pub. The handle on the back door was smeared with blood too and Joe prayed it belonged to Benny not Michael.

Gently, he turned the sticky handle and was mildly surprised to find the door unlocked. Joe pushed it open carefully, and cautiously slipped through, quickly surveying his surroundings as he eased the door closed behind him. The hallway was dark, with peeling wood chip wallpaper and a quarry tiled floor, but at the far end he could see a crack of bright light shining under a doorway which, from the sounds of laughter and conversation, he guessed opened into the lounge bar of the pub. To Joe's right was a steep wooden staircase, and on the banister were long slashes of still wet blood; a macabre trail which would no doubt lead to Benny Mottola and Michael.

Gingerly, Joe climbed the old staircase, placing his feet as close to the wall as possible to minimise the sound of the creaking planks, aware that at any moment he could be discovered. However, slowly but surely, he finally reached the landing, which was illuminated by the light emanating from behind the frosted glass of Benny's office door. As he edged towards it, Joe could again see blood on the handle and this time, on the glass too. He felt certain that Michael was in that room, possibly Benny also, but as to how many others he had no clue. All seemed quiet, although that could just be a ploy.

Joe took out the knuckledusters and slotted them over the fingers of his left hand, the pistol he pulled from his belt and gripped with his right. He then flattened his back against the opposite wall, took a deep breath and violently kicked open the office door. As it swung unsteadily on its hinges, he threw himself into the room, his eyes scanning for danger, the pistol moving in unison with them, ready for attack.

'What—? whassat, who is it?' Benny slurred groggily, desperately trying to focus through cloudy vision.

Joe stared at the man who had caused him so much grief, but who he'd never previously met: George Reilly's best friend; Frank Blades' master and Vic Cassidy's boss. Benny Mottola; the bane of Joe's life.

But Joe did not see the vile monster he had been expecting, just a bald, bloated and pathetic specimen of a man. A man who was drooling at the mouth, who was only half conscious and delirious with pain, his thick heavy features drooping lazily as he gazed uncertainly in Joe's direction, unable to distinguish the shape of the person standing before him.

'Who's that?' Mottola demanded again 'Maxie, is that you - is it you Maxie?' Dark red blood was seeping steadily from the holes in Mottola's chest and arm, he looked a mess and was surely close to death.

'No, Benny. It's not Maxie.' Joe replied coldly as he looked around and saw Michael curled up tightly on the settee, his attention snapped away from Gloria by his uncle's entrance. 'It's okay, son,' Joe said softly, 'You're safe now.'

'Cassidy!' Benny exclaimed, 'It's you ain't it? You've bloody well come to fetch 'im aintcha?' Suddenly he went for the gun on his desk, but in his weakened state he fumbled it and the revolver slipped from his grip, bounced on the edge of the table and spun off onto the floor. Benny's tattooed hands, one which had love scrawled on the knuckles, the other which had hate, desperately searched the table top for the weapon, but to no avail.

'It's on the floor,' Joe said flatly, enjoying the other man's pain as he strolled over to the desk.

'I'll getcha, ya bastard - don't you worry,' Benny growled back with a spray of saliva. He span in his chair and flung himself to the floor as he tried recklessly to find the gun. However, he landed badly, catching his injured arm on the bottom drawer of the desk and a flash of intense pain shot up his wounded limb. Darkness came crashing in on him and he passed out, his huge body sprawled awkwardly on the worn carpet.

Joe walked around the desk and stood looking over Benny's massive form, regarding the man he had wanted to kill for so long. He cocked the pistol and pointed it at the back of Mottola's huge head and slowly tightened his grip on the trigger, coaxing it steadily backwards. Then he remembered the boy.

Michael had already been through enough, there was no need for him to witness this too. Besides, Ray had probably killed Mottola already, judging by the amount of blood. He just wasn't dead yet.

After a moment's consideration, Joe released the trigger, tucked the pistol back in his belt and walked over to the settee where Michael sat cowering with fear. He lifted the boy up and briefly held him to his chest, 'It's alright, boy,' he said 'It's all over. Let's go home.'

As he put the lad over his shoulder to carry him, Joe heard the sound of a police siren and gunfire as all hell broke loose downstairs.

*　*　*

At eight fifteen, acting on a tip-off from an anonymous informant, Inspector Charlie Roberts was poised to give the signal for his men to enter the pub. He had found Benny's car and the dead man in it, parked recklessly on the pavement, and knew that Mottola must be inside the building. He'd also seen the trail of blood that led to the back door and, other than the dead girl he had been told about, wondered what else he might find of interest at the Black-eyed Pea. As a precaution, he posted two of his constables by the rear entrance, just in case Benny tried to escape.

Three police cars had been positioned facing the pub and twenty officers wearing riot helmets awaited the signal which took the form of a police siren that Charlie switched on from the central car. The men piled into the pub and almost immediately the shooting started. From his secure position behind the open door of the police car, Roberts lifted the loud hailer to his mouth and shouted 'This is the police. We have you surrounded, come out with your hands up!'

*   *   *

Joe heard the message loud and clear and made for the office door. He walked quickly back towards the stairs, but realised that the police would surely have the back door covered. Joe had no wish to return to prison, which he surely would if caught at the pub, with a shot and probably dying Benny Mottola.

He ran back along the landing, past the office, and found a small, black painted out window at the end of it. Peering through one of the scratches, he could just see the flat roof of the pub kitchen some six feet below. He tried the window latch but it was stuck fast having seized up with years of neglect. Thinking quickly, and with no time to put Michael down, Joe ran back into Benny's office, not noticing that Mottola had roused and was watching him starry eyed from around the side of the desk.

Joe looked about trying desperately to find something he could use to break the window, and quickly decided on a wooden chair that sat in the corner of the room. He swept it up and bolted once again for the door, but Benny had found the revolver and unsteadily pointed it in the direction of the figure rushing from the room. He squeezed the trigger as hard as he could and was rewarded with a loud crack of gunfire.

The bullet missed its target, striking instead the enamelled metal lamp shade, hanging above, with a deafening clang, sending the light dancing wildly about the office. Joe spun around and glared at Mottola, wishing he had killed him when he'd had the chance. But now there was no time - he and Michael had to make good their escape before the law got to them. With the boy still over his shoulder, Joe ran back onto the landing and along to the window, which he smashed with the wooden chair.

The police had gained the upper hand in the fracas and had managed to force their way to the door that led through to the quarry tiled hallway and rear stairs. Joe heard the door open and the sound of men pouring through it.

He lifted Michael down from his shoulders and noticed immediately that he wasn't making any attempt to support himself, his body all loose and floppy like a rag doll. Looking into his pale face, Joe was suddenly appalled to see a horrific gash in Michael's right cheek and bright red blood spurting from it. He'd been badly hit, the bullet from Benny's gun obviously ricocheting off the light fitting and striking him a glancing blow on the cheek, ripping through the skin like butter and scraping the bone as it past.

There was no time to check if Michael was alive or dead as Joe could hear the police already piling up the stairs. So, in desperation, he bundled Michael's limp body under his arm and ducked carefully through the window. Crouching for just a second on the sill to judge the drop, Joe, clutching his nephew as tightly as he dared, then silently leapt off into the night.

Eight

Ranch life suited me well. The days were long and sunny, starting early with a couple of hours with the horses before breakfast. After eating, it would be straight out to the corral again for another full day, which would invariably end long after dark. The highlight of the day was a huge supper which everyone attended - even Louretta herself. It was always lively and entertaining with the dining table abuzz with witty repartee and hilarious stories, each person competing with the other to tell a funnier, more amazing tale than the last. After three years with these warm, welcoming people, I felt as though I was part of the family, and I liked it.

Louretta sold her horses for vast amounts to buyers all over the world and among her clients were kings, princes, sheiks and movie stars, so the standards had to be very high. However, it was because of these rigorous standards that her success in this field had far surpassed that of her acting career and had gained her respect the world over. By her own admission, she was single-minded and demanded much from her staff, but no matter how tough she was on them, they all adored her and trusted her judgement on virtually everything, myself included. And she proved this very early on in my time at the ranch, when I was summoned to her office for 'a chat.'

Louretta was sitting behind her big desk, all business, her

face as serious as a heart attack. 'Okay, kid,' she said, 'You've been here eight weeks and you're fittin' in just fine. You're a good hard worker and I like ya. More to the point, Hank likes ya and he don't like no one.' Hank was the wily old hand who had been instructed to supervise me.

'But now it's time to cut the crap. If you're gonna stay on I need to know the truth.'

Suddenly I was flustered, surprised by this unexpected attack and her accusatory tone. Had I been found out, had I been tracked down? 'I don't know what you mean! Up against what?' I blurted, my thoughts racing wildly.

'Listen Kid, I can smell horse shit, I've been around it for years - and you're full of it. Sure you're good with horses, real good - but before you came here you'd never trained one in your life. They're my business son, so I know. Now, that said, I like ya and think you're basically a good boy. I'm willing to help, but I need to know what I'm up against, so I want the truth kid and I want it now. No more fairy tales.'

For the short time in which I'd known Louretta Wild, I'd come to recognise a quality in her which I instinctively trusted. She was a very straightforward down to earth woman, who although strict and demanding, had a keen sense of humour and a quick intelligence that made her extremely likeable. Her persona was much like that of a wise mother hen who defensively guarded her brood against all predators, a brood which I found myself pleased to be a part of.

For some reason, I felt I could tell this woman anything, and she would understand. Perhaps because she'd had such an eventful life herself. Born into poverty in Poland, arriving with her family as an immigrant to America and then losing both parents to tuberculosis before she was sixteen. She changed her name, and by financing herself through several demeaning and badly paid jobs, single mindedly pursued a career as an actress. This resulted in her becoming a world famous movie star and millionairess by the time she was thirty. In 1947, she retired from film at the peak of her popularity and as the highest paid female star of her time, to enjoy further success as a breeder of quarter horses.

She'd been married and divorced three times and had a child by each husband. Her daughter, Victoria, was now a movie actress in her own right, and both her boys had lucrative careers behind the camera.

Yes, I trusted Louretta Wild and felt that whatever I told her would not be repeated.

I sat up straight in the luxurious leather chair, cleared my throat, and told her my story, leaving nothing out. It was as if I was in the confessional booth, I felt the weight lifting from my shoulders and the burden I'd been carrying with me for all those years slowly fade away. I'd found absolution and I couldn't help but spill out the whole sorry tale, enjoying the freedom I felt in doing so.

Concluding the story with my arrival in Newport Beach, I looked Louretta directly in the eyes and said 'So that's it, that's the lot. You now know everything there is to know about me.' I felt cleansed and not in the least bit concerned about what the consequences might be as a result of my honesty. I just felt relieved at finally being able to tell someone.

'What are you gonna do now?' I asked.

Louretta's eyes told me nothing, not a trace of what she was thinking. She was a very tough lady and it was hard to gauge what her reaction was going to be.

'Where's the money now?' She asked, 'The money you been carrying around in that bag of yours?'

'Under my bunk,' I answered, 'It's been there since I got here. I didn't know what else to do with it.'

'You'd better go fetch it then,' Louretta ordered coolly.

'Fetch it?' I queried. 'Are you gonna turn me in?'

'No son, I ain't gonna turn you in,' she replied, 'But I am gonna put the bag in my safe where no one can stumble on it by accident. It's a whole lotta dough kid, and even though I trust everyone here, that kinda money just ain't easy to resist.'

'So, you're not gonna turn me in?' I said again.

'No. Like I said, I just wanted the truth. I'm a pretty good judge of character and I believe what you've told me. Sounds as though you've had it real rough and I'm sorry for you. For your girl and your buddy too. But now I know what I'm up against, maybe I can help. Heck, I've lived one helluva life kid, and I know how tough it can be, but you also need friends if you're gonna survive and maybe that's what we can be here. I don't want your money - hell, I don't even care about your money, and I certainly don't care about some crime you're supposed to have committed back in London. I know you, or at least I reckon I do, and I'm pretty sure you're as innocent as you say you are.'

She winked at me and gave me one of her best smiles, the sort I remembered her giving as a kid, looking up at her on the cinema screen on a Saturday afternoon with Joe and my mum, then said, 'Now go get that bag. You can have it back whenever you want but for God's sake get it out from under that bunk!'

'Yes Ma'am!' I said, still in a state of shock.

'Call me Louretta, son—' she smiled at me again, '—I reckon we're acquainted enough now.'

Nine

Virgil's movie career took off in the summer of sixty-two. He'd been playing bit parts for several years, but not really getting anywhere; once or twice he'd been chosen to speak a couple of lines of dialogue, but that was about it. However, a female studio executive who had been spending the weekend with her family in Newport Beach had noticed him strutting along the beach with a harem of giggling girls giving chase. Immediately impressed by his rugged good looks and bronzed physique, she approached him, unaware that he was already an actor, albeit not a particularly accomplished one, and asked him to audition for a film she was casting.

After an immensely successful screen test, he was given a three year contract and hired to play third lead in a romantic comedy starring none other than Victoria Wild - Louretta's daughter.

The film was a huge smash and the critics all agreed that Virgil showed great potential. On the strength of these reviews, he was signed to two more movies, with a further three in the pipeline. As yet, he'd not achieved top billing, but those in the know said it would not be long before he did.

Virgil still spent weekends at the apartment in Newport Beach and remained completely unaltered by his new found fame and fortune. His only extravagance was a new surf board with a custom paint job, but aside from that, he was the same old Virgil; laid back, cool and decidedly unaffected.

I was curious to know what he'd thought of Victoria Wild who, as yet, I'd not had the chance to meet. She'd only paid two short visits to the ranch since I'd been there and both times I was hard at work in the corral, unable to catch even a glimpse of her. All Virgil would say was 'Wild by name, wild by nature,' which only served to arouse my curiosity even further.

*   *   *

I arrived back at the ranch late on the Sunday night, after a particularly debauched couple of days with Virgil. He'd had one of his famous parties, which started on the Friday night and was still going strong when I left on Sunday evening. By the time I got back to Wildwood, late Sunday night, I was hungover, exhausted and urgently in need of sleep. In just a few short hours the sun would be up, the horses would need tending and I would have to be fit and ready for work.

I coasted into the driveway with the engine off, anxious not to wake up the whole house, and steered around the floral island in the centre. As I hopped off the Indian and began pushing it in the direction of the bunkhouse, I felt relieved that nobody was around to witness my less than sober condition. In fact, the whole house was in darkness apart from one upstairs light.

It was then that I noticed a beautiful blue Corvette parked in front of the house, its smooth lines and shiny chrome trim gleaming in the moonlight. Even in my tired and inebriated state, I couldn't help but appreciate it and wonder, jealously, who it belonged to.

Gazing at the car, I was suddenly aware of a tune playing in the background, it was Elvis' Return to Sender, which had only just been released and not the sort of thing that anyone in the main house would be playing, but that's where the music was coming from.

I looked up to the room with the lights on, the source of the sound, and saw a wondrous sight.

A fabulous looking woman, who I recognised immediately as Victoria Wild, was standing there, on her balcony, in her underwear, drinking a bottle of beer and swaying in time with the music. If I'd had to guess, I'd have said that it probably wasn't her first bottle, as she looked free of all inhibitions. I remembered what Virgil had said about her, 'Wild by name, wild by nature.' But no matter how appropriate his evaluation seemed, I couldn't help but stare. She was stunning.

She had not yet seen me standing there in the darkness leaning on my bike, and I purposely remained silent, guiltily watching, entranced by the beauty that I had only previously seen on a movie screen.

Her white, lacy underwear contrasted brightly against her deeply tanned skin, as did her long platinum hair, which was tied up in a pony-tail. Her body was slim and curvy with firm breasts and a smooth flat stomach. She was swaying her hips slowly in time with the beat, rhythmically, sexily, alluringly. And I was transfixed.

I was balanced, leaning against the Indian, my backside on the seat, my feet planted firmly out in front, taking the full weight of both me and the bike, which was, by now, leaning at quite a severe angle. Suddenly my foot slipped with a loud scratching sound as the heel of my boot slid along the tarmac and I felt the Indian fall as the balance was misplaced. Quickly, I twisted around and grabbed the handle bars, my feet thankfully finding purchase once more, preventing the bike from falling. But by then, it was too late. When I looked up again at the balcony, checking to see if my clumsiness had given me away, I saw of course, that it had.

Victoria Wild stared down at me, her large neon blue eyes fixing me hard with accusation and surprise. Yet her superbly crafted cheeks, clearly visible in the moonlight, were not at all flushed, and on her full red lips I definitely saw the beginnings of a mischievous, almost brazen smile. She made no attempt to cover herself as we stared at each other, and as we did, the record finished and started again. Then, with a flirtatious twinkle in her eyes, she raised her bottle in salute to me and took another long swig.

Then, still keeping her eyes on me, her hips began to sway from side to side once more. It was a clear invitation for me to continue looking and, lasciviously, my mouth watered and my excitement grew.

A moment later, she reached up and pulled the ribbon from her hair, shaking it out to allow the long locks to cascade down her back.

It was the most erotic display I'd ever witnessed and I was completely under her tantalising spell, only barely aware of my noticeable and pronounced arousal. She was clearly loving every second, knowing without doubt that she had control of my very being and becoming obviously turned on at the thought.

Suggestively she caressed her thighs and stroked the flat of her stomach, thoroughly enjoying the power she had over me. The record played through almost to the end, but I knew I couldn't contain myself much longer. My heart was pounding and blood pressure pumping, my jeans were almost at bursting point and my fearsome erection was throbbing painfully.

Then, without warning, my foot slipped again, but this time I was unable to stop myself from falling. I lost my grip on the Indian which keeled over and crashed noisily into the side of Victoria's brand new Corvette, breaking off one of its shiny chrome wing mirrors, denting the door and leaving two deep scratches down the waxed metallic paintwork.

As I sprawled awkwardly half on the tarmac and half over the engine of the bike, I again looked to the balcony, just in time to see Victoria Wild storm furiously back into her bedroom and slam the french windows behind her.

*   *   *

I was obviously a whole lot drunker that I thought, because in the morning the whole episode was a bit of a blur. I certainly couldn't remember Victoria screaming the house down, waking up the entire ranch shouting 'Peeping Tom!' and 'Intruder!' at the top of her voice. Nor could I recall Hank carrying me back to the bunk house or throwing up on Jarvis, the ranch manager's, bed, but I know I did, as I'd seen the evidence. I'd also been shown the damage I caused to Victoria's car, which would take a fair chunk of my wages to pay for.

Thankfully, the only mark on the Indian was a slight graze on the cherry red paintwork which I could polish out, but apart from that, she was, much to my relief, as beautiful as ever.

Feeling lousy and hungover I was sitting in Louretta's office drinking black coffee shame faced. I'd embarrassed myself and had let my boss down. Never before had I not been fit for work, but on that morning, with my head pounding and every muscle aching, I was in an awful state. To make it worse, I had to sit and listen as Louretta gave me the full treatment, reprimanding me for the unforgivable events of the previous evening. On top of that, Victoria Wild was sitting in the chair next to mine, a disgusted expression on her face, her large neon eyes staring daggers at me as if I were some loathsome pervert, which according to her version of the story, I was. She had great delight in telling the whole lurid account to her mother, while I was powerless to disagree. My recollection bore very little similarity to hers, which portrayed me as the villain of the piece and her as the innocent victim, but how could I object when I wasn't sure myself; my memory was cloudy to say the least and all I wanted to do was return to bed.

After a tortuous half hour, my ordeal ended. Victoria, clearly pleased with her latest performance, stood up and bent purposely over the table in front of us to kiss her mother lightly on the cheek, deliberately thrusting her bottom out, in her tight denims, for me to look at. I tried not to, but couldn't help it.

When Victoria was certain that I'd had a good look, she stood up straight and said 'Thanks for taking care of it Mom, I just felt so dirty knowing he was out there staring at me.' She then turned and looked at me with her back toward her mother, and gave me a victorious little smile, the corners of her mouth turning upwards vindictively. This was obviously a girl who was used to getting her own way, but the mischievous glint in her eyes told me that this was far from over; it was just the opening round.

When she had left the room, I smiled apologetically at Louretta, trying to convey how sorry I was. What she did then surprised me. She leaned across her desk, straining to see out of the door, making certain her daughter was gone, then she grinned back at me and gave me a wink, 'Don't sweat it kid, I know Vicky's games, but I play along to keep her happy.'

'You mean this has happened before?' I asked incredulously.

'Not exactly like that, but let's just say I got wise to her stories a long time ago.'

'So you and me, we're still alright?

'Sure, kid - we're just dandy!' Louretta said warmly.

'But the car—' I said hesitantly.

Louretta waived her hand dismissively, 'Forget the car. She's got hundreds of goddamn cars.'

'But I—' I offered, but again she waived her hand.

'Don't worry about the car, worry about yourself.' Louretta laughed at my predicament, 'She's got her sights set on you, I can spot it a mile away - and what Victoria wants, Victoria gets!'

'I don't believe it!' I said modestly, although I already knew what she was saying to be true.

'Oh, believe it! Louretta replied, 'But be careful - she's like dynamite!'

'Tell me something I don't know' I thought to myself as I got up to leave the room.

Perhaps I didn't feel so bad after all.

Ten

Soon after the Peeping Tom incident, as it became infamously known, Victoria left the ranch to start a new movie which was being shot in Hawaii, so I figured for the time being at least, I had escaped her devious but deliciously alluring wiles - although I have to admit I was slightly disappointed.

Life soon returned to normal and I threw myself into my work. Virgil was also off making another movie, so even at the weekends I stayed on the ranch.

Some of the boys had rigged up an old leather punch-bag in one of the barns and, most Saturdays, I'd bang away at it, reliving my days at the Golden Gloves gym. Often we'd have proper matches which were always good natured, but still punishing, and quite regularly someone would get accidentally knocked out. Nevertheless, the ranch hands were all tough men who loved a good scrap and when the adrenaline started pumping anything could happen - and usually did. However, these bouts, and my strenuous work schedule, had put me in great shape. The years at Wildwood had made me lean and hard with every muscle perfectly defined, and, even though I say it myself, I was the picture of healthy masculinity.

Occasionally we'd have boxing tournaments with a neighbouring ranch, meant for fun of course, but with pride at stake, they had become very competitive affairs. Unfortunately though, as I was currently the Wildwood champion, I had been forcibly volunteered to represent the ranch in the forthcoming contest.

These tournaments were carnival days which the competing ranches alternately hosted, and on this particular occasion, the event was to be held on the plush green acres to the front of Wildwood's main house. Anybody could attend these galas, and most of the surrounding population did so. There was picnicking and dancing and people would spend the day getting happily drunk, then they would watch as the two contenders knocked seven bells out each other. The perfect end to the perfect day.

*   *   *

The phone call came two weeks before the contest.

I was in the corral with Hank when Blanche, Louretta's maid, came rushing from the stable block and told me I had an urgent telephone call.

'A phone call, for me?' I queried 'Do you know who it is?'

'Somebody from England,' Blanche replied, 'Some guy called Joe.'

I ran to the house to find Louretta standing in the kitchen holding the telephone out, waiting for me to collect it, knowing I'd be anxious to speak to my friend. Snatching it from her grip, I nodded my thanks and put the receiver to my lips.

'Joe! How y'doin'?' I yelled.

'I'm fine Sean. Just fine. It's good to speak to ya.' Joe's gravelly South London accent was music to my ears, but I caught something in it that told me this was no social call. Instinctively I sensed he was phoning with bad news and I felt a stirring of dread in the pit of my stomach.

'What is it Joe?' I asked, immediately dispensing with the pleasantries and getting straight to the point. 'Is it Sarah?' I looked at Louretta, who had recognised my anxiety.

'No, Sean,' Joe replied. 'It's Michael. He's been shot.'

*　*　*

Thankfully, the boy was alive, although I felt sick when Joe told me of his injuries. His face was damaged and would never again look completely normal, even though the doctor had apparently done everything in his power to repair it. When the bullet passed through Michael's cheek, it had sliced an inch wide strip of flesh completely away, leaving the doctor little alternative but to pull the two remaining flaps of skin together as he sewed them up, distorting the boy's face slightly. The bullet had also displaced Michael's jaw, giving him an unattractive grimace which would tragically become a permanent feature of his already unsettling appearance.

My first instinct was to return home, but Joe warned against it as there were still posters of me all over London; the police having not lessened their efforts in searching for my whereabouts. This was mainly down to Lord John Tailby who was still waging his crusade, making certain that neither the public, the authorities or the press forgot about my crimes. He was as determined as ever to bring me to justice, convinced I was responsible not only for the killings of Jez Mottola, Vic Cassidy and Jimmy Feathers, but also for the rape of his mistress and the robbery of his apartment.

It had been ten years, yet the events of that night were still just as newsworthy, with speculation over my disappearance filling several column inches every couple of months.

That was one reason why I could not go home to care for my son. The other reason of course, was Benny.

Benny had been arrested, and although badly injured, his wounds had not, as it turned out, been fatal. This meant he was still a very real threat to all of us, even from the hospital wing of Broadmoor where he could still wield his sword of power. He would never rest until the deaths of both his brother and his best friend had been avenged.

More worrying, was that Benny now knew Sarah and Michael's whereabouts, and Joe was pretty certain he also knew where I was too. Ruby had discovered the envelope which had contained the letter stolen by Gloria, which Joe suspected had been given to Benny. My letter. The one that led to Michael's abduction. The one which had caused the near death of Ray Reece - the man to whom I was deeply indebted for the bravery he'd shown in trying to rescue my family, the same man who had taken on the role of father to my son. It was my letter that nearly killed them both.

Ray would now have to permanently walk with a stick, even then with a severe limp. The wounds to his knee and ankle assured him of that, although those in his arm and shoulder would heal perfectly in time. He would also have to live with only half an ear on one side, which, according to Joe, would not impair his hearing, and I was grateful for that at least.

With all this distressing information came the realisation that Wildwood was no longer safe and I felt deeply saddened at the prospect of having to leave.

*   *   *

Louretta and I sat in her plush office considering my options, each of us with glasses of bourbon that had been filled several times.

'You know somethin' kid?' Louretta said, her voice a little slurry, 'I'm gonna miss ya. Call me sentimental, but it's the truth.' She raised her glass in a silent toast to me, then took another large sip of the dark golden liquid.

History seemed to be repeating itself as again a woman I'd grown extremely fond of was toasting my farewell. Just like that night at Ruby's ten years before.

Louretta had friends in Montana with whom she regularly

supplied horses to and she was confident that she could secure me work on their ranch. Montana was rich and beautiful with wide open expanses of pasture land, it had mountains and lakes and a man could stay there forever maybe without ever being found. The down side was that Montana was not California. Sure, I could expect hot summers, but Louretta told me the winters would fall to below freezing and when that happened, the work would be hard and punishing, starting well before dawn and finishing long after night fall, often spending the night on the plains under a snow filled sky, wrapped in a sleeping bag with only a horse and a herd of cattle for company. I never did like the cold, I certainly wasn't keen on cattle; the primary source of income for the ranch, and the idea of not seeing my bed for nights on end didn't inspire me too much either. But Montana it would have to be. In Montana I would be safe.

'I'll miss you too, Louretta,' I said, and raised my glass in a salute to her. But then, as I did so, it suddenly hit me; a feeling of anger, of injustice, of mad stupidity. Perhaps it was the alcohol but it occurred to me that no matter where I went, whether it be in Palm Springs or Montana or even Outer Mongolia for that matter, I'd always be running. Sometime I was going to have to make a stand, to fight for the life I wanted, - and I wanted to live in California.

'Bollocks to it!' I said, drunk but aware of what I was saying, and more importantly, the implications of it, 'I'm gonna stay. If they want me, let 'em come and get me! I'll be ready.'

'Good for you, kid!' Louretta applauded, 'I was wondering how long it would take ya to reach that decision. For a moment there, y'had me worried!'

'You don't mind then?' I asked, knowing that me being at the ranch could potentially cause trouble for my employer.

'Course not. You know me, I like a bit of action - if they come for ya, we'll be waiting.' She raised her glass again, as did I. It was going to be a long night, and for the second time in just a few weeks, I wouldn't be fit for work the next morning, but then again, neither would Louretta.

What we didn't know, was that trouble was already on its way.

*   *   *

Two weeks later the day of the big fight finally arrived. I was in good shape and feeling pretty relaxed as I stood in the barn waiting to be called to the ring. I was bare-chested, wearing just jeans and cowboy boots, with a pair of brown leather boxing gloves on my hands that had been tied on with string. Whilst I waited I shadow boxed with Jarvis, who had assumed the role of trainer. Whilst not in Alfie's league, he meant well and had a reasonable knowledge of the sport, giving me some encouragement, if precious little else. However, there we stood; the hopes, and more worryingly, a substantial amount of the ranch hands' wages stacked firmly on 'our' shoulders. Our opponents were from an outfit called The Bluestone Horse Company and the desire to win in either camp could not have been more intense. It was a matter of pride and I had been left under no illusions about the importance of the battle. Even Louretta had given me a speech about 'doing it for the ranch' and had wagered heavily with the owner of The Bluestone as to the outcome.

Their challenger's name was Moses Brown, nicknamed 'Mighty Mo,' and the moment he stepped into the ring I could see why. He was the reigning champion and had easily won the last two encounters between the ranches, but I could see in his eyes he was hungry for another victory.

Mo was a huge black man with skin the colour of polished mahogany. At least six foot six with a shaved, shiny bowling ball of a head and a strong dark face that was illuminated by a smile of brilliant white which he beamed confidently in my direction. His impressive, supremely muscled physique was concealed only by a pair of sun-bleached denim dungarees that were loosely turned up at the bottoms to expose his naked ankles and feet. Looking at him, I felt slightly daunted by the enormity of my task, knowing that his huge gloved fists could inflict a great deal of damage to my face, which over the years, I had become quite fond of. I stared incredulously at his massive arms, each thicker than one of my legs, and knew that I was going to have to keep him at a distance if I was to stand any chance of winning. I guessed that I'd have speed and agility on my side, hoping that his sheer size would make him slow and an easy target. My strategy was to hit and run and to hopefully escape with all my teeth.

The capacity crowd - there must have been well over five hundred people - were all baying for blood. They had spent the day enjoying the carnival atmosphere; eating and drinking and having a good time, but now they were restless and ready for action as the two contenders stood in the ring.

I could feel the eyes of the crowd burning into me as I nervously awaited the bell that would signal the beginning of the fight. One set of eyes however belonged to a man who had an entirely different agenda. He too wanted to see me fight, but to him I was prey and he was studying me for weaknesses. Weaknesses which he could exploit later. He watched from a discreet distance, eager to see how I would perform against a man such as Moses.

The bell rang and Mo hurled himself forward, quick to attack. He was like lightning and from the very first second I knew my strategy was flawed. Not only was my opponent incredibly powerful, but deceptively light on his feet and I felt my meagre amount of confidence slipping away as he clubbed the side of my face knocking me instantly to the floor.

The fight was not like a conventional boxing match, there were no rounds and no adherence to any particular set of rules.

The main object was simply to stay on your feet longer than the other guy, because if you went down for longer than ten seconds you would be counted out and the fight would be all over.

I sat on my backside and rubbed my cheek, wondering how I'd managed to find myself on the deck so early.

'One, two, three...' I heard the referee shouting in my ear, I could also hear the sound of booing coming from the disapproving audience. 'Four, five, six...' I momentarily considered staying where I was, knowing that I'd be far better off doing so, but then I remembered Louretta's 'do it for the ranch' speech and something responded inside me.

'Seven, eight...' I jumped to my feet and I was given a rousing cheer from the relieved crowd.

I was determined not to take such a sucker punch again, and reverted to the training Alfie had given me years ago at the Golden Gloves, I could hear his voice shouting 'Move, boy! Use yer jab, duck and weave!'

It all came flooding back and I landed several shots, both to the head and torso of the man before me. My confidence started to rise and for a moment I thought I was winning. Then bang. I didn't even see it coming and I found myself on the canvas once more, this time with blood pouring from my nose.

Again, I heard the ref counting, but he'd only reached 'four' by the time I was back on my feet, my anger just starting to rise. I tucked my head down and began to work slowly with the jab, getting through Mo's guard several times. It was starting to come back, it had been a long time since I'd been in a proper fight against a good opponent and I was rusty, but slowly I was loosening up.

For a split second, I saw my opening and landed a blistering upper cut under Mo's jaw, rocking him backwards and for the first time he was on the ropes. Again I heard the audience roar as they suddenly realised that perhaps I was up to the challenge after all. I drew strength from their encouragement and launched a full scale attack, but Mighty Mo just kept his guard up, waiting for me to tire. I'd fallen into the trap I'd used many times myself, my arrogance blinding me to the obvious ploy and I was punished for it. As the intensity of my attack weakened, my defence slipped and all of a sudden a crunching blow smashed into my ribs cracking at least one. Breathless and momentarily stunned, I was unable to do anything but watch as the punch came that knocked me to the floor for a third time.

Everything went quiet, my vision was filled with brightly coloured lights and I could just see the referee's mouth as he gave me the count, but it wasn't audible, I couldn't hear a thing.

Each second seemed like a minute and eventually my eyes cleared. I stared into the crowd and saw their angry faces, filled with blood lust as they shouted insults at my prone form; others were cheering, obviously believing that I was finished, looking forward to receiving their winnings. I looked at Moses, his back toward me with his hands locked together above his head in a victorious salute. Again I looked to the ref and saw him mouth the word 'seven,' then, in a crescendo of sound, my hearing came back and with it came my rage. I felt it surge around my body, racing through my veins as the anger that had been locked away for ten long years suddenly reared its head. As the referee shouted 'nine,' I sprang to my feet, gobbed a ball of bloody spit onto the canvas and raised my gloves.

Mo turned to face me and I saw the surprise in his eyes, and as he read the intent in mine, I also saw fear. I charged forward, a different fighter from the one I'd been just seconds before. My attack was hard and accurate, instinct taking over, I moved with a grace and assurance that I'd previously been lacking; each shot counted and blow after blow hit home. Moses put up an excellent fight, but I was in a league of my own, something had snapped inside me, perhaps it was the guilt I felt from Michael's injuries, or the anger at the person who caused them, but something took me over and I was fighting like a demon. Eventually, after taking such a barrage of hits, Mo's hands dropped to his sides and I launched the killer blow, but, as my gloved fist connected with his face, I felt a violent burst of pain shoot up my arm. It was sharp enough to snap me instantly out of my frenzy and as the red haze cleared from my eyes, I caught sight of Mighty Mo crashing to the canvas, he was out cold and totally oblivious to his defeat.

As soon as the ref had officially counted him out, there was an enormous roar as the crowd went wild. Moses' corner had to drag him to safety as the ring filled with hoards of people and I was lifted high on the shoulders of men that I'd never seen before. But as the realisation of what I'd done sunk in, my right hand started to throb badly.

*   *   *

The man who had been watching so intently now had the information he needed. Satisfied, he turned and walked in the direction of the barn, gently smoothing his long Mexican moustache.

*   *   *

I was carried around for quite some time, being passed from one group of people to the next, each person patting me on the back or eagerly shaking my hand which, by this time, had become extremely painful and I was making a concerted effort to keep it out of their reach. Eventually though, when the furore died down and I had been placed back on the ground, I made my way to the first aid tent, to find the doctor. After telling him what was ailing me, he carefully cut the string that was tied around my wrist and gingerly pulled the battered leather glove off, causing me to wince sharply with pain. My hand had swelled to twice its normal size, and there was a large purple and yellow bruise surrounding my wrist.

After a thorough examination, the Doctor decided I had a severely sprained wrist, which would apparently be useless for at least a week. Expertly, he wound a bandage around my hand, wrist and lower forearm, tight enough so that I could not move them to cause more damage. He also cleaned a cut above my left eye and applied a band-aid, then wiped blood from my nose and checked it for fractures - although I knew from experience that it had not been broken. Finally, he wrapped another bandage around my aching torso to support my cracked rib, then sent me on my way.

By the time I'd walked the short distance back to the house, the last of the guests were departing and I took a moment to enjoy my victory; I was tired and my muscles were stiff, but I felt good inside and pleased about my decision to stay. It was hard to imagine ever being unsafe at Wildwood, my troubles in London all seeming very far away.

I walked through the house and into the large kitchen that was the focal point of the whole household and as I opened the door, a loud cheer rang out and a little ripple of applause welcomed me.

At the head of the table stood Louretta, 'Hail the conquering hero!' She toasted, and lifted a glass of champagne high into the air, as did the twenty or so others sitting at the long wooden table.

'Thank you fans!' I said, in mock arrogance, lifting my good arm above my head, then bowing as low as my aching ribs allowed.

'Siddown, Sean, have some champagne!' Louretta invited. 'We're gonna do some serious drinkin' tonight kid - and guess what? You don't even have to start work until nine in the mornin' - just a token of my appreciation!' She joked, knocking back her drink.

'Gee, thanks Boss!' I replied. 'Hey, where's Jarvis? Surely he should be given the same deal - after all, he was responsible for training The Champ - I'd hate for him to miss out on your generosity!'

Louretta smiled at my sarcasm, 'He's in the barn, probably sweepin' up some of that bullshit you're full of!'

I couldn't help but laugh, 'I best go and fetch 'im then, that job's never ending - keep that champagne on ice, I'll be back in a minute.'

Leaving the party, I opened the back door, and made my way towards the barn.

*   *   *

For a moment, I thought he'd had a heart attack and I ran to his side and knelt down by his motionless body, my ribs throbbing from the sudden movement. Then I noticed the slight trickle of blood as it crept slowly from under Jarvis' hairline and down passed his temple. Puzzled by what could have caused the injury, I checked his pulse and was relieved to find that the old man was alive. I looked about, trying to see what had knocked him unconscious, but I didn't have to look too far, because as I turned round, I saw the man standing about ten feet away from me, a short leather cosh in his hand.

The man spoke in a quiet, but controlled tone, a sadistic smile on his chiselled face 'Hello, Mr. Reilly, I've been looking for you.' I suddenly felt sick. 'Let me introduce myself,' the man continued, 'My name's Blades. Frank Blades. But if you're a good boy, I'll let ya call me Frankie.

*   *   *

Immediately I knew I was in trouble. Joe had told me about this man, about how tough and dangerous he was; 'a cold-blooded killer who enjoys hurting people,' he had said. Aside from that, I was still exhausted from the battering I'd taken that afternoon, with my torso bound so tightly I could hardly move with my right hand swathed in bandages it made it impossible to clench my fist let alone punch. Blades had chosen his moment well, yet even at the peak of physical fitness, I could not be certain I would be up to the challenge of the man standing before me. The smart money would undoubtedly be on Frank.

'I've got no argument with you, Blades' I said, trying to buy myself a little time as I climbed to my feet 'We don't have to—'

Blades was fast. He darted forward and quick as a flash, whacked me around the head with the cosh, knocking me painfully to the ground and not for the first time that day I saw stars.

'I don't remember giving you permission to speak, boy,' Frank said, his tone calm and matter-of-fact. The thick Cockney accent sounding strangely out of place with the surroundings.

'But—' I tried again. This time he kicked me in the guts, winding me and making it difficult for me to breathe. Instinctively, I screwed myself into a tight ball, defensively trying to protect my already damaged ribs.

'Not got much sense 'ave y' boy. Now, if y' wanna speak to me, y' gotta ask permission' Frank was enjoying himself.

'Fuck you!' I spat breathlessly as he kicked again, connecting hard with my mouth and splitting my lip, breaking a tooth. I spat it into the dust, a trail of blood filled saliva in its wake.

'Not very quick on the uptake are ya Reilly - or shall I call ya Sean. A pretty name for a pretty boy.' He smiled wickedly, 'I'm gonna have lots of fun with you before y' die.' Then he frowned 'Or are y' gonna play hard to get? - I do hope so.'

I nearly threw another insult, but thought better of it, concentrating instead on trying to get my strength back.

'I can't let you off lightly for killin' a lovely bloke like Jez Mottola, can I now?' Frank sounded almost friendly, which strangely made him sound all the more menacing, 'Bet y' didn't know that me and 'im used to be close did ya? Real intimate y' might say, that is until he left me for some scrubber and broke me heart. Still, a lovely bloke nonetheless. Then you went and killed 'im dincha? And 'im being Benny's brother an' all. Like I say, not too clever are y' boy?'

As Frank talked, I slowly pushed myself up onto my knees, my eyes never once leaving his and for the second time that day I felt the red rush of anger pulsating through my body.

Blades continued, 'Course, Benny don't just want y' dead. He wants the money you took too. He reckons that because ya nicked it from Vic and Jez, that it should, by rights, belong to 'im, and he wants it. All of it. Now, the sooner y' tell me where it is, the better it's gonna be for you. But the longer y' take, the better it's gonna be for me. It's been a long time since I've had someone as pretty as you, and I intend to make the most of it. So try to put up a fight eh? Show a bit of backbone.'

By this time, I was squatting on my toes, ready to pounce should he make a move.

Frank wrapped the fingers of his free hand around the cosh and worked them up and down suggestively. He took a step towards me and said, 'It's your choice pretty boy.'

Seeing my only chance, I desperately threw myself at him, grabbing him around the waist with my right arm, putting my injured hand behind his back, trying to keep it away from further harm. My head was down under his right armpit and I punched him as hard as I could in the ribs. My movement was restricted, but the force of my attack knocked him off balance and he staggered a couple of steps backwards, tugging roughly on the bandages that were wrapped around my back to steady himself.

Quickly, Frank regained his footing and as he did so, he brought the cosh down hard on my shoulders and I felt a severe jolt of pain as it rattled around my wounded body. In retaliation, I swiftly punched him twice more, although the power I'd shown against Moses Brown was sadly lacking in both shots. I was a spent force, the battle was already lost and there wasn't a damn thing I could do about. I knew it and Frank knew it. My defeat was inevitable and I hated my tired limbs for letting me down, all I could hope for was to hurt Blades badly, to try and prevent the fate he had planned for me.

I felt another blow, this time on the nape of my neck, and briefly I saw bright white light, but I kept my feet. Again I punched, this time a little more effectively, my fist smashing into his kidneys and I felt him wince at the pain. I tried it once more, all the time the two of us dancing around in some strangely grotesque waltz, but as my knuckles connected with his side, he simultaneously brought down the cosh, finding its target on the exact centre of my skull and suddenly everything went black.

*   *   *

When I awoke a minute or so later, I was confused, not entirely sure where I was. Then I heard his deep but strangely effeminate voice. 'Oh, good. For a moment there, I thought y' were gonna sleep through it - miss out on all the fun.'

Suddenly, it all came flooding back and my body tensed as I looked up at his evil face; the grinning moustached mouth, the cruel smile and missing front tooth, the crooked nose that had been broken by Joe. And in his piercing blue eyes I could read his vile intent.

Out the corner of my eye, and just behind and to the right of Frank, I saw Jarvis sit up. He looked around, dazed, much as I had a few seconds before, and I prayed that he wouldn't say anything to attract Frank's attention. Thinking quickly, I tried to distract Blades, 'You realise I'll never tell you where the money is don't you?'

'Oh, you'll tell me,' Frank said confidently 'But I'm hoping it'll take a while before y' do.'

Stupidly, I tried to stand, but this made Frank angry again.

He marched over to where I lay and kicked me hard in the face. I felt a violent crack and immense agony as my nose was broken yet again. Blood poured from my nostrils and I saw coloured lights as the blackness threatened to surround me once more.

'Down, boy!' Frank ordered, as if speaking to an excited spaniel. Then, for good measure, he booted me in the ribs, again knocking the wind out my sails. 'That's for talking without permission.'

As I lay groaning on the dusty floor of the barn, looking up at him with bleary, semi-conscious eyes, Blades dropped the cosh and smiled again as he deftly popped open the top button of his jeans. He then reached into his pocket and pulled out a flick knife with a polished wooden handle. He pressed the release button and the blade sprung out with a sinister click. 'Now, sweetheart,' he said with a lascivious twinkle in his eye, 'It's time to pay the piper.'

Jarvis suddenly appeared behind Frank's left shoulder. He held a shovel high up over his shoulder and was poised to bring it crashing down onto Blades' skull. But somehow, Frank knew he was there and span round, catching the handle of the shovel with one hand and thrusting the blade of the knife into the old man's chest with the other. 'Enguarde!' Frank shouted delightedly, easily wrestling the shovel from Jarvis' grip and tossing it aside. Jarvis looked at me with an expression that was half surprise and half apology, then slowly fell backwards; the knife making a sucking sound as it withdrew from his body.

Before the old man's wiry little frame hit the floor, Frank had spun back around to focus once more on me, a look of smug satisfaction on his face. Slowly, he undid the buttons of his black cotton shirt, then opened it wide to reveal his muscular chest and hard flat stomach, both covered in dark curly hair.

'Alone at last,' he whispered evilly.

I spat a mouthful of blood into the sand, 'Not quite,' I growled, nodding to the person who had crept silently up behind him.

Again Frank turned, but this time he was not quick enough and the shovel hit him squarely in the face. As he fell to the floor, Louretta shouted 'Eat that, asshole!'

*   *   *

Louretta had come to find out where Jarvis and I had got to. The party was getting into full swing and it was time the guests of honour made an appearance. As she approached the open barn door, Louretta witnessed Jarvis being stabbed and quickly ducked out of sight before Frank saw her. Then when his back was turned, she had silently crept up behind him and picked up the shovel.

She had hit Blades so hard that his remaining top front tooth had been cleanly knocked out leaving a wide gaping hole. His nose, broken again, had almost been flattened by the force of the shovel and a large egg shaped swelling had sprung up on his forehead making him look decidedly odd.

When certain that Frank was unconscious, Louretta ran to Jarvis, but there was nothing she could do, the little old man who'd been with her for over twenty years was gone, he had not stood a chance.

As she turned to me, I saw the tears in her eyes, 'Sean,' she said, 'Jarvis is dead.'

'I know Louretta,' I replied helplessly. Another good man had lost his life trying to protect me. First Eddie, then Dog Tooth and now Jarvis. When in God's name would it end?

Unsteadily, and with blood pumping from my nose, I clambered to my feet. Louretta put my good arm around her shoulders and together we staggered to the house.

The sight of me caused uproar among the assembled staff and Louretta had difficulty making herself heard above the row, but eventually, when she had quietened them down, she told them about Jarvis. The news was greeted first by disbelief, then by incredible anger. Many of the hands wanted vengeance and headed for the barn to find Blades - ready to lynch him for what he had done.

Louretta rushed to the phone and rang the Sheriff's Department, saying only that an intruder had attacked and killed one of her staff. However, half way through the call, one of the hands' returned from the barn saying Frank Blades had vanished and so, it seemed, had Hank's truck.

Eleven

Hank's truck was discovered ten miles from the ranch, but the Sheriff's Department found no trace of Frank Blades. He'd gone, disappeared but not, I suspected, for good.

It had been an awkward time for Louretta as she was forced not only to deal with the loss of her dear friend, but also to withhold vital evidence that could have brought his murderer to justice. But she never mentioned Blades' name for fear of incriminating me. If she had told the Sheriff all she knew, it would most definitely have led to a more thorough investigation. In the event of that happening, my true identity would not have been too difficult to discover, and my subsequent arrest and deportation almost a certainty.

As it was, the police assumed they were looking for a drifter with no motive, except perhaps to get closer to a former movie star.

I was interviewed as were the rest of the staff but again it was thought that I was just the unfortunate who had disturbed the intruder, not his intended victim. I said that I had never seen the man before in my life, which in itself was not a lie, but what I neglected to tell the Sheriff was that I knew only too well of him and that I was certain at sometime in the future we would undoubtedly meet again.

*   *   *

Jarvis had been buried under a large eucalyptus tree overlooking a particularly beautiful canyon on the Wildwood estate. The only people who attended his funeral were the staff and hands of the ranch who, it seemed, were his only family, but he could not have wished for a more idyllic resting place.

Louretta had been a tower of strength throughout the whole sorry episode and proved without doubt what a good friend she was. I had been devastated by Jarvis' death, as had she, but whereas I had been all for giving up and running away again, she had remained calm and sensible making me understand that no matter what had happened, I was not to blame. She had also tightened security around Wildwood to make it as difficult as possible for Blades, or anyone else, to try anything again.

However I knew better than anyone what Benny Mottola and Frank Blades were capable of and was equally sure that neither would rest until they had got what they wanted.

*   *   *

Three months after Jarvis's funeral, Joe wrote to me with excellent news; he was sending Ray, Ruby and Michael to California for a much needed holiday. When I told Louretta of this, she insisted they stay at Wildwood, using it as a base for the duration of their visit. When I tried to tell her it wasn't necessary, she merely raised her hand in a gesture that told me her mind was made up and I knew nothing in the world would change it.

Both Ray and Michael had recovered sufficiently from their injuries and the doctor had deemed them fit enough to travel. I was delighted at the prospect of meeting my son for the first time, who would celebrate his tenth birthday during the holiday. I was also looking forward to seeing Ruby again, hearing her thoroughly raucous laugh and enjoying her bawdy sense of humour, which, over the years, I had missed more than I realised.

Ray was someone I was keen to meet too. In his many letters,

Joe had told me much about the man he had come to respect more than any other and I was eager to find out if I would like him as much. Together with Ruby, he had already assumed the difficult role of raising my son and if nothing else, I wanted to thank him for that.

My only sadness was knowing that neither Joe nor Sarah would be accompanying them on the trip.

There was no way Sarah could come as she needed stability and security and to take her abroad would have been unwise. She'd had enough upset and no one wanted to cause her any more, so for the duration of her visit to California, Ruby had arranged for Sarah to stay at a private nursing home where she would receive the best possible care.

Joe was busier than he had ever been, what with the firm and Ironclad to handle - the latter becoming more successful with every passing day. Needless to say, when I spoke to Joe on the phone, inviting him out to the ranch with the rest of them, he said there was just no way he could spare the time for a trip to the States as he was working on a major investment scheme which could prove to be incredibly important for all of us. He said he'd tell me all about it if everything went as hoped but, until then, wouldn't burden me with the details. That was fine by me as I was far too fired up about seeing Michael to think about anything else.

*   *   *

I was nervous, far more so than I had anticipated; excited too, even though my guts were churning and I was beginning to feel sick. What would Michael make of me I wondered. Would he like me? Would he look like me? Would he sense that I was his father? At any moment, he was going to walk through the gate and my mind was racing with all these inane questions. I had arrived at the airport two hours early, just in case the flight was ahead of schedule, but of course, it was not. In fact, it was slightly late and

I had been impatiently pacing the terminal, eager for a glimpse of my boy. Eventually though, a robotic voice announced that the flight from Heathrow had finally arrived and at last the passengers started to filter slowly through the gate.

Tortuously, the minutes ticked by as person after person entered the terminal, but none of them I recognised. Then, with the last few stragglers, I noticed a man who I had never met, yet knew instantly. There could not have been anyone else who fitted the description; wild red hair, pointed goatee beard, waxed spiky moustache and, of course, the eye-patch. He was also walking with a stick and had a pronounced limp, which left me in no doubt. I was staring at Ray Reece.

Ray was every bit as impressive as Joe said he was. Even in his diminished capacity, he was an imposing figure that you could not fail to notice - particularly with the shirt he was wearing, which was a brightly coloured Hawaiian number - the sort that only the most confident of tourists would have the balls to wear. With the shirt he wore navy tweed trousers and shiny black brogues which made him look unquestionably English. But what he lacked in style, he more than made up for in presence as he surveyed his surroundings, savouring his first trip to America; in fact, his first trip to anywhere outside England.

Watching Ray, I barely noticed the pasty-faced child at his side. The boy was only small and quite skinny, standing just above waist height to Ray who was protectively holding his hand, but I realised it was Michael, and my heart leapt. I strained to get a better view of him as he was partially hidden from me by the other passengers who were still milling around in Arrivals, but I could only see the mop of thick black hair, the same shade as his mother's, and his pale skin, like alabaster, that gave him a sickly pallor. Then, as he came fully in to view, he turned, and for a second I was fixed by his dark eyes which, although very similar to both Sarah's and

Joe's, were chillingly different. They seemed to be somehow devoid of all emotion; totally cold, and a small shiver of foreboding ran down my spine. I then noticed his damaged jaw line and the ugly blemish on his cheek that was wide and shiny; still pink with the new growth of scar tissue and my heart went out to him instantly. Only then did I fully appreciate the ordeal that he must have been through. Only then did the guilt of being absent in his time of crisis truly hit me.

His appearance was strange, certainly not what you would call healthy, but he was my son and I was overwhelmed to finally see him.

'Michael! Wait for me luv!' I heard a familiar voice shout. It was the unmistakable sound of Ruby, although as yet, I could not see her.

'No. I wanna see America. You're too slow, I'll never see it if I wait for you - just hurry up, so we can get going!' Michael's high-pitched voice was sharp as he snapped irritably at Ruby, and Ray looked down at the boy, giving him a look that suggested his displeasure, but there was no reprimand. Michael was a difficult child and the airport was no place for a scene.

Reading his thoughts, Michael sulkily said, 'So? She is slow, why can't she walk a bit quicker?' Ray simply shook his head, refusing to be drawn into an argument.

Then I saw her. She still looked beautiful to me. The years had been kind, although she had gained a little weight and her orange hair was now obviously dyed to disguise the grey, but it was still her, still Ruby, and I smiled with joy.

'Ruby!' I shouted, and she turned to look at me. For a moment, I could tell she didn't recognise the tanned, blonde Californian calling her name, but slowly it dawned who I was, and her whole face lit up with pleasure. Her eyes sparkled and she beamed her devastating smile at me, the smile that had turned the legs of hundreds of men to jelly. Wearing a skin tight mini skirt and impossibly high stilettos, she looked brazen, brassy and way over the top, but she was a feast for my eyes, and I loved her for it.

'Sean!' She cried back, and ran as fast as she could toward me, tottering expertly on her heels with her enormous bosom wobbling jelly-like in a low cut top. By the time she reached me, tears were streaming down her face smearing her mascara, but she didn't care. Throwing her arms around my neck, she planted a huge wet kiss on my lips and another on my cheek, leaving two thick lipstick tattoos.

'Ruby!' I said, 'It's great to see ya! How ya doing?'

'Christ, boy! Yer sound like a bleedin' yank, but you're a sight for sore bloody eyes. Gimme another hug!' As we embraced again, Ray and Michael came up behind her. Releasing me, Ruby turned and said, 'Sean, luv, this Ray. He's the nearest thing to an 'usband I'm ever likely to get, and I love 'im to bits.'

I held out my hand and Ray shook it firmly. 'Please to meet you at last, Ray,' I said honestly, 'I've heard a lot about ya.'

'Same 'ere son,' Ray replied, giving me a knowing wink 'Both from Vinnie and Joe. Sounds like we'll get along just fine.'

'Sorry about Vinnie' I offered.

'Thanks, kid. Me too,' he said simply.

'Sean,' Ruby interrupted, 'I'd also like you to meet Michael. Michael, say hello to your—'

'—Uncle' I butted in, 'Uncle Sean - pleased to meet ya Mike,' I said holding out my hand. The boy studied it for a long moment, then looked away. 'My name's Michael, not Mike,' he said pointedly, 'Where's your car, I wanna go?'

'Er, yeah sure, Michael,' I stammered, withdrawing my hand, 'It's er outside, in the, er, parking lot.' I was not sure what sort of response I had expected from the boy, but it certainly wasn't this.

He was completely oblivious to the pain he had so callously

232

inflicted, but Ruby sensed it and she took my arm. 'Don't worry Sean, he'll come around. He's tired that's all.'

'Course he is' I said disguising my disappointment, 'He's had a long journey, bound to be a bit jet-lagged and all that - still, a few days at the ranch and we'll be great mates,' I enthused. But something told me that was wishful thinking.

Changing the subject, I said, 'Where are your bags?'

'Some bloke's bringin' 'em,' Ray replied, 'Ere he comes now.' He gestured to an airport trolley that had an enormous pile of matching suitcases on it. The trolley was stacked well over head height and was being pushed slowly in our direction. As it arrived, I said, 'You'd better give the guy a tip, they live on tips over 'ere.'

'Tip!' The man behind the trolley exclaimed, his face hidden by the mountain of luggage, 'I'll give 'em a bloody tip - don't pack so many flamin' cases next time!'

I would have known his voice anywhere. 'Joe?' I said, 'Is that you?'

Suddenly, my best friend stepped clear of the suitcases and smiled warmly at me, 'As I live and breathe' he replied 'How ya doin' Sean?'

Joe held out a large powerful hand and I grasped it hard, squeezing it firmly. As I did so, I pulled him towards me and we embraced like long lost brothers, patting each other on the back, delighted at being reunited after all the years apart.

'Jesus Christ! What the bloody hell are you doin' 'ere? I asked, gobsmacked by my friends' surprise visit.

'Just a bit of business - y'know, to do with that investment thing I was tellin' you about. I'll explain later, don't worry,' Joe answered mysteriously. 'But first, I wanna see you ridin' an 'orse, I could do with a good laugh!'

*   *   *

Louretta had loaned me her bright red Cadillac convertible,

all polished and sparkling with acres of chrome and white wall tyres, which she thought Michael might appreciate. And, sure enough, as soon as he set eyes on it, I noticed an admiring smile. Silently I thanked Louretta as my dampened spirits lifted a little, perhaps there was a glimmer of hope after all. Maybe the boy and I had just got off on the wrong foot.

After storing the luggage in the vast trunk, we set off for the ranch. The drive was immensely enjoyable with never a dull moment thanks to the banter between Ray and Ruby which was fantastic; their stories and anecdotes, even the way they commented on some particular object we happened to pass, were laced with the droll humour that was unique to South London. Needless to say, I spent most of the journey in stitches with tears of laughter streaming down my cheeks. The experience was also strangely surreal. There we all were, a motley bunch to be sure; a piratical wild-haired rogue; a bawdy madame of a high-class brothel, the boss of one of London's most notorious gangs, and a father and son who had only just met. We were cruising along with the hot desert sun setting behind us, sitting in the best automobile America had to offer, heading towards the palatial home of an ex Hollywood movie star. The weirdest thing was, that apart from being a little apprehensive about my relationship with Michael, I was not even slightly concerned. It all seemed perfectly normal and I felt more comfortable than I had in years.

Only as I pressed the intercom on the newly installed security gate that barred our entrance to the ranch, did I feel a slight prick of trepidation. It occurred to me that there was a great divide between Louretta's world, which although I knew she had worked damned hard for, could appear pampered and spoilt when compared with the grim, unforgiving and quite often brutal streets of South London. But I should have known better than to worry.

When we had been cleared by the guard on the other end

of the intercom, who was a member of a twelve strong force now permanently patrolling Wildwood, the gate slid silently open and I steered the Caddie smoothly up the long driveway, allowing my guests to take in the staggering beauty of their surroundings.

'Bleedin' hell, Sean! These bloody yanks know how to live, don't they?' Ruby said as she looked about her in amazement.

'Christ, it's unbelievable!' Joe agreed.

'This is just the beginning,' I replied, 'Just wait 'til you see the house.'

As soon as Louretta Wild's magnificent home came into view, Ruby, Ray and Joe all gasped in wonder as they stared awe struck. I even heard Michael catch his breath, who had remained silent for the whole journey, my attempts at conversation being either ignored, answered with an unfriendly grunt or just a lazy shrug of the shoulders.

As I brought the car to a halt next to the steps that led to the wide elegant front doors, Louretta came rushing out with a warm friendly smile on her face 'Hi, you guys! Welcome to Wildwood.'

'Ello, luv. You must be Louretta, I'm Ruby, pleased to meet ya,' said Ruby, completely unfazed by the fame of the person to whom she spoke.

'I've heard a lot about you honey, good t'meetcha at last,' Louretta replied shaking her hand warmly. 'I reckon you and me will get along just fine.'

'You know what luv?' Ruby smiled, 'I got the same feelin.'"

I completed the introductions, Ray was thoroughly charming with a flirtatious glint in his eye that Louretta found very attractive, although suspected, quite rightly, that he was a one woman man. Michael did actually give her half a smile and uttered one or two words of thanks after receiving a nudge from Ray, but Louretta had already got the measure of the boy.

Finally, when she shook hands with Joe she said, 'My God,

I was told you were good looking but you're a goddamn heart stopper. If only I were ten years younger...'

Joe flashed her one of his stunning smiles, which had been known to render women of a weaker constitution utterly helpless, 'Thanks for inviting me,' he said, 'It's good to put a face to the voice. I hope us all stayin' 'ere ain't too much of an inconvenience.'

'What! And miss out on a knockout like you?' Louretta gasped in mock horror, 'You gotta be kiddin'!'

'Hold on a minute' I accused Louretta, 'You invited him, you knew he was coming?'

'Sure, kid,' she replied with a smile, both her and Joe looking at me conspiratorially, 'We don't have to tell you everything, do we? 'Sides, we're gonna talk some business, which might mean ya see a bit more of your old pal here.'

'Business, with Joe?' I queried, 'What sort of business?'

'Nothin' for you to worry about tonight. We'll tell ya all about it in the mornin' - now, lets get somethin' to eat,' she said, smoothly changing the subject, 'I'm starving!' Louretta linked her arm through Joe's, and led him into the house with everyone else following closely behind. All that is, except me. I simply leant back on the car and stared after them open mouthed in a state of total shock.

Twelve

'Whaddaya think, Sean?' Asked Louretta, sliding the architect's drawings to me along the marble and glass coffee table. The drawings were of a proposed development on a prime piece of Las Vegas real estate, right on The Strip, for a fabulous hotel and casino. With them were the plans, local maps, an overview of the site and a full list of proposed amenities.

Confused by why they thought I should be interested, I picked up the drawings and looked them over, aware that both Louretta and Joe were watching for my reaction.

'The Las Vegas Villa Continental' it said on the bottom of the first drawing, then below it, in smaller type, 'Hotel, Lounge and Casino.' I scanned the detailed and brightly coloured artist's impression, the drawing showing a huge twenty storey hotel complex designed in the Mediterranean style. As well as several large free form swimming pools, it featured stone balconies, flowery trellises, flagstone walkways and ornately carved waterfalls. On the next sheet there was several more drawings, of coffee bars, pavement cafés - even what looked like a small shopping mall offering a range of quality boutiques, all in and around the hotel.

All very impressive, but I was still no wiser. I flipped to the next sheet, to see an illustration of the magnificent casino; Grecian in design with white columns, marble statues and huge urns filled with flowers. Blackjack, roulette and poker and crap tables all laid out on the spacious, marble floors together with row upon row of chrome slot machines all shining brightly in the cool, sumptuous splendour.

The next page featured the lounge where top flight stars such as Sinatra, Martin and Davies would hopefully be persuaded to entertain. Diners were illustrated sitting in their own private booths being served by leggy but elegant waitresses. The lighting in here was darker, more ambient and relaxing with hundreds of candles twinkling in the manufactured moonlight. Utterly dazzling and incredibly well conceived. And so it went on. Each page highlighting a different, yet equally impressive, aspect of the enormous complex.

I gave the plans and the rest of the documentation a summary once over but, after I'd looked at everything, I was still in the dark.

'Fantastic,' I said, 'Absolutely bloody marvellous. But I dunno what it's supposed to mean. Are you goin' there on holiday Louretta?' Frankly, I was extremely puzzled.

'No, Sean, she's not goin' on holiday,' Joe replied smiling.

'What then?' I was getting slightly annoyed and feeling a bit stupid 'What do you want me to say?'

'How do ya fancy ownin' a piece of it?' Louretta asked.

'Eh? What do you mean?'

'We mean,' Joe replied simply, 'how do you fancy ownin' a third share in it. Louretta and me are gonna put up the other two thirds.'

'But how the hell am I gonna afford—'

'Ironclad,' Joe interrupted.

'What? It's doing that well - enough to buy a place like this?'

'Oh yeah. Or at least with Louretta's third it is. Enough to buy it, develop it and build it up into one of the biggest, best resorts in Las Vegas.'

'Christ, that's amazing. I never thought—'

'I know, nor me. But this is our ticket Sean. Yours and mine. This is our chance. With Louretta's help we can make this work - all of us together, as equal partners.'

'It's a good scheme Sean. A good investment. Joe and me are sure of it - and we've both done our homework.'

'You've been discussing it without me knowing?'

'For months now,' Joe said. 'Louretta approached me and we've been talkin' on the phone ever since. We didn't say anything to you because we wanted to surprise you - and we didn't want you to be disappointed if it didn't come off. Both of us know how important this could be to you - it could mean you seeing a lot more of Michael. Maybe even, someday, Sarah could be well enough to make the trip—' Joe suddenly clammed up, knowing in his heart that his sister would probably never see his dream and the realisation, the sadness, quite unexpectedly threatened to overwhelm him.

Louretta came to his rescue. 'We've studied all the details, Sean, looked at all the angles, and we're more convinced than ever that it can work. We can make it something to be proud of. Whattaya say?'

I looked at them both. 'So you two have been conspiring behind my back. Plotting and scheming about building some great big bloody hotel in the middle of the desert. And now you're asking me, after just a quick glance at the plans, to invest a huge chunk of my money into it?'

'Exactly,' Joe said.

'Damn right,' said Louretta.

' Well alright then,' I said.

* * *

Louretta had been planning to build the Villa Continental for years but had never been able to find the right business partner.

She knew many people who had the money; movie stars, film producers and the like, but no one who had the balls to take on the other casinos. The reason was that Vegas, in the main, was run by organised crime and it was considered foolhardy, by the potential investors she had approached, to start up an enterprise on mob turf without fear of intimidation or recrimination.

Louretta not only needed a partner she could trust, but also someone tough enough to deal with the opposition; a business partner who would not be put off by threats or scare tactics.

After hearing my stories about Joe, Louretta became convinced that he would more than fill both criteria. She had been intrigued by his strength, loyalty and sense of honour, also the way in which he had regained control of South London after Vinnie's passing. It was clear to her that Joe was a man who was prepared to fight for what he wanted and had an ability to get things done. She was also impressed by his financial acumen and, after talking with him on the phone, had no doubts that he would make the ideal partner.

Joe I could tell, was very excited by the project, as were Louretta and myself, but it soon became clear after several discussions that we needed to employ someone to oversee the development - to be the 'visible face' of the Villa Continental. Joe saw his future in London not Las Vegas and Louretta was kept constantly busy at Wildwood. As for me, well I was supposed to be in hiding, so being the visible face of anything was not entirely practical.

What we needed was someone we could trust to act on our behalf, who could make decisions about the development of the project, who could oversee construction and ensure the high standard of materials. More importantly, we needed someone capable of handling the Vegas mob, who could talk their language and smooth out any potential problems. Eventually, this person would be expected to run the Villa, so they would need to be charming as well as tough. Firm yet fair, with enough charisma and foresight to bring in the high-rollers, as well as the average guy in the street.

Louretta assumed this person would be near impossible to find, but Joe already knew exactly the right man for the job.

*   *   *

Ray, Ruby and Michael were due to stay a month, Joe would remain for an extra four weeks to make sure our plans for the Villa were fully underway. Joe, Louretta and myself all planned to drive out to Vegas as soon as the others had returned to England, but until that time, I was determined they were going to have fun.

All my friends loved the ranch, and all but Michael made the effort on most mornings to get up before sunrise to witness the magnificent dawn. They also delighted in watching me and the other hands at work with the horses and were all speechless the first time they saw me break a wild bucking horse. Even Joe had been impressed by the skills I had learned since leaving London.

I taught both Ray and Ruby to ride, or at least, to stay on comfortably, and they happily explored the surrounding area on horseback with either myself or Louretta, who particularly enjoyed their company, acting as a guide through the beautiful but rugged terrain.

My progress with Michael was slow and I found him very difficult to get to know, a problem Joe had already come across, but I did so want him to like me, and I was trying desperately to like him, but it was hard. He seemed more than happy to be alone and showed very little interest even when I offered to take him to Disneyland for his birthday. Nevertheless, I took him anyway, although thankfully I was accompanied by Ruby, who made what could have been an extremely trying day a little easier. When I tactfully asked her about his surly attitude, Ruby apologised for him and said he was probably tired or a little overawed by the excitement of the day. It was as if she was unable to see his faults and completely blind to his spoilt and rude behaviour.

I thought about telling her, but Joe advised against it as Michael was Ruby's whole life, and he viewed her as his mother. As for me, well I could never be the father he wanted, besides, he already had Ray for that, who was fairing very well under the circumstances. As much as it grieved me, it was no longer up to me to decide on the best way to raise the boy. I had forgone that privilege before he was born. The best I could hope for was to be someone he visited every year or so, an uncle perhaps who, one day, he could hopefully call a friend.

Aside from my disappointing relationship with Michael, I was thoroughly enjoying the time with my friends, particularly with Joe. Even though we had both changed dramatically in the last ten years, our personalities had remained the same and we still enjoyed the easy rapport that had made us so close all those years ago. And, with the new Villa Continental venture, it was clear that we would be seeing a lot more of each other. This, I suspected, had a great deal to do with Joe's willingness to get involved in the project and, knowing Louretta as I did, probably had a lot to do with her choice of Joe as a partner. My life may not have been simple, but I did have some very good friends.

*   *   *

Having enjoyed their stay so much; visiting Beverly Hills and Malibu Beach and taking the bus tour around the stars' homes, Ray and Ruby decided to extend their stay by accompanying Joe, Louretta and me to Vegas, much to Michael's chagrin, who was becoming more surly with each day that passed.

Once in Las Vegas, the three of them immediately set about seeing the sights, whilst the three of us set about sizing up the competition. From the blazing neon of downtown's Glitter Gulch with the Lucky Strike, the Golden Nugget and the famous fluorescent cowboy that towered above the Pioneer, to the new ultra modern and rapidly growing Strip. The Strip was lined with fabulous, innovatively themed hotels such as the Desert Inn, the Tropicana, the Stardust and the Sands and all of them held a wealth of delights. They offered a stylish, fantasy lifestyle with glamour, star names and spectacular acts all part of the allure.

And the Villa Continental had to be right up there with them. We didn't just want to compete, we wanted to be the best.

On the morning of our first full day there, I was awoken, having slept in the largest, most comfortable bed I had ever been in, by the buzzing of the white courtesy phone that stood on the walnut dressing table of my sumptuous hotel suite. Reluctantly leaving the luxury of the red satin sheets, I staggered sleepily over to the telephone and picked up the receiver.

'Hello?' I said groggily.

'Sean, it's me, Ruby. Meet me in the lobby in fifteen minutes.'

'But, I—' I started to say.

'Sean, it's important' Ruby interrupted with an unusual urgency to her voice.

'Sure, Ruby,' I replied, 'I'll be there, but what—?'

'Good.' She butted in again, and then added 'And make sure you put on a suit!' Then the line went dead.

Very confused, I did as she asked and was down in the lobby in under ten minutes; washed, shaved and dressed in a beautifully tailored black suit that Joe had loaned me for the many meetings we had scheduled over the next few weeks. Joe and Ray were waiting for me downstairs, both looking as smart and as confused as I was. Then with a 'ping' the elevator doors opened and out stepped Ruby looking absolutely stunning. She was wearing a fabulous ivory silk dress with lace trimmings and her hair was adorned with small white flowers. Around her neck was a simple gold locket that set off the whole ensemble. I had never seen her look so beautiful -

even next to Louretta, who stood beside her in a chic blue twin set.

'Ruby?' Ray said, overawed by the vision before him, 'What's goin' on?'

Ruby walked slowly over to him, her expertly made up eyes sparkling as she stared into his bewildered face. When she reached him, she kissed him lightly on the lips, being careful not to leave any trace of her glossy red lipstick. 'I've decided that it's time you made an honest woman of me,' she said, 'I love you, and that's all there is to it. I wanna get married - whaddaya say?'

Ray was visibly stunned, but very gradually, his mouth cracked into a beaming white smile, exposing a set of perfect teeth, 'Darlin',' he replied, his face flushing with emotion, 'It'd make me the proudest man in the world.'

Everyone started to applaud, Louretta wiped a tear from her eye, and even Michael, who was smartly dressed in his Sunday best, was smiling and clapping. For a moment I watched the lad; it was the first time I had seen him truly happy since the day I had met him and it pleased me immensely.

*   *   *

The wedding took place by the swimming pool of the Sands hotel, in a simple but romantic ceremony that had been arranged in secret by Ruby and Louretta. It was wonderful, the warm desert sun shone as Michael acted as page boy, Louretta the matron of honour, Joe the best man and I gave away the bride, an honour which I was proud to perform.

Afterwards, we celebrated into the early hours, having had a day which none of us would ever forget. It was a day which, for me, was the best I'd had since leaving London. Surrounded by my closest friends, in a paradise far away, I felt as if I scarcely had a care in the world, and for a brief time, I didn't.

*   *   *

Four days later, the vacation was over. Ray, Ruby and Michael drove back to LA for the flight home. We said our goodbyes, I shook hands with Ray and hugged Ruby who bravely fought back the tears. Then, I clasped my son by the shoulders, feeling the emotion welling up inside me, not knowing how long it would be before I saw him again. 'Goodbye, Michael,' I said, my stare intense as I willed him to see what was in my heart, desperately wishing I could tell him he was mine, that I was his father, that no matter what, nothing would change that. But I could not, it was utterly futile, he already had a family, and like it or not, they were far better equipped to take care of him than I was. But one day, no matter how far distant, he would know he was my son, I would make certain of it.

'Bye,' he said coolly, completely oblivious to my pain. He climbed onto the back seat of the car and I watched as they drove away. Michael did not once look back.

*   *   *

For nearly five weeks, Joe, Louretta and I worked ceaselessly on the plans for the Villa. We had meetings with architects, planners, interior designers and structural engineers, theatre managers and restaurateurs. We also met with the Sheriff's Department and the Gaming Commission for our all important gaming license, without which we couldn't run or operate a casino at the Villa.

We visited the site almost daily, which was situated right in the centre of The Strip in a prime location; land which Louretta had had the foresight to purchase at a bargain price nearly twenty years before.

Eventually, when we considered that we had done everything that could possibly be done at this early stage of development, Joe decided to return home. He needed to tactfully approach the man he had lined up to oversee the project and who would hopefully run the Villa Continental for us upon its completion. It was a fabulous opportunity, and one which would normally have been jumped upon, but first Joe needed to iron out a few complications.

The night before Joe's departure, he and I went out for what we intended to be a few drinks, but it soon turned, rather predictably, into a drunken crawl. At around midnight we strayed away from The Strip and took to the more seedy joints that did not particularly welcome tourists, especially not two very loud, extremely inebriated Londoners. Eventually, we found ourselves in a small 'redneck' bar frequented by a bunch of die-hard regulars, who were busy drinking and playing pool. We sat at the bar drinking bottles of beer, reminiscing about old times, unaware that with each remembered adventure, our voices were getting steadily louder.

'Goddamn English pussies!' One of the locals shouted, and for a second, I saw Joe's eyes flash with anger, but almost immediately it vanished and we resumed our conversation, oblivious to the attention we were now attracting from the eight big men standing around the pool table.

Inevitably, our discussion got onto the subject of women, and Joe was amazed by my story of Victoria Wild, and the wonderful display she had put on for me that night on the balcony. I told him that since that night, I could not stop thinking about her and he said he knew exactly how I felt. Joe then described Rachel Davenport to me, how even though she was Carl Napier's girlfriend, he could not help how he felt about her.

He told me that since their first meeting, he had become almost obsessed by her and had found himself on more than one occasion, sitting outside her flat in his car. Then, two weeks before he left for America, he said that she had seen him from her window and smiled, but guilt ridden by his betrayal of Carl, he had sped off into the night. However, temptation had got the better of him and the following evening he had returned. Hating himself for it, he had purposely sent Carl on a business trip to Manchester, knowing that he would not be back until the next afternoon.

He knocked on Rachel's door, part of him hoping that she wasn't in. But she was, and when she opened the door the two of them stared at each other for a long moment until finally Joe spoke. 'I had to come. I had to see you again.'

'I hoped you would,' she replied. 'I've thought of nothing else since seeing you yesterday. I prayed you'd come back.'

'I've sent Carl away. I lied to him, it was wrong but I had to—'

'I know,' she interrupted breathlessly, 'I'm glad you did.' Rachel then took Joe by the hand and led him into the house and shut the door. 'I'm glad you did,' she said again, then lifted her chin and kissed him softly on the lips and Joe responded instantly. Suddenly, Joe said, they were kissing passionately, hungrily, as if feeding off each other, their hands searching the other's body, ripping at the other's clothes in mad, wanton desire. First, Joe's hands were in her long auburn hair, then on her firm, ample breasts, then on her tight, round bottom. Meanwhile she was tearing at his shirt, then at his belt buckle, then wrapping her long stockinged legs around him, writhing up against him, her skirt hoisted up around her waist in lustful insanity.

At last, with all inhibitions and guilt gone, he slammed her up against the wall, ripped aside her scant underwear and took her for the first time. Violent, shameless sex; a dramatic release for all the pent up animal attraction that the two had felt since their first meeting.

Somewhere along the way, Joe said, they made it to the bedroom where they made love again and again, long into the early hours.

'I tell ya, Sean. It was bloody amazin' - she's bloody amazin' - it's like she's some kinda drug and I can't get enough of her!'

'Sounds like she's a goddamn whore to me, whadda you say boys?' The slow American drawl of the lead redneck sneered behind us, his pals laughing appreciatively.

Joe looked at me, and again I saw the anger flash in his dark eyes, in return I gave him a small understanding smile. He turned his head away and looked down at his beer bottle, fighting to keep his temper under control, but both of us knew what was coming, we'd had years of experience in dealing with situations such as this.

'Hey, boy!' The redneck spoke again, this time his voice loud and cocky, 'I said, your girlfriend sounds like a whore.'

Joe shot another glance at me, his eyes almost red with fire, his mouth tight with rage. Desperately he was begging for my approval, knowing only too well what the repercussions could be for me if the Sheriff was called. But I knew these men wouldn't be ignored. 'Okay Joe,' I said.

In unison, we rose to our feet, both of us standing over six feet tall and in peak physical condition, our backs towards the eight protagonists. Again Joe looked at me and I saw him smile slightly. He was enjoying himself and, strangely enough, so was I. We understood each other perfectly as we slowly turned to face the opposition.

*   *   *

We arrived back at Sands sometime around six in the morning, both of us now almost completely sober, although the amount of alcohol in our bloodstreams would no doubt have suggested otherwise. However, at more than any other time in the previous two months, the last few hours had probably been when Joe and I had been at our closest; fighting side by side in that scruffy bar. It felt just like old times, with the years apart making no difference to the unique understanding we had between us. Somehow, we just knew what the other one was doing, which as Vinnie and Alfie had noticed previously, made us a highly effective team. Needless to say, we had emerged victorious from the bar, both with black-eyes, but fairing much better than our opponents who we had left in a dazed heap on the floor. As we walked out, Joe said to them, 'Thanks boys, I enjoyed that,' and I nodded my agreement, I knew exactly how he felt.

Afterwards, we decided to head back to the bars on The Strip, where a couple of British tourists would be far less conspicuous.

A few beers later and again the memories came back, as once more we reminisced about old times. Eventually the subject of Sarah came up, and I explained to Joe how my love for his sister had not altered in all the years I had been away but how, after a long period, it had faded enough to allow me at last, to have strong feelings for another woman, although I had no guarantees that those feelings were reciprocated.

It occurred to me that Joe might take exception to this, but I shouldn't have worried, he understood completely. He told me that Sarah was still in a very fragile state, that she still would not acknowledge even him, her twin brother, let alone anyone else, so he held out little hope for a full recovery anytime soon. Even though Joe refused to believe it, I gathered from what he was saying that the doctors suspected her condition may be permanent, which made me very sad.

Joe told me that I should pursue Victoria Wild, if I thought I had a chance at happiness, and whole heartedly gave me his blessing.

We also spoke of my mother's house, which I still owned but couldn't bring myself to sell. It was useless to me now, except for the memories it held, but for that reason alone I had to keep it. Also, maybe one day, my dad's hidden lock-up under the stairs might prove to be useful again. Presently, Ivy Reynolds took care of the house and would accept no money for doing so, but Joe, who had a set of keys for the place, would always leave a box of goodies for her whenever he called by. He left things like chocolate and bath salts and tins of biscuits, all of which she gratefully accepted.

But she would never take money. Mum's friendship had been too precious to her for that.

*   *   *

As we approached the front desk, the clerk sitting behind it said, 'Mr. Cassidy - there's a telegram for you sir!'

Joe took the small buff coloured envelope from him, which had the Sands palm tree logo printed in green on the bottom right-hand corner, 'Bit early in the mornin' for a telegram, ain't it?' He said to me.

'You'll be lucky if you can see it, let alone read it,' I replied, suddenly feeling tired and glancing at my watch to see it was nearly time for breakfast.

Joe ripped open the envelope, took out the folded message and opened it whilst scratching the fresh growth of stubble on his chin.

As I watched, I noticed his weary eyes widen as he became immediately alert, 'Oh shit' he said softly, automatically handing the telegram to me.

I took it from him and read its chilling message:

Mottola escaped . Two men dead . Come home soon . Phone me ASAP . Ray.

Thirteen

This time, there was no changing my mind. I had been foolish to think myself safe at the ranch and that foolishness had cost Jarvis his life. My decision to stay at Wildwood after his death had always felt unwise and slightly selfish and now Benny had escaped those that I cared for on the ranch faced yet another threat.

He could be anywhere, especially with his network of connections and virtually limitless funds. He would easily be able to buy a new face and a new identity. If Frank Blades was in the States there was a good chance Benny was too.

Now, for me, there was no other choice. I had to move on and this time I would not be persuaded otherwise.

I intended to stay in California, which I had fallen deeply in love with, but instead of staying in one place, I would travel up and down the coast, picking up casual work along the way, moving on every couple of months or so. Not an ideal situation, but at least I would be able to call in on Louretta and Virgil from time to time, which would make the pill a little easier to swallow.

Louretta tried to make me stay, but this time I could not be persuaded, so instead, I just gave her a hug, kissed her lightly on the cheek, then got on the Indian and rode out of Wildwood, the place that had given me so much. With a heavy heart, I headed for the highway, my life once more thrown into turmoil, with a future that was by no means certain, but at least my friends would be safe.

*　*　*

For Joe, also, it was a time for change. He arrived home to the news that he was going to be a father. Rachel was eleven weeks pregnant. Unfortunately, these tidings, which under normal circumstances would have made Joe ecstatically happy, were related to information that was far less welcome: Rachel had already told Carl that the baby belonged to Joe. Needless to say, Carl had not taken this news well.

Napier had suspected something was wrong when Rachel's attitude towards him changed. She became cold and distant and he had not been welcome in her bed since her first passionate night with Joe. The feelings she had for Carl, which were already uncertain, had all but evaporated and her treatment of him became increasingly hostile and intolerant. He was an annoyance who just would not go away; all she wanted and all she could think about was Joe.

Of course, Carl tried his hardest to please her, but everything he did was wrong and only seemed to make her more angry. If only he knew what was wrong, he felt sure he could help her, and time and again he begged Rachel to tell him, but flatly, she refused. It broke Carl's heart that the woman he adored, the woman who he wanted to spend the rest of his life with was slipping away from him, and he was powerless to prevent it.

When the doctor told Rachel she was pregnant, she cried with joy. Knowing, even without doing the maths, that it was unquestionably Joe's. Conceived the night before his departure to America.

Rachel kept her pregnancy secret, knowing it to be unwise to tell anyone, but it was killing her to do so and she was finding it increasingly hard to resist the temptation.

Finally, two days before Joe's return, Rachel and Carl got into a furious argument. He had refused to drop the subject of what was troubling her and she was sick of making lame excuses. All of a sudden her patience snapped, and she told him. She told him about Joe, how he made her feel, how that when he made love to her he took her to heights she had never previously imagined. She cruelly told Carl that what she felt for him was nothing in comparison to what she felt for Joe and when she saw the hurt she had inflicted she felt no guilt, just a glorious release of pent up emotion. 'Oh, and by the way,' she said triumphantly, with Carl still reeling from the first devastating revelation, 'I'm pregnant too - but don't worry, you're definitely not the father.'

Carl Napier's grief was complete. He left Rachel's flat a broken man and had not been seen in the forty-eight hours since.

*   *   *

Alfie strolled into the small back room at the Golden Gloves, which, three years previously, had become Joe's 'temporary' headquarters. It was past ten o'clock at night, but Joe was still working. It was his first day back and there were a hundred things to catch up on, although Carl had done a brilliant job in his absence, making certain that everything ran smoothly. He really was a good man; reliable, hard-working and loyal. Joe once again felt the guilt stir in his belly as he was reminded of his own treachery.

Alfie placed a glass tumbler on the desk in front of Joe which he duly acknowledged before properly examining the contents. However, when he eventually did so, he saw it was half full with at least two generous shots of whiskey.

'Are you tryin' to get me pissed?' Joe asked, smiling affectionately at his good friend.

'Not especially,' Alfie replied, 'But it might 'elp if you 'ave a stiff drink inside ya, there's somethin' y' oughta know.'

Joe felt his pulse quicken, 'What?' He demanded.

Alfie cleared his throat, then said, 'Napier's in the bar. He's out of 'is 'ead, drunk as a skunk and gettin' very mouthy - tellin' everyone he's gonna kill ya. Sayin' what a back stabbin' bastard you are—'

'Okay, Alfie,' Joe cut him off, 'I'll deal with it.'

'He needs shutin' up Joe, before he says somethin'—'

'I said, I'll deal with it,' Joe barked, then, instantly ashamed of himself, added apologetically, 'Sorry. It's been a long day. I understand what you're sayin,' and I'll sort it.'

*   *   *

Carl had a captive audience as the bar of the Golden Gloves was full, regulars mainly, most of whom had some connection to the firm, which was fortunate for Carl. If he had been discussing either Joe, or any of his affairs with strangers, his offence would be far more serious, and the repercussions much more severe.

'I'm tellin' ya,' he slurred, 'He's a two-faced, double-crossin' bastard. Cassidy's been screwin' my missus behind my back, and all the time pretendin' to my face that he's my friend - the dirty, lyin' cheat.' Carl had his back to the door that led through to the rear of the pub, and didn't see Joe enter the bar as he added, 'I'm gonna kill 'im for what he's done to me, the fuckin' bastard!'

'Okay, Carl, that's enough,' Joe said firmly, startling Carl, who span around to face him. Napier stared hard at Joe, his eyes watery and his jaw trembling with anger. For a second, neither man said anything, then Carl took a deep breath before defiantly addressing the riveted onlookers once more.'Like I said, a dirty, lyin' cheat!' The room was silent as Carl stumbled a step closer to Joe and hissed, 'You fuckin' bastard. How could ya do that to me, do I mean nothin? Are my feelings not worth anything to you?'

Joe moved towards him, 'Carl—' he started. But Napier, his defences heightened with rage, and his temper fuelled with alcohol, swung a right hook that caught Joe hard on the left cheek. Then, after a brief pause, and without witnessing any noticeable reaction from Joe, he swung again, this time with his other fist. 'Bastard!' He shouted loudly, as the blow found its mark, just under the right eye.

Joe saw both shots coming, but allowed them to land; he knew he deserved them. But now he had to end it before it got out of hand.

'Alright Carl,' Joe said in a low controlled voice, leaving the other man in no doubt as to his intent, 'I owed you the first one, and the second one was for free, but the next one comes from me.'

Carl did not heed the warning, he was too drunk to read the signs, too full of hostility to see reason, so he threw another punch.

Joe easily dodged the sluggish missile by simply ducking his head aside, but his response was lightning quick as he butted Carl on the forehead, using exactly the right amount of force so as not to cause any serious injury. Napier dropped like a stone, out-cold, unaware that he had even been hit.

*   *   *

Carl awoke to find himself laying face down on the tatty green velour couch in Joe's office. His head ached, his eyes throbbed and his mouth felt as though a small creature had slept in it. Gingerly, he turned himself over, and was immediately blinded by the bright morning sun that shone in through the large sash window. Holding a hand up to his brow to shield his eyes from the glare of the rays, he saw the unmistakable silhouette of Joe, who sat with his back to the light behind his old mahogany desk, staring down at him.

'What time is it?' Carl asked groggily.

'Nearly midday.'

'You hit me, didn't you?'

'Yes,' Joe stated honestly.

'Thought so.'

'Carl, we need to talk.'

'I know,' Napier agreed, then added sarcastically, 'We've got loads to catch up on ain't we, mate.'

* * *

Three cups of strong black coffee and two cigarettes later, Carl was ready to talk, but he was still very angry. 'You couldn't bloody stand it, could ya?' He sneered at Joe, 'Out of all the women you could've had, you had to 'ave mine dincha? What was it, couldn't ya bear to see me with a good lookin' woman, or was it that you just had to prove you could get anyone ya wanted?'

'It wasn't like that, Carl,' Joe said calmly.

'No? Then perhaps you'd better explain why I'm feelin' like some piece of shit that you've wiped off yer shoe.'

'There's nothing I can say to you that'll make what I did right,' Joe said, 'But the simple fact is that Rachel's with me now and we love each other, she's carrying my baby and nothin' and nobody is gonna change that. All I can say to you is that neither she nor I intended for it to happen. Neither of us wanted to hurt you, in fact that's the last thing we wanted. You're a good friend Carl, and I'm sorry for what I've done to you, but for whatever reason, it's happened. Now we've got to deal with it.'

'Yeah, that's easy for you to say. You with all your money and power and me with nothing. What am I gonna do now, where am I s'posed to go from here?'

Joe smiled and said 'How about Las Vegas?'

* * *

Carl hated Joe for what he had done. He hated Rachel too for the way she had so easily been seduced by Joe's wealth, power and good looks. However, Carl was no fool and realised the potential of the proposition that Joe had put before him. It was a golden opportunity to become just as rich, just as powerful as his mentor. Away from Joe, away from London, he could do anything he wanted; Las Vegas was a city where fortunes were won and lost at the roll of a dice, but as the manager of a casino, the dice would

256

always be weighted in his favour.

Carl made Joe sweat for a week before giving him the decision he had made within just hours of hearing the deal. He would go to Vegas and he would supervise the construction of the Villa, then when it was completed, he would run it and make damn sure it turned a healthy profit. He would make himself some money and some influential friends, then, when the time was right, he would see about getting even with Joe Cassidy and Rachel Davenport.

Carl accepted the offer with a smile on his face as he shook Joe's hand gratefully. He said that he was happy to let 'bygones be bygones,' professing their friendship to be as strong as ever, but his eyes were cold and his heart was hard as the glorious thrill of revenge twisted in his stomach.

Fourteen

Joe and Rachel were married at Lambeth Registry Office on February 14th 1964. It was a small informal ceremony witnessed by just a few close friends. As for family, Sarah was the sole representative of the Cassidy's to attend and Rachel's eldest brother, Danny, was the only member of the Davenport's. Rachel had four brothers in total, all older than her, but Danny was the only one she got along with. The other three she had not spoken to since leaving home at thirteen; two weeks after her parents had been killed in a car crash.

All the brothers were wild, rough men; Stuart, the youngest of the four, was currently doing time for smashing in someone's skull with a ball-peen hammer, whilst the two middle brothers, Keith and Tommy, had just finished a three year stretch for the brutal assault of a landlord who unsuccessfully tried to tell them that his pub was closing for the night.

At one time or another, the brothers had all worked for either Jack Anderson, Benny Mottola or Vinnie Reece, but presently acted independently. However, Danny had always been tight with Big Jack and was still an occasional member of The Twenty Ones. Whilst probably the most amiable, Danny was also the most volatile and his furious temper was well known on both sides of the river. Nevertheless, he alone had always kept a close watch on his little sister and remained the only family member she had any time for.

Joe knew the Davenport brothers, especially Danny whom he had met through Vinnie several times, but he had not known, until he started dating Rachel, that they had a sister. Danny and Joe had a mutual, if grudging respect for each other, but that is where it ended. The other three Davenport brothers were not worthy of Joe's attention, but for Rachel's sake he kept his opinions to himself.

The wedding ceremony, went without a hitch, even the reception, held of course, at the Golden Gloves, featured none of the punch-ups which had become almost a traditional part of South London weddings. No one would risk upsetting the 'Godfather of Gangland' as the newspapers had rather theatrically taken to calling Joe, whose fame was growing rapidly.

As a wedding gift to his new wife, Joe presented Rachel with a beautiful three storey house in Camberwell, ready for the arrival of their baby, two months later. 'The Castle,' as Joe had christened it, was a huge red brick Victorian town house surrounded by high fortress-like walls. It had an enormous rear garden, but a much smaller one at the front with a short slabbed path leading up to a wide front door. Access to the property was gained only through a tall wrought iron gate, or from the garages at the side, which had room enough for at least four big cars. Inside, the place had been extensively renovated and modernised whilst retaining many of the original features, such as large, ornate mahogany fireplaces and a polished black Aga that was the centre-piece of the huge kitchen. The house had six bedrooms, two living rooms, four bathrooms, a snooker room and adjacent to that, a sumptuously appointed study which was to become Joe's new headquarters. Last but by no means least, and dominating almost the entire top floor, was a brightly decorated nursery, crammed full of toys and essentials, ready for the much anticipated arrival of Joe's son. For Joe, there was never any question that he would have anything other than a boy.

*　*　*

At two minutes past midnight, on the ninth of April, 1964, at the height of the most ferocious storm that London had seen for almost thirty years, he was born. As he let out his first scream, an almighty bolt of lightning struck the main power cable with a deafening crack, shattering many windows and plunging everything into darkness. It was a sign that Brett Vincent Cassidy had entered the world.

*　*　*

A couple of weeks later, Joe was sitting in his office at The Castle, reclining in his plush leather wing-backed chair, behind his recently delivered rosewood desk. He was waiting for Jack Anderson to arrive who had specifically requested a meeting, and although reluctant to comply, Joe was curious as to what he had to say, so granted him a brief audience. Joe was fully aware that Jack knew about Vic's visit to Sarah on that fateful night, and whose lack of action had cost Sarah her sanity, Eddie his life and Michael his father. The only reason that Jack was still alive after contributing to all these things was solely down to the fact that he was Vinnie Reece's cousin - if he had not been he would be dead, and Jack knew this as well as Joe. Nevertheless, Anderson's skin was thick and Joe's interest had been piqued so the meeting had been duly arranged.

*　*　*

Once again, things had not gone Jack's way. At first, his plan had worked like a dream, Benny had been arrested and sent to prison for the murder of Gloria Coombs and he, as planned, had taken over the Mottola organisation. But Jack was just starting to reap the rewards and to earn some real money when Benny escaped. Furthermore, Jack had been told nothing of the breakout until after it happened, he had not been trusted with the information and for some unexplained reason, it had all been organised without his knowledge. He could not help but wonder if it was because Benny was wise to his treachery and, if so, contemplate what price he would pay as a result of it.

As if to add weight to this theory, the power Jack had accumulated in the short time since Mottola's incarceration had suddenly evaporated and all he could do was watch as it slipped through his fingers.

Benny was obviously pulling the strings once more, but nobody had told Jack from where. Nobody had told him why he was no longer required or why he had not been kept in the loop. He assumed, it was because Benny knew of his betrayal - a frightening scenario which would have him undoubtedly marked for death.

In nearly twenty years, Jack had hardly got anywhere, which for an extremely ambitious man like him, was nothing short of total failure. He had got a few clubs and ran a few scams, but what he wanted was a bigger piece of the action. He thought he had hit pay dirt when Benny went inside and that all his troubles were finally over, but it had all gone wrong and now he was worse off than ever before. So against his better judgement, and swallowing a large amount of pride, he was now going crawling to Joe, to beg him for another chance.

*   *   *

'Hello, Joe,' Jack said, standing in front of the rosewood desk, 'Long time no see.'

'Whaddaya want Jack?' Joe replied, immediately dispensing with the niceties, 'I'm a busy man, what can I do for you?'

Jack choked down the last remnants of his pride, there was no evidence that Joe could see of the old Jack, the devious one with the hidden agenda, none of the usual body language signalling his deceit. All Joe saw was a sad pathetic figure, and as Anderson spoke, he felt nothing.

'I want in Joe. I want another chance. I know that in the past things have been a bit strained, but I wanna forget that, make a fresh start, whaddaya say?' He sounded desperate.

'What, and let you double-cross me, like yer double-crossed Vinnie? I don't think so Jack, do you, really?' Joe feigned astonishment.

'But things will be different between us, I've never done anything bad to you.'

'You mean, like when you didn't tell Sean that my sister was bein' attacked by Vic, and that two other blokes were waitin' to 'ave a go when he'd finished - is that what ya mean by done nothin' bad?' Joe was getting angry, 'You mean that, by my best friend 'aving to leave the country, never bein' able to see his kid or his missus, just because you decided not to tell 'im what you knew - surely that's what you must mean Jack - am I right?' He was now shouting.

'No, I.. I just thought that—'

'What did you think Jack? That because you were Vinnie's cousin it would mean somethin' to me? Or because you thought I might need the help of that ridiculous bunch of no hopers, The Twenty Ones?'

'I just thought I could be of some use—'

'You, Jack?' Joe made a look of disdain, 'You're less than shit to me. You're lucky that I even let you exist. Now get out of my sight before I forget my manners and kill ya.'

Jack made to reply, then thought better of it. Bitterly he turned and walked to the door and as he opened it, he looked back at Joe, his pride re-surfacing with a rush of disgust at the depth of his own degradation. Hidden behind the hideous gold-rimmed sunglasses, hate filled Jack's eyes. 'You've made a big mistake here today, Cassidy,' he said under his breath, 'This won't be forgotten.' Then arrogantly, he walked out.

Fifteen

Joe had taken to fatherhood exceptionally well. He would feed and bathe his son and even change dirty nappies in an effort to give his child the love that he never had from his own father. It was important to Joe that Brett grew up to like him, to feel that he could go to him with any problems, or just for a bit of parental advice. The boy brought out the best in Joe and the two of them would play for hours together, Joe spinning the lad around or throwing him up in the air and catching him again, Brett's delighted giggling urging his father to do it more and more. Then when completely exhausted, Joe would put his son to bed and read him a story to lull him to sleep. If Brett woke in the night, Joe would get up, make him a bottle of warm milk and feed it to him until he finally nodded off once more.

Rachel tried to be a good mother, although she was not a natural parent and Brett was never a mummy's boy. Whenever he cried or was upset, there was only ever one person he wanted, and that was Joe. Rachel would take it in turns to get up in the night, but the lack of sleep made her irritable and short tempered. She did not cope well if she did not get a full eight hours, and occasionally, when really tired, she would snap. If Brett was tearful or particularly restless, instead of trying to comfort him, she would shout at him to shut up, which invariably served only to make him more agitated. If it did, then Rachel would smack him, sometimes leaving a red hand print on his little leg or arm, once even on his cheek.

Fortunately, these incidents did not happen often, but they did trouble Joe and were the only thing that marred an otherwise idyllic family life.

*   *   *

Every Saturday afternoon, Joe and Rachel would go to the local park, where they would stroll arm in arm, proudly pushing their son's pram, showing him off to the world. Joe would always have at least two minders on hand who would walk several yards behind him and his wife. This was merely a precaution, but since Benny's escape, Joe had stepped up security. He did not believe in being too careful where his family were concerned.

Richie Noakes, Alfie's eldest son, now a strapping young man of twenty-five, was Joe's driver and permanent shadow. Wherever Joe went, Richie went also, forever on guard, always watching his boss' back. Richie had been born for the work, learning through years of watching his father, he knew exactly his function, and performed it perfectly. He was also extremely tough and had won many trophies for his boxing prowess, coached, of course, by his very proud dad. He was the ideal choice for the job of minder; trustworthy, discreet and loyal with a right hook that could flatten an elephant.

The other man, who acted as Richie's lieutenant, was Stan 'The Man' O'Keefe, also known as 'Manno.' Manno was a traditional, no-nonsense hard case, only about five foot six, but almost as wide and every inch pure muscle. However, unlike a lot of tough guys, Manno had brains to match the brawn. Also twenty-five, he too was incredibly loyal and would not hesitate to lay down his life for those he protected.

Richie and Manno, were like Joe and I; they were best

264

friends and worked effectively as a team, each knowing the others strengths and weaknesses and able to compensate accordingly. A truly formidable pair, who would always accompany Joe, Rachel and little Brett on their Saturday afternoon excursions to the park. Richie's primary task was to protect Joe whilst Manno's was to guard Rachel and the baby.

On one particular Saturday, shortly after Joe's run-in with Big Jack, the Cassidys had finished their normal circuit of the park and were heading back to the car, which Richie had parked just opposite the entrance on the other side of the street. He crossed the road ahead of the others and opened the rear door of Joe's gleaming dark green Bentley then, after carefully checking both directions, he nodded to Manno, who, on his partner's signal, ushered Joe and his family across the road.

As they approached the centre of the wide road, a white Jag, which had appeared to be seemingly harmless just seconds before, screeched away from its parked position and headed at top speed towards the small family group. As Joe turned to face the speeding vehicle, he clearly saw four men inside it wearing stocking masks and his stomach churned with dread as he noticed the barrel of a sawn-off shotgun sticking menacingly out the front passenger window.

'It's a hit!' Joe shouted, before grabbing hold of Rachel with one hand and scooping Brett effortlessly out of his pram with the other.

Richie and Manno had also seen the threat and had both drawn pistols from the shoulder holsters under their jackets. Manno stood solid as a rock in the centre of the road and coolly took aim at the on-rushing Jag. Bang! The first shot rang out as Manno squeezed the trigger. The bullet punctured the windscreen of the car and shattered the glass in a three inch radius around the hole before burying itself squarely in the forehead of the man sitting behind the driver and killing him instantly. Manno's second shot smashed the windscreen completely, this time catching the already dead man in the throat. Before he could squeeze off another round, the driver of the Jag pointed a small black revolver through the vacant gap where the windscreen had been and fired back. The shot hit Manno hard in the thigh and he span off balance as he desperately tried to throw himself clear of the car which was headed straight for him.

Richie, who had run forward to protect Joe and his family as they rushed across the road, was also firing. Aiming at the man with the sawn-off, he had put two holes in the passenger door before finally hitting his target in the left shoulder. The injury jolted the man's aim at the moment of firing, and the shotgun, which had been trained on Joe, jarred upwards and emptied both its barrels harmlessly into the air. A fourth bullet from Richie hit the steering wheel and caused the driver to swerve as a reaction. This fortunately prevented the Jag from flattening Manno, and instead merely caught him a glancing blow on the backside as he tried to avoid the full force of the heavy vehicle.

Joe was virtually carrying his screaming wife with one arm wrapped tightly around her tiny waist and her feet barely touching the tarmac as he dragged her across the road. With his other arm, he was clutching the boy, his hand forcing Brett's face into his chest, with the lad's body tucked safely under his arm. Joe dived behind the Bentley and landed painfully on his back as he tried to protect his wife and child from injury. They fell heavily on him but as soon as they were down he rolled on top of them using his body to shield theirs.

In the heat of the moment Joe was unaware of the bullet that hit his shoulder, which had been fired from the pistol of the second man in the back of the Jaguar. But as the car raced past, Richie returned fire and hit the shooter fatally in the chest, although not before the would-be assassin had fired again. His shot should have caught Joe in the back of the head, killing him instantly. Instead, Richie hurled his large bulk selflessly into the bullet's path and it struck him in the side, breaking two ribs, before exiting through his back. It finally came to a halt in the plush beige leather of the Bentley's open rear door as Richie crashed painfully to the tarmac.

The white car ploughed violently into the baby's empty pram, the force of impact tossing it high into the air. As it flew, one of its wheels whirled off and span discus-like into the driver's window of the Bentley, smashing it noisily to pieces.

Manno, now lying on his stomach by the curb of the opposite pavement, fired two more times as the Jag careered down the street at break-neck speed. The first shot snapping off the chrome wing mirror and the second, Manno was certain, hitting the driver either in the shoulder or back.

As the bent and broken pram returned to earth in a crescendo of sound, landing with a metallic clang in the centre of the road, the Jaguar screeched into a side road and vanished from view. The whole episode had lasted less than thirty seconds.

After a moment, Joe slowly rolled over and Rachel, who had been almost paralysed with fear, suddenly let out a hideous scream as she pointed in horror at her six month old son.

As Joe looked down at his boy, his heart almost stopped as he saw what Rachel was screaming at. The baby's black hair was damp and sticky and his face and clothes were covered with a wet coating of bright red blood. The boy's eyes were shut and his body was motionless, and for the first time in his life Joe knew the meaning of absolute terror.

Then, miraculously, Brett opened his eyes looked up at his father and beamed a wide, gummy smile. With an immense sigh of relief, Joe felt the tide of panic subside, but there was still the matter of where the blood was coming from and frantically he checked over his son. Only when completely satisfied that the boy was unharmed did Joe consider the possibility that it was he who was injured and not Brett.

The moment this occurred to him, he became aware of the dull throbbing in his shoulder and when he placed his fingers on the source of the pain he felt the blood pumping from the small bullet hole. He needed medical attention, as did Manno who was limping across the road towards him. Then Joe turned his head to check on Richie who was propped up on one arm, a horrific red stain spreading steadily across his white shirt. He was hit hard but his concern was not for himself but for Brett who he too had thought was dead.

Very carefully, Joe climbed to his feet. Then, still clutching his son, he helped Richie up. Rachel was sitting on the curb, shaking uncontrollably, her face white as a ghost and tears streaming down her cheeks. The violence and the ferocity of the attack had devastated her more than anyone could possibly know. When the shots started firing she had been convinced she was going to die. Then, when she had seen Brett covered in all that blood, it had terrified her, but thanked God it was him and not her. There was no guilt to her thoughts just an overwhelming sense of relief mixed with the continued feeling of intense fear. Even when Brett was found to be alive and well she could feel no joy as the shock of the attack had rocked her to the very core and erased all rational thought. Joe helped her to her feet and tried to calm her, but apart from a few words of comfort, was not in a position to give her his full attention. He had no clue as to the depth of the damage the ordeal had caused her, nor any idea of the disastrous path upon which Rachel had just embarked.

*   *   *

Time was of the essence, Joe knew that they had to move fast before the police arrived. Also, he, Richie and Manno needed to see the Doctor as soon as possible, as each of them were losing a lot of blood, particularly Richie, who, from what Joe could tell, was undoubtedly the most seriously wounded.

Rachel, even though the only one fit to drive, was in no fit state as she was barely coherent, so Joe climbed painfully into the driving seat with Manno sitting beside him. Between them, with Joe steering and working the foot pedals and Manno operating the gear stick, they got the Bentley underway and headed towards Wandsworth and the Doctor.

As they got into a comfortable driving rhythm, Manno asked 'Who was it, Boss? Who was behind the hit?'

Joe's black eyes flashed with anger as he coldly replied, 'Big Jack Anderson - and believe me, the bastard is gonna pay.'

*   *   *

Joe phoned Ray from the safe house in Wandsworth, who came at once to pick up Rachel and Brett. The Doctor had given Rachel some tranquillisers to calm her nerves, and, at Joe's request, had allowed her to keep the bottle on the proviso she not exceed the dosage.

When Rachel got home, she settled the baby, then told Ray she was going to bed. He, in turn, went to the kitchen to wait for Joe. However, when Rachel was certain that Ray could not observe her, she crept into Joe's office, opened the drinks cabinet and removed a large bottle of vodka.

Once safely back in her bedroom, she stripped off her clothes, and, as she had done many times before, studied her naked form in the full length mirror. Her reflection gave no indication that she'd had a baby just six months before as her figure was just as slim and firm as it had been before the pregnancy. Her body and looks were the only things she had ever been able to rely on; the two things that had kept her from poverty and self-destruction, and it calmed her and reassured her to gaze upon them. She noticed a bruise on her thigh and another on her shin, there was also a slight graze on her elbow, but she knew, unlike her fractured emotions, that they would heal. She stared closer at herself, searching for any sign of the utter panic and absolute hysteria she felt inside, but there was none. Still unconvinced, she lifted her right hand, and holding it in front of her face, she saw the terrifying truth. It was shaking violently, and even when she concentrated, she was unable to stop it.

Snapping it quickly away from view, she walked over to her bedside table where, with trembling fingers, she unscrewed the top from the bottle of vodka. She lifted it to her lips and took several long slugs, feeling the warmth of it as it entered her body. Then she opened the bottle of tranquillisers and tipped a small pile of them into her quivering palm, a tear spilled down her cheek as she lifted her hand and threw the pills into her mouth before quickly swallowing them down with another long swig of vodka. When the pills were gone, she took yet another couple of swigs, then screwed the cap back on the vodka and hid the bottle under a pile of knickers in her bedside cabinet.

Rachel stood for a moment, composing herself as she let the alcohol and drugs take effect. After a couple of minutes she looked at her hand again and noticed that it had stopped shaking. Rachel managed a little smile, she now knew how to hide her fear. Soon though, the vodka bottle would be empty and the pills would be gone. She would have to get more, much more.

Sixteen

There were twelve of them altogether. All hard, tough men, all extremely skilled at their work, all knowing exactly what had to be done. None of them having cause to even slightly question their orders. Each man wore a dark suit, a white shirt and a plain, sombre tie - the unofficial uniform of gangland.

They arrived in three big cars, which were parked discreetly at the end of the one way street, ready for a quick getaway. When the engines had been switched off, and all passengers had vacated the vehicles, the drivers popped open the boots of their respective motors to display an assorted arsenal of weaponry. The selection included sawn-offs, pistols, knives, bats, chains, knuckle dusters and pipes, each one of the twelve being invited to choose their preferred implement.

The two leaders of the group waited until each man was properly armed, then started to walk toward the dimly lit building at the end of the street, the rest of the crew falling in behind them.

The pair at the head of the pack, were characteristically calm and relaxed, showing no signs of emotion. But inwardly, both were gripped with a bitter determination, adrenaline pumping through their veins, more than ready for what was about to happen. In truth, they each thrived in these situations, it was work that they knew well and had a natural talent for. They were easily among the ten toughest men in London and, in their heyday, would have undoubtedly been in the top five. By reputation alone, they struck fear into most men, and only the very brave, or very foolish would put them to the test.

As they reached the end of the street, the first man walked up the steps to the garish red double doors, and in a very business-like fashion, pulled them open, placed a large paw around the throat of the unsuspecting goon who was supposed to be minding the entrance, and dragged him out into the street. Before the guard could make a sound, he was coshed on the back of the head and knocked out cold. His legs buckled, but before he fell, his assailant caught him and guided him silently to the ground. Then the attacker, opened the door wide to allow the other eleven men through, and in turn, followed the last man into the building.

The small force then quietly climbed the short flight of stairs that led up to yet another set of double doors, which opened into the club proper. After the two leaders made certain that all members of the squad were accounted for, they exchanged an understanding nod and burst violently through the doors.

As predicted, it kicked off straight away. The club was busy, as was only to be expected on a Saturday night. The punters were mostly men, all of whom, without exception, were villains who were armed with some sort of weapon. The twelve announced their presence with a shotgun blast which shattered the nicotine stained mirror ball that hung over the small cocktail lounge just inside the entrance. They then piled into the club, the thirty strong opposition, although caught by surprise, rallied quickly to defend their territory. Fighting broke out all over the place, in the bar, on the dance floor, even on the stage. Tables and chairs were being smashed over people's heads, shots ricocheted around the room, and the few women present were screaming with terror, all that is, except for the rather 'over-the-hill' stripper, who stood in the wings, wearing nothing but an expression that suggested she had seen it all before. Glasses and bottles were being broken by the dozen as bloodied and bruised men were thrown around the room.

The twelve protagonists were all still standing, the opposition, although greater in number, were not proving to be up to the challenge and within minutes, over half had fallen, many with horrific injuries. Knife wounds, or cracked skulls, broken jaws and lacerated faces, the victims of knuckle dusters or chains. Most of these men deserved what they got. The vast majority would have undoubtedly inflicted similar injuries on others over the years, and now they were getting their comeuppance. It may not have been pretty, but it was long overdue.

The two in charge left the brawl and went in search of the prey they were specifically hunting. In the far corner, behind the bar, was a wooden door with the word private painted on it in chipped gold lettering. The smaller, broader one of the pair kicked the cheaply veneered entrance hard, near the lock, and it smashed open. As he did so, a bullet, which was fired from within, ripped through the rotten door frame sending a shower of splinters into the air as it passed within a hair's breadth of the intruders. Another shot hit the door itself, and another ricocheted off the already broken lock. The burly pair, not at all put off by this, merely stood aside, drew their guns and waited for their victim to empty his weapon. Three more blasts rang out in quick succession, and then nothing. Before allowing their quarry to re-load, both men stormed through the doorway and down the short corridor, firing shot after shot as cover, not giving the enemy a chance to fire back.

At the end of the passage, there was one room only, its door wide open. Inside, cowered the man they were looking for. He was crouching down beside the door frame with his back against the wall, shielding himself from the twin assault. Even in the squat position he was enormous, like some great silver backed gorilla, his vast bulk, most of which was muscle, ready to pounce the moment his attackers came through the doorway. He was out of ammo and out of luck, he had been expecting some sort of retribution, but was surprised it had taken this form. He had been convinced that the end would come unannounced, the victim of an assassin's bullet. Quick, silent and lethal. Not like this, a noisy, bloody offensive on his home turf.

When the two aggressors dived through the door he lunged at them, using his considerable weight to good advantage and grabbed them both around the waist. As he forced them backwards and pinned them up against the far wall, one of the men nearly lost his footing as he was unable to walk without the aid of the stick. However, when his back hit the wall, and the gorilla was unable to push him further, the man was no longer disabled and instead became an almighty force. First he brought down the solid silver ball of his cane, which had been fashioned in the shape of a clenched fist, striking hard the gorilla's skull. Then he kneed him in the balls.

As he squealed in agony, the gorilla looked up for the first time to see his adversaries and was astonished by who he saw; they were not at all who he expected them to be and was perplexed as to their presence. However, he recognised both of them instantly; the man with the walking stick was an almost legendary figure in London whereas the other, the one with the fearsome hooded eyes, was among the most powerful, and just one look into their faces told him enough. He was in serious trouble.

What he could not fathom, was why? He had said a few things that certainly would not have gone down too well, but surely nothing that deserved this, not now at least.

It was then that the man with the hooded eyes brought down a cosh to the side of the gorilla's head, which sent him, starry eyed, to his knees. The one with the limp then punched him hard on the cheek, sending him sprawling unconsciously to the floor.

When he awoke, some moments later, he made to get up, but was immediately punished by a kick to the ribs and another to the stomach.

'What 'ave I done?' The gorilla asked desperately.

'You're 'aving a laugh aintcha?' Said the man with the stick. 'You know exactly what you've done and now you're gonna pay.' With that, he kicked his victim brutally in the face, splitting his lip and knocking out two of his teeth, the blood now flowing in a steady stream from his mouth.

'What did ya think?' Said the man with the hooded eyes 'That ya could pull a stunt like that and not pay the price?' This time it was his turn, and he bent down and landed a powerful punch on the gorilla's nose, splitting it instantly and sending his precious glasses spinning across the tacky red linoleum.

The man on the floor was now almost begging, 'Please, just tell me what I've done, tell me how I can make it right?'

The one with the limp curled his lip, exposing his perfect white teeth and snarled, 'Don't fuckin' insult us you devious bastard.' Slowly, he walked around the prone form, using the stick to support himself. He reached the open door, which was blocking his path, 'We've come to deliver a message, a message we trust you won't forget.' He then slammed the door loudly and all that could be heard from outside the room, was the dull thud as feet and fists connected with their defenceless target.

* * *

When finished, the two attackers walked from the room, the one with the hooded eyes purposely stepping on the hideous gold sunglasses, crushing them under his foot.

They left the man on the floor, his face black and blue from extensive bruising, with blood seeping from his split nose and mouth, and unable to open his puffy swollen eyes. Suffering from three broken fingers, a broken arm and three cracked ribs, he painfully squinted at the door, only barely conscious.

There, almost dead, having suffered the beating of his life, Big Jack made his promise. In a whisper, only just audible through bruised lips he pledged, 'Watch your back Cassidy, 'cos one day I'm gonna fuckin' kill ya.' Then, he passed out.

*   *   *

As Ray Reece and Alfie Noakes walked back into the main room of The Pontoon, they saw that their men had made short work of The Twenty Ones. Not one of the opposition was left standing, whilst Joe's crew had sustained very few injuries. All in all, a very successful night's work.

'Well, Ray,' Alfie said, lighting a cigarette, 'I'd say Jack got the message, wouldn't you?'

'Y'know Alfie,' Ray replied, 'I'd be surprised if he didn't.'

Alfie took a long drag on the cigarette, then dropped it onto the carpet. He watched it for a second or two as it started to smoulder, then, when he was sure it had taken, he and Ray led their men from the building.

*   *   *

What neither of them knew, was that Big Jack was not responsible for the hit on Joe.

They had got the wrong man.

Seventeen

It had been an unsettled time for me. In the space of two years, I'd had nearly fifteen jobs. Jobs with no prospects and offering very little in salary. Louretta, using her contacts had managed to find me casual work on several ranches, but nothing permanent, nothing lasting longer than three months.

Since the early part of 1964, I'd washed floors, flipped burgers, cleaned offices and pumped gas. All menial jobs but they kept me out of trouble and the money I earned just about paid for motels, food and the up-keep of the Indian.

However, the most interesting work I had was the short time I spent with a circus as a motorcycle stunt rider. It started as a bit of fun, something to do for excitement more than anything else, but as it turned out, it was an occupation that would prove to be the making of me.

I had spotted the poster that the circus had put up in the window of a gas station asking for a 'part-time dare devil,' and thought it might be interesting if nothing else, so duly applied. Apparently, I was the only applicant, which naturally improved my chances, and when I told them I knew how to ride a motorcycle, which until then, I had never considered a qualification, they offered me the job on the spot.

It appeared that the usual rider, the circus owner's son, had broken his leg in practice and would be off for at least two months, which was fast becoming my accepted term of employment, but the wages were okay and food and lodgings were thrown in so I decided to give it a go.

The work was an adrenaline rush quite unlike any other and involved a bit of bike jumping, over barrels and through burning hoops and such, as well as a 'wall of death' show, four times a day. Although none of this was particularly death-defying, it did require a certain knack, especially when riding the wall, but I picked it up quite quickly and soon learned to love it.

Sadly though, it only lasted six weeks, as the original rider came back sooner than expected and I found myself, once more, out of work.

Depressed and needing a break, I decided to pay Virgil a visit at his new home in Beverly Hills. In the twelve months since I had last seen him, Virgil had become a hugely popular actor and now lived in luxurious style at his fabulous Hollywood mansion. He had a pool, a sauna, a tennis court, countless bedrooms, numerous bathrooms and a garage full of classic cars - he even had his own cinema!

However, success had come at a price. No longer could he pursue his passion for surfing or, at least, not without the media photographing his every move, nor could he go to a bar and enjoy a drink unnoticed. With celebrity, he had lost his anonymity, and this he found very hard to come to terms with.

When I arrived, Virgil was delighted to see a friendly face. Usually he was surrounded by agents, stylists, lawyers, free loaders and sycophants. Of the women he went out with, and there were many, very few were genuinely interested in getting to know the man, all they wanted was the movie star and Virgil felt very much alone.

He told me I was welcome to stay as long as I wanted which,

after the previous couple of years, was a very tempting offer and I was certainly ready to put down roots again. Since leaving Wildwood, I had covered my tracks pretty well. Never stopping in one place long enough to be traced, always using a different name and never returning to the same town twice. I had ridden the whole west coast, travelling up as far as Oregon and right back down to San Diego again and, whenever in the vicinity of Palm Springs, I always found time to spend a few days with Louretta before moving on again.

If either Benny Mottola or Frank Blades had tracked me down, I would have been very surprised. For the time being I was certainly safe, but I did not consider it fair on Virgil to sponge off him indefinitely.

He was currently shooting in Hollywood which, for him, was a nice change. He had been on almost permanent location for the last three years and he was glad to be spending at least the next six months in California. Being constantly away from home had made him feel even more isolated from reality and he was thankful to be back.

Every morning I would accompany Virgil to the studio where, between takes, we would chat or play cards. We would lunch at the studio diner alongside stars such as Cary Grant, Doris Day and Bing Crosby, which was completely surreal, and I was often left feeling completely star-struck. Virgil would just smile, understanding exactly how I felt, and admitting that, even now, he found it hard to believe when someone like John Wayne asked him to pass the salt.

Virgil was filming a cowboy movie on one of the backlots where a replica of an old western town was built. I recognised the set from numerous other films and it was amazing to actually be there, watching the whole movie making process. Sadly though, the production was fraught with problems, and it appeared that I was the only person enjoying the experience. Already the director had been replaced twice, and the leading lady, who had been arriving consistently late on set, having kept the crew waiting several hours before gracing them with her presence, had finally been fired. The studio, already infuriated by her prima donna antics, had eventually snapped when she turned up drunk and unable to speak her lines coherently.

Fortunately, she only appeared a few times in the scenes that had been filmed so far, and her close-ups could easily be re-shot with a different actress. The remaining images of her could be carefully edited out of the existing footage and her voice dubbed by the new replacement who, as yet, had not been cast.

In the meantime, the latest director decided to work around this by shooting the action sequences, most of which, did not require the leading lady. In the scenes that did, a stunt double would be used, and again, the close-ups featuring the new actress, added later.

This did not trouble Virgil as he was very easy going, which his popularity with the entire production crew proved. Unlike his former co-star, he was still very much a regular guy and did not play on his star status at all. Virgil introduced me to everyone and, very quickly, I felt at ease, particularly with the stunt people who, in my view, were the true heroes of the movies. They did for real what actors only pretended to do. They, too, were horse people and because this was a western there were many beautiful animals on set which I would always admire. I found myself talking to the stunt crew more and more between takes, or when Virgil was learning his lines, and discovered that I had a great deal in common with them. However, in a stupid attempt to impress, I told them of my prowess as a horseman and, for some reason, felt the need to boast further by informing them of my former 'career' as a stunt motorcyclist, embroidering the facts more than just a little.

They seemed to take this as provocation and immediately threw down the gauntlet, challenging me to a good-natured dual which, childishly keen to show off, I readily accepted. Little did I know at the time, that my quick decision would alter the course of my life.

*　*　*

My opponent was Brad Booker, Virgil's stunt double, who, like the man he impersonated, was tall, blonde and athletic, yet facially bore little resemblance. Brad was not so handsome, his features were heavier and more weather beaten and his eyes were a dirty grey not the dashing blue so revered by Virgil's admirers. However, on camera, and if not in direct shot, Brad could easily carry the illusion off for the audience.

Booker had also devised the challenge, which gave him a distinct advantage, but it was all in the name of fun, so I did not complain. The contest he conceived had been designed specifically for my 'talents,' the idea behind it being to beat me at what I was supposedly good at, and then to gloat at my inevitable humiliation. This would prove, without question, that they were the professionals, whilst I was just an enthusiastic amateur. It was not malicious, in fact Brad himself was an extremely nice guy, but there was a definite edge to the contest and I suspected he was keen to prove his superiority. I understood this, and happily entered into spirit of the occasion by betting outrageously on myself. However, all the smart money was on Brad.

The contest, which was to take place out in the Mojave desert over twenty miles of the roughest terrain, had been designed in two sections. The first section would be a straightforward dirt bike race, the course incorporating high sand dunes, near vertical drops and numerous natural jumps, ending with a quarter mile flat race to the finish. Without a break, we would then leap off our bikes and onto the back of a waiting horse, signalling the start of the second section. The idea of this section was to collect four orange flags, placed just above ground level, without either dismounting or reducing speed. Among the obstacles this time around were several high jumps and an exceptionally steep, soft-sanded dune, which a horse would struggle to climb even without a rider. Once again, the section ended with a mad dash to the finish; the winner being the first person to cross the line and present all four flags to the judge who, everyone agreed, should be Virgil.

The race was held early on a Saturday morning and the entire production crew had turned out to see it.

I was nervous, more due to the occasion than to lack of confidence as I was fairly competent on a motorcycle and riding a horse was now second nature. I knew, however, that my opponent was an equally good, if not better horseman, and was also far more likely to be able to get the most out of a bike.

Although I had been riding the Indian for years, it was a big, heavy machine, built more for cruising than for racing. My only experience with the lighter, faster bikes had been at the circus, which although an intensive learning curve, could never compete with Brad's skill and experience. In his capacity as a stunt man, he had raced, jumped, leapt off, and blown up more motorcycles than I had even seen, let alone sat on. I did not kid myself that the challenge would be easy, but I knew it would be fun and I was eager to get on with it.

Getting a good start was vital to my plan. I felt that if I could get ahead of Brad on the motorcycle part of the course, I had a more than average chance of winning the whole race, knowing that on the horse section, I could increase my advantage and, with luck, cross the line victorious.

As we sat revving our bikes, both of which belonged to my opponent, waiting for Marilu, Brad's girlfriend, to wave the starting flag, I glanced across at the assembled crowd and, for just a second,

I thought I caught a glimpse of someone I recognised. The face was hidden behind a pair of dark glasses and slightly obscured by another person in the audience, but I could see the distinctive long platinum hair billowing in the wind and I was almost certain I knew to whom it belonged. Temporarily forgetting where I was, or my purpose for being there, I strained for a better view, but at that very moment, Marilu waived the flag and Brad roared away.

Cursing myself for the lack of concentration, I pulled back the throttle and popped open the clutch, but in my haste to catch Booker, I released it too quickly, causing the bike to rear up high and charge off wildly on its back wheel, the front wheel spinning freely in mid air. The sheer angle of the upright machine caused me to slip from the saddle and I had to run along behind the bike, desperately holding onto the handlebars as I tried to wrestle the powerful 500cc beast back onto two wheels. The crowd thought this was hilarious and even over the din of the engine I heard their laughter.

Finally, after an enormous struggle, I managed to close down the throttle and bring the bike back down to earth. Quickly, I jumped back on the saddle and regained control, instantly opening the accelerator again, but with a little more care, and blasting off in pursuit of the other bike.

Looking up, I saw Brad had a good two hundred yard lead, and I berated myself again for the costly lack of concentration. It had not been exactly the kind of start I had hoped for and all I could do now was get my head down and hope for the best.

My bike roared under me, responding to my every demand, but Brad would be hard to catch. The dust and sand kicked up from his bike hung like a cloud behind him, obscuring all but the most fleeting glimpse of his back. I tore after him, blasting through the gears like a mad man, spitting out the dirt that spattered my face and smeared my goggles, finding my way at break-neck speed through muddied vision. But I was determined to catch him, determined to make up for my costly mistake and prove myself to all those who had laughed.

We charged around the course, the distance between us slowly narrowing. The bikes were really being put through their paces; one moment they would be flying through the air as they launched off the top of a dune, the next, they would be crashing down hard on their suspension as gravity pulled them down.

It was gruelling and hard but massively exhilarating and at times I wanted to laugh out loud for sheer enjoyment. With every corner, every jump, I was edging closer to Brad, then I lost sight of him as he vanished over the top of a particularly large mountain of sand. As I flew from its summit a few seconds later, I saw him sprawled at the base of the hill yards from his bike. He had misjudged the landing and I smiled at his error. I was airborne for what seemed like an eternity as Brad scrambled to his feet. Then my front wheel started to dip and I knew, like Brad, that I too had misjudged the jump. Too late to avert the inevitable, I braced myself for impact. The front wheel hit first and I was catapulted over the handlebars and headlong into the soft sand. The bike bounced right over me and cartwheeled out of harm's way. Brad was now running towards his machine as I sat on my backside and quickly checked myself over. I was fine but had to get to my bike before Brad roared off again and left me floundering in his wake. Fortunately though, Booker's bike had stalled but the engine on mine was still purring like a sleeping lion. Seeing my chance, I jumped up and made a run for it.

Brad was now back on his bike, pumping the kickstart desperately, trying to revive his dead machine. Just as I jumped back on mine his roared into life and, without another wasted second, he sped off. Immediately I gave chase; still in the losing position but with valuable ground made up. More to the point, I still had my best chance yet to come and if I could just keep close to Booker, I felt sure I could take him on the second leg, which was more suited to my talents.

On the final quarter mile charge, I crossed the line less than three seconds behind my opponent. I skidded the bike to a halt and handed it quickly to a helper, then sprang onto my waiting horse, which also belonged to Brad. Much to his credit, he had given me the pick of the animals owned by the stunt company he worked for, and I had chosen a particularly fine grey called 'Jasper.'

Giving him just a gentle dig in the ribs, he shot off at a blistering pace and I knew I had made a wise decision. Booker was now only about ten yards from me, his beautiful chestnut mare, Venus, also racing flat out. Laying as low as possible along Jasper's back, I placed my head against his neck and encouraged him to run like the wind which he responded to eagerly.

As Jasper came within touching distance of the other horse's tail, I saw the first pair of orange flags, one for each competitor. Brad slid his backside out of the saddle and removed his feet from the stirrups, then gently lowered himself down to the horse's flank, one leg wrapped vice-like under his mount's belly, the other clamped over its back. Still travelling at full gallop, Booker gripped the saddle with his left hand and, at full stretch, dangled his right one just inches above the ground, demonstrating a truly remarkable piece of horsemanship. As he approached the flag, he snatched it up and immediately placed it safely between his teeth. Then in one deft movement, he hoisted himself back into the saddle, returned his feet to the stirrups, and continued without having altered pace; the whole manoeuvre, swift, skilful and effective.

Using the same technique, only on the opposite side, I snatched up my flag, but as I attempted to pull myself back into the saddle, my leg slipped from Jasper's hips. Fortunately, I managed to gain a grip with the side of my knee, pressing it hard down as it slid across the horse's buttocks. This was just enough to keep me on, although I had to fight hard to regain my seat, which I did after an enormous effort. But, once again, I had lost ground to Brad.

We picked up another flag, this time with more success on my part, just before descending into a rock gully, where we had to slow our horses down to near walking pace in order to safely navigate the loose, uneven terrain. However, Jasper was fearless and we managed to claw back some distance, with Brad emerging from the gully mere seconds before me.

By the time we had reached the third flag, the horses were almost neck and neck as we thundered along at an incredible speed. There was only about a mile to go, and I felt my confidence rise, but in the distance, I could see the most difficult and potentially hazardous part of the course.

Between us and the finish line was an extremely steep dune, with deep, soft sand that the horses would find incredibly tough to cope with. Also, because of the sheer incline of the dune, Brad and I would pretty much have to hang off the front of our animals to counter balance the weight, preventing our horses from falling backwards. To dismount was an immediate disqualification and neither of us wanted that.

The last pair of flags had been strategically placed on the summit. The first person to snatch theirs up would just have to negotiate the small slope on the opposite side of the dune and then make a mad dash for the finish, just three hundred yards away.

We hit the base of the hill together, and both of us charged up the first part of it with relative ease, which was at a less severe gradient than the rest. The horses though were well over ankle deep in sand, which had slowed their movements dramatically. Both animals were snorting loudly as the ever increasing incline and cloying, energy absorbing ground sapped their strength. They were already tired, with frothy white sweat shining wetly on their glossy coats, but the hardest part was yet to come, and we urged them relentlessly onwards.

I was forcing myself as far forward as possible, with my head almost in front of Jasper's neck, his panting jaws just above my eye line. As the hill got steeper, Jasper's movements became more erratic, his strides more and more laboured as he tried to leap from one unsteady foothold to the next.

Glancing across at Booker, I noticed he was having an even harder time than me, the chestnut mare grunting and protesting as Brad desperately spurred her on. I too was constantly coaxing Jasper, shouting words of encouragement to him, forcing him onwards and, very slowly, we were creeping ahead.

As we came to the steepest part of the dune, I heard Brad's horse whinny loudly in high-pitched protest, then as I turned to look, I saw her rear up and fall backwards, tossing Booker from the saddle. Watching both horse and rider tumbling down the hill, I knew I had the race in the bag. Jasper must have sensed victory too because, as I nudged him gently in the ribs with my heels, he made one final assault on the dune and launched himself heroically to the top.

Having reached the summit, I allowed myself a last brief look down the hill, gloating at my adversary's downfall. I was relieved to see that the mare was alright, although Brad was still face down in the sand at the foot of the slope. There was no way he could win now and I smiled with malicious glee as I leaned down and pulled the fourth flag triumphantly from the dirt.

Steering Jasper down the shorter, gentler side of the dune, we cantered unhurriedly along the home straight towards the finish line where I could see the large crowd in the distance cheering us onward.

About fifty yards from the finish line, a troubling thought entered my head. What if Brad is injured?, What if he is laying

287

there unconscious, slowly suffocating in the deep sand?

I twisted in my saddle, looking back down the course, but there was no sign of Booker. I was now starting to worry. 'Whoa, boy!' I said to Jasper, pulling hard on his reigns, bringing him to a sharp halt.

Slowly I brought him around so that we were facing the large dune, and I could hear the shouts from the spectators behind me, urging me to cross the line. But I waited, and still there was no sign of Brad.

'Bollocks!' I cursed out loud, already knowing what I had to do. I kicked Jasper lightly into action, and we galloped urgently back. Skidding to a stop at the brow of the hill, I leapt from my horse's back and quickly scanned the steep incline. Sure enough, Brad was still where I had last seen him, face down in the sand and Venus was sniffing at his hair, distressed by her master's lack of movement.

I threw myself off the summit and landed halfway down, but the momentum pitched me over and I rolled and bounced down the remainder of the hill, eventually coming to rest in a dusty heap at the bottom. Although a little dazed, I jumped to my feet and rushed over to where Brad lay. The first thing I noticed was that his left leg was broken with his foot facing the opposite direction to the knee, and I winced in sympathy.

'Brad!' I shouted, 'Are you okay?' No response.

'Booker!' I tried again, 'Can you hear me?' Still nothing.

Very carefully, trying hard not to disturb his injured leg, I lifted his face out the dust and twisted it towards me. His lips sagged limply apart and a long stream of sand emptied from his mouth. 'Booker, wake up!' I ordered, but there was still no signs of life. 'Booker!' I shouted again.

In desperation, I slapped him hard around the face, trying to revive him and was rewarded with a very faint groan, but it was enough to give me hope and I slapped him twice more.

'Brad, wake up, open your eyes man!'

Suddenly, his eyes sprung open and he stared directly into my face, then almost immediately he started to splutter and cough violently with tears rolling down his face. With each cough he brought up handfuls of sand, retching maybe five or six times before finally ridding his stomach completely.

When it was all out, he wiped the saliva from his lips, then with eyes red and puffy, he turned to me and croaked, 'Thanks, Sean.'

Just as the first of the curious crowd members appeared around the side of the dune, Brad screamed with pain as the hideous injury to his leg made itself known.

He may have been hurt, but he was alive and I smiled to myself. Life saving was far more rewarding than winning races.

*   *   *

Brad getting injured, presented two problems. The first was that Virgil no longer had a stunt double, at least not one in full working order, and the second was that they needed someone to replace him.

As the stunt team sat pondering the problem, I realised that Brad had been the only one of their team who even slightly resembled Virgil. All the others were either too short, too tall or too stocky.

Then Virgil himself piped up, 'What about Sean? He's about the same height and weight as me, he's even got the same colour hair. Almost a dead ringer I'd say,' then added with a smile 'Course, not so handsome.'

Rocky Costello, the movie's stunt co-ordinator, threw his hands up in the air, 'Of course!' He exclaimed, 'We must be goin' blind - you and him could be goddamn brothers!' Everyone nodded their agreement, all that is, except me.

'Now hold on a minute!' I spluttered, 'Why me? Why not a professional? There's gotta be someone else who looks like Virgil—' I was struggling. 'Why me?' I asked again weakly.

Rocky pierced me with his dark green eyes and his jaw hardened as he replied, 'Because it was you Brad was racing when he broke his leg, and you who boasted just how good you were on a horse, and you—' he pointed a thick, powerful finger directly at me, '—who owes us a favour. Now, whattaya say?'

'Well,' I said, not eager to get on the wrong side of Rocky, who was built like a truck, 'When you put it like that, I can hardly refuse.'

Eighteen

Brad and Rocky started training me immediately, the former shouting instructions from his wheelchair. Starting with the basics, they moved quickly onto the things I would be required to do in the movie in place of Virgil; stunts which I would have to have down pat if I was to be taken seriously by the studio as Brad's replacement. My two instructors were experts in their field and made the work look so easy when, in fact, it was an extremely difficult and precise art.

Fortunately for me there was a break in filming as the director of the movie had shot all the footage he could without the presence of the new leading lady, who was still yet to be cast. Rumours were rife about who it was likely to be; Carroll Baker, Sophia Loren and Ann-Margret had all been seen with the casting director and, as usual, the book had been opened on who the successful candidate might be; the initial favourite being Sophia.

During this break in shooting I threw myself into training. I was taught how to stage fight, how to crash through a saloon window and how to fall from a building, which on the first time of trying was the scariest thing I had done in my life. I learned how to roll, land, jump, even how to 'die' properly. But by far the most important piece of instruction, which was emphasised throughout my training, was how not to get injured. There is always an element of risk in any stunt but with careful rehearsal and precise calculation, the risk can be minimised. However, there are always exceptions.

In the three weeks that passed before we actually started filming again, I became a trained, fully paid and accepted member of the stunt crew and, although still very much a novice, could not have been more proud. Even more importantly, the studio approved me as Virgil's double, which made it official.

I was not the only recent hiring as a new actress had apparently been cast, although there was still no confirmation about who it was. Only a few select people knew for sure and one of these happened to be Virgil. But he was keeping very tight lipped on the subject and refused to be drawn, anxious not to spoil the outcome of the sweepstake until the announcement had been officially made. Much to my annoyance he would not even tell me, and I had a hundred dollars riding on Carroll Baker.

Eventually the day came for me to prove myself in front of the cameras, shooting an action sequence. I had rehearsed it a thousand times with the aid of Rocky, Brad and his wife, Marilu, a professional stunt woman in her own right, who also featured in the shot. I was as ready as I ever would be.

Dressed exactly the same as Virgil in full cowboy regalia, I was to climb out of the saloon's first floor window, run along to the end of the balcony, jump the ten feet from there to the ground and then leap onto the back of Jasper, the grey horse from my race with Brad. Once in the saddle, I would gallop to where Marilu would be waiting, dressed as a saloon girl and wearing a blonde wig to disguise her bright red hair. Sweeping her off the ground and up onto the horse, she would wrap her arms around me and kiss me on the cheek. Then, together, we would ride around the corner and out of shot. The blonde wig gave me the idea that my bet on Carroll Baker was a shrewd one, but all Virgil would say was, 'Wait and see.'

When the director eventually yelled 'action', I climbed out of the window and ran along the balcony as instructed, trying not to let my first-time nerves show. When I reached the end I hopped over the rail, jumped to the ground and leapt swiftly up onto Jasper's back, relieved that everything so far had gone as planned.

As I spurred Jasper into action, I glanced at the assembled crew who were all watching out of camera shot and, rather worryingly, saw Marilu standing with them, dressed in her normal clothes. She was shrugging her shoulders and mouthing the word 'sorry'. Confused, I stared up the street to the place where she should have been and saw another woman there, dressed in costume and waiting to be lifted onto the back of my horse. I recognised her immediately. It was the same woman who had distracted me at the start of the dirt bike race. The one who had caused me to lose concentration - and here she was doing it again.

All of a sudden I was angry, I forgot all about the cameras and nudged Jasper cruelly in the flanks, launching him up the street. As I approached the bogus saloon girl, I could not help but be dazzled once more by her beauty, and just for a second, my heart skipped a beat.

She held her arms out, expecting me to whisk her up onto the saddle into the position behind me, as the script dictated. But suddenly I wanted revenge and decided to take matters into my own hands.

As I reached her, I pulled Jasper to a halt, making him skid and kick up a thick cloud of dust that enveloped her and made her cough.

'Cut!' I heard the director shout through his loud hailer.

Without heeding his instruction, I leaned out my saddle, grabbed her securely around the waist and scooped her off the ground.

'Cut!' I heard the voice shout again, but I was oblivious.

Looking into the glorious neon of her huge round eyes I very nearly lost my resolve; temporarily entranced by her lovely face. But then I saw it, just as I had at Wildwood; that glint of mischief and the hint of petulance. She was daring me. Daring me to do what I so badly wanted to, not just at that moment, but since the very first second I had laid eyes on her.

The script required her to give me a light peck on the cheek but I decided that if there was any kissing to be done, then it was me who was going to be doing it. Although somehow I sensed that was exactly what she wanted.

Still holding her firmly, I planted her bottom down on my lap. Then with my other hand I grabbed a handful of long platinum hair and pushed her face toward mine. Half-heartedly she fought against me, but she was only play acting and both of us knew it.

When our lips touched she struggled a moment longer, squirming in my embrace, then without warning she surrendered. Suddenly eager to comply, she opened her luscious wet mouth to allow my tongue in and I felt hers wriggle hotly in willing response. She in turn now had a handful of my hair, whilst her other hand was clasped against my cheek preventing me from breaking away, her plump breasts pressed purposely against my chest, resulting in my immediate arousal. We were locked together for several seconds, completely rapt in the heat of the moment before we both remembered what it was that we were supposed to be doing. I released first then, after a second or two, she pulled away also. However, as she did so, she maliciously bit my lower lip and I winced as warm blood flowed into my mouth and spilt onto my chin. Victoria Wild then smiled; the little spiteful smile that I had seen in her mother's office, the one that told me she had got her own way once more.

The anger flared inside me again and I threw her bodily over the saddle in retaliation; her head and arms dangling one side of the horse, her shapely rear end and legs the other; the skirt of her costume and white frilly petticoat blowing freely in the wind.

'Cut, cut, cut!' Came the instruction for a third time, the director obviously becoming more and more exasperated.

Unable to resist, I bawdily slapped Victoria hard on the backside and she squealed with the sting as my hand made contact with her firm round buttocks. Then I nudged Jasper again and pulled sharply back on the reins, making him rear up on his hind legs and whinny noisily. Victoria screamed with genuine fright as we hung there for a precariously long moment, until I flicked the reins once more, giving Jasper the signal to return to all fours. Then, with the barest touch of my heels, Jasper took off at a blistering pace. I felt Victoria being thrown about as she wriggled helplessly over his back, but she was never in any danger, and I allowed myself a small smile as we rounded the corner, knowing that I had won a small victory.

For the final time, and in a tone that suggested he might be on the verge of a heart attack, I heard the director shouting through his megaphone, 'Cut, cut, for Chrissakes cut!' And, slowly it dawned on me, that my victory, nor indeed, my fledgling career, was likely to last long.

* * *

Thankfully I had a very good friend in Virgil who, using his considerable clout, managed to talk the director out of firing me. Much to my surprise even Victoria Wild, who had won the lead in the movie over a dozen other actresses, came out on my side. She convinced the director that the deviation from the rehearsed scene was her idea, and that I was just following instructions. She did it, she said, because she thought it would be more believable. The director, unwilling to upset another star, or to risk yet another costly break in filming, diplomatically agreed and, after seeing the pre-edited footage, admitted that she did have a point. More importantly, although reprimanded for my disobedience, I hung onto my job.

Against my better judgement, I decided to pay a visit to Victoria's trailer, to thank her for defending me to the director and to try to ease the tension that had been building between us since our first encounter. The simple truth was however, no matter how I tried to justify it, that I was desperate to see her again and this was the perfect excuse.

I strolled up to her enormous chrome Winnebego, which was her private quarters when on set and the place where she relaxed between takes. All the main cast members had these and saw them very much as status symbols: the bigger the trailer, the bigger the star, and Victoria's was the biggest.

Apprehensively, I tapped on the door.

'Who is it?' A deceptively sweet voice asked from within.

'Sean,' I croaked, my throat choosing that precise moment to dry up.

'Who?' She asked again.

I coughed to clear the dryness, 'Sean Noakes. You know, the guy with the horse. The stunt man.'

The lock clicked and the door opened and Victoria stood there looking stunning in a baby pink silk robe with black fluffy fur around the collar and cuffs. It was knotted loosely around her middle emphasising her minute wait, and fell to just above the ankle, hiding her long, slender legs. Her glorious platinum hair was tied up in a pony-tail and held by a black velvet ribbon, allowing me an unhindered look at her classically carved face; the sculptured cheek bones and the smooth, feminine curve of her jaw. She was wearing just the right amount of make-up; just enough to show off the striking neon of her eyes and the deep red of her lips.

'Ah! The Peeping Tom from the ranch you mean,' she said. The words stung but there was a smile on her face and a mischievous glint in her eye and I could tell she was pleased to see me.

I smiled back and said, 'Yeah, I guess it is, I don't know why I didn't say so.'

She laughed, which was the first time I had properly heard her do so, and it was lovely. 'What can I do for you, Tom?' She teased, 'Or have you just come to spank me again?' There was a delicious element of danger in her voice.

I touched the cut on my lip, remembering the events of the previous day, and smiled again.

'Sorry about that. I think I got a bit carried away - are you okay?'

'Hey I'm fine, I need my ass spanking sometimes to bring me back down to earth,' then added with a wicked grin, 'Sides, I quite enjoyed it.'

'In that case, I'm not sorry,' I said, flirting almost as outrageously as her.

'So, how can I help you today?' She asked, batting her long eyelashes, 'Come to inspect the bruises?'

A marvellous image of her naked bottom flashed across my mind. 'Sadly no.' I grinned, 'I just came to thank you.'

'Is that so,' she replied, 'In that case, you'd better come in where you can do it properly.'

The innuendo hung in the air as I stepped up into the trailer and as Victoria closed the door behind me, I had the feeling I would not be leaving for some time. The inside of the Winnebego was pure Hollywood decadence. Upholstered in rich red velvet with matching taffeta trim and polished walnut panelling. To my left was a plush living room that led onto a superbly appointed kitchen. To my right, behind a half-opened door, I could see a luxurious, very inviting, bedroom.

'Drink?' She asked.

'Thanks. Scotch.'

Victoria took a decanter and two glasses from a nearby cabinet and fixed us both a drink. 'So you came to say thanks?' She said, matter-of-factly.

'Yeah. What you did, stopping me from getting fired, it meant a lot.'

'It did, huh?'

'Yeah.'

She handed me a very generous measure in an exquisitely cut crystal glass, our fingers touching as I took it from her, although she held onto the glass for just a fraction longer than necessary to make certain she got my attention. 'What about the kiss you gave me?' She asked quietly, 'What did that mean?' She was looking directly into my face now, with those incredibly alluring eyes and standing so close that I could almost hear her heart beating. Her expertly painted lips were glossy and tempting and the delicate scent of her perfume filled my nostrils. Suddenly I was lost, swept up in her beauty and I downed the whiskey, hoping to drown my desire but it merely acted as fuel to the burning passion within. I fought against it, tying to concentrate on my response to the question, 'Oh, the kiss!' I said lamely, 'That was er... sort of on the spur of the moment. I thought it might add something to the scene. Thankfully, it paid off.'

Still looking deeply into my eyes, she said, 'You did, huh?'

I nodded silently, knowing she had not bought it for a second. She knew what was going on in my mind, just as clearly as I did hers. 'Then I guess I should consider myself lucky,' she whispered, 'Cos it was one helluva a kiss.' She held my glare for a moment longer, watching as the words sunk in then, as she turned and walked towards the bedroom, she said, 'Why don't you make us both another drink and come on through?'

I watched as she sashayed sexily away, her pert bottom

moving rhythmically under the silk of her gown and my desire growing with every step she took. I did as instructed, pouring two generous shots of scotch before following her into the bedroom. I took a deep swig of my drink, then placed both glasses on the beside cabinet, not trusting my hands enough to hold them steadily.

Victoria sat down on the satin sheets of her enormous bed and took a pair of black stockings from the bedside unit. Rolling one of them, to make it easier to put on, she said, 'So you're gonna be Virgil's double?'

The whiskey was slowly taking effect and I had regained some sort of control although, unavoidably, my pronounced excitement was starting to show, 'Guess so,' I replied.

Victoria flapped open the lower part of her robe to expose her long shapely legs and, very slowly, extended one into the air, pointing her toes like a ballerina. Then, seductively, she pulled on the first of the shear silk stockings and gradually brushed it up to her smoothly tanned thigh before taking from the cabinet a pink frilly garter, also made from the finest silk, and looping it over her tiny foot. She pulled it up and snapped it securely in position, then shot me a look that positively sizzled, 'What about love scenes?' She asked.

'What about them?' I said, my mouth watering as she applied the same hypnotic treatment to the other leg.

'Are you gonna do those too?'

'Depends what you mean,' I replied, sensing with growing eagerness where this line of questioning was leading, 'Do you mean on set, or in real life?'

'Well then, let's say in real life,' she said, giving me a vampish look as she slipped her feet into a pair of high black stilettos.

'Then I do them myself,' I replied, my throat once again hoarse as I watched the beguiling performance.

Victoria then downed her scotch and stood up. Her huge

neon eyes once again fixing on mine as she slowly undid her robe and let it fall to the floor. 'What about now?' She asked huskily.

Her naked body was magnificent, even better than I remembered from that night at Wildwood; firm, smooth and curvaceous, 'Well, Tom' she teased again, 'Are you just gonna peep, or are you gonna make love to me like I know you want to?'

She was right, I did want to, more than anything else in the world and hungrily I took her into my arms; our mouths meeting as the passion between us exploded in heat filled frenzy. Madly, violently we kissed; our hands desperately exploring each others body's, our fingertips searching for the things we had for so long wanted to touch. Victoria grabbed the front of my shirt and ripped it open; the buttons scattering as they popped off. Her hand slipped down to unbutton my jeans, to free me from the restraining material, and she let out a soft gasp as she took me in her hand. Gently I eased her down onto the bed, studying her nakedness for just another moment, taking in the reality of what I had only previously fantasised about. Then, Victoria Wild reached for my hand and pulled me lustfully down on top of her. 'Make love to me Sean,' she demanded breathlessly, 'Make love to me now!' And willingly, I obliged.

Nineteen

In the spring of '66, The Villa Continental had its grand opening. Where once was just wasteland, now stood a glittering palace capable of competing on a world-class scale. A huge, sumptuously appointed hotel incorporating restaurants, bars, boutiques, a state-of-the-art theatre and an enormous casino. The complex was a masterpiece of design that exactly echoed the architecture of the small Mediterranean towns it was purposely trying to emulate.

There was no denying it, Carl Napier had done a terrific job in over-seeing the development and it was he, in no small part, who was responsible for its opening some three months ahead of schedule which, on a project of that size, was some feat.

As a reward for his efforts, Louretta and Joe presented Carl with a beautifully hand sculptured watch, crafted in white gold and platinum with a pearlised oyster face and diamond set digits. It was the only one of its kind, made exclusively for Louretta by Cartier, and was therefore totally unique and worth an absolute fortune. An incredible gift which more than demonstrated their immense appreciation of his achievement. Carl loved it, and immediately placed it on his wrist where it would forever stay.

The guest list for the opening weekend, who came at Louretta's personal request, was just as impressive and included movie stars, entertainers, politicians and other such people of wealth, power and notoriety.

Amongst all the high flyers were Joe and I who never thought, not even in our wildest dreams, that we would be mixing in circles such as these. I had actually met many of the actors on the list, thanks to my new role as a Hollywood stunt man and my association with both Virgil and Victoria, but few of them would remember me. However, had they known I was having an affair with one of the hottest stars around, they undoubtedly would have, but Victoria and I had chosen to keep our relationship quiet. If photographed together, there was a chance that I would be recognised which, in turn, could lead to my arrest and subsequent deportation. If that happened, Victoria's career would collapse under the media storm that would surely follow; the scandal of dating a wanted murderer not sitting well with her glamorous image and the Studio unlikely to stand by her. I had told her everything about my past and, together, after discussing all the options, we agreed secrecy to be the best way.

Victoria was very different in reality from the persona she presented to the world. She was undoubtedly a ballsy, confident woman and did set out to get what she wanted, but underneath that, behind the gloss and the glamour and the sometimes petulant temperament, she was kind and sensitive and understanding. In many ways she reminded me of Louretta; strong and sassy, but warm-hearted and a lot of fun.

Since our first illicit liaison, two months previously, Victoria and I had spent virtually every free moment together. I was hopelessly in love for the second time in my thirty-one years and it felt fantastic, further more, my feelings were reciprocated and we just could not get enough of each other. The very fact that our affair was secret made it all the more intense, with the risk element just an added thrill to an already extreme adrenaline rush.

Apart from Virgil and Louretta, the only other people who

knew of our torrid romance, were Joe, Rachel and Ray who, together with Michael and little Brett, had all come over for the opening of The Villa. Ruby had stayed at home with Sarah, and both were being watched over by Richie and Manno who, by now, had recovered fully from their injuries.

Joe had considered leaving Rachel at home too, because of the history she shared with Carl, whom she had not seen for nearly three years. But Rachel had seemed so unhappy of late, so low, that he did not have the heart to leave her behind. Besides, he thought the break might do her some good. Also, The Villa Continental was something Joe was very proud of and he was keen to show it to his wife and son.

*   *   *

The opening night was a hugely extravagant affair with a fabulous stage show held in the hotel's Napoli lounge. The room had been cleverly designed to give guests the feeling that they were eating outdoors on a balmy Mediterranean evening; the vast domed ceiling painted black and decorated with thousands of tiny lights that twinkled like stars in the night sky. There were flagstone floors and fountains, candles and pergolas, hanging vines and colourful scented flowers all adding the finishing touch to an incredibly romantic setting. The whole concept worked brilliantly and, had I not known, I would have believed myself to be enjoying an open air banquet in Italy.

At our table sat Ray Reece, Joe, Rachel and myself. Sitting at the adjacent table were Louretta, Carl Napier, Victoria and her companion for the evening, Virgil Nash, who was allowing himself to be used as a decoy for the press. Also, it was excellent publicity for the film which was close to completion. There was nothing like the hint of an affair between co-stars to boost box office receipts. Privately however, Virgil knew that Victoria was with me and I never once had reason to question his intentions.

303

As I scanned both tables, enjoying the company and, indeed, the success of my friends, I studied their faces as they watched the show. There was Virgil; impossibly handsome with the Californian golden boy looks; a Hollywood movie star with riches and fame beyond his wildest dreams but as yet still struggling to come to terms with the loss of his anonymity. Thankfully though, he was coping much better in the last few months. Next to him sat Victoria; stunning in a white, off-the-shoulder, silk evening gown; her platinum hair flowing gracefully down her back. She turned and saw me staring at her and smiled. Then mischievously, she winked and blew me a silent but very discreet kiss. Looking at her, as she turned back to watch the show, I felt immensely proud and had to stop myself from standing up and shouting out that she was with me, that I was the one she had chosen, but somehow I managed to control the urge.

I turned my attention instead to Louretta, and saw immediately the definite resemblance between mother and daughter. Still beautiful and extremely classy, Louretta looked every inch the star, as indeed she was, particularly on that night. It was very much her, together with Carl who were the glamorous hosts of the evening and both were in their element. Louretta unashamedly using all her feminine wiles and very sharp wit to make her guests feel extremely welcome and at ease.

Sitting next to Louretta was Carl, who I remembered from the old days when I was working for Vinnie.
I did not know him well, even back then, but he was evidently well suited to the role Joe had given him; cool, capable and confident with the ability to get things done. He was stylish and well dressed; not especially good looking but his gregarious personality more than made up for his physical shortcomings. His silver tongue and genial manner had won him a remarkable amount of influential friends in the short time he had been in America and he was

fast becoming one of the major players in Vegas. Joe and I were staggered at just how many people he seemed to know, particularly those of significant wealth and power, which gave some clue as to how he had managed to get The Villa completed so quickly. Carl knew how to use people to get what he wanted and how best to exploit them for his own benefit. This was certainly a useful talent, but not one I whole-heartedly approved of.

Although Joe trusted Carl, believing their problems to be in the past, I was not so convinced. I don't know what it was about him that I did not like, but there was definitely something - maybe it was just because he was too cocky and too self-assured. It troubled me also that Carl knew my true identity, although Joe assured me there was nothing to worry about. Rarely did I doubt my friend's instincts, but with Napier I sensed he may have, just this once, got it wrong.

In stark contrast to Carl Napier, my regard for Ray Reece could not have been greater. As my eyes wandered over to our table, I saw him sitting at the opposite end to myself, strong, powerful and imposing, yet the man I knew was also eccentric, warm and friendly. However, his enemies, of whom he had few remaining, saw a different side to Ray, one which I had on good authority could be very scary indeed. To me though, his obvious sense of humour and extreme love for life oozed from every pore. It was good to see him again, and of course, although not present that evening, to see Michael, who was now an awkward and gangly thirteen year-old.

Ray and Ruby had worked wonders with Michael since our last meeting. He seemed a different lad from the one I had met before - he even greeted me with a smile and a handshake at the airport. Still obviously very shy and, I suspected, extremely conscious of his damaged face which, I noticed, attracted many stares from passers-by. But nevertheless, I sensed he had become generally more amiable; not so arrogant and spoiled. This change in him which, according to Joe, was purely down to Ray, led me to think that maybe one day, we could possibly become friends. For that, amongst many other things, Ray Reece had my gratitude.

Smiling, I looked to the man sitting next to him. At thirty-two, Joe was fitter than ever. His punishing daily exercise regime, which was bordering on the obsessive, kept him in peak physical condition. Sitting amongst all the movie stars he could have quite easily passed for one himself. It seemed as he got older, he grew even more handsome, and I noticed more than one female celebrity's head turn as he sat down at our table. Even Victoria had commented on how attractive he was, and not for the first time, I felt a small pang of jealousy at the many physical gifts my friend had been given.

As always, he exuded an assured confidence, his manner calm and composed. Forever suave and stylish, Joe was immaculately dressed in a dinner suit tailor made for him in Saville Row. He gave no outward indication of what was actually going on behind those deep black eyes. No sign of the concern I knew he felt for Rachel. For some time, his marriage had been strained; what had started out as blissfully happy, had somehow turned sour virtually overnight. It had been getting steadily worse since the assassination attempt, with her attitude changing rapidly from loving to icy cold. More worryingly, she had become almost dismissive of Brett's needs. She had become introvert, withdrawn and moody; her weight had dropped noticeably and her once lustrous skin had lost its healthy glow. She was still beautiful and took great care with her hair and make-up, but it could not fully disguise her sickly pallor.

Their sex life too, which once was passionate and steamy, was now almost non-existent. They had made love only twice in the last six months, both times just briefly, enough to momentarily quell Joe's desire, but there was no enjoyment on her part and she was clearly just going through the motions.

Since then, Joe had not pushed Rachel. He loved her and wanted her well, and if that meant waiting until she was ready, then so be it. However, Joe had also noticed how much she was drinking and, on top of everything else, that concerned him too. He hoped the trip to Vegas would make her feel better; help lift her spirits and set her on the road to recovery.

He confided these hopes to me and, for his sake, I wished the same. It troubled me to see my friend so upset for although he would never let anyone else see it, his concerns for Rachel were tearing him apart and, unlike most other things in his life, he was powerless to do anything about it.

Midway through the show, Louretta and Carl stood up and made their way towards the stage in order to thank the assembled guests. Upon passing our table Carl smiled graciously at us, although his focus was most definitely on Rachel and, as he went, her eyes followed him. Her face took on an almost wistful expression as she watched him and I wondered for a moment if maybe seeing her ex-lover, in his glamorous new role, had sparked something within her, but I dismissed it almost immediately as a ridiculous notion. However, as the evening wore on and with the more wine Rachel consumed, I noticed how many times her eyes searched for Carl Napier. He pretended to be oblivious of course, but in reality he was all too aware of her attentions. Conversely, I noted that whenever Joe spoke a look of disdain appeared on Rachel's face, and when he tactfully mentioned that drinking too much could make her feel ill, she snapped, 'I'm not drunk! How dare you even suggest it? I'm just trying to enjoy myself, that's all.' Her voice was overly loud and carried clearly to nearby tables causing people to whisper behind their hands. 'Of course,' Joe replied trying to calm her, 'My mistake.'

Some minutes afterwards, when the fuss had died down, I

saw Rachel furtively take several pills from her purse and swallow them down quickly with a swig of chianti. I noticed her doing the same an hour later and once more again after that. Joe was obviously right to be so worried, although I guessed Rachel's problems were even worse than he'd feared.

*   *   *

By the end of the evening, Rachel was seriously drunk and, I suspected, pretty high too. Her words were slurry and her movements clumsy and she had become an embarrassment. Joe had tried to distract her from the wine, as had Louretta, Ray and myself, but all to no avail. Joe had, more than once, suggested they get an early night, but at the mere mention of it Rachel began to make another scene, so he had quickly backed down.

However, her reluctance to leave soon changed when, at the end of the evening, thousands of balloons were dropped onto the dance floor. The guests, in their revelry, began popping them in drunken abandon which, to Rachel, sounded just like the crackle of gunfire. She began shrieking hysterically with tears streaming down her cheeks and, with her hands clamped on her ears, she cried out maniacally, 'Get me out of here, get me out of here now!'

Joe, visibly shaken by his wife's reaction, swept her up in his arms and ran with her from the lounge, her sobs clearly audible all the way to the exit.

As I watched my friend leave, I could not help but feel sorry for him. It was a night that was supposed to be a glorious personal triumph, but it had turned into an absolute disaster, with repercussions so terrible that none of us could ever have begun to imagine.

*   *   *

I was not aware of it at the time but was told many years later that, as Joe ran with Rachel from the room, there was a smile on Carl Napier's face.

Twenty

Joe was in another meeting, the third one that day. It seemed that was all he did just lately; speak to people behind closed doors, locked away with his tightly-knit group of friends. This was supposed to be a holiday, yet all Rachel had seen so far was the inside of a hotel room and very little of her husband. The hotel doctor had said she needed rest to fully recover from the ordeal of the opening gala and that is exactly what she had been doing for the last three days.

Now however, she was heartily sick of resting and of being stuck in her suite with only Brett to talk to. It was like being in prison, albeit a very luxurious one, and she was about ready to climb the walls. She wanted her freedom and she wanted some company, but more than anything, she wanted a drink.

For three days she had drunk nothing but water and coffee as Joe had surreptitiously removed all the alcohol and forbidden room service to deliver any more.

Fortunately she had her tranquillisers which had helped, but they alone were not enough. By now, she was also using a number of other pills, acquired for her secretly by a girl friend. Uppers and downers and drugs that helped her control her emotions. Pills to make her sleep, pills to help her stay awake and pills that numbed her fear; anything her friend got her Rachel took. All without Joe's knowledge and all to make her life more bearable.

But seeing Carl Napier again had brought all her insecurities and misgivings about her existence crashing in on her. He had looked so dashing and so assured in the splendid environment he had created. Carl's life was so different from hers now and she envied him for it. He had made a successful career for himself; popular with everyone; a friend to the stars and people of influence, with scarcely a care in the world.

Whilst in contrast she was trapped in a gothic fortress in London with a gangland boss for a husband and a child she had lost interest in; she was sick of the whining, of changing shitty nappies and of wiping up puke. She hated her child, she hated Joe and she hated her life. If only she had stayed with Carl Napier things could have been so different.

When Rachel had first met Joe she had been bowled over by him. She had not fully appreciated what she was getting into or just how violent and dangerous his world was - a world in which people shot at you and tried to kill you, a world where terror reigned supreme.

She had escaped that once. Her father and brothers were very violent men as were their associates and often Rachel and her mother found themselves in the middle of vicious scraps that would leave their house wrecked and their men bloodied and scarred. It was a life filled with hardship and fear and one which she vowed to escape at her earliest opportunity. This presented itself at thirteen, when both her parents were killed in a head on car crash. Within just two weeks of the accident, and whilst still devastated by the traumatic loss of her mother, she left home, slipping silently away without telling anyone.

Months later she wrote to her eldest brother Danny, and the two of them began to see each other occasionally; awkward meetings in greasy cafés where very little was said over a cup of tea and a bacon sandwich. Danny, a dark, brooding figure with the scarred features of a regular brawler, never asked her how she managed to survive on the streets on her own, although had a pretty good idea. He preferred not to think about it as he was certainly no one to judge, but she was still his sister after all.

By sixteen, Rachel, who had always been extremely attractive, had slept with many men, all of whom having paid handsomely for her very thorough services. By seventeen, she was living in Kensington with a wealthy older man in his late seventies who financially took care of her every need; all he required in return was to be made 'happy' twice a week. Even though she detested this kind of existence, it gave her the things she craved and acted as a stepping stone to the kind of life she wanted. Furthermore, had her elderly gentleman lived until his eightieth birthday, when he was to make her his sole benefactor, Rachel would have inherited a fortune.

However, that was not to be; his heart had stopped two months too early, as Rachel brought him to climax a little too vigorously. A wonderful way to go, but from Rachel's perspective, a very untimely end.

Suddenly finding herself alone and vulnerable, she was kicked out of the old man's apartment by his money grabbing family who left her penniless and with just one suitcase full of her best clothes. Depression set in. She felt unable to face Danny and what little money she had was frittered away on booze and cigarettes. She drunkenly sold herself cheap to all kinds of low life scum in order to get money to eat, being beaten up more than once by several of her more 'speciality' customers. She stood this for three months, sleeping on a sofa in a tiny little flat owned by another whore in Bethnal Green.

By now she was at an extremely low ebb and wallowing in self pity and self loathing, her nerves and mind not coping well with the sudden change in circumstances and she was close to suicide more than once. The thought of having nothing, of having no one to care for her or to comfort her was almost too much to bear. Then one morning as she stood staring in the mirror, contemplating her future, a miracle happened. She realised that no matter what she had been through, she was still very beautiful; she had lost everything else, but not her looks. They were her salvation, and using them, together with her incredible body, Rachel woke up to the fact that she could get virtually anything she wanted. She scrubbed herself thoroughly, applied exactly the right amount of make-up, put on her best clothes, and set about improving her life.

Not letting her lack of work experience worry her, she found employment at a chic Soho boutique, getting the position after giving the manager a blow job in one of the changing rooms. After promising similar services on a weekly basis, she also persuaded him to allow her to use a vacant flat that he owned in Camberwell as a home until she got herself back on her feet.

Less than a month later, and quite by accident, she ran into Carl Napier, whom she had met as a child during the war. Impressed by his success and attracted to his charming personality, Rachel readily accepted his invitation to dinner. Six weeks after that they were engaged; her past life a secret from him and her drinking under strict control.

For a while, Rachel was content with Napier, and genuinely more fond of him than she had been of any man, but then she met Joe and instantly she knew that it was he, not Carl, who she wanted.

For the first time in her life she was in love - an emotion she had previously believed herself to be incapable of, and with Joe, she felt calmer, safer and happier than she had in years. He was not some old man on his last legs who would die on her and leave her all alone in the world; he was young and virile and strong and with him she would forever be protected.

However, the assassination attempt had categorically proved otherwise, with the events of that day having rocked her to the very core. The attack had completely terrified her, and the love and respect she'd had for Joe before then, had since all but evaporated.

Now she was in Vegas, away from the grime and the filth and the violence of London. Away from the would-be-assasins and the stench of the underworld; away from those that knew her and of what she had been, safe from the ever present threat of being discovered. Here, in her deluded, drug-addled mind, she fantasised of starting a newer, happier life, and since seeing Carl Napier on the opening night, she had convinced herself that he was the one to turn her dreams into reality.

With this in mind and the likelihood of Joe being in his meeting for several more hours, Rachel put on her most alluring dress, popped a couple more pills and slipped out of the penthouse suite, to go in search of the man she now believed to be her saviour.

*   *   *

Rachel had intended to search the whole hotel if necessary, but instead she had found the bar. She had been sitting on the same stool for the last two hours and was very drunk. Her speech was slurred and she was starting to get abusive. A gentleman, enjoying a drink before lunch, had been concerned for her welfare and had enquired if she was 'okay,' she in turn, had told him to 'Fuck off and mind his own business.' The man was a United States Senator, and one of Louretta's oldest friends.

Every now and then, she would burst into tears and babble incoherently into her vodka. Moments later, she would laugh out loud for no apparent reason, as if she had been told some wildly funny joke, then within seconds, Rachel would be silent again, staring at her glass with a pained expression on her face, as if wrestling with her inner demons. Troubled by her behaviour

- partly because she was annoying the other guests, but mainly because he knew her to be the wife of one of the owners - the bartender picked up his phone and summoned the hotel manager.

* * *

'Hey there, Baby,' Carl Napier's velvety voice whispered in Rachel Cassidy's ear as she was slumped almost comatose on the bar, mascara and lipstick smudged on her tear stained face. 'Why so sad? Why don't you come with me and tell me all about it?' Napier's smooth tones were now consciously less Bermondsey and more Beverly Hills, but the change had somehow added to its appeal.

'Carl?' Rachel lifted her head off the bar and looked into his face, 'Oh, thank God! I've been looking for you.' Suddenly she turned on the bar stool and threw her arms around him then, still seated, she pushed her head into his chest and began to weep. Carl, a little embarrassed by this very public show of emotion, put a comforting arm over her shoulders and placed another around her waist before gently coaxing her to her feet. Slowly he managed to steer his former fiancé away from the bar and towards the elevator. When it arrived Carl pressed the button for the top floor penthouse suite - his own very luxurious bachelor pad.

Once there, Rachel almost immediately started to relax and Napier could see she was visibly impressed by his ultra modern, expensively furnished home. Holding her hand, he led her across the white, varnished ash floor and down the three small steps to a sunken seating area that had a huge glass coffee table as its centrepiece. She sat down on one of the soft black leather sofas facing floor to ceiling windows that ran the whole width of the room, giving a spectacular, panoramic view of the desert city. Even drunk the sight was breath-taking.

'Best view in Vegas, Baby,' Carl said, skipping back up the steps and over to the hi-tech, open plan kitchen. 'And the most expensive,' he added, unnecessarily.

As he fixed them both a drink, triple vodkas with ice and lemon, Carl studied the woman he had once loved - immediately seeing why. She was a beautiful woman, although much less so now, he noted, than she had once been. Her body was too skinny now - he preferred her before, with a bit more meat on her bones - when her tits were fuller and her arse rounder. But she would still do.

In truth, he was thankful now that he had not married her; the romantic, loving side of him having died long ago in the aftermath of their break-up. But what had lived on, was the hurt and the bitterness and the hatred; his thirst for vengeance never abating. Looking at her now though, he was surprised to find he actually wanted her - as the growing swelling in his trousers was beginning to testify - but it was not love - not even lust - but revenge that was fuelling his desire. It was time for her and Joe to start paying for what they had done to him, and he had no doubts that they were going to suffer but, eyeing Rachel lasciviously, he was also damn sure he was going to have some fun in the process.

Rachel, already incredibly drunk, was now lying on the sofa unaware, but also unconcerned, that her dress had ridden up, allowing Napier an unhindered glimpse of her pink satin underwear. She was his for the taking, but he had to choose his moment well.

After handing her the drink, which she readily accepted, Carl sat down opposite her, 'Tell me what's the matter Baby,' he crooned, 'Perhaps I can help.'

Rachel did not need much persuading and, over tears and vodka, spilled out everything. She told him how terrified she was and how she feared for her life; she showed him her hands and how they shook, and said how she wished she had married him, not Joe. With only the slightest amount of coaxing, she also admitted to taking pills and drinking to excess, claiming that the drugs and alcohol were her only release.

Sensing that his moment was approaching, Carl wandered over to the sleek black cabinet which housed his music centre and switched on some Sinatra, low. Then, from a concealed drawer, he took out a small square mirror, a short glass straw, a razor blade and polythene sachet filled with white powder.

Coming back, he sat down beside her and kissed her delicately on the cheek, his fingers running up the length of her smoothly stockinged thigh until they found the lacy straps of her suspenders. He could have taken her there and then - he certainly wanted to, but intuition told him to wait. He took his hand from her leg, there was plenty of time after all.

Carl placed the mirror on the coffee table, then tapped out some of the white powder onto it. Rachel was still talking, now telling him about how hard her life had been before she had met him. 'In what way?' Napier asked as he sifted and chopped the cocaine with the razor blade, shaping it in to two neat parallel lines.

'You wouldn't believe me if I told you' Rachel replied drunkenly.

'Try me' Carl said, his voice low but still velvety smooth.

'I've been a whore' she blurted out.

Carl, not immediately recognising the truth of the statement, said 'Of course you haven't, you've just been unlucky that's all.'

'No, you don't understand,' Rachel slurred, about to unwittingly drop the bombshell that would ultimately help to destroy her, 'I've been a whore since I was thirteen. I've slept with more men than I can remember - done things with them that you can't even imagine.' Carl could imagine a lot. 'Filthy, dirty old men,' she continued, 'who'd pay almost anything - anything just to fuck me and do the things their wives wouldn't let them. I did it to survive, and because it was easy, and if I had to, I'd do it again.'

316

Napier was momentarily dumbstruck. He had courted Rachel for over a year - had even asked her to marry him, and yet he had no idea about what she had been. He was stunned and astonished. Was there no end to her deceit? To think, he could quite easily have ended up married to a whore and not known anything about it. Goddamn lying bitch. What the hell sort of a mug did she take him for?

'Does Joe know?' He asked, 'Does he know all this?'

'No. No one does. You're the only one Carl, the only one I can trust. You understand don't you?'

Oh yeah, he understood alright. She had played him for a fool. Joe too. 'I bet if Joe found out he'd—' Slowly, he started to realise just how explosive this knowledge could be, and what it would do to Joe if he ever discovered his wife's dirty little secret. 'Christ, it'd kill him. What man could stand hearing that sort of news?' Carl smiled to himself as he contemplated the potential repercussions. He then became aware of just how stiff he was - knowing that Rachel used to be a whore actually turned him on. Previously, when they had been dating, it had been straightforward sex, nothing kinky - and definitely no weird stuff as he'd never thought her to be up for that. But it turned out he was wrong, she was obviously not so fussy and, provided the price was right, she could apparently get down and dirty with the best of them.

'Do you understand Carl?' Rachel asked tearfully.

'Yeah, Baby, I understand.' He turned and looked directly into her eyes. 'I really do.' He leaned in and kissed her lightly on the lips. It was meant to be a peck but she opened her mouth and suddenly they were locked passionately together. She pushed her tongue hungrily into his mouth, making soft mewing sounds as if dining on the finest caviar. His hands found her breasts causing her nipples to spring out like bullets from under the silk of her dress. Her fingers clawed at his face and scraped through his hair, her drunkenness forgotten as she pressed her lips hard against his. Suddenly, unexpectedly, Carl pulled away, 'Wait, Baby, wait. We've got plenty of time,' he said, 'Let's make the most of it. I've got something here that'll make the moment much better - you'll see.'

'But—' Rachel was almost begging, the disappointment audible, the need for him clear to see in her eyes. She was offering herself up completely and Carl knew she was his to do with as he pleased.

Picking up the glass straw, he said, 'Just trust me, Baby. It'll make it better, I promise.' Then, as she watched, Carl bent over the coffee table, placed one end of the straw at the beginning of a powder line, and the other end up one of his nostrils, then snorted a nose full of cocaine, showing Rachel exactly what to do.

'Here ya go, Baby,' he said, offering her the straw, 'Believe me, it's the key to your freedom.'

Shakily, Rachel took it, then, very slowly, she eased herself onto her knees and bent over the table, showing Carl her slim, but still shapely rear-end. She put the straw to her right nostril and tentatively took a small sniff. The sensation was alien and it tickled, but the effect was almost immediate, 'Fuck!' She gasped, rubbing her nose with delicious pleasure, 'That's amazing. Weird but—, but Wow!'

'Do it again, Baby, but this time do it properly,' Carl encouraged, lecherously fondling her round buttocks as he spoke.

Rachel, enjoying his attentions, nestled her butt comfortably into the palms of his hands, then again placed the straw to her right nostril and took another sniff. This time she took in the remainder of the line. 'Wow!' She said again, 'That's unbelievable.'

'I know. It feels good doesn't it - do it again! Carl had now lifted up her dress so that it rested around her waist and was, with one hand, gradually easing down her expensive satin panties. His other hand was wrestling with his flies.

318

Rachel filled her left nostril and, just as Carl had promised, her problems evaporated. Her head was in the clouds and her body was tingling expectantly, so when Napier finally entered her, she squealed with delight. She pushed down onto him, wanting to feel him deep within her - wanting to feel thrust after glorious thrust; each one further erasing every trace of her life with Joe.

Even though Carl's love-making was violent and rough, Rachel was beyond caring. The drug had accentuated her sex drive and heightened her desire, causing her to scream wildly with exhilarating abandon. She felt wonderful, ecstatic, bullet-proof - but that feeling would not last long enough and soon she would be desperate for more of the magic white powder. As for Napier, his smile was wide and his satisfaction immense, for with every thrust, he was causing untold pain to Joe Cassidy. He was exacting the ultimate revenge, using his enemy's wife for his own delicious pleasure. With that, together with the information he now had in his possession, Carl believed he could bring Joe to his knees.

*   *   *

Joe and Rachel were scheduled to stay in Vegas for eight weeks. By the end of the fourth, she was hooked on cocaine and he, unknowingly, had lost her for good.

Within thirty days of stepping off the plane, Rachel had become a junkie and a whore who'd do pretty much anything for a hit, whilst Carl had become her pimp and supplier - of both drugs and sexual partners. But Joe was blind to it all. He was pleased to see his wife so relaxed and happy - convinced that she was on the road to recovery. They had even made love for the first time in months, which she genuinely seemed to enjoy. Little did he know that she had been high at the time and that an ageing oil baron from Denver had been with her less than an hour before.

Napier was now plying Rachel with cocaine on a daily basis and using her to indulge his many sexual fantasies, but so long as Rachel got her fix, she didn't care. The drug not only relieved her of her inhibitions, it also gave her an almost insatiable desire for sex, and she welcomed any chance to perform. The first few times it was just the two of them getting high and screwing - but soon Carl began inviting friends to join them, although only the most trusted and the most useful of course. Sometimes Carl would stay, at others he would go, but by this time Rachel had no specific preference. All she required in order to participate was yet another line of coke, which fortunately, Napier had an endless supply of. No one he had ever known had taken to the drug so quickly or so willingly as her. It was as if her whole life was consumed by it and to wean her off now would do more harm than good. Without it she would go into shock and suffer massive withdrawals which Joe would not fail to notice. If he became involved then the whole situation could potentially blow up in Carl's face; questions would undoubtedly be asked, fingers most certainly pointed and Carl's very existence put in jeopardy. Furthermore, if she overdosed, he could find himself implicated.

He hadn't expected things to happen so quickly. He'd only intended to have some fun - a bit of payback for what she and Joe had done to him; make them suffer and squirm and live through hell for a bit. Then, well, he wasn't actually sure about that - but it certainly didn't involve anyone winding up dead. But that's the way it was going to end. He knew it. Rachel was a runaway train and it was only going to be a matter of days before she crashed and burned.

That's why he had to find himself an escape route, and that's where Alvin Staedtler came in.

Alvin Staedtler was a middle aged shoe manufacturer from Wisconsin. He had a wife, a dog, a brand new Cadillac and a seat on the church council. He also had a couple of million dollars in the bank and a minor coke habit. For fifty-one weeks of the year, he lived the life of a model citizen, but every summer, he and a couple of his buddies would hit Vegas for a week of gambling, drinking and whoring.

Carl had met Alvin the year before at the Sahara, where the latter was losing a good percentage of his hard earned cash at the roulette table. Not wishing to see good money wasted in someone else's joint, Napier quickly extended the hand of friendship, together with an invitation to visit his brand-spanking new hotel when it opened. So, this year, Alvin was staying at the Villa Continental, where he and his pals had been fixed up with a fancy suite, a stocked bar and a pound bag of cocaine, courtesy of the management.

Carl arrived with Rachel when Alvin's last night party was in full swing, she being the promised entertainment. Just for kicks, Carl had brought along a point-and-push camera, saying that he thought the guys might like to take a few snaps. Naturally, when the party was over, Napier had the photos discreetly developed for them - as a little souvenir of their stay at The Villa, neglecting to tell them that he had kept a duplicate set for himself.

There was one shot, a particularly masterful composition, featuring Rachel straddling a pot-bellied salesman named 'Red,' whilst Alvin Staedtler sodomised her from behind. The expression on all their faces was climactic. Carl had taken the photo whilst he lay masturbating, on the couch. His face, as with all the shots, was not visible in the picture, but his white legs and spurting erection were clear to see; captured for posterity in the foreground. Napier smiled at the artistry of his work.

The third man should not have been Carl at all, but a marketing exec called Duane, who was the third member of Staedtler's party. But Duane had swallowed some bad shrimp at a seafood joint the night before and was too busy throwing up to take part in the orgy. The waiter who had spiked his meal had done an excellent job and Napier considered it a thousand bucks well spent.

Of course, no one would ever know Carl had taken Duane's place, nor the reason for doing so, which was to gain himself a very graphic, very convincing, insurance policy.

Twenty-one

For the first few weeks at The Villa it was hectic. Joe, Louretta and myself seemed to be constantly stuck in meetings of one sort or another, over-seeing everything and making sure it all ran smoothly.

With us so busy, the girls, Victoria and Rachel, seemed happy to amuse themselves. Victoria, I know, spent her time enjoying a much needed break after the strenuous movie shoot, which had only wrapped just days before we left LA. Whilst Rachel led Joe to believe that she spent her time shopping and sunbathing.

Ray and Michael on the other hand, flew up to Frisco to do a little sight-seeing. Once there they picked up a rental car and did the whole tourist bit - checking out the bridge and the wharf and anything else they could focus a camera on. They then took the coastal route through towns like Monterey, Carmel and Santa Barbara; taking a few days out at Anaheim to visit The Mouse - which, this time, Michael enjoyed. From there they cruised down to San Diego, then headed east, back to Vegas.

Their return coincided with the conclusion of Villa business, allowing me, at long last, to spend some time with my son. However, after a few days of trying, and failing, to start up a lasting conversation, I realised my efforts were just not working. Vegas was no town for a kid and Michael was obviously bored, so, thinking it might cheer him up, I suggested another road trip. This time to the Hoover Dam and the Grand Canyon - a three day tour designed to bring me and him together. I asked Ray along for the ride too because he was good company and it just didn't feel right to leave him out. After all, he was more Michael's father than I was - at least in all the important ways.

At Rachel's behest, Joe said he'd come along too, she having convinced him that she was fully fit and eager to spend some time alone with Brett. More time alone with the magic white powder is what she really meant, but in Joe's eyes she did definitely seem better, and as if to prove it, on the night before we left, she had begged him to make love to her. When he did, he found her wild and passionate and damn near insatiable. Her finger nails clawed at his back, her teeth bit at his ears and neck and she screamed with unrestrained ecstasy as she writhed, snake-like under him. When he was spent and unable to satisfy her any longer, she used her own fingers to bring herself to climax over and over again until Joe could rouse himself once more.

Delighted with his wife's apparent recovery, Joe had few remaining doubts about leaving her behind. Besides, it was only for seventy-two hours - what could possibly go wrong in that time?

*　　*　　*

Ray's sense of humour was the ideal antidote to a month of business meetings and put us all at ease right from the start of the trip. Michael seemed glad to be doing something again and appeared to be having a good time, even though he never said much, but that was just his nature.

At thirteen, his body and mind were in a state of continual development; his arms and legs had grown long and gangly and, like any other teenager, his attitude was shy and awkward. He was also noticeably round shouldered and nearly always walked with his head bowed. The reason for this, I guessed, was that he was self-

324

consciously trying to hide from view. Sadly, the scar on Michael's cheek had not faded with the passing if time, in fact, if anything, it had become even more pronounced, and formed a bright red blemish on his pale porcelain-like skin. His skewed jaw had also become more noticeable and when the poor lad tried to smile, it was awkward and lop-sided.

The only time he ever enjoyed being the centre of attention was at school, in the classroom, where he excelled. Proving without question, that his mind was razor sharp and far superior to that of most other students. Unfortunately he didn't fare so well in the playground, where, with no friends, he suffered at the hands of cruel bullies - although he never told Ray or Ruby.

He was also at the age when he was starting to notice girls, but because of his decidedly odd appearance, they, unfortunately, were not noticing him, or at least not for the right reasons. This further dented his confidence, making him even more self-conscious and painfully introvert.

Nevertheless, over the course of the trip, and after a good deal of coaxing on my part, he and I did manage to have a few very productive chats. He seemed particularly interested in stunt work and wanted to know all about staging fights and falling off buildings. He was also quite a movie buff and was very impressed by my friendship with Virgil Nash and Victoria Wild, who were, by this time, as famous in England as they were in the States. By the end of the three days, Michael was more open with me and far more relaxed, and I felt, at long last, we had finally made a start on forming some sort of friendship.

The only thing about Michael's behaviour I noticed that did sadden me, which I had picked up on even before we left Vegas, was his attitude towards Joe. The two of them had never really bonded, although it wasn't for lack of trying on Joe's part, who had done everything he could to be a friend to the boy. But Michael just wasn't interested; his contempt for Joe was obvious, and whenever he had to speak to him, which was, by choice, as little as possible, it was by using the fewest possible words, delivered in the iciest of tones. Joe himself was also acutely aware of this, and quite naturally, it troubled him.

The fact of it was, that Michael blamed his uncle for the scar on his face and the crooked line of his jaw. He had been shot and Ray had been crippled all because of Joe's connection with gangland.

Michael also knew how Joe had stolen Rachel away from Carl and this, to him, seemed like a despicable thing to do. Carl was one of the few people, outside of his family, who had ever shown him any respect, and as a result, he had become one of Michael's only friends. But his uncle had wrecked Carl's life too, then sent him away, with little regard for what he had done.

In his Michael's eyes, Joe Cassidy had an awful lot to answer for.

*   *   *

Aside from that rather disturbing observation, the trip overall was a resounding success. We had gazed in awe into the vacuous depths of the Grand Canyon, stared in amazement at the vast, concrete magnificence of the Hoover Dam and, having spent three nights under the stars, eaten some of the best damned camp-fire food we had ever tasted.

However, all too soon, our return to Vegas beckoned, where unknowingly, in the time we had been away, our lives had changed forever.

Twenty-two

As soon as Joe opened the door the smell hit him. It was strong and pungent and made him feel sick. 'Jesus Christ!' He exclaimed as he walked into the spacious lounge area of his hotel suite, 'What the hell's that bloody stench?' Quickly crossing to the french doors that led onto the wide balcony, he slid them apart to air the room and breathed in several lungfuls of clean, fresh air.

There was no sign of his wife, 'Rachel, it's me, I'm back!' He shouted, but there was no reply. 'Rachel, I'm home where are you?' Still no response. Joe then heard a laugh, 'Rachel? Is that you?'

'Dada, Dada!' Brett's excited voice chirped from his room, followed by a happy little chuckle, pleased that his Daddy was home.

'Brett!' Joe called to him delightedly, 'I'm home lad, but where's Mummy, and what's that horrible smell?'

Joe's second question was answered as soon as he walked into his son's bedroom.

Brett was in his cot, covered in dried excrement and sitting in a pool of his own stale urine. His face, hands, arms, legs and body were all smeared with hideous brown faeces, as was his nappy and bedclothes. He was holding his drinking bottle, which contained no liquid, but smelled of curdled milk, whilst a plastic bowl lay upside down on the floor outside his cot, the contents of which had spilled onto the carpet, and had already started to grow mould. The fur on Brett's teddy bear was also matted with excreta and liberal daubs of it coated his other toys.

It was obvious he'd been there, completely unattended, for quite some time, and Joe's anger rose hotly. For all anybody cared, his son could be dead and no-one would have known. Where the hell was Rachel? And what could she have possibly been thinking to leave Brett alone?

The boy was in a truly disgusting state, and the heavy stench surrounding him made Joe gag. Nevertheless, he cautiously picked up his son, careful not to get any shit on himself.

'Dada!' Brett giggled again.

'Hello, lad,' Joe said sympathetically, trying desperately not to throw up, 'What's happened to you, where's Mummy gone?' He shouted her again, this time at the top of his voice, but there was still no reply.

Becoming more concerned about his absent wife by the second, Joe took the boy into the bathroom and sat him carefully down on the tiled floor while he turned on the shower and adjusted it to the right temperature. Once that was done, he removed the lad's extremely heavy, and very full nappy and threw it in the waste bin under the sink. Then, Joe slipped off his shoes and, holding his son tightly in his big hands, stepped fully clothed into the shower.

Meticulously he scrubbed every inch of his son, carefully making sure that every trace of the excrement was washed away. Afterwards, Joe stripped off his wet clothes and put on one of the hotel's complimentary bath robes, which had The Villa Continental embroidered in blue cotton on the left hand breast pocket. His thoughts were still racing. What had happened? Why wasn't Rachel there? What could have possibly caused her to leave her son alone? All these questions flashed through his mind, but as yet he had no answers.

Ten minutes later, Joe placed Brett, wrapped in a fresh warm towel, on the large Italian rug in the centre of the living room, surrounded by soft cushions and plenty of toys. He was very nearly sparkling with cleanliness. But, even with the balcony doors open, there was still a God awful smell in the room, as if something was dead or rotting.

After making the lad some warm milk, which his son took greedily, Joe then fixed himself a large whiskey before slowly walking into his bedroom.

As he entered, the sight that presented itself, scared him more than anything he'd previously seen in his life. The whiskey glass slipped from his hand and smashed noisily on the floor, sending fragments of sharp glass across the marble tiles. Ignoring the splinters of crystal that cut his bare feet, he ran to the phone by the bed, grabbed up the receiver and hastily dialled for help.

'Hello?' I answered.

'Sean, it's me, Joe, I need you. Now!'

'Where?' I asked, noting the desperation in my friend's voice.

'My room, quick. Please - be quick!'

Then the phone went dead as Joe threw down the receiver.

*　*　*

I turned the key and entered the suite I was sharing with Victoria, although as far as the press knew, it was hers alone. She was laying on the cream chaise longue in our enormous, extravagantly upholstered bedroom, staring dreamily out the window, unaware that I had even entered the apartment. Her thoughts were clearly elsewhere.

She looked stunning and for a long moment, I silently admired her. I couldn't believe how fortunate I'd been that she had picked me over all the men she could have had. She was certainly one hell of a woman; headstrong, determined, sexy and passionate. And I loved her. I'd only been away for three days, yet I had missed her as if it were three years.

I walked over and stood behind her, she was still oblivious to my presence. 'Hello,' I said, but she didn't hear me, she was too deep in thought.

'Hello, it's me! The wanderer has returned.' I saw her shoulders jump as my voice startled her out of her trance.

'Hey there, Honey,' Victoria replied warmly, 'I didn't hear you come in, I must've been miles away.' Turning to face me, she continued, 'Did you and the boys have a good time?'

'Yeah, we did - I'm thinking of changing my name to Davy Crockett - king of the wild frontier,' I joked.

She laughed, then said sarcastically, 'Sure, I bet you were a real boy scout!'

I bent down and gave her a kiss on the lips, 'What about you, what have you been doing?'

'Oh, I've had a blast. The studio called and told me I'd gotta dub in some more dialogue for the movie, so while you were off playing Grizzly Adams, I had to fly to LA, work for two solid days, then fly back to Vegas so I'd be here when you returned.'

'Thanks, that's nice' I said, feeling quite touched, 'But you needn't have done, I'd have understood.'

'I know, but I wanted to. Besides, there's something we need to talk about.'

'Oh dear' I replied, feeling a little stab of dread in the pit of my stomach, 'That sounds ominous, what is it?'

'It'll wait,' Victoria shrugged off the question easily, 'First I wanna know how you did with Michael.'

Instantly dismissing my concerns, I launched into a full report on the whole trip, leaving nothing out. 'I think him and me are finally getting somewhere,' I concluded, ' - and I get the feeling that maybe one day, I'll be able to tell him he's actually my kid - can you imagine that, Vicky? Me a proper father after all this time. Who knows, one day he might even come and stay with me in Hollywood.' My enthusiasm knew no bounds, 'How about that Vicky? Just me alone with my son.'

'That's great Sean,' Victoria said honestly, but her tone sounded a little melancholy and I picked up on it immediately.

'Not just me and him, Vicky, but you as well. You know I meant that, don't you?' Suddenly I felt very guilty and inconsiderate. It hadn't been my intention to upset Victoria, I was just letting my hopes run away with me. 'You do understand, don't you?'

'Yes Sean, I understand, it's okay,' she said bravely. But it wasn't okay, I could tell and as if to prove it, a single tear ran down her cheek, and her beautiful neon eyes filled with water.

'What is it then?' Suddenly I was concerned 'Is it me? Have I upset you?'

'It's nothing,' she responded, feigning a slight smile, 'Just me being silly, that's all.'

'If it's me, just tell me what I can do to make it up to you. Ask me anything, and I'll do it,' I begged, desperate to be forgiven after my thoughtlessness.'

Victoria put her arms around my neck and pulled me down towards her, 'Make love to me, that's what you can do.'

*   *   *

We lay in the enormous bed afterwards, wrapped in the cream satin sheets, Victoria's head resting on my chest and her arm draped around my waist. Neither of us spoke, it was enough just to be in each others company. I'd just started to close my eyes, feeling fairly tired after the trip, when I felt a little trickle of water run down my chest and onto my stomach. Victoria was crying. 'What is it, what's the matter?' I asked, lifting her chin and staring into her tear stained face, 'Whatever it is, you can tell me.'

'I'm not sure that I can,' she sniffed.

'Of course you can, really. It'll be okay, I promise.'

'I think you're gonna be mad.'

Oh, Christ. She was going to break-up with me. 'I'll be fine - honest. Just—' I swallowed down the lump in my throat. '—Just tell me.'

'Okay then.' She took a deep breath. 'Here goes.'

'Okay then,' I repeated, bracing myself.

'Sean.'

'Yes?'

'I'm pregnant.'

'What?'

'I'm pregnant,' she repeated.

'Sorry, wh.. what?' I spluttered, utterly astonished at what I was hearing.

'You're gonna be a father. While I was in LA I saw my doctor and he confirmed it.'

'You're pregnant?' Slowly it was starting to sink in.

'Yes,' she said, 'I'm sorry, I know you wanted to spend some time with Michael, but—'

I placed a finger gently over her lips to quieten her. 'You're pregnant,' I said again, this time it wasn't a question, more of a statement and my mouth split into a wide grin. Suddenly I started to chuckle. I jumped out of bed, swept Victoria up into my arms and began dancing naked around the room, both of us laughing wildly.

Through, her giggles, Victoria said breathlessly, 'I take it you're pleased then?'

'You bet I'm pleased,' I exclaimed, collapsing onto the bed, '—in fact, I couldn't be bloody happier!'

Victoria then turned serious for a moment, 'I'm happy too Sean, ecstatically happy - even more so now that I know you are, but what the hell am I going to tell the studio? - I'm contracted to two more movies this year.'

'Don't worry,' I said, 'We'll sort it out, let's not worry about that now. Let's just enjoy today - the best day of my life!'

Tragically, it was just about to turn into one of the worst, because at that moment, the phone rang.

* * *

Rigor mortis had already set in and her body was cold, stiff and grey in colour. The smell emanating from the two day old corpse was vile and nauseating and lay heavily in the darkened room. Rachel was on her back with large amounts of dry blood caked around her nose and mouth. The blood was mixed with dark brown oily vomit that had hardened into a sticky crust, and several fat blue-bottles were feasting on it. Only the yellowy whites of Rachel's blood shot eyes were visible as they stared blindly at the ceiling; her pupils having rolled back into her skull. Underneath her eyes were deep grey smears, which with her sunken cheeks and gaping mouth, made her face look grotesque.

Her skinny body was completely naked with every rib clearly defined; her pelvic bone jutting out sharply like that of an under nourished victim of famine. Her breasts, in death, looked like empty sacks that lay limply on her chest. Around her nipples, on the areolae and on the very tips, were several black cigarette burns. More would later be found on the insides of her thighs and the cheeks of her bottom. Across her breasts, stomach and buttocks were long red welt marks, as if she had been lashed with a whip, and her torso was covered in purple bruises.

Rachel's genitals were also lacerated; the blood from the wounds mixed with semen. Semen, now dry and flakey, was also visible on her face, chest and belly as well as matted in her pubic hair. An autopsy would later prove that it belonged to three different men, all of whom had penetrated her, not only vaginally, but anally too. The autopsy would also find that Rachel's injuries, although horrific, were not the cause of her death. She had actually died from an overdose. An inspection of her stomach contents revealed that she had consumed large quantities of vodka and tranquillisers, but it was a lethally impure mixture of cocaine and heroin that killed her. First she had haemorrhaged from the nose, then almost simultaneously, suffered a massive heart attack. According to the doctors, her death, would have been almost immediate.

The first thing I saw as I rushed into the room was Rachel's naked body sprawled on the bed. In one hand she still held an empty glass and, in her other, were the few pills that she hadn't managed to swallow before death took her.

Joe was kneeling by the side of the bed, his legs and feet bleeding from the small cuts inflicted by his own broken whiskey glass that he'd dropped just minutes before. He was bent over her body, his shoulders heaving and, although there was no sound, I knew he was weeping.

Joe wept for Brett also; his twelve month old son who would grow up without the love of a mother, just as Joe himself had. He swore that would never happen to a child of his, but it had, Rachel was dead and he blamed himself for it. He was guilt ridden and distraught, convinced that if he had stayed at The Villa and not gone on the trip, this terrible thing would never have happened.

I walked over to my best friend in a bid to comfort him, but I could find no suitable words. I simply placed a hand on Joe's shoulder, then stood quietly beside him and watched over him while he grieved.

Twenty-three

The newspaper hit Benny Mottola's desk and slid across the polished veneer, very nearly knocking a steaming hot cup of coffee into his lap. 'Hey, what the fuck do ya think you're doin?' He shouted angrily at Frank Blades, his quick and very violent temper flaring instantly.

'Sorry Boss,' said Frankie, 'But I think you might find the photo on page three very interesting.'

'Yeah? Well I'd better for your sake,' said Benny cooling a little. He opened the paper and looked at the photo which appeared underneath the headline:
THE VEGAS VILLA OPENS TO THE STARS.

As he studied it, he was bewildered as to why he should be the least bit interested in a picture of Victoria Wild, Virgil Nash and a host of other celebrities he couldn't have given a damn about.

'Yeah, so what am I supposed to be lookin' at?' He snarled.

'Look at those two men in the background, right on the edge of the picture. You know them, so do I. I'd know them anywhere,' replied Frankie.

As Benny looked closer at the image in the newspaper, his face cracked into a broad smile. 'Well, well, well,' he exclaimed delightedly, 'Joe Cassidy and Sean Reilly, what a pleasant surprise, and both of them together as well. Two for the price of one, how absolutely bloody perfect.' Then with an evil sneer, and actually talking to the photograph, he added, 'Hello, boys. It's been a long time - but I think maybe now it's time we got re-acquainted.'

Benny, his interest now well and truly piqued, went on to read the couple of paragraphs that accompanied the photo, about how The Villa Continental was run by an English entrepreneur named Carl Napier, a man who Benny knew from way back. Napier was pictured with 'movie legend' Louretta Wild, who was rumoured to have a part share in the hotel, together with a mysterious businessman, who was thought to be from overseas. 'That would be a certain Joe Cassidy, I'll wager,' Benny said, speaking aloud but talking to himself. Subconsciously he rubbed the scars on his arm and chest, remembering the last time that he and Joe had met. Then he thought about the night that his brother Jez was murdered and how badly he wanted to make his killer pay.

Looking up, he smiled at Frank, who in return grinned wickedly back, 'I think it's time we paid a visit to Vegas, don't you?' He said.

* * *

Benny was now living in Miami. He had changed his name and had undergone some cosmetic surgery to alter his appearance - nothing too drastic, but enough to avoid being casually recognised on the street. But anyone that really knew him would be in no doubt as to who he was, his big, bullish frame easily betraying his true identity.

For nearly two years, he had been over-seeing operations in Miami for his uncle; one Tito Vincenzi, ambitious boss of one of the smaller New York crime families. Vincenzi had his sights set high and had been steadily expanding his business interests into other parts of the country. Benny's arrival in America had coincided nicely with this expansion plan. Tito knew what his nephew had achieved in London, and thought him to be exactly the right type to represent him in Florida. So, after proving himself with a successful number of stick-up jobs, truck hijackings and drugs transactions, Benny had been put in charge of the Miami operation.

Miami soon became the biggest jewel in the Vincenzi crown, and cocaine its main trade. The rise, and subsequent success, of this side of the business was entirely down to Benny who, with the aid of Frank, had cultivated a reliable, very lucrative network of suppliers and dealers. And in Miami, there was a never ending demand for what they were selling.

However, Benny was still every bit as ambitious as he always was, and had, for some time, been looking for an opportunity to get into Las Vegas, the place where real money could be made. Vegas was built, owned and run by organised crime, at least in the most part, and he saw no reason why he shouldn't jump on the band wagon. Drugs, hookers, gambling - it was all there - a neon oasis of sleaze, just waiting to be harvested. All he needed was a little bit of luck and a plan. Both of which he now had.

*　*　*

Mottola and Blades arrived in Las Vegas the following afternoon, together with another man who was known simply as Wolf. He was younger than both his superiors, but supremely confident with attitude and ambition in abundance. His role was that of bodyguard and enforcer - a cold-blooded killer who neither questioned what he was asked to do nor required a reason for it.

Wolf hoped one day to take over from Frank as Benny's right-hand man, a role for which he thought himself to be perfectly suited and one he desperately lusted after. Frank, however, had other plans, he had no intention of relinquishing his position just yet - he may have been getting older, but there were still very few men tougher. Wolf wasn't yet close to taking the title but one day he definitely would be.

Wolf's physique was hard and muscular. He was also quite handsome in a cruel way, with piercing steel-blue eyes, a cold, evil smile and a tight thatch of white-blonde hair. Dressing very much in the hip Latin style, he strutted about in Cuban heeled boots, figure hugging tee shirts and tight leather hipsters - the contents of which Frank ogled lecherously.

Like Frank, Wolf found the male form very attractive, particularly if it was as well defined as his, but he didn't think of himself as homosexual, nor indeed heterosexual. He saw himself as a stud, a sex-god at whose alter only the most beautiful were permitted to worship; male or female, but his tastes were a little too rough for most he met, and few came back for more.

Wolf's job in Vegas was one of surveillance at The Villa. He played the slots, roamed the tables, chatted to waitresses and hit on showgirls, all to glean any information which Benny might find useful. Soon, Wolf was on first name terms with pit bosses, bartenders and dealers, and taking off-duty security guards for drinks. He even banged one of the chorus girls from the Napoli lounge for a whole week, just for the merest snippet of dressing room gossip. He was thorough and very good at his work, building up a complete dossier on the marks Benny had targeted with the contributing staff none the wiser.

Within the contents of his final report to Benny, were details of Rachel's drinking and erratic behaviour. There was a note, too, of Carl Napier's interest in her, and of their drug fuelled orgies. An ex-maid, who made up her wages by hooking part-time, had told Wolf of her participation at one of these parties. She had not known, however, that the other girl there was Rachel Cassidy, but the description of her, particularly the English accent, corroborated with what a guy from room service had seen. Wolf had simply added two and two together.

Benny, scanning the file, couldn't help but smile at Napier's deceit. Joe was the man to whom Napier was once so loyal, to whom he had remained faithfully beside, even after being offered several lucrative positions with both Benny's organisation and Big Jack's. How times had changed and Mottola was aching to find out why.

* * *

Carl Napier was in the main foyer, leaning against the front desk, studying the floor plan for the evening's entertainment in the Napoli lounge, when someone came up beside him and whispered in his ear. 'Well, well - if it ain't me old mate, Carl.' The voice was gruff, yet chillingly familiar, 'Long time, no see.'

Carl span around, instantly recognising the sinister tones from the old days, but the face he saw was not entirely the one he remembered. The features had been altered and the greasy balding hairline had turned a little greyer, but there could be no doubt about it, the voice belonged to Benny Mottola.

Benny was accompanied by two men, the first he recognised as Frank Blades, one of the meanest villains in London. The other man he did not know, but could tell it was someone he shouldn't upset. Both men stood intimidatingly behind their leader, looking menacing and aggressive, positively oozing violent intent and Carl sensed all too clearly that this was something more than just purely a social call.

'Benny!' Napier exclaimed, rather over-playing his false enthusiasm, 'What a nice surprise, welcome to The Villa Continental.' He sounded like an annoying concierge angling for a big tip and immediately felt stupid at his transparent pretence, knowing that Benny the Bull could see right through the act.

'Careful Carl,' Mottola smiled, glancing casually about him, making certain that no one was within earshot, 'We don't want to let everyone know who I am, do we? Too many ears about, know what I mean?'

'Yeah, sure, sorry Ben—, I mean, well, you know,' Carl said, mildly flustered, curious as to what the hell Mottola was doing in Vegas. But he recovered well, 'How are you doing?' He asked sounding almost genuine, 'It's been years. You too Frank - good to see you - both of you.'

'Sure it is Carl,' said Benny, not buying any of it, 'Is there somewhere we can talk?'

*　*　*

They stood in Napier's penthouse, sipping whiskey and staring out of the tall windows at the city below. The Desert Inn, The Stardust and The Sands all visible; their giant neon signs advertising the big name stars appearing within. The conversation was light and good humoured. 'You've done well for yourself, Carl. This is some set up,' Benny commented appreciatively.

'Thanks, it's okay.' Carl said.

'Yep. Some set up alright. Guess you've hit the big time, huh?'

'No. Not really - it all looks good, but we're just startin' out. Depends on how well things go before we can think about anything else. But I think we're gonna do okay.'

'We?'

'Yeah.'

'Oh, you mean that movie star - whassername—?'

'Louretta Wild, Boss.' Wolf piped up. He and Blades were sitting on the soft leather sofas of Napier's sunken seating area, smoking his finest cigars.

'That's it, yeah. Louretta Wild - she is the owner right?' Benny asked, turning to face Carl.

'One of 'em - but she's sorta in the background. It's mostly my operation. I pretty much get a free hand as long as I turn a profit - and judging by these first few weeks, it don't look like that's gonna be too much of a problem.'

'Sounds like a sweet deal.'

'I ain't complainin' - an' it sure beats the hell outa Peckam.'

'I bet it does,' Benny agreed. 'I bet it does indeed.'

They were quiet for a moment, both men sipping their drinks and admiring the view before Mottola spoke up again. 'So, Carl, do you ever see Joe Cassidy?'

Frank Blades blew a smoke ring, 'Now ain't that a question?' He chuckled under his breath.

Napier, by now, was suspecting this to be the reason for the visit, and smiled at the lack of subtlety, never one of Mottola's strong points. 'Sure I do Benny, all the time. But of course you already know that, otherwise you wouldn't be here, would you?'

It was now Benny's turn to smile, Carl was still as sharp as ever. 'Straight to the point eh?' He said, 'Well, let me be equally direct, let's say you're right, maybe I do know. Maybe I also know that Cassidy and his buddy, Reilly, are partners in this joint. Maybe I know too that, until this mornin', them and that fuckin' pirate Ray Reece were here in Vegas and that all of 'em 'ave gone on some fucked up campin' trip. I dare say, if you wanted to know, I could even find out what colour their goddamn sleeping bags are too!'

'Okay, let's assume that's all true,' Napier agreed, 'What is it you want from me?'

'A piece of the action.' Benny said bluntly.

'And what makes you think I'd be willing to give you that?' Carl asked incredulously.

'Because Carl, me old mate,' Mottola was now enjoying himself, 'You've been bangin' Cassidy's missus and havin' parties with her and all your rich pals - and I'll make sure he finds out if you don't cut me in for a slice of the action. You been caught with your pants down boy, now it's time to pay the price.'

Carl smiled again, but now there was sweat on his top lip, obviously he hadn't been so discreet in his liaisons with Rachel as he'd thought, but he played it cool, 'Sorry, Benny. You must have me confused with someone who gives a shit.'

'Hey, good answer. But you know as well as I do what Joe'd do if he found out.'

Carl did know. Joe finding out was not part of his plan. This whole situation was not part of the plan. He'd just wanted some vengeance, that's all. Now Benny was involved, and unless Carl played ball, it would be game over.

'Where's your proof Benny?' He asked, his throat drying. 'I mean, it's just your word against mine.
Who's Joe gonna believe, you, his enemy, or me, his trusted friend?'

'Some friend!' Blades offered from behind them.

'Shuddit, Frank,' Mottola barked, before turning again to Napier. 'He's right though ain't he Carl? I never thought you'd do the dirty on your bosom buddy. What happened between you guys anyway?

'Nuthin.' It doesn't matter. The bastard had it comin' - that's all.'

'Sure he did. You don't have to preach to the converted. But he'd still rip yer fuckin' head off if he found out what you been up to.'

'Like I said, Benny. Where's your proof?' Carl was angry now, staring directly into Benny's eyes. Testing him. Not a wise thing to do with Benny the Bull, but this was Carl's turf, Carl's hotel - what the hell could Mottola do?

Benny smiled. 'Show 'im,' he said to Wolf.

Wolf sauntered up from the sunken seating area and unzipped his brown leather bomber jacket. From inside it he pulled out a burgundy file and handed it to Napier. 'Take a look,' he smiled, 'it's a good read.'

Carl felt his bowels shift as he opened the file. In it was a complete listing of his and Rachel's movements over the past few weeks. There were names and addresses of staff who had all witnessed certain things - things which to them seemed innocent, but when put with the other accounts, made for extremely incriminating evidence that would be impossible to refute. There was also a couple of glossies of Carl and Rachel entering the private elevator that led to his penthouse. Another, which Wolf was particularly proud of, showed the two of them, with Alvin Staedtler, leaving his suite. Carl had his hand down Rachel's top, Staedtler had his on her backside.

'Okay,' said Carl feeling sick, 'so you got proof. What is it you want from me?'

'That's the spirit,' Benny said cheerfully. 'Like I said. I wanna piece of the action. I wanna get into Vegas, an' you, me old mate, are my golden ticket.'

'Maybe I can swing a bit of something your way,' Carl said defeatedly, 'But it'll be tough.'

'Hey - it'd better be a whole lot more than a bit - an' it ain't gonna be half as tough as the alternative. Besides, think of it this way - you got a grudge against Cassidy, what better way to get even than by stealing his hotel out from under his nose?'

Carl hadn't thought of that.

That sounded good.

'You know what Benny? Maybe I can work something out.' Carl didn't know exactly what yet as his bosses were no fools and they would surely notice if he was skimming the profits, but he would think of something. It was his hotel after all. 'Leave it to me,' he added, 'I'm sure I can make it happen.'

'You'd better fuckin' believe it partner.'

'Partner?'

'You betcha,' Benny grinned, 'You belong to me now boy. You're my man on the inside - my key to the city - an' I'm gonna take it to the fuckin' cleaners!' They all laughed, even Carl.

After a few moments, when all their glasses had been refilled, Benny placed one of his huge arms around Carl's shoulders. 'Now we got that sorted,' he said, 'why don't you tell me everything you know about Sean Reilly?'

*   *   *

They were all pretty drunk by the time Rachel knocked on the fire escape door - her secret route to Carl's apartment.

Napier opened it ajar and saw her standing outside in the corridor. 'Not now baby,' he began, knowing the trouble she'd be in if Benny saw her, 'This ain't a particularly good—' but she was already through the doorway.

'Thank God, Carl,' she blurted breathlessly, 'I couldn't wait any longer, I need something now, I need it real bad.' Rachel was obviously desperate.

'I'll bring some down to you in a minute, just—'

'No now, baby. I need it now. If I don't get it I'll die!' She reached out and placed her hand on his crotch, rubbing it seductively, 'I'll give you somethin' in return. Promise.'

'What about the kid?' Carl asked, desperately trying to keep her from entering the room. 'Where's he? Shouldn't you be gettin' back to him?'

'He's fine. I've left him in his cot with some lunch. Worry about me. Not him!' She answered, sliding past him and into the room.

'Wait - Rachel—' but it was too late. She was in and the three men sitting on the sofas were eyeing her like a pack of hungry dogs.

'Oh, you've got company,' she exclaimed, though far from disappointed. She had come to realise that when Carl had 'friends' over, her enjoyment was far greater, with the cocaine and alcohol flowing much more freely. 'I do hope I haven't interrupted anything,' she added, extremely flirtatiously.

'Far from it, darlin'' Mottola said, a big, Cheshire cat grin on his face. 'So you're Rachel. Carl's told us all about you.

344

'All good I hope.'

'Extremely,' he added with relish 'In fact, we've all been dying to meet you.'

*　　*　　*

An hour later and Rachel was dancing naked on the glass coffee table, having consumed large quantities of vodka and cocaine. She was drunk and high and she didn't give a damn, her inhibitions having vanished long ago. She was being groped and fondled by Benny and Wolf, both of whom were in various states of undress. Frank Blades was still clothed, and remained unimpressed by the drunken slut on the table. However, he was aroused, although his focus was on Wolf, whose large erection was on full display.

Benny was almost foaming at the mouth with desire as he watched Rachel dance and, unable to control himself any longer, grabbed hold of her and forced her head down to his crotch. She didn't complain and took him willingly into her mouth, but Benny liked it rough and, after taking hold of her hair, rammed himself violently into her. She whimpered and choked slightly but had been subject to such treatment by numerous other men and knew the kick they derived from it, besides, the drugs and alcohol had sufficiently anaesthetised her gag reflex.

With Rachel now on her knees, and motivated by his boss's lead, Wolf crawled up onto the table top, clawed her buttocks apart and forcibly entered her from behind. Rachel grimaced with pain, but was powerless to stop him as Benny was still holding her firmly by the hair.

Carl saw this and, knowing things had turned ugly, wanted to stop it. In a bid to entice the others away, he'd opened a fresh new sachet of coke, hoping this might help them to forget about the girl.

Over the last few weeks he'd watched many men have sex with

Rachel, and had enjoyed seeing it, but these men were different. These men were dangerous, vicious and cruel and didn't care if she lived or died.

'Okay, okay!' Carl shouted, trying to end it, 'That's enough, let's not get carried away - we don't wanna damage the goods do we?'

But the only response he got was a contemptuously knowing little snigger from Frank Blades.

'Hey Benny!' Carl tried again, this time his voice loud and authoritative, 'Give it a rest will ya, come and have a drink, take some coke, let the girl have a break for cryin' out loud.'

Blades raised his eyebrows, impressed by the force of the demand, and was interested to see what Benny's reaction would be. He knew from bitter experience that his boss didn't tolerate being shouted at.

Mottola, jolted out of his trance, stopped what he was doing and fixed Napier with a fiery glare, his expression murderous. 'C'mon Benny,' Carl said, this time in a more placatory tone, 'This is good stuff - the very best money can buy - no point in lettin' it go to waste.' Slowly, the fire went from Mottola's eyes and his temper subsided. Carl had fortunately caught him on a good day and Frankie was disappointed.

Finally, Benny grinned and said, 'Sure, why not - what's the point of rushing, we got all night, right? Hey, Wolf,' he added, as he pulled up his silk boxers, 'Take her in the bedroom for a while will ya? I don't wanna hear all that slurpin' and slappin' while me and Carl, here, are tryin' to talk. Knock yourself out, enjoy yourself - we'll take our turns in a little while.'

Carl felt his heart sink, his attempted rescue had failed. The look of delight in Wolf's eyes as he pulled Rachel off the table and dragged her towards the bedroom made his stomach churn. What had he done?

Rachel was swaying and staggering, drunker than hell and high as a kite, but just before she reached the bedroom door, she broke free of Wolf's grip and tottered unsteadily back to where Carl sat. For a moment he thought she was trying to escape, and his spirits temporarily rose, but he was mistaken. She was merely coming to get another fix. Bending over the table, she snorted up a line of the freshly chopped coke, 'Fuck!' She said, as she felt the rush, her fingers stabbing at her nose as the wild sensation burned up her nostril. 'Wow!' She was seeing stars and her blood-shot eyes began to water, but by now she was incapable of rational thought. Placing the straw up her other nostril, she repeated the whole routine. She gasped again, and cried out, rubbing her nose frantically as if stung by a bee. A trace of blood trickled down her nostril but was quickly sniffed back up. No one but Carl noticed, and he was concerned that she might overdose.

'Fuck, that was good!' She exclaimed, before wobbling back passed Wolf, straight into the bedroom. Wolf grabbed his cigarettes, then followed her in, shutting the door behind him.

A feeling of dread filled Carl's stomach. What the hell had he done? Had he turned into a goddamn monster? How could he have allowed this to happen?

All the time Benny was watching Carl's face, and he could see the guilt he was feeling and loving every delicious minute of it. 'Reckon Wolfie's gonna show her a real wild time, wouldn't ya say?' He said lasciviously.

'Yeah, I bet he will,' Carl answered without enthusiasm.

*   *   *

Forty-five minutes later, Wolf emerged with a wide grin on his face, more than pleased with his performance, 'Who's next then?' He asked.

'That'll be you then, Carl' Mottola announced.

'No thanks Benny, I think I'll leave it, I've been there already'

Napier tried to bluff his way out, his conscience now eating him alive.

'Rubbish' dismissed Benny, clearly enjoying the other man's discomfort. 'You get in there my son - all for one and one for all!'

'No, honestly, I'm fine really.'

'Perhaps you don't understand' sneered Benny, tightening the screws, 'You either get your arse into that bedroom,' Mottola pointed at the one Wolf had just vacated, 'Or Frankie will take you into that one,' he nodded to the spare room, 'It's your choice, her or him?'

Carl glanced over to where Frank Blades was sitting - a huge, queer predator, just waiting to pounce. Blades winked and blew him a kiss. Carl knew he was beaten, there was no way out. 'Okay Benny, you win, if it makes you happy, I'll go with the girl.' He stood up and reluctantly wandered into Rachel's bedroom, and started to close the door.

'Oh, no you don't, Carl!' Mottola exclaimed, a cruel smile on his face, 'We wanna see, we wanna make sure you do it, don't we boys?' Frankie and Wolf nodded their agreement, both of them smiling with anticipation.

'Benny, please?' Carl protested 'Gimme a break?'

Mottola was having none of it, 'You can either do it on your own or with Frank's help, it makes no difference to me.'

Faced with a no alternative, Napier left the door open and walked over to where Rachel lay. When he saw her he was stunned. 'Jesus Christ, what's that bastard done to you?' He whispered, looking down at her bruised body; the cigarette burns red and weeping; her most intimate areas bleeding and sore. 'I'm sorry' he said, 'Please forgive me.'

Rachel was oblivious, completely spaced out, almost unconscious, 'That's okay, baby' she slurred, neither caring nor comprehending what was happening to her.

Carl tried to get it over with quickly, but he was unable to. He found it a struggle to get hard and when he eventually did, it took an eternity for him to reach climax, particularly with three men watching his every move and shouting encouragement from the bedroom door.

When he had finished, he felt filthy. He felt low and disgusting and hated himself.

'Looks like it's just me to go then,' Benny laughed, 'I hope you boys have warmed her up, cos I'm raring to go!'

Mottola was with Rachel for ages, maybe an hour or more. At one point, Carl heard the sound of Benny's thick leather belt as it whipped her fragile body, but she made only the slightest moan.

At last, the bedroom door opened and Mottola's fat, hairy body appeared; wet with sweat and glistening in the lamp light; his face red from exhaustion and effort. His cotton-reel sized penis hanging limply above his big hefty legs, completely spent and lifeless. Benny was so worn out, he was wheezing; his massive shoulders heaving as he gasped for breath. He even had to wait a few minutes before he could summon the energy to get dressed. Sitting naked and sticky on Napier's leather sofa, he resembled a big bull elephant gathering strength after an arduous battle. 'You can get that whore out of here now boys,' he said to Frank and Wolf. 'Now we've had our fun, Cassidy can 'ave her back.' His voice was thick with fatigue, but somehow he still managed to sound extremely satisfied.

Frank and Wolf lifted Rachel off the bed and when Carl saw her he nearly threw up. Her whole body was covered with bruises and lacerations, and blood was leaking from her vagina. She looked awful, but amazingly, she was still conscious and as she passed Carl, she slurred, 'Well, baby, did I do well? Were you pleased with me?'

Napier felt sick, 'Yeah, Rachel, you did great,' he replied.

At that moment he hated Mottola - he wanted to rip him limb from limb - but he knew actually that Benny had only foreshortened the inevitable. Even without the injuries, Rachel would not have survived much longer than her next line of coke. Better to end it now, Carl thought, whilst Joe was away, whilst he had time to sort things out, to organise his story and get his insurance policy into action. He thanked God for having the foresight to arrange that. Had he not, things would be much grimmer than they already were.

Rachel was no good to anyone now - not even herself. He had to end it, for everyone's sake. Especially his own.

They dressed Rachel in a bathrobe and led her to the private elevator, but before leaving the penthouse, Carl went to a drawer and took out another fresh sachet. He'd had this one for a long time, having kept it for just such an emergency. It contained an impure mixture of cocaine and heroin, and was totally deadly. He also took the glass straw from the coffee table.

The Cassidy's apartment was only two floors below, and the three men were very careful not to be seen. Blades opened the door with Rachel's key then he and Wolf turned and left; their work was done. Carl's, on the other hand, was not quite finished and he led Rachel into her luxurious bedroom.

He was completely clear on what he had to do. It was the only way.

He opened the plastic sachet and tipped some of the powder onto the glass top of the bedside table and moulded it into two thick lines. Then, with his handkerchief, he carefully wiped the straw clean of fingerprints and placed it beside the coke. He snapped his fingers in front of Rachel's face, forcing her to focus through the drugged haze. She was swaying precariously, but lucid - just. 'Rachel, listen to me,' he said, 'Listen to what I'm saying. There's some coke here for you - good stuff. A reward for doing so well.

Take it - I promise you it'll blow your mind.'

'Wild,' she replied, her voice just a slurry whisper, 'sounds like a blast.'

'I'm going now. I gotta get back, but I'll check in on you later, okay?'

'Sure thing, baby - see ya later,' she said, her eyelids heavy.

Carl kissed her lightly on the cheek, 'Goodbye, Rachel, I'm sorry,' he said, but she was no longer listening. He left her in her room and went to stand by the door to the apartment, watching quietly to make sure she did as instructed.

Rachel's head throbbed and she needed a drink. Unsteadily she went into the living room and fixed herself a large vodka from the bar, completely blind to Carl standing motionless by the door. She took a long swig then wandered back into the bedroom to stand in front of the full length mirror. She let the bathrobe slip to the floor and studied herself, as she had done so many times in the past, although the image was blurry. Where so many times before she had seen beauty, this time she saw ugliness. Bruises and burns and lacerations and blood. She looked like a freak, like a hideous Frankenstein's monster. And it horrified her. What on earth had happened to her? An image of a belt whipping her and of a cigarette burning her flashed through her damaged mind, but she could no longer detach fact from fiction. Did those things actually happen, were they what caused her injuries? She couldn't be sure. All she knew for certain was that she was no longer beautiful. She was ugly and haggard and damaged. For the first time since she was fifteen, she could see nothing of any worth whatsoever, and she began to cry.

For many minutes, she stood there feeling sorry for herself, then she remembered the cocaine.

*   *   *

She managed to snort only one line before the pain became

too great. Her face felt as if it was on fire and her nose was burning hot like a furnace with blood pouring from it. Her vision turned red and her whole body began to tremble. Then she vomited. Hideous brown slime dredged up from the depths of hell.

Scared out of her wits, Rachel desperately grabbed her tranquillisers from the bedside cabinet and stuffed a handful into her mouth, hoping they would quell her anxiety and stupefy her senses. She washed them down with the remnants of the vodka, but still the pain persisted - like a knife sticking directly into her brain and being slowly twisted.

She lay on the bed in an effort to calm herself but promptly started to convulse. Rachel was terrified beyond anything she'd ever known, her body shaking with violent spasms, totally out of control. Then, after long, tortuous seconds of utter panic, it ended.

Without any warning, her heart stopped, and finally she was free from pain.

* * *

With a tear in his eye, and the suffocating grip of guilt in his throat, Carl quietly slipped out. But he would never forget the horror of what he had just witnessed.

* * *

The suite was completely silent for almost half an hour before little Brett woke up and started to cry.

Twenty-four

Joe went wild. 'Why the fuck didn't you wait for me?' He hollered, 'I wanted to do it - I wanted to be the one to make those bastards pay!'

'Sorry Joe,' Carl said guiltily, 'I just thought it'd be for the best. You know, to get rid of 'em as quickly as possible before they skipped town. 'Sides, I was kinda mad too. Rachel, well - she and I used to be engaged and well - I guess I just lost it.'

'Yeah, well, ya shoulda still waited for me.'

'I know, sorry.'

'You got 'em all - you sure?'

'Yeah. All. Positive.'

'Where are the bodies?' Joe asked.

'In the desert. Buried. No one can trace 'em back here - they'd already checked out - were on their way home. But I got the fuckers good. They ain't doin' that to no one ever again.'

'I wish I'd been there.'

'Sorry, Joe.'

'I hope they rot in hell - the filthy, fuckin' animals!' Joe looked at the photo again - the one that showed Alvin Staedtler and his buddy Red having sex with Rachel. The one that, according to Carl, a maid had found behind Staedtler's sofa. Irrefutable evidence that proved these were the men behind Rachel's death.

Even though Carl could not have foreseen Benny Mottola showing up, nor his contribution to events, his idea to set Staedtler up for the fall was inspired. And the timing perfect. For Carl to pin the blame on Alvin and his pals was easy. The photo was all the proof Joe had needed, which was shown to him only after Alvin, Red and Duane, the supposed photographer, had been disposed of.

Carl, Wolf and Frank had driven them out into the desert and put a bullet into the back of each of their heads. Their bodies were buried together in a deep, unmarked grave. They would never be found. Just another suspected statistic of Las Vegas crime. The police investigated their disappearance as they did Rachel's death, but, with no knowledge of the photograph that tied the two incidents together, they could not make the link and both cases came to unsatisfactory conclusions. In Joe's eyes, Rachel's killers received the justice that no court could give them, he only wished that he had dispensed it.

As for Rachel, her autopsy report had been stamped 'death by misadventure.' The coroner said, that despite the injuries sustained, she had ultimately died from snorting impure cocaine. The sadistic sex and physical abuse by 'persons unknown,' were contributory factors but did not kill her. Joe was not convinced.

'I woulda cut their fuckin' balls off,' he said.

'Don't worry. I made 'em suffer,' Carl replied.

'I hope you did Carl. I really hope you did. But I still wish I'd been there.'

*   *   *

With his mission to get a foothold in Vegas nicely underway, Benny and his two henchmen returned to the comparative safety of Miami. But Benny would go back, and when he did, The Villa Continental would belong to him.

*   *   *

Joe's Las Vegas dream was over and he had to take his wife's body home to London to be buried. We said our farewells at the airport, and I told him that should he need me, he knew where I'd be. He smiled his understanding and we embraced. I didn't know it at the time, but it would be the last I saw of my friend for several years. Joe chose to be alone with his grief.

* * *

Upon his return home, Joe threw himself into the dealings of the firm, believing it to be his true destiny. He had tried to escape it by doing everything possible to diversify his interests - he'd even built a glittering palace in Las Vegas in a bid to be free of his criminal ties. But all his hopes and dreams had ended with the death of his wife. If a gangland boss was all he was meant to be, then he'd make damn sure there would be no one better, no one tougher and no one more successful.

For the next four years, Joe would rule the London underworld with a reign of terror, spewing out the vengeance he so wished he could have inflicted on Rachel's killers, purging himself of it at every opportunity, ridding himself of the guilt he felt for not being there to protect her.

Alongside him stood Ray Reece, Richie Noakes and Manno O'Keefe, with Alfie acting as chief advisor. Together they formed the backbone of the Cassidy Firm. Nothing could stop them and nothing could stand in their way.

As commander in-chief, Joe was rock solid, an immovable and emotionless wall, without either fear, pity or compassion. All he cared about was Brett and Sarah, the two most precious things in his otherwise solitary pursuit of power. It would take him four hard years, but by 1970, he would be the undisputed king of gangland and his firm would run the largest criminal network London had ever seen. There would be others more well known, who courted more publicity and made a larger show of the violence. But they all

355

knew who the true boss was.

Joe Cassidy was the man who pulled all the strings and not many would dare to argue with him, but there were still a few.

*   *   *

Danny Davenport was sitting in a café on the Mile End Road when he found out his only sister was dead. Her face staring at him from the front page of The News of the World as he ate his bacon sandwich. Danny wasn't the type to cry into his coffee, but he did feel her loss deeply. Lighting a cigarette, he read the accompanying story. It featured heavily on the drink and drugs, but predominantly focused on the sex. It painted Rachel as a cocaine-crazed nymphomaniac, and portrayed Joe as the uncaring, unsympathetic husband. To top it all off, next to the photograph of Rachel's dead body, was an inset shot of Joe. It had been taken three years previously at a friend's party, although all other guests had been carefully cropped out. In it, he was smiling broadly and looked as though he didn't give a damn about anything. Nothing was further from the truth, but who cared about truth, that didn't sell newspapers.

Danny took a long last drag on his cigarette then stubbed it out. 'That's it you bastard, you keep on smiling,' he said silently to Joe's picture, 'Cos one of these days I'm gonna wipe it off yer face for good.'

*   *   *

The Villa Continental only barely survived the scandal surrounding Rachel's death. It was publicity of the worst possible kind, which Louretta's celebrity friends just couldn't afford to be associated with. Takings plummeted and the problems escalated with the casino turning quickly into something resembling a morgue. Only a handful of rooms were occupied at any one time and our star-studded line-up of entertainers suddenly found they had other more pressing engagements.

We fought long and hard to make it work, but ultimately it all came down to money. If The Villa was to stay afloat, then we needed to inject more. Much more.

Six months after its grand opening, Louretta, Joe and I decided that we had no alternative but to sell off a percentage of our shares in order to raise the additional collateral.

Carl Napier suddenly saw the chance he'd been looking for. He'd been skimming off as much revenue as he could - although nowhere near enough to placate Benny, but with The Villa's flagging fortunes there just wasn't the money there to be had. Now however, a chance presented itself which had the potential to reap fantastic rewards for both Mottola and himself. Like Benny had said once before, it'd be like stealing the hotel out from under Joe's nose.

Claiming that he fronted a wealthy group of investors, Carl offered to buy all of the fifty-one percent of shares available. However, much to Napier's annoyance, Virgil Nash bought three percent of those - convincing us that he could persuade the Hollywood fraternity to come back to The Villa - and with them the general public. It was a good bet.

Nevertheless, Carl Napier did indeed manage to buy forty-eight percent for his backers, a consortium calling themselves Nevada Gaming and Leisure Associates and, with its finances revitalised, The Villa was set on the road to recovery. Within a year it would be back to full health.

Upon investigation, the NGLA seemed to be a completely legitimate organisation, but had we delved a little bit deeper, scratched that bit further under the surface, we'd have found that their chief executive was one Benito Vincenzi, AKA, Benny Mottola.

Twenty-five

Having just played a major role in wrecking Joe's life, Benny didn't wait long before he decided to have a little fun with my mine. In fact it was barely a week after Victoria and I got back to LA from Vegas that things started to go wrong, although, at the time, I didn't know Mottola was to blame.

We were asleep in the enormous bed in the centre of the lavish bedroom of Vicky's Beverly Hills 'cottage,' the place where she resided when not on location or visiting Wildwood. It was just after seven in the morning when the phone rang. The noise was shrill and irritating and I needed to shut it up.

I stretched over Vicky and grabbed the receiver, 'Hello?' I growled, clearly resenting the wake up call.

'Good morning,' came the reply, 'Would I be speaking to Mr. Reilly by any chance?'

'Eh?' For one horrific moment I thought that the man on the other end of the line had said the name Reilly. Since leaving London, I had been using the name of Sean Noakes, no one knew me by my real name, at least no one I wasn't close to. Surely I had misheard.

'Is that Mr. Reilly?' The man asked again. This time it was crystal clear. Suddenly I was wide awake and feeling nauseous. 'N-no, you must have the wrong number,' I stammered, 'There's no one by that name here.'

'This is the home of Victoria Wild is it not?'

'No, it's not,' I lied, 'I'm sorry, goodbye,' and slammed down the receiver.

'Shit.' I exclaimed, leaping out of bed in panic. 'Vicky, wake up! We've got trouble. Big trouble. The bastards 'ave found me - they've bloody found me!'

Victoria began to stir, 'What? What's the matter? Come back to bed and stop making all that noise.'

Then the phone began to ring again.

'Shit, Vicky! It's them again, they've found me! For cryin' out loud, will you please wake up. This is important.'

'Go away,' she pleaded sleepily, 'Whoever it is, just please tell 'em to go away.'

Finally I lost my temper, I grabbed her shoulders and shook her vigorously. 'Victoria. Wake up, wake up now.'

At last she opened her eyes, 'What's so goddamn urgent? It's barely dawn for chrissakes.'

'On the end of that phone—' I said through gritted teeth and pointing at it angrily '—there's a guy askin' for a Mr. Reilly.' I glared at her as I spoke, enforcing the gravity of what I was saying. 'He's askin' for Mr. Reilly, not Noakes, so whoever it is, they know who I really am - do you understand?'

Thankfully, at last she did and she stared at the ringing phone in utter astonishment. 'Oh shit, Sean. Whatta we gonna do?'

'Pick it up,' I said, 'But don't tell 'em I'm here. Deny all knowledge of me. We've gotta buy some time to think of a plan.'

Gently she lifted the handset and put it to her trembling lips, 'Hello?' She said nervously.

'Victoria? Is that you?' The voice came back.

'Yes, it's me, who's this.'

'It's me Vicky, Beau - Uncle Beau!'

The relief, was obvious, 'Uncle Beau? Is that really you?'

'Sure is honey!'

'Oh, thank God,' Victoria sighed as the weight lifted from her shoulders, 'For a moment I thought it was someone calling with bad news. I'm so glad it's you - how are you?'

'I'm fine, honey. But I'm afraid you were right about the bad news. I've got some for you - you and your gentleman friend. Perhaps you better siddown.'

*　　*　　*

Beauregarde Brewster was a big bear of a man. A larger than life Texan with a huge personality and a heart to match. He was a multi-millionaire whose financial interests ranged from oil and cattle to real estate and industry but his primary concern was newspapers. Across the States he owned ten major publications and had sizeable stakes in dozens more. Paramount among these was the Los Angeles Citizen, one of the most influential papers on the West Coast, and his own personal baby.

In fact, it was his love for this particular newspaper and his eagerness to work all hours of the day and night in order to make it a success, which caused the break-up of his marriage. A marriage that had ended because of his and his wife's hectic work schedules. He being an incredibly busy newspaper tycoon, and she being a beautiful, high-profile movie star by the name of Louretta Wild.

They had stayed close over the years, even though she had married and divorced twice more. But it was Beau who had been a constant friend and he who had become Victoria's godfather. Beau and Louretta's son, Jake, an assistant director working in Burbank, was Victoria's half-brother. She also had another half-brother, Martin, from Louretta's second marriage, who was a TV exec in New York.

I had not previously met Beau, but had seen him at the ranch so knew him as a tall man with silver side-burns and a spotlessly white ten-gallon hat. This was always accompanied by a western style suit, lariat tie and polished cowboy boots. He was a dandy and an extrovert but he did it with enormous style.

As previously warned, what Beau had to say was indeed, bad news.

Apparently, an anonymous tip had been phoned through to one of the journalists at The Citizen. It was information about film star Victoria Wild's illicit affair with a wanted murderer from England by the name of Sean Reilly; a man who now called himself Sean Noakes.

This news was explosive. Not just for me, who could be carted off in chains and shipped back to England, but also for Victoria, whose career could be damaged irreparably in the fall-out. She was having an affair with, and carrying the child of a suspected murderer, a scandal which even the most broad-minded studio head would find difficult to ignore - regardless of how good an actress she was.

Fortunately, the reporter who received the anonymous call was no fool and knew that the story he held was extremely volatile. He took it directly to his editor who, in turn, took it straight to Beau Brewster, knowing of his relationship to Vicky.

Beau was experienced enough to know that if he put a block on the story it would still break somehow, either on the front page of a rival paper or on the TV and, once the scent of scandal was in the air, there would be a feeding frenzy of fact, accusation and lies - all of it beyond Beau's control.

However, if he ran with the story, he could govern it. By using his influence and trading on the respect he had within the industry - as well as by calling in many favours, he could pretty much dictate what got printed and what did not. But for that to happen, even though it would break his heart, it would be vital for his paper to break the news first. Before that though, he needed to know all the facts. He didn't want any surprises after going to press.

It was for this reason he had phoned Victoria so early in the morning. Brewster himself had been given the story just after midnight and since then had been considering all the options. Now though, he needed to speak both with his god daughter and myself so that we may clarify or refute what he had been told.

*   *   *

Beau arrived at Victoria's cottage just after eight-thirty - time was of the essence as bad news travelled fast, particularly in Hollywood where the gossip mill worked on overtime.

I shook hands with him, but his attitude was frosty. In his eyes, I was a killer. The first thing I had to do was convince him otherwise, so we sat down together and I told him the whole sordid tale. When I had finished, his opinion of me seemed to have changed suitably, although it helped when I told him that Louretta knew all about my past. The fact that she believed me obviously carried a great deal of weight and he began to look upon me in a different light.

Next, we had to convince him that our affair was something more than a casual fling and that we were in fact, deeply in love, which he in turn said was 'clear to see,' although the news of Victoria's pregnancy came as a complete shock. On hearing this information, Beau sat back in his chair and thought in silence for several minutes, visibly re-arranging his thoughts as he considered this new piece of the puzzle.

Finally he spoke, but what he said offered us little comfort. 'As I see it, someone is gonna have to be thrown to the wolves. We can either focus the story on you Vicky, which will steer the attention away from Sean and his dubious past, making him out to be little more than a sperm donor - pardon me for speaking so directly,' he said, apologetically, before continuing, 'That way, we might just get away with not mentioning the name Reilly at all. Of course, we'll need photos of you,' he said looking at me, 'But you're older now, and with a cap and shades, no one from home should recognise you.'

'Or?' I enquired, not overly impressed with the first option.

'Or, we could focus the story on you. Make you out to be the bad guy, reveal your past and your true identity and portray Victoria as an unwitting pawn who has been badly used. Try to gain her the sympathy of the people, to get them on her side - at least that way, she might just hold on to her career. The Studio will still be madder than hell, but I'm goddamn sure they won't go against the wishes of the movie going public. Shit, it might even give her career a boost! I can see those fat cats down at the Studio trying to capitalise on her misfortune, casting her in roles for down-trodden housewives and fallen women, lining their pockets from all the free publicity.'

'Why would you have to reveal my true identity?' I asked naively.

'Because son, if we don't, somebody else will, and if that happens, they'll control the story and we won't be able to do a damn thing about it. If we lay it on the line right from the word go, we can portray what happened as a crime of passion, not cold-blooded murder, which on the face of it, it certainly looks like. Believe me, I've already studied the archives from London and according to the press there, you're public enemy number one.'

I was confused, 'But surely if you focus the story on Vicky, they'll still come after me, look into my background and discover who I really am won't they?'

'Not necessarily. If we sell it right, they won't even be interested in you. Victoria Wild's the star, she'll take the fall. You'll just be some nobody stuntman, who'll disappear into the background.'

I could sense Brewster's bitterness. He obviously cared a great deal for Victoria and resented me for putting her into this situation. I didn't blame him, I felt sick with myself for allowing this to happen.

'Okay,' I said, 'There's no question. Focus the story on me - there's no way Vicky's gonna take the fall.'

'Hold on Sean!' Victoria interjected, 'Don't I have a say in this? What's going to happen to you?'

'I'll be fine, I can take care of myself. Don't worry,' I said with false bravado.

'Oh, well, that's alright then. You'll be fine. Well what about me and your baby, what's gonna happen to us when they ship you back to England? When they lock you up and throw away the key? What am I going to tell this child I'm carrying when it grows up and asks where Daddy is?' She was obviously angry.

'I-I-er, I dunno—' My mind went blank as I tried to think of a convincing answer.

'No that's right, you don't know do you? Well listen buster, I do - and it's not gonna happen.'

'But—' I tried again.

'But nothin.' All I am is a movie star. So what if the Studio find out I'm pregnant? They're gonna find out soon enough anyway. So what if they fire me or the fans turn against me? It ain't the end of the world. What's important is that this baby grows up with both its parents, with a mother and father in a happy loving home. That's all that matters - everything else is just bullshit and you know it as well as I do.'

I was stunned, as was Beau. Neither of us daring to say a word. Both of us knew Victoria too well and once she'd made her mind up there was no changing it. Of course, I would try, but ultimately it would be futile. She was prepared to take the fall for the sake of me and our baby. It was incredibly selfless and courageous, what she had to lose was immeasurable. Her fall from grace would cost her dearly; her career, her image, a large amount of her fortune and more importantly, her respect. The reputation, the star status, the world-wide acclaim and public adoration, all that would be gone almost before the newsprint was dry. She was prepared to risk it all for the chance of a real family.

*   *   *

It was awful. Far worse than either of us expected. The press were like savages and treated us - Victoria in particular, like scraps of meat they were fighting over. Even though we had braced ourselves for the glare of the spotlight, nothing could have prepared us for the media hysteria that greeted us on press day. The phone was ringing off the hook, and the cottage was under siege from hordes of reporters and photographers - all straining to for a glimpse of the movie star carrying the illegitimate baby.

As Beau suspected, the press weren't really interested in me, the fact that I was a stuntman and worked in Hollywood had some novelty value, but they didn't delve into my past. My photograph was all over the papers, but it didn't really look like me, very few people from the old days would recognise Sean Reilly beneath the sunglasses and baseball cap that I wore at all times, even in the house.

Soon, I was history and, as instructed by both Beau and Victoria, I slipped quietly into the background.

It was agreed, albeit very reluctantly, that I was to have no immediate contact with Victoria for at least six months, not until some of the furore had quietened down. All I could do was watch from a distance as the press devoured the woman I loved. They hounded her every movement and called her every name they could think of. Her picture was everywhere and the critics were having a field day. The fickle public, convinced by the media that she was everything they accused her to be, turned against her, and her latest movie was withdrawn from circulation due to poor audiences.

The Studio suspended her for two years without pay stating that she was in breach of her contract. Apparently, in the small-print, it said that she was not to become pregnant without their prior consent. Now that she had, her inability to work, and her unpopularity with the movie-going public was costing them money. They said she was lucky they didn't fire her.

She didn't feel lucky.

For nearly three months the attention was almost constant. Her weight plummeted and she found it difficult to sleep even though totally exhausted. On top of that she suffered severe bouts of morning sickness and was unable to hold anything down, which made her terribly weak. Because of the immense amount of stress and the lack of a good diet, her bowels very nearly ceased up and she was rushed into hospital after collapsing with severe stomach cramps. Fortunately, after a few days of bed rest, she recovered, but even in hospital she was not safe as the press set up camp in the grounds.

Louretta, as usual, was a rock and stayed with Victoria throughout the whole ordeal, as did Virgil, who put his own career on hold, and on the line, to show his support for her. No other stars, however, would dare even mention her name for fear of a backlash.

Beau offered encouragement via the phone as did I, but that felt utterly useless.

It was, without doubt, the most harrowing ordeal a person could live through, even the death of a loved one would pale in comparison to the trauma that Victoria suffered. But she was tough and she endured it.

Finally, a month after the baby was born, the media spotlight faded from her and she was at last left in peace. A month after that Beau told us it was safe for us to be together again.

*   *   *

All we wanted after that was privacy and security and a place where our child could grow up out of the media spotlight. With this in mind, Vicky and I moved back to Palm Springs with our daughter, Olivia, in the late January of 1967. We were married a month later in a secret ceremony. It was to be a fresh start, a new beginning, but the trauma of what Vicky had been through, and the months we had spent apart, had already damaged our relationship irrevocably, although it would be many years before either of us recognised it.

* * *

It was a miscalculation on Benny's part, phoning the tip through to the Los Angeles Citizen. He had not been aware that the paper was owned by Beauregarde Brewster nor that the media tycoon was Victoria Wild's godfather. As it was, he was only mildly disappointed that the press focused their attention on the movie star and not on her boyfriend but, nevertheless, he and Frank had enjoyed pouring over the papers each morning, devouring every snippet of delicious scandal with relish.

Benny had toyed with phoning another newspaper - one not associated with Brewster - to tell them exactly who the person was screwing the famous actress, but he had decided not to. There would be plenty of time to have some more fun with his Hollywood 'friends' in the future. In the meantime, he would just monitor events closely then, when the circumstances were right, he would strike again - but next time, he would cause much more pain.

PART THREE

One

Lovingly, I polished the Indian, which had become my Sunday morning ritual. The big motorcycle looked just as good as it had the day I'd bought it thanks to a complete restoration. It was now almost twenty years old and considered to be a classic. Even though the bike had not been used since the mid-sixties, at least not for anything other than the odd nostalgic trip down memory lane, I couldn't bring myself to sell it. It was a part of me and to be without it was unthinkable.

Helping me, as always, was Olivia, who liked tinkering about with the bike almost as much as I did, although she usually ended up covered in oil and grease. However, my daughter, with her elfin face, curly blonde hair and the prettiest, bluest eyes imaginable, was a tomboy who loved getting her hands dirty. Today though, we were in trouble. It was her fifth birthday and this afternoon we were celebrating with an enormous party. I had been specifically asked to keep her clean, but I had failed. She was now going to have to be bathed and scrubbed and brushed all over again. Also, at her mother's and grandmother's insistence, she was going have to wear a dress - just like a proper little girl. This did not fill her with delight, although the party with its three hundred guests, and the possibility of three hundred presents, certainly did.

The ranch had been decked out in streamers and bunting

and balloons. We had children's entertainers, games and organised events; there would be music, dancing, an all-day barbecue serving hot dogs and burgers - and even a mini fairground to keep the kids happy. Victoria and her mother had gone completely overboard with the preparations, but it was worth it.

I had bought the Bluestone Ranch back in sixty-eight with the profits I received from The Villa. It had previously been a horse breeding ranch, and was the one that Wildwood so often competed against in boxing tournaments, such as the one I fought in against Mighty Moses Brown.

Moses now worked for me. When I purchased the ranch, I gave all the hands the option to stay on, which, I'm pleased to say, most did. Even though the ranch was no longer used for breeding, we still had a number of fine animals, but these were stunt horses, like Jasper and the chestnut mare Brad Booker and I had used in our race over six years ago.

Brad and his wife Marilu also worked for me now, as did Rocky Costello and a number of other excellent stunt workers. Coincidentally, around the same time that I bought the ranch, the company we had all worked for went into liquidation. So, faced with the prospect of redundancy, I decided to form my own company called Bluestone Stunts. This, thanks to the backing of big stars such as Virgil, quickly managed to establish a successful niche for itself and by 1971 we had become the preferred stunt crew of most of the major studios.

Mighty Mo, now bigger and stronger than ever, was far better suited to the role I had given him than to that of labourer, which was his previous occupation. He was now permanent minder to my family as well as security chief for the whole ranch, over-seeing a twelve strong force who protected the Bluestone and those who lived there. This included Victoria, Olivia and my son, Josh.

When we discovered Vicky was pregnant again I was ecstatic

but my wife was less enthusiastic as she'd really been hoping to return to work as soon as possible. Needless to say, the studio's position was the same as before and Victoria was suspended for a further two years. The second suspension hit her hard, but she put on a brave face and threw herself once more into motherhood. Josh was born in March 1968.

Josh, now three, was a bright kid with a sunny personality and had the same curly blonde hair as his sister, although his eyes were just a shade darker than hers. Josh was fearless too and cried little; he'd already started riding, something which the whole crew adored him for, and because of this, they'd taken him on as an honourary stuntman. A position he positively relished.

It was Olivia's day however, so Josh had been ordered to be on his best behaviour.

My other son was at the ranch too, although Michael was still unaware that I was his father. As far as he was concerned, Ray and Ruby Reece were his parents. He had not once asked who his true father was, and regarded Sarah, the woman whom he knew to be his real mother, as little more than an annoying house guest who demanded too much of Ruby's attention. Michael himself had never tried to talk to Sarah or to be respectful of her, and had, on numerous occasions, said some very nasty, spiteful things about her to Ruby, even when his mother was in the same room. Things that, if by some chance Sarah had heard and understood, would have upset her terribly.

It was as if Michael didn't care. He had no interest in either Sarah, or whoever his biological father happened to be, they were simply not important to him. In his opinion, Sarah didn't even know he existed and his father had disappeared long before he was born, so why should he concern himself with them when they so obviously didn't give a damn about him?

This was my son's view and it hurt me deeply, but looking

from his perspective, I could see his point. He was almost nineteen now and I knew he deserved to know the truth, but I was afraid it may spoil the fragile bond which had formed between us over the last few years. Since I'd bought the Bluestone, he'd visited often - at least once a year, sometimes twice, and slowly I was building up the courage to tell him what I knew I must. But Michael had grown into an awkward, shy and quite introvert young man, which made it almost impossible to tell what he was thinking, so finding the right moment was tough.

His intelligence though was never in question, and, because he was so clever, Ruby had managed to get him into an excellent school. He'd rewarded her by finishing top in all of his classes, with his grades among the highest ever recorded in the school's long history. However, his social skills were not so great and his teachers expressed some concern about his obvious lack of friends. Nevertheless, friends or not, he'd won himself a university scholarship and was currently at Oxford, impressing his masters' there.

Furthermore, Michael was now quite a wealthy bachelor. The trust fund I'd set up for him, with the guidance of Louretta, had paid out when he'd hit eighteen, although he had been led to believe Ruby was to thank for this, not me. That's not to say Ruby hadn't provided for him herself, because she had. She'd invested the money I'd left for Michael wisely, and that too had matured on his eighteenth birthday. With his new found wealth, he'd bought a luxury apartment in Oxford and a trendy flat in Chelsea that he used at weekends, driving between the two in his brand new MGB sports car.

The money though he'd have given up in the blink of an eye, just to look just half normal. He was still very conscious of his crooked face and odd appearance which severely hampered his success with the opposite sex. At nearly nineteen, he was still a virgin and, so far, had not even kissed a girl.

The person he blamed for this, and for all his other problems, was Joe, and over the years his hatred of him had grown into something all consuming. One day, Michael promised himself, he would see his uncle suffer as badly as he had.

He felt the same way about Joe's off-spring, and resented Brett's presence at the Bluestone.

Even though I'd not seen Joe in almost six years, his son had visited us regularly. He would always accompany Ray and Ruby when they visited, but this time, for the first time ever, Michael was acting as his guardian, the two of them having made the trip alone. Michael regarded this as a chore and despised having to look after his uncle's brat, although, in truth, he had no intention of looking after him at all.

Fortunately, Brett Cassidy was not the sort of child who needed mollycoddling. At almost eight, Brett seemed far older than his years and was more than capable of taking care of himself. He was the image of his father in almost every way; dark hair, olive skin and the trademark black eyes that were destined to break the hearts of many women in future years.

He was an extremely bright boy, although not an academic. He hated school and was forever in some sort of trouble there, whether it be his fault or not. Brett was always to blame as far as his teachers were concerned. But Brett didn't mind, school wasn't really his thing anyway. He liked being at home with his dad, and although Joe would make a show of being angry with his son for getting sent home, he liked him there. The two of them were close, just like two peas in a pod.

Joe could have sent Brett to an expensive boarding school, given him the best education available, but he chose not to. He decided instead to send him to the local primary school in Peckham, where he would learn about real life. Not a privileged, pampered one, but one in which you had to earn respect and fight for what you wanted. Joe believed this was the way to turn his boy into a man, and so far, he'd not been disappointed.

In order to help with Brett's upbringing, after Rachel's death, Ruby and Ray had moved into The Castle. Ruby had even closed down her thriving business in order to care for the boy. Joe had given them the whole ground floor, which included a small apartment for Michael, and a light airy room with french windows and a sun terrace for Sarah. This room had an extra bed, just in case a nurse was ever needed to stay overnight, and various medical paraphernalia in readiness for any emergency.

Joe and Brett lived on the top floor, but shared the same kitchen and dining room as Ruby and Ray. The middle floor was strictly for company business. Joe's office was located there, as well as the board room, bar and snooker room. This was the headquarters of the Cassidy Firm and the central hub of Joe's business empire.

Although Joe and I hadn't seen each other since sixty-six, we had kept in constant contact, either by mail, Joe resuming his normal regime of writing at least one letter per month, or by phone. So we both knew exactly what the other was up to.

Whilst I had found total happiness, Joe had not. He was still haunted by Rachel's horrific death and the unforgettably graphic photo of her with Alvin Staedtler and his pals. In the picture she looked to be having a wild time and there could be no doubt that she was enjoying herself. Those fat, bloated middle-aged men certainly didn't appear to be forcing her to do anything against her will. So why was she doing it?

Obviously she had been a drug addict, the coroner had proved that, an alcoholic too - but why the sex? Was she so unhappy with Joe that she felt the need to go with other men - and if so, did they pay her?

Initially, Joe wasn't sure if he wanted to know but, in the end, he had become so enraged by his wife's duplicity, so consumed by the questions surrounding her whole existence, that he'd asked Ray to discreetly check out her mysterious past to see if any answers lay hidden there.

Sadly Ray had found it all too easy to piece together her rather sordid history. He had spoken with the family of the old man who Rachel had lived with in Kensington, also with the owner of the Soho boutique who had received her sexual attentions as payment for rent. Ray had even managed to locate the woman in Bethnal Green who Rachel had whored with for a while.

All Joe's fears became reality. He had been a blind fool.

At first, when he found out, he felt anger, disgust and loathing, tried to deny to himself that he'd ever loved her, resented Rachel for all the lies she told and the charade she enacted throughout their farcical marriage. He felt betrayed and desperately he wanted to hate her. But eventually, he realised that he couldn't. The truth was that he had loved her and believed that she had once loved him, even if only for a short while, and in the end, that was all that mattered.

If it wasn't for Rachel, he wouldn't have Brett, and for that he'd always be grateful.

*   *   *

At thirty-seven, Joe had achieved everything he'd set out to. He had influence, money and respect. His legitimate business interests were hugely profitable and his underworld activities were, by far, the most successful in London. But now he'd had enough of gangland. It had made him very rich and very powerful, but it was a dirty, nasty, way of life. It had helped to purge the raw, painful memories of Rachel's death and to exorcise the violence that had raged within him, but now he felt empty.

Also, gangland had changed. Now it was all about drugs. The

market for them had been growing for years, since the fifties even, but now they were big business and everybody wanted a piece of the action. But not Joe. He refused to get involved. He had seen first hand the damage they could cause and wanted no part of them. But others did, and no matter how powerful Joe's influence was, he couldn't fight it for ever. And didn't want to.

He was sick of it. Sick of seeing his face in the papers and of his name being associated with all things dishonest - even the drug related crimes which were nothing to do with him. And he was concerned for his son. What kind of example was he setting Brett?

He was number one, of that there was no question and he had taken good care of those who had cared for him. Ruby, Ray and Alfie, also Peggy Reece, Vinnie's widow; none of them would ever want for anything again. He had done a good job, an exceptional one, but now it was time to get out. It was time to pass the reigns over to those who still had the stomach for it. Richie and Manno would be the ideal choice and he knew they were up for it.

The only question was, would he be able to just simply walk away? This was something he had pondered many times, particularly when he thought of the enemies he'd made along the way. Would they allow him to quit? Only time would tell.

*   *   *

After a workout and a sauna, Joe showered and put on a robe. He then went to his study, poured himself a large glass of Brandy and sat down in his favourite chair. He missed his son. Looking at his watch, Joe made a note of the time difference, then picked up the phone and dialled the number of the Bluestone.

Although they'd never met, Joe phoned Olivia every year on her birthday. He always sent her an enormous gift and ever since she was able to talk, she had insisted on speaking to 'Uncle' Joe. It had become something of a birthday ritual.

After a long conversation, in which Olivia described her

whole day, Joe was then put on to Brett. The two of them spoke to each other more like good friends than as father and son. Brett preferring to call Joe 'Pop' rather than Dad, something which he picked up in America on an earlier visit, but Joe didn't mind. When they had finished speaking, the phone was given to me. My friend and I talked for a while, but he wasn't his normal self, he seemed melancholy, maybe even depressed and I sensed that he might be lonely. However, when I asked him about this he said he was 'fine', although he didn't sound too convincing.

Eventually, we said our goodbyes and hung up. I went back outside to find my kids, but I couldn't help feeling a little troubled by my friend's manner.

Joe, meanwhile, poured himself another brandy and sat back in his chair. What I had said had made him think. Perhaps he was lonely. Sure he had Brett and Ray and Ruby, they were almost constantly with him. But he didn't have anyone he could be intimate with. He hadn't since Rachel and before that, since Rose.

He closed his eyes and not for the first time in recent months, thought about the woman he had loved almost twenty years ago, 'I wonder whatever happened to Rose?' He said out loud in a tired, world weary voice, just before he fell asleep.

Two

There was four of them. All in their mid-twenties, all drunk, all leering lecherously at her chest. But she was used to this. Working behind the bar of a busy pub meant attention of that kind came with the job.

'Show us yer tits sweetheart!' One of them shouted as she poured a pint.

'Not tonight luv, I'm a bit busy,' she quipped, well used to dealing with idiots.

She bent down to grab a packet of crisps for another customer from the box on floor, 'Nice arse, Darlin'' another of the drunks shouted as he admired her rear end in the tight fitting jeans.

'Yeah, I wouldn't mind sinkin' me teeth into that,' agreed the leader of the group, 'Or even me cock for that matter!' He added loudly, to much raucous laughter from his pals.

'Have a good look,' she replied, 'Cos it's as close as you'll ever get!'

His friends sniggered at the comment, 'She had you there, Daz!'

'Yeah,' Daryll said under his breath, 'Well we'll see about that, won't we?'

Rose Mason had worked at the Fiddle and Flute, her aunt and uncle's pub in Northamptonshire, for nearly eighteen years.

She had fled there from London aged just eighteen - and pregnant. Her relatives had taken her in without question or judgement and given her a new life and a loving home. Sadly her aunt passed away in '63, and Rose had taken over from her as landlady. When her uncle died four years afterwards, she was left the pub in his will and had been running it successfully ever since.

Owning a pub was not the career she had planned on, especially because as a young girl she had been so shy, but serving pints and dealing with drunken punters had soon cured her of that. Now she couldn't imagine doing anything else.

Rose looked nowhere near her thirty-seven years. She had no lines or wrinkles and not a trace of grey in her long auburn hair. Her body was still firm and curvaceous - even more desirable now, in fact, than it had been as a teenager. Her legs were long and slim and looked fabulous in the skin tight denims she always wore, especially when accompanied by the brown suede boots that she'd chosen to wear with them on that particular evening. On her top half was a figure hugging white tee shirt with a big yellow 'smiley' face printed on the front. Casual, but as usual, very sexy.

The four drunks were getting louder and louder and Rose was pleased it was nearly closing time so that she might finally be rid of them. She could take so much, gladly have a laugh with anyone, but when it started to get a little too personal, as it had with those four, it made her angry.

After she'd rung the bell for last orders and served those who were desperate for one last drink, including Daryll and his cronies, Rose walked around the other side of the bar and began to collect glasses. She had let her bar maid leave a bit earlier because her boyfriend was home from the army, which meant Rose was left alone to clean and lock up. Normally this wouldn't have bothered her, but on this night, she was eager for everyone to leave as Daryll and his buddies were giving her the creeps.

Whilst her customers supped up their beer, she busied herself collecting glasses and emptying ashtrays, then, as the pub slowly cleared, she began putting chairs on the tables, so she could vacuum the carpet first thing in the morning. Suddenly, she felt a hand grab her backside and thick fingers slide between her legs. Like lightning she span around to see the grinning face of Daryll and his slobbering friends. Without thinking twice, Rose slapped Daryll hard around the face, wiping the smile completely off and leaving a big red hand print in its place.

'That's it, you filthy creep!' She spat, 'Get out and don't ever come back!'

Daryll automatically made his hand into a fist and very nearly threw a punch, just managing to stop himself at the very last moment. 'Well now,' he said, 'Aren't you the little bitch.'

'That's right, I am. I'm also the owner and if you don't want me to call the police you'll get lost now!'

Daryll thought about making another clever remark, perhaps even daring her to phone the police and calling her bluff but thought better of it. 'Okay, darlin,' we'll go,' he said, 'But we ain't finished with you yet.'

'Yeah, yeah. If you say so,' Rose replied bravely but feeling more than a little intimidated.

'Oh, I do say so. In fact you can count on it.' He then laughed, 'Come on boys, let's leave this prick teaser alone.'

As they walked towards the door, Daryll gave Rose a little wink and said, 'See you soon, darlin.'

*   *   *

After they left the pub, along with the remainder of the other customers, Rose hastily ran over and bolted the door behind them, immediately feeling safer once it was locked. Then, working as quickly as possible, she tidied up, washed all the glasses and filled two big bins with rubbish. It was midnight, by the time she eventually finished. All that remained for her to do was to take the bins out to the yard, lock the back door and go upstairs to bed. It had been a long night and she was exhausted.

She opened the door and tottered up the few concrete steps that led to the back yard. The dustbins were always left at the far corner, just in case the smell from them wafted down to the kitchens, which were situated at the rear of the pub. It was only a short distance, but late at night it always made her nervous and after Daryll's attentions she was more uneasy than usual.

It was a cold, crisp night and she felt her nipples spring out in protest to the frosty air, making two horn like bumps on the smiley face of her tee shirt.

Rose put down the bins and span on her high heels, eager to get back inside, but the moment she turned round she saw Daryll. He was standing just in front of her, barring her way. One of his pals closed the back door, clumsily smashing one of the empty milk bottles that stood beside it on the ground. Another mate stood at the bottom of the steps and the last one was to her right, about the same distance away as Daryll. All had the same lustful expression on their faces. Rose was in trouble. Big trouble, and she knew it.

Daryll looked admiringly at her breasts, immediately noticing her erect nipples, 'Well now,' he said, 'Either you're pleased to see me, or you've dropped a couple of peanuts down your top!'

'I'll scream' Rose said boldly, 'Lay a finger on me and I promise you, I'll scream my bloody head off.'

'Oh, you'll scream alright darlin,' but it'll be with pleasure, when I'm shagging you.'

'You sick bastard,' was all Rose could think to say, the tears welling up behind her eyes, panic starting to take over.

'You say that now, but afterwards you'll be wonderin' how you ever lived without me. Well actually without all of us - I mean, why just have one when you can have us all?' Daryll smiled and looked across at the man closest to him. 'Andy, if you'll do the honours.'

Andy made a grab for Rose and she managed to let out only a short scream before his hand covered her mouth. She struggled furiously, but Andy held her tightly and quickly Daryll's other two mates, Ash and Spencer, came to help him out. Within seconds Rose could hardly move.

Daryll walked slowly up to her and grabbed her breasts with his big hands, squeezing them hard and pinching her erect nipples between thumb and forefinger, making her whimper. He ripped her shirt up and admired her red silky bra gleefully before yanking it down, 'Let's 'ave a look at those fabulous tits of yours, shall we?' As her breasts flopped out he took a firm handful, 'Not bad,' he said, 'not bad at all.' He bent and licked them with his wet tongue, his rough, unshaven chin scratching her soft flesh. 'Mmm,' he said with delight, 'She tastes good, boys.' Daryll then reached down and snapped open the button of Rose's jeans. She involuntarily flinched as he smoothly slid down the zip to reveal the red silk of her knickers. 'Wow, matching underwear. Just what I like to see - an' my favourite colour too!' His voice was gruff and thick and filled with lust as he tugged the jeans down to her knees, then he stepped back and undid his own trousers. He slid them down to show a pair of cream Y-fronts, his obvious arousal forming an unimpressive pyramid at the front.

'Hold her tight boys,' he growled.

Rose was almost paralysed with fear, powerless to prevent what was about to happen.

* * *

The handsome young man slowed his motorbike to a halt, turned the engine off and put the perfectly tuned Triumph Bonneville onto its kick-stand. He then slid his leg over the tank, stood up and helped his girlfriend off the pillion. 'How about

384

asking me in for a coffee?' He said, his voice full of assured charm.

The girl smiled. He truly was irresistible, but her parents were still up. She gave him a long seductive kiss, 'Not tonight' she jerked a thumb to the downstairs lights of her home, 'They're still watching telly - but if you fancy chatting to them I'm sure they won't mind.' She giggled, knowing exactly what sort of reaction she'd get from her boyfriend.

'Nah, I think I'll pass, Suzie. It is getting late after all.' He smiled at her, and she playfully thumped him in the stomach as he pulled her to him and kissed her again.

They had been going out for eight months and were clearly made for each other. Suzie could have been a model; slim, curvy and blonde with perfect bone structure, whereas he was like a rock star with long, shoulder length hair, carefully sculpted side burns and finely chiselled features. His looks were inherited from his mother, yet his eyes were dark, very nearly black, just like his father's - although Matt Mason did not know this, as he'd never met the man.

Matt was incredibly stylish and naturally cool, in flared hipster jeans and a suede bomber jacket. At almost twenty, he was probably the hottest guy in town; envied by the guys and lusted over by the girls.

He had left school with excellent exam results and now attended the local technical college studying mechanical engineering. On free afternoons and at weekends he worked at a garage, helping to fix cars, for which he had a natural talent. As for his long term career plans, he was keeping his options open.

He had taken up karate in his early teens, mainly for fitness but also, because he was the only man of the house, as a way of protecting his mother. He had become very good and had become a black belt at just seventeen. Because of the rigorous training he was also very fit; his body lean and hard.

Rose had never actually told Matt who his father was, but had always described him as an extremely honourable and good man who, through no fault his own, had been unable to be a part of Matt's life. She would say no more than that, even when pressed, which made her son even more eager to one day meet the man of whom she so glowingly spoke.

Matt gave Suzie one last kiss, then kicked his bike into life and roared off into the cold, clear night. It was almost midnight and he had college the next morning.

A few minutes later he came to a halt on the forecourt at the front of the Fiddle and Flute and, as he turned off the engine and put the Triumph on its stand, he heard the church clock chiming twelve. 'Time I was in bed,' he said to himself. However, as he approached the narrow alley that led to the back yard, he heard the sound of breaking glass, then he heard voices, but couldn't make out what they were saying. Suddenly someone let out a short scream and Matt knew instantly that his mother was in trouble. Quickly he sprinted down the alley and burst into the yard. As he took in the scene, he charged forward with gritted teeth and a blood curdling growl.

* * *

As Daryll slowly slid down his revolting piss stained underpants he smiled at his friends, Andy, Ash and Spencer; all of them positively drooling with expectation. But as he looked back at Rose, he caught a flash of horror in Andy's eyes and almost immediately, heard the inhuman growl.

He turned in time to see Matt flying through the air, one leg extended in front of him and the heel of his shoe crashing into Andy's face. Andy dropped like a stone before Daryll could even move.

Landing lightly as a cat, Matt took out Ash and Spencer with two lightning punches.

Daryll, hurriedly pulling his trousers up, tried to make a run for it, but Matt was too fast. Spinning around, he whipped his right leg backwards and up, his powerful body perfectly balanced as his heel made contact with Daryll's chin. The kick was so forceful that Daryll was launched off his feet and propelled backwards through the air until he smacked hard against the back wall of the yard, his head crunching against the brickwork. After he crashed to the ground his body went limp.

Matt ran to his mother's side. 'Mum, are you alright?'

Rose, hurriedly straightening her clothing, looked up at her son, her gratitude clearly visible, 'Yes. I'm fine,' she croaked, before breaking down in tears.

'It's okay Mum, everything's gonna be okay.' Matt put a comforting arm around her and let her cry.

Slowly, Rose's attackers started to regain consciousness, all, that is, except one. They were groggy and weary and suddenly very guilty.

'Get out of here, you bastards!' Matt shouted, his arm still protectively wrapped around his mother's shoulders, 'And if you ever come back 'ere again, I'll bloody kill you!'

None of them dared argue, but as they turned to walk away, Matt called after them, 'Don't forget this one!' He pointed at Daryll, who still hadn't moved.

The other three were already at the entrance to the alley. 'Fuck 'im!' Andy shouted back, 'This is all his fault - he can come when he's ready.' And with that, they disappeared.

Matt made certain Rose was okay, then walked over to where Daryll lay.

'Right, c'mon. Get up an' piss off.' Matt nudged the man in the ribs with his foot, but there was no response. 'C'mon arsehole, move!' Still nothing.

Matt bent over and tapped Daryll on the cheek with the

palm of his hand. 'Get up, c'mon!' Suddenly, Matt felt sick as he noticed the awkward angle at which the man's head lay and the utter stillness of his body. And as cold fear filled his belly, the awful truth struck him; Daryll's neck was broken. 'Oh, Jesus,' Matt said as he fell to his knees. Desperately he put an ear to the man's mouth and a hand on his chest, searching for any sign of life. 'Oh Jesus Christ, no!'

'What's the matter?' Rose asked, concerned.

'It's this bloke Mum. He's..., I mean, I think he's—'

'What Matt? What's wrong?' The alarm bells were starting to ring inside Rose's head.

'He's dead, Mum. He's bloody dead.' The tears were already in Matt's eyes as the realisation of what he'd done began to sink in.

'What the hell am I going to do?' He asked, hoping desperately that his mother had the answer.

'I don't know son. I just don't know,' she replied. But already her mind was ticking, somewhere in the back of her brain, the answer was screaming at her.

Three

The phone had been ringing for some time before it woke him. It was almost one thirty in the morning, normally a time when Joe would still be working, but he'd actually managed to get an early night for a change and had been in bed since eleven.

'Yeah?' Joe answered groggily, knowing it was Ray calling his extension.

'Sorry boss, I know you were asleep.'

'I was, but I'm awake now. What is it?' He was obviously annoyed.

'There's a woman on the phone. Says you know her, says she's in trouble and that it's important.'

'Tell her to call back in the morning,' Joe was less than sympathetic, 'Tell her this isn't the bloody Samaritans!' He looked at the clock by his bedside, 'Christ almighty, has she got any idea what the bleedin' time is?'

'I know, but she sounds really desperate,' Ray was not one to over dramatise things.

'Look. It's late. I'm tired and it's half one in the morning. Tell her that whatever it is, there's nothing that I can do about it tonight.'

'Okay, boss. Whatever you say.'

Ray was just about to put down the receiver, when Joe

stopped him.

'Hold on a minute,' he said.

'Yeah?'

'What's her name?'

'Rose,' Ray replied, 'Rose Mason.'

* * *

Just over two hours later, Joe, Ray, Richie and Manno were in the middle of Northamptonshire, sitting in the kitchen of the Fiddle and Flute, drinking steaming hot coffee.

Rose was sitting opposite Joe, staring into the face of the man she'd never stopped loving. For her, there had never been anyone else. It always had, and always would be, Joe Cassidy.

He had changed little in twenty years. He'd filled out a bit perhaps, and had a few crow's feet around the eyes, maybe just the slightest hint of grey hair, but nothing drastic. The only things that were notably different were his clothes, which were now impeccably cut and made of the finest materials - probably costing more than Rose made in a year.

On the phone, scared and panicked, Rose had just blurted everything out. It had taken her less than two minutes to tell Joe what she'd been meaning to say to him since a month after he went to prison.

Upon discovering she was pregnant, she left London to start a new life in Northamptonshire. She did this, she said, to protect Joe, fearing that if he found out about the baby the news would destroy him. If he could not be with his child, she thought, he would surely lose the will to live. By the time she realised that it would have given him the reason to live, it was too late. Too much time had passed and it was impossible to turn back the clock.

She told him then about Matt, his son, not all about him, just the important things, like how much she loved him and what a good lad he was; that he wasn't a trouble maker or a bully, but a responsible, hard working lad who kept himself to himself. She said that if Matt hadn't been protecting her, none of this would've happened. Finally she told Joe about Daryll; about how Matt had accidentally killed him and how they had dragged his body into the shed, where no one could see it.

Rose was thinking clearly enough to realise that Daryll probably wouldn't be missed until daybreak at the earliest, but after that, it was anybody's guess. She begged Joe for his help, certain that he would know what to do. His was the first name she had thought of, he was the most reliable person she knew. He was Matt's father.

What she didn't say was that Matt was unwittingly following in Joe's footsteps, it was history repeating itself and it was breaking her heart all over again. She couldn't bear for her son to go to prison too.

Joe was still reeling from the shock, his emotions running the full gamut of anger, surprise and happiness. However, there had been no need for Rose to beg. All she needed to have said was, 'It's Rose, I need help,' and he'd have been there in a heartbeat. No questions asked.

*   *   *

Whilst Joe, Rose and the rest of them were in the kitchen drinking coffee, discussing what to do, Matt sat in the bar alone. He was deep in thought, trying to come to terms with what he'd done. He knew it was self-defence and that if he hadn't acted as he had, his mother would have been raped. That ultimately, he was in the right, but somehow, it didn't seem to help.

He also knew who the man in the kitchen was, although Rose hadn't actually said as much. But he knew. He felt it, and he wasn't sure how he was supposed to react. Nothing about this night made sense. The only thing he knew for certain was that a man was dead and as a result, his own life had changed forever.

In the kitchen, Joe nodded to Ray, Richie and Manno, signalling that it was time to put the plan they had conceived into action. Obediently, they left through the back door leaving Joe and Rose alone.

Joe waited for the door to close, then turned to Rose and said sincerely, 'I wish you'd told me about the baby.'

'I know. I'm sorry' came the equally earnest reply.

'My life—' Joe paused to re-phrase, 'Our lives—' he looked directly into her face, '—could have been so different. If only I'd known.'

Rose placed a hand over his, 'Please believe me. There's been so many times I've wanted to tell you. Countless times that I've picked up the phone and dialled your number, but put the receiver down before it started to ring. Once though, I did let it ring, but a woman answered, so I pretended to have the wrong number. Another time, I actually came up to London with the sole purpose of telling you, I waited across the road from your house for ages, trying to build up the courage to face you. Finally though, the front door opened and I watched from a distance as you appeared. You looked so handsome, and for a second my legs turned to jelly and I nearly lost my resolve,' she paused and smiled at her own silliness, 'But I kept my nerve and walked forward. Just as I reached the curb though, a beautiful woman pushing a pram followed you out, and you smiled at her, the way you used to smile at me. You were obviously so happy so content, I just couldn't spoil it for you.'

Joe smiled his understanding, 'It was my wife you saw.'

'Yes.'

'You're right, I was happy. But that was a long time ago, things change.'

'Yes.'

'My wife... she—'

'Yes. I know, I saw it in the newspaper. I sent flowers, although

I left the card blank.' Rose placed her other hand on Joe's forearm, sensing his pain, 'It must have been a tough time for you.'

'It was, but I had Brett, my son, and together we got through it.'

'I understand. It's the same with Matthew and me. We look after each other.' Rose realised the truth of her last statement and how relevant it was to what had occurred that night and suddenly she began to weep as the horror of it all flooded back.

'Don't cry Rose, it'll be okay, I promise you,' Joe was deadly serious, 'Matthew's my son too, I know that now and I'll make sure he's safe, don't worry. I guarantee, no harm will come to either him or you.'

Joe put a finger under Rose's chin and lifted her head up so he could see into her lovely tear-filled brown eyes. 'You have my word,' he said and Rose managed a slight smile. She knew his word was stronger than oak.

*　　*　　*

With Daryll's body in the boot of the car, Ray pulled into a lay by next to a railway embankment on the outskirts of town. Then, making certain that they were not seen, he, Richie and Manno carried the body from the car and hoisted it over the wooden fence that separated the grass verge at the side of the road from the steep incline of the embankment. 'After three,' Ray whispered, as they all took a firm grip and began to swing the corpse to the count. 'One, two, three...'

As they let go, the body sailed over the barrier, then hit the long grass on the opposite side with a heavy thud and began to roll. Down it went, picking up speed by the second, bouncing and spinning in an ungainly manner until it at last came to rest half way across the railway track, Daryll's head laying face down between two sleepers. It stayed that way until the train came along some fifteen minutes later, severing it completely from the body with devastating force.

Hopefully, it would be seen by the police as death by misadventure, just a drunken accident with nobody else involved.

After watching the train pass by, Ray and the others climbed back into the car and headed back to town. Behind them, the horizon was already starting to glow with orange and the first strains of the dawn chorus were beginning.

*   *   *

The door that led from the kitchen to the bar opened and Matt looked up to see the tall dark haired man silhouetted in the opening.

'May I come in?' Joe asked.

Matt shrugged his shoulders, 'Sure.'

Joe walked slowly over and sat down beside his son. This handsome, unassuming young man who, until today, he didn't know existed. He was so like his mother; high sculptured cheek bones, perfectly carved nose and full sensitive lips. His teeth were white and his jaw was firm. But his eyes were all Cassidy. Joe looked at him with undisguised pride. 'You okay?' He said.

'Oh yeah, I'm just great,' Matt replied sarcastically, his emotions temporarily getting the better of him. However, almost immediately, he realised how selfish he sounded. He had no intention of being disrespectful as he was well aware of the trouble he'd put this man to. It was also a testament to Joe's feelings for Rose that he'd dropped everything to help her.

Matt had recognised Joe instantly, from the very moment he'd stepped out of the car. He had seen his face in the newspapers many times, the accompanying story usually associated with some illegal activity. The Godfather of Gangland was how they always referred to him. Although whenever Rose had seen any of these stories, she had always dismissed them as 'rubbish,' saying that it was just 'malicious gossip' or 'pure coincidence,' more often than not describing them as 'downright slanderous.'

On one particular occasion, when a large photograph was printed on the front page of the Daily Express, of the man attending his wife's funeral, holding a little boy in his arms, Matt had witnessed his mother crying silently to herself as she read the article.

When Rose had made the phone call just a few hours earlier, saying she knew of only one person who could help them, Matt had instinctively known to whom she was referring. Furthermore, when his car pulled up and Joe got out, Matt was anything but surprised, he had expected it.

Guiltily, Matt apologised for his surly behaviour, 'Sorry, it's been a long night. I suppose I'm doing okay - under the circumstances.'

'That's good, I know what you must be going through, but we need to talk.'

'I know.'

'Do you know who I am?'

'Yes, I do,' Matt said without hesitation. He turned, and for the first time looked into Joe's face, 'You're my father.'

Joe placed a hand on Matt's shoulder and said, 'That's right son, I am and we're gonna get through this problem together.

*   *   *

Matt and Joe talked for quite some time, Rose hovering near the door, just in case she was needed, but after twenty minutes, the two men were still in deep conversation with not so much as a hint of a raised voice. Rose began to feel a little easier as she had desperately hoped they would get along and, so far, it was looking hopeful, which is more than could be said for her future at the Fiddle and Flute.

Joe had already told her that it would be best if she and Matt disappeared for a while, until they could be sure that Matt wouldn't be implicated in Daryll's death and Rose was in complete agreement. With all that had happened that night, the pub had suddenly lost its appeal and Rose would be glad to get away from it.

After almost an hour, Joe and Matt wandered back into the kitchen. Ray, Richie and Manno had all returned and were drinking more coffee. Joe stood in the centre of the room and said, 'Boys, I want you to meet Matt,' the three men all nodded their acknowledgement, before Joe added, 'Take care of him, he's my son.'

Ray very nearly choked on his coffee, whilst the other two just stared open mouthed in amazement.

Joe then turned to Rose and Matt and told each of them to pack a bag.

At eight-thirty Matt rode off on his motorbike to Suzie's. By nine-thirty he had returned with her on the pillion clutching a small suitcase. Her parents were already at work, but she'd phone later and let them know she was safe and that she'd be back in a few weeks to finish off her college course work. They would understand.

* * *

Ten minutes into the drive back to London, with Matt and Suzie following behind on the Triumph, Rose said to Joe 'I wonder how Sean is doing? I'd love to see him again.'

Joe just smiled and said, 'You'll find out real soon, because that's who you, Matt and Suzie are gonna be staying with for the next few weeks.'

* * *

From that lunchtime, The Fiddle and Flute would be run by a temporary landlord; a certain Mr. Alfred J. Noakes, who would eliminate any potential repercussions from Andy, Ash and Spencer.

Four

Joe, his spirits now soaring, was completely re-invigorated, his life suddenly flush with new meaning and fresh opportunities. Eager to make the most of these and to spend more time with Rose and Matt, Joe accompanied them, along with Suzie, to America. To the Bluestone, where he would have the daunting task of introducing Brett to his newly discovered sibling. When the time came, however, it went much better than Joe had hoped, with Brett actually quite excited by the prospect of having an older brother, especially one as cool as Matt. Joe had taken Brett for a long walk to explain everything fully, making certain that he understood that Matt's arrival did not effect their relationship in any way. Although he need not have worried as the thought never even entered Brett's head.

After a short time alone, Joe and Brett returned to the ranch house, where the rest of us were slowly getting to know each other, all of us that is, except for Michael.

Upon hearing who Matt was, Michael stomped off to his bedroom and began throwing things into his suitcase. For him, one Cassidy son was enough, but two and the father was far more than he could take. To get away from it he decided to borrow a car and take a trip out to Vegas. He'd stay at The Villa for a couple of weeks until the excitement of Rose and Matt's arrival had died down. Come back when their sickening celebrity status had waned.

*   *   *

I envied Joe and his new acquaintance with Matt. I saw immediately the potential they had for forming a good strong relationship and knew that my hopes for a similar outcome with Michael were all but lost. He certainly didn't need me and, with his departure on that afternoon, it finally sank in.

*   *   *

Two days later Michael was sitting on a sun-lounger by one of the huge pools at the Villa Continental sipping an ice cold glass of lemonade. He wore a lime green pair of swimming trunks that did little to complement his fair skin, which under the intense heat of the desert sun was already beginning to redden. He'd been sitting there for less than half an hour but had noticed the girl almost immediately and had been surreptitiously staring at her from behind his black plastic sunglasses ever since. He thought he was being very subtle, very discreet and was confident that she hadn't noticed his attentions, but he was mistaken. She had felt his eyes boring into her, could sense his desire and for the last twenty minutes had been deliberately playing to a captive audience.

Moira Simmons was only just fifteen but looked much older. She had a body to die for and a face to match, with glossy red lips and sparkling green eyes. Wearing the skimpiest of string bikinis that showed off her plump breasts and pert round behind to perfection, she pranced around the pool on her long tanned legs positively sizzling with sex appeal. And knew it. She knew too that she could have any man she wanted and the service she gave was very skilled and highly practiced.

However, sleeping with Moira was not only memorable but also very expensive, as her many lovers had all discovered to their cost. After sex, she would always drop the age bombshell. Informing them that rather than her being the eighteen year old nymphet that they had believed, she was actually still only a minor and if they didn't give her a little cash to keep her quiet she wouldn't hesitate in crying rape.

Unfortunately, Moira's God fearing parents were oblivious to her ample charms and vampish ways which she had learned to use long ago to get what she wanted. And what she wanted, more than anything, was money. She had the ability to smell it a mile away and Michael was giving off a decidedly wealthy aroma. Every so often, Moira would glance over at him, making certain that his focus was still on her, although as soon as she made eye contact he would look away quickly, hoping she hadn't noticed his voyeurism.

She cavorted noisily in the pool with her six year-old brother, using him to gain as much attention as possible. Purposely jumping up and down to make her tits bounce and her ass wobble. Occasionally she would wipe herself down, letting her hands linger over her perfectly tanned curves, enjoying the reaction of those watching from behind their sun specs, each of them squirming uncomfortably on their sunbeds.

But it was Michael who Moira wanted, not because of his looks, which repulsed her, but because of the things that separated him from the other lechers on the sun deck. Things like his Cartier watch, Gucci sunglasses and Yves Saint Laurent swim shorts. Quite by chance she had also seen Michael arrive at the Villa in a sparkling new Porche convertible, another sure sign that this boy, ugly as was, had money. His looks instinctively told her that he would be inexperienced with the opposite sex, and therefore an easy target. Few women would have the stomach for him even with the lure of the money, but Moira was not so fussy, and when at last the Simmons family left the pool area, she gave Michael a long meaningful stare that even the most stupid of men would have interpreted. This time he held her gaze and slowly it dawned that this goddess was actually interested in him. She was blatantly declaring it, there could be no mistake and he felt his manhood stir in anticipation of the delights that her wondrous body promised. As if to clarify this, Moira winked at him seductively, then slowly turned and walked away.

Michael was elated, for the first time in his life, a girl had seen beyond his damaged exterior and recognised him for what he truly was: a normal, heterosexual, young man. So flattered, so delighted was he that the thought that she might only be concerned with the contents of his wallet did not even enter his head.

*　*　*

Over the years, Michael and Carl had become close, having developed an easy friendship that started in the early days, long before Napier's departure for Vegas. Since then, each had allowed the other to learn a little of their feelings toward Joe and, because of their mutual dislike for him, had become even closer.

Until Benny Mottola's visit to Vegas, Carl had not known who Michael's father was. However, since discovering the truth, Napier had, on many occasions, toyed with telling the boy although, as yet, he'd resisted the urge. His grievance, after all, was not with Michael's father but with Joe and until such time as Carl could see a specific benefit in revealing this closely guarded secret, he had decided to keep it to himself. He could see no point in causing Michael any unnecessary suffering so in the meantime set about making his visits to The Villa enjoyable.

*　*　*

Carl, seeing his friend by the pool, walked over to the bar and grabbed two cold Buds. Michael was again laying on a sun lounger, hoping to catch another glimpse of the gorgeous girl he'd seen the day before but, as yet, there was no sign of her. 'Thought you could do with a drink,' Carl said as he sat down on the bed next to Michael's.

'Oh, yes, thanks,' Michael replied, his accent no longer that of a Londoner thanks to his public school education.

'See anything you like?' Carl gestured to the assorted array of women, all of different ages, dotted around the sun deck.

'Haven't really been looking.'

'Yeah, sure you haven't.'

'Honest Carl, I really haven't—' As the words left Michael's mouth, Moira Simmons walked by and smiled. He just stopped and stared, completely oblivious now to Carl's presence.

This time Moira was all alone. She chose a bed just four away from Michael's, and quickly slipped off her tee shirt and incredibly short denim cut-offs, revealing yet another skimpy bikini.

Michael couldn't help but watch as she began to slowly oil her body with sun-tan lotion; his crooked mouth very nearly dribbling saliva from its lower lip. Napier grinned, immediately reading the situation, he understood exactly what was going through both Michael's and the girl's minds. He recognised Moira straight away for the gold-digging temptress that she was, but he was not too concerned as he thought Michael deserved a bit of fun.

Carl stood up, glanced at the white gold and platinum watch that Louretta and Joe had presented to him six years before, its pearlised oyster face gleaming in the sunlight, then, in a voice loud enough for Moira to hear, he said, 'It's no good, Michael. I can't stay here gassing with you, I've got a hotel to run, but help yourself to drinks. Have whatever you want - it's all on the house.'

'Thanks Carl,' his young friend replied, but his focus was elsewhere.

'No problem. I'll see you later.' Then before he walked away, Carl bent down and whispered in Michael's ear, 'Have fun, but be careful - she's jail bait.'

Michael nodded but hadn't heard, he was so focussed on Moira.

A few seconds after Carl left, Moira looked up and saw

Michael staring and he quickly looked away but it was too late. He'd been caught red-handed. Moira smiled; it was going to be like taking candy from a baby. 'Excuse me,' she said in a sweet voice.

Michael peered at her out the corner of his eye to see that she was addressing him. 'Y- yes?' He replied nervously.

'Hi,' she smiled seductively, 'Would you mind rubbing some oil onto my back?'

'P-pardon?' Michael couldn't believe his ears.

'Would you mind rubbing this on me?' Moira's posture in the string bikini was purposely provocative as she held up the bottle of oil and the twinkle in her eyes was positively obscene.

'Er - yeah - I mean no, I mean - sure. I'd be happy to.' His face turned crimson with embarrassment, knowing that she must have thought him to be some sort of idiot.

Michael stood up and walked over to where she lay, Moira spotting instantly the growing bulge in his shorts. She smiled to herself; already she had him. Close-up, his face was uglier than she had initially thought, but she ignored that and focused on the money, that was all that mattered, nothing else was important.

She handed Michael the sun oil and rolled over onto her stomach, 'Put as much on as you like,' she instructed.

'Okay,' he replied, perching his bottom on the side of her bed.

He poured a liberal amount of the lotion onto her deeply tanned shoulders and slowly began to rub it in, his fingers and palms caressing her soft skin as they smoothed in the oil.

'Mmm, that feels so good, your hands are so strong, yet so sensitive,' Moira cooed.

Gradually, Michael moved his hands down until they encountered the string that fastened her bikini top and momentarily he paused. 'Undo it if you like, I don't mind' she invited.

Slowly, with his fingers trembling nervously, he pulled at the bow that held her top on and easily, without any protest, it fell open allowing Michael to see the side of one of her white untanned breasts, the garment having hidden it from the sun. Desperately he wished he could see it all, but it was concealed by the sun bed.

'By the way,' she said, 'What's your name?'

'Michael,' he replied, his voice barely a whisper, his eyes still on the pale breast that was pressed almost flat against the bed. Then, as if in answer to his wish, Moira lifted herself up and twisted around allowing him a clear view of both her perfect breasts, the small brown nipples hard with excitement. She smiled intoxicatingly as she took his hand and shook it, 'Hi, Mike. I'm Moira.'

Michael was normally irritated by the shortening of his name but in this instance he couldn't have cared less as he was too busy gazing at the glorious sight of her bosoms. He knew it was wrong but he couldn't help himself. Moira smiled again, this time wickedly and as she spoke her voice was heavy with sexual intent, 'Tut, tut, tut, you naughty boy, I know what you're thinking.' She looked around furtively to make sure they were unobserved, then, still holding his hand she guided it down and rubbed it over both her breasts, her erect nipples passing between his greasy fingers, making them glisten with oil. She held his hand there for a few moments longer, then carefully removed it and placed it down on his lap.

'If you're good, we can have some fun later, would you like that?' She asked, already knowing the answer. Michael could barely manage a nod, the bulge in his shorts now threatening to burst through the fabric. 'Well okay then,' Moira continued, 'But for now, why don't you go get us both a drink?'

* * *

By the time they got back to Michael's suite they were both pretty drunk - even though neither of them were old enough to drink alcohol in the States. Fortunately though, thanks to Michael being Carl's special guest, they didn't have to worry about that as they staggered into the room and fell onto the soft cushions of the luxurious sofa giggling wildly.

Michael lay on his back and Moira sat astride him, purposely positioning herself where she could feel his excitement through her skimpy shorts.

'Well now, somebody's woken up haven't they?' She remarked lewdly.

'Sure has,' Michael replied proudly, his inhibitions long since vanished.

'Probably needs some attention, wouldn't you say?' She said, beginning to slowly gyrate her bottom, enjoying the power she had over him.

'Oh yes, I'd say so,' he nodded eagerly.

Moira continued to gyrate for a few moments longer, until she knew he could bear it no more, then, like the expert tease that she was, she lifted herself off him. Taking the small purse she had with her, she crossed over to the armchair opposite and sat down; her long shapely legs wide apart; the cropped denim shorts barely concealing her femininity. Michael was watching her every move, squirming with desire.

From her purse she took out a pack of Lucky Strikes and placed one between her teeth. She struck a match and lit the cigarette, letting the smoke from it curl slowly upwards from her painted lips. Moira knew Michael was ready to kill for her, he would do anything she asked of him, anything just to have her.

'Okay, Mike,' she said, her voice deep and husky, 'Show me what you've got.'

'What do you mean?' Michael was now aching with lust.

'You know what I mean Mike, I wanna look at you - I want you to strip for me. So show me what you've got, lover boy.'

Normally, Michael was not comfortable with his body; he

felt ugly and very conscious of it and would have much preferred to undress in the dark. But the alcohol and desire had all but banished his anxieties with only the slightest hesitation remaining. 'C'mon, Mike. I wanna see,' Moira goaded. The bulge in his shorts was enormous and curiosity was getting the better of her. She really did want to see. 'Show me what you've got - then, maybe, I'll show you.'

Very nervously, Michael rose to his feet and slowly slipped off his tee shirt. Then, after a brief pause, he removed his shorts and pants, not catching Moira's astonished gasp as she laid eyes on his giant erection.

He stood there completely naked and totally exposed, being inspected like some piece of meat, feeling a strange mixture of intense embarrassment and incredible excitement, hoping that there was some way in which she could find him even slightly desirable.

Moira stubbed out her cigarette and studied him. Facially he was hideous, even with the alcohol she was finding his crooked features difficult to look at. His body, although reasonably muscular was white and unimpressive. However, what was sticking out from between his legs was unbelievable. It was huge, something the size of which she'd never encountered before, and her mouth watered as she considered it.

'My, my... What a big boy you are!' She remarked lustfully, 'You'd better let me have a closer look.'

Michael apprehensively took a step towards her. 'Closer,' she said. He took another pace. 'C'mon, closer, I wanna real good look,' she demanded. Michael cautiously stepped forward until he was standing directly in front of her, his manhood only inches from her face as Moira bent to inspect her prize. She liked what she saw and, with her eyes wide with delight, she began to caress the inside of his thighs.

Michael, could feel Moira's hot breath on him as she spoke. 'Do you want me Mike?' She cooed softly, wondering what it would be like to have something that big inside her. Aside from a couple of high school fumbles with boys of her age, her previous lovers had all been old men, but none had been anywhere near so well endowed as the guy who stood before her now.

'Do you wanna go all the way with me, Mike?'

'What?' He asked, unsure if his ears were deceiving him in his high state of ecstasy.

'Do you wanna do it with me Mike, do you wanna fuck me?' She quickly pulled off her tee shirt and bikini top, letting her marvellous breasts fall into view.

'Yeah! Yeah. I want to, I really want to!' Finally, he would no longer be a virgin.

Moira was eager too. She wanted to feel him inside her, yet she had not yet laid out her terms. She stroked her breasts provocatively with the tips of her fingers, looking at him with her big round eyes, teasing him mercilessly, 'Are you sure?' She whispered.

'Yeah, I'm sure.' Michael was very nearly drooling with desire.

'It's gonna cost you.' She sprung the trap.

'What?'

'It's gonna cost you Mike. These goodies don't come for free.'

What was she doing, he wondered, was she playing? Was she serious? He didn't care. Not now at least. He just had to have her. 'How much?' He asked croakily.

Moira was pretty sure he would have paid anything, but she decided to err on the side of caution, no point in blowing the deal by being too greedy - besides, now she wanted him as much as he did her.

'Two thousand dollars.'

'Two grand! Jesus!' He exclaimed.

'Take it or leave it,' she bluffed, making a show of re-fastening her bikini.

'Stop. Don't do that. I'll take it, I'll take it!' Michael had never wanted anything more.

Moira smiled sweetly, 'Seems like it's my lucky day' she said. And with a mercenary glint in her eye she wriggled out of her tiny shorts.

*   *   *

Moira awoke a little after 10pm. Groggily she looked at her wrist watch but her eyes were still blurry and failed to properly register the time. Totally naked, she was wrapped in the navy blue satin sheets of the enormous bed, which were soft and smooth and felt good against her skin. Just for a moment she revelled in the luxury, but then, suddenly, she remembered where she was and turned to see Michael's grotesque, smiling face staring at her from the pillow opposite.

'Hello, sleepy head,' he said, 'I was hoping you'd wake up.'

'Were you?' Her voice was flat and disinterested.

'Yeah, because someone else has woken up too,' his eyes gestured to the growing bulge beneath the sheets.

'That's nice for you' she said sarcastically, but he didn't pick up on it. Moira pulled back the sheet and made to get out of bed but before she had time to move Michael threw himself on top of her and kissed her on the mouth, his tongue trying to penetrate her tightly closed lips and his hands fumbling at her breasts.

For a second she thought she might vomit and quickly she turned her face away, breaking free from the suction of his crooked wet mouth. 'Get off me!' She demanded, forcefully pushing him off and springing hastily from the bed.

'Moira, what's the matter? Have I done something wrong, have I upset you?' Michael was confused.

'No, you've done nothing wrong,' Moira replied impatiently,

as she pulled on her panties, 'I've just gotta go that's all.' She looked at her wrist watch again, this time though it was in focus and she saw how late it was, 'Christ! I've really gotta go - my parents are gonna kill me!'

By now, Michael too was out of bed and he rushed over to Moira and put his hands on her shoulders and made to kiss her again, 'Please don't be cross - come back to bed. Let's just talk about it.' His whiny voice sounded pathetic to her and, pulling free of his grip, she suddenly snapped.

'Listen, Mike, just forget it alright, just pay me my money and I'm outta here.'

Michael's face was blank, 'Money?' He asked.

'Yeah, money. The two thousand dollars you owe me, remember?'

'But— I thought that was just a game,' he replied, although not certain.

'You're kidding right?'

'B-but,' he stammered.

'Pay up, Mike - I'm running late.' Moira was now fully dressed and standing in front of the mirror arranging her hair.

'But I thought you liked me, I thought—' Michael said, his eyes watering as he realised his own stupidity. He had been gullible and naive to think that a beauty like Moira would fall for a beast such as him and now he felt sick, used and ridiculous.

'Yeah, sure, my heart bleeds - now get me the goddamn money so I can get going!' Her voice was sharp and bitter and Michael felt his anger rising.

'No way! I'm not going to pay you a single cent - you little bitch!' Michael grabbed Moira by the arm and tried to shove her in the direction of the door, 'Get out!' He barked, but she refused to budge.

'You don't get it do you, you fucking freak, if you don't pay me, I'm gonna walk out this door and shout rape!' Moira's face was now all contorted with hatred, as she regarded Michael's naked body with obvious disgust. 'Get the idea now, rich boy?'

'Rape - you're joking, right?' He was incredulous, 'Unless you're forgetting, it was you who seduced me - and apart from you being a complete whore, there's no crime in that, we're both adults!' Michael was at boiling point.

'That's where you're wrong you hideous fucking ghoul, you may be an adult, but I'm only just fifteen and in the good ol' U.S. of A., that makes me a minor and you a filthy, child molesting rapist!'

This information struck Michael straight through the heart. 'You're lying, you've got to be bloody lying, there's no way you're only fifteen, no way... you're too... too—'

'Yeah Mike, I know, I'm just too damn grown up, but it's the truth, what can I say. I'm just sweet lil' fifteen - and believe me, for a jury, I can make myself look it. Now get me my money you snivelling creep and I'll be on my way.'

Tears were running down Michael's face as the information sank in. Devastated, he turned away from her, his head bowed, utterly defeated. Moira beamed triumphantly and, with greed at last getting the better of her, she said, 'I'll tell you what, let's make it an even four grand and if I need any more, I'll be in touch.' She smiled at how clever she was being, but the smile quickly vanished as Michael turned and glared at her. The red rage of anger swept over him as he grabbed hold of her hair with one hand and took a fistful of her tee shirt in the other. More out of hate than of lust he covered her mouth with his, the saliva on his lips dribbling down her chin as his tongue forced its way between her teeth. However, Moira bit down hard on it, tasting his blood as it filled her mouth, and he pulled away in agony.

'Bitch!' He shouted, slapping her hard around the face, 'Fucking bitch!' He yelled again as he brought back his hand, smacking her violently across the jaw. Moira fell backwards, the thin fabric of her shirt ripping in Michael's grip as she fell and his fingernails involuntarily clawing at her soft skin. Her head crashed harshly against the large mirror behind her, shattering it into a random mosaic of razor sharp glass. And, as she slumped unconsciously towards the floor, her beautiful face slid down it, the deadly shards ripping at the flesh on her cheek.

She came to rest on the cold Spanish tiles; her bruised face was lacerated and covered in blood as was her neck and chest. The remains of her white tee shirt revealed one of her shapely breasts, but it was scratched and bloodied and had lost all of its former allure.

Michael was still panting, his anger only just beginning to subside. He stood over her, stark naked with sweat glistening on his pale porcelain skin, the knuckles on his left hand cut and bleeding. He looked down at Moira and suddenly the anger was replaced by panic. What the hell had he done?

For a brief moment he thought Moira was dead, but then, with relief, he saw her breathing. Thankfully he had not killed her, but his predicament was still grave and the realisation of it hit him with the force of a car crash. His life was over, washed away in one utterly stupid afternoon of pure lust. In his hotel suite, he'd had sex with an under age girl - raped her in the eyes of the law - after first getting her drunk. Then he had smashed her face into a mirror and quite possibly scarred her for life.

Not for the first time in his pathetic existence, he wished he was dead.

Five

Carl Napier was speaking to Benny Mottola on the phone in his office above the casino. He was puffing on a fat Cuban cigar; his feet resting on his enormous desk.

Carl had filled out a little in the last six years and now needed to wear glasses, which were large, gold-rimmed and tinted. His hairline had receded, although he'd grown it shoulder length at the back and now sported a set of Elvis Presley bushy side burns.

Carl had done well; he'd turned the Villa into a fabulous success and had amassed a considerable fortune in the process. However, his association with Benny Mottola he now bitterly regretted. Since joining forces with him to buy shares in the Villa Continental, Carl had managed to keep Mottola and his mob backers at a workable distance. But that distance was getting tougher to maintain as Benny was forever pushing Carl, pressuring him to get the other half of the shares. Benny wanted it all, the whole operation, not just half, and his patience were wearing thin.

But Carl knew that any takeover had to be legal, or, at least, appear to be so, and finding a way to relieve the other parties of their shares was difficult. Mottola, however, did not appreciate the intricacies of the process and at every opportunity reminded Carl of his growing impatience; the threat of violence never far away. But if Benny took over Carl knew his position, and indeed, his life, would be far from secure, and the stress of this weighed heavily.

Carl's antidote to this was cocaine. He was not certain when recreational use ended and addiction began, but as far as he could remember, it was shortly after the death of Rachel Cassidy, who had haunted his dreams ever since. However, the drugs had screwed up his mind, and often he was uncertain as to who his true enemy was. Was it Joe? Was it Benny? Or was it himself? Sometimes it was all three at once. But mostly it was unclear. However, when he was trying to placate Benny, as he was now, it was always Joe.

Mottola, or Benito Vincenzi as he was now known, had already fared very well from his association with The Villa. Since buying his piece of it for the Vincenzi crime family, in the guise of Nevada Gaming and Leisure Associates, things had been going very well indeed. Many things could be attributed to this, the all important foothold in Vegas definitely being one, but the main reason was because of his marriage. He had married at the back end of '66 as a personal favour to his Uncle Tito. His bride, Lucia, was the daughter of Carmine Carboni, boss of one of the bigger Miami families. The wedding had been designed purposely by Tito and Carmine to unite their two organisations by blood, thus making them both stronger. Tito needed Carboni's muscle, whilst Carmine needed a gateway into Vegas, which was to be graciously supplied by his new son-in-law.

Lucia was short, fat and had a moustache to rival a man's, but somehow Benny forced himself to consummate the marriage; the result being twin sons, Vito and Guisseppe - Jez for short, born in the summer of 1967. The boys were now five and Benny worshipped them, as did both their grandfathers. They were the rock upon which the Vincenzi and Carboni partnership was built and, provided nothing happened to them, the union would remain strong.

After the twins were conceived Benny never slept in his

wife's bed again. Although he made it abundantly clear that if his disinterest in her ever reached Carmine's ears, she would end up the victim of an unfortunate accident. Lucia wisely took this on board and contented herself to be the best housekeeper and mother she could be, two jobs in which she excelled, but her husband never noticed.

Yet another reason for Benny's meteoric rise to success was his very lucrative narcotics operation. He and Frank Blades had sourced a reliable supplier from Colombia whose high quality merchandise they were importing for the lowest possible price. Then from his secret warehouses in Miami, Benny distributed the cocaine not only across America but overseas also. London was high on his list of targets and his operative there was none other than Big Jack Anderson, who had been delighted to find himself once again back in favour. But in London, as in Vegas, Benny knew his plans for expansion would be thwarted by Joe, who would do everything in his power to prevent Mottola's narcotics business from prospering and that presented a problem.

On the English side of the Atlantic, Joe was the one who held the balance of power and to go up against him, at that time, would be a serious mistake. With this in mind Mottola decided that he needed somebody inside Joe's organisation who could distract attention, spoil plans and sabotage business deals and give him more to worry about than Benny and Jack's little drug operation. Not to mention the quiet re-birth of the Mottola firm in London.

In a flash of brilliance, Benny had thought of Michael, which was why he had phoned Carl. Napier had told him of the lad's hatred towards Joe and he felt confident he could exploit that given the right motivation. He needed to find a weakness in the boy that he could use to his advantage, something that would enable him to manipulate Michael to such a degree that he would be willing to do his dirty work. A filthy little secret for which Michael would rather sell his soul than to have made public.

Benny smiled at the prospect of becoming Michael's puppeteer; all he now had to do was find out what the boy had to hide - something which surely Carl could uncover for him.

*   *   *

When Carl finally put the phone down, he felt decidedly uneasy and had to snort a line of coke to calm himself. Napier didn't like the thought of selling Michael down the river but if it meant keeping Mottola sweet, then so be it. He took another line, then lit a cigarette. What the hell could he find out about Michael that he didn't already know? If he didn't come up with something soon, Benny was going to be really pissed off. And that wouldn't be good.

As he sank back in his executive chair to contemplate this, the telephone rang again.

'Yeah?' Carl said, his voice almost a whisper.

'Carl? It's me, Michael. I'm in trouble. Big trouble. I don't know what to do and I need your help!' He was obviously crying and in a state of extreme panic.

'It's okay, Michael. Calm down and tell me all about it,' Carl's voice was as smooth as silk.

Michael did as instructed and, as he related his whole sorry tale, Carl couldn't help but smile.

*   *   *

Moira was conscious by the time Carl got there. Sitting on her bottom with her knees up under her chin, a hand pressed against her lacerated cheek in an attempt to stem the bleeding. More blood trickled from the split in her lower lip and the bruises on her face were beginning to turn purple. She looked dreadful, like she'd done ten rounds in the ring at Caesar's.

As Carl looked over to Michael, he noticed that the boy's eyes were red and puffy, still full of tears and his face still wet from crying. The lad was now dressed in a vest and a pair of trousers, his feet and arms bare as he shivered uncontrollably; a sad, pathetic figure desperately out of his depth.

'Right, Michael,' Carl said, immediately taking control of the situation, 'Go and get in the shower and don't come out 'til I tell ya.'

'But I—' Michael began.

'Do it now Michael,' Carl snapped, his vision focused on Moira, 'Don't worry, I'll deal with this young lady,' the contempt he felt for Moira was undisguised and she visibly squirmed as his eyes bored into her.

Michael opened his mouth in order to say something else, but Carl, still not looking at him, but sensing the boy was about to argue, shot out a finger and pointed it towards the bathroom. The gesture was firm and decisive and Michael knew better than to disagree. Meekly, he took a last guilty look at Moira, then did as he was told, quietly shutting the bathroom door behind him.

Napier sat down on the bed and waited until he could hear the sound of the shower running before he spoke to the girl on the floor. His voice was calm and even but the underlying menace was unmistakable.

'Look at me.' He began, but she ignored him. 'Look at me,' he said again, this time though, it was not a request but a command and Moira was unable to resist. When he was certain that her full attention was on him, he spoke again.

'This is how it's going to be. There'll be no arguments, no discussions. This is how it's gonna work, pure and simple, do you understand?'

Moira could tell he wasn't a man to disagree with and without a word she nodded her understanding.

'Good, I can tell we're on the same page,' Carl gave her a little smile, but not the one he reserved for lovers, movie stars or senators. It was a smile that said, 'Mess with me and your dead,' and Moira read it with frightening accuracy.

'Here's the story,' he continued, 'A guy attacked you in the parking lot, tried to rape you. He smacked you around a little and tore your clothes but, before he could do anything more serious, one of our security guards chased him off. The guy got away and neither you or the guard got a good look. It sucks but it happens, what can I tell ya, life's a bitch.

That's it. That's what happened. No deviation, no elaboration. You're too shocked to remember any more and that's the way it'll stay. If it does, then by way of compensation the hotel will pay you and your family twenty grand. You personally will receive another twenty on your eighteenth birthday, which, I think is fair to assume, is some years away, am I right?' She nodded again, but this time her eyes were sparkling, the mention of money had excited her.

'The Villa will also pay for a surgeon to fix your face - make it look like nothing ever happened. In return - and this is important to remember - you will never utter a word of what went on here tonight. It doesn't leave this room, understand?'

Again she nodded.

'If either me, Michael or any of my associates ever hear of this again, from anywhere—' Carl hotched forward, pushing his face nearer to hers, '—You die. I hunt you down like a dog and I kill you. This is non-negotiable. Tell me we have a deal.'

Moira swallowed hard as she digested what he had said.

'D-deal,' she stuttered.

'Good girl,' he replied, 'Now get up, we've gotta go and see your parents and you'd better hope they believe what you tell them, otherwise all bets are off and your credit is cancelled. Do you follow?'

Once more she nodded her acknowledgement, a tear spilling down her cheek as the gravity of her situation finally hit home, 'They'll believe me, I promise they will,' her voice was small, barely a whisper as she desperately hoped what she had said was true.

'Good girl.' Carl said again, then walked over to the bathroom, opened the door a jar and spoke through the gap. 'Michael, give it five minutes, then come out. Get yourself dressed and don't do a thing until I come back, alright?'

'Alright,' he replied weakly.

'Alright?' Carl asked again to make certain.

'Yes. Alright. I'll be here, I promise,' his voice came back stronger this time.

'Good boy,' Carl said reassuringly, before shutting the bathroom door once more.

*   *   *

Michael stood under the shower, the warm water hitting him on the back of the head and neck. He had his forehead resting against the cold white tiles, his palms also pushed against them on either side of his face. The tears that were streaming down his cheeks mingled with the hot spray and his shoulders heaved as he sobbed deeply. Panic was mixed with shock. He felt hurt, useless, idiotic, scared. What the hell was he going to do?

He knew what Carl was saying to Moira, that he was trying to smooth things out, trying to make the problem go away, maybe even offering cash in return for her silence. He knew it and he hated himself for it. But would she go for it? Michael was extremely aware that if Carl couldn't sway Moira, he'd be looking at a prison sentence, and there was no way he could face that. He wouldn't last five minutes - he'd heard all the horror stories - the things that happened to the weaker inmates; the beatings and the rapes and the humiliation and he swore it wouldn't happen to him, he'd rather be dead.

He berated himself for his weakness and for his foolishness in getting enticed by Moira.

'You hideous fucking ghoul!' Moira's words echoed in his

head.

That's exactly what he was, a hideous, pathetic, weak-willed ghoul, who was good for absolutely nothing, a worthless freak whose sad existence was nothing more than a feeble joke.

Moira was a vindictive, spiteful bitch but the insults she'd hurled at him were true. How could he have been so stupid? The more Michael thought about it, the more he began to doubt Carl's ability to help him, panic washed away any hopes he had of Carl resolving the situation. It was useless, what was the point of even trying? Moira, the little bitch, would enjoy telling her parents, just to see him squirm, just as she'd threatened, then it would only be a matter of time before the police arrived and arrested him. Then he would go to prison.

As Michael stepped out of the shower his eyes fell on the towelling bath robe hanging on the wall hook beside him. As he noticed the long, thin belt threaded through its loops an idea suddenly occurred to him; a horrific, terrible idea, but one that, to him, was more acceptable than the utterly appalling prospect of prison. Pulling the belt free of the robe, he tugged it hard a couple of times to test its strength and was satisfied with the results. Then, with his hands shaking, he made a loop in one end and tied a knot.

He had found an escape.

*   *   *

It had gone just as Carl had planned. Moira's parents were rightly outraged that their daughter should have been attacked in the hotel parking lot, but at the mention of the money, their attitude changed dramatically. They became far less concerned about Moira and much more interested in the compensation.

Her father was quite clearly a compulsive gambler and Carl knew that by morning the cash he'd handed over would be safely back in the casino's care.

As for the twenty grand he had promised Moira on her

418

eighteenth birthday, well that was three years away and a lot could happen in that time, particularly to a girl as promiscuous and as careless as Moira. As for the plastic surgery, Carl knew a doctor that owed him a favour, it wouldn't cost him a penny.

Having been gone less than half an hour, Napier made his way back to Michael's suite, smiling with satisfaction. But the moment he let himself in to the suite, his expression turned to one of horror.

Michael was hanging from the chandelier by a length of towelling belt, an ornate dining chair laying on its side below him. The boy's face was purple and his eyes were bulging grotesquely, his mouth was contorted with pain and he was growling in agony through gritted teeth. His body was jumping around erratically on the end of the towelling rope like a puppet on a string, his legs dancing wildly in the air. Michael's hands clawed desperately at the noose around his neck, trying without success to free himself from the tightening knot, knowing the moment he kicked the chair away that he'd made a terrible mistake.

'No!' Carl shouted as he ran to him. In desperation he grabbed Michael around the legs and lifted him, taking his weight to relieve the pull of the belt. Quickly he took out his pen knife, the one he used to trim cigars and sift cocaine, then reached up and carefully sliced through the towelling noose.

When it severed, Carl eased Michael down, the boy wheezing and gasping for breath. But he was alive. Carl had saved him, and quite possibly himself in the process.

Twice that night the boy had been in trouble and twice Carl had rescued him. Now Michael would have to repay the debt.

*   *   *

At the hospital some hours later, Michael was sitting up in bed, his swollen and badly burned neck encased in a thick, white brace. His voice was croaky and sore, his vocal cords seriously bruised. Sitting next to him on the edge of the bed was Carl Napier, the man who had saved his life. The man who he considered to be his best friend in all the world.

'Thank God you arrived when you did, Carl,' Michael wheezed, 'I dunno what I was thinking - I just sort of, well, panicked. I couldn't think of a way out—'

'Hey, don't sweat it,' Carl smiled, 'Glad to be of service.'

'Yeah, but you saved me. I owe you and if there's anything I can ever do, well, you know, just ask.'

This gave Napier the way in he'd been waiting for. 'Well, now that you mention it, there maybe is one thing you can help me with - but feel free to say no if you think it's too much.'

'Anything. I owe you remember,' Michael replied croakily, but eager to be of use.

'I've been hearing rumours,' Carl began carefully, 'Rumours that Joe has been bad mouthing me and wants me out. Apparently he's been trying to dig up dirt on me, trying hard to ruin my reputation, to bring me down so he can take over the Villa now I've turned it around. He wants it all for himself Michael and I don't figure in his plans.'

'That two-faced, double-crossing bastard!' Michael whispered vehemently, 'It doesn't surprise me, anything's possible with that arrogant piece of shit!'

Carl kept his expression dour as he continued, 'That's why I need you Michael. I need you to be my eyes and ears in London. To watch Joe's every move - even to make friends with him if necessary. But I want you to tell me everything, right down to the tiniest detail, of what he does. It's vital to my very existence that I know these things, so I can stay one step ahead of the game.' Carl was deliberately making himself sound desperate as he looked Michael straight in the eyes, summoning up his most honest, most unquestionably sincere expression, playing his hand to perfection,

'Whattaya say kid, will ya help me?'

A broad grin appeared on Michael's crooked face, then in a hoarse but clearly audible voice he said, 'You know Carl, I don't think there's anything I'd like better. You've got yourself a deal.'

Six

At the Bluestone, Joe and Rose's love affair picked up from where it had left off over twenty years before, with the passage of time doing little to diminish their feelings for each other. The only differences were that Joe was now much richer and Rose was a little more worldly-wise, but they were still basically the same people they had been all those years ago.

Matt and Brett, the two half-brothers, were hitting it off too, having quickly become friends - which was a great relief to everyone. Matt was a very amiable, easy to like kind of person and Brett took to him almost immediately, obviously enjoying the novelty of having an older brother. Particularly an older brother who had offered to teach him karate. And, so it was, the two of them would go off to the barn every morning for lengthy training sessions. Brett was a quick study and, with each day that passed, he became ever more proficient. Most mornings, Joe would join his two sons, working out alongside them with a set of weights. Even I got in on the action by rigging up a punch-bag and blasting away at it like I had in the old days at Alfie's gym. It felt good to be there with my extended family and during the six weeks of that summer, in that barn, we all bonded, especially Joe and his boys, who became very close; something that was enormously rewarding for him as well as Rose.

For me personally, it was great to have my best friend around and in such obviously high spirits, with the spectre of Rachel's death having finally left him. I was pleased for Brett too, as Matt seemed to have added what was possibly missing in his life, and it was wonderful to watch their friendship grow.

I felt Brett was almost like my own son, and in Matt I found a young man with whom I had much in common; we were of a similar character and became friends instantly. Although often, when I looked at him, I guiltily thought of Michael and wished that he and I could enjoy the same kind of relationship.

I tried not to let my melancholy over my eldest son's departure spoil the time I had with Joe and the others, but it was difficult. A couple of weeks into their visit, we received a brief telephone call from Michael, telling us that he would not be returning to the ranch from Vegas, but would instead fly back to England in order to continue his studies. This saddened me greatly, but there was nothing I could do to change his mind.

* * *

After two months at the Bluestone, Joe and his family also returned to London. At first, Joe had been dubious about Rose and Matt going back to England so soon, considering the circumstances under which they had left. But it was perfectly safe, according to Alfie, who had been monitoring the situation in Northamptonshire closely; the investigation into Daryll's death had been closed and the police had thankfully concluded it to be accidental.

Matt and Suzie were going back to finish their college courses, after which they would return to California. I had offered Matt a job as a mechanic on the stunt team, keeping all our vehicles in good working order. Suzie, meanwhile, was going to work as a personal assistant to Victoria, who was planning her come-back as an actress. It was a dream come true for Suzie who would be working in the very heart of Hollywood.

Rose was to stay in London with Joe, where they planned to marry as soon as possible. Joe then intended to transfer the reins of power to Richie and Manno and retire from the gangland scene. He had done his time and fulfilled his promise to Vinnie Reece. Nothing more could be asked of him. It was Rose who he now owed, her and Sarah and Matt and Brett; his family. They, and his legitimate business interests would be the focus of his attention from now on.

That was the plan. However, as usual, nothing was ever that easy.

Seven

Richie Noakes and Manno O'Keefe operated out of the Galaxy Club in Peckham. It was Joe's place but they took a heavy slice of the profits and ran it as if it was theirs. Joe didn't interfere as there was never any need. However, on one particular Saturday night, a couple of well known heavies arrived at the club looking for a fight. Normally, trouble-makers would have been dealt with by the Galaxy's more than able bouncers, but these men were the brothers of Rachel Cassidy. They had once been related to Joe and nobody wanted to get on his bad side by denying them entry to the club, so they had been allowed in. But now, as feared, they were getting rowdy and upsetting the other customers. Things were starting to get out of hand and action had to be taken swiftly to prevent it.

Richie and Manno suspected that Joe couldn't have given a damn about Keith and Tommy Davenport but they needed to hear it from him before forcibly removing the brothers from the club. Reluctantly, Manno made the phone call, knowing full well that Joe had left strict instructions not to be disturbed. Having just got back from California, he and Rose were exhausted from the long, tiring flight and had gone to bed early to sleep off the jet-lag. The last thing either of them needed was for the telephone to ring.

Joe was groggy, his voice little more than a mumble as he

fought to think coherently. He was angry too at being awoken from an almost catatonic sleep. 'Jesus, Manno!' Joe snapped, his irritation undisguised, 'It's your bleedin' club. If they step out of line, get the bastards outta there. I don't care how ya do it. They mean nothin' to me. It's your call - now can I please get some sleep?'

*　　*　　*

Keith and Tommy Davenport were already drunk when they arrived at the Galaxy Club. They were celebrating the imminent release of their youngest brother, Stuart, who was due to finish his ten year prison sentence the following day.

The club was not a usual haunt for the Davenport's, but they had visited most other places on their day long binge and were now looking for some action; preferably the type that was young, female and willing. Something which they knew could be found in abundance at the Galaxy.

Each had a pint of lager with a whiskey chaser and were currently trying to chat up two large breasted eighteen year-olds, but without much success. Both men were pushing forty and looked extremely punchy, with broken noses, facial scars and barely a full set of teeth between them. They were rough, hard men and the women they attracted were usually the ones who couldn't afford to be too choosy.

After a few minutes, the girls' boyfriends appeared, understandably taking exception to the fact that Keith and Tommy were muscling in on their women. Needless to say, this was just the excuse the Davenport's were looking for and immediately started swinging their fists.

Quick as a flash, two of the Galaxy's bouncers, Lenny Stroud and Two-Ton Tony Briggs, piled into the fray, closely followed by Richie and Manno. Swiftly, the young lads' and their girlfriends were pushed clear as the four Galaxy men wrestled the two Davenport's from the club. Within seconds, all six men were out in the street; the punches flying fast and furious.

Keith and Tommy were like a couple of wild tigers with the scent of blood in their nostrils; this was what they lived for, but their opposition was more than equal to the challenge. They all scuffled violently on the steps of the club; heads clashed, fists collided and bones cracked, but the Galaxy crew were quickly gaining the upper hand. Tommy's nose had been broken and his brother had lost another tooth, but the Davenport's, Keith in particular, refused to be beaten.

Somehow, he and Two-Ton Tony had split away from the rest of the pack and were having their own private war some yards away. Tony had Keith's head in a tight lock under his arm, 'Give it up, Keith,' he said, not wishing to hurt the man further. But Keith's eyes were full of alcohol fuelled rage.

'Never!' He shouted. Then from his pocket, away from the other man's line of sight, Keith pulled out a murderous looking flick knife, popped open the shiny metal blade and drove it into Tony's kidney. As the big bouncer squealed in agony, Keith cruelly twisted the knife to cause maximum damage before jerking it free. Suddenly Tony's grip loosened allowing Keith to escape the neck hold and once free he stabbed again. This time the blade sliced between Brigg's ribs and Davenport smiled with glee as he caught the look of shock on the other man's face as the reality of imminent death registered in his brain. Tony, by now, had lost all feeling in his arms and legs and as he collapsed to the ground, he took his final breath.

'Not so big now are ya?' Keith sneered viciously as he stood over the body.

Manno, Richie and Lenny Stroud were in the process of finishing off Tommy, when Tony hit the cobbles. 'No!' Lenny shouted, as he saw the evil smile on Keith's face and the knife in his hand. 'No, you bastard - no!' He shouted again as he hurled his big frame at the sadistic figure of Davenport.

'C'mon then,' Keith goaded, waving the knife threateningly in front of him. But Stroud was too quick; he grabbed hold of Keith's wrist and twisted it hard, snapping the bone. Davenport cried out with pain as the flick knife loosened in his grip and Lenny snatched it from him. Then, without conscious thought, Stroud reversed the blade and thrust it six times into the bloated beer gut of Keith Davenport; the man who had just murdered his best friend.

After the frenzied, impassioned attack, Lenny took a step backward and dropped the knife; suddenly aware of what he had done. Keith looked down at his stomach and saw his blood spurting through the six holes in his red and bloodied shirt. He then looked up in disbelief. Everything had gone quiet, Richie and Manno had released Tommy, who was sitting on the floor ten feet from his brother, horrified at what he'd just witnessed.

'Jesus Christ, Keith' he said, 'You're... you're—'

'Tommy?' Keith's voice was full of alarm, 'I'm fuckin' dead, Tom. I've been fuckin' killed!' His astonishment was clear as he studied his wounds again. Then, slowly and with surprising grace, he pitched forward in death, his body landing with a loud slap next to that of Tony's.

Before Richie and Manno had time to react, Tommy pulled a pistol from out of his jacket and fired off three shots in quick succession. Richie and Manno immediately dived on him, but as the three men wrestled on the ground, a fourth shot blasted out and suddenly all struggling ceased.

After many seconds, Richie slowly rolled away from the other men, he was covered in blood and, for a moment, he thought it was his own but then he looked down and saw the bullet wound in Tommy Davenport's stomach. His blank eyes were staring up at him and his tongue was lolling hideously out of his mouth; he was dead, there could be no doubt. But Manno was trapped underneath the body and urgently Richie pushed it off. The bullet had passed clean through Tommy catching Manno hard in the shoulder. He was still alive but the wound was pumping out masses of bright red blood and if he didn't get to a hospital soon, he would most certainly die.

'Call a fuckin' ambulance!' Richie yelled to Lenny, but as he looked over to him, he saw that Stroud had been hit by all three of Tommy Davenport's bullets; one in the shoulder, one in the throat and one in the centre of his forehead. He wouldn't have known a thing about it and Richie was at least thankful for that. 'For Christ's sake - somebody call an ambulance!' He yelled again, this time at a crowd of onlookers who had come out of the club and were now standing gawping on the pavement.

For what seemed like an age, Richie sat there on the cold ground nursing Manno's head in his lap, the blood seeping through his trousers as he waited for the ambulance to arrive. Eventually, he heard a siren, then the thunder rumbled and the heaven's opened.

Richie sat there getting soaking wet, 'Fuckin' Davenport's,' he cursed.

*   *   *

Stuart Davenport's release was postponed for another two months, until all the furore had died down. He was not even allowed to attend his brothers' funeral, but Danny did.

Stuart was finally given his freedom, when the authorities considered it to be safe. He was picked up outside the prison gates by his only living relative and as he got in the car, he looked at Danny and said, 'Somebody's gonna pay, right?'

To Danny it was a clear cut decision; Joe owned the Galaxy Club, the men who killed his brothers were on Cassidy's payroll and, according to word on the street, Joe himself had given the order.

'Oh, yeah,' Danny replied, 'Somebody's gonna pay alright,

and I know just the man.'

Eight

Joe and Rose eventually got married some two months after they initially intended, on the very same day in fact, that Stuart Davenport was finally released from prison. This was unintentional with Joe only finding out a week before his wedding day, but he opted not to cancel as the Davenport's had already caused him enough trouble. They had murdered two of his best men, people who had been with him since he took over from Vinnie and he believed he owed it to Lenny Stroud and Tony Briggs not to rearrange his life because of their killer's brothers.

There would be no honeymoon though, at least not for the time being as London was too volatile a place to be left at present. Joe suspected that there could be reprisals from what had happened at the Galaxy and with Manno still recovering from his injuries it would be unfair to leave Richie and Ray to run things alone. Joe decided to stay until things quietened down a bit, but then, he promised himself, he would be out.

He had informed Richie and Manno of his intended retirement from the Firm and his desire to hand all matters related to it over to them. He realised that it would have to be a gradual process, but he was determined to do it. He had to do it.

The ways of the underworld were changing fast; now it was all about drugs, porn and filth - things that could eat away at a man's very soul if he got into them too deeply. Joe had already seen what cocaine could do to a person and he despised it. As far as he was concerned, coke, heroin, LSD, they were all bad news and nothing good could come out of dealing in them. As for Richie and Manno, they would have to do as they saw fit, make their own choices, but Joe trusted them to do the right thing. They were good guys - villains the pair of them who would take no shit from anyone, but in their world, the underworld, they knew what was right and what was wrong.

*　*　*

Since his return from America, Joe had been pleasantly surprised by Michael's change in attitude towards him. Far from being the aloof, obnoxious, almost monosyllabic youth he used to be, he was now friendly, considerate and eager to help.

With Brett also, Michael was making a definite effort. Previously he had barely spoken to the boy, but now he was interested in what he had to say, taking the time to get to know him and Joe had even witnessed Michael kicking a football around with Brett in the back garden. Brett, whilst being genuinely delighted at his cousin's apparent metamorphosis, remained more than a little sceptical about the reasons for it, but kept his reservations to himself. He knew how much it meant to his father for him and Michael to be friends and had no wish to spoil his pleasure now that it finally appeared to have happened.

However, for Joe, the transformation was amazing, and it pleased him beyond words. Michael was his nephew, his troubled sister's only son, and he desperately wanted to be a part of his life.

Michael still owned the flat in Chelsea, but lately his weekends had been spent at The Castle, where he appeared only too keen to assist Joe; running errands, filing and doing general office duties, although kept strictly away from anything connected with The Firm.

However, not wanting to rebuff his nephew's enthusiasm and eager to build on their budding relationship, Joe decided he could well do with someone as bright as Michael to assist with his legitimate business interests. It would be a perfect opportunity from which they could both benefit. Joe would get a quick, intuitive and intelligent young man who, as part of the family, would steer his interests in the right direction, whilst Michael would gain valuable work experience and put his considerable academic skills into practice.

Joe put this idea to Michael who readily accepted. The Oscar winning performance he'd put on for his uncle's benefit, playing the part of the loving, attentive nephew had worked and now that he'd been properly accepted into the fold, it was time for him to really get down to business.

Carl Napier would be pleased.

*　*　*

On the other side of the Atlantic, Frank Blades had finally got what he wanted too. He was now number two in the ever growing Mottola empire thanks, in no small part, to his very astute initiative.

It was he who had made first contact with the Colombians and he who had introduced them to Benny. Then together with his boss, he had helped thrash out the all important deal and subsequent supply chain that secured Benny Mottola's future in the Vincenzi crime family. Frank was also the man who had diplomatically pointed out to Benny the obvious benefits of marrying Lucia Carboni.

Mottola was far from stupid, but sometimes his hot-headedness and volatile personality got in the way of good sense. Frank was the only man who dared stand up to him and, ultimately, it had paid off. Benny sometimes lacked the sanity and clarity of thought that would let him see reason, and on these occasions,

Frank was the only man who could get through to him.

Quite uncharacteristically, Benny had been very grateful for Frank's guidance, especially in dealings with the Colombians and, as a result, had actually begun to respect his opinion on other matters. This was a previously unheard of phenomenon and clearly underlined Frank's position as Benny's most trusted confidant.

Because of Frank's sway with his boss, he was able to sort out a number of things that had troubled him in the past.

Wolf was one of these things. Frank had previously perceived him to be a very real threat to his future and it was clear that Benny had been grooming him for greater things. Things that Frank had ear-marked for himself. However, with his new found status, Blades could very nearly get Benny to do anything he wanted and that included disposing of Wolf or, at least, getting him out of the way.

Blades was not blind to Wolf's skills though and reluctantly appreciated his ample talents. Therefore, he persuaded Benny to send Wolf to California on a long-term assignment. Whilst there he would cultivate new outlets for the Vincenzi cocaine industry, building an increasing source of demand and generating lucrative new contacts.

But Wolf was also given another directive that was much closer to Benny's heart.

He was to infiltrate the Bluestone Ranch and report regularly on his findings there to Frank, who would fly out periodically to check on his progress. The information gleaned would allow Blades and Benny to determine exactly the right time to strike. A time they would purposely choose to cause maximum devastation.

*   *   *

In his capacity as Benny's lieutenant, Frank was also ordered to keep a close watch on how things were going in London. Once a month he would fly over to check up on Big Jack, to see how his end of the distribution chain was holding up.

So far, things weren't going too badly as Jack had found an ever willing customer base for his highly addictive merchandise. Everyone knew though that there was a much bigger market for their product, one in which profits could be doubled or even tripled, but presently progress was being blocked by one man. However, plans were in the pipeline to dispose of that particular blockage.

*   *   *

Big Jack considered himself very lucky to have been given a second, or maybe even a third chance and this time he was determined not to blow it.

When Mottola escaped from prison, Jack had been kept completely out of the picture. He was not told of the proposed escape or consulted about how Benny should be hidden. The reason for this, he had assumed, was that Mottola had discovered his treachery, and, as a result, had been convinced that at any moment, he would be the victim of an assassin's bullet. But the hit never came and as the years went by, he began to feel just that bit safer.

It was just possible that maybe Benny didn't know.

Then the phone call came from Frank Blades and all of a sudden, Jack was back in vogue, being given the biggest opportunity of his life - he was home free and he grabbed the opportunity to redeem himself with both hands.

As it transpired, Benny had suspected Jack's betrayal but no evidence was ever found of it, and, over the years, not even the slightest question about his loyalty had been raised. So, after much deliberation, Mottola decided to give Jack another chance. After all, he was still a very useful man to know and the ideal choice for the kind of work Benny had in mind.

Jack still operated from The Pontoon, which had been totally refurbished since the fire - started by a cigarette butt on the night of Ray Reece and Alfie Noakes' invasion. The same night that Jack had been beaten to within an inch of his life. It had taken him almost eight months to recover and he would never forgive those responsible. In his mind, it was an unprovoked and unwarranted attack, not just on his person but also on his turf which cost him a great deal of credibility and very nearly wiped him out.

If it wasn't for the help of a few close friends, like Danny Davenport and a handful of The Twenty Ones, he would have gone under. But he refused to be beaten, Big Jack Anderson was a fighter, not a quitter and he rallied support from many old associates, calling in all his debts. Finally, after a turbulent time spent in the wilderness, he got himself back in business. He gave The Pontoon a face lift and turned it into one of the most popular night clubs south of the river.

He reformed The Twenty Ones and slowly built up his strength and influence, perhaps to an even greater degree than before. Purposely, he stayed clear of the Cassidy Firm, he had no wish to tangle with them again - at least not yet, but his business with them was definitely not finished.

When the telephone call came from Frank Blades and his proposal was laid on the table, it was like manner from heaven. All of a sudden, Jack's future looked very rosy indeed.

In order to give this new enterprise his full attention he delegated some of his other operations to his newly appointed second in command; Danny Davenport.

Danny had always been an occasional member of The Twenty Ones and, more recently, he had stuck by Jack in his time of need, proving without doubt that he was not only a true friend but also that he was trustworthy and reliable. The very man for the job.

Jack took Stuart Davenport under his wing too when he was released from prison. Anderson knew he was at last heading for the big time, so why not take a few friends along for the ride? Besides, like him, the Davenport's had a particularly large grudge against the only man preventing them from reaching their goal and, to Jack, that could only be a bonus.

Nine

The first time Sarah emerged from her dream-like state, it had been for a little less than five minutes. It had been dark and she was alone in her bedroom and almost immediately she had begun to panic, her mind quickly shutting off once more, sending her again into the safety of her closeted world.

The second time, she had remained responsive for almost an hour, even building up the courage to get out of bed and tentatively wander over to the window.

Over the years, it wasn't as if Sarah didn't function, because she did. She washed herself, dressed herself, wandered around the house and garden by herself. But she just didn't react to anything or anyone - like she was in a trance or sleep-walking. She didn't talk or interact and remained a completely closed book, almost totally emotionless unless under extreme duress. It wasn't that she couldn't speak, she hadn't lost the ability, doctors just said that she chose not to, as if her mind had just closed down, refusing to allow anyone in and refusing to allow any emotion or response out. It was, they thought, a subconscious choice, a self-styled safety device to protect her from further harm.

But on this night, for the second time, she was having a moment of complete clarity.

Like the first time, it was, again, dark, but peeping through the curtains she could see that it was very close to dawn and as the first strands of sunlight crept into the sky, she caught a glimpse of the wonderful garden - the garden she had been in many times before but never really seen.

Sarah was staggered by its beauty and spent a long time gazing in awe, just studying the colours and wide variety of flowers; taking in, for the first time the path - completely unaware that she and Joe walked on it every morning. Finally, she closed the curtains and turned back to face the darkness of the room. As she did so, she noticed the reflection of a woman she thought she recognised in the mirror. The woman looked older than she remembered, and thinner, but there was something about her eyes that were familiar and it took some minutes for Sarah to register the truth of what she saw.

The woman was her. She was old. What had happened? How long had she been asleep? Then she remembered Vic Cassidy and once again everything started to close in. She tried to fight it, although her head was swimming, awash with unanswered questions and she barely managed to stagger back to the bed. What had happened to Joseph, was he still in prison? What about Sean and the baby? Again she remembered Vic Cassidy and the horrific events of that fateful night and even though she fought hard to resist it, her questions finally evaporated and she found herself once more back in the safety of her idyllic, make-believe paradise. However, this time, one image remained of the real world - it was that of the clock on the wall that faced her bed. It was not the time that was important, but the date, which appeared on a rotating dial on the centre of the face, which had burned itself into her sub-conscious. It was 1973, somehow she had lost over twenty years of her life.

As Sarah drifted away again, she inexplicably knew, that this time, it would not be for so long.

Ten

Matt finished his college course in the Summer of '75 and before heading to the States to take up his new job at the Bluestone he went to London to stay with Joe and Rose for a few weeks to spend as much time with his father and step-brother as possible before departing. He even got to know Michael a little, although he sensed that his new cousin did not appreciate his presence in the house at all.

During his stay at The Castle, Matt continued with Brett's karate tuition, and made him promise to continue with his training after he had gone. Brett assured him that he would and Matt didn't doubt it as the lad was a very talented student with a natural gift. Joe too continued to train with his boys and the bond between the three of them grew ever stronger which, Matt thought, may have accounted for Michael's coolness towards him - perhaps he was jealous, although he had no reason to be.

In the short time he had known him, Matt had grown to like Joe very much and was glad to have him as his father, regardless of the gangland reputation. Contrary to what the papers and, indeed, a lot of the facts clearly suggested, Matt felt that Joe was honest, at least in his heart and especially with the people he cared for. He was a man of honour who always kept his word and his loyalty to his friends, as he had already proved, was beyond question. That was the Joe Cassidy Matt knew.

However, Matt's faith in his father was soon to be seriously tested with the horrific power and true violence of gangland about to strike with all the force of an unstoppable freight train.

* * *

Suzie came up to London to stay with Matt every weekend and they would spend long happy hours planning their lives together in the States. Suzie couldn't wait to begin her new role in Hollywood as Victoria Wild's assistant and Matt was eager to get started at the Bluestone.

A few days before their scheduled departure, Joe announced that he was taking his son and Suzie on a shopping spree, to buy them all the clothes they would need for their American adventure. It would be his treat and there was to be no arguments.

Five of them went, Suzie, Matt, Ray Reece and Joe, plus another man on the Firm's payroll called Owen Tate. Tate had been around for years and was slightly older than Ray whose driver he now was. He had gone prematurely grey in his mid-twenties and ever since had been known affectionately as 'Uncle.' He was a good man though and could be relied upon.

It was Saturday afternoon and the King's Road was mobbed, full of tourists as was the norm, but being from out of town, it was the place where Suzie specifically wanted to go. It was famous for all its high fashion boutiques and she excitedly ran from one to another, both Ray and Matt, laden down with her shopping bags trying desperately to keep up. Joe though, was holding tightly onto her arm, clearly enjoying himself and determined to spoil his surrogate daughter as much as possible.

Uncle was crawling along in the Roller a few paces behind, trying to keep a close watch on Joe's party, although with the hordes of people swarming the street, it was proving to be difficult, not to mention hazardous as he narrowly avoided running over careless pedestrians.

The Ford Cortina had followed them all the way from Camberwell, always keeping a discreet distance so as not to be noticed. It too carried four men, but the last thing on their minds was shopping.

It had driven past the Rolls Royce several times since they had been on the King's Road, but neither Uncle or anyone else had noticed, however had they done so, they would have undoubtedly recognised at least two of the men inside.

Oblivious to the surveillance, Suzie led Joe into yet another boutique, and her entourage settled down for what promised to be a long wait as she carried armfuls of trendy clothing into the dressing room. If her pattern in this shop resembled that of the previous ten, she would try every outfit on at least twice.

'We're gonna be 'ere bloody ages, ain't we?' Ray said to Matt, bitterly regretting his decision to accompany them. He had gone along solely to buy Ruby a birthday present, hoping to take advantage of Suzie's opinion in order to gain a female perspective when choosing the gift. Stupidly, he thought they would only be gone for an hour, two at the outside. It was now four in the afternoon, they had been out since ten and still there was no end in sight to this unrelenting tedium.

'At least an hour, I'll bet,' replied Matt, raising his eyebrows and searching for somewhere to sit down, but as usual, there was nowhere. Women's shops weren't designed for bored men to wait in.

Uncle turned off the engine, lit a cigarette and opened his newspaper. He had a wife, so he understood how these little shopping excursions worked. Only Joe seemed unaware of how long things were taking, or perhaps he just disguised it well as he greeted each change of clothes with as much enthusiasm as the last. Matt, the man Suzie was hoping to please in these outfits, had

442

lost interest ages ago and made no such pretence, all he wanted to do was sit down and rest his weary feet.

The men in the Cortina were bored too. Parked directly across the street from the shop, they were getting twitchy and nervous, having waited most of the day for a clear shot, but no sooner had their target emerged from one shop, than he was dragged into another. They were feeling frustrated and irritable, their patience evaporating with almost every second that ticked by.

Finally, after what seemed like an eternity, Joe and Suzie stepped out of the shop and onto the pavement, the glass door of the boutique swinging closed behind them. Ray and Matt were still inside, trying to figure out how to carry all the additional shopping bags.

The pavement had cleared somewhat as it was now well after five and most shoppers were heading home. This afforded the men in the Cortina a clear view of their prey and a chance they were anxious not to squander.

Joe was looking back into the shop to check on the whereabouts of the others as Suzie glanced up and just happened to notice the three pistols pointing out of the car window on the opposite side of the road, aimed directly at her and Joe. At first she was puzzled by such an odd sight, then her brain clicked into gear and the true horror of what was about to happen hit her with a jolt.

Thinking only of how devastated Matt would be if he were to lose his father so soon, she leapt instinctively in front of Joe. She opened her mouth to scream a warning but her voice was stolen by the first bullet which ripped into her throat. The second and third shots struck within an inch of each other in the centre of her chest, the force of them launching her backwards. More bullets hit her in the stomach and abdomen as she slammed back into Joe, the pair of them crashing through the plate glass door of the boutique. Still there was the crack of gunfire as yet more shots tore into Suzie's legs and genitals as she and Joe stumbled to the floor of the shop in a shower of shattered, razor sharp glass. Only then did the gunfire stop, the sound of it replaced by that of screeching tyres as the Cortina sped away.

Uncle, alerted by the shots and having witnessed the whole dreadful scene, had not even had time to exit the Roller as the other car made its getaway. But as it passed, he got a clear view of the men inside it, recognising two of them instantly, however he would never be able to tell anyone, because at the exact moment he registered their identity, a bullet blew the top of his head off, instantly turning his wife of thirty years into a widow.

The assassination attempt was over incredibly swiftly, although more than fifteen rounds had been shot, all men firing in furiously quick succession, hoping to hit the target with as many bullets as possible. Which was staggering, because all had missed, mainly due to the amazing sacrifice of Suzie who had taken the brunt of the attack, her body acting as a human shield, protecting Joe from harm.

For a long moment, everything was quiet, almost eerily still, then as shock gave way to horror, one of the shop assistants let out a loud piercing scream. This triggered a chain-reaction among the other witnesses who almost simultaneously began crying and screaming too.

During the attack, both Ray and Matt had dived to the floor to escape the hail of bullets. Both had been hit by flying glass and had a few scratches, but thankfully nothing more serious and slowly, although still dazed from the onslaught, they began to stir.

Joe was laying on his back, alive but unconscious. Suzie's head had collided with his as they landed, knocking him out cold. Tragically, she was far less fortunate.

Suzie's blood soaked, mutilated body lay lifelessly on top of Joe's. Her arms were twisted under her and her bare, bloodied legs were riddled with bullet wounds. Jagged door glass jutted horribly out of her back and she had small holes all over her, from which rivers of blood were forming a large black lake on the navy blue carpet floor tiles.

Matt lifted his face off the floor and turned over to sit on his bottom. Groggily he surveyed the scene, looking first to the shattered door, then to the appalled, wailing faces of the gathered crowd. Finally he noticed the bloody couple laying just a few feet away from him. It didn't click who they were at first as Joe's face was turned away and Suzie's was unrecognisable. He was in shock, still not registering what had actually happened.

He studied Suzie's corpse, something about it looked familiar but he couldn't think what. His eyes wandered over her hideous wounds, never before had he seen anything so ghastly. Then Joe stirred and turned to face Matt who was now able to identify him, and suddenly he was confused. What was his father doing down there, lying under that poor dead girl?

Matt turned to look at Ray, who was now sitting up and facing him.

'Don't look at her boy.' Ray warned, his face full of anxious concern, 'Don't look at her, you can't do anything for her now.'

'What?' Matt replied, very slowly beginning to understand.

He turned back to face the body of the woman, his eyes drawn to a clean area of pattern on her otherwise blood covered skirt. It was the skirt Suzie had worn on their first date and suddenly the horrific, gut-wrenching truth of what had happened finally dawned, hitting him with a devastating stab to the heart.

His strength immediately drained as he weakly struggled to his feet, managing only to stagger a few paces before collapsing to his knees in a pool of his girlfriend's blood. With a look of absolute terror and utter disbelief, he surveyed the grotesque, mutilated corpse that was once Suzie's beautiful body and the tears finally came. He gritted his teeth, making his hands into fists and glared up to the heavens,'Why?' He screamed loudly, the emotion cracking in his voice, 'Why her you bastard!, Why her?'

He then turned away from the girl he loved, unable to look any longer at her sickening injuries and threw up on the carpet.

Joe, now fully conscious, looked up at Matt from where he lay, still trapped underneath the body of the girl that had saved his life. Unlike his son, he didn't have to ask why. He already knew.

Suzie had died because of him.

*   *   *

After the hospital, Joe, Ray and Matt were taken to the police station where they were interviewed separately, although it was more like a thorough and particularly nasty interrogation.

It seemed to Matt that the detectives weren't particularly concerned about Suzie or the dreadful way in which she had died. They didn't care that she was young and beautiful, that she was happy and in love, never once asking about her family or the ones she left behind. They were far more interested in Joe, about whom nearly every question was related. The police showed no sympathy for Matt's loss, in fact, quite the opposite, especially when it became known that he was Joe Cassidy's son. This was treated as some delicious morsel that they could not wait to feed upon and they made the most of every loaded question, stopping just short of accusing Matt of murdering Suzie himself.

It was a harrowing, demeaning and insensitive ordeal, but Matt fought to keep his cool, although inside he was at boiling point. He wanted to lash out, to shut these heartless, stupid, uncaring bastards up for good so that he could be left alone to grieve for the girl he had loved with all his heart. But he couldn't and he knew it, he just had to sit there and take it, because when they had finished, he knew ultimately that they would have nothing.

*   *   *

When they were finally allowed to leave the station, they found Richie waiting outside for them in the Bentley. Ray chose to ride up front, closing the glass partition behind him to allow Joe and Matt some privacy, but it only served to make the drive back to The Castle more insufferable. Neither Joe nor Matt knew quite what to say to each other. Joe, filled with an enormous sense of guilt, was able to find few words other than 'sorry', to adequately describe the absolute sorrow and deep sympathy he felt for his son. Matt, on the other hand, could not look at his father directly, for fear of venting the terrible anger bursting inside his chest.

As they pulled up at the house, Matt finally spoke.

'You own London, right?' He asked, his voice almost a growl.

'What?' Joe replied, caught slightly off guard.

'You own London, you're the boss - is that true?'

'Well... I—'

'Yes or no, are you the boss or not?'

'Yeah. I suppose I am.' Joe knew this was not a time for evading the truth.

'Prove it then,' Matt snarled, his anger bubbling over, 'Find the bastards who—' he choked for a second, before he continued, 'Find the bastards who did that to her. Find 'em and kill 'em.'

'Matt, I don't think—' Joe began.

'Can you do it or not?' His son interrupted.

Joe sensed Matt's irritation and felt his obvious animosity. 'Yes, I can do it,' he said simply.

'Good,' Matt replied, and got out of the car, slamming the door behind him.

∗ ∗ ∗

At the airport one week later, still wearing the dark suit he had worn to the funeral just a few hours before, Matt stood in the departure lounge of Heathrow airport. In his right hand he held a small holdall, which was his only luggage, in the left, he gripped his boarding pass. He had to getaway, to escape before doing something he would certainly regret. He had not spoken to his father since the day of Suzie's death and could not get the thought out of his mind that had it not been for Joe Cassidy, his beautiful girlfriend would still be alive. Matt needed space and time to sort out the swirl of thoughts rushing around in his head, to get his emotions in check, because if he stayed in London, he was bound to explode.

*　*　*

Rose found the note by her bedside when she returned from the funeral. It was from her only son, telling her that he was leaving. She knew why, and she understood, but it didn't stop her from crying. All she could hope for was that time would help heal the rift between father and son, and that somehow, some day, they could be a true family once more. She put her trust in the Bluestone, confident that Matt's stay there would help mend the wound. I prayed that her faith was not misplaced.

Eleven

Joe was standing next to Ray, who was lighting a fresh cigarette from the stub of his last one. It was cold in the warehouse and, apart from the single light that illuminated the small section in which they stood, it was also very dark. Snow was falling steadily through a broken skylight in the galvanised tin roof of the derelict building and forming a neat mound on the icy concrete floor.

As Ray lit the cigarette, Joe studied him. The old pirate was approaching sixty; his shock of bright red hair now liberally streaked with strands of grey, but still sticking out at all angles like a wild mane. The trademark eye patch was also still in place, and, as he clutched the solid silver fist that sat on top of his famous cane, he looked every bit as imposing as the moment Joe had first laid eyes on him.

Married life had tamed him a little, but on a night such as this one, Ray was still the man to have around. Ever reliable, ever dependable and always resourceful. It was he, using his wide network of informants, who had discovered the identity of one of Suzie's killers; the very person who was now tied to a chair in the deserted warehouse.

Stuart Davenport's arms were bound behind his back with wire, his ankles fastened to the legs of the chair in the same manner and his upper body strapped in place by a thick leather belt. Stuart was naked apart from a vest and a pair of underpants with his pale flesh looking almost blue with cold in the glare of the solitary yellow bulb that hung limply from an overhead beam. He was soaking wet, as was the ground around him, as Richie poured freezing water from a rusty tin bucket into his mouth. Manno, holding him tightly by the hair, forced his head back and his mouth open, making Stuart cough and splutter as he fought to save himself from drowning. He had held out well and, as yet, had only revealed the name of the driver of the Cortina; an inconsequential villain who would be dealt with in due course, but what Joe really wanted to know was the names of the other two shooters.

'Who was it Stuart?' Ray asked calmly, as Richie eased off on the water.

'I can't— I c..c.. can't, they'll f.. f.. fuckin' kill me!' Davenport screamed, the panic clear to hear as his body shook violently with cold.

Ray nodded to Richie who resumed pouring the water, causing Stuart to gag. 'Who was it Stuart?' Ray said again, blowing a smoke ring. Richie stopped pouring for a moment to allow his captive to speak.

'Alright!' Stuart spat, the icy liquid gargling in the back of his throat, 'Alright, I'll t.. tell ya.'

Richie watched expectantly for Ray's instruction.

'I don't just want the names Stuart, I want the whole story. Y'know it's not gonna be good for you if I have to ask you again,' Ray warned, his voice still betraying no sign of impatience.

'Okay, okay... I'll t.. tell you, I'll t.. tell you it all!' Davenport coughed, and both Richie and Manno looked at Ray, who thought for a moment before signalling for them to rest a moment.

'Okay, Stuart, you're on. Don't let me down now,' he said.

Davenport gasped for breath, spraying water from his purple lips as he blurted, 'It was D.. Danny. Danny, my b.. b.. bruvver...' he was shivering uncontrollably, 'Him and F.. Frankie B.. Blades. They was the ones, th... they was who else was in the c..c.. car.'

Joe was not at all surprised by the name of Danny Davenport, if Stuart was involved, then it was sure to follow that Danny would be too. But Frank Blades? He hadn't expected that.

'Blades?' Joe spoke for the first time, until then he had merely been an observer, 'You're tellin' me Frank Blades was in that car?'

For a second, Davenport remained silent and Richie made to lift the bucket once more, but Joe held up his hand to stop him.

'Let go of 'im,' Joe ordered and immediately Manno did so. Stuart was at last able to avert his gaze away from the light bulb. He looked ghastly, his eyes were pink, swollen and puffy and his skin icy white. His dark purple, nearly black lips and yellow teeth contrasted horribly against his frozen complexion. Soaking wet, Davenport's sodden hair was covered with a thin coating of snowy dew and tiny icicles hung down onto his forehead. A frosty mist was rising from his body as it trembled uncontrollably in erratic spasms; he was in a very poor state, but Joe felt no pity.

'Why Blades, Stuart?' Joe asked, turning up the collar of his expensive cashmere overcoat and adjusting the soft leather cuffs of his hand-stitched Italian gloves. 'What was he doing in the car and what's he got to do with Danny and you?' Joe realised that if Blades was tied in with the Davenports, then it was odds on that he was also in cahoots with Big Jack - and that spelled trouble.

Joe moved closer to the man in the chair and looked hard into his eyes, 'Tell me, Stuart. Tell me now, or never say anything else ever again.' Joe's voice was soft but firm, clearly conveying that he meant every word he said.

Stuart Davenport had never previously met Joe Cassidy, but had no wish to test his former brother-in-law's sincerity. He knew that if he didn't talk, his options lay somewhere between drowning and freezing to death; neither of which appealed. 'Okay,' Stuart said with a gulp, his teeth chattering audibly, 'W.. w.. whattaya w.. wanna know?'

*   *   *

With periodic prompting from Joe, and an occasional bit of 'persuasion' from Ray and the lads, Stuart, under immense duress, eventually revealed everything he knew.

He told of Danny's association with Jack, then of Anderson's involvement with Blades and how it came about. He also went into detail about Frank's employers, about Benny and the Vincenzi's and their Colombian supply chain. Joe learned vital information about Mottola's operation, about where it was based and where its vile merchandise was shipped to.

The final piece of intelligence that Stuart related was about a huge shipment of cocaine that was due to arrive from Miami within the week. Cocaine that was to be sold via The Twenty Ones, to as many different outlets throughout London as possible. This would not only net Blades, Mottola and the Vincenzi family an enormous profit, but also go a long way to securing a sizeable chunk of the market for the ever increasing demand. Effectively giving them the monopoly over London's drug scene.

By the time Stuart had finished he was close to death. He was barely able to talk, his whole body stiff with cold and the water which covered it had frozen into a thin white crust. Joe could have had him rushed to hospital, or at the very least, had him wrapped in a blanket or two. That would have probably been enough to save him. But all Joe could think of was Suzie and Matt, and the happy life which the scum before him had snatched cruelly away from them.

'What do you want us to do with him Boss?' Richie asked.

'Make it look like an accident,' Joe replied as he turned and walked away, his heart as cold as Stuart Davenport's body.

Twelve

'Don't worry, Benny. It'll go like clockwork I'm tellin' ya. Nothin' is gonna happen to that shipment, not while I'm in charge, it'll be sweet as a nut - I promise.' As he spoke on the phone to his superior, Frank Blades lay in the double bed of his plush, Park Lane hotel room, enjoying the feel of the silk sheets on his naked flesh. He was gently rubbing his groin, heightening his already extreme arousal. As he did this, he watched with delicious pleasure the pretty young eighteen year-old whom he had picked up just an hour before, in the members only club he frequented whenever he was in London.

The boy, totally nude, stood in the bathroom brushing his teeth, well aware of Frank's attentions and enjoying them to the full. He liked dominant, powerful men and the one lying in bed, whose lascivious, ogling eyes were boring into him was certainly that. He also showed signs of being a bit of a brute, someone who liked to play rough and would think little of using violence to increase his pleasure. A thought which appealed to the boy in a mouthwateringly masochistic way.

For Frank too, the boy was everything he could have hoped for; young, of course, but also very slim and feminine, slightly built with little sign of muscle and virtually no body hair. Blades smiled leerily at the thought of his big, strong hands caressing that smooth, delicate skin and his breathing quickened when he imagined the damage he could inflict with just the minimum amount effort, he found the excitement and near electric sense of anticipation almost unbearable. There was only one thing spoiling his pleasure and that was Benny Mottola. Frank had to get him off the phone fast.

Benny was fretting about the shipment of cocaine, which was expected to dock within the next few hours. It was an enormous consignment, with a street value of millions and he was quite understandably anxious about his investment.

Frank though, was less concerned. The shipment was worth an awful lot to him too and would increase his personal wealth considerably, but he had confidence in Big Jack and Danny, feeling certain that they could handle the situation by themselves.

As soon as Blades had met the boy he knew he wasn't gong to make it to the docks. For him, he needed all night, not just a few measly hours. This one deserved to be savoured. Besides, it was a filthy night, sleeting heavily and the roads thick with slush from the sporadic snow showers of the last few days. The last thing Frank wanted was to leave the comfort of his luxurious suite and the considerable delights of his young companion to meet some rust bucket of a ship on the cold, windy docks, regardless of its cargo.

No, he felt sure Jack and Danny could handle it alone. He would go down in the morning when it had been off-loaded, perhaps it might have stopped sleeting by then.

Of course, Blades had no intention of telling Benny any of that. As far as Mottola was concerned, Frank was going to be there to welcome the ship's arrival and to take delivery of the valuable contents in its hold. He had managed to convince Benny of this very easily and as he finally put the telephone down, he thought how clever he was. He had finally cracked it; there he was in the lap of luxury, whilst two underlings were doing his dirty work, work which in the fullness of time, would reap him untold rewards, and as for Benny, well, what he didn't know, wouldn't hurt him.

Frank smiled with satisfaction as he lifted the sheets allowing his young friend to slide into bed, it had all the makings of a truly momentous night.

*   *   *

Joe and Ray had been sitting in the Jag since the early hours of the morning, watching from a discreet distance all that had ensued. They were parked, unseen by those involved in the dramatic scenes across the river, nearly a quarter of a mile away from the EeZee Freight warehouse where the action was taking place. Both men were armed with powerful binoculars and enjoying themselves immensely.

Ray had telephoned the police anonymously the day before, tipping them off about the shipment. This behaviour went against all the unwritten laws of the underworld, which stated that never, under any circumstances, should you grass up a fellow criminal. But this was drugs - a massive consignment - and these were the men responsible for Suzie's murder, so, in this case, Joe decided to make an exception. Rules didn't apply when dealing with the likes of Danny Davenport, Jack Anderson and, more especially, Frank Blades - although, as yet, he was a no show.

Joe and Ray were wrapped in blankets and warm clothing, keeping the cold at bay by drinking hot coffee from a large flask which had been lovingly prepared for them by Rose.

From their secret viewpoint, they had witnessed everything from the moment the ship entered the dock. They had seen its cargo being off-loaded and watched as Big Jack and Danny inspected the goods, then they saw Anderson hand over a briefcase to the captain of the ship, which they knew to be full of cash.

But the best bit, the bit which was the whole reason for them being there, was when the police swooped in, seizing the shipment of cocaine and catching Jack Anderson, Danny Davenport and the captain red-handed. The raid had happened so quickly that none of the culprits even had time to draw their guns before they were over-powered by the combined forces of the police and customs units, who performed their parts extremely efficiently.

Joe would have paid good money to see again the expression on Jack Anderson's face as he was handcuffed and thrown in the back of the police van. Davenport was even better entertainment as, unlike Jack, he made quite a show of resisting arrest, but eventually he too was bundled into the van and whisked away to the station.

After the main characters had left, Joe and Ray continued to watch as the police cordoned off the crime scene and set to work on assessing the extent of their hoard. The drugs were hidden in what looked like stacks of car tyres, which in reality were cleverly disguised outer shells made from moulded plastic and coated in black rubber. Even under close scrutiny, these would have fooled many a customs officer, but fortunately the authorities had been told exactly how the narcotics were concealed and knew precisely what to look for.

Joe and Ray finally lost interest around 8.30am, even though the docks were still a hive of activity and would be for a good time yet. But they were tired and hungry and looking forward to one of Ruby's marvellous cooked breakfasts which she had promised them upon their return. It had, however, been a very eventful and rewarding night. Jack Anderson and Danny Davenport were off the streets, at least for the time being, and a large dent had been put into Benny Mottola's finances, as well as those of the Vincenzi crime family's. Also, theirs and Benny's designs on the London drug scene had suffered a serious set-back. It was a blow that would not be taken lightly.

Joe's only disappointment was that Frank Blades hadn't

turned up for the party, having been conspicuous by his absence. Joe was not too worried though, he knew he would catch up with Blades sooner or later and when he did, he would not get off as lightly as Jack and Danny. Prison was far too good for an animal like Frank Blades.

*   *   *

Frank awoke early and glanced over at the boy beside him. He stroked the lad's face with the back of his hand, running his thick fingers over the purple bruise he had inflicted in the throes of passion. The lad groaned with pleasure, still asleep but blissfully aware of Frank's touch, enjoying the feel of the rough, working hands on his face.

Frank looked at his watch, it was 7.45am. He got out of bed and peered through the curtains, it had stopped sleeting and the sun was just starting to show itself above the morning mist. He turned and looked again at the slim, almost irresistible form of the boy in the bed and for a moment was sorely tempted to slide back beneath the sheets and wake him up. But he knew thoughts of that nature would have to wait until later, now he really had to get to the docks as he'd delayed it long enough. Besides, the boy would still be there when he returned.

By now, the shipment would have been off-loaded and within a few short months he would be reaping huge financial rewards from the sale of the valuable merchandise. With that kind of money, he could buy as many young boys as he desired, this one, although beautiful and beguiling, was just the first of many that would undoubtedly form part of his new affluent lifestyle. But, for now, Frank needed to make sure that everything had gone smoothly before phoning Benny with the good news.

Once showered, Frankie put on a clean shirt and a freshly dry-cleaned suit. He then plucked a silk rose from the arrangement on the chest of drawers and placed it on the pillow next to the boy, who was still sound asleep. Then silently, Frank left the room.

The Mercedes he had hired was a joy to drive and he promised to treat himself to one, maybe even two when the money started rolling in. The automatic gearbox was as smooth as silk as the luxury car sped him through the busy streets towards south London.

Five minutes out from the docks, Frank was over-taken by a police van, then by two panda cars and two police motorcycles with their sirens blaring.

Alarm bells began ringing in his head too, especially when he approached the entrance to the docks and another two police cars pulled out in front of him and sped through the gates. Frank felt his stomach churn with dread, instinct and a strong sense of survival told him what had happened but he had to be sure.

Parking the Merc safely out of sight, Frank covered the remaining distance on foot being careful not to be seen. When he arrived at the dock, his worst fears were confirmed as he spied the police units and customs officials swarming around the EeZee Freight warehouse. The shipment had been rumbled, the consignment lost and all thoughts of his wealthy future suddenly evaporated.

Blades hung around unseen for another ten minutes or so, just watching the ensuing action with unbelieving eyes, trying to come to terms with the enormity of the loss and the repercussions that would inevitably reverberate from it. With a sick feeling in his guts, he finally returned to his expensive hire car and when the door closed, he roared with anger and despair. What in God's name was he going to tell Benny and the Vincenzis? They had millions tied up in that shipment. They had put their trust in him and he had blown it. What could he tell them? That instead of checking on their investment and making sure everything went without a hitch, he had decided to spend the night with some pretty little queer with a penchant for rough sex. That was the truth, but there was no way he was telling them that.

Frank had given Benny his word. He had promised that he would personally supervise the whole operation. Mottola had put his trust in him and he had squandered it. Now he would surely pay the price.

As he turned the Mercedes around and began the drive back, he wondered what fate had befallen Jack and Danny and whether it was them who had grassed about the shipment to the law. But instantly he dismissed it as they, like him, had too much to gain from the sale of the merchandise. Stuart Davenport, on the other hand, didn't and Frank thought him to be the most likely culprit. He hadn't been seen for a few days either, which made his treachery all the more likely. Conspicuously guilty by his absence it could be said.

As Frank pulled up at the traffic lights, he noticed a silver Jaguar passing in the opposite direction, driven by Ray Reece with Joe Cassidy sitting in the passenger seat. Both were laughing at something obviously very funny, neither noticing Blades as he watched, seething in silence. Suddenly everything made sense; Frank had no proof, but it was as clear to him as the hairs on the back of his hand.

Joe had obviously caught up with Stuart for the death of that girl, Frank deduced, and the weak willed fool had talked. That would certainly explain Davenport's disappearance and meant Cassidy was responsible for the loss of the shipment. He was the one behind it. Again he had prevailed and ruined Frank's life. But this was the last time, he would do it no more. Next time Frank would be the victor. Next time Blades would kill Joe Cassidy.

* * *

By the time Frank arrived back at the hotel he was in a cold sweat. The crisp, pristine shirt he had put on only an hour or so

459

before was now nothing more than a perspiration soaked rag, the tie that accompanied it, pulled loose and hanging at an untidy angle.

Frank was panicked, uncertain which way to turn. He suspected that no matter what he said to Benny by way of an explanation, it would not be enough. His actions, or lack of them, were inexcusable and his instincts told him that Benny would respond accordingly.

Neither Benny or Tito Vincenzi were big on failure and, with something so catastrophically disastrous, so financially damaging as this, they would be looking to vent their considerable displeasure swiftly.

Frank could tell Benny that Joe was behind the raid but he was not sure even that information would be enough to get him off the hook.

Blades entered his hotel room, incensed by the turn of events which he knew instinctively to be Joe's doing. Frank had despised Cassidy for years, but now it went further than that, much further indeed. The hate he now felt was so intense that it threatened to overwhelm him and banish every rational thought from his head. The fine line between sanity and madness had always been a thin one with Frank and, with this final humiliation, it all but evaporated.

As he crossed quickly to the bathroom, glancing over at the young boy still in the bed, he felt a strong prickle of irritation at his presence. The lad serving as an all too clear reminder of what Frank had lost in the short time since leaving his side. All his hopes and dreams had been washed away; the affluent lifestyle of flash cars, fancy clothes and willing young men that he had so confidently dared to fantasise about, had been destroyed, gone almost in the blink of an eye.

Blades wanted to be alone, he had to think, to form some

460

sort of contingency plan and having the boy there, with his young, slim, provocative body was not helping. It was a hindrance he resented and needed to be rid of.

Frank could hear the sound of his own heartbeat as it thundered in his ears, his palms clammy as he ran the cold tap. He cupped his hands together and let the water fill them, then bending over the sink, he splashed his face, repeating the process several times, hoping it would calm his frayed nerves and allow him some clarity of thought. But it did not.

As Frank stood up straight, he noticed the boy standing behind him, naked except for a smile, his mop of unruly blonde hair hanging untidily over one eye. He had just woken up and the sleep was still in his eyes, but he had heard Frank come in and was more than ready for a repeat of the previous night's performance.

The boy gazed dreamily at Blades in the mirror as he placed a slim feminine hand on his shoulder, the long delicate fingers beginning to play with the dark mahogany curls on the base of the big man's neck. Frank felt his ire rising even further, his face turning almost purple with rage as he looked back at the boy's beautiful face reflected in the glass. As he stared, he became convinced that the boy was taunting him, ridiculing him for the loss of the shipment and laughing at his incompetence. Frank's whole body started to tremble and he grabbed for the basin to steady himself. His right hand fixed on a hard plastic hair dryer which he gripped with all his might, his knuckles turning white with the force of it.

The lad, oblivious to the agitation he was causing, nuzzled his nose into Frank's hair, lightly kissing the nape of his neck, the fingers of his other hand gently caressing his buttocks.

'Want some more fun?' The boy asked in a husky whisper.

'Fun?' Frank was appalled, barely able to speak through gritted teeth. How the hell could he think about fun at a time like this?

461

'Fun?' He repeated. 'Are you takin' the piss or are you just fuckin' stupid?'

'What? No, I.. I.. just thought you might like some—' the boy was unable to finish as he saw the murderous look on Frank's face. Usually the boy liked it rough, enjoyed getting smacked around, he even got off on it, particularly when the violence was filled with lust. But that emotion was no longer present in Frankie's eyes, not as it had been the night before. What the boy saw in its place was hate, loathing and madness. The insanity was now plain to see and it sent a shiver down his spine.

'I'll give you fuckin' fun you little poof bastard!' Blades roared as he span around, lashing out wildly with both hands, the left one balled into a fist, the right one still clutching the hair dryer, the mains lead whipping freely in its wake.

The very first blow knocked the boy to the ground but Frank's eyes were red with fury as he continued to land blow after crushing blow, bending almost double to reach his target. Kicking and punching like a crazy man, totally incensed, sickeningly oblivious to the severe damage he was inflicting as the lad's face turned slowly to pulp. 'Not so much fun now is it you little prick!' Blades shouted in mid-attack, but it went unheard by his victim.

The force in which the hard plastic hair dryer connected, easily smashed the boy's skull and long before his attacker's temper was spent, he was dead. He lay awkwardly, no longer recognisable, in a pool of dark red blood, a spongy yellow goo seeping through a wide gash in his forehead.

Frank's suit was wet with blood and his hands were stained crimson. The hair dryer had fragments of skull and brain stuck to it and chunks of flesh were clogged in the end.

The rage at last subsided and Frank looked down exhausted to examine the heinous thing he had done. He knelt down and carefully lifted the boy's shattered skull, holding it easily in one of his huge hands, whilst with the other he stroked the bloody remains of his lover's destroyed face. 'Not so much fun now,' Frank said wistfully, his voice thick with remorse and a tear running down his cheek into his droopy Mexican moustache. 'Not so much fun now,' he repeated as he considered his own, increasingly more difficult situation.

*   *   *

Almost two hours later, the dead boy's corpse still lay on the bathroom floor where it had fallen, Frank's footprints clearly visible in the blood which he had trodden into the bedroom carpet.

Blades was sitting on the bed studying the macabre trail, although his thoughts were elsewhere. He still held the telephone receiver in his hand from the call that had finished abruptly over five minutes before. The dialling tone having now been replaced by an annoying high-pitched siren as a reminder for the caller to replace the handset. But Frank was not concerned with that, the noise was the least of his worries, which had dramatically escalated since his phone conversation with Mottola.

Blades had lied to Benny in order to hide the unforgivable truth of why he hadn't personally met the shipment, but Mottola didn't buy it. He didn't believe a word. Frank had no convincing answer as to why Jack and Danny had been caught at the scene but not him. And to Benny that stunk of deceit.

Even when Frank related his sighting of Joe and Ray near the docks Mottola seemed dismissive and just viewed it as another excuse, another attempt by Blades to cover his gross incompetence.

In the end, Benny placed the blame for the enormity of the loss entirely at Frank's feet. His whole handling of the situation had been disastrously inept and because of it Mottola and the Vincenzis had lost millions. After a long, scathing tirade, Benny was calling for Frank's blood. He told him to start running and to never stop, because if either he or Tito Vincenzi ever caught up with him, his

463

life would be over.

'I'll rip your fuckin' lungs out through the top of your worthless skull you incompetent prick!' Were Mottola's exact words, and even though Blades begged for a second chance, his boss was having none of it. 'I'm speakin' to a fuckin' dead man!' Benny yelled before finally slamming the phone down.

Frank was in shock. Even though he had expected Benny to react much in the way that he had, a small part of him hoped that he would be able to talk him round. After all, he and Benny went back over twenty-five years which he thought would surely have accounted for something. But no, he was out and his life was in danger. Now he had to get away, to avoid capture either by Mottola or the law, who would want him for the murder of the boy.

There could be no doubt in the minds of the police that Blades was the killer, as the hotel had been booked in Frank's name; his bloody footprints were all over the carpet and his fingerprints all over the hair dryer. Also the doorman had seen Frank enter with a slim young man, which he would testify to in a court of law. With the evidence stacked against him, a jury would find him guilty as charged and this time they would send him down for life.

There was no way he was going back to prison. Not in a million years.

Finally he was starting to think clearly again. The initial panic was over and he now knew what he had to do. Give it time, he told himself, let Benny cool off, then, when he had, take him a prize that would ensure his forgiveness: the head of Joe Cassidy on a silver platter. Frank's mood brightened as he savoured the thought - how ironic that his most hated enemy would be the one to bring about his own salvation.

After throwing a few items of clothing into an overnight bag, Frank Blades slipped out of the room and left the hotel by the rear entrance. He would not be seen again for many months.

Jack Anderson and Danny Davenport had done well in Benny's eyes. Neither man had disclosed Mottola's name to the police and both were doing time because of it. As a reward for their loyalty, he hired the very best team to represent them. Although, ultimately, the ridiculously inadequate four year sentence that was finally handed down, was not down to any cunning legal chicanery but to Benny's influence over the judge and most of the jury, who had all been 'persuaded' to be extremely lenient. With good behaviour, Jack and Danny would be out in two years. Needless to say, they were both extremely relieved and grateful.

Whilst serving their sentence, both men would learn that Joe was responsible not only for their imprisonment but also for the death of Stuart. And it would not be forgotten.

Thirteen

By 1977, Matt had been at the Bluestone for four years and was proving to be a valuable employee. He seemed to know almost everything about cars and bikes and kept all the stunt vehicles running remarkably smoothly. He fitted into our team well; Rocky Costello and Brad Booker, his two immediate superiors, finding him amiable and hard working whilst also keen to join in the boisterous fun that played a large part in the average day of the Company. Rocky and Brad were also notorious practical jokers so it helped if those who worked with them were game for a laugh.

It had taken Matt over eight months to come to terms with Suzie's death and at least another eight to be able to smile and enjoy himself without feeling guilty, but at last he had returned to his old self. Once more he was the confident, cool and easy going young man I'd met a few years before.

In the years that Matt had been at the ranch, Rose had visited Palm Springs with Brett several times, but Joe had not, preferring to give his eldest son the space he so obviously needed. However, in the meantime, Matt was working hard and I was very pleased to have him at the Bluestone.

* * *

Another recent employee was a personal chauffeur for Victoria who went by the name of Roberto DeSilva.

DeSilva performed his duties well enough, although did not socialise with the rest of the staff and was extremely secretive and guarded about his activities outside the ranch. In retrospect that should have aroused my suspicions, but I innocently assumed him to be nothing more than a harmless loner - besides his references, which I had thoroughly checked out, were excellent and Victoria had no complaints about his conduct. As long as she was happy, I had no interest in DeSilva's life away from work which, as it turned out, was a big mistake.

Unbeknownst to me, the name Roberto DeSilva was just an alias. Our chauffeur's real name was Wolf, and his extra curricular activities included frequent trips to LA and San Francisco, to oversee the Vincenzi narcotics operation on the West Coast, which he had been doing quite successfully for the last couple of years. Chauffeuring Victoria was merely a sideline, a little surveillance job on behalf of his true boss; Benny Mottola.

Originally, Wolf's brief had just been to keep a periodical check on what was going on at the Bluestone, but since the loss of the drugs shipment in London, which Frank had said Joe was behind, Benny thought it prudent to keep a closer watch on things.

When a vacancy for a chauffeur came up, Mottola ordered Wolf to apply for it, supplying him of course with all the relevant reference letters and work history that any potential employer could not fail to be impressed by. Sure enough, we fell for it and Wolf was hired; the consequences of that fateful decision still, as yet, to unfold.

*   *   *

The scandal of Victoria's pregnancy had taken its toll, as had the attitude of the studio and its appalling treatment of her. Some of the letters she received from the general public were mercilessly cruel too with very few actually offering support. It seemed her once loyal fan base had all but disappeared and that rocked her once unshakeable confidence to its foundation. Also, it hurt Victoria deeply that she was prevented from working. Acting was her passion and when she was suspended for the second time, it broke her heart, even though she made a brave attempt at disguising it.

During her years away from Hollywood, she took on a very different role, that of a housewife and mother. But it was not what she would necessarily have chosen for herself had things worked out differently. When she was not looking after the children she would busy herself around the ranch and on the surface she appeared to be leading a very busy, contented life. But I knew her too well, I knew it was not the life she craved, and suspected deep down that she was desperately unhappy.

Victoria was an actress and although she made a half-hearted attempt at protest, I persuaded her that as soon as her suspension was lifted, she should get back to it.

Sure enough, after years of being unable to work, Victoria's studio suspension finally ended and she was at last able to go back to what she loved, or at least she would have done had the studio not cancelled her contract. She was no longer, as they put it, a sort after commodity and had no wish to waste any more money on a star they considered to be washed up. Angry and disappointed but not put off, Victoria hit the audition circuit, determined to prove them wrong.

However, where previously she had been offered all the choicest roles, she was now forced to go for the smaller, not so glamorous supporting parts. Ten years was a long time to be away in the movie business and casting directors were afraid that the public had forgotten her.

With Louretta helping with the children, we made the decision that if Victoria was to stand any chance of finding work at all, she needed to be closer to the action. This meant she would temporarily move out of the ranch in favour of her cottage in Beverly Hills which was much more convenient for all the studios. That way, if an audition came up, she could be there in an instant. She desperately needed to get a decent part before her credibility and star status vanished completely. It was not about money, she had more than enough of that, it was about her need to work and about her pride too.

It was also, unconsciously, a significant turning point in our marriage as we had been drifting apart for years, since even before Josh was born. And, although neither of us were prepared to admit it, this work related separation was probably only a precursor to a much more personal one.

*   *   *

Victoria was far and away better than most of the other actresses on the circuit and she was getting to the point where she would do almost anything to prove it. She suspected that a lot of the younger girls were getting cast not because of their talent but because of their willingness to screw certain directors - a practice almost as old as the Hollywood Hills. There was one particular occasion when Victoria knew, without question, that she would have gotten a part had she been willing to do the same.

It was with a producer named Murray Lieberman, a particularly nasty and lecherous little man with a reputation for ruthless behaviour. Lieberman was renowned for womanising and gambling and regularly spent weekends in Reno, Vegas or Atlantic City where the pit bosses knew him well. Murray played high stakes poker and tales of his outrageous betting were legendary. Mostly he won, but on the occasions when he lost, he was a horrible person to be around and made the lives of those that accompanied him hell. He was a very, very poor loser, but the casino's loved him and always extended him an enormous line in credit. They knew he was good for it because Murray was very successful at what he did. His sure touch in movies had made him an extremely wealthy man; gambling was just one of his little perks - as were the women who came to audition for him.

Victoria's audition went particularly well and Murray phoned personally a day later to tell her that it was between her and a younger, less experienced actress called Christie Mathers. However, Victoria was led to believe that she would eventually be the one cast and, because of this, allowed herself to be quietly confident.

After a hellish, nerve-wracking, three day wait, Murray Lieberman finally called again asking Victoria to meet him at his office to discuss the part and although the conversation was fairly cryptic, Vicky felt a pang of excitement. This was it, this was her way back, at last she had been given a break.

When she arrived, she was ushered straight into his sumptuously appointed office, where Murray greeted her by kissing her on both cheeks. Then he stood back and quite deliberately eyed her up and down as if she was the main course at dinner. 'Mmm,' he said with approval, 'You look good enough to eat.' He then guided her to a polished green leather chesterfield and motioned for her to sit down.

'Drink?' He asked.

'Whiskey please, on the rocks,' she replied nervously.

Lieberman fixed her a drink and then sat down beside her, his leg touching hers.

'Well Vicky,' he began, 'I've got good news.'

Victoria felt her pulse quicken.

'The part's yours if you want it,' he said.

She couldn't help but beam with delight as Murray continued,'You do want it don't you?'

'Yes, yes I do. I do want it, thankyou.' She was almost laughing with happiness.

'That's good. I'm glad you do. There's just one thing that stands in your way....' Lieberman's hand was now resting on Vicky's knee and she could feel the dampness of his palm on her stockinged leg.

'Oh, what's that?' She replied, suddenly feeling a little deflated.

'Well, it's just that Christie Mathers so badly wants it too.'

'But— ?' Victoria was confused, 'I don't understand, if you're giving it to me then why—?'

'It's just that she's prepared to do certain...' He pretended to search for the right word, 'Certain things, shall we say, that make her just a little bit more appealing. That is of course, unless you can offer the same. I, in all honesty, have always preferred you over her, I just need a little bit more persuasion.' Murray's hand was now moving slowly up Victoria's thigh, dragging the silk of her skirt with it and threatening to expose her stocking tops.

'What sort of things?' She asked, although now understanding and knowing the answer all too well. Murray Lieberman was sixty-five with a bald, very tanned head and piercing grey eyes which peered at her from behind thick, black framed glasses. He was shorter than her with a large pot belly and his expensive three-piece suit smelled of stale cigars. When he smiled, which he was doing at present, he showed off a set of immaculately polished dentures that made him look like the letch that he was.

'Now there's a question,' he eventually replied, making a show of being embarrassed, although clearly not. 'Shall we say, a blow job, for starters?' He said, licking his teeth lasciviously.

Victoria couldn't believe the nerve of this vile little asshole. Did he think that just because she wanted a part in his movie she'd do anything he wanted? She could have slapped him, but played it cool. She'd teach the sonofabitch.

'Hmm. I dunno,' Victoria said flirtatiously,' You'd better show me what I've got to work with.'

Lieberman smiled broadly. It was all so easy. He stood up eagerly and unbuttoned his trousers, pushing both them and his blue silk under shorts down to display his puny manhood.

Victoria examined it closely, being careful not to touch. 'My God, Murray,' she said rising to her feet, 'Is that it? I guess you ain't got such a big part to offer me after all. If it's all the same to you, I think I'll pass.' With that, she sashayed over to the door and threw it open. Lieberman just stood there gobsmacked as four of his put-upon assistants got a hilarious look at his unimpressive penis.

'Oh, and as for your movie,' Victoria added before leaving, 'You can shove it up your ass!'

Murray's eyes burned holes into her back as he struggled to pull up his pants and, as the girls in his office giggled, he swore to one day get even with Victoria Wild.

* * *

Purely by coincidence, two weeks later Murray was in Las Vegas playing the tables at the Villa Continental, which he did every six months or so. Sitting next to him was Carl Napier, friend to the rich and famous. Carl was always on hand when Murray was in town, just in case he needed anything. For the amount of money Lieberman spent in the casino he was well worth looking after and for the two or three days he stayed at the Villa, Carl was his best buddy.

Carl supplied everything from helicopters and limousines to drugs and whores, not that Murray paid directly for any of these, but in the long run it cost him an absolute fortune.

On this visit however, Murray was not too interested in partying and seemed a little preoccupied, perhaps even slightly perturbed. When Napier questioned him about this he seemed reluctant to speak about it, but as the alcohol began to flow and, later, in Carl's penthouse, when the marijuana was thick in the air,

Lieberman began to loosen up.

He eventually told Carl what had been niggling at him for the past fourteen days; about the actress who had so badly humiliated him. When Murray finally revealed the name of the woman who had so embarrassed him, Carl smiled and said, 'Let me tell you a little story about Victoria Wild which might just interest you.'

* * *

When the phone call came, Victoria was stunned. Murray was full of apologies, saying that he hoped she could forgive him and that he had some news for her that he was sure would change everything, although he was anxious not to say too much over the phone. He wanted her to come down to see him at the studio as soon as possible, but Victoria could not forget so easily, and didn't see why she should be at his beck and call.

'How 'bout you come to me instead, Murray? Say tomorrow afternoon, at two?'

'That'll be fine,' Lieberman said, being uncharacteristically agreeable.

'Okay then,' she replied, genuinely perplexed by his attitude, 'I'll send my driver to pick you up.'

'Fine. Until tomorrow then. Bye.'

Victoria replaced the handset. What the hell was going on? What was the reason for Murray's sudden change of heart? Had she got the part after all? That had to be it, there could be no other explanation. She had stuck to her principles and won the part after all. Why else would Lieberman be calling her? Finally, things were going her way.

* * *

Wolf, posing as Roberto DeSilva, Victoria's chauffeur, delivered Lieberman at the appointed hour, showing him into the drawing room where Victoria, looking ravishing in a neon blue figure hugging silk dress, stood waiting for him.

'Thankyou, Roberto,' she said, 'That'll be all for the time being.'

Immediately, Wolf became suspicious, sensing that something important was about to happen and he was determined to find out what.

'So, Victoria, we meet again and my, how gorgeous you look!' Murray wasn't lying, she did indeed look absolutely stunning, proving that she could more than hold her own against younger actresses.

'Murray,' she nodded coolly, still a little amazed by his presence, 'For what do I owe this... pleasure?' Her sarcasm was undisguised.

'Straight to business, eh, honey?'

'Straight to business. What d'ya want, Murray? I'm busy.'

'There's only one thing that I want and you know what it is.' His pleasant manner changed instantly, his eyes becoming cold and Vicky felt a shiver run down her spine.

'You want me for the movie, right?' Asked rather hopefully.

'Oh, I want you alright, but as for the movie, we'll just have to see.'

It was over, the dream had ended and her anger flared, 'Listen, you filthy creep, like I said before, if that's what you want, you can forget it. Now get out, before I call the police!'

'Oh, but I haven't told you my news yet,' he was calm, totally unrattled, 'I think it'll interest you.'

'What could you possibly say that would interest me?' She was shaking with rage.

'It's about Sean.'

The words hit her like a bullet. 'What about him,' she hissed.

'Oh, nothing much,' his mouth slid into a satisfied grin, 'Just that I know his name is Sean Reilly and he's wanted for the murder of three men.'

It took a couple of seconds for the shock to register, then her legs buckled and she collapsed onto her large couch. The anger left her to be replaced immediately by horror. It was all going to happen again - her life would be in pieces once more and this time her faltering career would surely be over for good.

The room was silent for a long moment before she said, 'What are you going to do?'

'That's up to you' he replied.

'What do you mean?' It was an instinctive question as she already knew the answer.

'I want you.' His big white dentures gleamed at her and a little drop of spittle rested on his lower lip.

'And then?'

'And then we'll see, but for the moment it buys my silence. I might even get you the part in that movie if you're a really good girl.' As ever, Murray had his eye on the main chance, he knew she was the only one for the role.

'What do you want me to do?' Victoria had begun to tremble.

'Everything honey. I want you to do everything.'

Victoria had tried life as a housewife and life as a mother. But it wasn't anything like the life she'd had as a movie star, the life she'd had until circumstances forced her to give it up. She wanted to be an actress, it was what she lived for, the chance of being a star again, she needed it more than anything in the world.

She hesitated, then said, 'And if I do it, do you promise to get me the movie?'

'Oh, yeah, honey,' Murray replied breathlessly, 'I promise.'

After another long silence, Victoria finally said in a near inaudible whisper, 'Okay.'

*　　*　　*

Outside in the hallway, Wolf stood watching through the crack in the door, he had his flies undone and was relieving himself

475

vigorously by hand. He'd always had a thing for Victoria Wild and had secretly spied on her many times as she undressed, wishing he could do to her what Murray Lieberman was doing to her now. As Wolf climaxed, battling to suppress a loud moan of delight, he looked forward to the day, when Benny gave the word, when he could do just that.

Fourteen

They'd kept Benny down; Tito and Carmine. Ever since the huge loss of the drug shipment in London, thanks to the incompetence of Frank Blades, Benny's former lieutenant. Ever since then, Tito Vincenzi and Carmine Carboni had made Mottola work hard to win back their trust and confidence. Because of Frank's disappearance and their inability to find him, Benny had been the focus of their wrath, only just escaping a bullet to the back of the head.

For a long time they had forced him to suffer, keeping him been busy not only in Miami, but up and down the whole East coast of America. Twenty-fours hours a day, seven days a week oiling the wheels of the Vincenzi and Carboni crime syndicate. If the police started pointing fingers and began looking for someone to arrest, then Benny was the one set for the fall. Tito and Carmine would remain clean, whiter than white, completely innocent of all wrong-doing, although they, of course, were the chief architects of it all.

Benny had undertaken everything they had thrown at him, not with reluctance but with relish, eager to gain their trust once more. His performance had been faultless and his strategy flawless. Within a very short space of time he had recouped and doubled every cent that both he and his two mentors had lost on the London docks. So impressive were his accomplishments, that his slate had been wiped clean. He'd not only redeemed himself but had earned a great deal of respect in the process. However, the bosses were still wary of Benny, he was manic and clearly only just on the right side of sane so they would need to keep a watch on him to make sure he stayed that way.

But, with the heat finally off, Benny now had time to concentrate on other matters; things which had taken a back seat whilst Tito and Carmine had kept him so busy.

*　*　*

In the time Michael had been working for Joe, he had, through Carl, unknowingly fed some very valuable financial tips to Benny. Information about lucrative investments that Joe was considering as well as his uncannily accurate speculations on the stock market.

Mottola and Carl Napier had learned to trust this instinct and whenever they were told that Joe was either buying or selling stock in a particular company, they would follow suit. This had proved to be an excellent strategy and one which had swelled both their bank balances considerably, but for Benny it wasn't enough. He had grown bored. Money was one thing, but revenge was another and now that Tito and Carmine were off his back, it was time for some action, not just in London but in California also.

Benny decided that Wolf had been on the West Coast too long and it was time for him to return to Miami. Since ridding himself of Frank Blades, Mottola had been without the aid of a reliable lieutenant; a role which he knew Wolf would be ideal for.

Wolf would have to finish his business with the Bluestone ranch as soon as possible, to fulfil the task which he always knew lay at the end of his assignment; for him, the most enjoyable part. Then, when the work was done and all loose ends had been neatly tied up, Wolf would return to Florida to take up his new position.

Benny's thoughts then turned to London. Michael Walsh, whilst being an excellent stock market tipster, had not been such an inspired choice for the role of informant. Sure the financial intelligence was good, but nothing else was coming through of any worth. The boy was too weak and Carl far too soft with him; both needed a kick up the rear if ever Joe Cassidy was going to suffer.

Benny picked up the phone and dialled Carl's penthouse in Vegas. It was time to let Napier know just how disappointed he was in him and to remind him of the consequences should he continue to fail. He would also urge him to pass the message on to Michael.

The schedule had just been stepped up and if they couldn't do the job, then they could easily be replaced by someone who could.

*   *   *

Carl Napier had been partying far too hard of late and the effects of it had taken its toll on his weary body. The last two years had largely been one non-stop binge of booze and drugs, usually at the expense of the high-rollers who frequented the Villa on a regular basis. Carl liked to entertain in his penthouse, more often than not with a couple of showgirls, a case of champagne and copious amounts of cocaine.

Carl had not forgiven Joe but, thanks to the drugs, his mind no longer had the focus it once did and vengeance was no longer a top priority. Besides, why should he upset the apple cart when he was happily reaping the rewards from Joe's financial wizardry on the stock market - courtesy of his mole, Michael.

At least, that was what he had thought before the phone call, before Benny had upped the stakes. Before his life was put on the line.

For some reason, after a two year respite, Benny had suddenly taken a renewed interest in his old adversary and now, out of the blue, he wanted results. More to the point, he wanted Carl to supply him with them - and fast.

Carl knew he'd have to be tough with Michael in order to steel him into action. The boy was weak, not cut-out for the kind of work he had to do, but do it he must as Benny Mottola was not a patient man.

That much had just been made abundantly clear.

Fifteen

Michael had done all he could over the last few years to learn everything there was to know about Joe Cassidy. He'd had to get close to him; to pretend to respect him and admire him. He'd even made an effort to befriend his equally loathsome son, Brett, although that battle had been somewhat harder to win.

However, ingratiate himself to the Cassidys he duly had, exactly as Carl Napier had asked him to do and, on the whole, he considered himself to have done an excellent job. But apparently, for Napier, that was nowhere near good enough. Carl had spat words like 'useless, stupid and incompetent' down the phone at him and by the end of the call he did indeed feel like a combination of all three.

Of his few friends, Carl Napier was the only one who he could ever really talk to who truly understood. Never before had he so much as raised his voice to Michael let alone been angry with him. So why was he being so mean now? If Carl turned against him then it would be too much to bear; there would be no point in carrying on. Michael had to redeem himself and quickly. He had to win back the friendship and the respect of the man he had looked up to since he was a child, and he knew exactly how to do it.

* * *

Two years earlier, Joe had agreed to let Michael act as his

assistant whenever he was home from university, delighted that the boy seemed finally to have warmed to him. The arrangement was immediately successful, with Michael proving to be a reliable asset; his quick intelligence and intuitive business sense making him an excellent choice as aid. Over time, Michael's input and workload increased, as did Joe's confidence in him and quickly he became privy to nearly all of Ironclad's dealings. Now, two years on, he was one of Joe's closest confidants - at least in all legal matters.

However, there were a few files that Michael did not have access to which, he suspected, were the ones that Carl Napier might find the most interesting. Michael became convinced that these files held information relating to the more nefarious side of his uncle's business empire; the dirty, seedy side which Joe had always kept hidden from him, locked away in a private safe under the floorboards.

Fortunately Michael knew the combination.

He had watched his uncle open it many times and had made a mental note of the numbers, which he now knew off by heart. That was the easy part.

Unfortunately the safe also needed a key, which Joe kept in the drawer of his desk whenever he was in the office, but when he was out, he took it with him. This presented a problem. There was only one time every day when Joe was separated from the key for longer than five minutes and if Michael was to gain access to the safe, this was his window of opportunity; his only chance.

Sixteen

For almost the last quarter of a century, Sarah's eyes had been devoid of life, just blank, staring, and empty. Recently though, on more than one occasion, Joe had noticed them sparkle. For long moments, the fog seemed to lift and they were once again shiny, dark and alert. Whenever this happened he could almost swear that she knew he was there. He had tried to speak to her, tried to get through, but all too quickly the mists had returned. Even though disappointed, these occurrences gave Joe an optimism that perhaps one day, his sister would at last return to him.

Every morning, at precisely eleven, Joe would leave his office and walk arm in arm with Sarah around the large garden for half an hour or so. Sometimes it was more, sometimes it was less, depending on the demands of the day. Once the walk was over, he would return to his office and resume working. This had become a morning ritual and was the only time when Joe's safe key was in his desk drawer unguarded; the exact time when Michael knew he had to strike.

*   *   *

'Everything alright Mike?' Brett asked as the strapping twelve year old passed his elder cousin on the landing. Brett knew how much the shortening of his name annoyed Michael, but just couldn't help himself. He did it to get some sort of reaction, but invariably Michael would grit his teeth and ignore the obvious provocation. Secretly though, he would loved to have slapped the boy around the face for his insolence - if he wasn't so sure that Brett would hit him back. In a fight, Michael was certain that, even at twelve, Brett would be very tough opposition. God how he hated him.

'I'm fine Brett, thanks. Why do you ask?' He replied, trying to sound as relaxed as possible, when in truth the blood was pumping at a furious rate around his body.

'No reason. Just that you're sweating and look a bit flushed, thought you might be feelin' sick or something.'

'Er.. no. Just a bit hot that's all. Your dad's keeping me busy today.' Michael cursed his nervousness and hoped the lie hadn't been too transparent.

'Oh, right. That's good then. See ya later Mike,' Brett replied as he vanished down the stairs, already having lost interest in his cousin's answer.

'Bloody little shit,' Michael said to himself as he wiped his forehead with his handkerchief. Then after taking a few deep breaths in a bid to calm the jittery feeling in his stomach, he opened the door and strode as confidently as possible into his uncle's office.

He felt very conspicuous as he walked across to his desk, worried that his uncle might sense his treachery.

'You okay, Michael?' Joe asked, genuinely concerned. His nephew's face was still bright red and even though he'd mopped his brow just seconds before, he was sweating profusely.

'Yes. I'm fine, thankyou. What's up with everyone today?' Michael snapped with frustration, then almost immediately regretted it.

'Okay, okay. Just didn't think you looked very well, that's all.' Joe replied defensively.

Michael again cursed his nerves and his stupidity for arousing his uncle's suspicions. 'Sorry. I've just got a slight headache, but I'm fine really - thanks.'

'You don't want the mornin' off?'

'No, honestly. I'll be fine - really.'

'Well, okay, but only if you're sure.'

'I am.'

That seemed to do it. Joe nodded and smiled then returned to the paperwork on his desk. The time was nine-thirty, Michael had another hour and a half to wait. That's if the tension didn't kill him first.

It had been ten days since the unpleasant phone call from Carl. It had taken him that long to pluck up the courage to do what he must do this morning. He could put it off no longer, it was now or never.

*   *   *

Finally, after a tortuous wait and the loss of several pints of sweat, Michael watched Joe check his watch and stand up. 'It's eleven o'clock, Michael - you alright to hold the fort for a bit while I run yer mum around the garden?'

'Yeah, sure. No problem.' Michael forced a smile. Be cool, for Chrissakes be cool.

'Good boy,' Joe said to him, 'See ya in about arf an hour.'

After Joe left, closing the door behind him, Michael waited five minutes then slowly rose from his chair and tip-toed over to his uncle's desk.

His heart was in his mouth as he slid open the drawer. For a moment, he couldn't see the keys and he almost felt relieved. Then, just a heartbeat later, he spotted them under some paperwork and again the knot twisted in his stomach. Quickly he snatched them up and crossed swiftly to the space in the floor under which the safe was hidden.

Within seconds he had lifted the floorboards and inserted

the key. A moment later he was spinning through the final digits of the combination with little time to consider the consequences should his uncle return at that moment. Then it was too late as the door of the safe clicked open.

He was in.

*   *   *

Michael's hands were trembling as he systematically emptied the contents of the safe. There was no way he would have enough time to study all of it in depth, but hopefully he would discover something in the time he did have, with which to appease Carl. But where to start?

He selected a large, fat folder that looked promising. Inside, he found a planning application, some blueprints and an artist's impression of a large leisure complex. Nothing that was even remotely interesting.

He chose another folder of equal thickness and was disappointed to find that this one contained very much the same, except in this case it concerned a shopping centre in Walthamstow. It seemed that Joe's 'top secret' files were nothing more than a load of potential real estate purchases.

Surely there must be something more?

Hurriedly, Michael began opening and closing files and sifting through documents, his hands shaking, as he hoped to find something of importance. Finally his fingers touched upon a thick envelope, stuffed with what appeared to be personal papers. There were a few photos too, candid shots mainly of people Joe knew; some taken in London, some in California and some in Vegas. Michael recognised some of the faces but not all. He was about to discard the envelope as useless, when he noticed a small square print that was brown and faded. It was old, perhaps over twenty years, but there could be no confusion about the subject matter.

The photograph was of Michael's mother, Sarah, pictured as

a girl of perhaps eighteen. She was laughing and happy but her stomach was swollen with pregnancy. On her belly, a man's hand was pressed - the same man who was lovingly kissing her cheek and whose other arm was draped affectionately around her shoulder.

The man was young too, probably about the same age. He had definitely changed over the years, but there was no mistaking him and Michael recognised him immediately.

In the background there was a banner which read:

'Sean and Sarah - congratulations on your engagement!'

Michael was stunned. He had just discovered the identity of his father.

*   *   *

How in the hell could he have not realised it before? It had been staring him in the face all along. He was amazed not only by his own stupidity but also by the magnitude of his discovery. Everyone must have known. Everyone he knew, everyone who he had trusted, they had all kept the truth from him. Even Carl, he too must have perpetuated the lie. How foolish Michael felt. Foolish, and betrayed, but above all, alone.

Suddenly the telephone rang and Michael very nearly jumped out of his skin. The envelope he was holding jerked from his grip causing its contents to spill untidily all over the floor. Michael sprung up to grab the phone, kicking more papers and photographs across the office as he raced to pick up the receiver, but just as he got there it stopped ringing.

*   *   *

Joe fastened the buttons on Sarah's cardigan before opening the back door. It was a lovely morning but there was a slight chill on the wind and he didn't want his sister to be cold. As he took her arm and stepped out onto the terrace he took a deep breath of fresh clean air, anxious to blow away the stuffiness of the office. 'It's a beautiful day, Sis,' he said, 'Let's make the most of it, shall we?'

487

There was no answer, but Joe pretended not to notice as he slowly guided her to the path that encircled the entire boundary of the garden. 'Yep, a better day we could hardly wish for,' he continued, trying as always to provoke a reaction from his twin.

*   *   *

Ray rarely answered the telephone, especially if Joe or Michael were working in the office, but this morning he was standing right next to it in the hallway when it started to ring and without thinking he picked up the receiver.

It was Louretta calling from the States, wanting to speak with Joe about some stock that she thought he might be interested in.

'Hold on, luv,' Ray said, 'I'll go get 'im.'

*   *   *

Joe and Sarah had barely walked fifty feet before they were interrupted.

'Joe!' Ray shouted from the back door.

'What is it?' Joe yelled back.

'Louretta's on the phone - needs a word with you about something!'

Joe frowned and tapped the face of his watch, indicating that his time with Sarah was valuable. In response, Ray shrugged his shoulders apologetically and held up his hands. Louretta was on the phone, what could he do?

'I'm afraid our walk's gonna have to be cut short Sis,' Joe said shaking his head with annoyance, 'I'd better take the call, but I promise to make it up to you tomorrow, okay? Ray'll carry on the walk with you this mornin'.' He then left Sarah's side and jogged quickly back to the house.

Had he waited just two seconds longer, he would have heard his sister utter the words, 'Okay, Joseph.'

*   *   *

'Shit!' Michael cursed, knowing that the phone call would

488

undoubtedly be for Joe and realising with a sense of impending doom that there was a good chance he could return to the office to take it. Had Michael answered it, he could have dealt with whoever was calling, put them off or get Joe to call them back, but he hadn't answered it, someone else had, and that could prove to be disastrous.

For a moment he was frozen to the spot, waiting, praying, unable to move for fear of what might happen. Then, devastatingly, he heard Ray, from below, calling Joe to the phone and Michael almost began to cry as the terror of being discovered hit him like a brick.

*   *   *

'Sorry, Joe,' Ray said guiltily, 'But it's long distance.'

'Yeah. Don't worry about it. I'll take it in the office - sort Sarah out for me would ya?'

'Sure thing, Boss,' Ray replied as Joe marched past him, heading for the stairs.'

*   *   *

Michael turned back towards the safe and saw the utter devastation of the office. Panic set in. Papers and photos were strewn messily about the room and desperately he started stuffing them back into the envelope, squashing it all in as fast as he possibly could.

Then he was throwing files and folders back into the safe. He had no time to get things in the right order, no time to check if he'd missed anything, he just had to get the safe shut and the floorboards back in place before he was discovered.

He heard the stairs creak, Joe was on his way up to the office. He span the dial on the safe and turned the key, ripping it from the lock the moment it clicked.

He was going to get caught.

With fumbling hands, he roughly shoved the last of the

floorboards back into place and scrambled up, diving towards the desk drawer to replace the safe key. Just as he reached the desk, Joe strode in.

Michael froze with fear, his fist clamped around the key, the sweat from his brow stinging his eyes and his guilt ridden face flushing beetroot. He was dead and he knew it. Even a child would have been able to tell he was up to no good, as his deceit was clear for all to see.

However, good fortune was shining on Michael as Joe just grabbed up the phone, oblivious to his nephew's betrayal. 'Louretta? Hi, it's Joe. How's sunny California?'

Joe turned and sat on the corner of the desk as he spoke, not noticing the open drawer behind him, nor Michael as he silently dropped in the key and slid it closed.

Michael then stepped away from the desk and surreptitiously scanned the room. He could see no incriminating evidence to suggest he'd been in the safe, and he felt a wave of relief. But he was hot and sweaty and needed to splash his face. He had to cool off, to calm down otherwise Joe would surely suspect something to be wrong. Leaving his uncle to talk on the phone, Michael left the room and crossed to the bathroom, his heart still racing, but safe, at least for the time being, until Joe opened his safe and saw the mess inside.

Seventeen

Joe was on the phone with Louretta for twenty minutes before he noticed the photograph lying face down on the floor under his desk. After saying goodbye to his friend, he bent down and picked it up. As he turned it over to see the images it contained, he gasped and shot back in his chair with horror.

He had not seen the photograph for ten years, and even then he'd not studied it properly as its subject matter was too distressing, too dreadful to dwell on. It was the photo of Rachel with Alvin Staedtler and his pals in Vegas that Carl had told Joe he'd discovered in Steadtler's suite. The one that showed her with her killers - the men who now rotted under the sand of the Nevada desert.

Joe had kept the photo for all these years, not ever being able to bring himself to tear it up. He had hidden it in his safe, with other private photos and documents, away from Brett and Michael whose memory of Rachel would certainly be tarnished should they find out the awful truth.

But someone had. Someone had been in the safe and Joe suspected who, but he could not contemplate that now as his mind was awash with the vile images that the photograph conjured up. Those of Rachel being groped and fondled and penetrated by those sadistic, depraved monsters; of them laughing as they pumped her full of vodka and cocaine and semen. But even worse, the most lasting, most horrific image of all, was of Rachel lying dead, of her gaunt, white body bloodied and beaten and being feasted upon by fat blue-bottle flies. That was an image that would stay with him forever.

Joe's eyes went to the photo again and was surprised to find that time had hardened him to what it contained. Even though still extremely painful, for the first time he could actually look at it, to study it as he never had before. He regarded with disdain the smiling, lustful faces of Alvin Staedtler and his salesman friend, Red, as their hands poured over Rachel's skinny body. He was disgusted by the sight of the photographer, a man apparently named Duane, masturbating himself to climax just as the shot was taken, his face hidden from view. It riled Joe that he could not see it, that he could not identify the last of the three men responsible for the death of his wife. And for some reason that really began to matter. Something niggled him about this man that he could just not pin-point, something he recognised maybe that was momentarily alluding him.

Joe sat back in his chair and massaged the bridge of his nose with thumb and forefinger, closing his eyes to focus his mind. What was it he was missing?

He rested for a moment, then glanced at the photo again. He surveyed the whole thing once more, his eyes finally coming back to the photographer. Then he saw it and suddenly he felt sick as the sour taste of betrayal filled his mouth.

On the photographer's wrist was a beautiful watch, and even though the image was blurred somewhat, Joe would have recognised it anywhere. It was a watch that he and Louretta had commissioned to be made. A true one-off, crafted in white gold and platinum with a pearlised oyster face and diamond set digits. It was as unique as the man they had presented it to. A man called

492

Carl Napier.

*   *   *

Michael was pacing the bathroom, uncertain of what to do. What he had found out that morning was devastating and he was ill prepared to deal with it. His emotions were on a roller-coaster ride and threatening to speed out of control. He had also left his uncle's safe in a dreadful state which, when discovered, would land him in serious trouble.

He heard Joe open his office door and storm noisily across the landing, 'Ray, get up 'ere. Somebody's been playin' us for bloody fools!' He barked angrily down the stairs.

Michael's legs turned to jelly and his whole body started to shake involuntarily. Had Joe opened the safe already? Had he seen the mess and discovered his treachery?

'Oh, shit. I'm done for,' Michael gasped as he heard Ray rush up the stairs.

Joe closed the office door behind Ray and Michael, drawing courage from God knows where, tentatively opened the bathroom door and crept across the landing. He was sure he had been taken over by madness, and for the life of him couldn't believe what he was actually doing. But he had to know. He had to know exactly what his uncle and Ray were saying.

As he approached the office, he could hear a heated conversation.

'I'm gonna kill 'im, Ray,' shouted Joe.

'Oh, Christ, no!' Michael thought, becoming even more alarmed.

'If it's the last thing I do, I'm gonna bloody kill 'im!'

'Please God, don't let him kill me, please stop him,' Michael pleaded silently.

'Get me on a plane as soon as you can,' Joe continued, 'Today if possible. I don't care how many changes I have to make - just get me to Vegas!' He was obviously fuming.

'A plane? Las Vegas? What's this all about?' Michael was suddenly puzzled.

'Napier's a dead man, understand?' Joe was at the height of his anger, 'Ring Sean and tell 'im to meet me at LAX. Tell 'im I need his help.'

'Sure thing Boss,' Michael heard Ray reply.

'Oh my God,' Michael said to himself. 'It's not me, it's Carl he's going to kill.' Suddenly Michael was enraged. What the hell had Carl ever done to Joe?

Michael couldn't believe it. All thoughts of the safe and what it contained were forgotten, the only thing he could think of now was to warn Carl.

Eighteen

It had been three days since Victoria's stomach churning encounter with Murray Lieberman. Three days in which she had felt too guilty, too dirty, to even think about the movie role she'd landed.

Seventy-two hours she'd had to dwell on what had happened. Murray's shocking revelation had left her totally stunned and unable to think clearly. Had she been given more time to consider his threat and to gather her thoughts, then maybe she'd have acted entirely differently.

The memory of Murray's sticky, liver-spotted hands as they clawed at her breasts, the thought of his hot, wheezing breath on her face and his flabby, sweaty body as it jerked feebly on top of her was almost more than she could take. She had to physically block it from of her mind to prevent herself from vomiting. It was the most disgusting thing that she had ever endured.

However, by enduring it, she had effectively bought herself valuable breathing space. Time in which she could formulate some sort of plan to ensure Murray's silence and to get his signature on her movie contract. If she could do both of those, then perhaps all was not lost.

But Victoria knew Lieberman was not the sort to keep quiet for long as talk of his many sordid liaisons were rife in tinseltown.

She also knew that Murray would call on her again and again, wringing out every last trace of her pride, until a new, more exciting starlet caught his eye. When Murray finally lost interest in Victoria, his mouth would open and all the world would know her shameful secret. To prevent that from happening she had to guarantee Murray's silence - and the only way to do that was to kill him.

After he'd signed her contract of course.

*   *   *

It was late, around eleven-thirty and Murray was bored. He had just watched a disappointing rough-cut of his latest movie in his own private cinema which was only one small part of his enormous home.

Having been at the studio until eight forty-five, he had asked his housekeeper to make him a bowl of soup for dinner, it was too late to eat a big meal and he'd had a niggling indigestion all day that he didn't wish to make any worse.

After his soup, he dismissed his staff, who had their own annex at the back of the house. To Murray, servants were a necessary evil. He despised their presence, hated their ever watchful eyes and ever open ears. At the earliest possible opportunity, after they had performed the specific duties they had been employed for, he would banish them to their part of the mansion. Not off duty, or free to go about their personal lives, but just out of his sight until he needed them again. Little people, dull and uninteresting whose sole purpose for existing was to serve him, or at least that's how Murray saw it.

However, now he was bored. There was no point in going to bed as he was not tired. On the TV there was nothing but re-runs and B-movies, some of which he had produced and had no desire to see again. He glanced over a few screenplays, none of which held his attention, and scanned a couple of scripts which failed to do the same. He then picked up a small pile of documents and half-heartedly reviewed them, signing one or two, discarding others and making notes on several more. Finally he came across Victoria Wild's contract. His instincts had told him all along that it was she, not Christie Mathers, who was right for the part in the movie for which she had 'auditioned.' It was the perfect vehicle for her and one with which the studio could not lose. With Victoria in the lead role he knew the film would be a smash. The contract merely required his signature, along with hers, and the deal was done.

An evil smile spread across Murray's face as he thought of Victoria's immensely desirable body. He'd been able to think of little else in the three days since he had caressed it. He remembered its lustre and beauty and how soft it felt under his touch. How seeing her tears gave him a sense of power which excited him enormously. It was like a drug and he needed it again.

Murray glanced at the phone, somehow he had the feeling that his boredom that evening could soon be alleviated.

*   *   *

Victoria had just got back from an evening out. Virgil Nash had called her that afternoon, just to see how she was, and even though she had not said as much, he sensed she was feeling low and offered to take her to dinner. At first Victoria was reluctant, she didn't much feel like enjoying herself, but after a little gentle persuasion, she finally agreed. She and Virgil had always been close but, ever since her first studio suspension, they had become much closer. During that time he'd proved what a good friend he was, and she knew she could rely on him regardless of what level her career happened to be on, unlike some of her fair-weather friends who had made themselves remarkably scarce when things were rough.

In recent months, though, she had started to look at him in a different light - she'd always thought of him as attractive, but so too had half the women in the free world. Yet several times she'd caught herself wondering what would happen if she wasn't married to his best friend. What if she was single - would the two of them find happiness with each other? Neither of them were particularly happy with the way things were now. After all, they were both in the same industry and both shared a passion for it.

Virgil, however, unlike Victoria, was still one of the most bankable stars in Hollywood, yet remained unaffected by his fame. He didn't wear celebrity like a badge, and certainly didn't court stardom. He just got on with the job of acting. Victoria believed that if someone was to take all his riches away; the house, the cars, the yacht and the plane, even to some extent, the women, of which she knew there had been hundreds, he would probably be just as happy. No one could possibly have any hold over him because he just didn't care. He had no ties, no commitments, just him and him alone. And, Victoria thinking of her present predicament, envied him for it.

However, had she truly known, it was precisely the fact that he was alone which made him sad, a feeling he kept very deeply hidden. It was not that he'd never been in love, or found the right woman, it was just that the woman he loved was married to his best friend.

* * *

Virgil walked Victoria to her door, sensing that, even though her mood had lifted during the evening, she was still troubled. 'You okay?' He asked.

'Yeah, I'm fine. Just tired I guess. Thanks for the concern though and thanks for a great dinner,' she replied.

'Hey, no problem. Glad to be of service. You gonna be okay from here or is there anything more I can help you with tonight?' Virgil was just being flip, but was suddenly aware that it might have sounded like a line. 'God, that sounded so bad. Sorry - I just meant—'

'Don't sweat it, I know what you meant—'

'I mean your my best friend's wife - what kind of guy does that make me?'

'It's okay Virge. You're the best kind. The sweetest—'

Suddenly their eyes met and the moment became even more awkward as both read the others inner most thoughts. But it was Virgil who looked away first. 'Well okay then, as long as we're clear,' he made a joke of it, slapping himself lightly on the face, 'Must not make suggestive remarks to best friend's girl.'

Victoria giggled. 'No, guess not. He'd probably think it was a little outa line, huh?'

'Yeah, I guess he would.'

The two of them stared at each other again, both smiling, both sensing the spark but knowing that the line shouldn't be crossed. 'You sure you're okay? I can stay if you want - no funny business I promise?'

'It's okay, it's not you I don't trust, it's me! But really, I'm fine. You go home, get some sleep - you got an early call tomorrow. I'm gonna turn in too. I'm beat.'

'Okay. See you soon and take care.' Virgil leant in and brushed her cheek with his lips. 'Goodnight.'

'Goodnight, Virge.' He smelt so good and the touch of his lips sent a little tingle down her spine. 'And thanks for a great night - you really made me feel better, you know?'

'I'm glad, Vicky, I really am - sleep well,' he said, as he opened the door of his bright red Ferrari.

For a second Victoria wanted to tell him how she felt, 'Virgil!' She called, just as he started the engine of the convertible.

'Yeah?' He replied.

She looked at him for a long moment. 'Nothing.' She said. 'Just drive carefully.'

'Always. See ya soon, Vicky. And if you need me just give me a call.'

Victoria nodded and smiled, then stared after him as he sped off down the driveway. Away from her.

*   *   *

Virgil had cheered Victoria up, but once he'd gone her melancholy returned. As she walked into the kitchen, the phone began to ring. It was late but for some reason she picked it up.

'Hello?' She said.

'Hello, honey,' the man said on the other end of the line, 'I wonder if you could come over and do me a little favour.' It was Murray Lieberman.

*   *   *

Victoria had drunk far too much wine to risk driving herself, even though she felt quite sober. But on this night she did not want to chance being picked up by the police, so reluctantly asked Wolf to chauffeur her. Victoria realised that rather than involving her driver in her murderous plans, she could have waited for another opportunity; forced herself to surrender to Murray one more time; to wait until the next time when maybe circumstances would be perfect. After all, the filthy old pervert was bound to summon her again in a day or two. But to even contemplate that was more than she could stomach. It had to be now or never.

As Wolf pulled the limousine onto the cobble stoned driveway, Victoria touched the cold steel of the carving knife, which she had taken from her kitchen before leaving. Quickly she had made a small tear in the lining of her white fur wrap and slipped the long murderous blade into the opening. Once the expensive stole was draped around her shoulders, the knife was perfectly concealed from view.

'Wait for me, Roberto, I won't be long,' Victoria told Wolf as she exited the car, her face set with determination, knowing

500

precisely what she had to do.

Nineteen

Matt Mason had been in LA for the past three weeks working for Fox on a war movie with Brad and Rocky. They were doing the stunt work, whilst he was in charge of vehicle maintenance. The shoot had gone well, but his involvement in it was now over although Brad and Rocky still had one more day's filming to do. After that, the three of them, plus Marilu, planned to travel back to The Bluestone together in convoy.

Matt had enjoyed the adventure, his first time away with the boys, but now he was eager to get home. For the duration of the trip they had been staying in a small motel in West Hollywood, with him and Rocky sharing and Brad and Marilu in the room next door. But Rocky's snoring and smelly feet had somehow lost their appeal as had the sound through the paper thin walls of Brad and Marilu's nightly love-making marathon. Rocky usually snored loudly through the whole performance but Matt, unfortunately, could not, and after three weeks of it, he was exhausted and desperate for a good night's sleep. He decided that rather than to stay on with the others for one more night, he'd pack up his things and head for Beverly Hills, hoping that Victoria would put him up at the cottage. Silk sheets and an en-suite jacuzzi, perhaps even breakfast in bed in the morning. Perfect.

Matt phoned Victoria to let her know he was on his way, but

no one answered, she was obviously out. Never mind, he wouldn't get to her place until around midnight and she was bound to be back by then.

*   *   *

Wolf had received his orders from Benny. He was to finish his business in California as soon as possible, then return to Miami to take up his new position at Mottola's side.

He had known this for twenty-four hours and ever since had been planning his final, much dreamed of liaison with Victoria Wild. Afterwards, he would drive to Palm Springs to finish things off there, then, the following morning, board a plane to Miami, job done. He'd served his time on the West coast.

But in order to make his flight, he had to take care of Victoria tonight.

Wolf had meticulously worked it all out and was feeling particularly pleased with himself. But then that bloody playboy Nash had called and scuppered his plans.

Not one to be put off, Wolf merely re-scheduled, he would deal with Victoria upon her return from the restaurant instead. However, even that was not to be, because the moment she stepped back in the house, Murray Lieberman had phoned, effectively ruining that idea. The producer had called her over immediately - possibly, Wolf suspected, for a repeat performance of three days ago, when he had watched the two of them having sex. Wolf wanted her too, desperately so, and he could hardly bear to let her go to Lieberman's, but he had to, as it would appear too suspicious if she did not show. Wolf would once again have to wait, but no matter what, when they returned to the cottage, he intended to show her a better time than that old fart, and he was quite sure she would enjoy it too - at least until he killed her.

*   *   *

Murray answered the door in person, smiling widely with

503

his big white dentures sparkling in the moonlight. He was dressed only in a silk paisley gown and quite obviously naked underneath.

He ushered Victoria through into his vast living room which was decorated in strong masculine colours with furnishings made from luxurious leather and fake animal hide. An enormous tiger skin, complete with head, was spread out on the floor and made a striking, but intimidating centre-piece. Upon seeing it, Victoria felt her resolve waiver.

Murray fixed them both a drink without asking her whether she wanted one or not. She did though, and gratefully accepted the tumbler, taking a long slug and feeling the warm liquid instantly calm her nerves. After another couple of gulps she once again felt up to the task she had gone there to perform.

Lieberman wandered over to the coffee table and gestured to the contract sitting on it. 'There it is, Baby. There's the proof that the part's yours if you want it. All we gotta do is sign it and we got ourselves a deal - whattaya say?'

'What, no strings?' Victoria tried to sound surprised.

'Now I didn't say that, did I, Baby? Everything comes with strings attached, you should know that.'

'So what's the deal?' Victoria asked.

'Simple,' Lieberman replied, 'You sign it, then I sign it and then you thank me, in the way that I know you know how.' He was still smiling widely, looking slightly ghoulish in the dimly lit room.

'And what about my husband?'

'What about him? This is about you and me and as long as you continue to make me happy, that's the way it'll stay.'

There it was. Murray had just confirmed Victoria's worst fears. Her secret would only be safe until Lieberman no longer had a use for her. She felt her anger rising but she forced it down, she had to bide her time.

'Whattaya say, Baby? Do we have an agreement?' Murray

asked, already showing signs of excitement.

'Sure, why not,' she replied, 'Let's get right down to it.'

It was Murray's turn to feel surprised, but he was glad she was finally starting to see things his way.

The old man offered her his gold-plated fountain pen and she signed the contract in the appropriate place. Then she handed the pen back to him and watched as he did the same.

As soon as he had signed, Murray gave Victoria her copy and she slipped it into her purse, a little smile of relief on her face. She was an actress once more. The star of a new movie which she was sure would re-launch her career.

With the business completed, Murray slipped loose the belt on his dressing gown, exposing his flabby body and weedy manhood.

'That's it, Baby. Welcome aboard' he said without the slightest trace of sincerity, then added, 'Now, let's get down to it!'

As Murray ambled over to his large, zebra skin covered sofa, he took a swig of whiskey and winced painfully. The liquid stung as it went down, almost as if pouring gasoline onto the fiery heartburn that he'd been suffering from throughout the day. 'Dammit,' he hissed to himself. Holding the crystal tumbler, he felt an annoying prickle at the tip of his fingers and thought for a moment that he might drop the glass. 'What the hell's the matter with you man?' He asked himself.

He placed the drink safely on the wide arm of the sofa as he turned to face Victoria and all concerns about his health miraculously evaporated. She would make him feel better.

He sat down with his legs spread apart, the bubbly varicose veins on them forming broad, uneven roads on his calves and inner thighs. Not at all self-conscious, he beckoned her over using just the slightest movement of his head, making it quite clear what he expected her to do.

Victoria forced down the urge to vomit as she considered the hideous creature before her; this vile blackmailing letch who she was about to kill. But somehow she summoned a provocative smile as she stepped between Murray's legs and very carefully removed her fur wrap, deliberately keeping the lining, and what it concealed, out of his sight. She placed it on the floor, close to his foot where she could easily reach it. Purposely, she kept her long, elbow length gloves on. There would be no fingerprints.

As she stood there, the tips of her fingers just touched the hairs on his legs and she brushed them lightly up and down, magically increasing his desire. Murray closed his eyes and let out a slight groan of delight.

'That's it, Baby. That's it,' he whispered.

She continued brushing, tantalisingly increasing the length of her strokes, watching the goose bumps form on his thighs as she gradually knelt down between his legs.

'That's it, Baby. Do it now, do it now!' Lieberman was almost squirming with lust, his eyes still tightly closed.

Very, very slowly, Victoria, with her right hand, reached down towards her wrap. Her left took a gentle hold of his manhood and he thanked her with a gasp of pleasure.

The knife was now in Victoria's hand and she glanced down to see the rewarding flash of sharpened steel and briefly she froze, suddenly incredibly aware of what she was about to do.

'Don't stop, Baby. Do it! Do it now!' Murray was pleading.

But Victoria's mind was awash with conflicting thoughts, she was actually intending to commit murder, to kill a man in cold blood. Looking at the knife, everything was all of a sudden so real, she was there, she had the opportunity and the weapon, yet something was very wrong.

'Come on! What are you waiting for? Get on with it!' Lieberman was growing impatient.

'My God! Am I going insane? What the hell am I doing?' Victoria shouted to herself, appalled that she was actually holding the knife, stunned at how desperate she had become. Surely there was another way?

Then it came. The final straw.

'Hey, goddamit!' Murray shouted, slapping Victoria hard around the top of her head, his thick gold ring connecting painfully with her skull. 'I haven't got all fuckin' night y'know! Now get on with it before I have to revise our arrangement.'

He was glaring at her, his eyes hard and evil and she knew then that he deserved everything that he was going to get. The rage filled within her, more anger than she had ever felt in her life and she found herself shaking with hatred.

Her left hand clamped tight, like a vice around his weedy penis and she tugged it sharply, violently upwards causing Murray to shriek with the excruciating pain. His arms flailed wildly, knocking the drink from the arm of the chair and she knew he was utterly at her disposal, but she just squeezed tighter.

Then she brought the blade of the knife up underneath his scrotum, pushing the serrated edge hard up against the back of his balls, any false movement and she could sever them in one swift stroke. Instantly he stopped struggling, instinctively knowing what the sharp object was that she was pressing against his genitals.

'Oh, Christ, no!' He shouted. 'Please, no, don't.'

'Too late, asshole,' she spat at him, 'This is where you pay, you disgusting little pervert. It's time to kiss 'em goodbye Murray.'

'No, please, anything. I'll give you any—' Murray suddenly stopped in mid-sentence.

His heartburn had returned with a vengeance and he grimaced with pain, screwing his face up as he attempted to speak again, but his voice was strained and he started to splutter, the words getting lost in a spray of saliva. The burning sensation was far more intense than it had been before, this time accompanied by a crushing, unbearable tightening of the chest and upper body.

Murray then jerked violently, grabbing his chest, clawing with both hands at his saggy breasts, his face contorting into a hideous expression of agony with his eyes bulging from their sockets.

Victoria suddenly felt frightened as she watched in amazement, uncertain of what was happening. For a moment, she thought it was a ploy and she kept her grip on him firm. But then she saw how real his pain was, his whole body writhing in a series of wild convulsions, a gargling sound emanating from his throat. She released her hold when she saw the yellowy white froth bubbling from the corners of his mouth and even though she despised him, she somehow felt that she should try to help. But there was nothing she could do.

His face was turning a deep purple and the muscles in his neck were taught and prominent with no sign of the double chin that had been there just moments before.

All the time Murray's hands were still grabbing at his chest, his fingernails now unconsciously ripping the skin, making long bloody lacerations.

Then without warning, after a final, violent tremor, his body became totally still.

*   *   *

Victoria was utterly astonished and for a long moment was unable to move. Her disbelieving eyes were totally transfixed on Murray's lifeless body, which was now slumped awkwardly on the fake zebra hide of the sofa. She could not fully register, nor quite come to terms with what had just happened.

However, she rallied quickly, her brain finally clicking into action and she checked Murray's pulse, just in case her eyes had deceived her. There could be no doubt, he was definitely dead, yet amazingly, it was not her that had killed him.

Victoria had gone to his mansion knowing for certain that she would be leaving as a murderess, knowing that for the rest of her life, she was going to have to live with what she'd done, possibly in prison, if she was caught and convicted of the crime. The weight of that knowledge had been immense, but now the weight had been lifted. She had been granted a reprieve which, had she believed in God, could well have been convinced it was down to be some kind of divine intervention, sparing her from the task she had set out to do. Whatever it was, she was extremely thankful.

Victoria stood up and collected her thoughts, trying to re-trace her steps. It was vital that she left no sign of her presence at the Lieberman mansion, now even more so than before.

As far as she could recall, the only things she had touched were the whiskey glass, the fountain pen and the contract. Fortunately her evening gloves had prevented her from leaving fingerprints on any of these. The only mark she had made in the time she'd been there was the lipstick stain around the rim of the crystal glass tumbler. Victoria picked up the glass and dropped it into her handbag, she would bury it in her garden at the cottage later.

The fountain pen she placed on Murray's bureau along with his copy of the contract. There was a pile of other documents there too so it wouldn't look out of place. Finally, she picked up the carving knife and slid it back into the lining of her fur stole which she then draped around her shoulders.

Before leaving, she scanned the room, making certain that she'd missed nothing. What she saw, was what she hoped the police would see: An old man with a penchant for nudity, who had suffered a massive heart-attack whilst relaxing alone in the comfort of his own home.

The staff were in their quarters, they would never know

Victoria had even been there and, as she quietly clicked the front door closed, she breathed a sigh of relief. Murray had cheated her by dying in a much less painful way than she had planned, denying her the delicious revenge she had so desperately wanted. But now it was over, she was pleased that he had.

As she crossed the gravel driveway towards her waiting limo, she looked back at the huge mansion, the downstairs lights still burning brightly.

'Rot in hell, you vile bastard,' she said under her breath.

Twenty

Matt called in at a drive-thru and bought a burger, then leant on his bike in the car park to eat it. Whilst he chewed, he watched a bunch of girls who'd pulled up in a convertible beetle, obviously on their way home from a night out. One, who was easily the most attractive, was making eyes at him and maybe, if he'd not been so tired, he'd have wandered over and given her some chat. But he had not seriously chatted up a girl since Suzie and it still felt a little as if he'd be betraying her.

Eventually, the girls drove off and Matt felt a pang of regret. Some other time perhaps, when he wasn't so damn tired. He looked at his watch and saw that it was a quarter-past midnight. Time to make a move.

*   *   *

He arrived back at Victoria's and pressed the button on the intercom at the front gate. No reply. He tried twice more but each time was greeted with silence, she obviously wasn't home yet. Matt strained to look through the high, iron gates and up the long driveway, but the cottage was concealed by large trees so he could see no signs of life, all he could make out was the silhouette of the red tiled roof, some two hundred yards in the distance. 'Sure is some spread,' he thought as he turned away from the gates.

The cottage, as Victoria called it, bore very little resemblance to those that were dotted around the villages of England. It had six bedrooms, each with its own bathroom, four reception rooms, a screening room, an outdoor hot tub, swimming pool and a tennis court. Not exactly quaint, but certainly comfortable and Matt was already fantasising about how soft the beds might be. Surely he wouldn't have to wait too long for Victoria to return.

In Beverly Hills, the residents didn't appreciate strangers loitering outside their homes, nor was it tolerated by either the police or the private security firms that frequently patrolled the area. Matt realised that dressed in his battered leather jacket and jeans he looked exactly the type to be picked up by one of these patrols, so thought it best to stay out of sight until Victoria arrived home. Across the road on an immaculately maintained border was a bushy area, well-trimmed and clipped to perfection, which would suit him ideally. Quickly he pushed the Harley behind a tall topiaried hedge and lay down beside it so as not be seen from the road. Hopefully, he wouldn't need to stay there long as his eyelids were already beginning to close and even the motel in West Hollywood was preferable to a grass verge.

*   *   *

As Victoria reached the limousine, Wolf opened the rear door. 'Thankyou,' she said, but just as she stooped to get in he struck her hard across the back of the head with a leather cosh. Everything went black as Victoria collapsed onto the back seat, her fur wrap slipping from her shoulders to lay in a crumpled heap in the foot well of the car.

'My pleasure Ma'am,' Wolf replied, an evil smile on his face.

He leaned in next to her and checked her pulse. His years of practice had served him well and he'd judged the force of the blow exactly right. She was alive, but sleeping like a baby.

Unable to resist, Wolf ran his hands over her body. It felt so smooth, so firm, and so deliciously ripe. God how he wanted her.

He was sweating slightly and his mouth was full of saliva, it would be so easy to take her there an then in the back of the limo; to rip her clothes off and do all the things he longed to do, but he knew he must wait. The cottage would be safer, there they would be completely alone and have all night together, just her and him, just as he'd planned. Reluctantly, he got out of the car and sucked in a deep lungful of the warm night air then went to the trunk and took out some twine which he had stashed there earlier. Going back to Victoria, he tied her wrists and ankles together which would keep her secure on the drive back to the cottage. 'Soon, honey–' he said, running his big hands over her breasts one more time, '–You and me are gonna have a real good time.'

*   *   *

As she opened her eyes, Victoria felt a severe throbbing in her head and winced with pain. She made an effort to rub her temples but her arms were restricted by the tightly tied twine around her wrists.

'What the—?' she attempted to sit up, but again her movements were hampered and she realised that her ankles had been bound also.

'Hey Roberto! What's going on?' Victoria looked up to see Wolf smiling at her from the other side of the limo's privacy screen, leaving her in no doubt that it was he who was responsible for her current predicament.

Hotching herself awkwardly up into a sitting position, she banged furiously on the glass with her joined fists, 'Hey, you bastard! Untie me, let me go!' She screamed, but Wolf ignored her pleas and turned his attention on the road ahead.

'Let me go, goddamit!' She yelled again, but it was useless and she knew it.

Victoria started biting madly at the nylon twine around her wrists, trying desperately to free herself, but the rope was hard and impenetrable and quickly she realised it was useless. Then she made a grab for the door handle, if she couldn't break her bindings, she could at least escape from the car, whether it was moving or not. But Wolf had engaged the child locks, preventing her from going anywhere.

Victoria glanced out the window and was surprised to find they were driving through the gates to her cottage, and for a moment, thought she heard someone calling her name, but she was angry and hurt, still dazed from the blow, surely she was mistaken.

In desperation, she kicked at the walnut drinks cabinet in front of her, cracking the veneer, hoping that the blow would have some effect on Wolf, but if it did, he certainly didn't show it.

'You're fired, you asshole!' Shouted in complete exasperation, as if that was going to make some sort of difference.

*   *   *

Matt had been asleep for thirty minutes when he was awoken by the sound of the gates opening, and, still a little groggy, roused himself just in time to see Victoria's limo driving through them.

Quickly, he jumped up and ran across the road, 'Victoria!' He shouted, but the car just kept on going. 'Vicky!' He shouted again, but still it continued and just as Matt ran through the gates, the limo picked up speed and left him with too much ground to make up. He stopped running, knowing further pursuit was useless. He'd get the Harley and meet Victoria up at the house, but as he turned, he saw to his horror that the automatic gates were shutting.

Like lightening he darted back, trying to make it through the gap in the gates before they closed completely, but he was too slow, and they clanged shut just as he reached them. In exasperation, he rattled the bars violently, trying in vein to force them open, but it was no good, they were locked tight. He was trapped inside, whilst his bike was outside.

Reluctantly he turned back towards the house and began

walking up the slight incline of the long driveway. At least he was in, his bike would have to stay outside until the morning, he was just too tired to retrieve it tonight.

*　*　*

By the time the car came to a halt outside her home, Victoria was like a caged wildcat and as Wolf opened the car door, she pounced, kicking out furiously with both feet, aiming for Wolf's balls. But he was quick and dodged the impact of her sharp stilettos, which connected only with the fullness of his flares. To avoid a second attempt, Wolf grabbed the thin rope tied around Victoria's ankles and pulled her roughly out of the limo, her skull banging painfully against the sill of the car and her body landing hard on the cold flagstones of the driveway. However, Wolf pulled so hard that the twine snapped and Victoria's legs sprang free, but before she could kick out Wolf quickly took a firm hold of the twine tethering her wrists and jerked her forward so that Victoria spilled over onto her front. He continued to pull, walking steadily towards the front door, dragging her along behind, with elbows and knees scraping on the rough stones as she fought to be free.

Wolf threw open the front door and yanked Victoria forwards, but she was far from finished. Before Wolf could pull her inside, she knelt up on her scuffed knees and bit his hand, clamping her teeth firmly down on the meaty area below his little finger. He roared with agony and ripped his hand sharply away, snapping the twine as he did so and leaving a large chunk of bleeding flesh in Victoria's mouth, which she spat victoriously onto the ground.

Sadly, her triumph was short lived as Wolf brought the open palm of his other hand down hard across her cheek, sending her sprawling into the hallway of her home. But now she was running on pure adrenaline and she quickly shook off the blow. Realising that she was at last free, she hurried to her feet, eager to face her attacker.

Wolf was angry also, madder than hell as he stared in disbelief at the semi-circular gap in his hand.

'You, bitch!' He yelled, 'You fuckin' bitch - you're gonna pay for that!'

'C'mon then, asshole,' Victoria was pumped up, not at all scared, just downright furious, 'Bring it on, why don't ya?'

Wolf marched towards her and Victoria punched him hard on the nose, but he hardly flinched. She struck him again on the jaw, but he seemed impervious to the pain. Instead he fixed a vice-like hand around her throat and pushed her up against the wall, holding her there while he grabbed at her breasts with his free hand, groping them roughly. His fingers then moved steadily downwards, across her flat stomach and pelvic bone, finally forcing his strong digits between her legs, pressing them hard against her, hurting her.

'How do ya like that, bitch?' He snarled, 'Is that what you want, eh?'

'Fuck you!' She snapped back, her face contorted with hatred and pain.

His hand moved back up to her breasts which he squeezed cruelly, digging his nails into her soft flesh.

'That's what you like, ain't it?' He was smiling now.

Victoria slapped him across the face, but he just grinned wider. She slapped twice more, each time with the same result. It was useless. In desperation, with his large paw still fastened around her neck, slowly crushing her windpipe, she spat a large gob of phlegm into his eye,'Let me go, you bastard!' She shouted.

'Fuckin' whore!' He yelled, finally releasing his grip on her neck, 'Goddamn filthy bitch!'

With blood spurting from his damaged palm, he ripped Victoria's dress down the front in utter frustration, his sharp fingernails scratching one of her naked breasts as it spilled out of her dress.

Suddenly, he wasn't holding her at all, and seeing her chance, she bolted for the door. But just as she reached the opening, he caught her again and span her around to face him. Once more, she punched him in the face, this time hearing a rewarding crack as her wedding ring connected with his nose. This obviously stunned him, he could feel the blood as it gushed from his nostrils and for a second, it caused him to loosen his grip. Victoria turned again for the door, just clearing its frame before he fastened onto her for a third time.

*   *   *

It took a minute or two for Matt to reach the brow of the slope, from where he could at last see the house fully. Victoria was in the doorway although she was facing away from him, struggling with something which he couldn't quite see. Then she turned quickly, looking extremely distressed, and he saw that her dress was torn down the front, the ripped material hanging loosely by the waistband. So bad was the tear, that one of her breasts was visible and Matt could see three long scratches across its tanned surface. Victoria was fighting hard, trying to make it out the door, but somebody's hand was holding onto her dress, preventing her from running. The identity of the person from whom she was attempting to escape was blocked from Matt's view, hidden by the door frame, but, by the ease with which they held Victoria, he could tell they were very strong.

Suddenly forgetting his fatigue, Matt began to run towards the cottage, but before he'd covered ten feet, another hand reached out from inside the house and grabbed Vicky roughly by the hair, dragging her violently back through the doorway.

Matt's anger flared as he heard her squeal with pain. Then just after she vanished from view, he heard her scream with terror, and he desperately hoped he wasn't too late.

Wolf threw Victoria back into the hallway, and as she turned to look at his bloody face, she saw the murderous look in his eyes.

'My name ain't DeSilva, honey, it's Wolf and you'd better believe that I'm as big and as bad as they come,' he hissed, 'And this is a gift from Benny Mottola!' Aiming his huge balled fist at the side of her head, and just before everything went black, before she let out a final, blood-curdling shriek, she realised just how much trouble she was in.

Twenty

The first thing Matt saw as he burst through the open doorway, was Victoria's body sprawled awkwardly on the floor. Her bruised eyes were shut and there was a thin line of blood trickling from her mouth. Her dress was torn and the scratches on her naked breast were red and angry. Her dress was gathered up, exposing badly scuffed knees and around her ankles and wrists were ugly rope burns where the twine had been tied.

She was either dead or unconscious, Matt couldn't be sure which, but either way she looked like she'd been through hell. The obvious cause of her pain was standing above her, wiping his bloody face with an equally bloody hand, chuckling gruffly at his pathetic victory and Matt instantly recognised this creature as Roberto, Victoria's chauffeur. Briefly he was distracted, as he wondered what on earth the man's motive could be to do as he had, but then, almost immediately, the rage took over.

'What have you done?' He hissed.

Wolf span round to face Matt, his surprise clear to see. He'd assumed the house to be empty, that he'd be able to enjoy Victoria's pleasures uninterrupted, but now Joe Cassidy's bastard son had arrived to spoil things and yet again his plans would have to wait - at least until he'd disposed of this young pup.

'Hey now, whattaya know, a knight in shining armour' Wolf

replied with relish, 'Just in time for the main event.'

Matt stepped into the wide entrance, watching the other man carefully. Wolf had an excellent physique and was obviously very fit. Also, by the way he had adopted an attacking karate stance, Matt could tell he was also versed in the martial arts.

Wolf was prowling now, slowly edging ever closer, Matt very warily moving toward him also.

Suddenly, in a flash of lightning quick movement, Wolf sprung forward, his foot crashing into Matt's rib cage with devastating power. The kick sent Matt flying backwards through the door and, if he hadn't known it before, Matt certainly knew now, that he was facing an adversary of immense skill.

He landed badly, halfway between the house and the car, banging both his elbows as he tried, unsuccessfully, to break his fall. But even though the shock of it jarred his whole body, he forced himself to ignore the pain and automatically sprang to his feet for a counter offensive.

However, Wolf was waiting and sent another rocket-powered kick crunching into Matt's chest. Again, he was thrown backwards, the impact of the kick exploding throughout his upper body. This time he landed on the trunk of the limousine, making a deep dent in the polished black metal. He shook his head, momentarily stunned, his vision clearing just in time to see Wolf bearing down on him once more. Instinct took over and somehow Matt managed to effectively block two punches before rolling off the other side of the car. Staggering slightly, but staying on his feet, he turned around to see the other man heading straight for him.

Wolf leapt forward, one leg extended, his foot aimed directly at Matt's face, but this time Matt blocked him with a powerful forearm and, with his other fist, drove a brutal counter punch into his opponent's ribs. As Wolf landed, Matt span around and whipped his own leg out behind him, smashing the heel of his boot hard into the other man's nose. Wolf screamed as he felt his nose crack for the second time that evening, but he remained standing, although only long enough to receive a kick to the stomach, which sent him sprawling to the ground.

Quick as a flash, Wolf jumped up again, somehow switching off the pain to his broken nose, even though the blood from it was gushing over his mouth and chin, making a bright stain, like spilled claret, on his white shirt. He licked his mouth grotesquely and sucked up the blood, slapping his lips as he did so, relishing the taste. Then he smiled, his teeth coated in a dye of deep magenta; a hungry predator eagerly eyeing his prey.

Matt's retaliation had shocked him. He had not expected the boy to be so skilful, and for a moment, he allowed the slightest element of doubt to creep into his mind. However, it was dismissed just as quickly as Wolf was supremely confident in his own abilities. No young pup was going to get the better of him.

He used the pause to get his breath back, as did Matt, both men bracing themselves for the battle that was about to ensue.

'So, boy, looks like ya got some skills. I'm impressed,' Wolf said in his slow, Floridian drawl, 'But you'd better hope they're enough. 'Cos I'm comin' for ya boy, an' I play to win.'

'Ready when you are, asshole,' Matt replied, gearing up for the attack.

The two men came together in mad frenzy of spectacular combat. Both exceptional, both facing an opponent of equal skill. Punches, kicks, jabs, all accompanied by electrifying athleticism, each man fighting as they'd never fought before.

As the fight left the driveway and moved onto the closely cut lawn Matt unleashed a combination of kicks and punches that left Wolf reeling and slowly the younger man started to get the upper hand, his fitness proving to be better than that of his rival. However, the lawn sprinklers were on, and cascades of water showered down on them, soaking the ground, making it very slippery underfoot. Wolf was wearing rubber soled shoes which helped him somewhat, but Matt had on leather-soled cowboy boots that couldn't grip the wet turf, which hampered the effectiveness of his attack and allowed Wolf to get back into the fight.

Recognising the weakness, Wolf began aiming kicks to Matt's legs and feet, trying to knock him off balance. Matt had to retreat, his smooth soles treading precariously over the soggy ground, his clothing getting wetter and wetter as he inched ever closer to the lawn sprinkler, trying to beat off Wolf's bombardment. Then, disastrously, Matt's heel caught on the garden hose that supplied the sprinkler with water and he lost his footing and landed on his backside.

Seeing his chance Wolf launched a tirade of shots aimed at Matt's head and face. From his weakened position, Matt blocked the best he could but many shots found their way through his guard. All the time he was wrestling to get to his feet, but his efforts were severely hampered by the slippery boots. However, his fighting ceased when Wolf somehow managed to grab the leather cosh from his jacket pocket and whack Matt over the head with it, knocking him out cold.

Matt lay motionless over the metal and plastic lawn sprinkler, its nodules digging like spikes into his back and the water pumping from them shooting out at all angles. He was finished.

* * *

Wolf had done it. The boy had put up more of a fight than any man he'd ever faced. He was good, but not good enough, and Wolf smiled at his victory as he nursed his throbbing hand.

He stood there for a long moment, absolutely shattered and breathing hard, there was no way he could have fought for much longer. The boy was starting to get the better of him, he accepted that, but luck had been on his side, and ultimately he was the one who had prevailed, just as he always did. He was invincible.

He thought of Victoria and smiled again. Okay, so it had taken longer to dispose of the boy than originally planned, but now he was back on schedule, all he needed was a few minutes respite before he continued with his plans. However, at that moment, he saw Matt's head move. He was regaining consciousness and Wolf realised that the water from the sprinkler was helping to revive him.

'Shit!' Wolf cursed, 'What the hell has a guy gotta do?' Once more his plans were being hindered. He lifted the cosh again, intending, this time, to hit Matt even harder. But as he raised the cosh he noticed a gardener's wheel barrow close to the border of the garden. It was full of tools and suddenly he was struck by a delicious idea.

Wolf walked over to the wheel barrow and from a selection of hoes, rakes and other implements, he settled upon a long handled fork. 'That should do nicely,' he said.

He strode quickly back to where Matt lay and placed a foot either side of him, then he bent down and slapped him gently on the cheek, 'Hey, boy!' He said in his deep Miami lilt, 'Wake up, it's time to meet your maker!'

Matt blinked and Wolf slapped him again, 'Wake up, boy!' He repeated.

Slowly, Matt's eyes focused on Wolf's blood-smeared, sopping wet face. He was grinning evilly. 'That's it son, keep your eyes on me - you're about to see somethin' real good!' He laughed.

Wolf stood up and lifted the fork high above his head with both hands, aiming it at Matt's exposed throat, preparing to drive the sharp prongs straight through his jugular. Matt closed his eyes, unable to watch, as he prepared for what would surely be the coup de grâce.

'See ya in hell, boy!' Wolf growled.

Matt winced, held his breath and braced himself for impact, but nothing happened.

Tentatively he opened one eye. Wolf was standing there rigid, still holding the fork up high, still poised to land the killer blow, but his eyes were wide and staring out in front, bulging scarily from their red-rimmed sockets and his mouth was gaping open. Something shiny and metallic was sticking out of it, something which Matt could have sworn was a blade. Suddenly a thick river of blood started to flow from Wolf's gaping mouth, gushing over the metallic object and obliterating it from view. Then, very slowly, his body toppled forward, arcing majestically toward the wet turf before crashing face first with a loud splash beside where Matt was laying, the fork spearing itself deep into the grass, no longer a danger to anyone.

Amazed by what he'd just seen, Matt studied Wolf's prone form, which was now laying lifelessly beside him, and immediately noticed the carving knife sticking in the back of his head, its blade buried almost to the hilt.

'Are you okay?' Said a familiar voice.

It was Victoria, and Matt looked up, delighted to see her, although she looked decidedly worse for wear. She was swaying weakly in the soft breeze, her sodden and bloody fur wrap, which had concealed the knife, held by her side and the sprinkler showering her in cool water.

'Yes, I'm fine.' Matt replied, 'Are you?'

'What, me? Sure, I'm swell, honey,' she replied, before promptly passing out.

Twenty-one

O n the way to Palm Springs, Victoria checked that she still had the contract. She did. It was real. After all that had happened, she figured that she'd earned the part in the movie. Murray was just one of its several producers. It was a good script and a bankable story, if he knew that, then so did the others. The film would still get made either with or without him. And it was her name on the contract. She would be the star. Rightfully and legally.

In Hollywood, it was all about money, not about individual people and ultimately, after everyone had mourned the loss of 'one of tinsel town's greats,' they didn't really give a rat's ass, just as long as they made some dough.

However, for the moment, Victoria's movie career was on hold. She and Matt were heading home, where she knew she had a lot of things to talk about.

Matt was driving Victoria's El Camino pick-up, his Harley secured safely in the back. Next to it, under a tarpaulin, was Wolf's body. They'd bury it when they got to the ranch.

As they travelled, both swathed in bandages and surgical dressings, they talked. They talked about everything. They had formed a bond with the battles of the previous night having brought them together. They trusted each other. Neither one of them would have been there had it not been for the actions of the other and that meant a great deal to them both.

Matt was curious as to why Wolf should have attacked Victoria, but she could not offer any explanation other than that he revealed an association with Benny Mottola, a man who hated Matt's father and her husband equally. A man who would go to any lengths to see them both dead.

Matt winced when he heard this. He thought of Suzie and of her mutilated body, knowing she had died needlessly, a mere pawn in some vicious gangland vendetta. Now Victoria and him had almost been killed - how many more would have to die for what Joe Cassidy had done. Rose or Ruby? Maybe even Matt's niece and nephew at the Bluestone who were now like his own brother and sister.

'That bastard!' He spat. 'Because of my father and his seedy, underworld dealings, all of us are in danger. It's his fault, everything's his fault. Suzie, you, everything, I finally see it. I hoped it wasn't true, but now I finally get it!'

'What?' Victoria was appalled, unable to believe what she was hearing, 'Is that what you think?'

'Sure, what else can I think? There's no other reason for it,' he replied.

'Has no one ever told you?' She was incredulous.

'What? That my father's such a great guy, that I should consider myself lucky to call him Dad? Sure, they've told me, but they're like all the rest, scared of what he might do. I read the papers y'know, I'm not blind. I know what sort of a man he is.'

'Surely you don't truly believe that do you?'

'What else can I think? You just said it yourself. That guy Wolf tried to kill you 'cos Joe pissed off some bloody crime lord, just like when Suzie was murdered.'

'It's not like that at all, Matt. You've got it all wrong,' Victoria protested.

'Yeah? Well perhaps you'd better tell me how it is then, 'cos at the moment I'm ready to kill 'im myself!' He was angry and upset, the hurt he'd felt since Suzie's death which he'd tried hard to bury, had again risen to the surface, but now he had a clear target for his wrath, a target which he had at first been reluctant to find.

Victoria fell silent for a moment, composing her thoughts, deciding on what it was she was going to say. They had plenty of time. Time in which she was determined for Matt to understand the truth.

'Let me tell you about Joe and Sean,' she began. 'The story of your father and my husband.'

Victoria knew almost everything. More importantly, she knew it to be true and she told it to Matt as honestly as she could. She told of our humble beginnings, starting with our days running errands for Alfie Noakes; about Vinnie Reece and how we'd earned his respect by saving Alfie's life. She said about George Reilly and how Joe had killed him to save me and my mother. How he'd served time in prison because of it, which resulted in him unwittingly losing Rose and their unborn child, who now, twenty-six years later, was listening with great interest to the story.

Victoria then told of the death of Vic Cassidy, Matt's grandfather, and his rape of Sarah, Matt's aunt, and how my actions on that night led not only to the death of Jez Mottola and to a life long vendetta by his brother, but also to my enforced exile from England. She told of the Gladstone bag and about what became of Lord John Tailby's money. Then, of Billy Finn, and Ray Reece, of Frank Blades and of course, Benny Mottola. She mentioned Joe's release from prison and how Vinnie, dying of lung cancer, had placed his trust in him and how Joe had taken up the mantle of his mentor as a mark of respect and gratitude. She said how he had laid his own life on the line to save Michael from the clutches of Mottola with no regard for his own personal safety. Then Victoria

526

spoke of Wildwood and the Villa Continental, about the murder of Jarvis and the suspicious circumstances surrounding Rachel's overdose. She then described Joe's joy when he found Rose again, and the discovery of Matt, the son he never knew he had.

Finally, Victoria brought things up to date. After swallowing hard, she spoke of her degrading liaison with Murray Lieberman and the reason for it. She also told how she had intended to murder her blackmailer and how his heart attack had thankfully spared her from that.

In truth, she knew there was no reason to relate this last piece of information, but guilt was eating her up and confession was apparently good for the soul.

As for Wolf though, she could offer no reason for his attack, except that he was an associate of Mottola, which in itself, was explanation enough.

Victoria ended by saying, 'You see Matt, we have all lost something in this. You and me certainly have, as have your mom and Michael, but no one more than either Sean or Joe. But this is the important thing. This is what you really must understand. None of it was their fault. None of it. The blame lies with two men, Frank Blades and Benny Mottola. They're the ones you oughta hate.'

Matt was silent for a long time as he digested all he had heard. He knew it to be true. Not just because Victoria had told him, but because he felt it deep down in his heart. With this realisation came a surge of enormous relief accompanied by a large amount of guilt for what he had said previously.

'Victoria, I'm... I'm sorry—' he began, feeling very ashamed of himself.

'Hey, don't sweat it, we all make mistakes,' said Victoria coming to his rescue, 'But if you're gonna apologise to anyone, you'd better apologise to Joe.' He knew she was right, a reconciliation was

527

long overdue.

Again, the El Camino cruised along in silence until at last Matt steered it through the high gates of the Bluestone and asked quietly, 'Are you going to tell Sean about Lieberman?'

'I dunno, Matt' she replied apprehensively, 'I just don't know.'

Twenty-two

Ray stood at the front door with Joe. 'Be lucky, son,' he said, placing a fatherly hand on the other man's shoulder, then leaning closer, he added, 'And watch yer bleedin' back.'

'Don't worry, old man,' Joe replied with affection, 'I'll be just fine, but take care of my family while I'm gone, yeah?'

'Count on it - and less of the 'old man' yer cheeky git.'

Joe smiled as he climbed into the passenger seat of the Rolls, next to Manno who was driving him to Heathrow, 'See ya, Ray.'

'Yeah. See ya, son,' the old pirate replied, feeling uncharacteristically misty at the departure of his friend.

As he stood and watched the Rolls drive off down the road and vanish around the corner, Ray was aware of a strange sense of loss and an uncomfortable prickle of foreboding, almost as if he was saying goodbye to Joe for the last time. He walked back into the house, and was surprised to find that his one good eye had filled with water. Immediately embarrassed by his emotional over-reaction, he quickly wiped it before anyone could witness his girlish display. 'Silly old bugger,' he admonished himself, sucking in a deep breath of air and taking a moment to regain his composure. 'It's time I bloody retired!' He cursed. Then, with his unrufflable demeanour back in place once more, he marched into the kitchen as if he didn't have a care in the world.

Michael was in his apartment on the ground floor, listening at the door for his uncle's departure, still fuming over what he'd heard about Joe's intention to kill Carl Napier. He had to do something to warn Carl, he couldn't just sit back and wait for him to die.

The obvious thing, he decided, was to phone Carl, but he'd have to wait until it was safe. He gave it half an hour, until he was sure that everyone else was in the kitchen, then slipped out of his room and made his way silently upstairs to Joe's office. Quietly, he shut the door, walked quickly over to the phone and dialled Carl's direct line. Michael was sweating profusely as he waited for Carl to answer. He let it ring and ring, but there was no reply so reluctantly, he replaced the receiver. He stood for a moment and listened, but could hear nothing, he was still safe although the knowledge of that did little to calm his fragile nerves, if his treachery was discovered he would be in serious trouble. With a clammy hand, he picked up the receiver once again, this time dialling hotel reception. Immediately the phone was answered with a breezy but efficient, 'Good morning, welcome to the Villa Continental, my name's Janice how may I help you?'

Michael knew Janice from his many visits to Vegas. 'Hi, Janice,' he said in a hushed voice, 'It's Michael– Michael Walsh, could you put me through to Mr. Napier please.'

'Hi there, Mike, how are you?' The shortening of his name grated but he ignored it.

'I'm fine, Janice, but I really need to speak to Mr. Napier. It's urgent, very urgent.'

'Sorry to hear that Mike, but no can do I'm afraid. Mr. Napier is not in. He should be back in a couple of hours though, if you'd care to leave a message.'

Michael silently cursed. Why the hell did Carl have to be out? 'No, thanks, Janice. I'll try to catch him later.'

'Sure thing, Mike. Anything else I can help you with right now?'

'What?' He was distracted, his mind racing, 'Oh, no. Thanks, Janice, but like I said, I'll call again later.' He hung up. There was nothing more to do but wait. He'd give it another two hours then call again. Surely Carl would be in then.

Michael tentatively checked to see if the coast was clear, then quietly exited Joe's office and made his way back to his apartment, praying that no one would see him and recognise the guilt on his face.

* * *

Michael's heart rate had increased considerably and his clothes were damp with sweat, his wet hair sticking to his forehead. The last two hours had done little for his frayed nerves, he just wasn't cut out for all this cloak and dagger stuff.

Again, he sneaked out of his apartment and crept swiftly up the stairs, the door of Joe's office just making the slightest click as Michael closed it behind him.

* * *

Ray was dozing in the soft leather of the wing-backed armchair in the snooker room. This was his refuge, the place where he hid away from Ruby's watchful eye, a place that had helped him avoid all manner of housework and domestic chores. A hiding place which he naively believed neither Ruby nor Rose knew anything about.

In one hand, Ray held a tumbler full of eighteen year old, single malt whiskey, his chosen tipple for a lazy afternoon. In the other was a smouldering, hand-rolled Cuban cigar, taken as always from the case on the desk in Joe's office, which adjoined the snooker room. Between each luxurious puff, Ray's eyes would close and his head would gently nod, his chin moving ever closer to his chest. Just as he slipped completely into sleep, his chin would drop and the jolt would momentarily wake him up, causing the whole process to start again.

During one such moment, Ray was awoken by the click of the door in the adjacent room. Immediately he was awake, certain that Ruby had discovered where he was and had come to enlist him in the washing up. He froze, keeping dead still, hoping she wouldn't find him.

The door that led through to Joe's office was ajar, and Ray could easily hear the person in the next room walk across the polished exposed floor boards towards Joe's desk. Then he heard the slight 'ding' as the telephone receiver was lifted. He knew now that it wasn't Ruby and he relaxed, she would have used the phone downstairs in the kitchen. No doubt then that it was Brett calling his girlfriend, trying to avoid being overheard as he whispered his sweet nothings and wickedly, with a mischievous glint in his one good eye, Ray decided to eaves drop.

However, the moment the other person spoke, he knew it was Michael. He was obviously intending to make a business call, and Ray felt slightly disappointed that there was going to be nothing worth listening to.

* * *

'Hello, is that Janice?'

'Yes it is, how may I help you Sir?'

'It's me, Janice. Michael Walsh. I called earlier, remember?'

'Sure Mike, how are you?' Janice asked with false sincerity only barely remembering his previous call - he not being the sort of guy that stuck in her flittery mind.

'Yeah, fine Janice, is he back yet?' Again Michael was irritated by the shortening of his name, but he had far more important things on his mind than to worry about that.

'Is who back, Mike?'

Michael was starting to lose his patience, 'Carl! - I mean Mr.

532

Napier - is he back yet? It's very important that I speak to him.'

'Just a second Mike, let me check - I think he's out at the pool,' replied the girl, automatically placing Michael on hold.

'Shit!' Michael cursed with frustration, the pressure threatening to overwhelm him. Long seconds ticked by, each one seeming like a minute.

'Hello?' At last it was Napier's voice on the line.

'Oh, thank God, Carl, thank God it's you!'

'What Michael? What did you say?' Napier's voice was thick and groggy betraying the debauchery of the previous night.

'It's Joe,' Michael blabbed, 'I've got to tell you about Joe—'

Suddenly the line went dead and Michael stood gaping stupidly at the receiver, 'Hello? Carl, are you there?'

'No boy, Carl ain't there!' A voice growled behind him.

Michael span around in surprise, his heart threatening to burst through his chest in shear panic.

Standing there holding the telephone cord that he'd ripped violently from the socket, was Ray, his face blacker than hell, his expression meaner and more murderous than Michael had ever previously witnessed.

Ray was unable to restrain his anger. His disgust and disappointment in the boy almost beyond words. Throwing his cane aside, he marched briskly up to Michael and cuffed him hard around the face, nearly knocking him over, making him whimper like a puppy whose tail had been trodden on. Ray slapped him again with the back of his hand, catching Michael across the mouth causing a trickle of blood to spill over his lips.

'You... you–' Ray spat, but he couldn't bring himself to say the rest of the sentence, his words choking with emotion. He was trying desperately to rein in his anger, the veins in his thick neck taught and prominent. 'If only you knew what—' he was speaking through clenched teeth, finding it hard to swallow down his absolute revulsion, 'If only you bloody knew!'

Ray lifted his arm, intending to strike Michael again, but he held it there above him, almost paralysed, just looking into the damaged face of the boy, the boy he'd raised as his own and his heart broke. Ray was the one that had taught him, the one that had nurtured him - he and Ruby both. They had done their best, but that hadn't been good enough. They had failed. How on earth could Michael have turned out so bad?

Ray lowered his arm in defeat and turned away, his shoulders slumped and his head hung low. 'Get out,' he said in a whisper, 'Get out now, I can't even bear to look at you.' He bent down and picked up his cane then limped over to the open window, not noticing Sarah standing on the patio below. He closed his eyes and a tear ran down his cheek. His chest felt tight and his heart ached, suddenly he felt very old indeed.

Michael straightened up, he was snivelling but the fear was slowly subsiding. Anger was taking over, he could feel it building as he watched Ray. The old man was clearly upset and breathing heavily and it pleased Michael to see him suffer as he, too, had for so long. Why should he, Michael, be the only one to suffer?

He walked over to the door, then turned. 'Yes,' he said bitterly, 'I do know. I know all about my whore mother and my worthless father - the coward who deserted me when I was a baby. I also know all about your precious Joe and how he's ruined my life. But I promise you this - they're gonna pay - if it's the last thing I ever do, they're all gonna pay!'

Ray could stand it no more, he span around and threw the cane, the heavy silver fist at the end of it striking Michael on the temple, sending him crashing into the door.

'Get out!' Ray shouted.

Michael was stunned by the blow, but his temper made him immune to the pain. 'Okay, old man,' he hissed, 'I'm going, but don't ever think that this has finished. It's my turn now and I'll not rest until justice is done. Remember that.' Michael then strode from the room, slamming the door loudly behind him.

Ray turned back to the window and rested heavily on the sill. Today, he had lost two sons.

*   *   *

Less than an hour later, Michael left the house in his shiny new MGB sports car, the wheels screeching as he went. With his belongings stored in the Gucci luggage in the boot of the car, he believed himself to be driving toward a better life, but in reality he was driving straight into hell.

*   *   *

Sarah had heard every word exchanged by the two men and because of it, she too was crying.

No longer was she the emotionless drone that she had once been; she was now able to think, and more importantly, to listen, with total clarity of thought. The periods of cohesiveness that she had been experiencing for the last couple of years had been growing longer in length and becoming ever more frequent over the last few months. She had now been completely sentient and alert for almost a week and saw no signs of a relapse, but she had not shared this with anyone as she was still extremely fragile emotionally and did not want to risk being hurt so dreadfully again. She thought it best to keep this development to herself until she understood exactly what was going on, not daring even to tell Joe.

She feared it might only be a temporary state and didn't wish to raise his hopes or her own.

However, that was all before what she had just overheard. The argument between Ray and Michael had shaken her, woken her fully. She knew now, that somehow she would not be returning to that silent, safe world she had been inhabiting for so long. It was time for her to restart her life.

Because now things had changed.

Twenty-three

Carl Napier climbed out of the swimming pool and collapsed onto a sunbed, allowing the scorching Vegas sun to dry his bloated body. He felt like shit. He had been out with a client and it had inevitably turned into another long night of partying.

Booze, coke, a few hookers and a little bit of marijuana to take the edge off, just like the night before that and the night before that. In fact, like almost every night he could remember in recent months. It was burning him out and he knew it, but somehow he couldn't control it. What he needed was a vacation.

He rolled over onto his back and picked up the newspaper from the table beside him. He had read the headlines earlier but couldn't remember if it was a dream or reality, his mind had been fuzzy, still was in fact, but the swim had made him feel a little better and slowly he was coming around.

'*Movie producer dies of heart attack.*' Screamed the headline.

'Poor old Murray,' Carl said.

He and Lieberman were never friends exactly, Murray was far too unpleasant for that, but Carl always put on the 'best buddy act' whenever the producer came into town. He had been good for business and Carl would miss him for that reason alone.

Just then, a waiter handed Carl a phone, 'It's Mr. Walsh, Sir,' he announced.

'Christ!' Carl cursed, taking the phone, it was too early to speak to anyone.'

'Hello?' He said, but just as the boy started to speak, the pool bartender turned on the music system and Michael's words were lost in a loud burst of salsa. Carl glared angrily at the bartender who hurriedly adjusted the volume, but it was too late to hear the boy's message.

'What Michael? What did you say?' Napier asked, his patience already thin, but there was no one on the line, the phone was dead.

'Jerk!' Barked Carl as he slammed down the receiver, clicking his fingers for the waiter to come and relieve him of the telephone.

Feeling disgruntled, Carl turned his attention back to the newspaper and the story about Murray.

The funeral was to be in LA, in four days time. Everyone would be there, all the stars, all dressed in designer black, ever ready for a photo opportunity and a tearful comment for the press, all carefully rehearsed beforehand.

Of course, not all movie stars were like that, some of them were genuine, like Virgil Nash. Carl knew that Nash would be at the funeral as he'd headlined in three of Murray's highest grossing pictures and owed much of his career to him. This was well known in Hollywood, but Carl knew something else about Virgil that wasn't so well documented, something which Murray had once disclosed that Carl thought one day, might prove to be useful.

It happened, so the story went, in the spring of 1960, a couple of years before Virgil's big break. Apparently he was desperate to score some quick cash that would allow him to surf the whole summer instead of having to work, something which he tried to do at the same time every year.

Whilst at an audition, he met a guy who made 'adult films,' who in turn offered Virgil a part in his next production. The money was excellent for just three afternoons of 'work', and the film-maker seemed like an honest sort of guy. So, motivated by the thought of a carefree summer riding the waves, Virgil took him up on the offer, but it was a decision he would live to bitterly regret.

At first Virgil enjoyed the shoot, although it was a bit off-putting being filmed having sex - and taking direction on it, but it paid well, so he just went with it. However, on the final afternoon of the shoot he was to feature in an orgy scene in which 'the script' called for him to be tied-up and blind-folded then set upon by a band of nymphs. Very nice too, Virgil thought, although the thought of being blind-folded made him uneasy. Nevertheless, he put his concerns to the back of his mind and went ahead with the scene regardless. Virgil soon relaxed and actually began to enjoy himself.

It wasn't until almost the final reel, when his blindfold accidentally slipped, that the full horror of what was actually happening became clear. Between his legs, where he'd assumed he could feel the attentions of a girl, Virgil could see a large naked man who was performing an act on him so obscene, so utterly depraved that he felt sick to the stomach. To his side lay another nude man who was stroking and caressing Virgil's body whilst fondling his own. There were girls too, a whole bunch of them, all sweaty and panting and pleasuring each other, but Virgil couldn't think about them. All he could see were the men.

Suddenly he was desperate to be free and he kicked out wildly, his knee connecting with one of the men's balls causing him to cry out in pain. The other guy rolled off, but just as he did so, Virgil sat up and head-butted him, knocking him out cold. The girls began to scream and quickly scattered to safety as Virgil fought to rid himself of the thin rope tied around his wrists. He let out a deafening roar, as he tugged at it with all his might until, at last, it snapped. Immediately he ripped off the blindfold and jumped to his feet. The guy who'd got his balls kicked was writhing in agony on the floor and Virgil kicked him again as he barged off the set. He headed straight for the main camera which he wrestled from the cameraman and threw to the ground, hearing a rewarding smash as it hit. Then Virgil aimed for the director who was cowering behind one of his buddies who'd come for a peek. Virgil punched the friend on the nose who fell to the floor with a scream, then he grabbed the director by the throat and pushed him up against the wall, squeezing his windpipe in a vice-like grip.

'You lying, dirty creep!' Virgil growled, 'What the fuck do you think you're doing huh? I mean who do you think I am - some piece of meat with no life who you can just fuck with like it don't matter?'

'No, no, nothin' like—' the man squawked.

'Shuddup!' Virgil snapped, 'You're goddamn lucky I don't kill ya for what you've done here.'

'I... I'm sorry... I—' the guy tried again, but was once more cut off.

'Sorry don't cut it asshole, not this time, not with me. This time you've picked the wrong guy to mess with baby - and if this movie - this piece of shit excuse for a film - is ever released, then I will kill you. I'll hunt you down and destroy you - understand?'

The director nodded quickly. But that wasn't enough for Virgil, who punched him hard in the stomach and growled again, 'Understand?'

'Yeah,' the guy winced breathlessly, his eyes bulging with fear, 'I understand.'

'Good,' replied Virgil, before rendering him senseless with a well aimed upper-cut, sending him sliding unconscious down the wall.

Virgil then snatched up his clothes and bolted for the door, but as soon he stepped into the bright Pasadena sunshine, he threw up. He was disgusted, totally ashamed, but above all humiliated and he vowed never to tell anyone what he'd done - not even his closest friends.

That summer, Virgil took a job in a foundry. It was hot, heavy and unrelenting toil, but he worked harder and longer than he'd ever done in his life, to try and purge his memory of the ordeal.

By the end of '64, Virgil was a big name in Hollywood, already working on his second picture for Murray Lieberman, believing his past mistakes long since buried. Then, one day Lieberman called Virgil into his office and showed him extracts from a rough-cut that had arrived in his mail that morning. Even though it was very amateur, it was also very explicit and showed clearly Virgil Nash engaging in a number of obscene acts, most notably, in a scene featuring him blindfold.

Apparently there were four copies, all costing ten grand each - that supposedly being the price for silence. Murray bought all of them, his bright new star being worth every penny. However, just to be sure there would be no repeat demands, Lieberman hired a couple of goons who found the blackmailer and broke his legs. Upon searching his apartment, they also discovered another six cans of the rough-cut, together with the forty grand ransom money, but of course Lieberman didn't tell Nash that, who had already agreed to reimburse Murray from his movie salary.

Virgil swore Murray to silence, who in turn gave his word not to tell another living soul, it would be 'their little secret,' he had said. But then in his own loathsome, underhanded way, whilst enjoying a sauna with Carl in Vegas, Murray had told all. After a little sweet-talking and the promise of a particular showgirl the producer had his eye on, Carl even managed to persuade Murray to send him a copy of Virgil's dalliance with porn - and very interesting it was too.

The incriminating cine-film had been securely hidden in

Napier's safe for many years, but now, upon seeing the headlines of Murray Lieberman's death, he sensed an opportunity for which it could become very useful.

For sometime Benny had been pushing Carl to call on Virgil, to work out a deal with the movie star that would make them all a lot richer. It occurred to Carl that Lieberman's funeral would be the perfect excuse to do just that.

LA wasn't exactly Carl's idea of a vacation, but the break from Vegas would do him good. He'd do his deal with Virgil, then turn off the phones, snort a few lines and relax, just for a day or two, until his head felt better.

He picked up the phone and dialled Virgil's number to arrange their little get-together after the ceremony.

Benny would be pleased.

*   *   *

Virgil was no fool and as he put down the phone, he suspected something awry. He and Carl Napier had never been close, certainly not friends at least, acquaintances maybe, or business associates, but not friends. The only thing they had in common was the Villa Continental, which Napier and his consortium owned forty-eight percent of, whilst Virgil a mere three. However that three percent had always irked Carl and had been a source of much frustration. Of course he'd always tried to disguise it, but Virgil knew, and whenever they met the bitterness was almost tangible.

Now this request for a meeting, a demand nearly, with Napier's tone very knowing, very conspiratorial, as if he had a surprise up his sleeve which he was itching to reveal. He did say that it would be far more 'beneficial' to Virgil if he didn't say anything about their meeting to anyone, as the material he had to discuss was for his eyes only. 'Highly enlightening,' is exactly how Carl described it.

Virgil knew the meeting was going to be about the shares, it was obvious. But what more did Napier know? He glanced at his newspaper and saw the headline again, the story which followed it he'd read with disbelief earlier that morning. Could Murray's death have something to do with Carl's phone call?

Suddenly Virgil's stomach churned with dread. Lieberman could never be trusted, he'd known that over twelve years ago when the old man had got him out of that jam. His instincts told him though that Murray hadn't burned all copies of that film like he promised, but he couldn't prove it, he just had to hope that his fears were misplaced, and over the years, he'd believed that they had been.

But now there was this. Murray had died and Carl Napier wanted to discuss something - a secret he implied, which he was to say nothing to anyone about.

Lieberman and Napier had always appeared tight whenever Virgil had seen them in Vegas. Could it be that Murray had talked? A gut feeling told Virgil that he had.

Virgil smelled the dirty, cloying aroma of blackmail. The question was, what should he do about it?

* * *

The meeting went much as Carl expected it would. He held all the cards, he was in the dominant position and Virgil Nash had nowhere to go.

Carl enjoyed watching Nash squirm as he played him the cine-film on the projector he'd rigged up in his hotel suite. He squeezed every ounce of delicious pleasure from the other man's pain before he delivered the ultimatum, the only escape route open to Virgil if he didn't want copies of the film circulated to every TV station in California.

The deal was this: either Virgil turn up in Las Vegas in two days time and sign over his three percent of the Villa Continental to Nevada Gaming and Leisure Associates, thereby giving them the majority share holding, or, find himself back where he started; a penniless beach boy with nothing but his surf board and good looks for company.

To add weight to his threat, just in case Virgil hadn't considered him serious, Carl told him that the NGLA was merely a front for Benny Mottola and the Miami mob - and they, he emphasised, were people Virgil really shouldn't upset. He had forty-eight hours to decide which, Carl thought, was more than generous.

Hollywood movie star with riches beyond his wildest dreams or poor surfer living in a shack on the beach? Or maybe it was simpler than that; sell out his friends and live, or don't, and die.

Obviously, when presented with such a dilemma, Virgil just didn't have a choice.

Twenty-four

When I saw Victoria, I thought she and Matt had been in a car crash as they both looked so beaten up and bruised. However, my initial concerns were nothing like as grave as when Victoria related what had happened with Wolf. Matt then showed me the body under the tarp, which in the Californian heat, was already starting to smell badly, causing us both to gag. He needed to be buried quickly, that much was blatantly obvious.

Benny had planted him as a mole. Two years he'd been in our employ, two years in which he'd no doubt reported our every movement back to Benny Mottola. I had been a stupid, trusting fool and my wife had nearly been killed because of it.

Immediately, I picked up the phone and called Joe, but the number was unobtainable. I dialled the operator but she told me there was a fault on the line. I would keep trying, but first I had to dispose of the body. I had intended to do this alone, both Vicky and Matt had been through enough, but they wouldn't hear of it and insisted on coming with me.

We drove deep into the desert, the light already fading, and by the time Matt and I had dug a deep enough hole, deep enough so as not to be unearthed by scavenging coyotes, it was totally dark.

We threw in Wolf's corpse, wrapped tightly in the tarp, and began covering it with dirt. Half an hour later we climbed wearily back into the El Camino and headed home to the ranch. By the time we got there it was well after midnight and both my companions were asleep. The last twenty-four hours had been exceptionally tough for them and they badly needed to recuperate.

Reluctantly I woke Matt and pointed him in the direction of his apartment above the garage, then I carried Victoria up to our room and put her to bed. I kissed her lightly on the forehead before going back downstairs where I tried phoning Joe once more. Still the line was dead and my worries were growing by the second. Faced with no other choice, I turned in for the night, but slept sporadically, trying Joe's number whenever I awoke.

Still without any luck, I finally conked out about 4am, but would try London again before breakfast. It was imperative that I got through. All I could do until then was hope that everything was okay.

*   *   *

At seven-thirty, I picked up the phone in the kitchen, looking out of the window at the lovely sunny morning and taking a swig of hot black coffee. Just as I was about to dial the number, I noticed a car making its way up the driveway and was curious as to who could possibly be calling at such an early hour. As the car drew up outside the main house, I saw it was a very dusty LA cab.

The rear door opened slowly and out climbed a dishevelled, unshaven man with hair the colour of coal. He was wearing a pair of expensive dark shades which he removed before opening the trunk, revealing eyes that were as black as thunder.

Although I was delighted to see him, and more than a little relieved, I knew straight away, as he took his bag from the rear of the taxi, that Joe was not a happy man.

*   *   *

'I thought you were gonna come and pick me up!' He said as I went out onto the porch to meet him. 'Six bloody hours I waited at that soddin' airport. Six bloody hours!'

'Eh?' I replied, uncertain of what the hell my friend was talking about.

'I've been tryin' to phone you since yesterday evenin', but all it did was ring and ring. Finally I ended up gettin' a cab - cost me a bleedin' fortune. Didn't Ray call to tell you I was comin?"

'Eh?' I said again, not comprehending anything he had said.

Joe read my perplexed expression, 'You haven't got the slightest clue what's goin' on here, have you?'

I shook my head.

'In that case, we've got a lot to talk about - a lot's happened in the last couple of days.'

'You can say that again,' I responded and this time it was Joe's turn to look perplexed as he realised that I too had some news.

*   *   *

Ray phoned mid-morning, just as I was making some more coffee, to advise me of Joe's imminent arrival, 'Yeah, thanks for the warning Ray,' I said sarcastically, handing Joe the receiver.

'Silly old sod!' Were Joe's first words, 'I'm already 'ere,' but the irony of the situation was lost on Ray who seemed pre-occupied and far from his normal jovial self.

According to Ray, there had been some problems at The Castle which had resulted in the phone getting disconnected, but apparently it was all under control now. Joe asked Ray what the problem had been, but all he'd say was that everything would be explained when Joe got back to London. Joe tried to push him, suspecting that something was quite seriously wrong and hearing the barely controlled emotion in his friend's voice, but Ray wouldn't be drawn.

Troubled by the older man's uncharacteristically sullen mood, Joe thought it best not to pursue the matter any further, deciding that Ray would tell him when he was ready to.

Changing the subject from one troubling matter to another, Joe warned Ray to be extra vigilant because of what I'd told him that morning about Wolf. He advised him that it was likely Mottola was stepping up the pace and he wanted everyone to be prepared. Something big was occurring, he was certain of it, and he didn't want anyone to get caught off guard. Ray assured him that whatever it was, he and the rest of the boys would be ready.

Finally Joe said, 'Look after yourself, old man, I'll be home soon.'

Ray smiled, in a wistful, almost nostalgic way, again his one good eye filling with water, and he was thankful that Joe couldn't see him, 'Yeah, see ya, Son,' he replied, then replaced the receiver.

*　*　*

Ray made a couple more calls, the most notable one being to Richie Noakes, relating Joe's warning, then hobbled out of the office and shut the door. His ankle hurt him today and he was very tired, feeling all of his sixty-three years. Perhaps it was just all that business with Michael yesterday which he'd not yet recovered from. What had happened? He asked himself, had he become old overnight? A couple of days ago he was fighting fit, now he was weak and feeble and his emotions had gone all to pieces, whatever next?

The reply to the question came almost immediately, because as he limped to the top of the stairs and looked down them, he was suddenly giddy with his vision blurred and head swimming wildly. The stairs started to spin before his eyes like some mad ride at the fair and his legs turned to jelly. He knew he was going to faint but was powerless to prevent it. 'Oh, God, not this,' he said aloud, as the darkness came rushing in to consume him.

He made a desperate grab for the banister rail, but his hand couldn't find it in time. His legs gave way under him and instead of finding safety, he toppled forward into nothingness. The silver-headed cane slipped from his grip and hit against the wooden spindles of the banister, cart-wheeling down the steps ahead of him. But Ray heard and felt nothing as his heavy body connected with the patterned carpet at the bottom of the stairs. He had already been swept away into oblivion.

* * *

She knelt down by his side, being careful not to touch him. From her room, she'd heard the sound of him falling and had looked out of her open door just in time to see him hit the bottom of the stairs with a loud slap.

Without conscious thought, she had rushed to him, uncertain whether she'd find him dead or alive. Kneeling there, something in her memory told her that it was best not to move people until you knew the extent of their injuries, so instead she very gently tapped his face and asked almost in a whisper, 'Hello, can you hear me? - Are you alright?'

At first, she'd feared him dead, but then, just before the others arrived, she saw his chest move and noticed the slightest quiver of his nostrils as he unsteadily inhaled.

'Oh, my God!' Shouted Ruby as she bolted from the kitchen.

'What on earth—' gasped Rose, right behind her, neither woman being able to quite believe what they were seeing.

Slowly Ray stirred, letting out a long agonised groan before gradually opening his one good eye.

'Are, you alright?' The woman kneeling above him asked again.

'Eh?' He croaked, as he tried to focus on her face.

'Are you hurt?' She continued.

Then Ray recognised who it was that was speaking to him, but was confused, surely he was delirious -then something else occurred to him. 'Am I dead?' He enquired earnestly, the pain momentarily easing.

The woman smiled slightly. It was the first time he had seen it and it was beautiful, her eyes too, so clear, so dark. Unbelievable.

'No, you're not dead,' she replied.

'But you're... you're—' he wanted to say 'an angel' but instead he said, 'You're Sarah!'

'Yes, I am.' Again she smiled, this time widely.

'My God,' Ray exclaimed incredulously, 'You're alright.'

'Let's hope so,' Sarah answered hesitantly, still not completely sure of it herself, 'But what about you. Are you okay?'

'No luv,' Ray said with an anguished grimace, 'I don't think I am.' Then, almost as if testament to this, the blackness came again and stole him away.

Twenty-five

Joe needed a gun, something small but with a big enough kick to get the job done. I'd heard Rocky talking in the past, saying that he knew a guy who could get that sort of thing, anything from Derringers to Uzis he'd boasted, as well as fake IDs, Passports and other forged documentation, so I wandered down to the workshop and asked him for a quiet word.

I said I wanted a pistol for home security, but didn't want the hassle of going to the gun store and filling out lots of forms. He said he understood and that he'd ask his buddy, but it might take a few days, a week at most. That would be fine, I replied, although I knew Joe would have preferred to get the job done sooner. Nevertheless, it gave us some time to finalise our strategy. Time, as it turned out, which would prove to be vital.

* * *

Matt awoke at around lunchtime and came around to the kitchen from his apartment to be informed by me that his father had arrived earlier that morning. 'Where is he?' He asked.

'In the barn, doing some work on the bag,' I said. Joe needed to let off some steam, the anger he felt at Carl's betrayal was still fresh, still hot. If he was going to have to wait a week, then he needed to find a way to release it and the punch bag in the barn seemed to be the perfect answer.

Matt poured himself a coffee, then opened the back door with the intention of going to the barn.

'No offence, son,' I warned, knowing Joe's dark mood, 'But now might not be the right time.'

'No, Sean,' Matt replied, 'What I've got to say can't wait. In fact, it's long overdue.'

*   *   *

Matt could hear the thump, thump, thump of the leather gloves on the heavy bag before he reached the barn. He could also hear the grunting and puffing of his father and the creak of the rope from which the bag was suspended as it reeled away from each of Joe's devastating blows.

The door was open and as Matt stepped over the threshold, he saw Joe, whose back was towards him. For a moment the son watched the father and couldn't help but be impressed by what he saw. At forty-three, Joe was still in the peak of fitness. As he stood there, stripped to the waist, the sweat glistening on every sinew of his muscular physique, banging away at the bag as if it was filled with hot air, he could have passed for a man fifteen years younger. His hair, slicked back with perspiration, was still thick and black with only the slightest trace of grey and his skin was tanned and tight with no hint of ageing. Matt smiled, if he looked half that good in twenty years he'd be happy.

'Hi, Dad,' he said.

Joe landed one more punch, then steadied the bag before slowly turning around. The noon day sun shone behind Matt, silhouetting him in the doorway and Joe couldn't be sure it was him. It certainly hadn't sounded like him.

'Matthew?'

'Yeah, How ya doin?'

'Fine boy. Just fine... Say, did I just hear you right? Did you just call me—?'

'Dad. Yeah, I did.'

'That's what I thought.' Joe was clearly puzzled, it was the first time his son had ever called him that. 'Is er... everything okay?'

'Y'know what Dad?' Matt grinned, purposely using the name again, 'For the first time in ages, everything is okay. Very okay indeed.'

*   *   *

The two of them talked for a long time, maybe an hour or more, just chatting about things - things that should have been talked about before, but either pride, stupidity or circumstances had gotten in the way. Matt now fully understood what his father had been through and why he had done the things he had. He finally believed what the rest of us had been trying to tell him - that Joe wasn't some kind of vicious monster, but a tough and dependable ally who'd stand by you no matter what. Above all, he now accepted Joe as his father and trusted his word without question.

They spoke for the first time about Suzie and the men that killed her. Matt had already heard from Victoria about Frank Blades, so there was no longer any need to keep his existence a secret. It was a mistake not to have told Matt in the first place, Joe realised that now. The boy had a right to know who orchestrated the murder of his girlfriend and whatever he did with that information was entirely up to him. Joe filled in the gaps in Victoria's pretty comprehensive telling of events, details about Mottola and Blades and now Carl Napier, the man whom Joe had believed to be his friend. He concluded by saying that he and I were off to Vegas to settle the score, once and for all.

'I'll come with you, I can help,' Matt said.

'No, Son, it's not your fight,' Joe replied.

'But it is. You're my father - and if it's your battle, then it's my battle - besides, you might need some back-up.'

Joe could see the need in his son's eyes. It was evident that

Matt saw this as a chance to redeem himself, to re-earn the trust he felt he'd lost and to prove his worth to his father, who in reality had never doubted him. But to deny him now, would almost be to shun him and Joe had no wish to push him away, not now, not ever again.

'Well, alright. But I warn ya, it ain't gonna be pretty,' he said.

'Don't worry about me, I can look after myself,' Matt smiled.

'On that score, Son,' Joe beamed back, 'I've got no concerns.'

*   *   *

Things were happening fast. On the TV the news was full of Murray Lieberman's death, his body having been discovered the morning before by a housekeeper. He had, by all accounts, suffered a massive heart attack and had died alone in his huge Beverly Hills mansion. I remembered Vicky saying something about auditioning for a part in one of his movies and wondered how this would affect her chances of getting it. He was an old man and I felt sorry for him, but I was more concerned for Victoria. Surely she would be devastated when she found out he was dead. I decided not to wake her. I'd break the news to her gently when she came downstairs.

*   *   *

By the time she came down it was mid-afternoon. She was walking very carefully, her body obviously racked with pain from the beating it had taken from Wolf. The bruises on her face had now ripened into deep purple swellings which were concentrated around her eyes and mouth. She also had several small lacerations on her neck which marred her usually smooth, tanned skin and I felt the anger surge through me at the thought of what she'd been through. The very sight of her made me want to drive out into the desert, dig up Wolf's corpse and kill him all over again for what he'd done.

She had no make up on, her hair was only loosely brushed and for the first time ever, Victoria looked all of her forty years.

Somehow Wolf had robbed her of the ageless quality she'd always possessed and although I knew her wounds would heal, I felt that I had been robbed of something too.

'How you feelin'' I asked.

'Hey, I'm a tough broad - a Wild, remember?' She attempted a smile and tried to sound up-beat, as if her injuries were nothing more than mere inconveniences, but she was being brave, there was something more, something much deeper I could sense it. Victoria was an excellent actress but I knew her too well.

'Hey, it's me you're talking to. How are you really?'

'I'm—' her voice broke off, suddenly choked with emotion and I saw the tears well up in her eyes.

'Vicky?' I rushed to her and attempted to embrace her, but she turned away, unable to meet my gaze or accept my comfort. 'What is it? Are you in pain - is something broken?' I didn't know what to think.

'No, Sean, nothing's broken.'

'So what's—?' Then I heard the sound of the TV up in our bedroom and realised that she must have seen one of the hourly news bulletins which were all reporting the death of Murray Lieberman. Suddenly it all made sense and I cursed my stupidity for not disconnecting the television set. 'Are you crying because of Murray?' I asked.

'What?' She replied, immediately staring straight into my face, her interest suddenly intense.

'Are you crying about Murray?' I repeated.

'You know?' She seemed amazed as I nodded confirmation, 'But how—?' Her eyes were now full of concern, full of torment, almost haunted. I detected something else in them too; something which I could very nearly swear was guilt.

'Yes, I know.' I said, 'But it'll be fine I promise, everything's gonna work out okay, you'll see.' I smiled, then pulled her to me and this time she let me place my arms around her as she pressed her face against my chest.

'Oh, Sean,' Victoria gushed, 'I didn't think you'd understand. But I just couldn't let it happen again.'

'Ssh,' I whispered, 'It's alright, everything's alright.'

'I had to do it, you know that don't you? I had no choice,' she was weeping now.

'No choice about what?'

'Sleeping with Murray of course. But I knew, deep down, that it wouldn't be just a one off. I'd have to do it again and again, until he got bored. And then the truth about you would come out and my career would truly be over.'

Suddenly I went cold. I felt a clawing grip in the pit of my stomach and had to gasp for breath. 'You slept with him?' I was stunned.

'Yes, you know I did - I had to, but let's not discuss that any more, 'cos Murray's dead now and we don't have to worry about him ever again.' She pulled her face away from my chest and again looked into my eyes, but instead of seeing a kind, understanding expression, she saw my utter horror at what she'd just told me.

'Oh, my God,' she gasped, 'You didn't know did you? You had no idea—'

'No. I didn't,' I snapped. 'But I do now and I think you'd better tell me what the hell's going on!'

*   *   *

It was awful. Victoria told me what she'd done and exactly why she'd done it - in part, to save me, but also because she couldn't bear the thought of not having a career again, of spending another ten years, possibly a whole lifetime, in the Hollywood wilderness. I couldn't really blame her as I knew what she had been through before - which was rough, to say the least.

But it also transpired that the Bluestone, for Victoria, was not enough and apparently never had been. It was not the life she wanted - she'd grown up on a ranch, so she knew. The children, even though she loved them dearly, were not enough either and neither, so it seemed, was I. It all came out, all her disillusionments, her broken hopes and dreams.

She told me that she'd not truly been happy in years and I, too, had to admit the same. Our lives were too different, we wanted different things and I, with my past, was always going to be a potential hazard to her. In truth, we had grown apart and had probably stayed together for all these years because of the children.

Vicky confided to me that she was attracted to someone else. Strangely, this news didn't concern me, in fact, I was pleased as it somehow eased my guilt over Sarah, who, I admitted now, I had never really gotten over, even though I had desperately tried to. Vicky knew and understood. She'd always suspected, which was undoubtedly a contributory factor in the break down of our marriage.

It was clear that Vicky and I still loved each other, but in a platonic way, not as a man and wife should, and that was all that really needed to be understood. For that reason, after much agonising and many tears, Vicky and I at last agreed to separate.

The kids would be okay - we would both make sure of that. There would be no shouting matches, no law suits and no unpleasantness. Just an amicable, mutually beneficial, split.

Before nightfall, I kissed Olivia and Josh, and gave Victoria a hug, then watched them all drive off to Wildwood, where they would stay until things had been sorted out. The last thing Victoria said, before she climbed into the El Camino, was, 'I love you Sean and I always will.'

'I love you,' I replied. And I meant it too. Victoria Wild was one hell of a woman.

Twenty-six

What a day it was going to be for Benny Mottola. A day when he would finally own the majority share of a Las Vegas casino. However, it was not just any casino, but one he'd be stealing from under the noses of his two most hated enemies - and by far the most delicious aspect of the whole thing was that they would not know a thing about it - not until he had the pleasure of telling them afterwards of course, and he smiled with satisfaction at the thought.

So proud was he of what he was about to achieve, he'd even brought his twin boys along to witness it. Vito and Jez, now both ten, were the image of their father, strapping lads with heavy features and dark wavy hair. Benny's 'young bulls' as he liked to call them, who in the years to come would take their rightful places at the head of the Vincenzi and Carboni crime syndicates, truly uniting the two families. Even without Benny, their grandfathers would make it happen as the boys were the apples of their eyes. At ten years old, their illustrious futures were already sewn up - and the Villa Continental would be the rock upon which those futures were built.

According to Carl, Virgil Nash hadn't needed anything like the forty-eight hours given to consider his predicament, in fact Carl had only just got back to Vegas before the movie star was on the phone, obviously in a state of extreme panic, only too anxious to sign away his shares and save his own pitiful skin. People like that made Benny sick, they had no back bone and no loyalty and he had nothing for them but contempt, he'd see to it that Napier release Nash's porno flick anyway, that should teach the actor a lesson or two about selling out his friends.

Nevertheless, there they were, two days after Carl's meeting with Nash, sitting in Napier's sumptuous penthouse apartment at the Villa Continental, waiting for Virgil to arrive; Benny, Carl and three of Mottola's most trusted henchmen. Benny's two boys were in the adjacent room, waiting for their father to call them once the deal was done.

The meeting was set for twelve noon and at eleven fifty-nine, the elevator pinged, its doors slid open and out stepped Virgil Nash.

*   *   *

Rocky Costello had been as good as his word and exactly six days after I requested it, he presented me with the gun, a .38 snub nose, the kind used by cops and all those private eyes on the TV. Small but efficient and for what Joe wanted, ideal.

*   *   *

We arrived in Vegas the day after we got the gun, which was now loaded and tucked into the back of Joe's jeans, concealed from view by his black leather jacket.

I went to the front desk to enquire if Mr. Napier was still in his apartment. He was. 'Please don't announce my arrival, I'd like it to be a surprise,' I winked conspiratorially at Janice, the receptionist, as if I was some thousand dollar hooker that Carl had ordered. Nothing would have shocked Janice, she'd seen it all and knew when to turn a blind eye.

'Sure thing, Mr. Noakes,' she winked back. 'Nice to see you back sir.'

We were to travel up to Napier's apartment by the private elevator, leaving only Matt downstairs in the lobby. He'd take the public elevator to the fourteenth floor, then take the emergency stairs to the sixteenth where he'd wait by the fire exit door of the penthouse, in case Carl tried to escape that way.

I looked at my watch, 11.57am. The elevator pinged, its doors slid open and we stepped inside.

'Be careful,' Matt said to his father just before the doors closed and Joe vanished from sight.

'You too, Son,' Joe replied, but Matt was already one storey below us as the elevator made its way up to the sixteenth floor. Our date with destiny was just a few minutes away.

* * *

'Ah!' Benny said, as Virgil walked into the apartment, 'If it isn't Judas Iscariot - and right on time too. Sammy, Guido - search 'im!' At the order, two of Mottola's goons jumped to life and did as instructed.

Wolf should have been there too, but Benny hadn't heard from him in eight days so another goon, named Enzo had been brought in as a replacement. Enzo stood guard near Benny, his eyes on Virgil.

'He's clean, Boss,' Guido said.

'Good. Get 'im over 'ere.'

Virgil was frog-marched over to where Carl and Benny sat by the glass coffee table upon which Rachel Cassidy had once danced naked.

'This shouldn't take too long,' Carl said with a smug little grin on his face.

'Great, cos the air don't smell too good in here!' Virgil replied, getting a punch in the kidneys by Sammy for his insolence.

'Now, now, Nash,' it was Benny's turn to speak, 'This ain't Hollywood, you don't have to play the hero - not here. Besides, it's

560

a bit too late for that don't you think? Heroes don't sell out their friends now, do they? At least, not in the movies I've seen.'

'Okay, okay - you've made your point. Now where's the goddamn cine-film?' Virgil winced, trying to ignore the pain.

'Oh, there'll be plenty of time for that,' Benny interjected, 'As soon as you've signed over the shares.'

'No.' Virgil was firm. 'The film first.'

'Careful, Nash. You're in no position to barter—' Carl was going to say more, but Benny interrupted.

'Finally showing some back-bone, eh, Nash? Well good for you,' he said sarcastically. 'Enzo! Show 'im the film.' Then Benny turned his attention back to Virgil and added menacingly, 'It makes no difference either way,' he said, 'You will sign the papers.'

Enzo lifted a crocodile brief case and snapped it open. From it he pulled out a metallic film can.

'Give it to 'im, Enzo,' Benny commanded, nodding towards Virgil, who was still sandwiched between Sammy and Guido. He took the can and opened it, then pulled out a foot long reel of film and held it to the light. He studied it for a moment, then let it spool back into the canister. It was the movie.

'Satisfied?' Benny asked.

'Satisfied,' Virgil replied.

'Good, then let's get down to business.'

*   *   *

Vito and Jez, Benny's two boys, were in the bedroom, their little ears pressed up against the door, listening to the muffled sounds of what was happening in the adjacent room. Both eager for their father to call them, to tell them when the deal was done.

561

Twenty-seven

Like one of the magicians that appeared nightly on The Strip, Carl produced a thin wad of paper as if from nowhere, then from his inside jacket pocket, took out a shiny gold fountain pen.

'Okay, Nash,' he said, 'Time to make good your part of the deal.'

Virgil shifted uneasily, then, with a slight shove from Sammy, he stepped forward, a light sweat on his forehead. 'C'mon, Nash,' Napier sneered, looking at the pearlised oyster of his watch face, 'We ain't got all day.' He was getting irritable, his limbs becoming twitchy, it was time for a fix.

Benny thought he recognised the fear in Virgil's eyes, and savoured it, much as a wine connoisseur would a vintage Chardonnay. 'What's the matter Nash?' He grinned, 'Gettin' cold feet? Ya startin' to feel like the cowardly snake that you are? Well get used to it, cos you're gonna feel it every single day of your life. But it's too late now, there's no turnin' back - the buck stops here with you signin' those papers.'

'I can't,' said Virgil softly.

'Whassat? Did I hear you right? Did you say you can't?' Benny's voice was smooth, his manner almost genial, but the menace was unmistakable.

'Just sign the goddamn papers Nash - and let's get this over with!' Napier was starting to lose control.

'I can't - I really can't.' Virgil's voice was stronger now, his eyes more steady.

'Don't push it, son,' Benny replied, 'I'm not a guy you wanna upset.' The first signs of impending violence beginning to show through the cracks in his calm exterior.

'Listen, Nash,' Carl snapped, 'Do you really think that copy of the film you're holding is the only one? Do you really think we'd be that stupid?' Virgil looked directly at Napier, of course he knew there would be other copies, or at least he suspected there to be, and now it had been confirmed. It would not end here, that was for certain - even if he signed the papers, they would still have something on him and every time Napier or Mottola needed a little favour from their man in Hollywood, he would be at their beck and call, unable to refuse, just in case they released the damning footage of him appearing in a porno flick. His life would belong to them.

Virgil allowed himself a little inward smile of satisfaction, he knew now for definite that he'd done the right thing, not that he'd doubted his decision for a second, but it was comforting to know that he'd chosen the right path.

-'—Now for chrissakes—,' Carl was still speaking, '—pick up that fuckin' pen and sign your goddamn shares over to us!'

'No. That's what you don't understand,' Virgil was smiling openly now, there was no longer any need for the subterfuge, 'They're not my shares, not any more - you see, I've already sold 'em.'

*   *   *

We rode the elevator all the way up to the sixteenth floor and just before the doors opened, I nodded at Virgil. What he was about to do was risky, very risky, but he was adamant that he wanted to do it - he was a brave man and an exceptional friend.

Virgil had phoned me just moments after Carl Napier had put forth his proposal, the evening after Murray Lieberman's funeral, and he'd told me everything.

He'd told me about the porn movie and the alleged copy that had found its way into Carl's possession; about Napier's link with Benny Mottola and how the two of them were trying to blackmail him into signing over his shares in the Villa.

However, what neither Carl nor Benny had considered was Virgil's strength of character. What they failed to see was that he couldn't give a damn about stardom. He was a surfer, a beach bum, nothing more, nothing less and that's all he ever aspired to be. More to the point, surfing was the one thing he could still do whether news of his scandalous past broke or not. Money meant little to him, fame even less, so when Napier gave him his ultimatum, he didn't even have to think twice. Okay, so there was also the definite possibility that he could be injured or even killed, but Virgil thought what the hell, he was over forty, single and life just wasn't worth living without a little risk - indeed, perhaps that's just what his life was missing.

With that in mind, he drove to Palm Springs and signed his three percent of the Villa over to Louretta, Joe and myself, the shares divided equally. Twenty-four hours later he was in Vegas with us, his presence and volunteered participation at the very heart of our plans. If Mottola doubted that Virgil lacked backbone, he was about to be proved very wrong.

As the doors of the elevator opened, allowing Virgil to step out, Joe and I flattened ourselves against its wall, hoping that Benny hadn't stationed any of his goons immediately outside.

By now Joe had the .38 snub nose in his hand whilst I was gripping the handle of a Louisville Slugger. It was Josh's favourite bat but I suspected it was about to get dented.

As I heard Benny greet Virgil, I slid my arm across and

pressed the doors open button on the elevator control panel, then, like Joe, waited for our cue. My brow was wet and my hands sticky, it had been a long time since I'd done anything like this - maybe too long. I glanced at Joe and saw that he was calm, just as I would have expected, cool as a cucumber and ready for anything. For the first time in over twenty years, I was to be his back-up and I was determined not to let him down.

We listened to the banter and the threats being exchanged in the apartment, waiting for the moment, readying ourselves for when Virgil dropped the bombshell.

When he finally did, the explosion was every bit as fierce as predicted.

'You've done what?' Benny roared, lunging towards Virgil.

At that moment, Joe flew out of the elevator like lightening with me hot on his heels. I didn't notice at the time, but now when I think back, my edginess had already gone, no longer was I nervous but totally composed, the whole thing becoming second nature, just as it had been when we were kids.

'What the fuck—?' Benny growled, as he saw Joe flying towards him.

'Oh, my God!' Carl shouted with alarm, the colour visibly draining from his face.

Joe had always been quick, but on this day, he was like a man possessed, completely focussed and utterly lethal. Before Sammy had a chance to move, Joe raced over to him and coshed him around the jaw with the .38. Likewise, as Guido reached into his jacket for his gun, I hammered my foot into his balls and as he went down, landed a crushing blow to the side of his head with my balled fist. Neither goon would be bothering us again for a while.

Enzo had drawn his revolver from his belt but Virgil dived on him before he could use it and the two of them fell to the ground, wrestling madly for control of the weapon.

Benny was still aghast, stunned by the interruption, realising that his dream was crumbling away. 'Cassidy! You sonofabitch - you motherfuckin' sonofa—'

'Be quiet you fat piece of shit!' Joe spat as he sprang up onto the coffee table and kicked Mottola hard in the face, knocking him back onto the sofa with blood spraying from his thick pink lips.

With Benny down, Joe leapt onto Carl like a wild tiger. 'You killed Rachel you bastard, and now I'm gonna kill you!' He snarled.

Benny made to get up, but I slammed the baseball bat into his chest, driving the air from his lungs as he collapsed once more onto the sofa. 'Just give me an excuse to smash your skull in Mottola,' I said, 'one tiny excuse to kill you.' But Benny just glared at me with blood pissing from his mouth and hate in his eyes. I couldn't stand to look at him after everything he'd done to me and my family. So I punched him with all my might, squarely on the chin, and I couldn't help but feel good as I saw the pain spread over his face, like the shattering of a granite boulder. Then his body went slack and he slumped back onto the sofa, out cold. However, I had no time to enjoy the moment as other battles were still raging around me. Virgil and his guy were somewhere behind and Joe and Carl were scuffling on the floor beside me.

'No, Joe - please!' Napier cried, but his pleadings were cut short as Joe took a tight grip on his throat and whipped him around the head with the revolver. Twice, three times, Joe struck, smashing Carl's nose and breaking his teeth.

'Bastard!' Joe yelled, 'Treacherous, lying bastard!' Then, just as he whacked Carl around the ear again, the gun, quite by accident, went off.

The bullet missed Napier by a whisker and, instead, struck the ceiling with an almighty crack. A large chunk of plaster crashed down onto the glass coffee table, smashing a giant jagged hole directly through its centre. The sound of both shot and glass seemed to release Joe from his all-consuming rage, the blood lust finally subsiding. But Napier was oblivious as he'd lost all consciousness.

Joe, his shoulders still heaving with exertion from the beating he had just doled out, stood over Carl and pointed the pistol at his face. Joe stood there for a long moment, poised for the shot, aiming point blank at the man responsible for killing Rachel. Wanting to kill him.

I stood watching, unable to intervene, knowing that this was why we had come to Vegas. Knowing that Joe had come here to kill Carl. It was his call. His right.

It can only have been seconds but it seemed like much longer as I waited for the shot to ring out. But it never did. Joe couldn't kill him, not in cold blood, no matter what Carl had done.

Joe took his finger off the trigger and lowered the gun, his anger spent, his hate gone. He looked over at me and, in answer to a question that I never asked, said, 'He was my friend once. How can I kill him?'

This was the real Joe Cassidy. Not the newspaper version or the gangland version, but the real man, and at that moment, I respected him more than I ever had before.

As I turned away, a shot rang out and I thought for a second that Joe had changed his mind. Then I realised that the sound had come from elsewhere and I looked immediately for Virgil.

He and Enzo had been fighting for control of the gun, their bodies pressed together as they writhed violently on the floor. Now they were both still, the gun trapped somewhere between them and a pool of dark red blood seeping out from where they lay.

Twenty-eight

Both Joe and I made a move to help Virgil, but as we did so a familiar voice spoke up. 'Hold it there, you pair of bastards!'

Quick as a flash, Joe and me span around, Joe lifting the .38 as he turned. 'Ah, ah, ah - I wouldn't if I were you Cassidy,' the voice warned, 'Not unless you wanna get yer head blown off.' Immediately Joe read the futility of our situation. He was staring down the barrel of Benny Mottola's gun, an enormous .357 Magnum, which was aimed directly between his eyes.

'Drop the piece!' Benny barked, nodding at the snub-nose in Joe's hand. Joe didn't move. 'Drop it now or die. You too, Reilly. Lose the bat. Enzo! Cover Seanie boy will ya, and if he moves, kill 'im.'

Unbeknownst to either Joe or I, Enzo had climbed to his feet and was now pointing his pistol at me. I knew now that it was Virgil who had taken the bullet, not Enzo, and I looked at the floor to see my friend still laying there, blood pumping from a hole in his thigh. Virgil's eyes were open though, and he was looking at me. He nodded slightly, to let me know he was okay, at least for the short term, but I knew that if he didn't soon get help, he'd be in trouble.

'It's your move, Joe, but I'd say things ain't lookin' too good for you boys - wouldn't you?' Benny gave a throaty laugh, his teeth stained pink and his bulbous nose still bloody.

Joe took another couple of beats, then released his grip on the .38, letting it drop to the floor, all the time his eyes not leaving Mottola's.

I threw the bat down next to the .38. It was over.

*   *   *

Benny had a victorious smile on his face. 'Now then,' he said, 'Who should I kill first - the one who killed my brother, or the one who killed my best mate?' His big Magnum was now pressed against Joe's forehead whilst Enzo's smaller, but equally lethal pistol was pushed hard into my ear. Then Benny said, almost wistfully, 'Y'know, for a moment there, I thought you'd ruined my chances of gettin' my hands on this place,' he gestured at the room with his free hand, 'I really thought you'd got me, but then, even I can be wrong once in a while. Now, of course, standing here, it suddenly occurs to me that this way is better than I'd planned. Much cleaner, no loose ends, all my troubles swept away in one fateful afternoon. No more Cassidy and Reilly to stand in my way - and I guarantee with you two outta the way, your lady friend Louretta Wild ain't gonna need a lotta persuadin' to sell those shares of Nash's back to me. Betcha I get 'em at a real knock down price an' all. Hell, I might even grab a piece of her daughter's movie star ass while I'm about it - whaddaya say, Reilly? Bet she wouldn't mind for a friend of her old man's eh?'

'Yeah, sure thing, needle dick, whatever you say.' I snarled, 'Now why don't you get on with it and stop wasting our time?'

'Why not, indeed.' Mottola continued, 'And guess what? You've just made my mind up for me and it's you who's gonna get it first.'

'Yeah? Well I guess I'll see you in hell then you fat piece of shit,' I growled in one last attempt at bravery.

'I guess you might at that' Benny chuckled, 'Move away,

Enzo, unless you wanna get covered in blood and brains.'

Not liking the sound of that, Enzo quickly took his gun out of my ear and stepped aside as Benny moved the Magnum from Joe's head and aimed it at me.

Suddenly, there was a loud bang as the fire escape door burst open and Enzo, startled by the sound, swung around to see what was happening. Matt had been listening at the door and upon hearing how badly things were going had decided to take drastic action. He had kicked open the door and flung himself into the room.

*   *   *

Carl Napier had been unconscious for several minutes but now he was coming around. His eyes were gluey and sticky, his head ached and his face was wet with blood. He'd lost four teeth, his nose was smashed in, and he was completely deaf in one ear as a result of Joe's gun going off less than an inch from it. He was dazed and disorientated, but he climbed to his feet anyway. Seeing several other people standing close by, Carl moved gingerly toward them. His vision was blurred and he couldn't make out who the people were, but surely they could help him. He didn't hear the sound of the fire escape door bang open, nor the gunfire that immediately followed, but he felt an explosion of devastating pain in his chest as a bullet hit him and the sensation of flying backwards through the air. Then, before everything went black, he saw a stream of bright red blood being jettisoned in his wake.

*   *   *

Enzo fired twice as Matt charged across the room towards him, but his aim was poor and both shots missed. Matt took out Enzo with remarkable ease with two lightning jabs to the throat and a crippling kick to the groin, before spinning to face Benny.

Mottola also fired two shots, one of which struck Carl squarely in the chest as he staggered across Benny's line of sight, the other blasting a large round hole in the bedroom door.

Mottola, was about to fire again, but the distraction was all Joe needed to make his move. He grabbed hold of Mottola's gun hand and pushed the weapon away from Matt, simultaneously landing a thunderous punch to Benny's kidney's. But Benny was tough and as strong as an ox and he barely flinched. Furthermore, he kept a tight hold on the .357.

Joe hammered into Benny's kidney's again, but incredibly Mottola seemed immune, he even tried to hit back, swinging his chubby fist wildly and catching Joe a glancing blow on the chin. Again Joe struck home and at last Benny buckled under the pain, but he was still putting up a fight, all the time trying to wrestle the gun free. The two men rolled and turned, each trying to gain control of the huge black pistol, but then, suddenly, Benny stopped struggling, allowing Joe to easily free the gun. Now it was in his grasp, Joe aimed it point blank and prepared to fire the bullet that would blow Mottola's brains out.

But I had seen why Benny had ceased the struggle, and, more importantly, where his attention was now focussed. 'Joe, no!' I yelled. 'Not now. For chrissake not now!'

For a second, Joe didn't understand, then he noticed the horrified expression on Benny's face and the direction in which he was looking. Slowly Joe turned, and a chill ran down his spine as he saw what the rest of us had already seen.

Jez Mottola, Benny's son, was standing in the bedroom doorway. In his arms he held Vito, his younger brother by fifteen minutes. Half of Vito's face was missing - a testament to the enormous impact of a .357 Magnum, the gun which Benny had fired into the bedroom door just moments before.

Twenty-nine

I'd never heard such a gut-wrenching sound as the one Benny emitted upon seeing what he had done to his youngest son. It was the sound of utter despair.

For a moment I thought Benny was going to collapse, but somehow he managed to stagger over to where Jez stood and gently took Vito from him. Only then did he sink to the ground, carefully cradling his son in his big powerful arms, sobbing loudly as he studied the boy's ruined face. Jez stood by his father's shoulder, tall and proud, his face set in an expression as hard as stone, his eyes cold, dry and menacing, his unreadable emotions locked up tighter than a drum.

We no longer belonged there. Vito's death had ended it and Benny needed to be left alone with his grief and the knowledge of what he'd done. It was time for us to go, however, that all depended on Sammy, Guido and Enzo who were now all standing and eyeing us murderously.

Virgil groaned, and without thinking about the consequences, I quickly rushed over to him. But the moment I moved, all three of Benny's goons lifted their guns and my body stiffened as I realised my error.

'Leave 'im!' I heard Mottola growl. 'Leave 'im alone. Don't ya think there's been enough killin' today?' His voice was heavy and full of despair, but the authority in it was unmistakable and the three goons stood down.

I turned to Virgil, whose eyes were open, the pain he was in clear to see, but there was a laconic smile on his face. 'Guess I should leave the stunts to you huh?' He winced.

'Guess so,' I replied. 'You up to movin'?'

'Hey, if it means I get outta here in one piece, I reckon I could goddamn fly!'

'Let's not get too ambitious eh?' I smiled, then gestured for Joe and Matt to come over.

Very slowly, we lifted Virgil up. I draped one of his arms around my shoulders and Matt did the same, then we both held him firmly around the waist to support his weight. Joe stood guard, still holding the Magnum he'd wrestled from Benny, just in case.

On the way to the elevator, we passed Carl Napier's body. The power of the Magnum had thrown Carl backwards so that he was now sitting in the hole in the glass coffee table, his backside was touching the wooden floor below whilst his legs and arms rested awkwardly on the cracked glass table top in a very ungainly position. In the centre of his chest was a large, wet cavern the size of a saucer with thick black blood bubbling and oozing from it. A massive shard of razor sharp glass had sliced through his back like butter and now stuck grotesquely out of his belly.

*   *   *

Carefully, we crossed the room and although Virgil was in agony, he never uttered a sound. The room was totally quiet now, except for our footsteps on the wood, every eye on us apart from Benny's, who was still staring at the bloody mess that used to be his boy. He knew what was going on though, and just before we got into the elevator, he said in a soft, almost gentle voice, 'It's not over Cassidy. You know that don't you? You too Reilly. Keep looking over your shoulder 'cos I'll be coming for you.'

We both looked directly at Benny. 'Yeah,' Joe replied.

I just nodded. Would it ever be over?

*   *   *

We took Virgil straight from the parking lot under the hotel to an ex-surgeon friend of Louretta's who would keep quiet and not ask questions. He fixed Virgil up as well as any hospital could and the prognosis for a satisfactory recovery was thankfully good. He'd be surfing again in no time.

*   *   *

The Vincenzi and Carboni clean-up team had gone in to overdrive, keeping all word of the bloodbath at the Villa Continental out of the news. Carl Napier's body had been dumped in the desert for the coyotes and buzzards to feed upon, it would never be found by anyone. Louretta put out a story to the media saying that her hotel manager had been suffering from exhaustion and would be taking an extended leave of absence. Of course, he would never return.

Another story that appeared in the papers was of how Vito Vincenzi, son of Miami mob boss Benito Vincenzi, had drowned in a swimming pool whilst on vacation with his family in Las Vegas.

*   *   *

Benny was devastated by the loss of his son, the tragedy driving him ever closer to the madness he'd been fighting against for most of his life. However, he had enough clarity of thought left to know that Vito's doting grandparents would be devastated too and that they would not forgive what he had done. Even though it was an accident. That, coupled with Benny's failure to net them the Villa Continental would spell the end for him. The only possible way out was to tell Tito Vincenzi and Carmine Carboni that Joe was responsible for Vito's death and not him.

To this end, he made Sammy, Guido and Enzo swear to tell the same story. Then he ordered Sammy and Guido to follow Joe

574

back to London where they were to kill him. Benny would then report back to the two grandfathers and Enzo, should he be called upon for his account had been ordered by Benny to back up his version of events.

That might just be enough to help Benny survive their wrath.

But things didn't go quite to plan. The grandparents didn't trust Benny's story at all and immediately sensed the insanity engulfing Mottola when they spoke to him on the phone. They summoned Enzo straight back to New York for his account of things without the influence of Benny beside him. However, they decided Sammy and Guido should continue with their orders to kill Joe, just in case Benny was telling the truth. Sammy and Guido were Benny's men and therefore expendable, if they didn't make it back from London then it was no big deal, they wouldn't be missed.

Mottola, meanwhile, was ordered to stay in Vegas to clear up any loose ends and to get rid of any other witnesses, and was told, in no uncertain terms, not to fuck it up again.

After that they would get rid of Benny Mottola permanently. He was a liability and certainly not to be trusted with Jez's upbringing. He needed to have an accident soon, before he brought the whole family down.

Thirty

Frank Blades had been parked discreetly across the road from The Castle, watching the home of his most hated enemy and waiting for his moment to strike, when he had observed Michael storming out of the house after his argument with Ray. Blades had then followed Michael as he sped away in his MGB, and had tailed him all the way back to the apartment in Chelsea.

Later, after conceiving his plan, Frank had grabbed the boy as he came out of his flat. No one saw, and Michael's strength was no match for Frank's, it was easy. A lamb to the slaughter.

*   *   *

Blades had been laying low around Europe for a couple of years, the last six months in Marseilles where he had friends he could trust. But he was impatient, eager to heal the rift between him and Benny, and desperate to get even with Joe, the man who had brought about his downfall. Frank believed that he'd spent enough time skulking in the shadows and hoped that the time was now right to be accepted back into the fold, but for that he'd need a peace offering, a little sweetener to make his return that bit easier. There was only one gift substantial enough to guarantee his own safety and that, was Joe Cassidy's head on a plate.

The idea had been to grab Michael, then demand four million for his safe return. After Joe paid up, Blades would kill them both and take the ransom money to Miami as a gift for the Carboni's and the Vincenzi's in lieu of the drugs he had lost them on Rotherhithe docks. That, together with the news of Joe's death would surely be enough to secure his place at Benny's side once more.

However, no sooner had Frank taken Michael, when Joe disappeared. Of course Blades knew now why that was, as the boy had told him; he had gone to Vegas to kill that worm Carl Napier, which in itself was of no consequence to Frank as he never did much care for Carl. However, with Joe away it meant that Frank's schedule would have to be stretched, he would have to hold the boy much longer than he'd originally intended and that could be dangerous. But he had no choice, he was committed now and if he wished to continue with his plans then he'd just have to wait for Joe to return.

* * *

Frank had chained Michael up naked on a dirty mattress in a derelict garage in Brixton where he had beaten him and raped him, then left him alone to cry in the dark for over seventy-two hours.

When Blades went to check up on him on the third day, the boy had messed himself and the sight of it disgusted him. The smell was so unbearable that by the time Frank visited again, on the fifth day, he could bear it no longer. Wearing a pair of thick rubber gloves and using an old tin bucket full of cold water, Frank sluiced Michael down. It was filthy, nauseating work and he threw up more than once before he finished, although every time he did so, he slapped Michael hard for making him endure such a revolting chore.

On the sixth day, Frank returned to the garage, and before unlocking it, heard Michael yelling for help, for which he gave him yet another beating. To prevent him yelling further, Blades gagged him then shot him full of heroin, inducing a state of drug addled delirium from which he could not escape.

After that, the boy had done nothing but shiver and whimper, not even the heroin could keep him totally quiet, and Frank suspected that Michael perhaps had pneumonia, but he only needed him to last until Joe came back. Until pay day. Then all Frank's problems would be over.

Since snatching Michael, Blades had spent most of his time watching Joe's house, waiting for him to return. He had been gone eleven days now, and as the days dragged on, he was becoming more and more anxious. Michael seemed to be growing sicker by the hour, he looked malnourished and emaciated and there was some doubt in Blades' mind as to whether the boy would live long enough to be useful.

It was turning into a seriously bad situation and Frank was now desperate for it to be over. So impatient had he become that, on the evening of the ninth day, he had pushed a note through Joe's letterbox which he hoped Rose or Ruby might find. It stated that he had Michael and if Joe didn't come up with four million pounds ransom money within forty-eight hours, he'd start sending bits of the boy back through the post.

If that didn't make them call Cassidy home, nothing would.

But that was thirty-eight hours ago and there was still no sign that the letter had been received. Frank was starting to despair, his plan to redeem himself in the eyes of Benny was going very wrong indeed.

However, on the morning of day twelve, Frank was slouched in the driver's seat of his stolen, puke green Morris Marina, when he spied Manno O'Keefe pulling the Bentley up outside The Castle. He had a passenger with him, and as Frank blinked his tired, almost unbelieving eyes, he saw with enormous relief, Joe Cassidy climbing out of the car.

* * *

Frank Blades was not the only one with vengeance in mind.

578

After serving nearly two years, Big Jack Anderson had just been released from prison and was looking to get even with the man who put him in there.

As he lay in the enormous bed of the Mayfair penthouse his associates had laid on for him as a coming out present, he received a nice cup of tea and a blow job from the blonde who'd been instructed to make him comfortable. Afterwards he showered, put on a brand new suit and joined his friend Danny Davenport, for a full English breakfast; eggs, bacon, sausages, fried bread and tomatoes - the whole works.

Whilst they ate, Jack and Danny talked. They talked about what they had been planning for many long months in prison; the death of Joe Cassidy.

Only another twenty-four more hours to wait then, finally, London would be theirs for the taking.

*   *   *

Sammy and Guido travelled economy on fake passports, both had two days growth of beard and both wore dark glasses, baseball caps and sweat suits. They looked more like a couple of travelling gays than mafia hit men with a very pressing contract to fulfil.

However, they couldn't do anything until they'd met the guy with the guns; a small time operator by the name of Harry the Louse who, so Benny said, had a grudge against Cassidy from years back - something to do with his snooker hall getting torched apparently. But it made no odds, Harry would only live long enough to hand over the two 9mm semi-automatics, as per the order. That was the brief; no loose ends, and Harry was definitely that - whether he had a beef with Joe or not.

After they'd disposed of Harry, Sammy and Guido intended to go to their hotel to get a good night's sleep - maybe just a couple of beers first to help with the jet lag, then tomorrow, they'd do the job. They would be back in Miami within forty-eight hours. Easy.

*   *   *

Michael lay shivering on the soiled, stinking mattress in the derelict garage, his hollow eyes were watery and lined with red, his skin was blue and stained with purple bruises and his bare arms bore the needle marks of a junkie. But Michael was no drug addict, he was a captive, a mere pawn in a bitter feud between his uncle and the vile, perverted creature who referred to himself only as 'Frankie.'

Michael's moments of lucidity were few and far between, but when his head did clear, when he was capable of coherent thought, his mind and body were consumed by hatred and vengeance.

Thirty-one

Ruby was sick with worry. Michael had stormed out eleven days ago without a word about where he was headed and she'd not heard from him since. She had repeatedly called the flat in Chelsea and the apartment in Oxford, but she was getting no reply at either. Ruby hoped that he was alright, but, for the time being, that was all she could do.

At the moment she had to be with Ray. He was the one who needed her most. He was in a coma with a machine helping him to breath and his future uncertain.

The doctors suspected that a blackout, possibly brought on by the stress of Michael leaving, had caused him to fall down the stairs. Fortunately - and remarkably - he'd not broken any bones, but he had taken a severe crack to the head and, apart from those few seconds in which he'd recognised Sarah, he had not regained consciousness since.

How long he would remain in the coma the doctors couldn't speculate, but they did say that he seemed to be 'a very tough customer,' and Ruby, knowing that to be true, prayed that would see him through.

For nine days she had kept vigil at his bedside, going home only twice in all that time, just for a shower and a change of clothes, the rest of the time she'd stayed with him, hoping for some sign, but, as yet, it hadn't come. Ruby's first instinct had been to phone Joe, to call him home, but she'd resisted the temptation. Joe had other things to do, things that demanded every ounce of his concentration, and Ruby knew that any distraction from the task he'd undertaken could prove fatal.

Had it not been for Rose, she may well have crumbled. Ruby, who had been through so much and survived everything life had thrown at her, was finally exhausted. With Michael's disappearance and Ray's collapse, the strain had almost killed her. But Rose had been a rock. Not only did Rose travel to the hospital twice a day, she also took care of the house, of Brett and, more importantly, of Sarah.

Sarah, although fully rational now and getting more confident every day, was still uneasy about leaving the safety of the house. Soon enough she would be completely well, and free to restart her life, but, until then, she would confine herself to the house and garden. 'When Joe comes home' she told herself, 'he'll give me the confidence I need.'

Sarah now knew most of the story, of the things that had happened over the last twenty-five years, Rose had told her, although being careful to leave out anything too distressing. The most important thing however, was that Sarah now knew about Michael and it had become her dearest wish to see him. It was a daunting prospect though, speaking to her son for the first time, especially as Rose had warned her to expect some resistance. She had not, however, told her the depth of Michael's resentment towards her as Sarah was not equipped to cope with such information just yet.

Rose had told Sarah that Michael had gone away for a while. Indeed, Sarah had heard the argument he'd had with Ray for herself, but she had not let on. Rose thought Michael would be back soon, but Sarah was not so convinced, as it hadn't sounded like that to her. If he did not return, she herself would go and find him. Her son needed to be brought home, he needed to be reunited with her and his father, as did she.

*　　*　　*

Brett was missing his dad. Joe had been away for ten days and had not telephoned since first arriving at the Bluestone. This was not like him, but his son was thirteen now and old enough to understand, if not to fully appreciate the gravity of what was going on. Joe had taken him aside before he left, and whilst not dwelling on specifics, told him that the mission he was embarking on would be dangerous, but if all turned out as planned, then he'd be back soon enough. Brett didn't allow himself to doubt that he wouldn't, not for many days at least, but with all that had happened with Ray, he kept getting a niggling little worry. In Brett's eyes, both Ray and Joe were invincible, it was inconceivable that anything could ever harm them, but then Ray had fallen down the stairs and suddenly he had become mortal. And in so doing, Joe had too.

With each day that passed, Brett began to worry just that little bit more, although he never let it show. He had to be strong for Rose, stronger still for his Aunt Sarah. With Ray incapacitated, he was the man of the house and he'd be damned if he was going to go to pieces. Nevertheless, when the telephone rang on the morning of the tenth day, his cool facade vanished as he ran to answer it, desperate for it to be his father.

It was Ruby. Ray had opened his one good eye at around 4am, he'd turned his head and looked around the room, following the wall until at last his sleepy gaze settled directly on his tearful wife. Ray gave her a crooked smile, then, if possible with one eye, he winked at her. He was going to be alright, his brain was functioning normally and Ruby was overjoyed to have him back. Brett, speaking on the telephone in the hallway, near the front door, replaced the receiver then breathed a huge sigh of relief. He was just about to go to the kitchen to relay the good news to Rose and Sarah, when he heard the sound of the letterbox and turned in time to see a small, folded piece of paper float down onto the mat in front of the door. Brett picked it up, unfolded it and was just about to read the untidy, handwritten scrawl, when the phone rang again.

This time the call just had to be from Joe. With all thoughts of the note vanishing from his mind, Brett threw it face down onto the small table beside the front door, upon which the household kept their car keys, and snatched up the phone once more.

'Hello, boy!' A familiar voice greeted him, 'did ya think I was gone for good?'

'Watcha, Pop! Nah, I knew you couldn't stay away - how'd everything go - okay?'

'Yeah, fine son, just fine.' Nothing could have been further from the truth, but Brett was not the ideal person to tell. 'How is everyone - alright?' Joe swiftly changed the subject.

'Yeah, fine,' Brett said. He'd been told by both Ruby and Rose not to say anything about Ray, they said that Joe would find out when he got home and if he knew any sooner he'd only worry. 'Let him get home safely first,' they had said. Brett agreed. There was one piece of good news however, that Brett was desperate to tell, but again he had been banned from saying anything. Sarah wanted to surprise Joe with her recovery when he got back, much to her nephew's chagrin.

'When ya comin' home, Pop?' Brett too was adept at changing the subject.

'I'm on my way - I'm calling from LAX now as a matter of fact. Trouble is I've gotta change at Houston and then again at La Guardia - it's a pain but it's the best I could do. At least I'm movin.' Nothin' worse than sittin' around at airports - I did enough of that on the way out!'

'Whattaya mean?'

'Ask Ray. Somethin' to do with the phones being out - couldn't get hold of Sean to tell 'im to pick me up - God knows why not, but I waited ages at the bloody airport before I realised no one was comin' to fetch me. Actually, I'll 'ave a quick word with Ray before I go - just to make sure he's gonna be at Heathrow when I get there.'

'Er.. no. No, you can't-—' For a second Brett was thrown.

'What? What's the matter?' Joe picked up on it instantly, 'Is something wrong?'

'No, course not,' the recovery was swift, 'everything's fine. Ray's out that's all - gone up West with Ruby - but if you tell me when you're gettin' in I'll make sure he picks you up.' Brett hated the lie, but surely it was for the best, and it seemed to placate his father.

'Christ, I bet the old pirate's lovin' that - being hauled round by the wallet while Ruby tries every pair of bloody shoes on in Oxford Street! Alright boy, get a pen and I'll give you the details before the money runs out on this pay phone.'

Brett did as instructed, then exchanged a few more brief words before the money did indeed run out.

'Tell Rose I love her and give yer Aunt Sarah a kiss for me - see ya in about thirty-six hours, son. See ya!' That was all he had time for before the line went dead.

'Yeah, see ya Pop,' Brett replied to the dialling tone. He replaced the receiver, then strode off toward the kitchen to tell Rose and Sarah that Joe was on his way back. He also had to tell them the good news that Ruby had phoned with, about Ray's recovery.

The unread note from Frank Blades still sat face down, forgotten, on the table by the front door.

* * *

Joe first noticed them at a news stand at LAX as they pretended to leaf through magazines, clumsily trying to conceal themselves behind a book display, thinking that baseball caps and sunglasses would be enough to disguise them. They were not.

Initially, Joe thought that they were just making sure he caught his plane, but then, once he arrived in Houston, he spied them again, eating a burger at one of the fast food outlets, and he realised that their mission was more than that of simple surveillance.

At La Guardia he played it safe, concealing himself in a busy section of the departure lounge where he could watch the concourse from behind his New York Times. After an hour of watching anonymous faces strolling by, he saw them once more. Sweatsuits, caps and sunglasses. In Vegas they had worn Italian silk suits and stony expressions, looking every bit the mafia enforcers that they were. Not now. Now they were incognito, travelling light, just a couple of regular guys - anything but suspicious. But it was them, Sammy and Guido, no mistake.

Joe was fairly sure that had they wished to kill him on American soil, then they would have done so in LA and not chased him half way around the country. No, if they were going to attempt a hit, and Joe was convinced they were, then it would almost certainly take place in London. Probably within twenty-four hours of touch-down.

He made it safely to the Pan Am terminal, proving his theory, thus far, to be accurate. Thirty minutes later he was drinking an ice laden Jack Daniels in first class, the plane just taxiing to the runway. Joe hadn't seen either Sammy or Guido board, but he knew they had as he could almost feel their hot breath on the back of his neck. They were back there in economy somewhere, believing that he was unaware of their presence. But Joe was acutely aware, and he had the five hour flight, plus perhaps a very short time upon landing to do something about them. He glanced at his watch, hoping Ray would be on time - just for once in his life, because every minute after touch down would be vital.

As he pondered this, he drained the last remnants of his Jack Daniels then closed his eyes for a nap. If he was going to stay sharp then he needed to be fresh, and who knew when next he'd have the opportunity to sleep.

Thirty-two

As Joe disembarked, he glanced through an inch wide gap in the curtain that was supposed to prevent the first class passengers laying their precious eyes on the cramped hordes of economy. It took him just a few seconds to locate Sammy and Guido, stuck like a pair of sardines in the centre aisle. A woman with a screaming baby sat on one side of them and an elderly man with a hacking cough the other. The two hit men did not look at all happy and Joe allowed himself a little smile; he'd had almost four hours of uninterrupted sleep and apart from needing a shower, he felt quite refreshed.

Joe had collected his one small suitcase from the luggage carousel before the economy passengers had even arrived in baggage collection, so knew he had a good head start on his pursuers as he marched into Heathrow's main terminal. Quickly he scanned the dozens of faces for a wild haired man with an eye patch, but soon realised that Ray wasn't there and swore under his breath with frustration.

Manno, who at five foot six, had previously been hidden by a couple of tall students, finally swept them aside and waved to Joe. The two students, obviously disgruntled by the smaller man's insolence, thought briefly about making more of it, but upon studying him and the man he was signalling to, felt it best to keep quiet. These were definitely not men to pick a fight with.

'I thought Ray was coming,' were Joe's first words to Manno, his annoyance quite clear.

'He would've Joe, but—'

'I needed to see 'im. There's somethin' goin' down and I wanted 'im 'ere.'

'He couldn't come—' Manno tried again, but Joe interrupted once more.

'Whassamatter, couldn't he get outta bed?'

'Somethin' like that Joe, yeah.' Manno paused for a moment, then said, 'Ray's in 'ospital. He's had a bit of an accident.'

*　*　*

The news came as a terrible blow. Ray was his friend; a father; a man to whom Joe owed so much, but before he could think about him, he had to eliminate the threat that was following close behind.

Joe glanced quickly about him and immediately noticed a slightly built Asian man who was holding a sign saying 'mini cab.' The man looked tired, hungry and slightly impoverished, as if the next fare might just be enough to save his life. He would do nicely.

Joe strode over to him, noticing the look of anxiety on the cabbie's face as he saw him approaching - it was obvious that he'd been recognised - hardly surprising as his picture appeared in the newspapers on an annoyingly regular basis. However, Joe grabbed the little Pakistani by the elbow and led him a short distance away from the throng.

'Do you know who I am?' He demanded.

'Y... yes sir. Your the Godfather of Gang— I mean, that is, y... your Joe C.. Cass—'

'Okay, okay. So you know who I am, that's good.' Joe cut straight to the chase, there was no time for pussyfooting around, 'I need you to do me a favour - there's a grand in it for ya if you do it right and keep yer mouth shut. Nothin' dishonest - just a little bit of surveillance - interested?'

The Pakistani nodded eagerly. A thousand pounds before breakfast, now that's what he called a good day's work. 'W... what do you want me to do sir?'

'Not 'sir', just Joe, okay? What's your name?'

'Johnny, sir— I mean, Joe.'

Okay, Johnny, this is what I want you to do. In a minute, two men are gonna come walkin' through them doors,' Joe pointed to the doors he'd just come through, 'They're both dressed the same - sweatsuits, shades and baseball caps - you'll spot 'em no problem. What I want you to do is follow 'em, find out where they go and who they talk to, then phone me tomorrow and let me know - Manno there'll give you my number.' Joe took a wad of notes from his wallet and handed them to Johnny, 'Do a good job and there's another grand for you tomorrow, alright?'

'Yes, sir!' Johnny couldn't believe his good fortune. Two grand was more money than he'd ever had in his hands at one time and it could make a dramatic difference to him and his young family. There was no way he was going to blow the chance of getting it. 'You can count on me!' He declared confidently.

'Good man,' Joe said, then nodded to Manno, who handed Johnny a business card, before following Joe in the direction of the short stay car park.

'Where to?' Manno asked as he got into the Bentley beside Joe, 'Hospital?'

'Yeah,' Joe replied, 'Hospital.'

*   *   *

He stayed for three and a half hours but Ray didn't stir once. According to Ruby, who was still keeping her bedside vigil, he'd been awake most of the night and had finally fallen asleep just before Joe arrived. Neither he nor Ruby wanted to wake him. 'Let him sleep,' Joe said. He was shocked by how much Ray had changed in the short time they'd been apart and it unsettled him. Ray's hair for example, although still wild and unkempt, had gone from a vibrant red highlighted by streaks of grey to almost totally silver. His huge muscular frame too, that seemed to have shrunk and his cheeks looked hollow and empty. Likewise, the collar on Ray's pyjamas, even fastened at the top, gaped wide around his thin neck, making his body look far too small for his clothes. It was as if he had suddenly become old.

Joe, needing a shower, a shave and a set of fresh clothes, reluctantly left the hospital, promising to return later, and with Manno driving, he headed for home.

When they arrived back at The Castle, Joe jumped out of the car, eager to see his wife and son. But such was his enthusiasm to get in the house, he did not notice the puke green Morris Marina that sat across the street, nor the evil smile on the face of the man behind the wheel.

*   *   *

Joe walked through the door and was greeted by Rose and Brett, who both rushed up and flung their arms around him. Brett released after a few seconds, but Rose was reluctant to let go. Whilst Joe had been away, she had carried a heavy burden, not least the thought of possibly not seeing her husband again. She knew what he'd gone to do in Las Vegas and understood the dangers, but there were others who needed her to be strong, so she had hidden her distress and quelled her emotions. But now her man was back, he was safe, uninjured and back in her arms where he belonged and finally she allowed the mask to slip and the tears to flow.

'Hey, c'mon,' Joe whispered, 'It's over, I'm home, everything's gonna be okay now - you'll see. Everything's gonna be fine. I promise.'

Rose sniffed, then smiled, then kissed him. 'I know,' she said softly. After another big hug Rose looked up at Joe and smiled again, this time mischievously. 'Oh, I've just remembered, we've got a surprise for you - haven't we Brett?'

'You could say that,' her stepson replied with a huge grin on his face. He then stepped aside and Rose did the same, allowing Joe an uninterrupted view of the hallway. 'Close yer eyes, Pop,' Brett instructed.

'What-—?' his father began.

'Do it!' Rose ordered, trying to suppress a giggle.

'What's going on-?'

'Do it!' She demanded again, and this time he reluctantly complied.

'Keep 'em shut,' Brett said, 'until I say.'

'Okay, okay,' Joe was smiling now, 'But if it's chocolates, I'm eating 'em all myself.'

'It's not chocolates - just keep those eyes closed,' Rose chuckled.

'Keep 'em closed, keep 'em closed... okay, open 'em!' Brett announced.

*　*　*

She was standing at the other end of the hallway with her hair down. It was loose and black and shiny with a gentle curl. Her face, although pale, had been made up beautifully with just some lipstick and mascara. She was slim and stunning in a simple white tee shirt and faded Levis, and when she smiled her dark eyes sparkled.

It was her. It was Sarah.

She moved a step closer towards him, then spoke, and the sound of her voice was almost magical, a sound which he thought he'd never hear again. 'Hello, Joseph,' she said.

Joe suddenly felt weak at the knees and had to blink several times to make sure that his eyes weren't playing tricks. 'Sarah?' He gasped, almost in disbelief, 'Can it be true?' His vision was starting to sting from the well of tears that had risen up unexpectedly. 'Have you come back to me?'

Sarah nodded, causing a tear spill down her own cheek, and her mouth buckled as she tried to hold back a tidal wave of emotion, 'Yes, Joseph. I've come back and I'm well again,' she was crying now, '–Joseph, I've come back.'

Joe ran to his twin sister and grabbed her, holding her tight in an embrace that said more than any words could. His eyes were wet and his shoulders were shaking, but he didn't care, because today, Sarah had returned to him.

Thirty-three

The phone call came just after breakfast. Joe and Sarah were laughing, sitting at the table, him with his hand over hers, as if reluctant to break contact, just in case she left him again. He was telling her of all the things they would do together now she was able, of all the places they would go. Rose and Brett were listening, smiling, the warmth of the reunion effecting them too. Joe was enjoying his family, this was how life should be, this was how he wanted it to be.

But then Manno burst into the room and the moment was spoiled. 'Joe, there's a call—' he blurted.

'No. Not today. No interruptions.' Joe held up his hand, adamantly.

'But it's important, very important - you need to take it.'

Joe turned in his chair to face Manno, about to blast him out, but then he caught the look in Manno's eyes and knew instantly that this was no frivolous request.

'Who is it?' He barked.

'Company business.' Manno jerked his head toward the hall, his mouth tight and his teeth gritted together as if to emphasise the importance. Then, suddenly aware that the others were looking at him too, he relaxed his features, and said in a much calmer voice 'Sorry. It won't take long, but it's someone who can't wait.' Manno stared directly into Joe's eyes, willing him to see the urgency of what he was trying to convey.

'Oh, alright. But they'd better pray it's worth disturbing me.' Joe got up from the table, 'I'll be back in a minute,' he said to his family, and then to Manno, 'I'll take it in my office.'

* * *

'Who is it?' Joe demanded as soon as the kitchen door was closed.

'Wouldn't tell me,' Manno replied, 'but he said you'd know.' Manno hesitated for a moment, then said, 'Listen, Joe - this nutter's got Michael.'

'He's what--?'

'He's got Michael, boss. Says that if yer don't want 'im to get 'urt then you'd better bloody well listen to what he's gotta say. I thought it best not to say too much in front of the ladies, but the bloke sounds...' Manno's voice tailed off, as if reluctant to finish the sentence.

'What?' Joe asked, 'Serious? Tough?'

'Yeah, that and... well—'

'What? Tell me Manno, what does he sound like?'

'It's daft, I know boss, but the bloke sounds sort of...' He paused for a moment and then said, 'Evil. Like a bloody vampire or somethin'.'

'Well,' said Joe with determination, 'Vampire or not, if the bastard's got Michael then he's gonna end up in a fuckin' coffin - and that's a promise.'

* * *

'Who is this?' Joe demanded, now in his office with Manno beside him, listening in.

'Ah, now, that would be telling,' the voice was a hiss, snake-like with the slight rattle of a heavy smoker. 'Why don't you guess... surely it's not been that long?'

595

Joe knew instantly and a cold shiver ran down his spine. The voice was different slightly; still menacing, still strangely effeminate, but now with more of a psychotic edge to it.

'Blades!'

'Ah, how sweet, you remember. For a moment I thought you might have forgotten me - especially when you didn't answer my love letter.'

'Letter?' Joe didn't know what Frank was talking about. 'Forget bloody letters - where's Michael?'

'Ah, the boy. So ugly, so grotesque yet, oh, so succulent. I do believe he'd never had a real man until he met me. I do hope I haven't spoilt him - he squealed so loudly - oh, and the blood! I never thought it would stop.'

Joe felt his gorge rise, he felt sick and angry and he gripped the phone so hard that his knuckles turned white, 'If you've harmed him, Blades, if you've damaged one hair on his head—'

'Harmed him? Why would I harm someone whose been so, so... accommodating, shall we say? No, on the contrary, we've become very close - lovers you might say - although he does seem to have picked up a very nasty drug habit - y'know, I think he's pretty well addicted to the stuff—'

'Enough, Frank!' Joe could take no more, 'Whaddaya want? How much do you want for the boy?'

'Ah, the deal. The business man as always. Well now, let me think.' Frank was playing it cool, he gave no hint of the anxiety of the last two weeks, no inkling of the utter desperation he'd felt. In fact now he'd actually got to speak to Joe he was enjoying himself immensely. The thrill of the last few days had acted as foreplay and the realisation of seeing his plans finally come to fruition was highly intoxicating, even arousing. 'What I want, Cassidy—' he continued, '—is you. Your head for the boy's - that'll do for starters.'

'Okay, where?' Joe had no concern for himself, he just had to save Michael and he saw Manno frown at the apparent disregard for his own safety.

'Ooh, so eager - I love that in you, but let's not get ahead of ourselves—,' Blades was in heaven, speaking from a phone box just a couple of streets away, he could feel the swelling in his trousers as his excitement increased. The power he had over Joe now was all consuming and he couldn't resist making the most of it. He unzipped his flies to release himself and began to masturbate as he spoke, '—As well as your head on a plate, I want money. Lots of lovely money - Four million to be precise. I know you can afford it.' Frank's voice was hoarse, trembling with erotic abandon.

'Fine,' Joe didn't even flinch, 'Where?'

There was a little grunt at the other end of the phone as Frank shuddered with climax, the thrill was all too much.

'Blades, hello? Can you hear me?'

There was a long pause.

'Blades - are you there?'

'Yeah, yeah, I'm 'ere,' Blades said, lighting up a cigarette, 'Just... enjoying the moment.'

'Where?' Joe demanded again, 'Where do you wanna meet?'

'Rotherhithe Street, Surrey Docks,' Frank said, trapping the receiver between shoulder and neck as he re-fastened his fly. 'The old grain warehouse - eleven tomorrow morning. Got it?'

'I'll be there,' Joe replied.

'Just make sure you are. No pigs, no back-up. Just you, me, the boy and the money. Change anything, and the boy dies, understand?'

'Understand.'

'Good.'

The line went dead and Joe replaced the receiver.

*　*　*

Joe was back at the hospital by lunchtime. He had been

597

followed all the way by Big Jack Anderson and Danny Davenport, who Joe had clocked just minutes after leaving The Castle. He saw them again as he crossed the car park; white Capri with a black vinyl roof. Things were definitely hotting up.

*   *   *

By the time Joe returned to the ward, Ruby had roused and was massaging the stiff neck she'd awoken with. 'Hello, luv,' she said, 'This bloody chair's gotta be the most uncomfortable thing I've ever sat in - you been 'ere long?'

Joe gave her a kiss on the cheek, 'Oh, 'bout an hour, but I thought I'd let ya sleep, thought it'd do ya good.'

'It would've done if I had a decent chair to kip in - bloody thing. Never mind, 'spect I've re-charged me batteries a bit - thanks luv.'

'How is he?'

'I dunno, he's been asleep since this morning, but his breathing's steady and he looks peaceful enough - I suppose I could wake 'im - if ya like.' Ruby was trying to be helpful, and he did want to talk to Ray, but Joe could hear the reluctance in her voice, which was understandable. 'No, it's okay,' he replied, 'He'll wake when he's good and ready. I'll stay with him for a while though, if you wanna take a break.'

The thought of a hot bath suddenly flashed through Ruby's mind and it was almost irresistible. 'You sure?'

'Yeah, Ruby. Go home for a while. Relax, have something to eat, have a rest - you deserve it.'

'You sure?'

'Yes. I'm sure - now go!'

'Thanks luv,' Ruby picked up her coat, 'I'll be back in two hours.'

'Take as long as you want.'

'Two hours will be fine. If he wakes, tell 'im I'll be back then.'

'Okay. See ya - and don't worry, it'll be alright.'

'Okay.' Ruby kissed Ray on the cheek, then Joe. 'See ya in a bit luv,' she said, then vanished through the doors, leaving Joe and Ray alone.

*   *   *

Joe sat down in the battered hospital chair. Ruby was right, it was uncomfortable. He glanced around the ward which was empty except for an old guy at the other end of the room who looked dead. Maybe he was, Joe thought. Perhaps the hospital had left him there as an incentive for Ray, a sort of 'get better or else...' type of deal. Joe smiled at this ludicrous train of thought and turned his attention back to Ray. 'Hello, you old pirate,' he said. 'What ya tryin' to do to me, gimme a heart attack? I go out of the country for a couple of weeks and you decide to 'ave a blackout. Anything to get out of a bit of work - is that it?'

Ray snorted and appeared to stir slightly, turning his head to face Joe, almost as if he was listening to what his friend had to say, although his eye remained shut. Joe was silent for a moment, waiting to see if Ray would wake, but he didn't, although it did seem as if he'd heard him. After a few minutes Joe spoke again, 'You know, I could have done with you out there, in Vegas—' he paused again as he thought of all that had happened since last seeing his friend. Joe's mind then turned to current events; Sammy and Guido, Frank Blades, Big Jack and those who would suffer should they have their way.

'I could do with your help now too, me old mate,' Joe spoke again. 'Things are bad. There's serious trouble comin' and I'm in the shit pretty deep. Michael too. Coulda done with your advice, your council, your—.' Joe broke off once more as he studied his friend's shrunken frame again, his wasted body lost in the baggy pyjamas, not realising that his own eyes had become wet. '--—Your strength.' Joe bowed his head in sorrow.

Minutes went by, maybe five or more as Joe wrestled with both his grief and his dilemma. When he looked up again Ray had awoken.

The old rogue was there, glaring at him with a fierce intensity. His good eye boring into Joe's and even the empty socket where once his other had been, which was now pink and scarred, seemed to be staring too.

'Tell me!' Ray demanded hoarsely.

'Ray—?'

'Tell me now, son. Tell me what I can do.' His voice was croaky but strong.

How could Joe have ever doubted his strength. He smiled at his old friend, 'I have a plan,' he said.

Thirty-four

Joe got back a little after six. It was still hot, still sunny, a lovely summer evening, but he was too pre-occupied to notice. He called Richie Noakes and asked him to come over. Just as he put the phone down, it rang again, it was Johnny, the little Asian mini-cab driver he'd hired at the airport the day before. He had news. Joe listened and what he heard should have surprised him, but it didn't, it all just seemed to add up.

Johnny had followed Sammy and Guido to the Lucky Break Snooker Club in Walthamstow, not normally located on the general tourist route, especially not after a long haul flight. But Joe knew that his pursuers were no tourists. They had stayed about ten minutes with Harry the Louse - long enough for anybody before their skin started to crawl - and then left out of the side entrance. As they emerged from the alley, they were sniggering and Johnny saw a flash of metal as one of them shoved what looked like a pistol into his jacket.

It was then that they realised that the mini-cab driver who should have been waiting for them had long since departed - a situation which set Johnny off on a rant, half in Urdu, half in English, about how that was exactly why mini-cab drivers had such a bad name. 'It's why the tourists are told to take black cabs and to stay away from us. It's the reason why our business is going down the drain—!'

'What happened then?' Joe asked, getting back to the matter in hand.

'What—?'

'What happened next?'

'Oh, I'm so sorry sir, boring you with all this - it's just that people like that really annoy—'

'What happened next?' Joe asked again, this time with a little more steel.

'Sorry. Well, then they spotted me sir, sitting across the road, pretending to read my newspaper. For a moment I thought I was in trouble - especially when they came running over, but they just wanted a ride. I thought twice about it though sir, I really did. But a fare is a fare.' He was apologetic, as if guilty of a major crime.

Joe smiled at the other end of the phone, 'Where'd you take 'em?

'To a hotel near Tower Bridge - but they didn't leave a tip,' Johnny spat with disgust. 'I'm in a call box across the road from it now. Shall I wait sir?'

'No. But you've done well. Come round 'ere and I'll give you your money.'

Joe put down the phone with Johnny still expressing his thanks. He'd bung him another five hundred as a bonus, the guy looked like he could do with it. What the hell, he was getting soft in his old age.

He clicked on the TV while he waited for Richie and Manno and caught the closing headlines of the news. It appeared that a known villain, by the name of Harry 'the Louse' Armitage, had been shot dead in his Walthamstow snooker hall. The TV pundits were speculating that it was maybe the result of some gangland feud, although, as yet, they had no clue as to who might be responsible. But Joe knew. 'Those yanks don't mess about,' he muttered under his breath. 'Killed 'Arry with one of his own guns. Poor bastard.' He poured himself a scotch, and before taking a sip he lifted his glass skywards in a toast, 'See ya soon, 'Arry old son,' he said, 'See ya soon.'

*   *   *

When Richie arrived, he and Manno were called up to Joe's office. They were powerful men now, respected, admired and reliable. Joe's men; still loyal to their mentor, even though his kingdom now belonged to them.

'Hello, boys,' Joe greeted them with an easy smile.'

'Boss,' they nodded in unison, still using the title that was no longer his.

'Pour yourselves a drink and shut the door. We've got a lot to discuss.'

*   *   *

Richie and Manno left an hour later, Joe having told them his plan. They took it well, as he knew they would. They were good men and he would miss them.

Next up was Brett and what Joe had to tell him, and also, what he had to ask him, were the two hardest things he had ever done. But the boy was strong. Like father, like son.

*   *   *

That night, Joe held Rose in his arms, almost scared to let her go. He loved her so much and the thought of never seeing her again was unbearable. They stayed that way all night and, in the early hours of the morning, they made love, maybe for the last time, but only he knew that and the guilt felt sharper than a knife. Afterwards, Rose drifted back to sleep and Joe slipped out of bed.

The last day of his life had just begun.

Thirty-five

So as to give Virgil some much needed time to recuperate away from the public glare, I rented a bungalow for us in the mountains outside Las Vegas. I'd told Vicky over the phone what had happened in Carl Napier's penthouse and before I knew it she turned up on the doorstep, all concerned for Virgil and telling me she had come to help care for him whilst he recuperated. This left me in little doubt as to who it was she had developed feelings for and although it came as a surprise I was genuinely pleased for both of them.

As for me, I was ready to go home. Not to the Bluestone, but to England. Back to London to see Sarah, the woman I had never stopped loving in all the years I had been away. I could spend time with her and help take care of her and who knows, it might even do some good. It certainly couldn't hurt. I was still wanted by the police but Lord John Tailby had died some years earlier and without his constant pushing and lobbying interest in a thirty year old murder case had diminished. The people who died were all gangland villains and very few people mourned their passing even at the time - it was only Tailby who kept the case in the public glare and in the newspapers. But no one cared any more so if I was to return - albeit under an alias and laying extremely low, now was as good a time as any.

I was still determined to spend as much time with Olivia and Josh as possible but Vicky and me would work it out somehow and Louretta would jump at any excuse to have them so between us all things should turn out just fine.

However, the timing was not great for me to return to London just yet as things were still very hot and emotions running high in America - particularly after what had happened to Benny's son. The Vincenzi and Carboni families were unlikely to let matters rest and Mottola had already said that it wasn't over. Nevertheless Victoria wouldn't listen and insisted on being there in mountains with Virgil and that was that.

So I left Virgil in Vicky's loving care and took Joe back to Los Angeles for his flight home.

On the way, Joe and I got to talking about our lives and how things had turned out. Both of us were sick of looking over our shoulders and of burying people close to us. There were too many who had died as a consequence to Joe killing George Reilly and me killing Vic Cassidy. No matter how justified we were in doing so at the time. Billy Finn, Dog Tooth, Suzie, Jarvis, they had all died because of what we had done.

This had got Joe to thinking and he outlined a plan to me which had been buzzing about in his head for sometime.

A plan that sounded to me like it had some very clear merits.

* * *

After dropping Joe at LAX, I headed back to the Bluestone to pick up some supplies. After a coffee, a shower and a fresh change of clothes, I jumped back in the car and started out on the long drive back to Vegas to help Vicky take care of Virgil.

Little did any of us know that one of Mottola's underlings had followed Vicky to the bungalow and had already reported his findings back to his employer.

* * *

Benny Mottola was fifty-seven years old. He was still a powerful man but much of his muscle had turned to fat and trekking through the mountains, under the baking Nevada sun, was killing him.

There was only one approach road to the secluded bungalow and he couldn't risk using that through fear of being spotted. The only alternative was to park up as close as possible and hike the rest of the way over the mountains. But 'as close as possible' turned out to be five miles of mostly up hill scree and rock which, in this heat, might as well have been twenty. He was wearing street shoes, Italian, hand made and expensive. But totally unsuitable for the terrain he was attempting to cover. Benny slipped and fell numerous times and his finely tailored trousers were snagged and torn, his beautiful shoes scuffed and scratched. He was worn-out and irritable and sweating profusely, with his silk business shirt soaked through. But the madness was still in his eyes and the .357 Magnum he'd brought, in memory of Vito, was still tucked in his belt.

Benny had started his hike just before dawn, but now the midday sun was burning fiercely down on his ripening bald pate and turning his face crimson. He felt nauseous and had a severe migraine that just wouldn't stop throbbing. Sanity would have told him to find shade as quickly as possible, but he was way passed that.

As he staggered onwards he saw a vision of his dead brother and promised to avenge him. He saw his dead son too, but as he reached out desperately to him, blubbing almost uncontrollably, the boy disappeared. Then, he saw the men responsible, the two that he'd hated for all these years, who had so recently robbed him of his Vegas dream. They were laughing at him, pointing and taunting and fuelling his anger. He pulled out the Magnum and shot at them repeatedly but the bullets simply passed through.

Then, one at a time, his tormentors disappeared and Benny realised that they, too, were just hallucinations.

He laughed at himself maniacally. It didn't matter, they would both soon be dead anyway.

One of them probably was already, in London, and the other, Benny, himself, would be killing very soon. As soon as he got to the damn bungalow.

*   *   *

At last, as Benny came over a particularly steep rise, he saw it in the basin below. Maybe three hundred yards distant. A big sprawling bungalow, built in a luxurious adobe style, surrounded by mountains on three sides and facing a solitary dirt road that cut a swathe through the pass in front.

As he surveyed the scene, Benny dropped to his belly so as not to be spotted, shading his eyes from the vicious glare of the sun. On the drive was parked a red El Camino. In the back he could see a large pool deck, circled by a high mesh fence. And outside of that, the terrain was open with no brush or rock to offer any cover. On the deck, lounging by the pool, he could see a woman, the movie star Victoria Wild, he thought, although at this distance he couldn't be certain. On another bed, Benny could just make out the blonde head of a man who, he was pretty sure, was her husband. His target. The man who had murdered Benny's little brother, Jez, over twenty-five years ago. But the angle wasn't great and the back of his head was all he could properly see. And, even then, it was with blurred and patchy vision which was proving difficult to rely on.

Although his head was swimming, Benny knew an approach in daylight would be spotted before he'd covered fifty yards. He'd not anticipated such open terrain or the complete lack of cover, and even though he was sorely tempted to risk it with the smell of vengeance so ripe in his nostrils, he knew it was no good.

To be sure of success, he'd have to wait until nightfall. Which meant at least another seven hours under this scorching heat. It would be torture, but the end result would be well worth the wait.

Reluctantly, Benny slunk away from the rise and staggered over to a large rock out of sight of the bungalow, and eased himself down into its shadow, with his back resting against the warm red stone. At last, protected from the powerful glare of the sun, he shut his eyes, and prepared himself for the night to come.

Within minutes, he was asleep. But it was a disturbed, fitful sleep, full of visions and nightmares and horror. He chuntered and cried out as he slept, again seeing his boy, Vito, his ruined face held between Benny's own blood soaked hands. He awoke, several times, in delirium and twice vomited as a symptom of the sunstroke he had subjected himself to on his ill-prepared hike.

*　*　*

Victoria walked out onto the pool deck in her bikini, holding a couple of ice cold beers. Virgil watched her from behind his shades as she sashayed over and handed him one. God she was beautiful.

'To help with the recovery,' she said.

'Thanks,' he replied, 'Good ol' Doc Budweiser works wonders every time. Him and you.'

Victoria had arrived, unannounced, the previous day and Virgil had listened whilst she and her husband argued over all the reasons why she shouldn't have come. In the end, however, she had been the one to stay and he was the one who had sped off back to Palm Springs.

Victoria settled down beside Virgil on the opposite sunbed and took a sip from her Bud. 'Wow, that's good,' she said. 'So's seeing you, Virge. When Sean told me what had happened, I was so worried.'

'It's great that you came, Vicky. Really it is. But Sean wasn't joking when he said it was dangerous to be here. I mean, after what happened at the Villa, we're all lucky to be alive. But that Benny guy, he's gonna be real pissed off when he gets over grieving for his boy. From what everyone says about him, I'm surprised he didn't blow our brains out right there and then. Still, I guess killing your own son kinda messes with your head, huh?'

'From what I know of Mottola, his head's been messed up for a lot longer than that. You know he was behind all that shit storm that happened to me, right?'

'Yeah, Sean told me.'

'If it wasn't for my Uncle Beau, I don't know what would have happened. Except that Sean would have been arrested and most likely deported back to England.'

'I'm glad he wasn't.'

'Yeah, me too.'

'So what's the deal with you guys? Sean says you're breaking up - is that true? If it's none of my business just tell me and I'll shut up.'

'No. It's okay. Sean's right, we are breaking up. But it's all good - we're still friends. We just want different things that's all and I think we have for a long time. He never really got over Joe's sister and I, well, I guess I'm just too career driven. Sounds stupid, I know, but there's more to it. But like I said, Sean and me are okay with it. We're cool.'

'That's good.'

'Yeah, it is.' Victoria hesitated for a long moment, then added. 'You know you were part of it, Virge, don't you? You were not the cause, but for me you were definitely part of it.'

'Yeah, I sorta had an idea.'

'And, is that okay? I mean is that what you want?' Then she smiled with uncharacteristic embarrassment, 'What I really mean is, whilst trying not to make a complete fool of myself, am I what you want?'

Now Virgil smiled, 'Yeah. You're what I've always wanted, Vicky. For as long as I've known you. But we've got to take it slow. It wouldn't be right to jump right in.'

'Hey, I can wait. As long as I know you're there. I can wait. But not too long.'

'No. Not too long. Just until this goddamn leg gets better.'

Victoria smiled broadly. 'That's good. Now we both got a time frame to work to - and I'm gonna make sure it stays right on schedule.'

Virgil laughed and without warning she leant over and kissed him. The spark was instant and the passion hot and immediate. But then, after a few moments, she pulled away. 'That was just to keep you interested,' she said. 'You'll have to wait for the rest until that leg strapping comes off.'

Virgil smiled once more. 'Believe me, I'll wait. But I reckon this leg's gonna mend real quick.'

*   *   *

For the rest of the afternoon, they chatted easily by the pool, enjoying the intimacy of each others company although never allowing it to become anything more than just conversation. As the night closed in they went inside and Victoria made dinner. Then they sat side by side on the sofa and chatted some more. Victoria helped Virgil to bed just after midnight, giving him a lingering kiss on his cheek and drinking in his masculine scent, before leaving him alone to get undressed and into bed.

*   *   *

Benny slept sporadically for a long time and when, finally, he properly awoke, his head still throbbed and flashing lights still played tricks with his vision. The sunburn on his head, face and neck was tight and sore. But he didn't care as it was now dark and cool and it was time to do what he had set out to.

610

*   *   *

Before heading for bed, Vicky loaded the dishwasher and tidied away the dinner things. However, she accidentally knocked over a wine glass spilling the remnants of a full-bodied Barolo down her white cheesecloth blouse and cursed her clumsiness. Still wearing her bikini top underneath, she slipped off her blouse and took it down to the laundry room in the basement. She sprinkled some detergent onto the patch of red wine under the buzz of the blue-white strip light of the laundry room, and rubbed it well to make certain she got the whole stain. Then, after throwing it into the washer and hitting rinse, she snapped off the light and headed back up the short flight of concrete stairs to the kitchen.

*   *   *

Benny slipped down the mesh on the pool side of the fence, his fingers ripped and scratched from the climb over. He weighed in excess of two-hundred and forty pounds, so just getting over was some feat and the success of it fuelled a rush of excitement. On the way down to the fence, in the darkness, with the scree slope lit only by the half-moon and a solitary light from the bungalow, he'd felt extremely unwell. He'd thrown up again after just thirty yards and his head had felt as though it was going to explode. But the fence had focussed his efforts. It had been the only obstacle standing between him and vengeance and not being able to scale it would have caused a serious problem.

Now, thankfully, he was over, but he was panting hard and retched again, although there was nothing more to come up. Dehydrated and badly needing to take on water, Benny lay with his face over the side of the pool, cupped his hands and took a long, refreshing drink. The water was full of chlorine and had a nasty, metallic taste, but it was glorious. Again he drank and again. Then he sluiced his sore head and face, not even thinking that he might be heard from the house. But he wasn't. All the doors and windows were closed and the air-con was humming loudly enough to mute out anything else.

Eventually, Benny got back to his feet, dripping water all over the deck, feeling light-headed and euphoric. Suddenly, unexpectedly, he began to giggle and quickly clamped a hand to his lips to stifle the sound. He was going to kill Sean Reilly, the man he had hated for all these years and that filled him with joy. He was laughing, rocking backwards and forwards with tremendous glee, trying hard not to guffaw, his hand still pressed over his mouth to muffle any noise. He was now doing a little jig and without conscious thought, he reached into his belt and pulled out the .357. Then he held it aloft and was just about to fire a celebratory shot to mark what he was about to do. Then, a moment before pulling the trigger, he stopped. And the euphoria cleared. The madness temporarily suppressed. He was no longer laughing or dancing and carefully he eased the safety back on his gun. What on earth was he thinking? He had a job to do.

Keeping low, he crept across the pool deck towards the double french doors that led to the bungalow's spacious lounge, the Smith and Wesson still gripped in his hand. He tried the latch and wasn't surprised to find it open. After all, who the hell would be around to break in to a place as remote as this.

Benny slipped in and stood for a moment to take in the layout of the place. The lounge was obviously the focal point, with a hallway leading off from it to the bedrooms and bathroom. The rest was fairly open plan, with both the kitchen and dining area separated from the lounge only by a breakfast bar.

A light was on above the sink in the kitchen, casting an ever decreasing glow across a circumference of about ten feet. The rest of the area remained dark - the occupiers, it seemed, were in bed.

But then Benny heard the door opening in the kitchen from the basement, and quickly he ducked out of sight, away from the moon lit french doors, into an area of heavy shadow. He saw the woman, Victoria Wild, step into the light, and watched as she finished loading the dishwasher. She was pretty and slim and she hummed happily as she worked. When she was done she turned on the dishwasher, turned out the light over the sink and, without noticing the open french doors, headed up the hallway in darkness unaware that she was being watched. And stealthily, Benny followed.

*   *   *

In her bedroom, Victoria put on her bedside light and took off her bikini. Then she went into her bathroom, switched on the light and brushed her hair and teeth. Five minutes later, she turned off the light and left the bathroom. As she crossed to her bed, she felt a cold shiver run down her spine and suddenly, for no apparent reason, she was frightened. Instinctively she span round and saw the intruder there, pressed against the wall beside the bathroom door, and she opened her mouth to scream. But it was too late.

*   *   *

I turned my Chevy Blazer onto the dirt road that led to the rented bungalow just before midnight, it had been a long round trip and now I was ready for bed. Ten minutes later I pulled onto the drive, swinging the Blazer in next to Victoria's cherry red El Camino. The house was in darkness, so I assumed them both to be in bed. Then it occurred to me that they might actually be in bed together and no matter how okay I was with their blossoming relationship, I had no wish to stumble in on that, but I was dog tired and needed sleep badly.

So, to save everyone's embarrassment, I reluctantly grabbed a blanket out of the Blazer and headed around back to the pool deck. I'd get my head down on a sunbed for a few hours - it was a warm night and they were nice, big comfortable beds, so I thought what the heck - I'd certainly slept in worse places.

I noticed something wasn't right straight away. At the far end of the deck the mesh fence was bent and misshapen - like someone had climbed over it. And, more worryingly, the french doors were open. But what concerned me the most was the wet footprints that led from the pool to the doors and continued on into the dark interior of the bungalow.

Benny left the woman on the floor where she had fallen. She was just practice and not who he had come for. Again he began to laugh, the feeling of euphoria threatening to overtake him once more at the thought of how easily he'd managed to get into the house. But he controlled it. He could laugh later.

He was vaguely intrigued to find that the woman hadn't intended to sleep with her husband. What a waste he thought. She was a real stunner.

Benny's head began to throb again. He had to move on, to get the job done. Moving away from the woman's bedroom, he crept up the hallway, carefully checking two more rooms, and finding them empty, before hitting the jackpot.

His victim was asleep in bed, the sheets pulled up over his face and his blonde hair laying messily on the pillow. Benny stood for a moment and watched him sleep, savouring the moment. Tasting victory. The lights were still flickering in his eyes and his head still throbbed but he didn't care. His moment was here.

Slowly he aimed the .357 an inch from his target's temple, knowing that from this distance the head would explode like a melon hit by a grenade. But he wanted mess. He wanted blood and brain and skull. He wanted his most hated enemy to die a nasty, blood-spattered death.

He touched his finger to the trigger of the Magnum and caressed it lovingly. 'This is for my brother, Jez. And for my boy,

Vito.' He said.

'No.' I said, behind him. 'You killed Vito, not me. And this, is for you!'

Startled, Benny span round, just in time to see me smash him around the head with Victoria's solid silver hand mirror. Stunned by the impact, he staggered backwards and fell awkwardly onto the bed.

Virgil awoke with a start, ' Hey what's going—' he began, but was cut short.

'Reilly?' Benny said, a confused, befuddled expression on his bleeding face, clearly surprised to see me standing there and not laying in the bed as he had thought.

'Yeah, you sonofabitch, Sean fuckin' Reilly and this is for Michael!' I spat, smashing him again around the side of the face with the mirror.

Weakly, he tried to raise the gun, but I hit him again, 'And this is for Vicky!' And again, 'And for Sarah,' and again, 'And for Joe, and for Rachel—' Then Virgil was pulling me back. He grabbed the mirror and gripped me around the chest as he forced me back out of the room.

'It's over Sean. It's over!'

I looked down at Benny Mottola's bloody, smashed in face and saw the man who had ruined our lives lying dead on the floor. He wouldn't be hurting anyone ever again.

But Virgil was wrong. It still wasn't over.

*   *   *

Victoria had an enormous bruise on the side of her face where Benny had knocked her out with the butt of his gun. Another bruise to go alongside the others that were still healing from her encounter with Wolf. But, again, she had survived. She was a tough broad, just like her mother.

We all sat in the living room, drinking black coffee, discussing what needed to be done. Virgil and Vicky would go to Hawaii for a while, to recuperate, and to spend some time with Louretta and the kids. Just until things cooled down. But it was clear to me now that I couldn't just return to London in the hope that everything would be fine. Someone else would surely come looking for me, the Vincenzi's and Carboni's would see to it - and that time somebody close to me, one of the kids even, could get killed and I simply wasn't prepared to let that happen.

I thought back to the conversation that I'd had with Joe as I drove him back to LAX and remembered the plan he had outlined. He was right, it had to end, no matter what. This blood feud, this thirty year vendetta, had to stop and as far as I could tell, there was only one sure way to make this happen, the only way I could permanently protect those that I loved. I had to die.

*　*　*

Victoria followed me up the canyon road in her El Camino. When I reached the top I pulled the Blazer over and lugged Benny's heavy corpse out of the trunk. Vicky then helped me position it in the driving seat.

With the car in neutral, both of us put our shoulders to the rear of the Blazer and slowly pushed it over the edge into the ravine. It fell through the air for a second or two before hitting the rocks below with devastating force. It then cartwheeled three times, smashing heavily on several rocky outcrops each time. On the third bounce, it exploded like a bomb as a spark ignited the gas in the fuel tank, then glided like a lazy fireball through the air and eventually crunched to a halt in the dry riverbed at the bottom with an ear-splitting crash.

A short time later, the police got a call from someone who didn't wish to leave their name about a dreadful accident up on the canyon road. When they arrived at the scene, the actress Victoria Wild was found close to where the Blazer had left the road, clearly distraught. She had somehow managed to jump from the car as it ploughed, out of control, over the edge and into the ravine. Her husband, the stuntman Sean Noakes, had not been so lucky.

Paramedics gave her an ice-pack for the terrible bruise she had received leaping from the car.

After a few routine questions, the Sheriff's Department dropped Victoria back at the bungalow just before noon. Later that day, she would issue a statement to the press about the accident, through Beau Brewster, but she would not be available for comment. She wanted to be left alone to grieve and hoped the media would understand. Beau would do his best to make sure they did.

*   *   *

All that was left of the Blazer was a burned out shell. Inside were the charred remains of a body, to be recorded by the Las Vegas coroner as the charcoaled bones of Sean Noakes.

I was officially dead. Now it was over.

Or at least it was on this side of the Atlantic.

Thirty-six

Joe left the house early as there was still much to sort out before his eleven o'clock rendezvous with Blades. Before leaving, he crept into Sarah's bedroom and kissed her lightly on the forehead. She had only just come back to him and their reunion had been all too brief.

Sarah woke late. She glanced drowsily at the digital clock next to her bed and saw it was 10.15am. After a brief wash, she threw on some clothes and left her room. No one was around, Rose and Ruby already having departed for the hospital. Joe's jacket had gone from the peg too.

On her way to the kitchen, she noticed that the post had come, so went to collect it from the letterbox. As she pulled the wad of mail free, an electricity bill slipped out of her hand and glided under the nearby table. As Sarah bent to retrieve it she noticed a piece of lined note paper laying face down on the carpet next to it. She picked it up, turned it over, and, as she read the first line, promptly dropped the rest of the mail on the floor. The message, written in an untidy scrawl read:

Cassidy,

I've got the boy. Michael. Christ he's an ugly one, I don't know how you stand to look at him.

If you want to see him again - although I don't know why you should, then bring four million quid (I know you can afford it) to the Surrey Docks on Friday morning. Meet me at the old grain warehouse, 11 o'clock.

Any law and I'll post the boy back in bits. Any funny stuff, he dies. No question.

Be there or be square.

Love and kisses

Frankie B.

X

Sarah felt sick and light-headed and thought for a moment that her mind might shut down again, returning her to the closeted world of her last twenty years, but she fought against it, knowing that was the last thing her son would need.

Today was Friday, in forty minutes Joe would be meeting with Frank Blades, giving him four million pounds in exchange for Michael's life. If ever there was a time when her son needed her, it was now. She wouldn't fail him, not Michael or Joseph, she wouldn't crumble, not again, not this time.

The keys to the Bentley lay on the table next to the front door. Sarah hadn't driven for over twenty years, hell, she'd not even been outside the house on her own in that long either, but now wasn't the time to think about that. Now was the time for action.

Thirty-seven

Michael knew he was going to die as Blades had told him so. According to Frank, his plan was to blow Michael's brains out in front of Joe, and then after relishing the utter despair of his mortal enemy, after wallowing in the delicious triumph of bringing Joe Cassidy to his knees, to then kill him also. This Blades had told him many times over the last several days, or maybe even weeks - Michael couldn't be sure exactly how long he'd been held captive as the drugs had addled his mind, but he knew for sure that this was the plan.

Now he was in the boot of Frank's car, headed for the rendezvous with his uncle, knowing that when he next glimpsed daylight it would be for the last time. His hands had been bound with orange bail string, although not very well as Blades appeared to have lost all interest in his prisoner now, his focus totally switched on to the money and Joe. Besides, as Frank viewed it, the kid was spaced out on smack and half frozen with pneumonia, what threat could he possibly pose to a man such as himself?

Michael was indeed in a bad way, although not quite as bad as he'd pretended to Frank. Everything did ache and his body was weak - mainly through lack of food and the unbearable cold, which had taken its toll after lying naked for days on end in that dank garage. The beatings and sexual abuse were also contributory factors, although Michael preferred to omit those parts of his imprisonment from memory. Most of the time he'd been left alone in the dark, except for the daily administering of drugs - a procedure that Blades seemed to begrudge more with every day that passed.

Michael looked dreadful; his nose was thick with green slime; his eyes were yellow with gunge; black, blue and purple bruises covered almost the entire surface of his skinny body and the red polka dotted needle marks in his swollen arms bore testimony to his awful suffering. All this was easy for Frank to see, but what wasn't visible was Michael's new sense of determination, the will to survive, which had once been severely lacking in his life but now, since his enforced captivity, burned stronger and brighter than even Michael could have ever imagined. He wanted to live, for the first time since that bullet disfigured his face all those terrible years ago, he actually, truly, whole-heartedly wanted to live. After making that rather surprising discovery, the only question that remained to be resolved now was how.

*   *   *

Frank had chosen not to inject Michael with any heroin since making his arrangement to meet Joe - no point in wasting his precious stash any further, especially since he no longer had a need for the boy, or at least he wouldn't after today. Michael, in fact, had not been given anything for over forty-eight hours, which had allowed his thoughts to become more lucid, no longer tainted by Blades' poison. Since his final fix, Michael had begun to think more clearly, and although tired, ill and weak and suffering dreadful withdrawal effects from a lack of the drug, he was able to formulate some sort of plan.

He was warmer now, dressed in a loose fitting boiler suit that Frank had told him to put on. Also, the day was another scorcher, and in the boot of Blades' car it was well over a hundred degrees.

The heat however, was far more preferable to the cold of the garage, from which, in his weakened condition, he was still shivering. At first, he thought he was in total darkness, but as his eyes became more accustomed to it, he was gradually able to see small cracks of light, mostly where the top of the boot joined the actual hold. More interestingly though, he could distinguish where the rear passenger seat partitioned the interior of the car from the boot space, and, thanks to a careful tap with his elbow, how poorly fitted it was. It was an old car, clapped out and ready for the scrap yard, and Michael began to realise just how easy it would be for him to knock out the partition and crawl through into the car itself. As to how or when he could manage this without Frank noticing he hadn't quite yet worked out, but at least it was a start, a possible escape route, and its discovery had given him reason to hope.

*   *   *

Joe had the money. Not in a bank, not in a vault in Zurich, or even tied up in bonds. It wouldn't take him twenty-four hours to get it together like they always said in ransom movies and he certainly wouldn't have to call in any favours. He had it. It was safe, stashed away where only he and one other person could ever find it, over ten million pounds in mixed bills stacked in large bundles under the stairs at Rita's place, in George Reilly's old lock-up. Joe had been secreting money there for years, for us, just in case it should ever be needed. And now it was.

Frank had demanded four, but if all went to plan, he wouldn't get a penny.

Joe stuffed the ransom money into two large kit bags, their zips threatening to burst as he fastened them up. The money was a last resort, in case all else failed; four million pounds for the life of his nephew, which, if Michael came through unscathed, would be worth every penny, but Joe was damn sure he wasn't going to hand it over without a fight.

Joe locked everything back up then, being careful not to be seen, left over the back wall. The Rolls was parked half a mile away, the number plate, JC 1, ensured it would not be touched, as everyone knew to whom it belonged. The car was conspicuous, but that was precisely the idea. He stowed the bags in the boot, then sped off towards Rotherhithe. It was 10.40am.

*　　*　　*

Jack and Danny watched the Roller pull away, then followed at a discreet distance in their Capri. Both men were armed and ready; anxious to do what they'd been itching to do for years. Today was the day and they couldn't wait. As to what was in the kit bags, well that remained a mystery, but both were confident they'd find out in due course.

Neither man noticed the sporty blue Jensen Interceptor that pulled out after them.

*　　*　　*

Sammy and Guido checked out of the hotel early, picking up the paperwork to their Ford Granada hire car as they did so. They had a busy morning planned, after which, they had a long flight back to Miami, and a nice bonus awaiting them upon their return. Guido glanced at his watch as the two made their way towards the parking garage, it was 10.30am. 'Another coupla hours an' d'boss won't have to worry about that limey sonofabitch ever again,' he said.

'Yeah,' Sammy smiled, 'An' we'll be in clover.'

They saw the guy from Hertz waiting by the car, which was brown with a tan vinyl roof and sports wheels. An emblem on its side read Ghia, which in car-speak translated as fast.

'Nice,' Guido cooed, 'But too cool for you Grandpa,' he sneered at the old man with the Hertz badge who was holding the keys. The old man just smiled knowingly, the expression in his one good eye hidden behind black sunglasses, the eye-patch that he normally wore was tucked out of sight in his breast pocket.

*   *   *

The Surrey Docks, once a vital and thriving shipping hub, the very place from where the Mayflower had long ago set sail carrying the Pilgrim Fathers to America, was now a sad, run-down waste land. Rotherhithe Street itself dated back to Roman times and was still one of the longest streets in London. But now, almost all the great riverside warehouses which decades before had been the very backbone of the docks, had been demolished, making room for promised development which had never come. Joe himself had bought up many acres in the early seventies with the intention of building new modern offices and housing. It was a vision of the future that would transform the old stomping ground of his youth into a thriving and affluent business community. It was still a dream, but now it would be his sons who realised it and not himself.

He arrived dead on eleven. The grain warehouse was to his right and the river was to his left and Frank Blades was standing directly between the two, leaning on the bonnet of his puke green car stroking his chin with the barrel of his .38.

Joe pulled up about twenty feet away and turned off the engine.

Slowly, he got out of the car, his eyes, concealed by mirror shades, never leaving the man standing opposite him. 'Keep those hands where I can see 'em!' Blades yelled raising his gun.

Frank had changed: he was older, uglier, no more the strutting peacock that Joe remembered from prison. His body was in good shape though, still obviously powerful and strong - its size and stature mirroring Joe's own. He was like a waiting viper, coiled and brooding, readying himself for the precise moment in which to strike. One look told Joe that Blades was more dangerous than ever before and to underestimate him would be fatal.

'Where's the boy, Frank?'

Frank made a face of mock indignance, 'What - no hello? After all this time. Well I'm hurt.'

'Where is he Blades?' It was not so much a question as a growl.

'Oh, don't worry, he's safe - not a hair hurt on his ugly little head. But we're getting ahead of ourselves aren't we? Surely you've got something for me first - four million somethings I think it is.

'I've got it, but it's not yours until I see the boy.'

Frank squeezed the trigger of his .38. Bang! A shot blasted from the gun which struck the road about four inches from where Joe stood and ricocheted away. 'Not so bossy Joe old son - this is my show, not yours and it'd pay ya to remember that.' Frank was relishing his moment.

The shot made Joe flinch, nothing more, but his expression remained calm. 'The boy, Frank - where is he?'

Bang! Blades fired again. This time the bullet struck less than an inch from Joe's shoe and the ricochet caught the edge of his Armani trousers as it whipped away. 'You're just not listenin' are ya Joe? You're not in charge here, I am. Now talk to me with a little respect or the next shot's gonna take off yer foot.'

'Okay, Frank. We'll do it your way. I've got the money but before I hand it over, I'd like to see my nephew - please.'

Frank smiled. 'Tell ya what I'll do. You show me the money - an' I'll show you the boy.'

Joe knew he had little choice, he had to be certain that Michael was alive. 'Fine - you win. I'll get it.' Joe made to turn, but as soon as he did, Frank fired again. The bullet struck Joe hard in the left bicep, spinning him around onto the rear door of the Rolls. 'Shit!' He cried out.

'There you go again,' Frank sighed, 'Forgettin' who's boss.

You can't just do what you want without askin' me permission - that's not the way it works.'

'Shit!' Joe spat again, his arm hurting like hell and bright red blood pumping from the hole in it. 'Wait,' he told himself, 'Hang on. It's the boy that's important not you. Stay focused.'

Thirty-eight

Sarah, wrestling to control the huge car, put a long scrape down the side of the Bentley as she pulled out of the garage. She proceeded to kangaroo all the way up the street in first gear and only crunched into second after a mile or so, the gearbox whinnying in protest as she neglected to depress the clutch. By the time she'd hit seventy she had pretty much mastered the controls, although the break pedal wasn't getting much use and several cars had to swerve out of her way to avoid a collision. But Sarah didn't care about them, all she cared about was Joe and Michael and to save them she'd have happily ploughed into a dozen vehicles. Being out, in the car, away from all the security that had previously surrounded her, gave her a surprising sense of freedom. She did not feel unsafe or scared or timid, she felt brave, strong, exhilarated and even under the circumstances, she felt better than she had done in years. If there was ever a time to do what was needed, it was now, today and she was more than up to the challenge.

The gun, taken from the glove box, sat next to her on the passenger seat and every now and then she glanced at it, knowing that before the day was through she would quite probably have to use it. But even the thought of that didn't faze her.

* * *

Ray, wearing the badge that he'd stolen ten minutes earlier

627

from the Hertz rental guy, who was now tied up and gagged in the caretaker's office of the multi-storey, smiled at Guido as he handed him the clipboard. 'If you'll just fill out the paperwork and sign at the bottom, Sir, I'll get you on your way in no time,' he said.

Guido gave him a contemptuous look and Sammy smiled, studying the car from a few feet back, as if it was a thoroughbred race horse. Why didn't they just kill the old guy? That would save doing the paperwork. What difference was another dead Brit?

As Guido lent the clipboard on the roof of the car and reluctantly bent to the task of filling in the rental form, Ray undid his jacket allowing easy access to the silenced Beretta tucked into his belt. He held up the car keys to Sammy, 'You want these, Sir?' He asked in his best salesman voice, 'It's a beautiful drive, although you may find it a bit too quick for you.'

'Hey there, Gramps, I can handle anything you got. I like 'em fast. Trouble is with you Brits is you just don't know how to live,' Sammy laughed, then added, 'But one of ya is sure gonna find out how to die - ain't that right, Guido?'

Guido laughed along. Ray just smiled pleasantly pretending not to understand the joke then suddenly threw the car keys at Sammy. 'Catch,' he shouted as the keys soared through the air. Sammy made a grab for the keys but before he'd reached them Ray had drawn the pistol from his belt and fired two shots in quick succession. 'Handle this,' he said flatly.

Sammy went down like a sack of spuds squealing in agony, both his knees blown away.

Ray then span and fired at Guido, but his age and recent illness had made him just a fraction too slow. Guido darted aside and Ray's shot slammed into the car door. Guido had already drawn his gun and was pulling it up as Ray, with no other choice, threw himself at him causing both of them to fall to the ground.

After his hospital stay, Ray was barely eleven stone soaking wet, whilst, in contrast, Guido was a good eighteen stones and in excellent shape. The bigger man landed heavily on top of Ray, knocking the wind out of him and sending his pistol spinning across the cold concrete floor. Guido locked a huge paw around Ray's scrawny throat, pinning him down. In his other hand he still held his semi-automatic which he pressed hard against Ray's temple.

Sammy was still writhing and screaming in pain in the background, 'Kill 'im. Kill the motherfuckin' sonofabitch. Blow his fuckin' head off!' He cried.

'Ah, shut up whining ya big baby!' Ray yelled, trying to disguise the shame he felt for letting Joe down. Too damn old. Too damn feeble.

Guido grinned. A big toothy grin that exposed his nicotine stained teeth. A gob of saliva dripped from his lip and splashed onto Ray's grey, sickly face; the black sunglasses still hiding his empty eye socket.

'Better make it quick, boy,' Ray snarled, 'or I might just bite.'

'Y'got balls, Gramps, I'll give ya that,' Guido said with admiration, 'But now it's goodbye.'

Ray heard the slight click of the trigger and knew this was the end. 'Better this way than another bleedin' blackout,' he mused to himself.

*   *   *

The Jensen pulled up alongside Jack and Danny's Capri on a clear stretch of road just outside Bermondsey. Danny, who'd been so busy keeping Joe in his sights, hadn't noticed the other car until it slid up beside him. He casually glanced across, expecting it to overtake, but then, to his utter astonishment, he saw Manno O'Keefe grinning at him from the passenger seat and Richie Noakes behind the wheel.

'Oh, shit,' he gasped as he gazed in disbelief at the two new kings of the underworld, the kings that he and Anderson had been scheming to de-throne.

'Whassamatter,' Jack asked. Then saw for himself the midnight blue Jensen and the two men riding inside it. 'Oh, shit,' he said, echoing the words of his partner.

Manno, who was pointing a sawn-off out of the window, waved pleasantly at Anderson. Then, with Jack still staring in awe, he mouthed the words 'Bye-bye.' Before Danny had a chance to react, Manno shot out the front tyre of the Capri, blasting both rubber and metal to smithereens.

The Ford, travelling at sixty, careered out of control, Davenport fighting with the wheel but failing to restrain it. He and Jack were helpless as the Capri slewed wildly across both carriageways. Finally, it hit the curb on the far side of the street and flipped over, cart-wheeling nose over tail twice before pirouetting a full 360 degrees onto its side and sliding head long into a lamp-post.

Petrol was pissing in over Danny's shattered legs, his right foot severed by the accelerator pedal and both hands broken and mangled by the steering wheel. Blood was pumping from a deep wound on his forehead but he was still conscious. 'Jack,' he gasped. 'Help me Jack, I'm trapped. I'm fuckin' trapped - help me - please!'

Jack was dazed but conscious. He had bruising on his cheek and his chest hurt like hell, which had been crushed by his seat belt. His nose was bleeding and so was his chin, but apart from that he was remarkably unscathed. 'What?' He said, with a foggy head.

'I'm trapped, Jack. I need you to get me outta here.'

A flame flared up at the front of the car. It was going to blow and both men knew it. 'Quick, Jack. Quick. I'm covered in fuckin' petrol and this car's gonna go up like a fuckin' bonfire. There ain't much time.'

Anderson realised Danny was right. He shook his head clear

and snapped open his seat belt. The car was on its side and Jack, who was in the higher position, had to force his door open. It creaked and moaned but eventually he did it. He slid around in his seat, holding onto the head rest for purchase.

'Sorry, Danny, old son,' he said, 'I reckon this is the end of the road for you and me.'

'No! Jack - please. Don't leave me - if you could just release my legs—'

'Like I said,' Jack interrupted, as he placed a foot on Davenport's shoulder in order to boost himself out of the car, 'There's nothing I can do. There ain't no time. This is the end of the road. No hard feelings eh?' As he spoke, Jack hoisted his heavy frame through the open door. Once out, he squatted on the rear passenger door and prepared to jump free, 'It's just survival of the fittest, Danny. Nothing more.'

'Please, Jack, don't do it. Don't you leave me—'

'See ya around, Danny!'

'No! Don't you dare you bastard - don't you fuckin' dare!' Danny cried, the flames now licking around his trapped legs. But it was too late. Jack had already left him.

*   *   *

Although shaken, Anderson hit the ground running, but he'd covered no more than ten yards before the Capri blew. An ear-splitting bang followed by a huge cloud of oily black smoke and flame, the force of which sent Jack tumbling to the ground and his diamond studded shades, which had remarkably stayed on in the crash, went spinning across the tarmac.

Jack lay face down on the ground with his hands clamped over his head as the smoke billowed over him and the pungent smell of burning rubber filled the air.

Once the initial blast was over, Jack waited some seconds for the smoke to disperse before rising to his knees and crawling towards his glasses. He stretched out a hand to grab them, but a shiny black brogue crunched down on his fingers and made him cry out in pain. He looked up, eyes streaming from the acrid smoke, and saw Richie Noakes standing over him pointing a .38 directly at his forehead. Manno O'Keefe was by his side, the sawn-off aimed at the same spot.

'Hello, Jack,' Richie said in an amiable tone, 'Long time no see.'

'R-Richie. M-Manno. H-how y'doin' boys?' He said as coolly as he could muster. 'You wouldn't be after me, would ya?'

'Now whattad make yer think a thing like that?' Manno asked.

'Dunno, just a wild guess.' Jack smiled ironically through the pain, his fingers still being crushed.

'What y'doin' following Joe, Jack?' Said Richie.

'Joe? Where? I dunno what you mean boys - really I don't.'

'Good try Jack. Very good. Try again.' Richie pressed his foot down harder on Anderson's fingers making him whimper in agony. 'Try again. There ain't no reason why we can't throw you on this barbecue too.'

'Okay, okay. So me and Danny were followin' Cassidy. We wanted some pay back that's all. You know how it works boys. We ain't at kindergarten no more. We're grown-ups and we have to play tough to get what we want. That's all we was doin' - tryin' to get somethin' we want. You can understand that can't ya?'

'What do you want Jack?' Said Manno.

'A piece of the action, that's all. Joe has kept me out of it for so long - I just wanna be back in.'

'Thought you were workin' for Mottola now Jack. That's the word anyway.'

'I hate fuckin' Mottola. Always have. Sure I'll take his money - I ain't no fool, but the guy's a piece of shit, a total fuckin' head case an' I'd never trust 'im. Never. I'm like you. I'm a London boy, I couldn't give a shit about the mob, or Miami or the fuckin' Colombian drug barons, but over the last few years I just ain't 'ad the choice. I gotta live, I gotta earn and I gotta go where the money is. But given the choice, I'd rather be tied in with Joe an' you two.'

'You've had the choice before though,' Richie said, 'But you fucked it up Jack. Big time. No one did that but you.'

'Yeah, sure. I know I've been an idiot. The world's fuckin' biggest, but I've paid for my mistakes - I done time for my mistakes - lost my club because of 'em too. But I'm a fighter, I never quit. Never. I wanna be back in, boys. I want another chance - one last chance to make everything right.'

There was no doubt about it, Jack was a handy man to know - especially with his insider knowledge of the Miami mob, and he was good at working both sides. But could they trust him? Probably not, but a lot of what he said rang true.

Jack could see Richie mulling over the situation, 'Whattaya say, boys?'

Richie knew what Joe would say. He knew what Vinnie and Ray would say too, but he could see the sense of keeping someone like Jack around. He could certainly be very helpful in stopping the Americans from muscling in on their turf. Manno could see it also. 'Whattaya reckon, Rich?' He said.

Richie considered things for a moment longer then said, 'Okay, Jack. Come an' see us at the Galaxy next week. Maybe we can work somethin' out. Maybe. But if you fuck us—' Richie glanced at the burning Capri for added effect, '—you're toast.'

Jack couldn't believe his good fortune. Not only had he escaped a horrific crash and a bullet to the head, he'd also talked his way back into the fold. 'Thanks boys. Thanks a lot. I really mean it. I won't let ya down I promise.'

'We'll see,' Richie said.

'Hey,' Jack smiled, unable to disguise the relief, 'Gimme a hand up would ya?'

This time Jack wouldn't mess it up. This time he'd do things right.

*   *   *

Freeing himself, at last, from the bail string tied around his wrists, Michael heard Blades speaking to Joe. He sounded close to the car but he couldn't be sure. He heard his uncle reply but couldn't make out the words, but felt some sort of comfort that Joe was there, that he'd come to save him. And for the second time in his life he was glad of that. Perhaps he'd got his uncle wrong. Maybe, if he lived through this day, he should re-evaluate things a bit. Maybe.

It was dark in the boot of the Marina, but the faint light being let through from the crack in the rear seat panel allowed him a little visibility; his eyes now becoming accustomed to the gloom. He pushed his weight against the panel and felt it give. The crack of light increased by an inch.

A shot rang out and for a moment Michael panicked. His uncle might be dead, there would be no rescue after all. Then he realised Blades was speaking again, which meant Joe was still alive. Another shot was fired, followed by more talking, Blades was obviously having fun, but Michael had no idea how long that would last. He took a gamble and shoved at the back of the seat hard with both hands and miraculously it fell forward. Michael quickly poked his head out, his eyes blinking from the brightness, as he risked a peek out of the rear door window in time to see Frank fire his third shot. Michael watched with horror as he saw his uncle spin around, blood shooting from the wound in his bicep.

This wasn't going to work. Joe was going to die. He, Michael, was going to die too unless he did something to prevent it. He felt woozy and ill, everything ached but his determination was strong.

Stronger than ever.

Blades had left the drivers door open which was Michael's obvious route out. In between the front seats there was a steering lock bar, which was completely unnecessary in Frank's aging rust bucket, but it would make for a very useful weapon and Michael grabbed it eagerly as he clambered into the front as quickly, but as silently as possible. He slid awkwardly onto the front seat, keeping his eyes glued on Frank Blades, but as he eased his leg into a more comfortable position, his knee caught on the horn and it blasted loudly. Frank couldn't fail to hear and he span his head round to stare at Michael, the gun temporarily moving away from Joe.

Blades grinned with delight. 'Well, well, well,' he said, 'Looks like the young master has arisen.'

*   *   *

The Beretta slid across the floor of the parking garage and came to rest by a thick, square concrete pillar. The same pillar behind which the thirteen year old boy had been hiding. The lad bent down and picked up the chrome-plated gun, the polished silencer gleaming under the artificial lights.

Brett Cassidy knew guns, he'd grown up with them. His father had allowed him to clean his every Sunday and, when in California, he'd practiced shooting at targets from an early age. Now though, he had to kill a man. Two men in fact. It wasn't target practice, they weren't coke cans perched on a rock twenty feet away, they were men. Dangerous men, armed men. But Brett had no fear. He was Ray's only hope.

Joe hadn't wanted to involve Brett, neither had Ray, who insisted he was strong enough to go it alone. Joe sincerely hoped that he was but, in his heart, suspected that he wasn't. Ray had just crawled out of a hospital bed, he was weak and still ailing - although trying like hell to convince everyone otherwise, but it wasn't working and finally even he reluctantly admitted that he was not yet fully well. Against his better judgement he agreed to take Brett with him, but was adamant that the boy should remain hidden.

Joe could only afford to trust those closest to him and there was no one else who could back Ray up; Richie and Manno were on another equally important assignment, the women Joe had purposely kept out of the loop for their own safety and I was on the other side of the Atlantic. Only Brett remained. The boy who Joe was asking to be a man.

It was a big decision but Joe finally put it to his son. He explained it all. Everything. It was important now, no matter the outcome, that Brett knew everything that his father was. Warts and all. It was important, too, that he understood what he was being asked to do, and Joe emphasised the need for him to stay out of sight and not, under any circumstances, to put himself in harm's way. His role was to assist Ray, to phone for help should he get hurt. He was not to engage, whatever happened, as it was too dangerous.

Brett had agreed. He understood his role completely. But that was then. Now Ray was down and he was going to be killed, unless he, Brett, put a stop to it. The old rogue, no matter how tough he once was, was no match for Guido and, even if he was, Sammy was still armed and would shoot Ray before he could so much as move.

Brett didn't hesitate. He stepped away from the pillar, aimed the Beretta at Guido's temple and fired. He then turned and fired at Sammy, the bullet striking him between the eyes. Two dead. Should he feel anything? He didn't know. Maybe he would later. His only concern was for Ray who lay stretched out under Guido, breathing heavily.

'Jesus, boy! You don't mess about do you?' But even as Ray said it, he knew Brett wasn't a boy any longer. He was a man and forever he would be tainted by the vile stench of the underworld. Just as he had. Just as Joe had.

'You okay?' Brett's voice was calm, his emotions kept well in check. Like father like son. He was born for this type of thing, they all knew it, and Ray felt a twinge of sadness.

'Yeah, son. I'm okay - just bloody old that's all.'

Brett hoisted Guido's body off Ray and pulled him up. When the old pirate had dusted himself down he placed a large hand on the thirteen year old's shoulder. 'You've done a hell of a job 'ere today, son, an' I'll never forget it - neither, if he lives to the end of it, will y'dad.'

Brett gave an awkward smile and flicked the unruly mop of black hair out of his eyes, looking deceptively like the innocent young lad he would never truly be again.

Ray swore, that whether Joe lived or died, he would try to be a guiding hand to Brett, to steer him on the right path. He owed him that and far more.

If only he'd have the chance again to do the same for Michael.

* * *

Frank grabbed hold of Michael's arm and yanked him roughly out of the car, barley even looking at him let alone considering him to be armed or even a threat. Instead he kept his focus on Joe where the obvious danger was. Frank then forced Michael up onto his feet and pressed the gun hard into his neck. Meanwhile Michael had the steering lock bar hidden behind his back. 'You wanted to see 'im, Joe,' Blades shouted, 'Well 'ere he is! Ain't he just a little darlin'?'

If Joe had made a move to help, Frank would have shot them both before he'd covered two yards. Joe's gun was locked in the boot of the Rolls along with the two kit bags full of money. Maybe, if he ever got to open the boot, then he could get a clear shot at Frank but, for the moment, that was impossible.

Michael looked terrible. What the hell had Blades put him through? Joe tried hard not to think about it. For the moment it

637

was vital for him to concentrate only on Blades.'

Michael was willing Blades to move the gun, praying for a chance to put the lock-bar to good use.

'Now, where was we?' Frank continued. 'Oh, yes. The money. I believe, before our young friend 'ere so rudely interrupted, you was just about to show me the cash.'

'I've got it, Frank. All of it. It's in the boot - shall I geddit?'

'That's it, Cassidy. Talk to me nice. That's the way I like it. Yeah, I wanna see the money, but first I wanna know you're not armed. Open the jacket nice and slow - an' while you're at it, lose the sunglasses - you've got such beautiful eyes, it's a crime not to show 'em off.'

Joe tossed the glasses and opened his jacket, as instructed, his bicep hurting like a bitch.

'Very good. Now lift up the tails and turn around,' Frank ordered. Again Joe did it. 'Now, the trouser legs, let's get a look at those lovely tanned ankles.'

There was no gun. Michael couldn't believe it. They were both going to die!

Finally satisfied, Frank smiled. 'I'm impressed. You get a maximum score - but how're y'gonna do in the next round? Why don't you open the boot an' we'll find out. Remember, no sudden movements, or the kid gets it - hey, I've always wanted to say that.'

Joe turned to the boot of the car and stood there for a second or two. He looked from Frank to Michael and stared hard into his eyes, willing the boy to see what he was thinking.

Michael did see. He saw the intent in his uncle's eyes and read the message. He's got a gun. This is it. He's going to make his move! For the first time in their lives they had a connection. Michael changed his grip on the lock-bar and gave Joe the very slightest of nods to show he'd understood, then readied himself.

Joe pressed the boot release and lifted the lid, revealing the four million pounds and a loaded .45.

He glanced up over the lid of the boot and finally Blades did what he'd been waiting for. He took the gun away from Michael's neck and waived it at Joe. 'Go ahead, Cassidy. Make me rich!'

Joe grabbed up the .45. 'Move now, Michael - Move!'

Frank fired at Joe, but just as he did so, Michael brought the lock-bar down hard on his wrist, making him miss.

Michael then jerked out of Blades' grip, but as Frank fought to keep hold of him his gun fired again, hitting Michael in the back of the leg and he cried out in pain as he fell.

No longer having Michael as a shield, Frank dived towards the front of the Marina for cover, but as he moved, a bullet from Joe's .45 thumped into his ribs and he too went down.

Michael was wriggling, as fast as he could, around to the back of the Marina, his leg hurting like hell. Frank, blocking out the pain in his side, was still firing madly as he lurched towards the front, but before he could reach safety, Joe caught him again, this time high in the left thigh. Frank screamed as he threw himself in front of his car, leaving a spattering of fresh new blood in his wake. But he wasn't finished yet, not by a long way and whilst he re-positioned, Frank fired off a couple of wild covering rounds in the general direction of Joe. One shot took out the windscreen of the Rolls the other a headlight. Joe, himself was behind the Rolls, trying to pick the right moment to make a run for Michael, knowing that if Frank reached the boy before him it would be all over.

Blades was inching backwards, firing sporadically, as he tried to get around the back of the Marina to Michael. 'I can hear the boy, Cassidy!' He shouted. 'He's cryin' for his mummy. I think he's been hit pretty bad. Think I'll go see if I can help 'im out - how 'bout you coming too?'

'No, Uncle Joe! He'll kill you,' Michael yelled, in a pained voice. 'I'm okay. I can take care of myself!'

'Ah, ain't that sweet, Uncle Joe, the boy wants to save you. But who's gonna save him? 'Cos I know he ain't no match for me. You know that too, don't ya Joe? You know what I can do. Christ, I'll cut his balls off and send them home to his momma for Christmas - but I'll have me some fun before that. You know I will Joe. You know I will!' Frank shot twice more, both shots slamming into the bodywork of the Rolls, then he laughed, 'Come and get 'im, Joe - I know you want to - I know you're just dyin' to play the hero, just like always!'

'Don't listen to him—' Michael yelled again, '—I'll be fine - really I will. I can take care of myself!'

But Joe knew Frank was right. Even if Blades was badly wounded, Michael would be no match for him.

Joe had no choice but to go for it. He took a deep, steadying breath then dived out from behind the Rolls, keeping low. A bullet struck the tarmac inches from his right foot, another ricocheted off to the side. He was weaving as he ran, zigzagging towards Frank's car, firing all the time in a bid to keep Blades occupied, his shots splashing like hail stones into the Thames behind the Marina. Another bullet whizzed past his head, missing him by inches. He had five, six feet to go. He was nearly there.

Then he got hit. And he went sprawling to the ground.

Michael saw it all. As he looked on in horror he saw his uncle go down. He saw him die.

It was over and now Blades would kill him too.

Thirty-nine

The wheels of the Bentley squealed as Sarah turned onto Rotherhithe Street, taking the corner at sixty. As soon as she straightened up she pressed the accelerator to the floor once more and took off up the street, the River Thames, that ran parallel to it, nothing but a blue-green blur to her left.

The clock on the dash said 11.05. She was late. Joe and Michael were here. Frank Blades was here. And she was late.

The street was deserted, just the scars and ruins of a once thriving hub to the world, and in the distance Sarah could easily make out the shape of Joe's Rolls Royce. In front of that there was another car; a green one, but she did not recognise the make. Cars had changed a lot in twenty years.

As she drew closer, the Bentley's engine purring smoothly as it soared past a eighty, she saw the flash of gunfire and three figures huddling by the vehicles. Joe was behind the Rolls. Michael and the other man, whom she suspected to be Blades, at opposite ends of the green car.

Suddenly Joe sprang out. He was running, zigzagging, heading for Michael. He was shooting at Blades, Blades was firing back. Then, as his sister looked on with horror, Joe went down, hitting the tarmac hard; his arms and legs splayed.

'No!' Sarah shouted. 'No, you bastard, no!' She banged on

the horn, blasting it loudly again and again, deliberately aiming the Bentley directly at Frank Blades, using it like a guided missile which was approaching its target fast.

Blades hopped out from his hiding place, obviously injured badly; blood pouring from his side and leg. But he was smiling. No. Laughing. Laughing like a mad man. He raised his gun and took slow deliberate aim, the Bentley bearing down on him at top speed. He fired off three rounds in quick succession, then dived clear. The Bentley's brakes screeched loudly, but it was too late and it ploughed headlong into the Marina with an ear-splitting crash.

*   *   *

Michael, from his hiding place, was the first to see the approaching Bentley, although he could not see who was behind the wheel as his eyes were stinging with tears. Tears of pain and, to his surprise, tears of despair after seeing his uncle fall. He also realised, before Blades, where the Bentley was headed and he waited until Frank was fully committed before rolling clear.

The noise was deafening as the two cars collided; the big, heavy Bentley blasting the lighter, weaker Marina up into the air, tossing it like a child's toy into the muddy waters of the Thames. It bobbed gently on the tide for a moment or two, before the river finally found the open doors, and flooded in. Then it sank quickly, vanishing from view within seconds.

The dust and smoke kicked up from the impact was thick and brown and hung above the ground in a huge cloud, obscuring the Bentley and all around it from view. Nothing moved, nothing stirred, not for a long moment.

The silence was eerie and Michael lay motionless on the ground as the sun tried desperately to penetrate the gloom.

Suddenly, a tall figure arose from the dust; dark hair, dark clothes; broad across the shoulders. It was Joe, he was alive. Michael was saved. But as the figure became clearer, Michael knew he was mistaken. It wasn't Joe. It was Frank Blades, and he'd come to finish the job he'd begun.

'Heh, heh, heh!' The laugh was maniacal. 'Woo, what a rush! That was a close one.'

'Stay away from me you animal! Michael yelled.

'Hello, darlin'' Blades said, blood pumping from the wound in his side, 'You still kickin'?'

'Get away from me, I'm warning you! Don't you come near me.' Michael inched away, but suddenly his injured leg seemed heavy and immovable and he noticed a bright red puddle underneath where he lay. 'Stay away or I'll hit you with this!' He held up the steering lock bar, his only weapon. 'I mean it, I'll break your nose!'

'Ha, ha, ha. Aw, now that ain't very nice - not after all we've been through.' Blades' teeth were red, and magenta coloured spittle was dribbling from his bottom lip. 'Sides, I've had a broken nose a coupla times before - it ain't so bad. Then again, why should I be frightened of that silly little stick, when I've got this?' Frank held up the .38 and pointed it at Michael.

Michael did not waiver, he felt more courageous now than he'd ever felt in his life, 'You've just killed my uncle. You just killed Ray—' he'd wrongly assumed that it was Ray who had been driving the Bentley, '—and now you're gonna have to kill me, cos if you don't, I'll hunt you down and kill you like the dog you are!'

'Hey! Bravo, bravo. Well said, son. They was big words for a little man like you. And you're right, of course, I am gonna have to kill you. Not because you might 'hunt me down and kill me like a dog' - nice words by the way - a little bit Hollywood, but nice all the same. No, I'm gonna kill ya 'cos that's what I do. I kill. I like to kill and if I don't, I get all sort of irritable. It makes me a bad person to be around - can you believe that? Hard to imagine I know.'

'You're scum, you know that?' Michael spat.

'Oh, yeah. I know. Heh, heh, heh. But you're dead, darlin.' You're fucking dead.' Blades aimed the pistol at Michael's head, 'Goodnight sweet prince,' he said, slowly pulling back the trigger.

A millisecond before the gun fired, a shot blasted into Frank's chest; the impact rocking him backwards, ruining his aim and causing his chamber to empty harmlessly into the Thames.

Frank's face was aghast, uncomprehending. Then another bullet tore into his stomach and he staggered violently, clutching at the wound. Still he couldn't believe it, his eyes wide as he stared at the person who had shot him. 'Heh, heh, heh,' he laughed gruffly, forcing the sound from his throat, he coughed and red bile shot from his mouth. 'Well I'll be—' his words tailed off, blood pouring over his lips and through the gaps in his teeth. He stared for a moment longer, his eyes dark and menacing and filled with hate, then he fell back, disappearing into the dust cloud that still filled the air around them.

*　*　*

Michael looked up and saw two hands holding the smoking gun. His eyes then travelled back, up the arms and onto the face of the person who had rescued him.

'Sarah? Mother?' He had to blink twice to be sure. 'You—?'

'He was going to kill you,' Sarah said, still looking at the empty space where seconds ago Frank Blades had stood. 'I couldn't let him do it. I had no choice. I had no choice.' She had a trickle of blood on her temple and a graze on her cheek. The seat belt had saved her from serious injury in the crash and all Frank's bullets, that he'd shot at her speeding car, had miraculously missed. They'd shattered the windscreen, punctured the seat and smashed up the dash, but none had hit her.

'You saved me,' Michael said. 'You saved my life. I didn't think you could talk - didn't think you could walk, but—'

Sarah looked down at him and smiled. One of her fabulous

smiles. 'I couldn't,' she said. 'I couldn't do any of those things, not for a long time, not for far too long. But now I can. Now I can.'

She dropped the gun onto the tarmac and bent down to her son. She kissed him lightly on the forehead. The first time in all her life that she had kissed her son. The first time in all of Michael's life that he'd felt the warmness of his mother's kiss. The warmness of her love.

She took his hand and helped him to his feet. 'Are you back for good?' He asked. It seemed like a silly, childish question, but he really had to know the answer.

Sarah smiled again, staring into his crooked face and seeing only beauty. 'Yes,' she said firmly, 'I'm back for good.'

'I wouldn't be too sure of that if I were you, sweetheart,' a familiarly gruff voice said.

Sarah and Michael, startled out of their loving reunion, looked up to see Frank Blades standing before them. Sarah had not killed him. Like a phoenix from the ashes he had risen again, albeit unsteadily. But he was there nonetheless, his gun waiving threateningly in their direction and his evil intent clear to read. He was covered in blood. A bullet hole in his leg, a bullet hole in his side, another in his chest and one more in his stomach. He was in bad way, he knew that, yet somehow he was still talking, still breathing, still dangerous. And for the next ten seconds, that's all that mattered.

'How dare you think you can kill me,' he growled. 'Who the hell do you think you are? A pathetic, ugly brat and a crazy, simpering female.' He aimed the gun, fighting to keep his vision from blurring and the pistol from swaying, 'You can't kill me, you're not capable of killing me—'

Suddenly, the barrel of a .45 appeared out of the dust and was pushed hard into Frank's cheek.

'No, but I am,' said Joe, as he pulled the trigger.

Forty

Joe rang me to tell me to come to London, to tell me that Michael had been kidnapped and that Sarah was all better. But I never got the phone call because I was already on the way.

After disposing of Benny I drove straight to the airport and took the first available flight out. It was a long arduous journey, first we set down in Houston and had an eight hour delay there. Then, after arriving at JFK, I had a five hour wait for my adjoining flight. Finally, the British Airways flight to Heathrow was diverted to Charles de Gaulle due to thick fog and a connecting flight wasn't available until late the next day. But at last, after a thirty year wait, I made it back to London, the city of my birth. My homecoming was long overdue.

*   *   *

As I cleared customs, I noticed a little Asian man holding a homemade sign with my name written on it. Warily, I wandered over and asked what he wanted. He told me that Joe had sent him. Apparently my best friend had phoned Victoria and she had told him that I was on the way. The little Asian man, whose name I soon learnt was Johnny, had been asked to collect me and take me to my mother's old house before going anywhere else. It all seemed very mysterious but my instincts told me that Johnny was trustworthy, so I agreed.

Johnny dropped me off close to the rear entrance of the house as instructed but when I offered to pay him he said he had already been more than adequately compensated.

After watching him drive away, I approached the house from the alley behind. I took a deep breath then opened the back door and stepped inside. The house smelt fusty and old and in need of airing, the windows had not been opened in many years and no one had lived there for even longer. Not since Rita Reilly, my mother.

Being there seemed strangely surreal, like going back in time and the memories, both good and bad, came flooding back. Memories of Rita, memories of Joe and me as teenagers, memories of George Reilly and memories of Sarah.

My darling Sarah. I thought of her as I'd seen her the day I left, her life ruined by an abhorrent act over a lifetime ago.

*   *   *

I was in our old kitchen. The curtains were drawn but light was still finding a way in. And then the door to the living room opened and a tall, familiar figure came in.

'Hello mate,' Joe said, his face breaking into a wide, warm smile, 'It's good to see you.'

'Good to see you too,' I said, grabbing him by the hand, 'Although, I've seen you looking better.' Joe's arm was in a sling and he was clearly in some pain. 'You okay - looks like you've seen better days?'

'Ah, I'm fine,' he said, 'I'm bullet-proof, me.'

'Yeah, it looks like it. What happened?'

'It's a long story, I'll tell you all about it later. Sufficed to say I took one in the arm and another in the gut. Both clean shots. Hit no major arteries. I was lucky. The doc's seen me and says I'll live. But that's enough about me, what about you - how was the flight?'

647

'Don't ask. That Johnny's a character though ain't he? Showed me the sights on the way here.'

'I thought you might appreciate it, you being away for so long and all that - a little taste of blighty to make you feel like you were home.'

'Yeah, it did, thanks. It was great. This is all a bit cryptic though.'

Joe smiled. 'Yeah, I know. Sorry about that - everything will be explained soon enough.' Then he changed the subject. 'How's it feel to be back at last?'

'Good.' I said. 'Really good. Seems a bit strange being back here though, in this house.'

'I'll bet. You got no trouble at the airport then?' He asked.

'No, it's amazing what a tan, a few wrinkles and a baseball cap can do. I walked through customs without any problems.'

'That's good, mate. You should be safe enough as long as you're careful. There's been nothing in the press about you for years now, ever since Tailby died - so I reckon the ghost of Sean Reilly is long dead too.'

I smiled, 'Yeah, let's hope so! No thanks to Benny bloody Mottola though.'

'Yeah, bad business all that. Glad it's sorted though, Sean. Real glad, for all of us. Are Vicky and Virge alright?'

'Oh, yeah. More than alright, in fact - it's a long story. But the plan worked, it was a good idea of yours. I'm now officially dead!'

'Pleased to hear it,' Joe said with a grin. 'And more about that plan in a minute, but for now, let's just enjoy you being home.'

'Sure, why not,' I said. 'How's Michael, is he okay?' I was desperate to see my son again. It had been far too long - it was time for me to tell him the truth about who I was.

At that moment, another person entered the kitchen. 'Yes. I'm fine,' he said.

'Michael?'

'It's me. And I'm fine, thanks to Uncle Joe and—'

'Hey Michael - great to see you!' I said, rushing over and wrapping my arms around him. 'I'm glad you're here, there's something I need to tell you that just won't wait—'

'He knows, Sean.' Joe interrupted, 'Figured it out for himself.'

'He knows?' I looked at Joe, then back to Michael, 'You know?'

'Yes, *Dad*. I know.'

'Oh, Christ, Michael. I'm so sorry. I don't know what to say. There's been so many times that I've wanted to tell you - so many times that I should've told you, but somehow I always found a good excuse not to. I'm sorry, son. I'm so, sorry.'

Michael smiled at me. His mouth crooked and lop-sided, but it was a nice smile, a handsome smile which I'd finally noticed. No longer was he an ugly kid, all gangly and awkward. He had grown into his rather unusual features and even though he still had a nasty scar, he had transformed into quite an attractive young man.

'It's okay,' he said, 'I've been a first class arsehole all my life, I know that. I've been holding on to so much hate, so much bitterness, that I just couldn't see common sense. I know you did what was best for me, I understand that now. I know too what Mum has been through, and that none of it was hers or your fault. I've spoken to Uncle Joe and, well, we've sorted things out. He saved my life. Twice. And that's something I'll always be grateful for. Not that I realised that until a short time ago. I've been a fool, I've wasted my life and spoiled the lives of others and for that I'm truly sorry.' He bowed his head in shame, 'I hope you can forgive me,' he added softly.

'Oh, Michael. Of course I can,' I said, 'There's nothing to forgive, boy. We're flesh and blood. There's nothing that either of

649

us can do to ever change that. You are my son and that's all that matters and we've spent far too much time apart. All I want is what's best for you, whatever makes you happy, and if I can be included in just a small part of that then that's wonderful. But you've got your whole life ahead of you and you can do exactly what you want with it - the world's at your feet. But there's no need for forgiveness Michael, no need at all.'

Then, for the first time, I noticed he was on crutches and I nodded to them, 'You okay?'

'Yeah, I'll heal alright. It's just a bit sore that's all.' He also looked very pale, even more than usual, as if he'd been extremely ill recently.

'You sure? You both look like you've been through hell. What's been going on? How on earth did you both get so messed up?' I asked. 'And another thing, why are we meeting here? What's with all the cloak and dagger stuff - I could've met you at The Castle. No need to meet here, at Mum's, although it's very nice.'

'No. But I thought this place might be apt,' Joe said.

'Apt?' I said, 'Why's that?'

'Apt, because the two of us had a bit of help with our encounter with Frankie Blades, from someone who saved both our lives,' Joe said.

'Frank Blades? What encounter? Whose help? I said bewildered as Joe opened the door to the living room.

'Mine.' A female voice said from inside the living room.

I looked through the doorway towards the sound of the voice and saw her immediately.

Her hair was down and the sunlight streaming through the small gap in the curtains was lighting her whole body. She was wearing the small silver stud earrings of my mother's that I'd asked Ruby to give her if she ever recovered.

She was beautiful. More lovely than I ever remembered. An

angel.

'Sarah?' Surely I was dreaming. 'Is that really you?'

A tear ran down her cheek, 'Yes, Sean,' she whispered hoarsely, 'It's me.'

'But–?' suddenly I was breathless, ecstatic, confused, 'But Joe didn't say–'

'I thought I'd surprise you,' I heard Joe say somewhere in the background.

I felt weak with shock, my legs unsteady, but my need to get to Sarah fuelled my body and I strode over, stopping, just short of where she stood. 'Is it really true - have you come back to me?' I asked, my own eyes now wet. 'Have you really come back?'

'Yes, my darling,' she said, her big dark eyes twinkling with life, 'If you'll have me.'

And in reply I took her in my arms and kissed her.

My world was now complete.

Epilogue

Joe had decided that in order to get his life back and put an end to the life-long vendetta that had forced his destiny so many times, that he would have to die. It was his big plan which he outlined to me on the way to the airport from Vegas. I merely borrowed it when Benny Mottola tried to kill me. But the plan had worked for both of us. Joe Cassidy and Sean Reilly were now both officially dead.

*   *   *

Joe had burned off Frank Blades' fingerprints with the battery acid from the Rolls, then he and Sarah had loaded his body into the boot. Joe had replaced Frank's wallet with his own which contained his driving license, his credit cards and photographs of his kids.

To the world, it was Joe's body in that boot with his face blown off. To the Vincenzi's and Carboni's, to the police and to the media. To anyone, in fact, who had anything other than a loving interest in him. He had to get out for his and his family's safety and to be dead was the only sure way of doing it successfully.

Things had not gone exactly to plan, but the final goal was achieved.

His biggest regret was putting his family through so much heartache, but the grief at his funeral had to be real. It had to be convincing, for all their sakes. Not even Ray or Brett, who were such an important part of the plan, knew the whole story, they too thought Joe to be dead. Even poor Ruby, who was beside herself with worry about Michael, not knowing if he was dead or alive, was kept in the dark and Joe felt terrible about that too. But it was all necessary.

Only Sarah, the doctor and Johnny, the little Asian mini-cab driver knew the truth. Shortly, Johnny would be returning to Pakistan with his whole family and enough money for a new house and a brand new start. He was so grateful that Joe knew his silence would be assured. The doctor, too, had proved many times that he could be trusted.

But it was Sarah who had been Joe's go-between. She was the one who had driven her brother and Michael from Rotherhithe in the smashed up Bentley and who had got rid of it afterwards. She was the one who brought in the doctor from Wandsworth who had saved both their lives. She was the one who had taken the food and sleeping bags from The Castle and who had visited every day without anyone else suspecting. They were all too absorbed in their grief to notice.

No one was to be told until after the funeral.

Ruby, Ray, Rose, Brett and Matt now knew the truth as Sarah had told them. The men received the news well, especially Brett, who was over-joyed at the thought of having his dad back, but Rose and Ruby, were furious at the deception and through the tears and furore that followed, both threatened never to speak to Joe again. Nor Michael or Sarah either for that matter.

Of course, neither meant it, and soon both were buzzing about, looking forward to meeting up with their men again.

*   *   *

Ray and Michael resolved their differences and once again resumed their close relationship. Michael was devastated when he learned how close to death Ray had come and blamed himself for it. However, Ray was quick to forgive and was soon back to his old self in no time. I was grateful to have the old rogue on hand to act as my councillor because, to date, he had been a far better father to Michael than I had. I sensed too, that Ray liked to be involved and there was no way I was going to rob him of that.

*   *   *

Several years earlier, through one of Ironclad's subsidiary companies Joe had bought a large villa in Majorca whose ownership could not easily be traced back to him. His family, using passports supplied by Richie and Manno, would now vacate The Castle and head there as soon as they could.

*   *   *

As for Joe, Michael, Sarah and me, we travelled down to Dover in a camper van, which I'd bought brand new off the forecourt, cash. No questions asked.

We had the best part of ten million pounds stuffed in several large kit bags in the back of the van and all of us were travelling under false passports - again supplied courtesy of Richie and Manno.

Our aim was to take a leisurely drive through France and Spain, then to rendezvous with the others at Joe's villa in Majorca. From there we weren't sure exactly where to go. The Bahamas were mentioned, as was Australia.

Personally, I was eventually going to head back to the States - with Sarah, of course. Then maybe onto Hawaii, as I had to sort things out with Victoria about Olivia and Josh. I also had to think about what I was going to do about the Bluestone. Maybe I'd even sell it to Rocky or Brad.

I didn't know for sure how it would all pan out but felt confident that it eventually would.

However, for the present, I was going to take some time off, lay on a beach with the woman I loved and drink some sangria.

What could be better than that.

About The Author

Kris Lillyman is based in Northamptonshire, England and has worked as a freelance graphic designer and illustrator for over twenty-five years. He is married with two grown up children.

In addition to adult thrillers, he also writes and illustrates children's books - to find out more about these, please visit: **www.boom-boom-books.com**

Alternatively, search 'Kris Lillyman' in iTunes, Amazon, Barnes & Noble or most other online bookstores.

www.ingramcontent.com/pod-product-compliance
Lightning Source LLC
Chambersburg PA
CBHW030028030726
47500CB00001B/5